Storm Rising

The Beginning of the Storm

T.J. Farish Sr

Storm Rising: The Beginning of the Storm Copyright © 2018 by T.J. Farish Sr. All Rights Reserved.

All rights reserved. No part of this book may be reproduced in any form or by any electronic or mechanical means including information storage and retrieval systems, without permission in writing from the author. The only exception is by a reviewer, who may quote short excerpts in a review.

This book is a work of fiction. Names, characters, places, and incidents either are products of the author's imagination or are used fictitiously. Any resemblance to actual persons, living or dead, events, or locales is entirely coincidental.

T.J. Farish Sr.

Dedication

I have some very important women I want to dedicate my first book to. First and foremost is my mother. You have been gone twenty years but not a day goes by that I don't think about you.
Thank you, Mom, I wouldn't be the person I am today if not for you. You were always there in the good times and the bad no matter what I could always count on you.

I miss you.

And to my wife Donna. You are truly an amazing woman for several reasons. You raised our three wonderful children by my side and have stuck with me through life no matter what it dealt us.
You allowed me to take the time I needed to fulfil one of my lifelong dreams by writing this book. And finally thank you for loving me for I wouldn't have made it without you by my side.

I LOVE YOU!

And last, but in no way least, I want to thank my editor, Kerri Boehm. Your help in the editing process has been invaluable.

Contents

Title Page
Dedication
Prologue
The Deal — 1
The Pack — 12
The Guardian — 22
The Hill — 24
Nemesis — 29
The Tournament — 32
Compromise — 53
The Banquet — 58
Changing of the guard — 76
The Docks — 84
Chosen — 90
Aarya — 101
Ishani's Plan — 116
The Visit — 122
Testing — 126
Dorms and Detention — 137
Diron's Pack — 151

First Bonded	161
Nug Bars and Shattered Gems	170
Lunch	180
A Spies Confession	189
The Visit and The Shattered Door	195
Anastasia and The View	215
Disappointment and Rewards	219
Training and Class	224
The Hill and Family	230
Home and Heart	235
Diron's Warning and a Grizwolf	256
The Prophecy	279
Oak City	291
New Boots	298
A Warning from Beyond	307
Consequences	324
Mildred's Bargain	338
Long Time Coming	347
Dirk and Sorey	365
Unexpected Help	371
Healing and Explanations	377
The Miraga Stones	380
The Old Outpost	406
The Traitor	425
Rescue and Retreat	436
Pineral	446
Reunited	453
Ishani's Reprieve	464

The Thirteenth Bonded	466
Epilogue	482
Storm Rising	484

Prologue

Diron Storm was on his hands and knees, sweat and blood dripping down his body. He stared at the puddle of blood that had formed below him in the sand. A hot, dusty breeze blew by, causing the puddle to ripple. He raised his head and looked around, listening to the wind as it passed through the armor of the fallen soldiers surrounding him.

Struggling to breathe, he looked up at the sky, his entire body aching. A dark cloud of death floated through the air. The battle on the plains of Der-Tod was all but over now. He gagged from the stench of death that had been stirred up by the wind. The smell was attributed to the burning bodies and the viscera scattered around the battlefield.

He wiped bile from his lips with his shoulder, even though he hurt from every single movement he made. Sunlight slipped through the cracks in the swirling smoke in the air above. He could hear no sounds of birds singing on this day as he knelt in his own blood, gasping desperately for air.

The cries of the dying soldiers made his heart break. He got another taste of blood from the wound above his ear that he didn't remember receiving. It ran freely down his face and every time he licked his dry lips, the taste of iron caused him to gag. After he finally finished heaving up the last of the contents in his stomach.

He looked around at his fallen friends on the plains one more time. A wave of nausea overtook his body, causing him to fall forward, with only his elbows stopping him from crashing face-first into the puddle that had formed beneath him. He started to sway. After he stuck out his hands to steady himself, he shook his head, trying to remember something important. *Remember what?* he thought. He knew there was something important he was supposed to do. Diron couldn't remember why he was even there, for his thoughts were clouded. His vision blurred causing dizziness to almost overtake him. He shook his head, causing sweat and blood to drip onto the ground around him.

The clouds in his mind finally cleared away and he remembered that the mountains in front of him were the entrance to the underworld. It was the home of Zolun, the guardian of the underworld and the son of Zona and Marluna, the father and mother of the gods.

Diron also remembered that it was Zolun's greed for power that had brought this day to fruition. The cries of the dying finally ceased, causing him to look around again. He realized at that moment he was one of the last soldiers that King Jerard, ruler of Silver City, had sent to stop Zolun's madness. Looking to his side, he saw, lying next to him, slowly taking his last breaths, his best friend, Thadeus.

"Diron," Thadeus whispered.

"Yes brother?" Diron asked his dying friend.

"You must do what is needed, for the children!" Thadeus said as his last breath left his body.

"Yes, for the children," Diron replied as tears ran down his face. He didn't know whether his lifelong friend, his brother, had heard him or not. The tears dripped into the puddle below him. Diron was in pain seeing Thadeus lying there with clouded eyes. He stared at Zolun, who had just appeared several yards in front of him, in defiance.

"Give me the sword, Diron Storm!" Zolun's voice boomed.

Diron looked down at Harbinger still clenched in his right hand. His hand was trembling from pure exhaustion. "Kira, my love, I will always be with you," Diron said, realizing he was about to die.

He gripped Harbinger, the only weapon with the power to rid the land of Zolun, even tighter and thought back to when he had trained with his father Durkon. He had learned that the sword was a gift from Zona and Marluna. Zona had given it to the Chosen, the true protectors of the world Marona, to help aide in the fight against evil. The Storm family line was the one chosen to be the protectors of all races. Zona had chosen them for their selflessness and courage.

Diron had learned that their bloodline was the only one gifted with the power to wield the sword and use the powers it held within. Diron had freely devoted his entire adult life to the protection of all Maronans, which consisted of humans, elves, dwarfs, and many other races. He wanted nothing more than to protect them, especially his family, his wife Kira, their newborn son Dirk, and Diron's father. Durkon had been the Chosen before him. The responsibility passed from the Chosen to their heir either at the time of death or when the time was right for it to be handed down. Diron knew his father was still one of the best knights to have ever lived, but when Diron had turned eighteen years old, his father had passed the legacy on to him. He took on the mantle of the Chosen willingly and knew it was his blood rite to protect all Maronans. Kneeling here defeated at the end of his life, he started to have some doubts about the decisions he had made. All things considered though, he still felt that he would do everything the same way he had again if given the chance.

A thought struck Diron as tears fell from his eyes, whether it was caused by the timing of his death or the panic of his son having to endure what he had.

Could I betray my duty to the world and the gods? The deal Zolun is offering is so tempting. I know Harbinger has to be given to Zolun freely, not forced or taken for it to work for him. If I didn't give it to him freely the power would be lost, he thought kneeling before Zolun while looking at Harbinger. Diron's hands started to tremble even more. He knew weakness had filled his emotions.

The battle had taken so much from him, his best friends and all who relied on him to finish the job. Most of them he had known his whole life. Now they were lying beside him, their bodies broken and bloodied. Diron looked around again and their eyes, still open, seemed to stare into his soul. He turned and glared at Zolun with hate for what he was about to do.

"Will you take care of our families?" he asked through gritted teeth.

"I will give you anything your heart desires," Zolun replied with an evil grin. Diron gathered strength he didn't think he still had and pushed himself back up onto his heels. He rolled the sword in his hand, looking at it. He remembered the first time he had seen it.

How could such a beautifully made weapon be so deadly? he thought.

It was a single-handed broadsword with a marble handle that had a crimson diamond in its golden hilt. Smaller blue diamonds were embedded in the end of each cross bar. Looking at it now, he could see that the power in the jewels were completely drained from the battle. The beauty of this deadly weapon still amazed Diron to this day. It was three and a half feet long from tip to handle.

Blood dripped from his chin, splashing onto the silver blade. He watched as the blood glided down the blade, slipping across the runes that were engraved on it. The runes were lifeless now as well. He took a deep rattling breath as he threw his head back and looked into the sky one last time, letting out a scream. Then he lowered his head and started to give Zolun the sword. The betrayal he was about to commit would break the commitment his family had honored for generations. Diron hesitated pulling the sword back to his chest, then closed his eyes and shook his head.

He knew that it was his responsibility to stop Zolun, but he didn't see any other way around it. The only other option would be to take the sword and run it through his own heart to keep Zolun from getting it. But that would only delay what seemed to be the final outcome, he thought, still wavering on what to do. Zolun stood there confidently, watching Diron.

Diron didn't want to put this burden on his only son whom he had never met. He wouldn't be there to teach and instruct him the way his father had been there to prepare him. His father was capable of training his son the way he needed. Diron just didn't want to burden him with that challenge again.

With a sigh of regret, Diron started to hand the sword to Zolun again. Zolun laughed, seeing victory, and said in a deep thunderous voice, "That's right, Diron. Do the right thing, give me the sword and all your troubles will be gone, along with my meddlesome mother and father."

In the distance, just as Diron was reaching out a trembling hand to give him the sword, a deafening shriek vibrated through the air, making the ground shake. Diron stopped his arm inches from Zolun's hand. The sound had prevented him from moving any further. It made them both look to the sky.

Diron saw a crimson flame streaking through the air towards him. "No!" Zolun screamed as the rolling flame headed straight at them. Diron squinted to see what was causing the guardian of the underworld to panic. When Diron saw the phoenix, it was the most beautiful sight he had seen in a long time.

"Arial," Diron said. "I thought you were dead." She had been around him since he was a child. Arial was the phoenix that had been given to the Chosen by Zona. She was his friend and ally in this adventure. Arial, with flames rolling off her wings, soared towards the two. Diron's and the phoenix's eyes locked, and the connection with her was reformed in that instant, filling him with remorse. He felt shame wash through him for what he was about to do. He now knew what he had to do. Pride replaced that shame because he knew when he had made the ultimate sacrifice. His son would have everything he needed when the time came to face Zolun. Zolun, seeing the look in Diron's eyes, knew that if what he assumed Diron was going to do happened, it would be many years before his power was strong enough to make another attempt at his plan. He just couldn't wait any longer.

He reached for Diron's arm. Diron was filled with determination and newly added strength given to him by Arial. "Kira, my love, I will see you again." He smiled at Zolun and then lunged forward towards the ground with Harbinger placed at his heart. Zolun was too late by the time he reached him. Diron rolled over on his side, Harbinger was piercing through his chest. His vision blurring, he saw Zolun fade away like mist. One of his last thoughts as he looked to the sky was of Arial. "Thank you, my friend."

She reached out to him with her thoughts. *I will protect them.*

I know you will my friend. With tears falling from her eyes, she assured him that he had made the right decision. As Diron's heart beat its last few shattered beats, he looked into his best friend's vacant eyes. He reached over and clasped Thad's open hand smiling as he exhaled his last breath. The phoenix's cry could be heard throughout the plains.

Arial swooped down to where Diron and Thad lay landing close to her now-dead friends. She nudged Diron's face with her beak like a caress from a mother. She looked at Thadeus and nudged his face as well.

"You know what must be done," a godly voice said in the back of her mind.

"I do," she responded. Arial grabbed Harbinger in her talons and gently pulled it out of Diron's chest. With one last look at her friends, she took flight, with Harbinger grasped in her talons, and disappeared in a flash of fire.

Far to the north at the Storm Farm on the outskirts of Silver City, Kira was in the kitchen making a few potions and salves that she would sell at the market. Without the right potions and salves, some magic could only heal so much. It was one of the things that she did to occupy her time while Diron was away. The income from the sales helped to put a few more things they needed in the cupboards. Kira was strong in magic and a good healer since she was an elven female. Kira heard a sound of a baby crying in the background, causing her to smile.

Dirk is going to be restless tonight, she thought. Dirk being only eight months old, this was a typical night for her. He usually would do this for a few minutes after being put in his crib. Then he would ease off to sleep.

After several minutes longer than usual, Dirk was still crying. Kira began to worry so she went to his room to see what the fuss was about. She slowly cracked opened the door, trying not to get his attention. When the door was open enough for her to see his crib, she was startled by what she saw leaning against it. It made her heart wrench in pain.

"No!" She fell to her knees, heaving with cries of agony. Dirk cried harder after Kira had voiced her pain. What she saw leaning against his crib was Harbinger, his father's sword. Blood was dripping from the hilt. The jewels in the sword were void of light. Kira, shaking and crying, knew the love of her life, Diron, was gone. He had passed to the underworld. She knew this because that was the only way Harbinger would have appeared. Kira cried not just for the loss of her one and only true love, but for Dirk. She knew the burden of being the Chosen had been passed to her son. "He will never know the great man his father was," Kira said between sobs.

Kira thought that Dirk was crying because of the sword. What she did not notice until she got the strength to get up and walk over to comfort her son was a crimson feather in his hand. She dropped her head praying to Marluna. "Goddess, give us strength for that which is to come," Kira said while she reached for the phoenix feather that her son was grasping in his tiny little hand.

She took it, placed it in a silk handkerchief, and put it in her pocket. Kira would give it to him when the time was right for him to have it. Wiping away her tears, she noticed a little irritation around his nose. It must have landed on his face as the sword appeared and tickled his nose, causing the laugh that she'd heard. When she removed the feather, she could see a very small crimson mark on the palm of his right hand. Kira knew that it was left there when the power of the Chosen was transferred. She knew that as he aged, it would take on the shape of a tiny crimson phoenix. The transfer lasted only a few seconds and the power he had just received would lie dormant until the age of awareness was upon him. Thankfully, that was at least eighteen years away and she was glad for that.

Kira let her son grip her finger as she picked him up and nestled him in the crook of her neck. She rubbed his back, calming him down the way she always did and rested her head gently next to his. Tears started falling freely again at the thought that at the beginning of his life, his destiny had already been written. Kira felt comfort, knowing that how he got there was a journey of his own making. The choices he made though would be detrimental to the world. Unlike Diron, Dirk wouldn't have his father's guidance. He wouldn't be there for him. Kira kissed his forehead and he giggled. She eased him back, looking into his eyes.

Little flames were rippling in his emerald, green eyes, an effect of the power he now had. She smiled at him and kissed each cheek, making him giggle more. Kira, her heart still breaking from her loss, took him into the kitchen with her and sat in her rocking chair. She held him close, rocking him back and forth. He slowly closed his eyes and drifted off to sleep. She sat there with him in her arms for most of the night, thinking about the best way to help her son.

The tears had dried several hours as she lost herself in her thoughts. With a plan in mind on how to keep him totally away from his destiny for as long as she could, she placed him on her bed. Kira laid down next to him and snuggled him close to her. She would protect him as much as she could, starting right then and there, she thought, determined. She soon drifted off into the nightmare of living life without Diron.

The Deal

A warm summer breeze blew across the waters of Lake Fire, causing Dirk's hair to blow away from his face. His hair was always a mess, his mother Kira would tell him. He sat with his back up against the old tree at the top of the hill and gazed out at Silver city. It was The Pack's favorite spot. Tab and Linc sat beside him, taking in the scene silently. The Pack was what he and his friends were known as to all of the locals. Everywhere one went, the others weren't far behind. He laughed to himself, thinking how silly the name was. He didn't even know how or when it started. Their days as The Pack would soon be over, he thought. The others would be taking different paths than the three sitting on the hill. At least Dirk hoped so.

He pulled his knees up close to his chest and wrapped his arms around his knees, just gazing at the sight before him. Even though he could hear the boys breathing in the sea air, they were as silent as the gentle waves of the lake. He took in the sights and sounds of the sea birds as they glided up and down on the wind drafts that blew along the port. *It's a beautiful day in the capital of Reygn*, he thought. Reygn was the biggest country in Marona.

He gazed at the giant dormant volcano silhouetted behind the city. A few pillow-like clouds floated through the sky and seemed to circle around Mt. Blazire's peak like a halo. He thought it emphasized the giant volcano's importance. The giant mountain towered over the land as if it were a sentinel standing guard.

The summer was ending, and Silver City was swarming with activity. Silver City was the main place of trade for all of Marona. Dirk smiled, knowing today, the first of the month, was the biggest trade day. Dirk wanted to spend the rest of his life with Tab and Linc, having adventures and discovering new things in the world to sell at the market.

He grinned at the two beside him. They responded only with a nod. Reality for him, though, was that it was the start of a new class year at the school of magic and military academy. The General, his grandfather, wanted him to follow in the family footsteps, going to the school, learning to use magic, and eventually joining the military. But Dirk had different plans. He still had hope for the future that he wanted.

He thought about all the different races that would be there for the start of school. Dirk knew that he and The Pack would watch from this spot as they arrived in the city. The Elves would come by ship and the dwarves would come through the mountain trails. Merchants would flock in from the lands far to the west such as Oak City with their tobacco products and their products made from the ancient oak trees that surrounded their lands.

Dirk could see all of Silver City. The hill was located where they could see where every trade route converged on the city. He could also see the school and academy. They were both located together not far from the palace. Trying to stay positive, he thought about the traders from Korkin with their spices and animal hides. Tailors would buy the hides to make some of the best clothes, especially Mrs. Glan, El and Jonesy's mother. She was a clothes-maker and, from what Dirk knew, she was the best in the land. Her kids were two of The Pack members.

El was the protective mother hen of The Pack, and Jonesy, a big fellow, had saved Dirk and The Pack in many fights. El was nine months older than Jonesy but they were still in the same class in school growing up. He would miss them. He looked over at Tab, who was oblivious to Dirk staring at him. Tab would miss El. Dirk knew how Tab felt about her, even though he wouldn't admit it to anyone. Feeling that his thoughts were starting to betray him, he turned his thoughts back to the dwarves, who would come to trade their building materials. They were excavated from the edges of Mt. Jover, their home. The materials the dwarves brought were usually second-rate. They kept the best grade for their own use. Dirk was taught that the king of the dwarves allowed them to only trade what they couldn't use. The dwarves were very reclusive but still maintained a small amount of trade for access to items they couldn't grow in their mountains or the surrounding lands.

Dirk heard the call of a bird in the distance. It sounded like a battle cry. He picked up a piece of dead grass and put it in the corner of his mouth. He rolled it across his tongue to the other corner of his mouth, thinking about the strange bird cry.

"It must have been an eagle chasing its lunch," Linc said, bringing Dirk's attention to him.

"Aye," Dirk said, turning back to his thoughts of adventure and trading. The traders from Feriah could always be counted on to be there. Their land was to the south of Silver city. They would always bring the best fruits and vegetables. Dirk couldn't wait to see what they would bring this year. A sparkle on a grand building in the distance caught his attention. It was the high temple of Zona. He went there once a week to honor the gods.

The father of one of The Pack members, Gil, was Romus Jamous. He was the high cleric of Zona. The thought of him turned Dirk's smile into a frown. Dirk knew he was cruel and would beat Gil. Dirk had seen the evidence of it several times, but Gil had sworn him to secrecy.

When they first met Gil, he was a loner at school that El felt sorry for. She convinced the rest of the pack to let him join the group. Dirk and the rest of the pack could never say no to their mother hen, so they agreed. Soon though, they had become such good friends that it was soon forgotten why Gil had been admitted into the group to begin with.

Hearing the seagulls fighting over scraps of fish guts caused Dirk to turn towards the port. He hoped The Pack might see an Elf there from Elmwood, trading medicinal products. On rare occasions, they had seen a few of them trading for items that were produced from Mt. Blazire. Dirk really enjoyed seeing the Elves at the market. He was half human and half elven. His only other contact he had with Elves was with his mother. Kira had never told him much about her life before she married his father. Dirk was always curious to learn more about them, so he observed them every chance he could.

Venia and Vanguard merchants would also be there. They were cities from the south that was controlled mainly by King Cray, who wasn't the biggest fan of the north. He and King Jerard didn't see eye to eye on how people should be treated and were usually in conflict.

Dirk would hear The General discussing with his mother the horrible things the Vanguard would do to their people. The thought of the cities to the south always left a bad taste in his mouth. His father had died in the war with the Vanguard when he was a baby. At the moment, there was a time of peace between the two lands. He didn't hold a grudge over something he had very little information on, but he swore to himself that one day he would find out more about his father's death.

He let that thought go. He didn't want to waste any time on that at the moment as he watched the hustle and flow of the market. There were plenty of traders from all the lands flooding in. Travelers came from all corners of Marona, who held no allegiance to anyone but themselves.

"The food." Tab's stomach grumbled as Dirk licked his lips, thinking of the highly sought-after delicacies of the Mere people. Dirk and Linc laughed at Tab.

"Your always hungry," Linc said, matter of factly. Dirk agreed, not getting a response from a smiling Tab. He looked back towards the water, thinking of the Mere city delicacies, such as muscles and exotic fish, that were in high demand. The waters of Mere lake was the only place that these foods could be cultivated. He didn't know how the Mere people did it, but it was one of the things he hoped to learn in his travels.

It also was the only known place that could grow black pearls. These pearls were used in jewelry. Legend said that to own and wear a black pearl would bring good luck. He had never seen one but knew superstition was a hard thing for most people to get past. It was also what made these items so rare.

He could tell a group of nomads were entering into the market because everyone seemed to stop and watch them as they lumbered by to set up their wares. "Nomads," Dirk said and pointed them out to his friends as they followed his gaze.

To the south below Feriah was a vast desert wasteland. The nomad scavengers who brazenly roamed these lands would come across the discarded and long forgotten weapons of battles past and would bring them to trade at the market for needed items for their tribes, such as foods and clothing. The main reason for these battles taking place in such a desolate area was because of Der-Tod. It was said Der-Tod was the entrance to the underworld. The land of Zolun.

Of course, Dirk, like all other Maronans believed in the gods but had never seen one. He believed that the Vanguard used them as an excuse to prey on the areas surrounding their lands. He knew Zolun was the god of the underworld and that he was the son of Zona and Marluna.

There was a rumor that there had been a never-ending battle between the son and his parents for control of Marona. Unfortunately, the races of Marona had not only been the victims of these battles but the tools in the disagreement, whether it was true or not. The childish disagreement made Dirk furious because it had taken his father before he had gotten a chance to know him.

Mr. Little had taught Dirk, Tab, and Linc all about the nomads. Dirk loved working for Mr. Little in the summers at the trading company he owned. This job had been what had made the three of them want to be traders and adventurers when they got out of school. It was almost time to begin their journey.

They had learned from Mr. Little that being a nomad meant they would be constantly on the move so they would need certain things to survive. The monsters and beasts that roamed the nomads lands were extremely dangerous. The nomads knew how to kill most of these creatures, and their hides were valuable trading items. Another one of the things that Dirk, and the boys wanted to learn on their adventures was how to kill these monsters. He knew it was one of the hazards of being nomadic, but it was their way of life. The nomads knew how to handle themselves in those lands and they knew the signs and what to watch out for when traveling to stay safe.

Dirk had heard rumors that King Jerard used the nomads to keep an eye on events in that region. They kept him informed of anything happening that could be a threat to Silver City and its allies. The tribal leader was rumored to be a distant relative of his, but nothing could be proven.

Dirk got up and stretched. He had been sitting here for at least an hour, watching the busy market as he thought of the future. The boys had been there since the break of dawn. "I better head back," he said to Tab and Linc.

"You prepared to take on Kira?" Tab asked, pulling a piece of grass out of the corner of his mouth that he had been chewing on. Linc leaned back on one elbow and looked at Dirk, waiting on his answer.

He smiled at Dirk, "Yeah you better be ready for her because she will be ready for you," Linc stated.

Dirk looked at his two best friends. "I have a plan. Don't worry. In a few days we will be heading off searching for items to trade and building our company." He didn't sound too convincing.

Linc looked at Dirk. "I hope so. I can't stay in this town any longer."

Tab patted Linc on the shoulder. "Don't worry, brother. We will be on our way soon." Dirk confirmed what Tab said and told them he would see them later.

He headed down the hill, leaving his two friends talking about their plans, and he made his way home to face his mother. Dirk knew he was in for a battle with her. He hadn't told Tab and Linc, but he did have a backup plan if he failed.

As he slowly walked toward the Storm farm, the sound of the grass crunching under the weight of each step put him into a trance like state. He took in the colors of the leaves in the forest. The yellows, reds, browns, and greens swirled together, making the forest look alive. The chittering of the squirrels he'd watched earlier came into earshot. They seemed to hear his approach and the excitement in their voices took on a hurried pace. He smiled to himself at the sound. The thick forest surrounding his path home was literally untouched by any race. Dirk and his friends always had adventures to the north of the farm, but they rarely entered the southwest section due to the predators that lived in that area. The animals roamed freely, without worry of a hunter's arrow burying itself deep in their hide.

His thoughts drifted back to the market as his body automatically followed the trail home. He had traveled it his whole life. As he got to where the trail descended deep into the woods, he looked back and waved to his friends up on the hill, who returned the wave. From his viewpoint Mt. Blazire loomed over the city and his friends. He was amazed at the sight of the giant volcano. Silver City sat near the base of Mt. Blazier and was located to the left of Fire Lake.

Dirk had been taught that Mt. Blazier was the reason for most of the country's wealth. It had vast amounts of gold, silver, and iron ore deposits that were mined out of the mountain and used for various items. But these were not the most valuable, nor the only items produced inside the dormant volcano. The mined sapphires and diamonds were the most valuable traded items.

Dirk and Tab and sometimes Linc would trek through the woods that separated the farm from the volcano and hunt for them anytime they wanted, as long as the chores Dirk was responsible for were done. That was a luxury he took advantage of often since the Storm farm was right near the mountain. Dirk knew the gems were the main source of magic in Marona and that the more powerful ones were not found on a regular basis. They were hard to find and one of the main reasons Dirk and his friends to had a lust for adventure. He laughed to himself, thinking of the silly games they would play hunting for fortune and fame.

Kira had taught Dirk that the gems were linked with the worlds source of magic, The Core. He really didn't understand how the gems helped power everything, but he believed his mother. Dirk knew they were used for healing and all sorts of aspects of magic, good and evil.

Dirk continued walking towards the farm. Every now and then, a small mouse or rabbit would shoot across the trail in front of him. He slowed down, preoccupied with watching the animals as they hid from him and ran deeper into the woods. A wolf howled in the distance, eliciting several responses from the others in the area. Dirk stopped, gripping the knife at his side. After a few minutes of searching for any animals that might be stalking him, he continued on his way home. He wasn't too excited about the confrontation he was about to have. He let his mind wonder more on what other items he was looking forward to hunting down when their adventure began.

Lake Fire, he knew, had items of value in it as well. The red fish in the lake were the greatest delicacy in Marona. They were a rare catch and would grow to an enormous size, up to several hundred pounds. The lake was full of all types of fish, but the red fish were the main goal of fisherman. Someone might catch one of those fish once in a lifetime, if they were lucky. The reds, as they were known were highly intelligent. Not in a sentient way, but they were overly cautious about their surroundings. Dirk and the boys had seen one once when working for Mr. Little. A fisherman had caught it and the whole port was in an uproar, trying to catch a glimpse of it. Mr. Little had been the one to buy it, so the trio got to see it before he sent it off to the butcher. Having it cut up into smaller portions, he could sell it for a lot more than he had paid for it.

Lake Fire was attached to all the lakes and rivers in the world, making Silver City the port where everyone would come to trade, whether it be by land or sea. The port had direct access to the market. Obviously, Dirk knew they needed a ship for this because it is where their adventures would begin.

Dirk could see the fence that surrounded the farm ahead of him. Destiny was drawing closer. He didn't mind arguing for what he wanted, but he knew the counter argument his mom would give him would be strong. Silver City Military Academy and School of Magic was where students from all over would come to get their training in healing, battle, defense, agriculture, or just basic use of magic. It covered basically all the areas in which a mage could be trained.

"Your grandfather expects you to attend," is what Kira would say. "It is so important that the leaders of each province send their best and brightest to the school to train."

He let out a frustrated sigh. He knew the majority of students were trained in healing and the basics, but there were a few who were trained as specialists, who focused only on one power. Those students consisted of the Elves from the west. Which to Dirk, was a plus because of his thirst for elven knowledge. The dwarves from Mt. Jover, though they hadn't sent anyone to the school for years. Fork city, Oak City, Korkin, and Feriah would send kids every year to be trained, and occasionally one or two would come from one of the lesser-known provinces and surrounding islands. Dirk felt like he was betraying Tab and Linc by thinking that it might be good to attend for at least one year. It would only be to gain skills and knowledge of the people and their communities. He knew they wouldn't look at it that way though.

The schools were set up for a three-year course that specialized in magical training and military applications. The school year was seven moon cycles long, starting at the end of summer with a thirty-day break in winter and sixty-day break the following summer.

That was the part that bothered him. He didn't know if he could make it that long. Students were there until they graduated, flunked out, or quit. The courses were rigorous and mentally challenging. Only the most gifted were meant to survive all of the training. The leadership courses were the ones that were extremely hard and challenging and the candidates for those were selected after the first year of training was complete.

He passed the barn and sat on an old stump, in sight of the back door to his home. He was still thinking about how best to handle his mother. He couldn't quit thinking about his grandfather either. Dirk knew he owed him everything. Deep down inside he knew what he had to do, he just didn't want to face Tab and Linc. One good thing about going to the military academy was that it focused on army and naval training. This could be an advantage in their travels. With his head in his hands staring at the ground, he made up his mind.

He got up and headed into the house, knowing Tab and Linc were going to be pissed at him, he smiled at the thought that El, Jonesy and Gil would be very happy.

Dirk headed upstairs to wash and change after greeting his mother. He looked in the mirror trying to gain some confidence before the talk he had planned. The reward of growing up on a farm was his above average size and build that he saw in his reflection. He had dark brown hair. Usually tied back in a ponytail. He would wear it over his ears to hide their points in the city. His emerald, green eyes came from his mother.

The towns people always gave him the creeps when they stared. Most people in Silver City knew who he was and were cordial to him, but they still stared. He washed his face before he went to face Kira.

Dirk sat at the kitchen table, rubbing the red mark on his right hand. It would sometimes itch when he was upset. He never understood why it was there, but he had gotten so used to it that it was just a part of his life now.

He stared at it for a minute. It seemed to be growing and taking on a different shape lately.

He looked up at his mother, frowning when she came back into the kitchen. He knew he was a good kid who always did as his grandfather and mother requested but he felt he needed to stand his ground.

"Mom, I don't want to go to that school! You know I have other things I want to do." Dirk said.

"You know why," Kira retorted. "Your grandfather will not allow you not to attend."

"That's stupid Mom. Why do I have to attend anyway? I want to become a merchant trader with Tab, and Linc. You know we've been planning it for years," Dirk said, putting his face in his hands and leaning on the table.

"Dirk, your grandfather has given a lot to us and the kingdom in which we live. It would not do if the grandson of Durkon Storm didn't at least try to follow in his footsteps."

"I know that, but if dad would have been around, I bet he would have let me choose. That school is one of the reasons he isn't here to tell me what he thinks!" Dirk yelled.

Kira stopped washing the dishes and gave him a sad but determined look. "I'll tell you this. Your father was an honorable man and, yes, he would have wanted what was best for you. Maybe not exactly what you wanted, though. He had a high sense of duty and I believe he would want you to at least give it a shot." Tears formed in her eyes. "At least give the first year a try. Your father died in defense of these lands. You may never know how or why. So, in honor of him, you should give it a chance. You may find the answers you've been wanting to know for so long. Do you want to know?" Kira asked, playing on Dirk's curiosity. She knew it was a question he had wanted answers to for years.

"I do, Mom, you know I do. I just know Grandfather wants me to be like him. I don't think I have it in me to be like that. It's a lot of pressure you know. I am grateful for what he has done for us and I do sincerely love him, but I am different. I can feel there's something great out there for me, but I don't feel it's in the King's Guard," Dirk looked down at the table.

"You're right, Dirk, it may not be there for you. But at least when you go to the school, you will be tested for your abilities. With your elven blood, you have a chance for many abilities to appear. There may be powerful magic in you, more than one type, and that can help you, no matter what you decide to do," Kira said. "And if that's the case, you need to be trained properly."

Dirk thought about what he would tell Linc and Tab. Of course, he already had a plan, even before he talked with his mother. Tab he had a backup plan for, but Linc he knew would never go for what he had put in place for Tab. *I'll just have to convince him it is for the best,* Dirk thought. Then with a sound of defeat, Dirk said, "Mom I will go, but remember, one year is all I can promise, ok?"

"Dirk, one year!" Kira said and patted his back. He got up and she pulled him into an embrace. He looked into her eyes and he could see new tears starting to form. He knew he had to escape her hug, or she might figure out she had fallen into his trap. Before he had walked from that old stump to the back door, he had decided that one year would be the sacrifice he was willing to make.

He stepped back from her. "Ok then I'm going to go spend the rest of the day with the pack. Plus, I have to break the news to Tab and Linc."

Kira eyed him. "So, Tab is going to be there?"

"Yes, Mom, you know you love him."

"I do, just make good choices," Kira said.

"Mom!" Dirk embraced her in a hug again and headed out the door to meet his friends where he knew they would be waiting.

As Dirk headed out the backdoor Kira walked over to the kitchen window. A sadness overcame her as she watched him run to the woods. She knew deep down inside that Dirk would be at the school for more than a year. She knew his destiny had been plotted when his father died. She didn't feel it was fair, but their bloodline couldn't be changed, as much as she longed for it to be.

She let out a sigh, walked to the kitchen table, and began to work on some more salves she had been putting off. She thought about what Dirk didn't know. She already knew what abilities Dirk would have. His father Diron, like his father before, was the Chosen and Dirk didn't really have any choice in it. He was the next in line. Kira herself had been a protector once and was a very powerful magic wielder and healer. She thought about the secret she had kept from him about his father's death. She did not want Dirk growing up with more pressure than was needed. It would still be a few more years, hopefully, until his destiny would come into play. She wanted him to be able to make up his own mind when the time came instead of being forced into it. There was very little chance of that. She let out a frustrated breath.

While she was working on crushing some mushrooms into the salve ingredients, a weird feeling came over her to the point that she had to balance herself by putting her hands on the table. A warm sensation of happiness mixed with sadness engulfed her.

"Kira..." a familiar voice whispered.

"What?" Kira asked out loud looking around. In the corner, she saw a shimmering in the air. She just stared in disbelief at what she was seeing. The shimmer moved closer to the table as it formed more clearly. His eyes were recognizable the second they became clear. She had dreamed about those eyes for the last eighteen years.

Kira knew that she was seeing the man she had loved since she had first laid eyes upon him. Diron's ghost just smiled at her and reached out to caress her face. When his hand touched her face, it caused a cool chill to spread across her entire body. Kira instinctively reached to put her hand over his, but it passed right through his to her face. He just smiled at her.

"Kira, the time is at hand my love. Be prepared!" the voice said in a whisper.

"No, he isn't ready!" Kira said, fighting back the emotions her husband's spirit was causing her to feel. The man she loved leaned in closer and peered into her emerald, green eyes. Even though he was dead, his love for her had caused him to reach out to contact her.

"Kira, there are things happening again in the south that cannot be stopped. You must tell my father that they must investigate. Dirk must be ready when the time comes, or all will be lost. Zolun's minions are preparing for his coming. They are deadlier now than ever before. He has more support now. Even though his power to come back is still a few years away, his power is growing stronger every day. He will be more powerful than ever before when he breaks his chains. I'm sorry, my love, but I must go. I will pay dearly for this breach, but I had to warn you."

Kira just stared at him. "There must be another way," she pleaded.

"I miss you, my love, but that is all I can say. One last thing. I feel death pulling me back. There are dangers closer than anyone knows or realizes. Do not trust..." was all he could say before he disappeared, almost as fast as he appeared.

"Wait!" Kira yelled, reaching for the empty spot where her husband had just been. Realizing what she just had been told was very important, she knew she had to be on guard now more than ever. She would tell the General what she had witnessed and been told. Would he believe her? She sighed, put her head down on her folded arms, and began to cry again. She realized that maybe Dirk didn't have that long after all.

The Pack

As Dirk headed out the door, he was thinking, I can make it a year. But he wasn't sure about Tab and Linc. I hope they don't think I betrayed them.

The smell of manure blew on the breeze and hit him as he was crossing the yard to the gate that led to the woods. He wrinkled his nose. "Yes, one year and no more smells from this farm." Dirk's grandfather had retired sixteen years ago, and for his service to the kingdom, he had been given a grand estate with the farm attached to it. He had turned down the estate and told the king that he only wanted the farm. His grandfather was a very humble man. He believed that hard work got a person what they deserved. The king and Durkon had grown up together. When Durkon made the request, the king obliged him. He let him sell the estate and keep the money from the sale to live on and to purchase the things he needed for the farm, such as cows, chickens, pigs, sheep, and horses. He raised the animals for the meat and hides to sell at the market.

Dirk knew this firsthand for he had been the General's main workforce growing up. Along with selling Kira's potions and salves, they made a comfortable living. Dirk, on the other hand, had other plans. Number one was he did not want to work on a farm when he became an adult. He had had his fill of that growing up. He longed for adventure. He wasn't egotistical. He just wanted to make a name for himself, other than living off his grandfather's reputation.

The Pack would be waiting on him, especially Tab and Linc. They would want to know how the confrontation went. The Pack had been friends since primary school. They were all from different backgrounds but had the same thirst for fun and adventure. Tab and Linc were clearly his best friends. Since they had met, their shenanigans had put them in so much trouble. Dirk laughed to himself, thinking about some of the things they had done. *It's a wonder we made it out of primary school.*

Tab was an orphan who had lost his father to the war of the south, just as Dirk had. He had lost his mother a few years later. Tab would always say it was from a broken heart after his father's death that took her. Dirk knew how he felt about the loss. His own father's death had troubled Dirk his whole life as well.

Tab had been raised by the nuns of Marluna, a group of women who followed Marluna's teachings. It was an orphanage that was sponsored by the church. They received their income mainly from selling wool and mutton from the sheep they raised. They also received donations from several businesses and a portion came from the king's treasury. Dirk knew his grandfather had given them part of his land for their sheep. He would take a small portion of the profits each month, mainly because Mother Agnes, the head of the orphanage, had insisted. Truth be told, his grandfather was sweet on Mother Agnes. This was one of the reasons he had given the land to them so cheap. Once or twice a month, he would visit the orphanage to collect his small percentage of the profits.

During this time, he would usually trade it for a nice dinner with Mother Agnes. He told Dirk that he would trade with them just in case they hadn't made enough money for the orphanage. The times that he would collect, he would just sneak it back into their donation box. Dirk had seen him do it once, but he swore him to secrecy. Dirk went with his grandfather once before primary started. That was when he had met Tab for the first time.

As time went on, Dirk would see him at the farm working with the sheep. They would usually send five kids a day along with one of the Sisters of Marluna to work the flock. Mother Agnes would come quite frequently herself. Dirk would go out and talk with him after his chores were done. He usually ended up helping them to get the job done faster so they could talk. They both had similar interests and found they both wanted to be adventurers and travel the land. This was also when they had discovered the connection between their fathers.

With that in common, they became best friends and dreamt of adventure and discovery. Then they started primary school and were in the same classes since they were the same age. Their friendship grew along with their high jinx.

The others that formed The Pack were pulled into their misdeeds a few at a time. Linc was first. He had a talent for mischief. Tab had met Linc at the orphanage where they both lived. Linc was an orphan as well but not in the same way Tab was. Linc had never known his parents. This thought angered Dirk a little. At least he and Tab had one parent, in Tab's case only for a little while.

Jonesy was next. He had a strong dislike for Brock Little, who with his gang of thugs, were constantly terrorizing Dirk, Tab, and Linc. Brock was the son of Mr. Little, the merchant who employed the boys in the summer months. Truth be known, he was jealous of the relationship Dirk, Linc, and

Tab had with his father. This was the main reason that the pack and Brock's group were always getting into it. Jonesy was a big guy with a slight temper, so when he witnessed the gang beating up the boys, he stepped in and put a stop to it.

One of Dirk's fondest memories was the day Jonesy came to their rescue. From that day on, he was in the Pack. His sister, Elyse, joined the group just to keep an eye on her brother, but soon became enthralled with the Pack members and their deeds. Dirk knew she was a rebel at heart, but she was also the responsible one. Then finally Gil started hanging out with them at El's insistence.

Tab was waiting for him. Dirk knew he would be very disappointed with him soon. Tab was a little shorter than Dirk. He was thin with an average build. He had stringy blonde hair, brown eyes, and fair skin. He was very stealthy. Dirk had seen him sneak extra food at school in the lunch line. One time, Dirk watched Tab sneak into the school headmasters office to retrieve their side knives that had been absconded by their teacher. He was always able to sneak into places without being noticed. He had a natural act for blending in. That's what was so great about him.

"What took you so long?" Tab asked. "I felt my hair grow an inch waiting on you."

"You know," replied Dirk. He looked away from Tab, not wanting to tell him what he had committed to. He just kept walking down the trail. Tab grabbed his shoulder to stop him. Dirk did and lowered his head when he turned back to look at Tab.

"You didn't?" Tab asked heatedly.

Dirk took a breath. "Look you know I want to leave tomorrow, but I've been thinking about what kind of an advantage we can gain from being at the school for at least a year." Dirk waited for Tab to respond. He didn't, so Dirk continued. "The people we will meet, the things we can learn from the use of magic, and don't forget the tactical training we can get from the military."

"Awesome, you're just gonna let Linc and me go it on our own for a year?" Tab gritted his teeth.

Dirk took another deep breath. "Well Linc, maybe, but not you. I sort of asked the general to speak on your behalf to get you into school for a year." Dirk didn't want to lose his momentum, so he continued. "Look, I knew there was no way I was gonna get out of going to school for at least a year. Let's be serious here for a moment. The general would have disowned me if I tried and where would that have left Mom?" Dirk was pleading for his friend to understand. He paused and looked Tab in the eye. Tab was looking around trying to stay mad. Dirk knew Tab better than he did himself. He knew he would see the logic. "You know the school allows one local a year to join on a trial basis, to see if primary had it wrong on their positioning in life." Dirk looked at Tab with hope. He knew what Tab's reaction was going to be.

"No! We can't do that to Linc." Tab said angrily, shaking his head and beginning to walk away. Dirk grabbed his shoulder to keep him there. Tab turned back and looked at Dirk. "You know I hate the **military**. Look at what it cost us. And I very seriously doubt I have an ounce of magic in me."

Dirk grabbed Tab's other shoulder, turning him so he could look at his best friend. "I know, I do too, but it's just for one year. Everyone else is going, Gil, Jonesy, and Elyse. Linc can go ahead and set up the business. With the money we saved and with his black-market connections, he's the right one for that, and you know it. That's why I got my grandfather to secretly petition you in. I knew down deep that Mom would make me go at least for a year, so knowing a few of the general's secrets, I convinced him to help."

Tab looked down at the ground in thought for a moment. "Linc is still gonna be pissed. He'll think we're bailing on him," Tab said calming down.

"I will make it right with Linc. He'll understand. I know it. You're the one I was worried about. I'm sorry I didn't tell you, I had to have everything in place before I confronted Mom." Tab smiled. "Hey at least you will be around El a little while longer," Dirk knew Tab's weakness for her. Tab's eyes sparkled a little at the mention of her name. Dirk knew he had him then.

"All right, but what did Kira say?"

Dirk smirked in victory because at that moment he had accomplished two things. He had convinced Tab, and best of all, he had defeated Kira's attempt to keep them apart. "I didn't tell her. Tab, you know she loves you, but the trouble we tend to get into together has her a little worried. If she doesn't find out until the last minute, it will work."

"One year?" Tab asked.

"Yes," Dirk confirmed.

"You have to tell Linc and deal with Kira before we go. I don't want to deal with her wrath."

Dirk pumped his fist in the air victoriously. "You got it, brother."

Kira did love Tab, but she felt Dirk's choices might have been a little different if Tab wasn't in on the decision process. It was like the time the two of them decided to sheer some of the sheep the nuns owned and sell it to buy a fishing boat. They had wanted to start their own trading company at the age of eight. When they got caught, the General had to smooth things over with the nuns and stop them from shipping Tab to a different orphanage.

The General had given the nuns four months of profit to ease the cost of their loss because of what Dirk and Tab had done. Their brilliant plan was to blame it on thieves. They then lost the wool to a cunning young thief in the market who took advantage of them. It was the first time they met Linc.

He was what locals called a wharf rat. He grew up on the docks. He was raised off and on by a group of thieves who trained him to steal and con people from an early age. Dirk was glad Linc was their friend now, but he had conned them out of the wool. Linc felt guilty for what he done to them so a few years later, he helped them retrieve their lost money, two hundred coppers which equaled twenty silvers.

Dirk and Tab buried the money by the hay barn, so no one knew they had it. Linc told them he was forced to take advantage of them, but he hadn't wanted to do it. It was the first time Dirk had heard the name Ram Stockton. Ram was a cutthroat thief who used kids to do most of his stealing. Linc had been rescued from this situation by Mother Agnes. She caught him trying to steal her change purse one day soon after he had conned the boys. She convinced the magistrate to give her custody of him since no parents came forth to claim him. He ran away a few times, but when he was starving from hunger and it had almost killed him one winter, he vowed to stay with her until primary school was over. Linc became one of the Pack soon after.

Tab raised an eyebrow at Dirk, who looked like he was miles away. "What are you thinking about?"

"Linc. I'm sure he'll be fine. He's a survivor and has great instincts." Linc was a medium-sized guy around Tab's height with brown eyes and hair. He was very stocky from constantly pushing his body to its limits when they worked. He was much stronger than anyone would believe. He weighed a little more than average now and always ate like it was his last meal, just another byproduct of being raised on the docks. With his knowledge of stealth and cunning, the boys had learned a lot from him over the years. Tab smiled.

"Yes, you're right. He'll be all right. But you're still telling him."

"All right, I said I will," Dirk replied, patting his friend on the back. "So where is everyone else?"

"Linc said he had some business he needed to take care of, and he would see us later. Gil can't come because his father has him doing things around the church since he will be leaving soon."

"The High Moral one has him busy. Go figure," Dirk said, not surprised. He hated Gil's father because he was one who always judged everyone by their standing in life as a rule. He didn't like the Pack, but he put up with them because of the General and his reputation. Dirk knew his father allowed Gil some leeway with them. Gil was an even keel guy, even though he had a domineering father. Dirk didn't like the way Gil always wanted to please his father to the extreme, but he still had mischief in his blood. That's why they got along so well.

"Jonesy and El are stuck at home as well," Tab told him. Their dad was the main blacksmith for the military. It made them a little spoiled, but Dirk could tell having a dad who worked really hard for a living kept their egos grounded and just short of snobbish. He smiled thinking about Tab. Tab had been in love with El for years. It started in their fourth year of school. Dirk had caught Tab glimpsing her way when he thought no one was looking. Then Tab finally confessed his feelings to Dirk not soon after that. He never followed through with those feelings in fear of causing a rift within the Pack. Dirk told him that it was silly and that no one would blame him. She was tall, physically fit with long strawberry-blonde hair and beautiful waterfall-blue eyes. She had great hand-eye coordination skills. Dirk was astounded at how great she was with a staff and bow. He caught her eyeing the bow every time they were practicing at the general's training grounds.

She privately practiced every chance she could get with the bow. Early one Saturday, El had told everyone she was staying to talk with Kira. Everyone else except Dirk went ahead to Burk's Bakery. El asked Dirk to teach her how to use the bow and he did without any complaint. She picked up on it really fast, which didn't surprise him. He knew El was good at anything she wanted to do. Tab wouldn't admit it, but every time he was around her he seemed to get quiet unless he really had an opinion on something.

Jonesy was a big guy who took after his father. He was tall and towered over everyone, with deep red hair and a beard. He weighed about the same amount as a two-year-old cow. He didn't have an ounce of fat and was very strong thanks to working with his father. He loved to make things out of iron and various metals.

He was always the Pack's protector and Dirk was thankful for his big friend, especially when they got into scuffles with other kids. Jonesy would usually just stand up and the troublemakers, usually Brock and his crew, would back down immediately when they realized he was there. Sometimes people were foolish and thought he was slow, but he could fight. When a fight would break out, Jonesy would go into a trance like state, and it was as if he couldn't stop until everyone was down. El would usually have to get in Jonesy's line of sight to break the trance when this happened because no one else would get close. The rest of the Pack would just stand back and watch, catching anyone stupid enough to sneak up on him. Usually, he did all the work.

One time, they got into ruckus with some older kids, and it was a little more than they could handle. They all came out of that fight with bruises and broken bones. Tab had broken his right arm and Gil had broken two of his fingers. Dirk had some bruised ribs while Jonesy got a black eye, not to mention the ruined tunics that had to be replaced. Linc and El escaped without any damage luckily.

That taught Dirk a lesson he would never forget. Don't go into a fight without two plans: one for the attack and the other for the escape. Dirk hated that it cost the pack two week's worth of detention and a week of hard labor at the farm.

Jonesy loved his sister and was very protective of her. When it came to Tab, though, it was different. He had always known Tab had feelings for his sister and secretly rooted for him. He thought Tab was a great guy.

Dirk was brought out of his reverie by Tab. "So, where are we going today?"

"I say let's head to the base of Mt. Blazier and see if we're lucky enough to find a prize!" Dirk said, heading into the forest.

"Yeah right! Like either of us are that lucky," Tab exclaimed as he followed Dirk. It was a three-mile trek through the woods.

The branches hung low in some areas causing them to duck as they walked. The woods were made up of pine trees, oaks, cedars, and several other types of maples and birch, which gave the forest a wide variety of colors and smells. The variety of trees made the woods hard to see through. The trail was covered in pine needles and different kinds of leaves. The leaves crunched under their feet. The broken branches on the path didn't help either. They always tried to walk without stepping on them but never missed them completely. The sound echoed throughout the forest.

The noise in the forest today is louder than usual, Dirk thought. He could tell there was at least one predator out there, because the wildlife was making a lot of noise. The General had taught the boys that animals tended to do that as a communication method to keep every animal alert to the danger.

Most likely it's a wolf or bear, Dirk thought. Dirk and Tab both looked as they walked through the foliage but couldn't see or hear any predators stalking them. The boys had their bows and staffs with them, just as they always did when they walked through the forest. They were prepared for anything they may encounter.

Dirk was glad when they finally arrived at their usual stone-hunting area. They started looking around the mountain base for any signs of activity from the sleeping giant. They both knew that usually rockslides would provide them with a lot of rocks to examine in hopes of finding sapphires or diamonds. They usually found a lot of gray rocks but always tossed them since they had no value. They had found some small gems over the years, but nothing of great value. Kira had taught them that sapphires and diamonds were used by most people with magical abilities because they had innate power already in them, depending on where they were formed. The closer to the center of Mt. Blazire they were formed, the stronger they were. She also told them that these precious jewels were also formed at Mt. Lune, but it was in the center of a frozen wasteland to the north and people wouldn't go there because no one survived that trip. This didn't make sense to Dirk. How would anyone know if they hadn't been there before? But he didn't think about it too much. He knew one day they would go there themselves and find out.

They searched around for a little while but found nothing but the gray stones as usual. "I guess we'll have to go to the welcoming ceremony then?" Tab asked.

"Well that's where they will reward the winners of the tournament, don't forget. Plus, you know we have to now since we will be attending the school. The general is always there for the grand hoopla. You have to come since you're the one he presented for admission to the school. And who knows, one of us might win one of the competitions."

There was always a beginning of the school year tournament in which any kid in their age group could compete whether they attended the school or not. The events were in archery, axe-throwing, and combat.

"I guess Kira will be there?"

"Yes, Mom will be there. She's really excited." Tab gave Dirk a questioning look. "I think because of the elves that are coming to join this year. I think they're related to her."

"Who is it?"

"I don't know. She said something about her friend she hasn't seen in years and her daughter, Natia."

"Well tell me about her!"

"I can't. Mom doesn't really discuss her family or childhood friends much. You know since she is kind of an outcast for marrying a human. All I know about them is that they are related to the king of the elves."

"Wow that will be interesting. I guess that means your mom is friends with royalty,"

"I guess so," Dirk said without even thinking about it. "Look I…" Tab interrupted him.

"Hey, are we going to look for gems or talk?"

"Look for gems." Dirk replied.

"Then we better get started because now I have to go! Since I'll be attending school, I better get with Mother Agnes on my plans."

"I can just about bet you the general has already informed her."

Tab just smirked. "Yeah I bet you're right."

So, they continued looking a little while longer and found nothing but a few small gems. Dirk decided they would give them to Linc to sell to help set up the business. As they were leaving, they heard a commotion on the mountain behind them. They turned and a rock was rolling down the side of the mountain. It barreled toward them and hit Dirk's foot.

"Ow!" Dirk yelled, hopping around.

"What is it?"

"This rock just rolled into my foot and it hurt."

"Cry-baby." Tab laughed.

"Ok, it's not that small and it's a little heavy," Dirk said after picking it up. They both looked at it for a moment. It was the size of small ostrich egg. They had seen one at Trade Day one year and it really astonished them that an egg could be that big. Neither of them had ever seen an ostrich before so their imaginations had gone wild with what an ostrich looked like. "I'm going to save this and look at it later," Dirk said. The rock was black with what looked like dried lava on the outside of it. It was about six inches in circumference and round but not smooth. It had a very course layer around it. When he got home, he would put it on the shelf in his room and check it out later. He put it in his pack.

The boys were unaware of a shadow that had been passing overhead the whole time they were there, especially when Arial had dropped the rock from her talons. She had successfully timed it's fall perfectly so that it would catch Dirk's interest. The boys were used to shadows in the sky. So, they never noticed it or just accepted that birds were always flying by.

The boys then headed back to the farm, so they could get ready for the next few days' events.

Arial followed the boys back to the farm. She had always kept an eye on Dirk and Tab. Now that Dirk was approaching the age of knowledge, she had to stay closer than ever before to keep her promise. It was her duty to protect the sons of Diron and Thadeus as long as she lived. Several times, she had saved them from trouble, but they were unaware of it. She knew Briar Forest was full of deadly threats that were always looking for an easy meal, wild boars, wolves, bears, mountain lions, and even some dark forces, such as wood nymphs and Ratkes, the half rat half human minions of the Screel, Zolun's evil commander. The Gores, ape-like beasts with enormous strength, were known to be seen occasionally in the Dead Woods, not far from Briar Forest.

They were all loyal to Zolun. Arial kept them at bay though when it came to Dirk and Tab. Arial's ferociousness and power would scare most of them off because they knew she could incinerate them in the blink of an eye.

The wood nymphs had always watched Dirk constantly keeping tabs on him and his friends as their adventures brought them here. Arial knew the creatures would be rewarded by the underworld guardian if they produced a dead Storm or Clearwater. That was why she was never far away from Dirk or Tab.

The Guardian

High above Mount Blazire, while Kira and Dirk were talking, thunder rumbled through the clouds. A lightning storm could be seen brewing anywhere around Silver City. In the midst of it, where only a god could be, Zona and Marluna were deep in discussion.

"I think it's starting again," Marluna stated matter-of-factly.

"Yes, my dear, there is no doubt about it." Zona began to fume.

"What can we do to put an end to our son's madness."

"I do not know. We raised him right. This agreement I've engaged in has stretched my patience. I thought making him guardian of the underworld would please him, but it has only seemed to fuel his lust for power. A decision I wish I could undo," Zona said.

Marluna sighed. "One of these days, I'm afraid one of those Storms is going to kill our son!" She shook her head at the thought. She couldn't change what Zolun had brought on himself.

Zona looked at her, seeing the grief that would cause. "The people of Marona have to be able to protect themselves." Zona shook his head. "Marluna, you know the rules. I can't interfere unless he makes the mistake of interfering himself."

She knew too well what her husband was talking about. "He already has his human minions and those dastardly creatures of his keeping an eye on the Chosen." Marluna said.

"That is true, but Arial is making sure he is safe for now."

"You know her time is running out. She can't become his familiar like she had with the others."

"I know. I have a plan for that, Marluna. Since I am already skirting on the edge of breaking the rules, I believe it's time for Arial to have an offspring, it will be as powerful, if not more, than her," he said with confidence.

"That's the plan, is it?" Marluna said with mirth as she looked into the flaming eyes of her husband.

"Yes. It's time for Arial to give birth to the next guardian of the skies."

"Well, that's good! Arial is getting older, dear," exclaimed Marluna as Zona nodded sadly in agreement. "I have also skirted the rules and have had some say in which a particular elven princess has been raised." She smiled at her love.

"Marluna, you're sneaky. I've always wondered why you seem to disappear every now and then." Zona beamed at his wife. He knew there was no way he could have done this or his power over the realm would have been forfeit.

"Yes. I knew one day they would meet, and he would need her more than ever when he had to face our ill, wayward son. And that time is drawing nearer. Zolun has had plenty of chances to groom his people. It's time we stepped up our game and put an end to his lust for power. I believe he has involved some of his siblings this time, and he has never done that before," Marluna declared.

"Well, we will deal with whoever has been disloyal to us. They're not protected under the agreement like he is. You're right, dear. We need to step up our game and end this." Zona turned to face her.

"Well, I better go."

"Where are you off to?" Zona asked.

"Let's just say the less you know the better." Marluna kissed her husband and then disappeared.

Now that Zona was alone, he set to thinking about the things he had to do. With his mind made up he sent a lightning bolt through the air. Arial was not far away when she saw the lightning. There was the signal. She had been summoned. She immediately headed into the storm.

"Ah, there you are, my dear," Zona said to Arial as she landed on the perch that formed in front of Zona. It brought her almost eye-level with him so he could look into her eyes. "I have one last request of you before I am able to allow you to pass onto the next life." Arial bowed to the god, who she loved and honored. He told her his plan and she accepted it without question. A flaming ball of fire appeared in his hand. It burned brightly for a few seconds before dying down.

Arial looked at his hand where the flame had been seconds before. In its place was a crimson seed the size of an overgrown egg. It had a fiery shine to it. Zona leaned forward and caressed her neck with his free hand. She bent down and swallowed the seed. "You will know when the time is right my dear."

Arial squawked an affirmative and flew back into the storm. Zona soon disappeared as well, going off to put another plan of his into action.

The Hill

The day of the celebration and tournament was here. With dread, Dirk thought about the start of the new school year being a few days closer. He knew at the celebration; the tournament winners would receive their prizes and the new students would be introduced to all the honored guests.

The town was buzzing with excitement. The contingent of elves would soon be arriving at the port of Silver City which really excited him. The dwarves would be coming through the mountain trails. All the other people who weren't already here would be arriving either through the port or through the trails by Lake Fire. A few would come from the southern trails through Feriah.

The market was set up for trading. A whole bunch of activities would be taking place as well.

The younger children had games like corn bag toss and chase the piglets. There would be knife-tossing and log-climbing for the adults. All kinds of food vendors would be there. Dirk's stomach grumbled as he thought about the smoked pig, mutton, fish, mussels, and the variety of breads and sweets like honey sticky buns, taffy, and gum made from tree sap. Delicacies from all over Marona would be there. Dirk couldn't wait to try all of the foods. Tab was excited because he was going to be in the archery contest. He had decided to enter it after their treasure hunt the day before. El was excited about the new students. She hadn't quit talking about it for the last week. She was very interested in meeting new people, learning about their cultures and the contests.

El told Dirk that she had signed up for the archery contest but hadn't told anyone else. Jonesy was looking forward to the axe-throwing contest. Jonesy was gifted at throwing things. Dirk was just excited to see all of the contests. He could enter any of the contests because he had experience in a little of everything.

Dirk thought about the training the General had put him and the pack through for most of their lives. The General had definitely drilled them enough that they would be well rounded. Gil was great with a staff, so he was entering the combat competition. All weapons allowed in the tournament were wooden, so the staff was ideal for that. Dirk and Gil had discussed this extensively. Linc entered the throwing contest since he could use small hand axes. He didn't want to enter the combat because he knew Dirk would probably win that, even though Linc was very good, and could probably match Dirk. The contests started at ten in the morning, and they had decided to meet at their favorite spot before going to the tournament.

The contest would take place at the academy training grounds. Dirk was thinking about the events of the past few days while he and Tab went to meet their friends.

"What are you going to compete in?" Tab asked Dirk.

"I entered the combat tournament."

"Good, I didn't want to humiliate you in the archery contest." Tab laughed.

"The archery contest starts first, then the axe throwing, and finally the combat competition."

As they entered the market, the smell of all the fresh foods drifting through the air made Dirk's stomach growl. Fresh baked breads, baked fruit pies, sticky sweets made with honey, roasted meats, pork, beef, smoked fish, chicken, smoked sausages, roasted potatoes, meat pies, and everything he could think of was for sale. Even his favorite, smoked turkey was there.

"I think I'll grab a quick turkey leg and roll before we head up the hill."

"Yea, I think I'll get some roasted pork myself." Tab said, stopping at a vendor.

They got their food and began walking to the hill. As they walked away from the food vendor area, Dirk looked up at his favorite spot in the city. As they got closer to the hill, they could see Linc, El, Jonesy, and Gil sitting at the base of the tall elm tree.

Dirk smiled as he elbowed Tab. He motioned up ahead. Jonesy was eating at least two chickens, Linc was eating his weight in sticky buns. El was nibbling away at some cheese and bread while Gil was stuffing sausages into his mouth two at a time. They got within earshot of the group and both laughed at the sight.

"I swear, Gil. Where does it all go?" Dirk asked, walking up.

"I don't know; it's tasty," Gil replied, taking a drink from his water skin. Everyone laughed. Gil ate two times more than anyone and never seemed to gain any weight. "Father said I will die of gluttony one day." He had a sarcastic smirk on his face.

Dirk left that alone.

The subject of the high moral one left him looking for anything else to talk about.

"Have any of the visitors arrived yet?" Tab asked, sitting next to Linc.

"There were several arrivals earlier, but the elves haven't arrived yet," Gil said.

"Linc, I need to talk with you about our plans," Dirk said.

Linc looked at Dirk and smiled a knowing smile. "I figured that was going to happen. Your mom?"

"Yes, she made me swear to a one-year trial."

"Well, at least Tab and I can get started?" Linc said.

Dirk looked at the ground, shaking his head. "Well, I sort of got the General to help get Tab in as well. I knew there was no way you would want that." Dirk sounded like he was pleading.

Linc looked disappointed, but then smiled at the two of them. "You're right, so what's the plan?" Linc asked. Dirk really loved that about Linc. He was a fierce friend and could adapt to about any situation change as fast as it came up.

"Nothing other than us two not being there has changed. We will still give you the money to get set up. You just have to hire a few wharf rats to help in the beginning," Tab said.

"Well that will work temporarily, but you guys don't forget about me."

"Never!" they both said in unison."

Dirk walked over and grasped Linc's arms.

"You know we three have been talking about this forever, and I wish you could come with us."

"I know, brothers. Maybe it's for the best that you get the training to protect us, and I'll get the trade routes set up for when you're done with school." They embraced.

"We'll get with you tomorrow and help you get set up, since we don't start school for a few days." Dirk replied.

"That sounds good." agreed Linc.

"You guys have lost your minds," El said to them with tears in her eyes. They looked at each other and grinned.

"You're jealous," Jonesy said to El.

"Well, a little, but I love you guys and I don't ever want to lose any of you. We are family. I just don't want us getting separated," El said.

"We will always be together," Gil added. The rest of the Pack agreed. El pulled the boys into a group hug. Dirk leaned back and looked at each of them.

"This just feels right," Dirk said to his group of friends. They all looked at him. When he spoke, they listened. They didn't always agree but usually followed his lead. "Let's always stay close no matter where life leads us. You are my family. I love each of you and you know it. Let's never lose what we have. We have been through a lot together. I want us to stay close until the day we die." Dirk saw tears rolling down El's face as she looked at the group. Even Gil and Jonesy had to look away, pretending to cough, so no one would see them wiping away the tears.

El hugged each of them, Tab a little longer than the others. "Okay enough of this sappy stuff," Gil said to get away from the subject.

"Let's do what we came up here to do. Who's first?" Tab asked. They had agreed that since this was their favorite spot they would mark it. Dirk had come up with the idea to carve their initials into the old elm tree so that anyone who ventured here from now on would see whose place this really was.

"Ladies first," Dirk said smiling at El.

Linc pulled out one of his knives and handed her the blade. She took it and carved her initials into the ancient tree. "I'm sorry tree. This is just necessary and important to us. I hope you understand," El said as she rubbed the tree beside her initials.

Dirk watched as everyone took turns carving their initials. He was last and when he finished, he stepped back and looked at their work. Everyone had, intentionally or not, carved their initials to make a circle. "It needs one more thing."

Dirk stepped up and, in the center of the initials, added the words 'The Pack' and the word 'Family' underneath that. After that, he stepped back, and everyone saw what he had done. El put her arm through his and laid her head on his shoulder. A warmth filled Dirk.

"I love you, brother," she said.

"I love you too, sis," he replied. "Family is what we are, Family is what we will always be."

The Pack repeated his heartfelt words. They knew how Dirk felt about family. They were all his family, and they knew it. Everyone admired their leader. "All right, enough of this sappy shite like Gil said," Linc said "Let's just relax and see if we can see the elves or the dwarves arrive."

They all agreed and sat around the north side of the tree and gazed out over Lake Fire, talking about nothing in particular.

Dirk, as he had been the day before, sat in his favorite spot. He took a deep breath and smiled. Foods, sweets, and even the fishy smell of Lake Fire drifted through the air. The sounds of merchants pitching their wares were mixed with the sounds of the harbor.

On the horizon, he could see the outline of a ship sailing into view. It looked as normal as any other ship the Pack had ever seen. But the closer it got, the more he could see what it really looked like. It had three masts with three sails each. The biggest sail had a beautiful dark red falcon with yellow tints embroidered around the outer edge of its feathers. The two other sails had a beautiful tree with white bark and red leaves in the center of each sail. The boat, at least one hundred seventy-five feet long and fifty feet wide, was made out of a type of yellowish wood he didn't recognize. It had a curvature to it that looked impossible to make at the angles that it was. Dirk was determined to find out how this ship was made. The elven boat docked at the palace harbor, which was north of the regular port.

A contingent of about fifty elves, consisting of what appeared to be thirty guards in gold elven armor with five-foot-tall Glaives exited the ship. The procession was met by what looked to be the king and his royal guard and ambassadors. The elves were quickly escorted into the palace.

"That was interesting," El said with a look of confusion on her face.

"Yeah that was different," her brother agreed.

"Well, let's head to the academy now that the fanfare is over with," Dirk said to the Pack.

Just as they were heading down the hill to the tournament area, a loud horn sounded throughout the city.

"Dwarves!" they all said excitedly. They stopped and looked to the northwest. Just outside the city, they could see a band of ten wagons with about fifty children marching behind them. They were dressed in leather shoes and breeches. A steel-like mesh covered their chest. They wore metal helmets on their heads with ivory horns sticking out of the sides. They had beards down to their waist and battle axes attached to their backs.

Again, the royal guard was waiting on them at the gates. The wagons were allowed to travel through the gates. Some headed to the palace entrance and were escorted in just like the elves. The rest headed towards the market.

"Just regular people due now, so let's get to the tournament," Dirk said, starting down the hill.

Nemesis

As they were walking through the market El said, "I've got to go see mother before the tournament begins. I'll see you there."

"You better hurry up. I don't want you to miss me win the archery tournament," Tab yelled.

"I'll be there!" she said with a smirk on her face.

"What's up with El?" Tab asked Jonesy.

"Don't even get me started on what's on that girl's mind," Jonesy replied.

"That's something I would like to figure out." Tab grinned. As they were walking past the market towards the tournament area, Dirk heard cackling laughter that made him and the Pack cringe.

"Skylar," Gil growled. Skylar Sweet was the prettiest girl in town, and she knew it. At least she thought she knew it.

She was taller than the average girl with tan skin. She had long blonde hair that was always braided in a ponytail. She was a very athletically-built female with curves in all the right places and she always used it to her advantage. When she wanted something, she would stare at people with her light green eyes, and they were done. Using her looks to get what she wanted in life was a waste in Dirk's opinion. The problem wasn't only her. It was also her boyfriend, Brock Little.

Brock was Dirk's height with dusky black hair. He was in fair shape and had always looked down on Dirk's family. He referred to Dirk and his friends as the Wannabes instead of the Pack. Truth be told he was jealous of their friendship because anyone who was his supposed friend just wanted to be around his money.

Dirk hated the thugs that were always agreeing with everything Brock said. He would use them to do his work and never got his own hands dirty. That was how he kept his reputation clean with the teachers. This held true for Skylar as well. Brock didn't think the General was too bright for getting rid of the estate. He saw that as a weakness. He had told Dirk that one summer.

He was the son of Lord Little, the biggest merchant fleet owner in the land and the lord that had bought the estate from the General when it was up for sale. He was a smart businessman that had started his company in his youth and had turned it into a well-oiled machine. He was a good man, as lords come. He just had a blind spot for his son. Dirk, Linc, and Tab wanted to do what he had done with their business, but that would have to wait.

Gil and Linc had fallen for one of Skylar's tricks the year before. It had gotten them in big trouble with the port guards. She had talked them into stealing a package from one of Lord Little's ships. They had gotten caught by the authorities and when Skylar was asked about it, she lied and said they had stolen it on their own. When Skylar put on her act, most everyone believed her. Again, it took the General to smooth things over.

If Gil's dad had found out, it would have been over for him. The General handled it without the High One finding out. Dirk and the Pack would never forget that.

One day, they would get even with her and Brock for sure. Dirk never found out what was in the package, but at that point, it didn't matter.

"Come on, guys. Let's go around the market so we don't have to see that sprite Skylar," Gil said. Just as they turned to go through the lower city road, they ran into Brock.

"Well, well, well, look guys, it's the Wannabes," Brock said to his cronies. Stew and Larkin both laughed.

"Oh, look it's Brock and his butt sniffers," Dirk said, gritting his teeth and balling his fists.

"So, Stewie, did they decide you were too dumb to join the infantry yet, or did you apply at the stables to be the dung boy?" Linc said, laughing.

"You gutter rat!" Stew threw a punch at the side of Dirk's head. Tab, knowing their tactics, had already started to move. He pulled Dirk back just as Stew's roundhouse was about to connect. Unable to stop his attack, the punch caught Brock in the jaw, knocking him into Larkin.

"Ow! you bloody idiot!" Brock screamed.

"It's that rodent's fault!"

Larkin started to retaliate back as they all moved toward Dirk.

Jonesy stepped in front him. "Now boys, do you really want to get your butts kicked twice today?" Brock and his cronies weren't stupid. They knew they didn't want to get Jonesy riled up at. They would have to surprise him to have a chance.

"No, you're right, stumpy," Brock said to Jonesy, backing away. "You little wannabes will get what you deserve in the combat tournament. If you're brave enough to enter."

"Oh, you can bet your sweet ass we'll be in it," Gil said confidently. Brock and his cronies just laughed as they walked towards the training grounds.

"What in all of Zona's name has gotten into you?" Tab asked Gil.

"I'm just sick of him and his boys. Let's destroy them today."

"Ok, tiger, let's go," Jonesy said to Gil. The Pack all looked at Gil and laughed, then headed towards the training grounds, knowing with confidence that Brock and his boys would pay dearly today.

They walked through the market to get to the academy, talking to everyone they knew as they passed. The streets were crowded so they had to push their way through. Finally, the towers of the academy could be seen over the crowd. The sight gave Dirk a sense of dread. He didn't know why but he had the feeling that something in his life was going to change today.

The Tournament

When Dirk and the Pack arrived at the academy. It was like nothing they had ever seen before. There were men, women, and children all trying to get into the arena to get the best seats that their status would allow. Dirk had been told by the General that the noble part of the arena was roped off so that nobles and foreign dignitaries wouldn't have to fight the crowd. He could see that the royal guard had set up a perimeter around that entrance so that anyone not allowed could be directed to the regular entrances. They were jam-packed into a single file line. There were two guards posted at each entrance.

"The crowd shouldn't be too rowdy. The celebration doesn't start until tonight." Dirk said. They all agreed. "The entrance into the competition arena is through the school." The boys followed him around to the side of the academy. As they walked up to the entrance, they saw a bunch of contestants waiting in line to get in. The line was steadily moving. A lot of people were wearing cloth masks so no one would know their identity. *In case they do something bad*, Dirk thought.

He saw there were several elves up ahead. It looked to him that at least three of them were males and the rest were female. He pointed them out to Tab. There were five dwarves in line as well. They all looked to be male.

Several of the elves were wearing wraps over their faces to disguise who they were. Their faces were covered, but their eyes or ears were visible. The helmets they wore looked like a non-typical military helmet and seemed to fit right on their head like a skullcap. Their outfits were one-piece tunics the color of the forest with greens and browns swirled together.

The boots they wore were almost knee-high and they wrapped from their feet up to their knees around the legs. They were made of what looked like a soft leather with a type of flexible leather padding on the bottom. Three of the elves had katana's on each side of their hip. One carried a scimitar type blade, and the others had a glaive, like the ones that entered the port had been carrying.

"Did you see El?" Tab asked no one in particular. They all shrugged.

"Don't worry, she'll be here to see you embarrass yourself," Jonesy said, slapping Tab across the back.

Standing in front of the guys were the five dwarves. Dirk edged to the front to get a better view. They came up to Dirk's chest in height, wearing rough leather pants and vests. They had on wool shirts with padding in the arms and legs, and boots made of thick leather, good for hiking. They carried battle axes with dark wooden handles strapped across their backs. They weren't wearing the helmets that they had worn previously.

"Hey Gil, isn't the tournament wooden weapons only?"

"Yes, why do you ask?"

"Well I'm seeing a lot of weapons being worn by the contestants."

"Volar goes nowhere without his axe," said a deep voice behind Dirk. Dirk turned back around to see who was talking to him. He looked down. Staring up at him was one of the dwarves.

"And who is Volar?" asked Tab.

"I am Volar, human," said the dwarf gruffly.

"No offense," Dirk said quickly to diffuse anything from happening.

"None taken, human."

"I am Dirk, and this is Tab, Jonesy, Linc and Gil. Nice to meet you," Dirk said, holding out his hand.

"Good day to you, young man and friends" Volar, said shaking Dirk's hand and then bowing to them.

"Is it your first time in Silver City" Gil asked.

"Yes, it is. I have never been west of the Mt. Jover, nor east of Lake Monte." Volar said and laughed.

"So basically, you have never been anywhere?" Gil asked.

"Well I've been here, now haven't I?" Volar said.

"I really like you, friend," Dirk told him, laughing.

Volar smiled at Dirk. "This is Jangoo, Raga, Thelgra, and Fernen." All of them made a fist and crossing their arm over their chest, bowed as Volar talked to the group. They all shook hands and continued talking as they moved closer to the entrance.

Volar told Dirk about their adventure across the mountains and around Lake Fire. He told them about the wild animals and the things they had encountered on their travels. He told of the glow of Silver city at night from across Lake Fire.

"Did you travel across any of the water?" Dirk asked.

"No way, the closest to water we want to be is a water skin." Volar said with distaste in his voice. "We dwarves do not like being on the water. We'd rather walk through the underworld than cross any water." The Dwarves, biggest fear was dying in water. "Garga would not let us enter the Great Mountain, the Dwarven paradise, if we perished anywhere other than under a mountain or in battle."

Dirk knew Garga was the god of the dwarves, Zona's little brother. It was said that he was born inside Mt. Blazire and formed the other mountains of the world. The last and greatest, other than Blazire, was Mt. Jover. Home of the dwarves. His creativity was only paralleled by Zona himself. It was said that his tears were what had formed the mythril, the precious metal dwarves used to create their greatest weapons and armor. It was only found in Mt. Jover. Mr. Little had taught the boys about their beautiful cities of stone and marble.

They had a few farms at the edge of the mountain entrances for their goats and wheat fields. Wheat was their main staple next to goat products, such as meat, milk, and cheese. They used the hides to make their clothing. Their hunters would go out into the forest by Lake Monte, hunt for wild game and work the fish traps they set up in the lake. But that was it.

He taught them that the dwarven traders would go to the trading post by Mere city, a city-built half in Lake Mere and half on land. It was the home of the mere people. They would trade for other goods, such as medicines and different types of food and clothing materials like silk, wool, cotton, and leather.

"I like your axe," Jonesy said.

"Thanks" Volar replied.

"What's it made of?" Linc asked.

"Dwarven secret" Raga said with a growl, eyeing Linc.

"Now Raga, we are going to be sharing education and possibly battles with these men. There is no need to keep all secrets. We don't have to tell them how it was made," Volar retorted.

"You're right, kin's son, my apologies."

"What's a kin's son?" asked Gil.

"Just a name we have for the son of a clan leader. All I can say is that I am responsible for all their actions, good and bad," replied Volar.

"Wow. Wha…" Tab started to ask, but Volar held up his hand to stall anymore questions.

"That is a question I can't reveal the answer to. Maybe one day" Volar replied.

"Ok." Dirk held up his hand to the Pack. "So, what are you all competing in today?" he asked the dwarves.

"Combat and throwing of the axe" Thelgra answered.

"And you?" Jangoo asked.

"A little of everything. Gil and I will be in the combat, Jonesy and Linc will be in competition with you in the throwing of axes, and Tab will be in the archery contest." Dirk replied.

"Sounds like the archery is starting. We better get a move on then," Tab stated.

"Don't worry. You know, it's by age group so your group will be last." Jonesy said. Tab just shrugged and nodded.

"So how does that work?" Jangoo asked.

"Each year students, or anyone of that age, can compete against each other in the contest, usually about thirty for each age group. They start each event grouped in twos. They compete until there is one winner. The winners receive an award for winning. A special elven made bow for archery, supposedly made of white hickory which is said to be the best wood for bows. A set of throwing axes for the throwing contest. They said they were made by the dwarves."

"Aye they are. We brought them with us on our journey here," Volar said.

"A sword and shield is given to the combat winner, made here in Silver city." Dirk replied.

"Good, I can't wait to get started!" Volar replied as the line began to move forward.

Dirk and Volar continued to talk about each other's lives the rest of the way to the entrance. The dwarves, it seemed, were very much like them in a lot of ways. Ambitious and wanting adventure, especially Volar. He seemed to have something to prove, or someone to make proud.

Once inside the arena, Dirk led the group to the stands at the left where everyone competing in their age group was sitting. He looked out over the arena and could see that it was laid out in a square about one hundred fifty feet wide by four hundred feet long. He could see the king and the dignitaries were seated on the right side of the arena in the stands. The other three sections were set up for contestants on the end by the academy that he was in and the other two were for the rest of the townsfolk who came to watch the competition. The judges were sitting in bottom left-hand corner of the king's area, close to the contestants.

By the time they got into the tournament, it was already the finals of the twenty-year-old archery competition. There were only two people left. A human female, and male. The female was slender and tall. She was wearing soft light tan leather pants and a turquoise silk shirt. Her blonde hair was tied in a double braid that wrapped around the top of her head and met at the back converging into a single braid. Dirk recognized her as Princess Anastasia. He knew her well. They had grown up together. With the general always going to the palace on business for the king, Dirk would usually accompany him. Anastasia and Dirk became friends, always getting into trouble when he was there. Dirk laughed to himself at the memory. He was aware that everyone in Silver City knew her on sight. She was one of the most beautiful girls in Marona, the youngest child of King Thurmond and Queen Thea. She was a last-year student at the school.

The male was Kal James. He was over six foot with jet black hair. He was wearing a forest green tunic and matching pants. He was very muscularly built. Dirk knew Kal and Anastasia had been competing against each other since they had first arrived at the school. Kal's father, Kal senior, was a hunter in Fork City. He wanted Kal to become a military man to secure his future, the General had mentioned one day while talking with Dirk about potential leaders in the new classes. Dirk could see that Kal, and Anastasia were close by the way they were looking at each other.

Dirk sensed the restlessness of the crowd. A slight breeze blew through the competition grounds, kicking up small dust devils that quickly evaporated in the wind.

Kal stood, taking in the crowd. He smiled at Anastasia. She smirked back at him. "So, Stas, just you and me again"

She looked at Kal, glaring. "You know I hate that name."

"Yes, I have to do something to get under your skin, so I'll have a chance," he said with a wink.

"Don't even pretend you don't think you'll win."

He smiled at her comment. "Good luck"

"And to you," she replied and winked at him.

Dirk watched the two banter back and forth. He then listened as the judge explained the rules. The contest final was one shot each at three hundred-fifty paces. A gold coin with a hole cut in the center had been placed on the target's center. The person to hit the closest to the center of the hole would win.

Tab pointed out that the arrows they were using were made from pine. "If the arrow hits the target wrong, it will bounce off and not stick. That shot will take great marksmanship to score perfectly with that type of arrow." He also pointed out that Anastasia was using a bow made from ash wood with a silk string. It made it easier to pull back. The flexibility made it more accurate. Kal was using a yew tree bow with soft leather string. "It's a little more durable and gets longer distance due to the tension needed for long distance shots," Tab explained to the dwarves. "They will both shoot at the same time once General Harkin gives the go-ahead. General Harkin is the headmaster of the military academy."

The dwarves took in everything Tab told them. Dirk, like the crowd, was getting really excited. He knew they all loved Princess Anastasia. She was always helping in the city with the orphanage and helping the needy whenever she wasn't at school or out on patrol with the military.

Dirk had witnessed firsthand that being a princess had its perks. She was able to go out with the military when her brother Prince Thelon was on patrol. He was captain of the guard. Their father sometimes would let her go with him.

Dirk quieted Tab down as General Harkin stood up and waved his hands to the crowd. "Archers, to your mark!" Both Anastasia and Kal stepped up to the line with their arrows nocked, looking at the ground. "Raise your bows." They both looked up, bringing their bows to their desired angle. The crowd went silent, as if holding their breath. "Pull and aim!" the general bellowed. They both pulled back to the desired tension, adjusting the angles of their arrows. Dirk thought he could hear the sounds of an eagle in the distance. *The trees shaking with the wind was like a challenge to the competitors*, Dirk thought.

"Release!" the general shouted. The thrumming sound of the arrows being released broke the silence. The whistling sound they made through the air echoed throughout the crowd. As if they were ordered, Dirk and the entire crowd stood up as one, trying to get a view of where the projectiles would hit.

Anastasia's arrow hit the target a millisecond before Kal's. It was a perfect shot, right in the center of the coin. Then Kal's hit. Right in the center of his target. The crowd erupted into applause. The opponents both looked at each other and laughed. The judge on the field went to the targets to examine the contestant's shots. He wrote down their markings on each of the contestant's score cards.

Dirk watched as the field judge took the scorecards up to the judges in the stands to confer his findings with them. He watched the brief discussion that took place. The general, after conferring with the judges, stood up. "Well, this has never happened before," the general said over the crowd. Usually only one person would hit the target center.

If they hit the target at all from that distance, Dirk thought. The closest to the center would usually win.

"It seems we have a tie," Dirk, along with the crowd, went crazy, chanting their names. Anastasia and Kal both waved to the crowd and bowed to the king, who had a big grin on his face as he stood up and clapped. All the visiting dignitaries were congratulating him.

Kal walked over to Anastasia. "That was a great shot."

"Yours wasn't so bad either," she said, smiling at him and squeezing his hand. Kal held her gaze for a moment. He whispered just loud enough for her to hear.

"I love you, Your Highness."

Anastasia stepped a little closer to him, holding his gaze as well. "And I you, my love." That moment for them probably seemed to last for ages, but only mere seconds had passed. They broke their grasp and waved to their still-cheering fans. They stood and waited on the final announcement.

Dirk and the Pack were sitting in the top row of the contestant section, cheering with the crowd. "Isn't she the best?" Gil said to them all.

"Oh, wake up, silly idiot. You don't have a chance," Linc said.

"Yea, she's way out your league," Tab replied.

"Come on, guys, she's always nice to me when I've been around her."

"Well, isn't it the job of the princess to be cordial to all of her father's guests?" Dirk said, laughing with Linc.

"Well one can dream, can't he?" Gil said to no one in particular.

"Well, my young friend, I think that the princess is already taken, by the look that passed between her and her competitor," Volar said to Gil. They all nodded and slapped Gil on the back, laughing. "That was truly two great shots with those little sticks."

"Yes, no one has ever done that before that I know of," Dirk replied.

"So, what will they do?"

"Don't know. Look. General Harkin is getting ready to speak."

"The judges have decided, with the approval of the king, that we declare you both champions of this year's archery contest for the third-year student age group."

The crowd erupted into cheers and applause, once again chanting Kal's and Anastasia's names. They both looked surprised and happy, sharing a brief hug. The crowd, seeing this, really went wild. Dirk had heard rumors around town that when Anastasia was out doing her charity work with the city's less fortunate, Kal was usually around to help. Rumors of their relationship were abundant, but nothing was ever formally said.

"See Gil, the rumors must be true. You don't stand a chance!" Jonesy said, pointing to the princess.

"Just forget about it. You will see one day." Gil said, waving his fist at Jonesy, who was still laughing.

Up in the noble section of the stands, the king couldn't help but notice the close hug between his daughter and Kal. *Kal is a good man but not of royal blood. I will have to find out more about these rumors I have chosen to ignore*, he thought to himself.

After that, Dirk and the Pack's new friends watched as the nineteen-year-old archers competed. There was no drama in this group. Jake Fisher won that age group. Though he did not hit the center of his target, he was the only one to even hit the target from that distance. His father was Lord Fisher, one of the king's counsel.

Dirk and the group watched as the first three rounds of the eighteen-year-old age group archery contest went by quickly. Tab won his rounds. Larkin made it through his. Skylar and Sylvie were out in the first round. The semifinals were down to Tab against Larkin and one of the female elves against a female whose face was hidden by a purple wrap.

Dirk knew her the instant he saw her eyes. For the semi-finals, one had to shoot from two hundred feet and hit the stem of an apple placed in front of the target. The ladies went first. Dirk watched as the elf shot and hit the apple in the center instead of the stem.

"Wow, that was a great shot."

"Yes, but she hit the apple, not the stem."

The mysterious female in purple shot next and clipped the apple stem in half. Dirk smiled as the crowd went crazy. That was the first time in many years that anyone in first-year had done that.

The elf bowed to the girl in purple and, in a melodic voice said, "That was an excellent shot. Good luck to you!"

"Thanks, that means a lot coming from you." Dirk knew that voice. He noticed Tab trying to get a closer look at the mysterious girl.

Tab, leaning against the wall next to the contestants, said to Dirk "Have you seen El yet? I'm getting worried about her."

"She's here somewhere, I'm sure of it," Dirk replied with a smile on his face.

"You'll be fine without showing off in front of her," Jonesy said, laughing. Then they laughed together.

I just feel better when she is around, Tab thought to himself, not wanting to share that with her brother.

"Good luck," Linc said to Tab.

Larkin was first up. He was using the same yew bow Kal had used. He walked up to the line and shot when General Harkin had said. The arrow hit in the top right-hand corner of the apple. The crowd applauded. "Beat that, orphan scum!" Larkin whispered to Tab. Tab glared at him as he walked by. Brock and his cronies had always been good at keeping their misdeeds quiet and sneaky. They had the reputation of being good kids, but the Pack knew their secrets.

One day, dirt bag, all of Silver City will know just how scummy you are, Tab thought. Tab was using the ash bow he had gotten from the rack. It was not the same one Anastasia had used but very similar. He slowly walked up to the line, took a deep, slow breath, and pulled back the string after General Harkin announced for him to aim. He took another deep, calming breath and released the arrow. The crowd went silent and stood up to see the result. After a collective gasp, they all broke out into applause. Tab had cut the stem in half with his shot.

"Well, well, that's two in one day. Great shot, young man!" General Harkin announced. Tab was excited, not just from hitting the shot but from seeing the expression on Larkin's face.

Larkin had a look on his face of disgust and disbelief and skulked off without saying a word. The Pack was clapping and chanting Tab's name. Dirk watched the contest crew quickly get the field ready for the final contest.

"Good luck to you both," General Harkin said to the two finalists.

Tab looked to the mysterious girl beside him, "Good luck!"

She nodded back to him without a word. They both walked up to their marks. When the general gave the command, they released their arrows at the same time. Tab's hit the target first but was two inches below the coin. He quickly looked at the other target, but the crowd had already let him know what he would see. The mysterious girl's arrow had flown true and hit right in the center of the coin, just as the princess and Kal's had. His shoulders slumped in defeat.

The crowd was still going crazy in the background when the mysterious girl walked up to him. "That wasn't a bad shot for an orphan boy." she said, her voice filled with laughter. Tab knew that voice. He had heard it in his dreams many nights. He looked up into her waterfall blue eyes. "El?"

She nodded and took off her head wrap. "Yes, it's me."

Tab hugged her. "I didn't think you were here."

"I didn't want you all to know it was me if I did bad," she replied.

"We would never think that El. You were awesome! I can handle losing to you but at least I beat that ass, Larkin."

"I know I wanted to come and hug you, but I had to keep in disguise."

They walked over to the wall to wait for the announcement of the winner. The Pack was at the wall waiting to congratulate her and to tease Tab for losing to her. He took it in all good fun, laughing with them.

General Harkin cleared his throat to quiet the crowd. "Well, congratulations to Elyse Glan, our winner of the eighteen-year-old archer group. We look forward to great things from you, my dear. That was truly an amazing shot."

"Thank you, General." El said, bowing.

"And you, young Clearwater, that was a very impressive shot yourself. And to all the competitors, great job. Now, let's get ready for the axe-throwing competition." General Harkin turned to the crowd.

Dirk eagerly waited for the set-up. Jonesy, Linc, and all of the dwarves would be competing. Dirk looked over at Brock's group and he could tell they were planning something. They kept looking the Packs way while in deep discussion.

"Guys, we need to keep an eye on them," Dirk said, pointing discreetly towards Brock.

"They look like they're up to no good," Linc said. They all agreed. The general announced the throwing contest was ready to begin.

"Good luck Linc and Jonesy." El said, going to sit with Dirk, Tab, and Gil.

"Thanks," they both said.

They watched as the throwing competition went by pretty fast. The third-year axe competition was won by Lance Gains from Feriah. Second-year was won by Noah Macklin from Fork City. He was Kal's second cousin. First-year's first round went good for the pack and the dwarves. Dirk watched as Jonesy beat Stew, even after Stew had put some kind of oily substance on Jonesy's axe handle. The judges missed their high jinx, as usual, but Jonesy saw the handle before picking it up and wiped it off on his shirt tail.

The Pack cheered for Linc when he beat out Jarrod Gaines, a local from Silver City. They watched as the dwarves won their matches. The quarter finals had Linc facing Volar. Volar beat Linc by half an inch. Dirk and Tab congratulated him anyway. Jonesy won his round against Jacko Jenkins. The dwarves lost three of their matches, leaving Volar and Raga facing Jonesy and Brock in the semi-finals.

Raga, unfortunately, didn't see the slippery substance on his handle and before anyone could warn him, he threw his axe, missing the mark by three inches. Brock was one inch off the mark, making him the victor. Raga walked off, muttering to himself that vengeance would be his and sneered at Brock, who was laughing. Jonesy's and Volar's throws were both dead-on, with Volar edging the mark a mere quarter of an inch closer to the center. Jonesy was disappointed but happy with his performance.

Dirk made Jonesy sit with them to watch, even though he was mad at himself. "You did great, big guy," Dirk told him. Jonesy finally agreed. Dirk turned back to watch the finals. It was Volar against Brock.

"You can go first, my slippery friend." Volar said to Brock with disgust in his voice.

"Thank you, short man," Brock said.

"I am no man, you…" Volar was cut off by one of the judges who stepped between them because Volar was rapidly approaching Brock.

"Now contestants, this is a friendly competition," the judge said.

"Yes, you're right. Forgive my impatience with smaller-minded people. I am ready," Volar replied, stepping back.

"You may begin," General Harkin announced. Brock stepped up to the line first and threw his axe. It hit one quarter inch from the mark.

"Yes!" Brock shouted, pumping his fist in the air at his band of cronies. They were applauding and shouting unpleasantries to the dwarves, who were being restrained by Jonesy and Gil.

"Let them talk because that is all they are, talk," Dirk said to the dwarves.

"All right, there will be time to deal with them later." Raga said. The Pack and the dwarves began chanting for Volar.

"Garga, steady mine hand," Volar said in prayer with his eyes closed.

"Hurry up, short man. I want to get my winning celebration started." Brock whispered so only that Volar could hear him. Volar took a deep breath and released his frustration. He walked up to the line. In the background, he heard the order from the General. "Throw."

Volar released the axe with a lot of force. It whistled through the air and hit the target dead center. The Pack and the dwarves went crazy in the stands. Brock and his goons were mad and demanded a remeasurement because they didn't believe it was dead-on. Dirk watched as the judges did the measurement again just to appease them. It was dead center.

Brock and his crew cursed, yelling back at Dirk and the dwarves. "You will get what you deserve in the combat competition!"

"Yeah, yeah, we'll see!" Tab yelled back. General Harkin announced Volar the winner and the crowd cheered, much to the dismay of Brock's group.

"Let's get the field ready for the final contest," General Harkin told the judges.

The Pack and the dwarves congratulated Volar as the academy crew began to get the field ready for the next competition. "I wonder why the elves didn't compete in the throwing contest?" El said to no one in particular. She was still pumped up from winning the archery contest.

"They do not like axes." Raga explained. "The elves feel they are one with the forest, so they don't harm any trees without permission from the trees themselves. They mainly use fallen wood or wood given from the trees for their fires and weapons."

"I didn't know they were that close with nature," Tab said.

"Yes, it is their culture. A lot of their practices are mysterious, but every race in the west knows of their feelings towards trees."

"Okay, let's go see who is battling who in the combat competition," Gil said as they walked towards the brackets.

Dirk read aloud the combat scoring rules for the contest. "A total of ten points to win each contest. You get five points for a fake killing blow to the heart or the back of the head. Two points for anywhere else. You can lose two points for illegal blows to the crotch, face, or any area that could actually harm you. Using dirt or anything to blind your opponent while competing is illegal as well." The group listened to him and then walked up to the competitor's bracket.

"Well look at this, Volar," Linc said. "You get first shot at Brock in the competition."

"Ah, Garga smiles on me," Volar replied.

"Looks like I get Stew," Gil said looking at the brackets.

"Volar, are you the only one fighting in the competition?" Tab asked.

"I am the only one in combat today. We don't want to show all of our best-kept secrets today," he said, laughing.

"Dirk, you get Red Granger first," Tab said, looking at Linc and laughing.

"Hells," Dirk said, thinking he was about to lose in the first round. He watched Tab and Linc. Evidently, they thought so as well based on their reaction.

"What's he about?" Volar asked, bringing Dirk's attention back to him.

"Red is a big fellow and very good with a sword. He has a heroic reputation. He fought off a bunch of thieves that were attacking innocent people in Feriah. They were robbing the old and weak while they traveled between settlements. Red was traveling with his grandfather when the thieves came upon them and attacked. They say he beat back five bandits at the same time to save his grandfather."

"Well, that's impressive. Good luck master Storm." Volar replied, patting him on the back. Dirk frowned.

"Hey look at this. The elves are competing in the tournament. Three of them entered and it looks like Larkin is getting one of them in the first round. Her name is Nat S," Gil said.

"That's a weird name," El said.

"They seem to be very secretive, especially with their faces being covered. This should be very interesting," Dirk replied.

"It's about to start. Let's go watch the third-and second-years before it's our turn. We might learn some moves," Gil replied. They all agreed and headed back to their seats.

Dirk watched, amazed, from the stands. In the third-year finals, he got to see two swords versus a sword and shield. Princess Anastasia had gotten to the finals with twin wooden sabers, where she faced Raiden Finbar. Raiden was from Pineral. He was Kal's best friend. He used a sword and shield. Dirk heard Raiden promise Anastasia that he would go easy on her in a joking manner. Dirk saw a look in Anastasia's eyes that he knew well. Her resolve would take it as a challenge. Then he watched her beat Raiden in three masterfully executed strokes in under five minutes. First one to the right thigh which caused him to protect too low, then two quick fades to the right and a quick jab to the heart. The last move was beautiful. He charged at her, striking with his sword to her right side. She dodged it, then hit his leg as he finished the move.

This caused him to fall to the ground. She swiftly swung her left sword to engage his shield, then hit the scoring point with her other sword over the heart and then spun in a backwards summersault away from him.

She landed gracefully with a smile. Dirk just shook his head in amazement.

The crowd went crazy again and a humbled Raiden got up and he bowed, congratulating her.

"My princess, as usual, your grace and prowess amaze me," he said before he walked off the combat area. Dirk listened as General Harkin announced Princess Anastasia the winner.

Soon after, they began the second-year competition. Ronan Quinn from Oak City won his year. He was masterful with a sword, defeating one of the Weather twins. Patrice had tried to use the duel sabers, as Princess Anastasia had done, but she had been unsuccessful. It was a close match, coming down to who scored the final blow. Patrice tried a feint and was caught off guard when Ronan stepped into her before she could complete her move, scoring the final heart jab.

Dirk decided to remember that move so that he might one day use it. The crowd was applauding as General Harkin announced for the final competition to begin. Dirk decided to go out to the warmup area to loosen up and stretch before his match began.

Dirk got back in time to see the first round with Gil beating Stew after two solid knee strikes and a rib jab and finishing with a tap to the back of the head. Tara Silk, one of the elves in the competition, beat Sylvie by sweeping her legs on the final move and landing a jab to the heart.

Dirk watched the match between Nat S, one of the mysterious elven females and Larkin with fascination. It started out with Larkin getting seven points pretty fast through brute strength. He rushed in with his shield in front of him forcing her to use her dual blades to catch the assault and leaving him free to score a heart jab. He then quickly spun, catching her in the right thigh with his sword. Catching his rhythm, she flipped back to the amazement of the crowd.

Squatting in a challenging position, with her left leg bent back behind her right with her swords readied in front of her, she rose gracefully and moved towards Larkin spinning her swords in opposite directions. With a shocked look on his face, Larkin tried the first move again and stepping in. Nat spun her left leg around, hitting him in the arm with such force that it caused him to lose his shield. She quickly jabbed him in the heart. and followed up with a tap to the back of the head with another spin in the opposite direction.

Immediately after the head tap, she made the winning score with both blades hitting him over the heart again.

Larkin had to be dragged off the field by the judges because he was complaining that her moves were illegal. The judges affirmed her moves were not illegal and announced her the victor.

A couple of the pairings were regular army cadets against each other. In a match between locals, Landis beat Gregor. River Cask, a tavern owner's son, beat Burt, who was from Korkin. Then two of the elves faced each other, Aarie Frair against Sirien Sleigh. Sirien was the victor, though the competitors were evenly-matched.

Dirk was amazed at how Volar beat Brock hands down using a wooden combat axe and shield. Brock had used a regular wooden sword and shield but was no match for Volar's strength. Brock had kept swinging and missing. It looked like Volar was teasing him to attack. Volar repeatedly pounded Brock's shield, weakening him then score on Brock's legs and arms. Saving the winning blow to the back of the head, he knocked Brock to the ground and sent his helmet flying. Brock and his crew again complained that it was an illegal hit, but since it was the back of the helmet, it was ruled legal.

Dirk was close enough to hear Volar say, "Nice match, small human," as Brock was walking off the field. Volar smiled.

Dirk was ready by the time the final first-round match came around. It was him against Red. Dirk had decided to go with twin swords in the first round. He felt the shield would slow him down and he wanted speed against the big guy from Fork City. He kept his eyes locked on Red as they bowed to each other. They prepared for the battle, waiting on the announcement. Then General Harkin announced, "Begin!" The words echoed through the crowd.

He could tell everyone was excited to see him in competition. His father had never lost a match when he was at the academy so they were anxious to see what his kid could do.

"Let's go Red!" shouted one of the Fork City kids. The pack couldn't let that go without adding their own shouts of support.

Dirk smiled as he and Red circled each other in the center of the arena, sizing each other up. Red made the first move. He feinted left and came around with a circling swoop at Dirk's chest. Dirk caught the swing with both swords. A loud thump echoed through the arena almost breaking Dirk's hold on the swords.

The force of Red's strike probably would have broken my ribs if it had landed, he thought. He was straining to hold the swords in position. He relaxed his legs and rolled back with momentum from the swing. His arms shook as he stood up. *My swords won't survive another hit like that.*

He went on the offensive, moving in, while Red prepared himself for what he thought Dirk was going to do. Dirk moved swiftly, swinging both blades at his shield to get Red off balance. Red tried to back up from the attack, but Dirk was bombarding him with strikes so Red had to use both sword and shield to block them.

Dirk's strikes kept coming one after the other and he was starting to get winded, but he kept attacking continuously. Finally, one hit caught Red on the top of the left shoulder, scoring Dirk two points. Elated that he had finally scored a hit, he took a step back and slowed down his relentless attack to catch his breath.

"Oh hells!" Dirk realized it was a mistake. Red, seeing him slow down, pushed his attack stroke after stroke, left then right. Dirk missed one of the strikes and Red scored a fake killing blow to his chest, knocking him to the ground. If it hadn't been for the practice armor he was wearing, it would have seriously hurt him. Dirk quickly picked himself up off the ground and settled into a defensive stance. "Good one, big guy."

Red just shrugged off the compliment, glaring as he moved to attack. Now it was five to two in Red's favor. Dirk moved to the left as Red turned. Dirk scored a quick two-point thigh hit. Red, reeling from the fact that he had been hit, started his frontal attack again, scoring a two-point hit on Dirk's right arm. *Seven to four now,* Dirk thought.

He took a chance and charged Red, catching him off guard. Red went to block the strike, but Dirk rolled to the side and scored another thigh hit. *Seven to six now.* Dirk rolled to his feet as Red was responding with a thrust to the heart. Dirk deflected the thrust, but Red still scored a hit to the left arm.

Nine to six now. Next points could win, Dirk thought, trying to see a weakness in his defenses. Both of them were sweating and out of breath as they circled each other again. Red was breathing so loud the crowd thought he was going to pass out.

"You ok there, big fella?" Dirk asked Red, trying to intimidate him. Dirk knew it had worked when Red screamed.

Red bellowed and started running at Dirk. Dirk set his feet for the attack. Red swung with such force that it would have split Dirk's skull if it had hit. Dirk bent his knees as the swing came down just short of contact. Dirk took advantage of Red's position and dropping one sword, he jumped over Red, placing his hand on his shoulder, and flipping behind him. Mid-flip he swung his sword, tapping Red on the back of the head, scoring the winning blow.

Dirk landed in a kneeling position. With one knee on the ground, he bowed his head and silently thanked Zona that he had survived. He stood up as the announcement was being made.

"Dirk Storm, winner," General Harkin announced. The crowd roared with applause including the kids from Fork City.

"The best match ever!" Dirk heard someone say in the crowd.

"Did you see that move? I thought he was a goner," Tab was saying to the Pack.

Dirk looked into the crowd and spotted his mother. He nodded to her and she smiled and nodded back. Dirk stood and faced Red. Red walked up to Dirk with an outstretched hand. Dirk clasped his hand and gave a small nod of appreciation. "Sorry I let my anger get the best of me out there. I knew if I lost, it would be to you, I am honored to have competed against you,"

"I might have won this match, but you made me pay. If I'm ever in a fight, I definitely would want to have you by my side," Dirk said, shaking his hand. They embraced and headed back to the stands.

"That was very impressive, Master Storm," Volar said as Dirk was walked up.

"Do any of you know where a healer is? I think he broke my ribs," Dirk said in a non-joking manner. They all laughed, thinking he was joking around. Volar reached into a pouch he wore around his waist and gave Dirk what looked like a small pinch of grass.

"Here, put this under your tongue for a few minutes. Then chew and swallow it. That will help with the healing process," Volar instructed. Dirk, without hesitating, did as the dwarf instructed. He trusted Volar. The pain in his ribs subsided and Dirk felt much better.

"That was amazing. What is it?" Dirk asked.

"Jover moss. It grows on the walls of our mountains and is known only to dwarves. Please do not share this information with anyone."

"You have my word."

Dirk was glad the rest of the rounds went much easier for him until the semi-finals. He would be facing Volar. On the other side of the bracket, Gil had made it to the semi-finals against Nat S, who had destroyed all of her opponents in mere minutes. She was fast and smooth. It was like she could sense their moves and react with the right response. Gil lasted a little longer than most but fell to a leg sweep with and a jab to the heart.

Dirk had a difficult time with Volar, even though he had been studying his moves in the previous matches. He learned that Volar was rhythmic with his attacks and would do the same movements with each scoring hit. They were powerful attacks that caused a heavy strain on Dirk's resolve to fend them off. He was ready though and successfully blocked the attacks. Dirk finally scored two heart hits on Volar after deflecting the same move several times, earning him the victory.

"I am very impressed with you, Master Storm; I have rarely been beaten in test of skill. I look forward to our future contests so I may have the chance to learn from my mistakes," Volar said bowing to him.

"I am with you as well, my friend." Dirk clasped arms with Volar as they walked off the field. Even in defeat, respect had been formed, which would be needed in the future. Dirk was exhausted. The first battle with Red had taken its toll. Then the final battle with Volar had almost done him in.

There was a ten-minute break before the final contest. "Does anyone have anything to eat? I'm famished," Dirk said to no one in particular.

"Here eat this nug bar," Raga said.

"What's a nug bar?" Gil asked curiously.

"It's emergency food rations we dwarves make for long trips and hunting expeditions. It's made of dried goat meat, oatmeal, honey, and pine nuts. It'll give you energy temporarily," Fernen said. Dirk thanked him and ate the small bar. Immediately, he felt his energy reserves restored.

"Wow, that's great! How can we make them?" Dirk asked.

"Maybe one day we will reveal that secret," Volar replied.

Over at the other end of the stands, two elves were in deep discussion. "Will you reveal who you are to him?" Tara asked Natia, looking over her shoulder at Dirk.

"The time of revelation is not here. Though it will be soon for him to find out who I am. I understand he has not yet accepted his destiny, so there is no need to put the cart before the horse," Natia replied.

"As you wish my princess," Tara responded lightly bowing her head.

"Contestants, the finale of the combat competition is upon us," announced General Harkin, raising his hands to quiet the crowd. Dirk headed to the center of the ring. Already waiting there was the elf who had decimated all of her opponents that day. "Ready yourself for combat."

They turned and faced each other and their eyes locked. As they bowed to each other, Dirk couldn't help noticing her amber eyes staring back at him. All of a sudden, his fingers started to tingle. He felt a warmth spread over his entire body. It took his breath away. He gasped quietly and had to shake his head to clear his mind.

Stay focused, he thought. He closed his eyes and his senses heightened. He could smell the sweat of battle all around him and the sweetness of honey and almonds hung in the air. He felt his heartbeat slowing down, just as he had been trained. He opened his eyes and saw that her eyes were still locked on his. He sensed that she was acknowledging that something was happening to him. He focused on his task and could hear the crowd breathing with excitement. Somewhere in the distance, there was a shrieking sound that sounded like a war cry.

No one could see her, but Arial was circling high above, witnessing the first meeting between the two beings that the fate of the world would one day depend on.

Dirk took a calming breath. He heard a voice in his head say, *Let your core lead you*. He shook it off, dismissing it as the day's events weighing on him. He finally pulled his thoughts back to the moment. Dirk, unable to turn away from her stare, saw what looked like small flames come to life in her eyes.

"Begin,"

Dirk wanted to make his family proud, especially his mother. He knew of his father's reputation at the school, and he wanted to represent him well. This gave him more energy than the nug bar had. Dirk put up a good fight at first, scoring the most points on her that anyone had all day. She was just too quick for him; it was like he was moving in slow motion while fighting her.

She scored her first five-point jab after he had scored his first six points. He hit her right thigh for the fourth time and then she gave the final kill jab as a response. Dirk stood there with his mouth hanging open after her final attack. He could've sworn he had just seen her eyes flare again as she made the final move. He figured that his lack of strength had caused his delusion. The crowd still chanted his name regardless of the loss. They applauded even louder for the elf since she had been awesome in her performance.

"Ladies and gentlemen, I give you your first-year age group victor, Princess Natia Silver of the Elms Woods!" General Harkin announced. The crowd began to chant her name. The nobles and the king were all giving a standing ovation. Dirk just stared at her as she unwrapped her face scarf for the first time. A small breeze blew across the arena and she pushed a stray strand of hair behind her left ear.

Dirk's birthmark on his hand tingled, causing him to rub the spot subconsciously while he stared at her. Natia had light almond-colored skin and dual auburn braid hung down to her waist. She stepped a little closer to him. Dirk didn't notice because his eyes were transfixed on the princess's eyes, but she had rubbed her own hand in the same place at the same time.

"Don't be ashamed. You competed honorably today. Your elven blood showed in your movements." Her voice was authoritative yet alluring.

"How do you know I have elven blood in me?" Dirk asked stepping closer to the elven princess.

"Because your mother is my god-aunt," the princess replied as she edged even closer to him. They stood in the center of the arena, mere inches apart. Dirk was a few inches taller than her, so she was tilting her head slightly up and he was tilting his slightly down to gaze into her dreamlike eyes. The scent of battle still hung in the air around them. The smell of honey and almonds hit his senses again, but he couldn't figure out what it was.

Dirk's heart was beating hard. The closer she got, the faster it beat. He took a calming breath and slowly let it out. As the princess moved to within an inch of him, she raised her right hand up while still staring into his eyes. She casually caressed his face. Goosebumps immediately formed throughout his entire body.

The world could have ended at that moment and they wouldn't have known. The only thing to them was each other even though the crowd in the stands were still chanting her name.

Finally, after a few seconds of this interaction, she turned and walked away waving at the crowd, leaving Dirk still shocked and unable to say anything. He just looked at her in disbelief.

She stopped and looked back at him. "You look confused. Ask your mother, I'm sure she will explain." The princess turned away and waved at the crowd as she returned to the stands where everyone was beginning to depart.

To the crowd in the stands, it looked as if they were just talking as the victor was congratulating her opponent for a valiant effort. Kira knew differently, though. Everything she had been avoiding for years was coming ever closer. The vision of her husband lying dead on a battlefield killed every hope she had of keeping Dirk from his destiny. Now that he had come face to face with her god niece, it was inevitable. Her father in-law grabbed her hand and squeezed it lovingly.

Kira had informed him of her vision before the contest. He knew

Dirk's destiny as well. He had been the Chosen once and knew what that responsibility meant. He leaned close so that only she could hear. "We will prepare him better than anyone has been prepared before."

Kira turned and looked at him. "Thank you, Father," she said, embracing him in a hug.

Dirk's friends, which now included the dwarves, ran up to meet him as he walked off the combat area. "That was awesome! She was just too fast for anyone," El said. Tab patted Dirk on the shoulder.

Volar shook his hand, "Good battle, my friend. Just remember, all battles are not won in a single fight."

Dirk looked at Volar considering his words. "You're right, my friend, but losing a fight doesn't ever feel good." Dirk shook his head, still reeling from defeat. He smiled and looked around at his friends. "Thanks, I really appreciate all of you for your support. Right now, I'm really drained. I'm just gonna head home and get some rest before tonight's events."

Gil, El, Linc, and Jonesy said their goodbyes and left. Dirk turned towards Volar. "We'll already be inside when you arrive tonight. See you there," Volar replied as he and the dwarves headed out.

"What's wrong?" Tab asked as they walked out of the arena. "You really didn't expect to win, remember?"

"It's not that. The princess just informed me my mother is her god-aunt."

"What? You said your mother knew them, but I didn't realize it was that well," Tab said.

"Yeah, me neither. Meet me at the farm later and we can go to the banquet together. First I need to talk with my mother," Dirk told him.

"Okay. We can talk on the way to the palace. See you later," Tab replied. Dirk thought about everything that had happened the last few days as he walked home.

There is so much about my mother and father I don't know. When I get home, I am going to press her for some answers.

Dirk walked through the crowd and was congratulated for a great performance by the locals as he passed. "Dirk." A voice caught his attention. He turned to see Mr. Burk, the baker, running up to him with a small bag in his hand.

He stopped in front of Dirk, breathing heavily from trying to catch him. He finally caught his breath, stood up, and handed Dirk the small bag. "This will help in getting your strength back," Mr. Burk said, patting Dirk on the back. Dirk looked in the bag and it was one of his favorites, Mr. Burk's honey sticky buns.

Dirk smiled. "I'll eat it on the way home. Thank you." Mr. Burk smiled back.

"No thanks needed, Dirk. You made Sharay and me proud today." Sharay was his wife. They had always been very good to Dirk. Mr. Burk smiled and headed back towards the market. Dirk immediately scarfed down the sweet bun. Mr. Burk was right. The honey sticky bun restored some of the energy he had lost.

He smiled to himself as he licked the honey from his fingers and headed home.

Compromise

Dirk just couldn't stop reliving the words the elven princess had said to him, your mother is my god-aunt. It kept running through his mind as he made his way home. The aroma of trees was in the air. The woods always smelled like the trees and wild plants that grew in the area. Even the scent of death would occasionally float through the air from an animal who had fallen victim to a larger prey. Such was the way of life in the woods. At least that was what Dirk had been raised to believe.

He was on the road that was nestled next to the woods that bordered his grandfather's land and separated it from Mt. Blazire. As he continued home, he failed to see the pair of yellow eyes hidden in the darkness of the woods. They followed his every move.

Suddenly the snap of a twig echoed to his right, bringing him out of his trance. He stopped in his tracks and looked into the thicket of trees. His senses, sharper than a normal person's due to his training with his grandfather, made his gut twitch.

"Who's there?" Dirk yelled into the darkness. He scanned the area and thought he saw a pair of yellow eyes behind one of the big trees on the edge of the forest. His instincts put him on alert. He reached for the dagger that was always at his side. It was the dagger his father had worn as a child growing up. His grandfather had given it to him on his tenth name day. The eyes seemed to disappear.

An illusion or just the exhaustion from the day's events, he thought to himself. He put his dagger back in its scabbard and headed down the road to his home.

The black panther chided herself for stepping on the stick that had alerted him. She had been sent to keep an eye on the Storm boy, but she was to stay hidden. Her familiar would not be happy that she was almost exposed. *I'll just keep that to myself*, she thought. She continued through the woods stealthily following the half elf, making sure to pay more attention to where she stepped.

When Dirk finally got home, he quietly entered through the back of the house. As he walked in, he could hear his grandfather and mother engaged in a heated discussion in the kitchen. He stopped and eased the door open.

"He needs to know soon!" his grandfather was saying to Kira.

"I know, I just can't help but feel that it is still not the time. Even with everything that has happened, I think we should wait a little longer. We'll discuss this later. I think he just walked in."

Dirk walked in casually, acting like he didn't hear a word they had said. "Hi, what's up?"

"Just getting ready for the banquet," replied Durkon. "Did you discuss the situation with Tab?"

"I did, and he agreed."

"Good that's what he needs to do. It's what his father would have wanted."

Here it comes, Dirk thought, seeing the look on his mother's face.

"What are you two going on about?" Kira asked.

"Tab is getting a chance at the school with Grandfather's help," Dirk told her. Kira raised her eyebrow questioningly, looking at the general. "Mom, you're making me go and I won't do it without Tab!"

Kira just looked at Dirk. With a huff, she said, "All right, but you better keep yourself focused. Any shenanigans with you two and I will personally talk with General Harkin and we will see how much pull your grandfather has then."

"Thanks, Mom. By the way, I met your god-niece today." Dirk said casually, looking for a response from her. Durkon was standing there staring at Kira with an *I told you so look on his face*.

"Right now is not the time, Dirk. Don't interrupt," Kira said before he could speak. "Tonight, is a big night and I promise I'll tell you about her tomorrow," Kira held up her hand to stop Dirk from asking any questions. He knew once she threw the hand up, he would have to wait. She had made up her mind and there would be no changing it.

"Ok, but we are talking about her tomorrow," Dirk said with conviction.

"Ok," Kira said.

"You did very good today Dirk, I am sure Diron would be very proud of you," his grandfather told him.

"Yes, your father would be very proud you. All of your friends did very well. Elyse really surprised everyone with her archery skills, and Tab should be very proud himself even though Elyse beat him," Kira said.

"I think that's the only reason he was ok with losing. Because it was El who beat him," Dirk said, smiling.

"Yes, I forgot he's hopelessly in love with her," Kira responded with a laugh.

"Well I've got to go. I'm expected earlier than you two. The king's carriage will be here to get you, Kira. Be ready around six thirty. Dirk, I guess you will be meeting Tab and going with him?" the General asked.

"Yes sir, we'll be walking. I'm going to leave Midnight here." Midnight was Dirk's horse. His grandfather had given Midnight to him on his thirteenth name day. "Too many people at the celebration to ride him."

"Good idea. Make sure Tab is dressed appropriately. He is a representative of me."

"He will be. I'll take care of it."

"Good, got to go. Don't be late!" the General told him in that commanding voice of his.

"We won't be," Dirk responded as the General walked out the door.

"Son, I set out your crimson silk shirt, your tan leather pants, and your nice dress boots for tonight. Let Tab wear your green silk dress shirt and the dark tan pants if he needs anything," Kira responded. "I have to finish getting dressed now. Remember to be polite. There are a lot of people you will be meeting tonight. If any of the elves ask you questions, be courteous. Some of them I have known for a long time and they may be curious about you. I'll explain tomorrow."

"I love you, Mom."

"I love you too." Kira smiled, looking into his eyes. "Your father is proud of you. He is looking down on you at this moment and I know he would tell you the same thing." Kira pulled Dirk into a hug, kissing his forehead. He squeezed her tight.

"You're the best, Mom. I know there are secrets you have kept from me, but I'm sure it has been for my benefit."

Kira held him by the shoulders and smiled. "Now go take a bath and get dressed." She pushed him towards his room.

Kira headed to her room to finish getting dressed. She sighed. *Durkon is right. I should inform him tomorrow. At least about some of the things he needs to know. Not all but some, maybe.* As she walked into her room, she noticed the air start to shimmer as it had earlier when Diron had appeared to her. Kira closed her door quickly and stared at the shimmering spot near the window. Her husband appeared slowly.

This time, he was kneeling and looking up at her. His mouth was moving but she couldn't make out what he was saying.

"I can't hear you, my love," Kira said, kneeling down in front of the apparition. He reached out to touch her, and she extended her hand to his. As soon as their hands touched, even though he was an illusion, Kira's entire body was engulfed in pain. So much so that it knocked her backwards.

Kira, grasping her chest, saw the pain in his eyes. Tears were streaming down her face because of the agony that her husband's spirit was experiencing. The only words she could make out was, "Tell him!"

Kira nodded. "I will, I promise," is all Kira could get out before his spirit disappeared again. Kira wiped the tears from her eyes and decided that she would tell Dirk everything, not just some of the story, but the whole story. If her son were going to have a chance at the life he deserved, she would make sure he knew everything.

Dirk went upstairs to get ready after he had hugged his mother. He quickly took a bath; Kira had gotten the water warmed and ready in anticipation of him coming home. He quickly washed and dried off before he put on the clothes she had laid out for him. He decided to wear an amber sash around his waist and put on his necklace. It had a circular gold medallion with his family crest engraved on it. Two swords crossed over a capital S centered with crimson-tinted wings in the background.

Dirk never could get a straight answer from either his grandfather or his mother about what it all meant. They would just say that it would all become clear one day. He eventually quit asking them and accepted that, in time, he would know. He decided to also wear formal tan leather bracers on his forearms that matched the color of his boots.

"I'm leaving. Don't be late," his mother shouted up the stairs.

"Okay!" he yelled back. He was looking at himself in the mirror, thinking, *I look good!* when he noticed movement on the shelf above his writing desk. He walked over to get a closer look.

Hmm, the only thing that looks disturbed is the rock we found yesterday at Mt Blazire. He picked up the rock. It felt a little warm to the touch, but nothing else had changed. He didn't notice the hairline crack on the stone.

A knocking sound came a from downstairs. He set the rock back down hurriedly and went downstairs to see who was at the door.

"Tab, you're here."

"Who else are you expecting?" Tab asked sarcastically.

"Mom had me pick out some clothes for you if you want to wear them."

"She knows?" Tab asked.

"Yeah the General kind of forced my hand."

"How did she take it?"

"Better than I expected. Only one threat from her," Dirk said, laughing. "I kind of had her where I wanted her. She didn't want to answer any questions about the elves, so she let it go and I didn't push. She promised to give me more answers tomorrow."

"Good, let's look at those clothes. I love Mother Agnes, but these clothes are a little too old for tonight," Tab said.

Dirk looked at Tab. He was wearing a beige tunic shirt and brown pants that looked a little worn. "What about Linc?"

"He said he's covered for tonight."

"What's he up to, I wonder?"

"I don't know but we will find out later. Let me change and then we can go," Tab said, going up the stairs. Tab got dressed and they headed to the palace.

The Banquet

Daylight had completely faded as Dirk and Tab made their way to the palace. The streets were still busy with people celebrating from the day's activities when they got to Silver City. The city guard was busy keeping the peace and getting the drunks off the streets. A few fights were taking place outside of The Horned Goat, one of the seedier taverns in town.

When they got closer to the palace gates, they could see a small line forming at the entrances. There were two entrance gates to the palace. One off the main street that came directly from downtown, and the other one was closer to the northwest side of the palace. That one was for the nobles to enter through.

Dirk could see that the guards were dressed in their formal military dress instead of their usual daily uniforms. They wore red dress coats and black pants with black knee-high boots. Their swords had been replaced by seven-foot pikes. There were four guards at each gate. One guard was checking off names as they came up to enter the palace. Two guards on each side of the gate would cross their pikes, blocking the entrance after each person was let through until the next person had been cleared.

"Boy, tight security tonight," Tab said to Dirk as they got closer.

"Yes, a lot of important people here tonight."

"Next," said an older-looking guard with silver-streaked hair as he checked off names. "Names?" he asked, looking down at his list as they stepped up.

"Tab Clearwater and Dirk Storm," Dirk replied.

The guard looked up at them. "Ah, Mr. Storm and Mr. Clearwater, it is good to see you. I am Sergeant Brooks. I am the survival trainer at the academy." He marked their names off the list.

"Nice to meet you Sergeant." they responded and shook hands with him.

"You boys are the spitting images of two young lads I knew several years back. Well, we'll talk later. You better get going. Next!" Sergeant Brooks said, allowing them to pass. The guards uncrossed their pikes and let them enter.

"What was that about?" Tab asked.

"I haven't got a clue. I guess we'll find out later," Dirk answered.

As they walked through the palace grounds, Dirk thought about how beautiful it was there. It was full of exotic birds like peacocks, flamingos, and guinea fowl. The trees were tropical in nature with no branches, just big pad leaves at the top with various fruits dangling from them, bananas, coconuts, and some red round fruits Dirk wasn't familiar with. There were several water fountains placed throughout the gardens. Marble and dark wooden benches were set up in various places across the garden with a white marble walkway that wound its way throughout. There were so many blue, red, orange, and yellow flowers. The fragrance was overwhelming to anyone who had never been in their presence before. Tab sneezed, as if to prove Dirk's theory.

"You okay?" Dirk asked.

"Yeah, just these damned flowers."

When they got to the entrance of the palace, they saw a red carpet that started at the bottom of the steps and ended at the top.

Standing at the entrance was a single guard dressed in his fine formals as. He was directing people to the banquet hall. Dirk took in the floor as they entered the palace. The tiles were so shiny that Dirk could see his reflection in them as he walked down the hall. The armor that adorned the walls were polished to a fine finish.

Tab whistled, trying to touch the armor, but Dirk grabbed his arm just in time to stop him. "Don't. They take their shining armor serious around here," he said, pointing to the stiff-backed man who was watching them as they walked down the hallway. Dirk nodded and received an upturned nose in response. Tab took on a serious demeanor and followed Dirk.

"Thanks," he whispered. Dirk smiled and kept on walking. At the entrance to the banquet hall, a pair of guards were posted, opening the banquet hall doors as guests approached.

After they were let in by the guards, Dirk took in the view. The banquet hall was set up with a stage at the back of the room. On the stage, tables were set up for about twenty people to sit at. On the floor-level, Dirk counted about thirty similar tables, equally divided and set up to seat at least ten people each. There was an open area in the center that he assumed was probably for people to mingle and talk. He looked at the table closest to him and saw that the table had names written on tent-shaped cards. He looked around and saw that the other tables had similar cards on them as.

The third-year students were in the rows closest to the stage on the left side of the hall, followed by second-year and then first-year students. Behind them, the tables left were for the other guests. The right side of the hall was set up for the nobles and foreign dignitaries such as the dwarves and elves.

"Probably ranking from highest to lowest in status," he said to Tab, motioning to the tables.

"Everyone, please take your seats as soon as possible," announced a man standing on the stage. He was wearing a red tunic and pants and was draped in crimson robes.

"It's the king's aide, Mr. Stavers," Dirk told Tab. Dirk then scanned the room and noticed that the guards at the entrances on the inside of the hall were dressed in their formal battle armor, their helmets tucked under one arm. Their swords were at their sides with their shields leaning on the wall behind them. There was another pair of guards stationed at the back entrance where the king would be coming through once everyone had arrived.

"Over here!" A voice caught Dirk's attention. He looked around to see El.

"Our table is over here," El told them as they walked up. Sitting at the table were Jonesy, El, Gil, Linc, and four of the dwarves. Dirk and Tab walked over to the table. Dirk sat beside Volar. Tab sat between Dirk and Linc. The dwarves were dressed in brown silk tunics, brown pants made of some kind of hide, ankle-high polished boots, and a shoulder-to-waist length sash. Their hair was tied in ponytails that started on top of their heads and reached their waists. Their beards were tied into ponytails as well.

"I notice you're not wearing your axe," Dirk said.

"They're underneath the table," Volar said, pointing to his feet.

"I figured you would have them close. Where is Raga?"

"He didn't get so lucky with his seating," Volar replied, looking two tables over. Dirk followed his gaze. Raga had been seated with Brock and his cronies. He was seated by Larkin and looked like he was ready to strangle him. Fortunately, the elves had been seated there. One of the male elves was trying to talk with Raga, but it looked like he was barely responding to the elf's questions.

"I bet he wished he was over here," Gil said.

"You think?" Jonesy said.

"Yes, I'm sure we will hear about this later," Thelgra said in his deep voice. Jonesy and Gil were dressed similar to Dirk, with various colors of blue and red. Linc was wearing a nice beige tunic with matching pants and polished brown boots. El looked exquisite. She wore her hair in small braids that wrapped around her head, culminating into a single braid that ran down her back. There were pearls laced in them. A red sapphire sat in the center of the pearl necklace she wore with matching earrings. Her satin red sleeveless dress complimented her skin tone and open V-neck left no doubt she was a young woman. The dress was full-length with a cream-colored belt around the waist. She wore dark red flats to match.

"El, *wow*," Tab. "Ow!" Tab rubbed his ribs where Dirk had elbowed him.

"Don't stare," Dirk whispered into Tab's ear.

El blushed, trying not to look Tab in the eyes. "Thanks, Tab. You look very handsome tonight." That caused Tab to look away. His face had turned a shade of scarlet. Dirk smiled, looking at Tab, and had to put his hand over his mouth to hide his smile.

Dirk told El she looked great and then started looking around the room for familiar faces. He saw several of the town's local business owners that he recognized. Jonas and Eleanor Glan, Jonesy and El's parents, were sitting at the front of the noble's tables. Lady Weathers was sitting with them. Her nieces, twins Annise and Patrice, were in their second year at the academy. Lord Fisher was seated up front with the nobles. His son, Jake, was a second-year student. Most of the business owners were present as well. The Coupes, who owned the produce shop, the Burks, who owned the bakery, and Doc Green, the main healer of Silver City.

Dirk felt a sensation in his hand where his birthmark was located. He turned towards the stage and noticed a well-dressed noble seemed to be staring at him with a smile. He thought he recognized him as a trader from Oak City. He was seated next to his grandfather.

Dirk smiled with pride when he saw the General. He was dressed in his military formals. Dirk always thought he looked like a man of authority when he wore them. Kira was seated between the General and an elven woman. Kira and the elven woman were talking and laughing with each other like they had known each other their whole lives. Dirk smiled to himself. Kira was dressed in a peach-colored formal gown with her hair brushed down her back.

The woman she was talking to was probably one of the most beautiful elves Dirk had ever seen, with the exception of his mom. She was dressed similar to Kira with a light blue silk dress. She had light brown hair and her features looked very familiar. She wore a jeweled tiara on her head. Sitting next to her was an elven male who wore a silver crown on his head. He was talking to the man next to him, Lord Bracken Little, Brock's father. Lady Olivia Little was next to her husband. The High One, Romus Jamous, Gil's father was sitting next to her and having a discussion with her.

Several other nobles were at the table. Prince Thelon Jerard, the king's son, was dressed in his military formals. His wife, Princess Crystal, was next to him. Her father sat next to her. Prince Cistol, the ruler of Feriah and his wife, Crysta, was beside him. There were two dwarves sitting up there too. They were both similar in size, but he could tell who the king of the dwarves was. He was wearing a golden crown with all types of jewels set in it. The female wore a smaller crown of the same design. There were two empty chairs at the head of the table that were left for King Jerard and Queen Thea.

Dirk felt a tingling sensation in his right palm again. He looked down at it and touched the spot. Curiously, the mark looked to him like it had doubled in size since he had last paid any attention to it. He brushed the thought away. *That's not possible.*

As he rubbed the mark, he looked up at the stage. The man who sat next to his grandfather was looking at him with a raised eyebrow. Then he noticed that the man turned his head slightly toward the table where the elves were sitting. Dirk followed his stare.

One of the female elves was looking back at the noble sitting by his grandfather. Dirk noticed she seemed to be rubbing her palm as well. She had a smirk on her face. She turned slowly to look Dirk's way. Their eyes locked and Dirk got that warm feeling through his body again. It was Princess Natia looking back at him.

"Hey Dirk," Linc said, waving his hand in front of his face, trying to get his attention. The clouds in his head cleared and Dirk turned to face Linc.

"What?" he said a little too loudly, causing everyone at the table to look at him. "Sorry, I was just thinking about today. What do you want to ask me, Linc?"

"We're still on tomorrow, right?"

"Yes, we are. Tab and I will meet you in the morning before noon at the guard house that leads to the docks."

"Good, I don't want you to forget. Tonight might get crazy with all of these people and I want us to have a plan," Linc replied. Tab jumped into the conversation. The three of them talked about their plans but had to quit when Mr. Stavers walked to the front of the stage.

"Kings, queens, princes, princesses, lords and ladies, and to all of our guests, may I present to you, King Thurmond Jerard and our queen, Thea Jerard!" Stavers said, waving to the back entrance of the hall. Everyone in the hall stood up. Trumpets sounded from somewhere behind the stage. The guards at the back entrance came to attention as the door opened.

The queen walked through first, followed by several handmaidens who broke away from her and headed toward the kitchen doors. He turned his gaze back to the queen. She was wearing an elegant purple satin silk dress with white lace trimming. She was escorted from the stage to her seat by her son Prince Thelon, who had gotten up to greet her.

The king followed her in with only one maiden, who immediately made a beeline for the kitchen doors. He was dressed in a crimson tunic with crème pants. The crown of Zona sat atop his head. It was the crown that all of the kings of Silver City had worn since the beginning of the city. It was believed to have been made by Zona himself.

The king waved and smiled as he walked up to the stage. The crowd applauded as he came to stand front and center stage. "Thank you, thank you," the king said in his powerful voice while motioning for all of them to be seated. He looked around the hall. "Welcome everyone to this year's banquet of champions and the start of a new year at the Silver City school. We have a lot of new students starting the school as well as joining the military academy this year."

He paused and looked around the room. A concerned expression crossed his face. "In the coming years, I am afraid that we are going to need their dedication," There was some mumbling in the crowd. The king held up his hands up to quiet the crowd. "Now don't be worried by what I just said. I believe in keeping all of my citizens and allies informed. There have been a lot more skirmishes and activities over the last few months in the southern region."

Another gasp came from the crowd. "Is it the Vangaurd again?" someone in the crowd shouted.

"No, that is not what I am saying. Bandits and thieves are getting a little more aggressive and I just wanted to let you know that we are preparing for the rise in their criminal activities. Prince Cistol and his guard in Feriah have handled these issues well. We are just going to be building up our forces down there to help ease the strain that the skirmishes are putting on his army. I just wanted you to let you know, so that when you see the military movements in our city." There was a sigh of relief shared across the crowd. "Now again, thank you all for coming, and to all of you who competed today and to the winners of competitions, great job."

"There were some amazing feats I witnessed today and look forward to watching you grow in your careers." The king looked at the students. "Also, one last thing before I turn this over to General Harkin and Master Nabas. I want to thank King Askin of Elmwood city and his beautiful wife Queen Naira for being here. And for the first time in many years, we all have the pleasure of having King Horan and his wife, Queen Jada of the dwarves," he said, turning around and clapping. The whole banquet hall broke into applause.

After a few minutes of applause, the king turned. "Now, General Harkin, I suppose you are ready to pass out the awards to today's winners and announce the first-year cadets,"

"I am, My Lord," the general responded.

"Good, make it quick I'm starving," the king said laughing as he walked to his seat. Everyone in the hall laughed along with him.

General Harkin walked up to the center of the stage and a table was rolled up beside him. "When I call your names, come up to the stage and stand beside me to my left. I will announce each event separately, starting with archery, then throwing, and lastly combat," the general said waving his hand his left.

"Now, let's start with archery. Third-year winners, Princess Anastasia Jerard and Kal James." The crowd applauded as each winner was announced. "Second-year winner, Jake Fisher. First-year winner, Elyse Glan." Dirk's table roared with applause, causing El to blush as she walked to the stage. General Harkin paused as they all walked up to the stage with cheering from the crowd. Dirk noticed no one louder than King Jerard himself.

Dirk took in all the winners. They were dressed in formal wear. He looked at Anastasia, amazed at how her look had changed since the competition. The princess had her hair braided with small red and yellow flowers woven into it. She wore a crimson sleeveless dress that sparkled when she walked.

Gil stared with his mouth open until Jonesy punched him in the arm. "You're drooling, idiot. Close your mouth."

"That hurt!" Gil said, closing his mouth and rubbing his arm. Everyone at the table laughed. As soon as all four of the winners had reached the stage, General Harkin began passing out the prizes. The new archery bows and quivers that the elves had made for the winners. Elyse received her white yew tree bow and quiver to the applause of the crowd, as did Jake Fisher.

When he got to Anastasia and Kal, he held up his hand for silence. "Let me say something about the bows that Anastasia and Kal are about to receive. Everyone here knows we have never had a tie before, so we were one short. King Askin noticed this dilemma. He wanted to do something special for the two of you," Harkin said, looking at Anastasia and Kal. On the table, there was one bow and quiver set left, and something hidden under a cape. "King Askin and Queen Naira have generously donated their very own bows and quivers to you as your awards." The crowd gasped, especially the elves. General Harkin uncovered the two sets of bows and quivers.

Dirk focused on the bows. They were bone white and curved at each end. They had runes carved top to the bottom on each side. The grip in the center looked to be made of a soft black leather. They also had a strange-looking bow string. Dirk thought it was changing colors, depending on how the light hit it.

General Harkin presented them with their awards. King Askin walked up behind Harkin and whispered in his ear. "Yes, Your Majesty, go ahead," the general replied.

King Askin stepped forward, looking at both Kal and Anastasia. "I have not seen shooting like that in a long time. I just wanted to make it known that the two of you are very special, and I believe you deserve an even more special award. These bows were made for us upon assuming the elven throne. The wood is an aged white ash. The drawstrings were made from donated unicorn hair."

The crowd gasped again, loudly at this revelation.

"The fletching on the arrows are made from white eagle feathers. The runes on the bows were carved by elven elders. I do not know where the special ash tree wood comes from, but I do know that these are special bows, and we hope that they protect the both of you wherever you go for many years to come."

King Askin bowed to them. The crowd exploded with applause. King Askin presented the winners their prizes. Dirk watched with the crowd but couldn't hear what the elven king was saying to Anastasia and Kal when he handed them their bows. By Anastasia's reaction, it must have been heartfelt words because she hugged him in an unformal way. King Askin shook Kal's hand after the embrace with Anastasia. He then grabbed the original winner's bow left on the table and went back to his seat. He placed it on the floor beside his wife as he sat down.

Dirk watched as the winners walked off the stage. Kal and Anastasia raised their bows in the air and the crowd applauded so loud that General Harkin had to quiet them down so that they could continue the awards presentation.

"All right, congratulations to you all. Up next, we have the throwing winners," General Harkin said as the archery winners were leaving the stage, their awards in their hands. Elyse got back to the table and everyone wanted to look at her bow.

"Okay guys, but one at a time," she said, grinning from ear to ear. Dirk could see that the bow was a beautifully made yew long bow. The drawstring was made out of some kind of animal mane that was soft to the touch but supposedly unbreakable. It had three runes carved in the shaft on each side. Above and below the grip, there were two iris-sized red jewels.

"Ah, those are power stones," Volar said.

"You can pull strength from them in battle when you get weary. They are said to pull power straight from the gods a little at a time until they hold all that they can," Fernen stated.

"That's awesome, El," Jonesy told her.

"Well, I hope they explain these power stones when we get into school. I'm always hearing about them, but no one explains how they work," Tab said to the dwarves.

"They will. The wizards set it up as a part of our training," El said.

"Good," Tab declared as General Harkin started announcing the throwing winners.

Volar went up when his name was announced. The stage was filled by the time Volar got there. Dirk was looking around the room when third-year winner Lance Gains from Feriah and second-year winner Noah Macklin from Fork City received their dwarven made throwing axes. Dirk turned back to the stage when Volar received his prize. The crowd applauded when the general released them to their tables.

Dirk really liked the dwarves. He had a feeling Volar was going to play a big role in his first, and hopefully only, year at the academy. Harkin then started announcing the combat winners. Third-year again was won by Princess Anastasia. The second-year winner was Ronan Quin from Oak City and thee first-year by Princess Natia from Elmwood. They all received newly forged scimitars and shields, both made in Silver City.

It was more than likely that El and Jonesy's father had made them because he was the best smith in town. Also, because he was smiling ear to ear as they were passed to the contestants.

"Uh-hem!" Tab was poking him in the side and pointing to the stage. He hadn't notice when Natia had walked to the stage since everyone at the table was looking at Volar's axes.

She was walking gracefully back to her table, wearing a lavender one-piece outfit that had no sleeves. It looked kind of like a tunic with pants attached and a deep purple wrap around her waist. It was made out of a material that looked like silk. Her hair was slicked straight back, tied in a ponytail, and lined with small lavender jewels.

He looked around the room as she was accepting congratulations from the people she walked by and then it happened again. Their eyes met. Dirk started to get that warm sensation rushing through his body again.

He was saved by El, who was squeezing his arm and talking to him. "Wake up, dreamy."

Dirk looked at her questioningly. "What? What are you talking about, El?"

"I was saying how beautiful the elven princess looked, but I think you already noticed," El said matter-of-factly.

"You're crazy," Dirk replied.

"Oh, every time you look at her, it's like you're in a trance, Dirk."

Dirk leaned close to her so only she could hear what he said.

"I don't know what it is El. It's like when we look at each other, there is a connection. I get this warm sensation all over my body and it's like I'm in a dream."

El snickered. "Well, that could be your hormones. She is gorgeous, though. Just make sure your thinking with the right part of your anatomy." El glanced down at his waist. He just stared back at her in disbelief.

After realizing she was joking, he started to defend himself. "No. I don't think that's it. It's a sensation I get, kind of like when you know when someone is staring at you."

"Well, you have never met her before except in combat, so maybe you're just lovesick," El said.

"No, it's different."

"Oh, you're a master of love now? The Dirk who has never even talked about a girl, except when we were twelve." El began to giggle.

"Hey, that was infatuation. How was I supposed to know that Skylar was an evil snake?"

"Yes, you dodged that trap. Who knows? Maybe time will tell," El said as they both turned their attention back to the stage.

"Master Nabas now has some announcements before we can eat," General Harkin said, motioning for an elderly man with silver hair. He was dressed in light gray robes.

"Ah yes. Welcome everyone. First, I want to congratulate and greet all of the new students. Please stand when your name is called out," Wizard Nabas announced to the crowd. Dirk and El laughed at Tab because he really didn't like being singled out. There was a small grumble from most of the first-years at this announcement, but they quieted down fast when Nabas seemed to glimmer while staring in their direction. Wizard Nabas started calling out the first-years names. Dirk listened patiently. "Aaric Frare, Stew Carpus, Gil Jamous…" Wizard Nabas went through the names of all the first-years. Tab's name, however, was not called out, causing him to look a little perturbed. After Nabas had called out the student's names and each grade, he made a few more announcements. "Third-and second-year students need to meet at the lobby of the academy at eight on the first morning of class to get your schedules, room assignments, and training schedules. First-year students, Wizard Laseous will meet you at the entrance to the testing rooms around ten after the third-and-second years are settled in. There, he will give you your testing schedule for the day."

Nabas paused, looking around the room. "Oh yes, there is one more thing that I almost forgot. This year, the sponsored student chosen to attend the school is Tab Clearwater."

The room applauded. Tab blushed and ducked his head, feeling a little embarrassed by the attention. Brock and his cronies were making snide remarks at him from their table. The elves and particularly Raga didn't seem to care for what they were saying. They quieted down quickly when Raga stood up so fast his chair fell over. He sat back down after a few words from one of the elves.

"Well, since that is settled then, I think I hear the king's stomach so let the feast begin," Nabas said. The crowd, including the king, laughed.

Dirk eagerly watched as the door to the kitchen opened and servers started rolling out carts of food. His stomach grumbled and he received a smirk from Tab as the servers went to each table. He waited patiently' even though he was starving.

They put plates and silverware down at each place along with a goblet. Another set of servers came around behind them with the food. He could see, as well as smell, the roast turkey, pheasant, slow-roasted beef, chicken, fish, and even roasted goat for the dwarves. There were all types of vegetables; potatoes, beans, corn and cabbage and breads that smelled freshly baked. He saw that a special vegetable salad was made for the elves since they didn't usually eat meat. Fruits from all over the world were there as well.

The servers came around with carts and gave each person a choice of what they wanted. The red wine that was served was from Elmwood. The ale was from a local brewer as was the mead. After everyone was ready to eat, King Jerard stood and said, "May Zona forever bless us and this food."

Almost everyone in the crowd repeated his words. King Askin then stood up, "And may Marluna guide us with good health." The elves repeated his words.

Then it was King Horan's turn. "May Garga keep the ground at our feet safe from treachery." The dwarves all stood and repeated their king's words.

"Let us eat and enjoy, everyone," King Jerard said before sitting down to eat.

The sounds of everyone eating filled the hall. The kids at the table were saying the food was delicious as Dirk stared at those amber eyes that was staring back at him. Before the feelings could engulf him again, he looked away. Dirk was hungry but found himself not eating because his thoughts were on the night's events. *What is up with these emotions I'm having? Why was Princess Natia and the noble man on the stage looking at me strangely?* Dirk thought as he poked at his food.

Dirk kept looking around the room. He hadn't seen his mother that happy in a long time. Her and Queen Naira kept touching each other's arms while talking to each other, laughing and being very animated. Dirk smiled at the scene. He was going to find out this story tomorrow. As he turned, he noticed another elven woman at one of the dignitary tables smiling at him.

He smiled back, and she nodded. For a second, he could have sworn he saw a sparkle in her eyes. He dismissed it as the lighting and finally finished his meal.

After everyone had finished eating, Stavers walked up to the center of the stage. "Everyone, thank you all for coming. Feel free to mingle with the other guests after you have finished your deserts. Students, remember the next few days are going to be busy so get some rest. You are going to need it," Stavers announced to the crowd.

Once everyone had finished the deserts that were brought out by the servers, the group started getting up and moving about the hall to talk with other students and family.

"We're going to talk with our parents. We will see you tomorrow sometime. Maybe we can get lunch at the festival?" El said to the table.

"Goodnight," Volar said and all the dwarves at the table repeated him standing up and bowing. El and Jonesy waved goodbye to Dirk, Tab, and Linc.

"I have to go as well. I'll see you two in the morning, before noon, remember?" Linc said to Dirk before rushing off quickly.

"Yes, we will see you then," Dirk replied. Dirk knew Linc, and thought he was up to something as he watched Linc weave through the crowd. "Come on, Volar. Let's go save Raga and then all of you can come with me and meet my mother and grandfather."

"We would be honored for you to meet mine mother and father as well," Volar replied. Dirk looked questioningly at him.

"Hey, you all go ahead; I want to get a better look at El's bow," Tab said. The other dwarves had a similar idea and followed Tab.

"I bet," Dirk replied, laughing. Tab frowned at him with a hint of a smile and walked off with the dwarves in tow.

Dirk and Volar saved Raga and he followed them until Thelgra grabbed him and made him come and talk with Mr. Glan. Dirk shook hands with people and introduced Volar as they headed to the stage area where his mother was talking with Queen Naira, King Askin, King Jerard, Prince Thelon and Princess Crystal. Dirk looked back over his shoulder expecting Volar to be there as he stepped up onto the stage, but at the last second, he saw him break away to talk to King Horan, who was in discussion with General Harkin and Dirk's grandfather.

"Ah, here he is now," Kira said to the group. Dirk walked up to his mother, bowed, and kissed her hand. Kira smiled, patting her son on the shoulder.

"Dirk, that was a valiant fight today. You represented us well," King Jerard said in his commanding voice.

"Thank you, sire," Dirk said bowing to the king.

"No need for all that bowing, son. Tonight, we are all friends here," Jerard replied.

"Yes sir," Dirk responded.

"Yes, very good. You and your friends were fine competitors today. I look forward to getting them in the field. I believe Elyse Glan could challenge Stas and Kal with her archery skills," Thelon said to the group. They all agreed.

"Well, son, you'll have to wait a few years on these here. We don't want them out there too early," The king said, patting Dirk on the back. They all nodded in agreement.

"Well, we better go talk with the other nobles, Father. That is to be expected," Thelon said.

"Yes, Yes I suppose you're right. Askin and Naira, I will see you later, and of course, Kira, it is really good to see you my dear. We haven't had the pleasure of your company for quite some time. Please come around more," the king said giving Kira a hug that she returned.

"I will, Thurmond, I promise." Kira said. Dirk smiled. He had been around the king a lot when he was younger, going along with the general on his visits, but he didn't remember his mother ever going. Using his first name like that strengthened Dirk's resolve to talk to her tomorrow and ask more questions than he originally had planned.

King Jerard, Prince Thelon, and Princess Crystal all said goodbye and walked towards where his grandfather and General Harkin were talking.

"Dirk, I would like for you to meet King Askin Silver and Queen Naira Silver of Florendale. Naira is my oldest and dearest friend," Kira said.

"It is an honor to meet you both," Dirk said, clasping King Askin's arm, bowing in formal greeting, then turning to kiss Naira's hand as he had his mother.

When he bowed and grasped her hand, he felt a sensation of warmth and strength enter his body. He shrugged it off and kissed her hand. When he looked up, Queen Naira had a look of approval on her face.

"Well young Dirk, it is a pleasure to finally meet you officially." She grabbed his face and got closer, inspecting his eyes, "You are very much your father's son. The resemblance is uncanny." She leaned forward and kissed his cheek. Dirk couldn't move. He just stared back at his mother. The queen laughed and stepped back.

The elven king smiled. "Kira, I see there are things you need to discuss with your son. If you will excuse me, I feel I need to be in on that discussion your father-in-law and the king are having," King Askin said, politely excusing himself.

"Dirk, I am sorry it has taken so long to see you again, I have asked your mother for years for the two of you to come and visit her home again," Naira said to Dirk in her soft voice.

"I am sorry, I don't mean to be rude, but I don't remember ever meeting you," Dirk responded.

"Of course, you don't. The last time I saw you, you were just an infant. I guess, a year old?" Naira said with a questioningly look at Kira.

"Yes, that's about right, Naira, but I've never told Dirk about that. It was so long ago."

"Well it seems to me, my dear friend, we need to remedy that," Naira said, clasping Kira hands.

"Not now," Kira said sternly. "We have so much happier things to talk about tonight."

"Yes, you're right," Naira said, hooking arms with Kira and directing her and Dirk to sit down at the stage table that had been cleared of dinner. "So, Dirk I see you met your mother's god-niece in competition today."

He nodded. "Yes, she is very good. I didn't stand a chance."

"You lasted longer than anyone else. You did just fine. You'll get better once you have the chance to focus on your training instead of trying to be a trader," Naira responded.

"Mom!" Dirk said, looking at his mother.

"Naira, not now, please," Kira glared at Naira.

"Ok, I'll let it go. Besides, I need to get to know my godson better," Naira said with a motherly smile.

I really need to talk to my mother now, Dirk thought while faking a smile.

So, they sat there talking for several minutes, though it seemed like an hour to Dirk. Naira asked questions about his likes and dislikes and Dirk answered. That went on until a shadow walked up behind Dirk. He turned to see Natia behind him, smiling and walking towards Kira. Dirk saw a look that meant something unsaid between them. He watched as they hugged each other with tears falling down their faces.

After composing themselves, Natia said, "Aunt Kira, I am so glad to see you."

"Natia, It has been way too long! You have grown into a beautiful woman and, from what I saw today, an excellent fighter," Kira said, holding both of her hands.

"Natia, this is Dirk," Naira said to her.

"Yes, we kind of met earlier today," she said, bowing to him with her eyes locked on his. Dirk nodded back, starting to get that feeling again.

"Good to meet you, Natia," Dirk said. They both turned to their mothers at the same time. Natia and Naira began whispering to each other as Dirk pulled Kira to the side.

"What is it, Dirk?"

"Mom, I've had some weird feelings tonight that we need to discuss."

"Dirk, it needs to wait until tomorrow. There're too many listening ears here tonight. We need to discuss this in private," Kira responded.

"Well tell me this, who is that man talking with Brock's father?" Dirk pointed to their right.

Kira looked in that direction. She smiled. "That's Lord Philias Saint. He is a big supporter of King Jerard and he owns a big trading company in Oak City. Why do you ask?"

"Tonight, before the king and queen came out, I got a tingling sensation in my hand where that red mark is. I looked up and he was smiling at me."

"Well, that's just a coincidence," Kira replied nervously.

"That's not all, Mom. After I looked at him, he turned his gaze and I followed to see what he was looking at, and it was at Natia."

"Well, just how do you know that for sure?"

"Because she was looking at him and rubbing her hand in the same spot that I was. She then turned her gaze on me."

"Purely coincidental, that's all. You have had a very tiring day and I am sure you are imagining things. Look, we will talk tomorrow after you and Tab get done helping Lincoln. I promise. So, get out there, meet some new people, and head home early to get some rest," Kira held up a hand in a manner that meant, *don't ask anything else or argue*.

Dirk was frustrated from not getting any answers, "Ok, but I want you to meet someone first." Seeing that Volar was standing back from the conversation that he had been involved in, Dirk walked over, grabbed him, and he led him to Kira. "Mom, this is Volar, Volar this is my mom, Kira Storm."

Volar responded with a bow.

"It's nice to meet you, Volar of the Horan Clan," Kira said, bowing to him.

Dirk, confused, looked at Kira and then at Volar.

"Ah nice to meet you Kira of House Storm," Volar said respectfully.

"Ok, what is this talk?" Dirk asked them.

"It is proper etiquette to greet dwarven royalty in that manner."

Before Dirk could reply, Volar said, "Dirk, I am the son of King Horan. That is why your mother greeted me that way."

"Yes, we were introduced to each other at dinner, and we talked about the two of you," Kira explained.

"Oh, is that why you were referred to as kin's son?" Dirk asked.

"Yes, I told you that you would find out later," Volar replied, smiling. They talked for a few minutes before the other dwarf cadets came over and were introduced to Kira. After that, Volar took Dirk over and introduced him to his father and mother.

After talking with them for a while, Dirk decided he was going to take his mother's advice and head home and get some rest. He said his goodbyes and while he was walking to the door, he looked around for Tab. He had not seen him since he had left the table to go talk with El and Jonesy.

Someone grabbed his shoulder from behind. Dirk stopped, very weak in his knees. The blurred vision and sweats began to take over his body again. He shook off the feeling and turned to see Natia and an elderly elven woman standing there. "Oh hi," Dirk said sluggishly. That warm feeling was still with him.

"Hello, Dirk Storm. Are you okay?" Natia asked.

"Just tired."

She nodded. "I wanted to say goodbye before you left and introduce you to someone very important to me. This is Teyna. She has been my main trainer since I was five years old," Natia said, introducing him to the elderly elven woman.

"Hello, nice to meet you," Dirk said, bowing to kiss her hand as the custom required.

"No need for that," Teyna said rather brashly. "It is nice to meet the son of Kira. I should have met you years ago. I should have been involved with your training since you are half elven."

"Enough, Teyna, the past is the past. We will discuss that later," Natia said, dismissing Teyna. Teyna bowed and walked off towards the stage where Lord Saint was standing taking in the scene in front of him.

"What in all of Zona was that about?" Dirk asked Natia.

"She is very territorial when it comes to elven people being trained in the right way. Being from the house of Fleur Ian, your mother's family, she feels she should have trained you from the beginning," Natia stated.

"I don't get all the fuss. I'm just a normal kid, who is lucky enough to have both great races in his blood. I am honored that she feels that way, but I feel I would be a very disappointing student to her," Dirk humbly told Natia, avoiding looking her in the eyes. Natia reached out and grabbed Dirk's right hand and clasped it in hers.

Dirk started to resist her hand, then he looked up into her eyes. That warm rush spread through his body again. Along with Natia's touch, he gave into the struggle and let the feeling fill his body uncontested this time. For a moment, he could have sworn that he heard the war cry of a bird in the distance. He felt excitement and loss at the same time.

He heard Natia exhale and then clutch her chest with her free hand. "Dirk, you are not a mere normal person. The problem you have is that secrets have been withheld from you for a long time and for a good reason. The time is coming that you will know that which you did not know," Natia said, low enough that only Dirk could hear her.

As soon as she grabbed his hand, the rest of the world stopped moving. There was a fog surrounding them that no one could penetrate. He noticed Natia's thumb was rubbing a circle around the red mark on his palm. Every time she touched the spot, an intense sensation passed through his body.

Dirk looked up at her. Her amber eyes seemed to have flames flickering inside her irises. What he couldn't see was that his eyes were doing the same thing.

"What do you mean?" Dirk asked.

Natia looked away, releasing his hand. "The time for you to know is soon, just not tonight. I will see you in two days and if Kira has chosen to explain more to you, we will discuss this more. But if not, it is not my place to tell you that information. I must go for now."

Natia turned to walk away. Dirk grabbed her shoulder to stop her from leaving. Natia turned back and he could see a single tear slowly leaving the corner of her eye. Dirk took his thumb and wiped it away gently. Feeling out of control, he took a step closer to Natia. She defensively put both hands up to stop him from coming any closer. Dirk, for the first time, noticed Natia's left hand had the same red mark.

"Is that a red birth mark on your hand?" Dirk asked.

"Dirk," Natia said, pulling away and stepping back. "I have to go. I swear to Marluna that we will discuss this after, and only after, you talk with Aunt Kira," Natia walked away before he could respond. Dirk stood there with his mouth half-open and just watched her as she seemed to glide away like an angel. Not until he lost sight of her did he decide to head home, excited that he would get answers tomorrow.

Lord Philias Saint was standing in the corner of the banquet hall watching the sequence of events that were taking place between Dirk and Natia. *That seemed to be an interesting conversation*, he thought.

"Did you see what you wanted there?" an elven female came up behind him. Lord Saint turned to see Teyna walking towards him.

"Excuse me, my lady?" he said to her.

"It's just, I pay close attention to who is watching my Natia. It's my job to protect her from any threats my Lord."

"Oh, my lady, I can assure you I am no threat. I just love to see the goings on in the kingdom. It always helps in my business to be informed if there are any new alliances being formed," Lord Saint declared.

"I see. Just make sure your intentions are honorable and you have no need to fear me," Teyna told him.

"I can assure you that they are."

"Good, keep it that way," Teyna said, bowing and walking away to join Natia, who had left Dirk and was walking towards her parents.

Well that was odd, Lord Saint thought. He decided to continue his conversation with Lord Little, so he headed over to where he was talking with another group of friends.

"Lord Little, do you have time to finish our previous conversation now?" he asked, walking up to Lord Little. He agreed and after having a discussion for several minutes the two lords agreed on a small trading ship. Lord Saint made his reasons for having to head back to Oak City and left the banquet. He now had put one part of his plan into action. *The other parts will fall into place as time goes on*, he thought as he walked off the palace grounds. He flagged down a messenger and gave him a note to be delivered to Linc, telling him of his purchase and that he had a meeting with Lord Little in the morning.

Lord Philias Saint was always aware that he had been inhabited by Zona. In fact, he was a willing participant. He was very conscious for almost everything that Zona had done with the exception of the encounter with Teyna. Zona had sensed his wife but hadn't revealed he knew who she was. He would surprise her when the time was right. He didn't want Lord Saint to know what his wife was up to. Some things were for a god's ears only.

After Zona had disappeared from his body, Lord Saint went to the docks to prepare for the money for the ship to be transferred. He would then set sail for Oak City where he would have to get his new partnership set up at his offices. This would allow Linc to buy and trade at all of the ports as Lord Saint could. Lord Saint set out to do the task he needed to do. His intentions were definitely honorable, but were they what was best for everyone involved? *Only time will tell,* was his last thought as he left for the boat dock.

Changing of the guard

Dirk went straight home after the banquet. He came home to an empty house, so he went straight to bed. In the middle of the night he awoke to a cracking sound. Sitting up, he lit the candle by his bed and looked around the room to see what could've made that sound.

He got out of bed, walked to the window, and looked out to see if there was anything in the yard. Everything seemed to be quiet and still. He couldn't see anything that would have caused the disturbance. He took one fast look around the room and then sat on the bed, blew out the candle, and laid back down, thinking he had imagined the sound.

Up on the shelf above his desk, the rock he had found started to shake. If Dirk had looked closer at it, he would have noticed that the crack in the rock had gotten bigger. Just barely visible to the eye, a small shimmer of crimson light was beginning to seep through the crack.

The next morning, Dirk woke up early. *It's going to be a big day,* he thought as he got out of bed. He and Tab would help Linc get their business set up and then he would get some answers from his mother. He got dressed and went downstairs to eat breakfast. His grandfather was at the table, drinking caf and writing on the paper in front of him. His mother was cooking scrambled eggs at the stove. The smell of freshly cooked bacon had already hit Dirk's senses before he had even reached the stairs. He sat down at the table, his stomach growling. His grandfather looked up from his writing and smiled at him.

"Good morning," his mother said to him while putting some eggs and buttered toast in front of him.

"Good morning Mom. Good morning, Grandfather," Dirk said, grabbing his fork and shoveling down the eggs and toast.

"A little hungry, I see."

"Yes, I'm starving!" Dirk said while grabbing four strips of bacon.

"Ah good morning, son," his grandfather said, or rather grumbled.

"Whaath youv wooorking on vere?" Dirk asked his grandfather while shoveling food in his mouth.

"Dirk Storm! Do not talk while you are eating. It is very rude and unappealing," his mother fussed.

Dirk washed down his food with some juice. "Sorry."

His grandfather stood up, "That's it, I have to go the palace."

"Father, what's the rush?" Kira asked.

"I have a meeting with General Harkin about palace business. That's all I can say. Don't ask me anything else," he said, kissing Kira on the cheek before rushing out the door.

"Well, everyone always seems to be running off with secrets around here," Dirk said, staring pointedly at his mother.

"Dirk, there is more to life than knowing everything everyone else does. This life isn't just about you, young man!" Kira said, glaring at him. "I know we need to talk, but I, just like your grandfather, have to meet Naira and Natia this morning to catch up. We'll have this overdue discussion tonight at dinner, agreed?"

"Yes, Mom, but no more delays,"

"Ok, tonight, we will talk. What are you and your pack up to?"

"Nothing really, just hanging out and helping Linc with a few things. We start school testing soon, so we want to make sure he's set up."

Kira smiled and squeezed Dirk's shoulder. "Your grandfather did your chores for you this morning since you had a busy day yesterday. Thank him when he comes back." Dirk nodded. "All right. Clean your room before you leave and get your dirty laundry down to be washed,"

"Yes Mom."

Kira smiled and kissed Dirk on the forehead. "Now wash your dishes while I clean up the rest. Then you can get started upstairs."

After he finished eating, Dirk washed his dishes and headed upstairs. When he walked into his room, he couldn't believe the state of it.

"What is that smell?" The smell of burnt rock hit him. It was like rotten eggs that had been laying in the coop on a hot summer's day. He looked around the room but couldn't seem to find the source of the smell. His window was open and figured that the smell was coming from outside.

"Probably Mt. Blazire. I've got to hurry, I have to meet Tab and Linc in two hours," Dirk said to himself as he looked around his room and saw the mounting pile of clothes on the floor. He picked them up hand put them in the basket his mother had left by the door earlier. He made his bed, choosing to sleep on the sheets one more night.

I should leave the window open, so some fresh air can circulate that smell out, Dirk thought. He opened the window wider. A gush of fresh air blew in, causing the papers on his desk to flutter to the floor. "By Zona!" Dirk exclaimed and walked over to pick them up.

When he placed them on the desk, he noticed little black particles on his desk. "What is this mess?" Dirk said out loud, picking some of it up and rubbing it between his fingers. He looked around the desk, and on his shelf, he saw the rock from the other day. He picked it up.

It was about the size of his fist. He rolled it around in his hand, looking at it, and noticed that there was a crack in it. He picked up the small side knife he always wore, stuck the tip into the crack and wiggled the tip side to side. The rock was crusted around another object, probably another stone.

Dirk kept chipping away at the crust. Finally realizing that the crust was dried lava. "Hells," Dirk said, really excited. "The only thing that lava can crust around is a stone of power!" He frantically chipped away at the lava.

All of a sudden with a dull poof, the lava crumbled away. In his hand, he realized, was a gem. It was crimson in color with hints of yellow flames streaking through the stone. He got a warm sensation from touching it. He rolled it around in his hands, examining it closer. The loud screech of a bird sounded in the distance, as if it were on a hunt.

Dirk quickly ran to the window and looked up. In the sky to the west, flying towards Blazire, was a beautiful bird. It almost looked as if fire wafted off its wings. It flew higher and higher, chirping a sorrowful song.

Suddenly, a brown streak shot towards the bird. As if struck by an object, the beautiful bird rapidly descended at angle falling toward Mt. Blazire at a startling speed. Dirk grabbed his shoulder satchel, and without a second thought, he snatched the crimson stone up and put it inside the bag.

He grabbed his bow and arrows, put his knife in its scabbard on his belt, and raced out the front door. He headed straight for the path that led to the mountain.

He passed Tab as he was running out the door without even noticing him. "Hey!" Tab yelled as Dirk ran by him towards the trail that entered the woods.

Dirk didn't hear him because he only had one thought on his mind. He didn't know why but getting to that fallen bird was important. The most important thing he would ever do. It was a matter of life and death.

As he ran through Brier Forest, he noticed it seemed to be darker than normal today. There were no sounds, not any, no animals, or insects. It was deathly quiet, which put Dirk on high alert. The training his grandfather had drilled into him when he was young took over. The scent of death filled his nose as he ran deeper into the darkness of the woods. Pain, emanating from his birthmark, shot through his hand. Dirk shook the pain away and kept running toward his destination.

I can't remember the woods ever being quiet like this, he thought. It was like all the animals were gone or in hiding.

He jerked his head side to side as he ran, looking for the hidden danger he sensed was there. He looked at every tree as he passed. Even though he was searching closely as he ran, he failed to see the two figures in the shadows, who were watching him.

Dirk ran as fast as he could to reach Mt. Blazire. He still hadn't noticed the two forms that had been following him when he finally spotted the end of the trail. When he got to the base of the mountain, a searing pain ripped through his right side. *Is the frightened creature the cause of it?*

Dirk gasped and ran to the fallen creature, kneeling beside it. For some reason, he didn't understand yet, but he knew it was a phoenix, the most beautiful creature he had ever seen. A wooden arrow was sticking out of her chest.

Dirk's eyes met the phoenix's and a familiar sense overwhelmed him. He knew immediately that the bird was dying and there was nothing he could do to save her. "Who would do something so vile?" Dirk screamed to the sky as tears slowly formed in his eyes.

A rustling sound at the edge of the forest caught his attention. Dirk took up a defensive position over the phoenix and turned to see what had made the noise. There, standing between two trees were two figures. They were both about four feet tall with dark, rugged skin and sickening yellow eyes. Both were glaring at him, as if he had somehow made them angry.

"Wood nymphs! What do you want?" Dirk screamed at the two creatures.

"You wills nots beats Father. We's wills makes sures of this!" the creature on the left squeaked in a slithery voice. Dirk noticed the one on the right had an arrow, the same type that had shot the phoenix, aimed at his chest.

"What are you talking about, you idiot?" Dirk screamed. Not knowing where his defiance came from, he stood as the protector of the fallen phoenix. He glared back at the two wood nymphs. After laying the phoenix behind him, in one smooth motion, he stood up and nocked his own arrow. "I am not afraid of you."

"You cants hits boths of us," the nymph on the right said. There was a loud *thwump* and then a screech.

"NOS YOU ARES DEADS!" the wood nymph screamed, looking at his partner who was now nailed to a tree with an arrow sticking through its heart, its eyes void of life.

Now, I believe that there are two of us to your one," Tab said, out of breath, appearing from the trail with another arrow nocked and aimed.

"You wills pays. I promises the fathers wills makes you pays!" the creature said before he and his dead comrade disappeared in a rush of wind.

"What in the hell, Dirk. Wood nymphs?" Tab asked.

"I don't know." Dirk turned back to the dying bird.

Tab ran to Dirk's side, looking in awe at the phoenix on the ground. Dirk gently grabbed the phoenix.

Tab pulled the arrow out slowly and threw it to the ground. "By Zona that's a phoenix, isn't it?"

"It is," Dirk responded.

"I thought the stories were just wild tales," Tab said. Dirk agreed. Dirk stared at the beautiful bird, feeling helpless. Tears slowly rolled from the bird's eyes. The hole where the arrow had been closed almost immediately.

Dirk felt a rustling in his pack. He slipped it off his shoulder and set it on the ground. He stuck his free hand inside, and felt a warmth coming from the crimson jewel. He had forgotten that he had put in there. He pulled it out.

"What is that?" Tab asked, growing more perplexed by the minute.

"That's the rock we found on our last trip here," Dirk said with more force than he meant to. Not knowing why, he held the stone in front of the phoenix's beak. She looked into Dirk's eyes. When their eyes connected, the bond that had been there since his father's death came alive instantly.

Unable to cope with the visions filling his head, he fell to his knees. Tab caught his friend under the arm to steady him. Tab's touch formed a similar link with him. He was able to feel and see what Dirk was feeling.

Tab sank to the ground as well. They didn't know how long it took, but from the connection Arial, the phoenix, had with them, she let them see things through her eyes. Her reason for being, her connection to Dirk's father, their familiar relationship. The sacrifice that was made by Thaddeus, Tab's father and Diron's friend. The sacrifices made by his father. The reasons they had made those sacrifices.

And the realization that the stone Dirk was holding was not a stone at all. It was an egg, a phoenix egg. They now knew the purpose of the egg and why from this day forward they would have to protect it until it was ready to protect them.

As fast as it started, it was over. Tab and Dirk both exhaled at the same time, as if they had been holding their breath. The emotions that racked them were overwhelming. Tears were freely falling down their faces. It took a few minutes for the boys to gather their thoughts. They stared at each other for a moment, then at Arial. She blinked, seeming to acknowledge that they understood.

They both nodded in unison. Arial bent her neck forward and pecked the egg still in Dirk's hand.

In that instant, a bright crimson light expanded from Arial and the egg. It grew to engulf Dirk and Tab as well. They could feel raw power surging from Arial flowing into them and the egg. Dirk's body heated up, as if he were going to explode. The mark on his hand began to pulse and grow.

Tab made the mistake of touching the egg with his free hand. He was immediately blasted backwards and fell unconscious. The light soon faded, and Dirk looked at the bird in his hand. But she was gone, vanishing along with the light.

The egg was no longer an egg. The shell had crumbled into small pieces of ash leaving only a baby phoenix. The bird was crimson with an orange beak and talons. "You are magnificent!" Dirk said to the newborn phoenix. It's eyes caught Dirk's overall attention. They were emerald, green with yellow-orange streaks running through them.

Dirk's eyes felt warm, but so did his whole body. If he had a mirror, he would have noticed that his eyes had changed a little and were similar to the baby phoenix he now held in his hands.

Dirk realized that Tab was not standing by him anymore and he looked around. Tab was laying on the ground with smoke coming off his left sleeve.

"Tab!" Dirk's scream seemed to make Tab come around.

"Ow!" Tab groaned, trying to get up.

"Be still for a moment," Dirk said, walking over and bending down beside Tab's outstretched body. "You'll be okay. Just give the power a minute to diminish."

"Is that what that was?" Tab asked.

"A transfer, from Arial to the baby phoenix. Me and you got it as well." Tab eyes had changed, but just not the extent as Dirk's had. A little greenish flame, barely noticeable circled his retina.

"How do we know?" Tab asked, but he knew what Dirk was saying was true.

"I don't know, I just feel it," Dirk responded. Tab lay there for a few more minutes then started getting up, leaning on Dirk's shoulder.

"Why didn't you get knocked out?" Tab asked.

Dirk shook his head, clearing some of the cobwebs from the transfer. "I guess I was the conduit of the two. I was supposed to be touching them both. Not you, though. That was a little unexpected, I think. It should be okay since you're standing now." Dirk looked at the baby phoenix.

"I don't know what to think. Did you see everything I did?" Tab asked with tears in his eyes. Dirk grabbed Tab with his free hand and pulled him into a hug, overcome with the grief they were both feeling.

"Yes, I did. I am so sorry for what your father went through."

"Hey, it looked to me that they both made their choices, as I would make for you."

"Never! I will *never* let you give up your life for me." They had always loved each other as brothers but now that bond was even stronger, knowing what their fathers had meant to each other. "Family is what we are, family is what we will always be. This only proves that."

Tab smiled at Dirk. "Right you are, brother."

Dirk looked at the phoenix and smiled. He looked back at Tab, who was getting his legs under him. "I wonder what my mom knew?"

"I don't know, but from what I saw, she knows more than she let on."

Dirk agreed. The boys sat down on the ground and looked at the baby phoenix Dirk was holding, pondering everything running through their heads.

After a long few minutes, Dirk broke the silence. "This is a lot to take in right now."

"I think our future plans may have just changed," Tab said.

Dirk looked at the phoenix and then at Tab. "Are you okay now?"

"I don't know. It's a lot to take in all at once,"

"Only thing I know for sure right now is Linc is going to kill us. We better do something with our little friend here and go meet him," Tab said as they got up and started walking back to the farm. "Oh, by the way, why was that wood nymph trying to kill you?"

"I think it has something to do with what we just went through."

Tab nodded in understanding. "I always thought they were fiction."

"Me too, until about ten minutes ago,"

"So, fill me in on what I missed," Tab said. Dirk filled Tab in on everything that had happened that morning from the discovery of the egg to seeing Arial getting shot.

"What are we going to do with our friend here?"

"We better set her up in the barn. I think I can make a nest out of hay in the top of the loft and set it up with chicken feed and water. That should be good until we get back this afternoon."

Protecting the young phoenix in his arms with Tab beside him as an honor guard, Dirk started running to the farm as fast as he could.

Dirk felt like his heart was going to break leaving the baby bird alone, but it had to be done this one time. "I promise I will be back soon," he said to the little bird after setting the phoenix up in a safely in the loft.

Squeak, squeak. The phoenix was nodding to Dirk. He just smiled because somehow, he knew what she was saying to him.

"She is a, her," Dirk said to Tab.

"Of course, she is her, you dummy. She is always her." Wait a minute, who are you talking about?"

"The phoenix, it's she," Dirk said, smiling.

"How do you know?"

"I just do."

"You're right. I feel it too. Okay, I just don't know if this is going to work, but we need answers,"

"You're right and tonight we will have them,"

"I want to be there."

"You will be. Both of our fathers were involved and now both of us are too. I say you hide in the barn with the phoenix until I call for you. And when the time comes, you can walk in with the phoenix. Let's see what reaction we get from that."

"Linc is going to kill us. We better run," Tab said as they left.

The Docks

After they had set up the baby phoenix in the barn and made sure she was safe, Dirk and Tab took off toward the docks where they knew Linc would be waiting. They found Linc standing by the port entrance, pacing back and forth impatiently.

"Where the hells have you two been? I've been waiting for an hour!" Linc yelled at them.

"I know we're late, but there's a good reason," Dirk replied.

"It damn well better be. I have a lot to tell you both about what I was unable to last night," Linc explained. They looked at him with a *you have no idea look*.

"Well?" Dirk and Tab asked in unison. Linc told them a little about meeting Lord Philias Saint the night before.

"That sounds a little too good to be true, doesn't it?" Tab asked.

"Well, it certainly does, but stranger things have happened lately," Dirk replied smiling at Tab.

"Wait, what happened? I know that smile." Linc looked at both of them suspiciously.

"That can wait. Let's discuss you and Lord Saint," Dirk responded. Linc explained more about their meeting but was still vague about the merchant. Linc assured them that he was only looking for a new investment. Dirk and Tab, trusting Linc's judgement, finally took him at his word. They planned the best course to take and headed to Lord Little's office to secure a vessel first.

Dirk saw that the port was busy, as was usual for this time of the day. The fisherman, who had gone out early that morning, were bringing in their catches to trade at the market. A few of the cloth merchants had arrived that morning by ship and were heading to the trading area as well. They carried fine silks, expensive cloth, and even some very special hats in their inventory that they had bargained for at their last stop. Fur and meat trappers were heading in from the mountains.

The boys walked with an air of excitement in their step. They had talked about this their entire life, and it was about to happen. As they were walking around the corner beside one of the dockside taverns, Linc noticed a pair of eyes watching them.

Linc elbowed Dirk, nodding in the direction of the two skulking figures. The three of them, since they hung out so much together growing up, knew how to communicate without words.

Tab caught the nod and readied himself for the thugs that were heading their way.

"So, Louy? Wha do we ave ere?" boomed a voice in front of the boys. The boys stopped as the giant shadow seemed to appear out of nowhere.

Standing in front of them was one big-brutish looking guy and a smaller man with a patch over his left eye. "I don't have time for this right now, Kumbo," Linc said to one of the two men blocking their way. He instantly balled his fist. Both Tab and Dirk took up defensive positions on each side of their friend.

"Oy, look at the little dodgers, thinking they can step up to us," Louy said, laughing.

"Ram wan's a word wit you, little thief. You still have a debt, and he wants it repaid," Kumbo said to Linc.

"I don't owe him anything and you make sure you tell him that," Linc said. They both laughed. As if he had any choice in the matter.

"Well you're coming with us, whether you like it or not," Louy said. In that moment, several things happened at once. Kumbo reached out to grab Linc by the collar of his shirt while Louy drew his knife from his belt.

Linc ducked Kumbo's grab and swept his leg around, catching him in the right knee. He hit it with such force that there was a loud snap. Kumbo fell to the ground, grabbing his injured knee. "You little *bastard!*" Kumbo screamed.

Seeing all of this happen, Louy swung his knife at Linc's throat. Moving as one, Dirk and Tab reacted quickly. Tab caught Louy's arm as it was coming down and Dirk stepped in, punching Louy in the chest hitting him with such force that Louy dropped his knife. He was knocked back, collapsing on the ground unconscious.

If anyone had seen Dirk's eyes, they would have seen the flames flaring in them at the moment of attack.

Kumbo, not believing what he had just seen, said, "You're gonna pay little thief, and your little buddies will too."

"No, I'm done with all of you, and you can tell Ram that. I've been done with you a long time so leave it be," Linc said before kicking Kumbo in the head, knocking him out, and then the three walked away from the small crowd that had begun to gather.

Dusting himself off and looking at Dirk and Tab, he said, "Thanks, but what the hells was that Dirk?"

Both Dirk and Tab looked at each other and nodded in agreement. "Ok, we'll tell you why we were late, but like everything we do, this stays between us three," Dirk said. Linc looked between the two and nodded. Dirk and Tab told the story of everything that had happened that morning.

Linc looked at the two them with a grin on his face. "Ok, the joke's on me. That was just a lucky punch, huh?" Linc laughed at them. With a serious look in his eyes, Dirk grabbed Linc's arm a little harder than he meant to.

The connection sent a small spark into Linc's arm. "Ow!" Linc scowled at him and pulled away. A sudden realization came over him. He just stared at Dirk's eyes squinting, and then he realized that he could see flames rippling in them. He then looked at Tab and saw the same in his eyes. His mouth hung open in shock.

He realized at that moment that they were telling him the truth. "By Zona, you two have flames in your eyes!" Linc exclaimed. Dirk and Tab hadn't seen the flames yet. They looked at each other and confirmed what he had just told them.

"Probably because of the bond," Dirk said. They turned to Linc and smiled. All three of them looked at each other and started laughing.

"What does it all mean you think?" Linc asked.

"I don't know yet. But let's keep it between us for now. Remember just us three," Dirk said as they all grasped arms. What a strange sight that would have been, if anyone had been looking, but luckily at that moment the crowds walking by them paid little attention to them.

Soon enough they had arrived at Lord Little's merchant office. "Ah boys, there you are. I have been waiting for you," said a silver-haired man standing behind the sales counter.

"Sorry we're late, Mr. Little. We had a little trouble before coming to meet you this morning, but we sorted it out," Linc said, smiling at the other two. The boys had decided to let Linc do all the talking since he would be dealing with the everyday business of the ship.

"Ah, still having problems with Ram, I see. I can help with that if you will let me," Mr. Little told them.

"No thanks, we handled it, but we really appreciate the offer. It's better if we do it," Linc replied.

"Ok. If ever you change your mind, just let me know. Now, I believe you are here to pick out a ship, Linc?"

"Yes sir,"

"Now, you seemed to have already set up your first business arrangement with Lord Saint." Dirk and Tab looked at each other, still a little confused by Lord Philias Saint's interest. "He is a very shrewd businessman, so you must have impressed him young Linc."

"Yes, he said he was looking for a new business venture and I was in the right place at the right time,"

Mr. Little nodded in agreement.

"He has guaranteed to help purchase your first ship for your new business so what would you like?" Dirk and Tab were excited and not really paying attention to the last part of what Mr. Little said. "So, what will it be?"

The boys had discussed this at length and knew that they needed to start out with a smaller sloop. Since Linc was starting without Dirk and Tab, he would have to hire two or three crewmen so he needed a ship that a small crew could handle.

They had learned about different types of ships over the years working with Mr. Little. Small sloops had up to a twenty-five-hundred-pound cargo hold with two small sails and a sleeping cabin. It provided cover in the bad weather and was easily handled by that many crew members.

"I think we want a seventy-foot sloop, which a crew of four can handle," Linc replied.

"Well, let's see what I have," Lord Little said, opening the ledger he had on the counter in front of him. "I have a seventy-five-foot, eight-oar hole sloop with two sails that will hold up to twenty-eight hundred pounds of cargo. It is a little old, probably at least twenty-years old, but has just been reconditioned." The boys looked at each other and immediately agreed on it.

"How much do you want for it?" Linc asked.

"Let's see, two fifty for the ship, one twenty for the sails, seventy-five for the oars and tact. I'll throw in fishing rods and nets for twenty, ten empty barrels for water and storage, ten food crates, one thousand yards of rope, and three canopies. Four hundred and fifty silvers for the lot."

Dirk and Tab looked shocked. They knew they needed money, but this was a little more than they had planned for.

"I'll take it," Linc said with pride.

"Wait a minute," Dirk said before Tab could interject.

Link shushed them, "Guys, it's covered." Dirk and Tab looked at Linc like he had lost his mind. He just smiled. "I'll explain after we sign the agreement."

Lord Little had the paperwork drawn up and then they all signed the agreement.

"Well, remember if you have any trouble with the ship, bring it back and we can fix anything wrong with it. Also, since everything was arranged to be paid for by Lord Saint, there is still about two hundred silvers left." Dirk and Tab just stared at Linc, wondering what kind of a deal he'd gotten them into. "Do you want that now or do you need anything else?"

"No, sir, we don't need anything else right now. We'll take the difference now, so I can go to the harbor master's office and buy the permits we need for the ports," Linc replied. Mr. Little agreed. Linc could tell Dirk and Tab were about to burst with questions so he smiled and said, "When we leave, I'll tell you everything."

Lord Little gave them the ownership papers and the remaining silvers in a small leather bag. He then showed them where the ship was docked and shook all of their hands. "I envy you three, just starting out. Oh, the adventures you will have. I'm jealous. Linc, are you going to be able to handle this while they slack off at school?"

The boys laughed "Yes sir, we have a good plan, we believe," Dirk said.

"That's good. Just remember, I'm here if you need any support. You boys did a great job for me over the years and I'm proud to help if I can."

"Thank you," they said in unison.

"I only wish Brock could be as prepared as you three are." Lord Little either didn't know his son was evil or if he did, he chose to ignore it.

The boys left the shop and as soon as they were out the door, Linc was cornered by Dirk and Tab who demanded to know what was going on. Linc explained in detail about his run in with Lord Saint the day before.

"That's a little fishy, isn't it?" Tab remarked.

"Yes, but he checked out. I talked with a lot of the traders after I met him, so he seems legit," Linc explained.

"We're entrusting our future with you, Linc, and we trust your judgement," Dirk replied.

"Thanks, guys. I know what's at risk here."

"Let's get those permits and secure anything else you need, like a few crew members to start with," Dirk said.

They went to buy the permits and Linc got the required maps needed for his first trip. They talked with Stumpy Cask, the owner of the Falcon's Nest. He gave them the names of three men who were looking to join a crew.

River Cask, Stumpy's son, was eighteen years old and an experienced fisherman, so he would be valuable when finding fishing spots. River and the boys had always been friends, so it seemed to be a good idea to let him join the crew. Dirk and Tab both felt it was a great idea for Linc to have someone he knew and already trusted on the crew.

The rest of the crew was made up of Kaz Toped, Corky and Jerle. Kaz was the son of Marco Toped, the market trading manager. Linc thought he would be able to help move their purchases easier. Kaz had been in and out of trouble a lot, but Linc and the guys liked him, so they decided to give him a chance. Corky was an older experienced sailor, who liked the spirits a little too much, but he knew the waters really well. Jerle 'Jurly' was another experienced sailor. He was known for not taking orders well, but he was a good worker. He agreed to come aboard if Linc would take advice if he felt he needed to give it. Linc reluctantly accepted. He was really the best of what was left to choose from, Dirk told him.

With the crew assembled, they planned to purchase the items they still needed and then helped Linc plan a route to the Oak City port where Lord Saint's warehouse was located. Linc would be leaving in two days so they sat around for a while, talking about situations, and making sure he had a good plan to deal with whatever came up.

The guys left, satisfied with their plan. Linc made sure they would meet up in a few days to finalize any plans they missed and so they could fill him in on the confrontation with Kira. After coming to an agreement they headed their separate ways.

Chosen

Later that evening at The Horned Goat, one of the seedier taverns in Silver City, a meeting was taking place. A dark hooded figure sat at a table in the darkest corner of the bar. He was meeting with Ram Stockton and his first lieutenant.

"Your efforts to thwart young Mr. Storm's plans seem to be falling very short of my expectations," the dark figure said angrily.

"Aye, me lord, we have made a few mistakes I agree, but I have a plan in place to make up for previous failings," Ram said nervously while Monk, his first lieutenant nodded anxiously in agreement.

"Well, you better. I answer to a higher power and his patience isn't what mine is. I don't need to know how, but Linc can't be allowed to meet with Lord Saint in Oak City. You have failed to stop their initial meeting. Now, you foil the second meeting, or else! Do you understand me?!"

"I do, my Lord. It will be taken care of." Ram squirmed.

With that, the hooded figure rose and seemed to glide out the door without anyone noticing, or so he thought.

"You're an idiot!" Ram cursed as he slapped Monk on the back of the head. Ram was a tall man with a regular build, but he was a cutthroat and all of the people down at the docks knew it. Monk was taller than Ram and built like a troll, but he was terrified of the man. He had seen him do inexplicable things and knew he was not above being replaced.

"We had Linc. I don't know what happened. That Storm kid and his friend seemed to anticipate what Kumbo was going to do and almost broke his leg. And poor Louy has broken ribs from the altercation," Monk said.

"They just got lucky, that's all, huh?" Ram asked sarcastically. "You better make sure that ship they bought has been sabotaged so it doesn't make it to Oak City, or it might be the death of us, you understand?"

"I do, I swears," Monk said, heading out the door before Ram could slap him again.

In the other corner of the tavern, someone had witnessed the whole meeting. He got up quietly and headed out the door. Once outside the bar, when he had gotten far enough away to avoid being noticed, Linc pulled his hood down to get some fresh air.

"I knew he would be planning something dirty. I'll have to keep a watch out for something else to happen. I just wonder who that figure was? It's too bad I couldn't hear what he was saying. I'll have to let Tab and Dirk know about this when I see them tomorrow so they can be on the alert," Linc said to himself as he walked home.

Back at the Storm barn, while Linc was doing his undercover surveillance, Dirk and Tab were preparing to put their plan into effect. "Ok, the plan is you wait for me to stand in front of the kitchen window. When you see me, bring our little surprise in," Dirk said.

"Okay don't be too long. I'm starving," Tab said, holding the baby phoenix in his arms. Dirk softly rubbed the top of the phoenix's head. A small electrical charge crackled along his fingers as he did. Both the guys were amazed at what they were seeing.

"We just need answers," Dirk replied as he turned and walked out of the barn to the house. Dirk, who had been pretty tired after the day's events, felt very refreshed now and knew it was from the bird.

Dirk walked into the kitchen using the back door. Kira was preparing dinner by the sink. "Ah, there you are," Kira said. Dirk noticed she was making a fruit salad with mixed nuts. He walked over to his mother and gave her a hug. She seemed a bit startled.

"What's gotten into you?" Kira asked, putting her hands on Dirk's face. Turning his face to look at her, Kira just stared at him to make sure everything was all right. Then, as she looked into his eyes, she gasped loudly and pushed him back a little to get a better look. A smile crossed his face as she gazed into his eyes.

"What's all this noise in here?" the General said as he walked into the kitchen. "What is it, boy? What has happened?"

The general walked in front of them. After not receiving a response, he grabbed Dirk by the shoulder and turned him around to look at him. The general, eyeing Dirk up and down, finally looked at his face and saw the small flames rippling in his eyes. Realizing what had happened, he took a step back and smiled, his chest swelling with pride.

Kira stood there, looking at both of them with a hand over her mouth. A single tear rolled down her face.

"It has finally happened," his grandfather stated. "So where is Arial?" He looked out the window.

Dirk stepped in front of the window and looked at them. "She's not here, Grandfather."

"Preposterous! This couldn't have happened without her."

"Dirk, what happened?" Kira asked, finally regaining her composure. She sensed something was not right. At that moment, Tab walked in the back door with the baby phoenix nestled in his arms. All three turned at the sound of the door closing. The baby phoenix squeaked as Kira and the general saw what was in Tab's arms.

"No..." the general said, stunned at the sight of the tiny bird. He stumbled back. Dirk grabbed him and guided him to the nearest chair. Kira, her eyes now flowing with tears, walked over to the table, and sat down beside her father-in-law. She put her hand on his shoulder then leaned her head against it.

"Tell us what happened," the general said to Dirk.

Dirk, surprised by their reactions, walked to the table, and sat down. Tab sat beside him. Dirk put his hand over theirs and began to tell the story. When he got to the part about the dark wood nymphs, Tab jumped in and told his part. They both finished the story together, sharing what they had experienced and describing all of the emotions that had engulfed them.

"Wait a minute," Kira said, getting up. She rushed over to Tab, grabbed him by his face, and looked into his eyes. A sudden recognition came over her as she realized what had happened. She pulled Tab out of the chair and into a hug. Tab, having only one hand free, handed the phoenix to Dirk and then hugged Kira back, as any son would a mother.

"I'm so sorry Tab. I never wanted this for you," Kira said, hugging him tighter. "I know I have been rough towards you, but it was only because of my desire-for you to have a normal life." Kira paused for a moment and then took a calming breath. "Dirk's destiny was to have to deal with all of this Chosen business, not you. I knew what had happened to your father. Then your mother passed a few years later. I wanted to at least keep one of you away from all of this. I want you to know that I've always loved you like a son and I wanted nothing but the best for you." She began to cry again and squeezed Tab harder.

Tab, overwhelmed with emotions from the day and from what Kira had just said, began to cry. In that moment, the pain of many years dissolved away with that embrace. Kira grabbed Dirk with her other arm and pulled him into the hug.

The general, figuring out what had happened, cleared his throat loudly. The three embraced heard him and looked to the general. "Well, I guess there's questions to be answered now."

Kira kissed Tab's forehead. She released the boys and they all sat down at the table. Dirk, who was still clutching the phoenix, placed the baby in the center of table between them. He caressed its head before looking at the general.

"Boys, first, let me see your eyes." The general stared first into Dirk's, then after a few minutes, he looked at Tab's. "Well, this is a first. I have never read about the powers being shared before." The general held up his hand to stop the onslaught of questions that the boys were fixing to ask. "Let me explain."

He then told them the short version of the Storm family history, and about the Chosen and their connection to the phoenix. "It all began five hundred and twelve years ago with the first Chosen, Dorian Storm," He then briefly summarized the history up through Dirk's father, paraphrasing a lot in the middle, and assured them they would learn the rest in due time. Dirk and Tab sat listening to every detail that the General was giving them.

He explained a little about the protectors and the connections they had with the Chosen, the abilities that normally came from the connection, the power and the weaknesses, and the feelings from the union would cause.

"Now, I am not sure how Tab being connected will affect the union, but there has to be some limitations on you since it's not a singular bond."

They all sat there in silence for a few minutes, just staring at the baby bird. Dirk and Tab still had questions, so they started asking a few.

"You don't have to worry about those things right now. I'll be back in a few minutes." The General got up and left the room.

Kira, still looking at both boys, held their hands in hers. She had been quiet while the general spoke. "The first thing you two need to make sure is that you do not tell anyone," she said in a very serious tone. Dirk and Tab both squeezed her hand.

"Mom, you sure seem to know a lot about all of this," Dirk said.

Kira just smiled, "I'll explain later, but now you *must* keep this a secret."

The boys looked away from her. "Well, it's kind of little late for that. We told Linc today. But he swore he wouldn't tell anyone about it. And you know he won't," Dirk said before Kira could respond.

Kira released a heavy breath. "That's it, then. There will be a time later when you, Dirk, must share this with other people, but Tab, for your safety we must keep this a secret from everyone. It could mean the difference between life and death," Kira said seriously. "There are more evil things at play here. More than you know yet. You will both learn about those dangers later. Just remember, your secret should be maintained until the time is right. I'm sure you both will know when it is time to reveal it as the events of the future unfold."

Kira paused in thought. "You will learn from what I believe your grandfather is getting. There are other things more important to the future.

The first thing you both need to do is learn to control the flames in your eyes. It becomes visible when you're agitated, angry, or excited. It's kind of like a warning signal for danger, and if a strong emotion overcomes you." Kira looked at them for acknowledgement. They both nodded. "You have to relax and calm your emotions. Just close your eyes and concentrate on something that will center your focus. Do you understand?" Kira released their hands.

They both nodded.

"Now, both of you, close your eyes and think about something calming. Take a few deep breaths in and out."

The boys closed their eyes and concentrated. Kira could tell it was easier for Tab than it was for Dirk by their body movements. Tab had his father to focus on. He finally knew what happened to him. The pride he now had was calming.

Tab took a deep breath and envisioned his father, the hero, standing next to him. The sensation like a cool breeze blowing across his face, washed over him. He opened his eyes and looked at Kira.

"That's perfect, Tab. Now, remember that feeling. What happens usually is you'll feel a warm sensation in your eyes. When you feel it, your powers are easy to reach. Sometimes it could be a more forceful feeling, if the need is dire, but just keep practicing turning off your power every time you feel that warmth."

Dirk thought about what would calm him. Hunting in the woods, his friends, his new business venture, and the pride he had in his father. Nothing was working. He opened his eyes. "I can't do it!"

"Dirk," Kira said, grabbing his hands. "There is always something that switches the power off. Just close your eyes again and take a deep breath. It could be something old or something new. A hobby, an animal, or even a person."

"Ok," Dirk said, exhaling his frustration and closing his eyes. A few minutes passed. *Just relax, idiot.* Then a calming sensation passed over his entire body. All of a sudden, he could see a pair of amber eyes looking deeply at him. They were recognizable, but he couldn't quite make out whose eyes he was seeing. Then, as if stepping back, his vision zoomed out. He realized it was an elven female staring at him. She was talking to him. *This is the most beautiful creature I have ever seen.*

Then she smiled at him and two things happened to him at once. He felt a cool breeze blow across his face, and as if holding his breath, he let out a deep sigh of relief.

"Natia," he whispered to himself. It was the elven princess. Kira could feel the tension in Dirk's hands relax and she knew he had found his focus.

Dirk opened his eyes and had the biggest smile on his face. "That's good. You both found your calm. Keep what it is to yourselves. That way, no one can ever use them to distract you when it is needed."

Dirk looked at Tab and Kira. He noticed they had been watching him closely. A sound like a half-purr half-chirp came from the phoenix.

They all looked at her and realized she had almost doubled in size. A small ring of smoke was rising from her, and the little nest she had been in was now a pile of ash. Tab and Dirk looked at Kira, confused. "What happened?" they asked in unison.

Kira just laughed into her hand. "That, my boys, was your second and third connection to the power of the phoenix. She will grow as you grow; I think. Probably faster now since you'll begin using your powers. It'll be slow until you understand more. Do you understand?" she asked the boys.

They both nodded in agreement. Dirk watched as his grandfather walked back into the room with several things in his hands. One was his father's sword.

Both Tab and Dirk looked at it in wonder because the jewels in the sword were now glowing like a star at night, a pulse was coming from the center of each jewel. He set it on the table between Dirk and Tab.

Another thing he had was an exquisite long bow that seemed to be made of the same materials as the prizes from the archery contest. It was three and a half feet long and had seven jewels set into the wood, three small jewels on each side of a larger blue gem in the center and they were all pulsing faintly. The wood was white as bone, there was what looked like ancient elven runes carved into it, and the string seemed to sparkle in the light.

He placed the bow on the table as well. There was also a set of daggers in jewel-crusted sheaths. The handles had similar, smaller pulsing jewels around the hilts. He put them by the bow and sword. And the last thing he had was an ancient book.

"First thing to remember is you must learn slowly as well as making sure to document everything as you go. Second, you mustn't push yourself too hard either because we might not have the answers we need right now for what all this will do to you."

Both boys, nodded, "Yes sir."

The general and Kira both laughed at this.

"By Zona, boys. You're not in the military taking orders. I'm just passing on the knowledge you'll need," the general said, still laughing.

There was a loud growl coming from Tab. Everyone looked at him. "Sorry, I don't know about any of you, but with everything that happened today, I'm starving!"

Kira stood up. "Yes, that's very important, you'll learn. You must keep fed properly to be at full strength." The phoenix trilled in agreement. "I'll get her some cornmeal and finish making dinner for us." She placed a cup of water and a small pile of cornmeal in front of the phoenix.

While Kira was busy with dinner, the general explained the weapons that he had set on the table. The boys listened carefully. It seemed to Dirk that the phoenix was listening and nodding in agreement as she ate.

Tab picked up the daggers noticing that nothing happened with the blades and there was no reaction inside him. The general had explained that the weapon's powers were dormant when they were not engaged. This would save the power reserved in the gems. They were still deadly, but the magic wasn't active at that time. The gems would slowly gain strength when in proximity of a Chosen or a protector since they pulled their strength from the core of the Chosen. They didn't always need them for their power.

Dirk was inspecting the bow. "Grandfather, I've never seen the bow or daggers before. Where were they?"

"They were stored away from prying eyes," he said with a grin. "I know how you two are inquisitive, especially when you're here by yourself, so they were put away until they were needed. The blade was your fathers, as it was mine in my time as the Chosen. Its name is Harbinger," the general told them.

"The daggers are named Twinsuns. And the bow's name is Luna's Tears, named after its creator." The boys just looked at him in awe. The general could see that the boys were overwhelmed from everything they had been through that day. "That's enough for today. Let's put everything away for now and eat."

Both Tab and Dirk wanted to beg him not to stop, but they realized they needed to eat. They had gotten more information out of Kira and the general than they thought possible. "Tomorrow we will begin the basics so you can get a little understanding of what will happen. Agreed?" The last word was more of a statement than a question.

They both agreed as Kira was putting dinner on the table. The general grabbed all the items he had brought out and put them on the prep table behind the dinner table.

Dirk and Tab ate in silence, contemplating everything. The only one at the table making any noise was the phoenix. It was a comforting sound. It was a hum that somehow sounded happy and sad at the same time.

Dirk and Tab both knew it was more for the general than anyone else. He had lost a lifelong friend today, Arial. His mood had been somber since they had started eating. Now he seemed to be lightening up. Dirk put his hand on his grandfather's shoulder to comfort him.

"Thanks, son, it has been a trying day for us all. I'll be fine." The general smiled. That seemed to break the silence as they were finishing the chicken, salad, and vegetables Kira had prepared.

Kira started to get up and Tab and Dirk moved in unison. "No, Mom, we got this."

Kira sat back down in the chair and a small tear formed in her left eye. She shook the feeling away as the boys cleared the dishes and began to wash them. Dirk saw out of the corner of his eye that the general and Kira had pulled the little bird close to them and began to caress her neck.

Dirk elbowed Tab gently and nodded towards the table. Tab looked and smiled. "I didn't even think how much this would affect them," Dirk whispered.

"Me either. Well, it doesn't look like the phoenix minds the attention back there."

Dirk agreed. They continued cleaning the dishes and heard the phoenix begin to coo. The sound made Dirk and Tab smile. Kira and the general whispered amongst themselves while the boys finished cleaning up.

"What do you think?" Tab asked under his breath.

"I don't know. That's a lot to grasp ahold of. I still have our plans in mind."

"Yes, me too, but we have a responsibility here, it seems."

"I don't know, it's a big burden," They both decided to keep their minds open and take it one step at a time and finished the dishes.

"Tab, you stay here tonight. Tomorrow morning after breakfast and the chores are done, we can get started on the book and a few of the things you must know now," the general said. The boys agreed with him. The general then got up and hugged Kira and the boys. He caressed the phoenix and received a coo from her in return.

He then headed to the prep table, picked up everything he had brought out, and left the room. "See you two bright and early," the general said before he closed his door.

"Boys, listen to me," Kira said, forcing them to look at her. "I know this is a lot, but remember, you don't have to learn everything right now. You just need to learn the basics on how to keep your powers hidden until you need them. There will be changes that you'll have to get used to, but I think you won't mind. Don't ask now, we've talked enough tonight. You two get upstairs and make a bed for your new family member there."

Kira stroked the phoenix's back. They gathered the phoenix up and began to climb the stairs. "By the way, what's her name?"

They both stopped and looked at each other. "She doesn't already have one?" they asked in unison.

Kira just giggled. *I guess I'll have to get used to that*, she thought. *They probably don't even realize they're doing it.* "She'll tell you when she's ready. You'll learn more about that tomorrow. Good night."

The boys headed upstairs and began making a place on Dirk's desk for the phoenix between the twin beds in his room. Dirk had asked his grandfather to put an extra bed in his room after he and Tab had become friends. Dirk got a small blanket out from his closet and curled it up like a bird nest. The phoenix nodded in approval and Tab sat her in the center of the desk.

The bird looked at each one of them, then tucked her head under her wing, and seemed to go to sleep. "Well, that was easy," Tab said.

"You know I was just thinking the same thing," Dirk replied. "That's not the first time since the incident that we've had the same thought."

Tab just shrugged. "Well, we are around each other a lot so that's probably just coincidence."

"You're probably right," Dirk agreed, even though he didn't think so.

"Let's get some rest because tomorrow will be a big day," Tab said, getting a sleeping shirt out of the dresser.

"Yes." Dirk took his shirt off. He didn't like sleeping in a shirt and never had. He slept in just a pair of sleep pants and he was happy.

That night while they slept, their bodies started to go through a string of changes connected with the phoenix. What they didn't know was that the phoenix had already started sharing her power with them and that in itself started many changes.

At the king's palace, in one of the guest rooms, a restless Natia tossed and turned. She had broken out into a slight sweat. Standing over her with a concerned expression was Teyna. Zona appeared by her side. "What are you doing here?" Teyna scolded him.

"You think I didn't know it was you?" Zona said to Marluna.

"I did, you fool, I was just playing along," She smiled and kissed her husband.

"Did you feel it?" he asked her.

"I didn't need to. I could tell by her restlessness that something has happened.

"Yes, something has happened and quite surprising it is," he said with a smile. "I never thought that it could happen, but it seems our beloved Arial has thrown a twist of her own before her departure."

"You need to go before Natia awakens. I can sense she will soon."

"Okay but let me give you a little info first." He told her an abbreviated version of what had happened between Dirk and Tab.

"Really? What does it mean?" his wife asked as she changed into her godly form.

"I don't know. There's no telling. I guess we will see, since we're in unchartered waters now. I better go. She's waking up," Zona kissed his wife on the cheek before disappearing.

"Wha... Who's there?" Natia said as she tried to sit up. Marluna quickly transformed back into Teyna.

"There, there, dear, you were having a nightmare," Teyna said, sitting beside her to wipe the sweat from her forehead.

"No, Teyna. No nightmare. It has begun! I felt the power transfer, but it was different from what you told me to expect."

Teyna caressed her hair. "Well, it's different for every Chosen. At least that's what history has taught us."

"Maybe you're right. It just felt awkward and kind of divided, really," Natia said, wiping the sleep from her eyes.

"Sleep, child. We can discuss this away from here tomorrow."

Natia nodded in agreement and lay back down, knowing something was off. She knew they would have to make a trip tomorrow to see her Aunt Kira. Maybe her aunt would have the answers she needed. Natia knew her aunt had been a protector once, so she might be able to explain all of the feelings and changes that she was going through.

Teyna walked over to the spare bed in the corner of the room. She had slept in the same room as the princess since the day her training had begun. She could only help her so much with the rules that had been set up, but she would always do her best to give her as much information as she could.

She didn't sleep that night. She knew she had to tread carefully around the Storms. If they recognized her from the past, it could be a problem.

At that time, she had been known as Aliana, Kira's trainer from when she was young. And even though she looked different, her mannerisms wouldn't be hard to recognize. *I'll think of something*, Marluna thought.

The one thing that Teyna didn't know was that Natia had witnessed the entire incident at Storm farm. She couldn't hear what was said, but she knew something was off. She had seen Tab there, but since he and Dirk were best friends, that only made sense. She closed her eyes and went back to sleep.

The night would be filled with confusing dreams for them all.

Aarya

The smell of roasted pig caused Dirk to open his eyes. He looked around, confused. He was sitting around a fire pit with several people he didn't recognize. His mind raced trying to figure out what was going on. He gasped when he looked into the blue eyes of the elven female talking to him.

"Diron, are you listening to Thad?" Kira asked, squeezing his leg.

Dirk looked to the man sitting beside him. He realized it was Tab, only bigger, with a harder edge to his facial features. The signs of fatigue could be seen in the bags that hung below his eyes. Realizing they were in a forest at the base of a mountain that he didn't recognize, he looked around at the others. King Askin Silver and his wife Naira were there. A dwarven male was kneeling beside the pit adding wood to the fire.

"Hey bud, are you alright?" Thad asked concerned that Diron wasn't responding to his question.

Then his vision blurred and the sounds of steel hitting steel brought his eyes into focus. He was in the middle of a battle. An ape like creature was swinging a sword at his head. His instincts took over and he blocked the sword. A movement to his right jumped in stabbing the creature in the heart.

"You better be quicker my love. I don't want to carry you off this field." A silver headed elven female with a silky voice said. She put her hand on his face then kissed him.

Dirk's vision blurred again, and he was standing at the back of the guest house on the farm. An apparition of a man was looking at him. "Dirk, you must forgive him. He had no choice son. You will understand when the time is right," the man pleaded looking at Dirk.

He stared at the man talking to him. There was something familiar about the man, but Dirk couldn't quite figure it out. Then it struck him. "Father?"

Dirk woke up abruptly. He looked around. "Father?" Where was his father? He quickly realized the conversation that took place was only a dream. "Was it truly only a dream... or a premonition?" Sweat drenched his body. A coo sound cleared the fogginess of his head. He looked to the right and stroked the head of the phoenix. "It was a dream wasn't it?" he asked not really expecting a response. His eyes were blazing green fire that lit the room. He saw the phoenix nod her head. Dirk smiled knowing that she had understood. Tab mumbled causing Dirk to look at him. *He must be dreaming as well.*

Tab like Dirk opened his eyes and found himself sitting around a fire. He noticed a dwarf kneeling by a fire. He was telling a tale about a goat he once had. He was going to cook it and tried to catch it, but he slipped. Startled by his movements, the goat squirted him in the face with its milk. Evidently he had frightened it so bad that it acted in self-defense. Several people were laughing at his telling of the story. There were several other people gathered around. An Elven male and female, a man who looked eerily like Dirk. Confused he kept trying to make sense of what he was seeing, and then he noticed her. "Kira?" It was definitely her, but she was much younger, and he thought he heard her say 'Diron'. Tab shook his head.

Then she looked at him and said, "Thad". Tab's head was spinning so fast now that he had to lean forward and rest his hands on his knees. His stomach was churning. He felt like he was going to throw up.

After a few moments, his head cleared, and he found himself in the middle of a battle. Dirk was beside him blocking an attack from an ape like creature. He realized after staring at Dirk that it couldn't be him. Dirk's doppelganger had human ears instead of an elves. An elven female with silver hair then stepped in and stab the beast in the heart. He was shocked at how swift she had moved. Then she smiled at Tab and winked. He heard her say to Dirk that she didn't want to have to tote him off the field. Tab was so confused by what was going on. His head started spinning again.

Tab jumped with a start looking around. His breathing was strained at first. Then as if a breeze of fresh air blew over him, he took a calming breath. The room seemed to have a green glow about it. He was so drenched in sweat that the sheets felt like a towel after a bath.

"Having some weird dreams?" Tab startled by the question looked at Dirk who was rubbing the baby phoenix's head.

"Hell's your eyes are on fire!" Tab glared.

"Well I hate to tell you, but yours are too." Dirk laughed.

"Was that a dream?" Tab scratched his head still confused.

"Here, rub her head. It cleared my mind," Dirk said nodding to the phoenix.

As soon as Tab touched her feathers a small spark leapt into his hand. "Ouch," Tab said pulling his hand back. After a jolt of pain his head was clear now. "Thanks," he said to the phoenix, and he received a coo back in return causing him to smile. He looked to Dirk. "What did you see?" Tab asked.

Dirk then started explaining what he saw, but when he got to the part about his mother Tab interrupted him.

"I saw Kira." Tab smiled. "Though she was much younger."

Dirk smiled. "I know, and it kind of freaked me out. I saw your dad as well."

"It had to be the Chosen; don't you think?"

Dirk laid back down and put his hands behind his head and stared at the ceiling. "It had to be. Did you see the battle?"

"I did. Who was that beautiful dark-haired elf?"

"I don't know but she saved my life or whoever I was." Tab leaned closer to Dirk.

"It was you."

Dirk sat back up and looked at Tab. "What do you mean?"

"It looked just like you, only he had regular ears," Tab explained.

Dirk not having an answer flopped his head back down on the pillow. "I guess the general can maybe explain it more. We better get some sleep. Tomorrow, or later on today is getting more and more interesting.

"That it is brother," Tab said and laid his head down. Thinking of his father he felt the cool wave wash over him. The heat in his eyes dissipated and he slowly fell to sleep.

After their discussion Dirk felt the heat in his eyes disappear as he envisioned Natia. A smile crossed his face as he slipped into more dreams.

The boys tossed and turned, and it seemed the night would never end for them. Muscles were starting to grow larger where before they had been small. Senses were starting to become sharper. Over time, their senses would become significantly heightened.

When they finally awoke the next morning, the sun was just rising in the sky. The birds were singing. The usual sounds of the farm could be heard through the open window. A voice from downstairs shouted, "I think it's time you two got up! There is a lot to do today, and you also have to get ready for your testing tomorrow!"

The boys sat up at the same time and stretched. "Wow that was a weird night. Anymore dreams?" Tab stood and bent down to touch his toes stretching his back more.

"I did. But it's all jumbled," Dirk said while getting his tunic and pants. They both moved tenderly as they dressed.

"I'm sore all over!"

"Me too." Dirk moved his arms in a circle, loosening them up.

They both looked to the desk at the same time. The baby phoenix was just waking up. She stretched her wings and yawned as she flapped them quickly. The boys walked over to the desk, amazed. She looked like she had grown a little more overnight. The blanket she was resting on had small scorch marks on it. The soreness in their bodies seemed to disappear as they rubbed her neck. They both felt a spark pass between them and the phoenix.

"Well, that can be useful," Tab said.

"Yeah, I feel great now. We'll have to remember that."

After they both finished getting dressed, they headed downstairs with the phoenix in tow. Kira was just opening her mouth to yell for them again.

"Mom! We're here."

"Well, it's going to be hectic today so let's get a move on. Eat, then we will talk about today's schedule," Kira told the boys as they placed the phoenix on the center of the table and sat down.

After a small bowl of grain and a few strips of meat were put in front of the baby phoenix, they filled their plates with eggs and sausage. They ate quickly and then cleaned up their plates as was required of the inhabitants of Storm Farm. "Okay, now that you are through stuffing your faces," Kira said, looking at them both in amazement. They had eaten everything Kira had prepared without saying a word. "I'll take care of our guest while you two feed and water the animals. As soon as you get done with that we will sit down and discuss what needs to be done today," She began putting away the clean dishes.

"Where is the general?" Tab asked.

"He received an urgent letter from the palace this morning. He had to leave early to meet with the king, but he'll be back after lunch to answer your questions and start your training," Kira told them before pushing them out the door.

Doing their work as fast as they could, they made sure to do everything on the morning list. A few hours later, they practically ran into the house. Kira met them at the door. "Slow down and clean off your shoes before entering." She pointed at the mud on their boots. At least she hoped it was mud.

They both wiped off their boots on the outside rug and then took them off. As they entered the house, they noticed there was some freshly made guarve fruit juice and Dor berry bread with butter waiting for them.

The phoenix was sitting in the center of the table again with a bowl of oatmeal-like food in it. The boys **rubbed the phoenix's neck and received a light trill in return. Their weariness washed away at**

104

the touch. They sat down and ate greedily.

"Mom, when can we get started?" Dirk asked.

"We will as soon as you two clean up your mess and freshen up. You smell like a cow's backside," Kira said, pretending to pinch her nose with her fingers. The boys cleaned the table and dishes. They ran upstairs to get cleaned up. As soon as they washed up and exchanged their dirty tunics and pants for clean ones, they headed back downstairs.

Dirk saw that Kira had placed three mats made of some kind of cloth on the living room floor. Two of them were side by side while one was in front of the other two. The phoenix was on the floor between the mats. Kira had changed into a light green tunic and matching pants with a brown sash around her waist and soft light brown shoes that looked very flexible. Her hair had been rolled up into a tight bun at the back of her head.

"Nice outfit, Mom," Dirk said.

"It's an elven training outfit that allows for flexibility without discomfort. You'll get something similar to this at the academy." Kira walked over and sat on the single mat that was facing the other two. "Ok, I want the two of you to sit cross-legged on the floor, facing me."

After she was satisfied with their positioning, she began.

"The first thing to learn is how to find your core. That is where the power and abilities come from. The core is what connects everyone to the power of the world. It flows through every living thing. Only a few can really connect with it and use it properly. Everyone touches it in their own way. Most just don't realize that's what they're doing. You'll learn more in the first year at the academy about that." She paused to make sure they understood.

When she was satisfied, she continued. "The spot where the core flows into your body is located above your stomach right below the center of your chest, around your heart. It feels like a pulsing knot. After you two find that spot, we can work on turning your abilities on and off."

Dirk and Tab looked at each other and nodded. The boys were determined to find their core, so they did as Kira had instructed and started to concentrate. She told them to clear their minds and to take deep breaths in and out as she focused on them. The phoenix just sat and watched the boys with interest.

"First, hold your shoulders straight while keeping your eyes closed. Now breathe in slowly and then exhale, focusing on your core. It will feel like a warm tingle above your stomach when you find it. Let your thoughts guide you into your body. Start at your fingertips. Feel the blood flow. Follow it through your body. Imagine it running through your veins, circulating towards your heart. Stay relaxed and keep concentrating until you feel it.

Keep yourself focused and calm. When you find it. You will feel it. You will have a sensation of calm and clarity come over you. This will allow you to connect with your inner power."

Kira closed her eyes and found her core instantly. She could hear the boys breathing as she instructed, but she could also feel the struggle in their thoughts.

Dirk was having a really difficult time. Tab was having a hard time also, but his breathing was a little closer to the mark.

"Be patient and follow the flow."

The boys tried to do as they were instructed, but Dirk couldn't relax. He had a thousand questions running through his mind.

"You two have to relax. We will not be able to continue unless you totally relax. You can't walk before you crawl," Kira told them.

Dirk sighed, losing his concentration. "Mom, I just can't relax. There's just too many questions I need answered first," He opened his eyes and looked at Kira.

"I can't either," Tab said, exhaling loudly.

"Dirk Storm! Tab Clearwater!" Kira scolded. "That's what your problem is. You are always in such a hurry that you can't wait to get things done. When you want something, you must have it right then. If you do not learn patience, you will be dead before your twentieth name days. Now, take heed of what I tell you, for your lives and ours as may depend on you two learning patience. Do you understand?"

They both stared at Kira with their mouths hanging open and then they just nodded.

"I'm sorry, Mom," Dirk said softly, letting the weight of his mother's words sink in. "It just… there has been so many secrets. Now that some answers are being given, I guess I want to know as much as I can. And Tab, think about what the last day has been like for him. Everything he thought he knew about his family was a lie. These feelings we're both having, good and bad, are kind of making us feel like there is a storm brewing, pardon the pun."

Kira, taken back by her son's words, looked him in the eyes. His eyes were rippling with amber flames. Tab's eyes were flaming too.

"Boys, calm down and use the technique I taught you last night. Your powers are activating." The phoenix trilled in agreement with Kira. Both boys looked to the bird and, not realizing looked, at each other and saw what Kira was seeing. They both took a deep breath and tried to relax using the technique she had showed them.

After several minutes of concentration, the flames had disappeared.

"I'm sorry, Mom. I didn't mean to get worked up."

"Me either," Tab replied.

"That's why it is so important to find patience. Your powers could really hurt someone if you're not in control of them." Kira paused, letting her words sink in. "I'm sorry. I didn't want this either, but it seems destiny thinks otherwise. Okay we can take a break and I'll try to answer what I can, but your grandfather has the important information you need. I'll answer a few questions, then we will try the find your core again. Dirk, one question for now. Agreed."

They both nodded in agreement.

"Mom, can you explain how you're involved in this?"

"I will tell you this much. You come from a long line of Storms that were known as the Chosen. They are Zona's selected line of guardians. He created them to protect the innocent from evil. Zolun was the main reason for the Chosen being created. He has been trying to overthrow Zona for centuries. He wants to rule all the lands. Zona chose the Storm line to be the guardians for all races. More will be explained when your grandfather talks with you about the Book of Storms," Kira stated.

"But that doesn't explain you," Dirk said.

"I'm getting to that," she retorted. "I was once what is called a protector. The protectors are the guardians of the Chosen. Zona realized a long time ago that the Chosen must have a protector by their side to be successful. The protector and the Chosen were meant to stand together against the evil of Zolun. Believe me, you will learn, unfortunately, that there is a lot of evil in this world, not just Zolun himself. He has armies that do his bidding and evil creatures by his side. I was your father's protector for several years.

"We fought side by side, along with Thad. A protector is supposed to care for and protect the Chosen, not fall in love with them. That is what happened to me. I fell in love with Diron the first time I saw him. Eventually, after much debate and many long conversations, we decided for me to step aside from my protector duties and follow my heart."

Kira looked out through the living room window. She had tears forming in her eyes and the boys could tell there was heartache in her thoughts. "That's where my dad came into the scene, isn't it?" Tab asked, breaking the awkward silence.

Kira, coming out of the trance she was in, looked at Tab. She then leaned forward and put her hand on his face looking lovingly into his eyes. Tab was overcome with grief and felt tears pricking at his eyes as he gazed into Kira's eyes.

"Your father was Diron's best friend. We were all pretty close, as a matter of fact. They grew up together and were as thick as thieves, just as you and

Dirk are. That's the reason I tried to keep the two of you separated for all those years. I didn't want the same tragic end to repeat itself. I promised Millie I would protect you from that fate, but I guess I've failed in that task. The gods must have different plans."

"You knew my mother?" Tab asked.

Kira nodded. "We were all very close." She pulled her hand away from Tab. "Your father agreed to become his protector and allowed me the freedom to become Diron's wife. Like I said, he had been fighting with us for years. He had been very interested from the beginning about protectors, so I trained him in our ways through the years. At that time, the world was very peaceful. At least so we thought. I didn't hesitate to release my protector status to Thad."

Silence filled the room as Tab let this sink in.

"We had a small ceremony that we performed with Thad and Arial to give him my powers. Diron and I were married the very same night."

They sat silently for a few minutes. Kira, realizing the somberness of the room, decided to get away from that subject.

"But more about that later." Kira brought the boy's attention back to the task at hand. The phoenix cooed.

"Let's return to focus on touching your core. It might help to attain the link with the phoenix as well. The connection between you two and her will be vital to your survival. You'll be able to see each other's thoughts and feelings. The communication bond between you will be very helpful, especially if you're ever in danger. It will also strengthen the abilities you have been given. Now, since the bond is split, I am not sure how that will affect you. I thought if you could sense your core it might be safer before you have to get started on learning how to link with her," Kira told them. The boys were in awe at the phoenix in front of them.

Both of the boys rubbed her neck with the back of their fingers and felt a slight electric charge. Calm spread throughout the boys and they both relaxed.

"That will probably stop as soon as you two learn to find your core. Has she told you her name?" Both boys shook their heads. "Well, it's time you learn how to find your core. Her name will probably be known to you after you are able find it. It is the first step we need to do."

The boys resumed their positions and concentrate on finding their core. Kira could immediately sense what the boys were feeling as soon as she connected to her own core.

Dirk and Tab eventually began to relax and come to terms with the information they had been given. Their thoughts were still swirling with memories from the past. The vision of men and women talking and laughing came in and out of focus. As hard as they tried to touch their core, they would get close to finding it, but then it would slip away.

Focus on a happy memory. They could hear Kira in their thoughts.

Determination set in and they tried harder. Both of them finally relaxed, then they both felt a warm sensation in their chests. They also felt a presence, as if someone else had entered their minds. Then they heard a soft loving voice speak.

Aarya. My name is Aarya, the voice whispered.

All three of them opened their eyes at once. Kira looked at the boys and smiled. "Did you hear that?"

The boys looked at each other and then down at the phoenix, realizing that they were both still caressing the phoenix's neck. "Aarya," they both said at the same time.

"That's her name," Dirk said to no one in particular. Tab nodded in agreement.

Kira smiled at Aarya. "That was your first real connection to your core."

Aarya looked at the boys and communicated her happiness to them through their link. She was happy that they could finally hear her and that they would always be connected.

"Okay now since that is achieved, let's work on a solid connection to your core, using your connection to Aarya to achieve it."

They worked for several hours on the technique, only reaching their core a couple of times and only for a few seconds each time. Kira explained that the problem was that the dual connection was probably hindering their efforts.

"You both need to become one when trying to obtain your core."

"Become one?" Dirk asked.

Kira looked at her son. "I think your minds, at least right now, need to think as one. I want you and Tab to concentrate on each other and see if you can link your thoughts. Now grasp arms, close your eyes, and think of Aarya."

Dirk and Tab did as Kira instructed and after a few minutes, they felt the warmth spread through their bodies.

That's it. Do you feel the pulsing around your hearts? Aarya was communicating to them. They both found their cores immediately. Kira could feel that they had been successful. She smiled at Aarya receiving a head nod from the small bird in return.

"Now that you have achieved that, I want you to practice doing it on your own to get used to what it feels like," Kira instructed.

They continued to practice and had more success now with the link to Aarya established. They practiced until the general finally came back from his visit with the king. The boys were relieved to be able to take a break.

"Ah, sorry that took so long," the general told them. "So where are we at? Have you had any success today?"

Kira explained to him what they had achieved that morning. The general gazed at Aarya while Kira was filling him in. The phoenix stood up, stretched her wings, flying up to him and landing on his outstretched arm. She nudged her head under his chin and then looked into his eyes.

There was a brief flame in his eyes, disappearing just as fast as it had developed. A recognition came over his face. "Aarya." the general patted her head. Kira and the boys just stared in disbelief at her. "Ah I guess that is the first time she has flown,"

"That was amazing!" Dirk said, getting up and walking to the general.

"Yes, now that you can touch your core, and the both of you can link, her abilities will grow faster than yours. I did some research last night on the Book of Storm. When Arial first appeared, she was in an egg just like the one you described Aarya was in. I suggest when there's time, you look at the fifth Chosen, Durk Storm. That section explains the learning process he went through with her. It is well-documented and will be really useful to you. Her fast growth is an effect that she gains by being linked with the Chosen."

Tab's stomach grumbled. Everyone looked to him. He held up his hands in an 'I'm sorry' gesture.

"Time for a break,"

After lunch, the general told the boys to follow him outside to his workshop. Dirk had only been inside once before, and that was nearly ten years ago. He couldn't remember for the life of him what it looked like on the inside. He stared at it as they walked up to the shop.

It was a good-sized building, about the size of a small home. It was one floor with only one entrance and windows on both sides.

The boys entered after the general unlocked the door. A tingling sensation rippled through their bodies as they passed the threshold. Dirk and Tab just stared at each other, waiting for the general to explain. He didn't right away so Dirk looked around the room, taking in the layout.

Against the back wall was a bench, a worktable, and a couple of stools. Various tools hung in assigned spots on the wall above the table. There was a vise anchored on the left side of the table and a stool in front of it. On the left side of the room, instead of tools, the wall held swords, shields, lances, and many other weapons. One weapon in particular caught Dirk's eye. Harbinger was right in the center, kind of like a tribute.

Beside Harbinger was a crimson shield. In the center of the shield was an etching of an amazing phoenix and jewels were encrusted throughout the entire piece. The phoenix's eyes were amber, and the talons tipped with green gems. A red, heart-shaped jewel resembling a flame was on its chest.

On the right side of the room, there was a fireplace with a couch and several chairs placed strategically around an oval-shaped table. The windows were tinted so that they could only be seen through from the inside. The floor was red, polished hardwood.

The general walked over to the fireplace and put a single log into it. He bowed his head and said a few words, then a small flame burst from the log. The flames were bright, tints of green mixed with amber.

He went over to the window on the opposite wall and opened it. The room lit up instantly, as if daylight had filled the room.

Aarya landed on the windowsill, chirped, and then glided to the couch. The general sat in a chair, clearly his favorite, and motioned for them to sit on the couch with Aarya. The boys sat down, one on each side of her. The general set a book down. He turned it to face them and rubbed his beard, as if deciding where to begin.

"Ok, first, this building is enchanted. The tingling sensation you felt when you first walked in was the magic doing its job. The reason for this is so you can bring whoever you want in here but when they leave, they won't remember what happened or what was said in here unless you want them to."

Dirk looked at Tab and then at the general.

"I remember coming in here a long time ago but, for the life of me, I can't remember what was inside."

The general nodded. "Ah, that's the power of the enchantment. Let me show you."

He touched Dirk's forehead and said, "Rememoria."

A small light appeared at the end of his fingertip. Dirk felt dizzy for a minute and shook his head.

A realization came over him. "Wait a minute... I remember this room now. I was in here and I had a broken arm, didn't I?" Dirk asked, looking at his grandfather for confirmation. The general nodded. "I remember Arial being there and she was crying. She dripped her tears on my arm and she healed the bone, didn't she?"

"Yes. The thing about the phoenix tears is that they have healing properties. You took a nasty fall out of that big tree behind the barn and Kira was gone so I had no other choice than to bring you in here and let Arial heal you. It was unfortunate, but it needed to be done. Obviously, your memory needed to be wiped so that you wouldn't remember Arial and what she had done."

"That's amazing. I kind of remember that, even though I wasn't there," Tab said.

"Yes, it is," Dirk said.

"That's the power of the connection you now have with Tab. I believe that you both will have vague recollections of each other's memories and the memories of the previous Chosen and protectors. But since this is the first time that we have two Chosen at the same time, I am merely guessing. Understand?" the general asked them. They both nodded. "Now this room is to be only used if needed and only in certain situations."

They both agreed.

"The word for retaining memories is *memoria*. It is not discriminatory and affects everyone. It has to be said out loud so everyone in the room is affected. If it isn't said before you leave through the door, your memories will be hidden. If you ever want to restore someone's memory, the word is *rememoria*."

His first lesson was teaching them that by either saying or concentrating on a word, they could cast a spell. The more connected they became with their power, the easier and more powerful the spell would be.

"Okay, that sounds easy enough," Dirk and Tab said in unison.

"Well, it sounds easy, but trust me when I say it's not," the general told them. "You two try. Just say or think the word burno as you look at it this stick." The general placed a small twig on the table beside them.

They both sat up and a look of discomfort came across their faces as they both stared at the twig. Several minutes passed. Beads of sweat formed on their brows.

Finally, the twig started to smolder a little. Both boys exhaled the breath they had been holding.

The general chuckled. "Sounds easy, huh? Remember what your mother was teaching you this morning. Once you master connecting to your core, it'll become easier," He looked for a moment at Aarya and smiled. "Now, Aarya, why don't you help them with this? I want you two to touch the crest of her neck and focus on the twig again."

Both boys did as they were told and looked at the twig. The sweat formed again. After a few minutes, deep inside, Dirk felt a warm sensation in his chest. He felt a presence tell him to push that feeling onto the twig. He did, and a flame formed.

Both Tab and Dirk smiled at their success and sat back. "Wonderful," the general said, putting out the small flame with a thought.

"That was intense," Tab said. Dirk agreed with him.

"Did you feel that warm sensation inside your chest?" the general asked. They both nodded. "That was an effect of the fire spell. Each spell has a different sensation. For example, cold would feel cool, wind would feel like your chest was twisting, etc."

Aarya nudged both of the boys affectionately. They both caressed her neck, receiving a trill from the appreciative phoenix. "That's amazing! I felt like my insides were on fire. I don't think I would ever want to feel what casting a death spell would feel like," Dirk said casually.

"Never!" the general growled. Tab and Dirk both pushed their backs into the couch, their mouths hanging open. "You never want to do that! It would probably kill you!" He pointed a determined finger at them. "Do you understand that every time you cast a spell; it affects you as well. Death could be the cost of casting the death spell, *understand*?"

They gulped. "Yes sir."

"Never even think about it. Give me your word, or we will stop right now."

"You have our word," They both responded together.

"There are a lot of things that you will learn when you go to school about the use of your power and its effects. Just remember this one is the most important." Aarya chirped in agreement.

After that intense moment, the general let the boys get up and walk around for a few minutes to relax. The general just sat there and rubbed Aarya's neck. She had moved over to his chair, sensing his uneasiness.

Dirk stretched and got a glass of water from the pitcher the general had set on his workbench. Tab got one as well. Walking over to look at the weapons hanging on the wall, they mainly examined Harbinger and the shield placed beside it.

"That was Dad's," Dirk said, looking at the sword, while Tab ran his fingers over the shield.

"Do you feel that?" Tab asked Dirk as he put his hand on the shield as well. The moment he touched it both boys slipped into a dream-like trance. They heard the sounds of a battle. The screams of men and women dying. The shrieks of something hideous in the background.

"Diron, behind you!"

"No, Thad, don't!"

As if the force of the shout itself had blasted them back to reality, they were ripped out of their dream-like trance.

"Did you…"

"I did."

The boys stared at each other in shock as they pulled their hands away from the shield. The general walked up to them, noticing the look on their faces.

"You both just shared a vision from the past, I believe," the general said, pulling their attention to him.

They both looked at him and said, "Yes."

"That will happen quite often in the beginning and the more it happens, the more you'll come to understand your family's past. Now come and sit down. Let's discuss the Book of Storm." The General guided them back to the couch.

The Book of Storm sat on the table in front of the boys. Dirk picked up the book and Tab ran his hand across the face of the book. A small spark passed between them as both boys made contact at the same time.

"This is an abbreviated history of all of your predecessors," the general explained. Dirk examined the book more closely. The cover was made from a thick, hide-like material that he didn't recognize. On the dark cover were the words, *The Book of Storms*. Engraved behind the title was an emblazoned phoenix with its wings spread and talons extended, as if it were in flight.

"That's cool," Tab said. The general explained to the boys how the book was created as a log of the Chosen's names and exploits. Every Chosen's own history was in the book. The boys opened the book and on the first page was a name in the left-hand corner.

Dorian Storm 839az-876az was written there with a brief history of how everything had started with him saving a smith's family. Zona had witnessed the event and decided to pick the Storm line as the Chosen. Dirk, with Tab looking over his shoulder, flipped through the pages. They stopped to read significant things the general pointed out.

One big event was Arial being created by Zona as a protector and a companion since the era the general referred to as the Dark Times. Dirk quickly scanned through the rest of the five-hundred years of Chosen and protector history. By each name of the Chosen, there was a red mark.

"That's looks like blood." Dirk ran his finger over the mark curiously.

"That is exactly what that is. The book is made from magic, so the properties of it allow a person's history to be imprinted into the book through their blood. Once the Chosen and the protector write their names in the book, they put their print beside their name. This connects them to the book, allowing for their memories to be embedded in the book forever. This includes past, present, and future memories." He paused to make sure they understood. "So, what are you waiting for?"

They each looked at him, confused.

"It's time to put your thumbprint in the book, its tradition."

"Oh"

The general pulled his knife from its scabbard and handed it to Dirk. "First, write your name under your father's name and the date."

Dirk hadn't even thought about that. His father's history was in the book. He quickly turned to the last page with writing on it, but the only thing that was there was his father's name, dated 1315az-1335az, as the Chosen with his blood print beside it. His mother's name was listed underneath as the protector, dated 1315az-1330az. Then Tab's fathers was listed as the protector from 1330az-1335az.

"Wait a minute! It's blank below the name," Dirk and Tab said in unison.

"Well, that's because your father never got to enter his history there, but I imagine, as your power grows, you two will be able to fill in the blanks."

"Wait, you mean, we'll learn everything they went through?" Tab asked.

"Yes. Once your power is strong enough, you'll be able to touch his print with your thumb and the history will be shown to you."

They both nodded understanding. Dirk turned the page to leave room for their history and then wrote his name with the word Chosen beside it and the year. He then took the knife and nicked his thumb. When the blood spread enough to cover Dirk's thumb, the general mumbled some words and the cut healed. He motioned to the book and Dirk pressed his bloody thumb next to his name.

When his finger made contact with the paper, he heard a rushing sound in his head. The world seemed to spin for a moment, but then it was gone. "That was weird."

"That was the book embracing you to the connection. You will forever be linked now," the general told him.

Tab repeated the process, producing the same effect.

"That's enough for today. The book will stay here for now and you can come here in your free time to read it. Right now, you know the basics of everything and that should get you started down the right path."

Both boys began to complain but the general gave them his *enough* look and they kept quiet.

"You two need to get ready for school and there isn't much time for anything else. We can work on this on the weekends when you're free. Trust me, there's plenty of time to learn what you need. Right now, you need to focus on school and learning to use your core."

The general put the book back on the bookshelf in the corner of the room. They all headed out the door together after saying "Memoria," in unison.

Ishani's Plan

Zolun was deep in the underworld when he felt the book surge with power. It was the most powerful surge he had ever felt, and he found himself staggering backwards.

A few seconds after he had shaken it off, he felt it again. That was the first time he had ever felt it twice in a row. There was something different this time. He had to find out what was going on. He wasn't ready for the Chosen yet. His strength had not fully returned from the last battle at Der-Tod. His power in the land of the living wasn't fully restored.

He knew it would be a few years before he was at full strength. So he needed to put his legions to work immediately. They had already begun their plans, but he would need to speed things up now. *We need to start wearing down the Chosen and what he calls his pack*, Zolun thought. It was always a Storm, and the boy would be around the right age now to come into his power. But what was different this time?

Zolun walked out of the main torture chamber into the next room, where he would disperse his orders. "Ishani, you are summoned!" Zolun shouted into the air. There was a loud pop behind him. He turned around to see a black mist dissipating into the air.

Ishani walked over to her lord and bowed at his feet. "You summoned me, my lord?"

"Ishani, where are you at on training your spy?"

"My lord, he will be ready soon." Ishani stayed as close to the ground as she could. She knew that Zolun would not like her answer.

Zolun snatched the priestess up by her dark hair. She cried out in pain. "I have tolerated your insolence and failure far too long!" He bellowed as he wrapped his free hand around her throat, squeezing a little tighter with every single breath she tried to take. Her face turned red from the lack of air as Zolun stared at her, admiring her beautiful almond skin and the silver streak in her hair.

As Zolun squeezed, she grasped at his hand weakly. Her face was now turning scarlet red. She finally wedged one hand under his.

"What's that, Ishani? You wish to speak?" he asked her, a smirk on his face. Zolun loved torturing his leaders. He felt it was fear that kept them in their place. "Hmm, do you wish to try again?" Zolun released Ishani. She fell to the ground, gasping for air.

"Yes…. my…lord," Ishani said between gasps of air.

"Well, don't keep me waiting," Zolun said eagerly.

Ishani, straightening herself, bowed her head to him. "Here is my plan and timeline." Ishani laid out her plan.

"Your spy is in position?"

"Yes, my lord." Ishani said with more confidence than she had. "He still needs a few more enchantments that I will put on him before the end of the month. With his fear of loss and what we know about him, I know he will do our bidding well."

"You feel very confident, but I'm not as confident in you as you are with the plan." Zolun slapped Ishani across the face so hard that her jaw snapped, and she flew across the room.

After she landed, she took a moment to heal her jaw, something she had done many times before. She stood up with a hint of defiance in her eyes. "As I said, my lord, the plan will work. Draxen has been working on his contact. He has total control over him now. He feels very confident."

"Well, your pet lackey and the other slimy one you associate with have let me down many times before. This time, if they fail to come through, I fear none of you will live to ever make a mistake again. I have a special place set aside down here for you if that happens and trust me, it will not be a happy stay."

"Yes, my lord. By the way, one of your sisters has agreed to help, so that will make it a lot easier this time," Ishani said with a hint of a smile.

Zolun raised an eyebrow. "Dusa, I imagine."

Ishani nodded.

"She has been trying to get back in my good graces since her failure at the last battle," Zolun said, more to himself.

"Yes, we have a plan to turn one of the Chosen's friends very soon, which will help weaken his will." Ishani's faint smile turned into a devious grin.

"All right, everything better happen as you say and soon. The last battle with his father we should have won, but that damn bird ruined my victory."

"She is a problem no longer, my lord."

Zolun looked at Ishani with a smile for the first time.

"Tell me."

"Screel sent two of our eager wood nymphs to assassinate her, and I am assured that she has fallen. They got her with a magical arrow I'd made. If it didn't kill her immediately, the poison it was laced with did. It would keep her from healing."

"Are you sure?" Zolun asked.

"Yes, my lord. They shot her several days ago. Unfortunately, one of them was killed by the protector's son before they could witness it die all the way. But the one who returned said it fell from the sky and was definitely dying."

"Interesting. I wonder how Father took that." Zolun began to laugh hysterically.

"Well, we must make sure there is no evidence implicating me in these events. You know the rules," Zolun said after his laughter subsided.

"I know, my lord. The remaining wood nymph has met an early demise, as I knew our involvement could not be known by your parents."

"Good, now, go before I change my mind on allowing you to live, but remember, *do not fail*," Zolun told Ishani just before she vanished.

Zolun smiled to himself. That might make things a little more interesting. If it was ever found out, then I could blame Ishani for any misguided actions. That would keep me safe from Father breaking the deal. Zolun was amused at his own genius. "Screel!" Zolun shouted, summoning the dark and creepy leader of his army.

There was another whooshing sound. Screel appeared and kneeled down in front of Zolun.

"Yesth masther?" Screel slurred.

"Ishani has just left. She has told me the phoenix is dead. Can you confirm?"

"Yesth, masther. She no longer protects the boy from the skies. My Ratkes have been on alert for her, but she is nowhere to be found,"

"Good, good, good. That should be very advantageous," Zolun said, rubbing his chin. "Now, I don't believe Ishani's plan will work. Let's make sure our backup plan is in place."

"It is being prepared now, masther."

"Good, remember it has to look like raiders were responsible when we go down that road. And remember this is between us only! You understand?"

"Yesth masther"

"Now be gone, I have other business to attend," Zolun told Screel before he vanished with a whoosh. The sounds of screaming could be heard coming from the other room. "Hmm, now for some fun."

Zolun headed into the room where the screams were coming from.

"Now, Chosen Diron, where did we leave off?" Zolun asked the figure as he closed the door behind him.

"I will break these chains and help destroy you!" Diron's spirit surged forward, stretching the chains to their limit. Hatred blazed in his eyes.

Zolun laughed. "If you haven't noticed, you're already dead. You're just a pathetic spirit I won't let go to the underworld. I can torture you forever if I want."

"We will see!" the defiant spirit screamed as he strained against his chains, trying to get even closer to Zolun. "I will personally see you fall into the final abyss and we'll see who's laughing then!"

Ishani appeared back at her palace just as fast as she had disappeared.

"How did it go?" Draxen asked her, placing a grape in his mouth. Yellow electricity formed around Ishani's right hand and the yellow jewel in her bracelet began to glow. She jabbed her open hand at Draxen. A jolt of energy engulfed his body. Writhing in pain, he felt himself being lifted off the bed. Ishani whipped her hand around, dragging Draxen in the same motion. She opened her closed fist and pointed it at the wall to her right. Draxen's body slammed into the wall as the electricity bombarded into his body.

He collapsed to the floor, smoke trailing into the air. He moaned as Ishani waved her hand to dissipate the smell and the smoke from Draxen's burning clothes. Draxen got to his feet slowly and looked at Ishani timidly. "Bow, before your mistress!" Ishani demanded.

He bent down and put his forehead on the floor at Ishani's feet. "I am sorry, mistress. I felt sure with the death of the bird, it would be a praiseworthy visit."

"That's your problem, pet. You never think long term, just short term. You are to never be on my bed unless I invite you into it ever again. You are getting too comfortable around here. We need results and fast, or the three of us will be in Zolun's torture room far too soon." Ishani walked to the window that overlooked the Bay of Muerta.

Draxen stayed where he was until Ishani told him he could move. "Should I inform our captain to be ready with the plan we discussed?"

Ishani put her hands on the window ledge and stared at the water. The wind blew through the open window, billowing Ishani's clothes. She always wore silks and satins.

Draxen took a risk and raised his head so he could see every curve of Ishani's body. The light shining through her flimsy clothes left Draxen with no doubt as to what her body looked like. Draxen had lusted after her for hundreds of years. He would do anything for her, but he knew she could end his existence anytime she wanted.

"There is one change. I want the young captain to survive. I have special plans for him."

Draxen lowered his head as Ishani walked back towards him. "It must not have been a good meeting."

"The lord was not pleased with our progress and he showed me as much," Ishani said, rubbing her jaw and turning back to the window to stare out at the bay. "Go meet with your contact and make sure he is ready to do his part. Remind him of his folly if he fails. Make sure he knows we will be getting the boy soon for his final training." Ishani glared at Draxen until he nodded. "Now go, leave me."

Draxen got up and slowly walked to the door. "Mistress, I will not fail," he said to her as he walked out of the room.

Ishani leaned forward on the window ledge. She knew her plans were risky, but she wanted revenge for the things that had happened in her life. She had dealt with strife because of the Chosen. Their consistent luck had caused Ishani to be tortured by Zolun for failing time and time again.

"Oh yes, I will have my revenge," Ishani said out loud. There was a swooshing sound behind her. She lowered her head and smiled.

A figure stepped behind her and wrapped his arms around her waist. "My love, I sensed your distress," a strong male voice said. She laid her head on his shoulder.

"The time is close for this to end. I sense it," Ishani said, closing her eyes and breathing in the scent of the man she loved.

"Then I better make sure our plans are in place for the final stages."

"Yes," Ishani said, turning around pulling him into a passionate kiss.

She was glad that Draxen had left. If he had been there when her love had appeared, she would have had to kill him. She still needed him around for the plan to work.

Ishani's clothes were soon on the floor beside her lover's own. The love they shared was beyond this life, and soon the main cause of her distress would be dealt with once and for all. Then life could really begin for her and her true love.

In the candle-lit basement of a building in the center of Silver City, a cloaked figure appeared out of nowhere. An older man was reading a journal. The whooshing sound caused a disturbance in the air and some of the papers on his desk fluttered to the floor.

The older man got up, bothered by the sound, and looked directly at the figure. He began to tremble. The younger man removed his hood to reveal who he was. The older man bent down quickly to a knee and dropped his head.

"Lord Draxen." The man trembled.

"Calm down, man. I am here to make sure our plans are in place," Draxen said walking over to the bowl of fruit sitting on the man's desk. He picked up an apple and, before the man could stop him he took a big bite out of it.

"My Lord, that is bad," the man said with disgust on his face. Draxen, while chewing looked at the apple and realized he had bitten a worm in half. He just smiled and took another bite, finishing the apple without a word.

"No worries, I like the extra taste."

The man, still kneeling, felt his stomach began to turn. He swallowed down the urge to vomit all over the floor. "Yes, the plans are in place. The boy captain leaves tomorrow. I have secured his demise with a local man who has a score to settle with him."

"Good, we can't fail. It would mean the death of me. And I might add, you as well. I will not go down alone," Draxen said, throwing the core on the floor.

"Yes, lord, I have secured an understanding with the cutthroat."

Draxen was preparing to leave when he turned to face the man. "Stand up and look me in the eye." The man stood and looked down at Draxen. He was a little taller than the warlock. Draxen patted his shoulders. "By the way, we will come for the boy soon to finish his training."

"My lord he is ready. There is no more need to torture him," the man pleaded.

"Ishani wants to be sure," Draxen said with a smile. "Now if you want, you can plead your case with her." Draxen knew the answer already. A look of horror come over the man's face. He knew the terrible things she could do. He had been converted to the darkness thanks to her when he was young. He still had nightmares from the time under her care.

"No, lord, that's fine. He will be ready."

"Good choice, I'll be in touch in a few days," Draxen said, stepping back before disappearing.

The man sat down at his desk and put his face in his hands. He began to weep like a baby. "What have I done? I'm sorry. Please forgive me!" He knew the boy couldn't hear him, but his black heart felt slightly better knowing he had said it, though he could never say it to the boy.

The Visit

Dirk and Tab were leaving the general's workshop when Dirk noticed that they had company. Four beautiful white horses connected to a carriage were stopped in the front of the house. "Hey Grandfather, I think we have company." The general looked towards the house.

"Well, let's not keep them waiting," the general said, heading to the house. Dirk and Tab hurried behind him. Dirk knew it was someone important. The carriage and horses had the royal seal on them.

As he got closer to the house, he could hear raised voices. Dirk knew one of the voices well. He had heard it his entire life. It was Kira.

"No way! Not now! The timing is not right."

"But, Kira, now is the perfect time," a melodic voice was saying. Kira heard the door open and quickly decided to force a change in the discussion. She looked at the three coming into the living room.

"What have you three been up to?" Kira stood up from the couch that she was sharing with the queen of the elves.

"Just getting the boys ready for tomorrow," the general said, walking over to greet the king of the elves, who was standing by one of the windows facing the woods. Scanning the room, Dirk saw Princess Natia and her elven trainer, Teyna. The general shook the king's hand. "Didn't expect to see you so soon your highness." He bowed his head.

"I know, but there have been a few new developments to the south and I told King Jerard I would inform you since we were coming to visit your family," the king said.

"Let's head outside and we can discuss what you have learned," the general said. He bowed, kissed the queen's hand, and led the king outside. The king's four guards, which Dirk hadn't noticed standing in the shadows, followed him out the front door.

"General," Queen Naira said as he was exiting the house.

"What's going on?" Dirk asked no one in particular.

"The queen and I were just catching up," Kira told him, sitting back down beside her. Natia just sat there, staring at the two elven women. Teyna was standing at her side with a hand on her shoulder.

"Not now," Teyna whispered to Natia, squeezing her shoulder. She had asked Kira about the dream she had before Dirk, Tab and the general had come in. Kira had explained that it was just a dream, not a vision. Natia's mother didn't quite believe Kira, and she had been insisting on talking to Dirk about the Chosen's responsibilities. Kira had told them that Dirk wasn't ready and that he didn't know anything of the legacy. Natia was trying to control her impatience while sitting there and staring at the two women.

"Well, what have you three been up to?" Kira asked the boys again trying to diffuse the tension in the room. Dirk looked at Tab and then back at Kira and the queen,

"We were discussing the first day's expectations and what we could look forward to," Tab blurted out a little awkwardly. They all looked at him.

"Tab Clearwater, right?" the queen asked, looking at Tab with sadness in her eyes.

"Yes, my lady," Tab said, bowing to her.

"No need for that, we're all friends here. This is my daughter, Natia, and her personal trainer Teyna," the queen said, drawing attention to the two elves on the other side of the room.

Tab bowed to them. "My ladies." They each returned a greeting.

"Well, Dirk, I'm sorry we didn't get to talk a lot at the ball, but it seems now is not a good time either. I see your grandfather coming back in without my husband."

The general walked back into the room. "The king feels he needs to give King Jerard a report on our discussion as soon as possible."

"Nothing urgent, I hope. I was looking forward to getting to know my new classmates." Natia said to the general, finally breaking her silence.

At the sound of her voice, Dirk felt a warm sensation forming in his chest again. "Ow," Dirk said, rubbing his shoulder. Tab shot him a stern look.

"Dirk, are you going to say goodbye?" Kira had asked him for the second time.

"Sorry, been a long day." Dirk hadn't realized the queen and Natia were heading for the door.

"That's ok. That beating you took in the tournament probably left you a little slow, I'm sure," Natia said jokingly, walking up to Dirk looking him in the eyes. To Dirk, the world seemed to come to a halt. She leaned in close and whispered, "Our paths are intertwined. The answers I seek will come sooner or later."

She kissed his cheek, turned, and walked to the door. She stopped, turned again, looked at Tab, an eerie look coming over her. She smiled and nodded a goodbye. Teyna followed close behind her with a smile on her face. Dirk, feeling weak in his knees suddenly grabbed Tab's shoulder to steady himself.

"Dirk, we will talk soon," the queen said as she walked over and hugged him. Dirk hugged her back and felt an instant connection to her. She leaned back, holding him by his shoulders looking into his eyes. Before she got to see what she was looking for, Kira grabbed her shoulder and pulled her into a hug.

"It's been good to see you. I promise I'll come see you in a few days after the kids are settled in school and we'll have a long and uninterrupted conversation,"

"We will." The queen turned and hugged Tab. Shocked, Tab just stood there awkwardly, patting her back. "It's good to meet you as well. Any friend of the Storm's is family to me. Always remember that, Tab."

"Thanks," Tab responded.

"General," the queen said, bowing her head to him and walked out the door.

"Well, what the hell's was that about?' Dirk asked his mother.

"Not important right now. They were just trying to find out more information than they needed to know. General, is everything ok?" Kira asked.

"Just the southerners getting more aggressive. The king of Vangaurd has broken all trade agreements again. Nothing that needs discussing here. Now boys, you both have a busy day tomorrow. Tab, you're staying here tonight, right?" the general asked Tab, though he knew the answer. Tab nodded. "That's good, so that you two can go together." The boys knew they wouldn't get any more information, so they listened to the general.

"Anyone hungry?" Tab asked, rubbing his stomach. Kira smiled and told them to give her a few minutes and she would put together some sandwiches for dinner. She left the room. The general looked at them with a sadness in his eyes.

"No food for me. I must head back to the castle where I'll be staying tonight. Remember all the things you two learned today. The next few months will be trying. We won't see much of each other, I'm afraid. I have been called back into service at the castle. Your mother can handle your training for a while. Focus on the basics you learn at school. The rest will come in time." The general held up his hand to stop the questions. "Trust me." He hugged Dirk and then Tab. "I love you both." He walked into the kitchen to tell Kira what he had learned.

"What the hells?" Tab asked Dirk after the general disappeared into the kitchen.

"I don't know. More secrets, it sounds like to me," Dirk replied. Tab nodded his head in agreement. They discussed the events of the past hour and Dirk told Tab about the sensation that he had felt when he had encountered Natia's touch.

"I felt it too. I didn't know what it was, but my chest got a little warm," Tab explained. They brushed it off. It was probably their connection. Then Dirk explained more in detail the feeling he got from the contact with Natia. By the time he was through telling him, they both just sat there in thought, waiting on Kira to call them to dinner.

A few minutes later, they heard the general go upstairs, then come back down, and exit the house. Kira finally called them to eat. They could tell she had been crying. There were tears in her eyes. She wouldn't explain anything, so they ate in silence.

After the dishes were washed, Kira told them to go upstairs and get ready for bed. She had already gotten all their clothes and supplies needed for school and had packed their packs. She kissed them both and got an extra big hug from Tab before she headed to bed.

"I'll see you off first thing in the morning," were the last words they heard from her before she closed her bedroom door. The boys went upstairs and there, sitting in her nest of blankets, was Aarya.

"We didn't forget you, girl," Dirk said to her, sitting on his bed. She cooed in understanding. They got dressed for bed and laid down with Aarya between them on the desk. They talked until neither could hold their eyes open. Aarya just looked between the two, listening to the conversation.

Truth be told, she understood every word. She like the boys got sleepy as soon as they did and dosed off. Their night was full of dreams again.

Testing

Dawn came quickly for the boys. It seemed they had just fallen into a deep sleep when they heard Kira yelling at them to get up. "More dreams?" Dirk asked Tab.

"Yes, but more jumbled this time," Tab responded.

"Well, I, for one, am not going to worry about it today. Linc is taking off and to be honest, I don't want to think about this Chosen stuff today. What about you?"

"I don't know how I feel yet. Don't get me wrong I'm happy to know the truth about my family but this is a lot to take in. We go eighteen years thinking one thing, then overnight, the world as we know it has changed. I'm torn to be honest with you." Tab rubbed his face.

"Yeah, me too, but I still feel strongly about our plans for the future with Linc," Dirk said, finally getting up to get ready. Tab agreed. After washing and getting ready, they grabbed their things and headed down the stairs. Aarya flew out the bedroom window and glided down to the open kitchen window. She landed on the sill and began eating from the pile of food that had been laid out for her.

"Boys, there is a lot to go over this morning, so eat and we'll cover a few things before you leave," Kira told them while filling two plates with eggs, bacon, and bread. The boys kissed her on the cheek. They grabbed their food and sat down at either side of the table to eat.

Kira informed them that they would be hiring temporary help for the farm since school was beginning and the general would be working at the palace. Bart Thane, who had been a farmer his whole life, and his wife, Carly, had agreed to help while Dirk was away at school.

Their farm in the south had been falling on hard times with all the bandits in that area. They had moved to Silver City looking for an opportunity. The general had met Bart when he was at the market looking for work. Kira explained that they would live in one of the guest houses behind the main house while they were there.

"Mom, what about Aarya? Won't they see her?" Dirk asked.

"Aarya can make herself invisible to anyone she doesn't want to see her, if she is like her mother. It was one of her powers."

"Wow, that's cool," Tab said. Aarya let out a trill of agreement.

After Kira laid out the training that they would get on their brief visits away from school, both boys gathered around Aarya and touched her neck. "We'll be back soon. Take care of Mom and yourself while we're gone,"

Aarya nudged their hands and nipped each boy affectionately acknowledging them with a shriek. The boys smiled as she flew out the window and into the sky.

"I wonder where she's going," Tab said out loud.

"Remember, she's growing. She's probably just stretching her wings and getting used to her surroundings," Kira said. "Now give me a hug. I won't be able to see you for a few days. Remember to learn the basics. It's so important," Kira said, hugging them and saying goodbye. She hurried out of the room as the boys grabbed their things. Kira's heart had still not accepted that her boys were changing already. She hoped that the pain of what they would go through would come later, not sooner, because it would be overwhelming.

The boys met Bart and his wife as they were leaving the farm. "They seem nice," Tab said to Dirk while they were walking down the trail towards the city.

"Yes, they did. My grandfather is a good judge of character so I'm sure they'll be fine."

It took them half an hour to get to the spot where they had agreed to meet Linc that morning and then they went over the plans one more time. Linc didn't tell them what he had witnessed at the shady pub. He was keeping that to himself for now. He knew the burden that had been placed on Dirk and Tab and didn't want them running off too early.

"Everything's ready. We sail out in a few hours," Linc told them. The three of them clasped hands.

Dirk looked at Linc. "Remember, our future is in your hands. If you need us, no matter what, get a message to us and we'll be there as soon as we can."

"I know. You two go learn some magic. I'm sure it'll be needed one day. I'll handle this part," Linc said confidently. They grasped each other in a hug and then Linc headed to the docks while Dirk and Tab headed to the other meeting spot they had set up with the rest of the Pack.

As Linc was heading down the main path to his new ship, he looked up. There was a bird circling high in the sky. He couldn't make out what kind it was. He heard it make a shrill sound as it flew off. Linc smiled. His chest warmed and he knew at that moment who and what that bird was.

Aarya circled over the three boys. She knew danger was close by, but she couldn't intervene yet. She understood the boys thought of Linc as a brother, so she had decided to keep an eye on him as well.

Dirk and Tab met El, Jonesy, and Gil a few blocks from the school in front of Mr. Burk's bakery. They wanted to get some treats one last time before they stepped onto the academy grounds.

"Where have you two been? We've been waiting half an hour for you!" El said as they walked up.

"Sorry, we had to say goodbye to Linc," Dirk explained.

"Well, if you want to get one last sticky bun, you better hurry. Mr. Burk said that they had a rush on them this morning, but he saved us a few," Gil told them, licking his sticky fingers.

"Okay, okay," Tab told them as he and Dirk went into the shop to get the last buns of the day.

"Hurry up! We can't be late!" Jonesy told them as Tab and Dirk came back out stuffing their faces. He was nervous already. He wouldn't see them much since his training would be different.

"Stop pacing, you. Everything will be fine. You'll see," El told her brother.

"Ok, if you say so, but you know that sleazy Brock and his thugs will be looking to take advantage of you since I won't be around all the time."

Dirk patted Jonesy on the shoulder, feeling sticky sweat transfer onto him. "Don't worry, big fella. We'll be ready for them." Dirk smiled and looked at Tab.

Tab just laughed and said, "Yeah, we will be ready for them," as he wiped off the stuff Dirk had accidently smeared on Jonesy. El and Gil just looked at the two with concern.

"What have you two got planned?" El asked.

"Nothing. Honest, we're just not taking any more of their crap. Let's get to the school before we're late," Dirk said, heading off and the Pack followed.

Dirk saw that there was a line of about fifty kids, a mix of boys and girls, waiting to go inside the academy. All races were represented. Volar and the dwarves were the first that Dirk and the Pack ran into. They talked while the line started to move and split, guiding the new students in the direction they needed to go. Some went to the left for the military induction while the rest went to the right for magic testing. All the dwarves went to the military academy except for Volar. He went to the right with Dirk, Tab, El, and Gil. Jonesy said his goodbyes after much hesitation.

At the entrance of the school, a single wizard was gathering students around him. "I am Wizard Laseous. I am here to explain where you need to go from here. There are five rooms set up for the testing. The four elements and Health. Healing, water, earth, wind, and fire will be written on markers above each door, representing which room is for what testing," he said. "Each student will go to each room and be tested on each power. Your main area of study will be in the area in which you do best in."

"Each room will have two wizards sitting behind a table. Once your inside sitting down, a single gem will be set up between you and them. Each color represents an element: red opal for fire, blue agate for water, green emerald for earth, quartz for wind, and light blue aquamarine for healing.

"All you need to do is pick the gem up, place it in the palm of your hand, and concentrate. It will light up, revealing the inner power you have. The brightness of the light depends on the innate strength you have. The wizards will use a grading scale of one to five, one being the lowest and five being the highest potential." He looked around seeing that they understood.

After explaining the instructions, he started sending them through to do their testing one at a time. Dirk waited patiently, talking with Volar and Tab to pass the time. As they got closer to the front, Dirk heard the wizard say, "Next."

"Volar Horan," the dwarf said, stepping up when he and his friends finally had gotten to the front of the line.

"Ah yes, Master Horan. Room three, I believe, will be a good place to start." Volar entered the building and headed to the center door down the hall.

"Elyse Glan," El told the wizard.

"Yes, Miss Glan, room two." El smiled and headed to her room.

"Gil Jamous," Gil said, stepping up.

"Ah, Master Jamous. Hope your father is well?" the wizard said to Gil.

"He's fine," Gil responded.

"Good, tell him Wizard Laseous gives his regards. Now room one for you." Gil shrugged and headed to the room.

Tab stepped up.

"Ah Tab Clearwater."

"Yes," Tab replied.

"Now, you understand that being General Storm's appointed student, you'll have to really apply yourself and maintain your grades. If not, it's off to the military school. Understood?" the wizard asked.

"Yes, I understand," Tab said a little too sternly.

"Keep that attitude in check while you're enrolled here. You wouldn't want to find yourself in detention on the first day," the wizard scolded, looking at Tab with fire in his eyes.

"Yes sir."

"Now, room four, I believe." Tab looked back at Dirk and smirked as he headed to room four.

"Dirk Storm! As I live and breathe," Laseous said sarcastically. "I will give you some free advice as well. You and your friend's misdeeds are well known to us here at the academy. I don't care who your grandfather is. One toe out of line while you're here and I'm sure the military could use another grunt. Do I make myself clear?"

"Well, I wouldn't want you kissing my ass like you did Gil's," Dirk said, a hint of flames beginning to circle his eyes. He lowered his head. He could feel the fire beginning and he knew he had to control his temper. Lately, it didn't take much to set him off. He would have to talk with his mother about that.

Laseous took his glasses off and closed the book that he had been using to check off the student's names in as they arrived.

With a pointed finger, he leaned towards Dirk. In a powerful and stern voice, he said, "Mr. Storm, I see I was right about you. That language will not be tolerated here. Tonight, after dinner, come to my office so I can lay some ground rules down for you. It's right next to the head wizard's office. Now, go to room five and wait your turn. You need to contemplate my words." The wizard pointed towards the room.

"Yes sir," Dirk said through gritted teeth. He didn't really want to be here anyway. His thoughts were on Linc. That was where he truly wanted to be, with Linc and Tab starting their adventures, but he had promised his mother and then the family legacy thing had been thrust upon him. He still didn't know what to think about all of that, but he had made a promise.

Here we go, he thought, heading to the room. He could still feel the fire that had kindled in his eyes. There was something about Laseous he didn't like or trust. He would have given him a chance, but the way he talked to Tab had made him angry. Feeling his eyes tingling, he stopped in front of door five and took a deep breath. Thinking of the calming technique his mother had taught him, he relaxed. His eyes cooled down and he could feel the magic subsiding.

Dirk waited patiently behind some big kid he didn't recognize. The boy wouldn't even look his way. He must have been nervous because he heard him cough every few minutes. After a while, it was finally his turn.

He walked through the door and there, sitting at the table, was a middle-aged female wizard with silver-streaked brown hair curled into a bun on top of her head. She had a radiance about her that Dirk could sense. It was her inner power, definitely, and he could tell she had a lot of it. He didn't know how he knew, he just sensed it. She wore silk amber robes and glasses that were made of a thin gold wire attached to a linen strap. Sitting next to her was a young girl in student robes who had a very solemn look about her. She was fair-skinned with blond hair braided down her back.

"Ah, Dirk, please come have a seat, dear," the wizard said. Dirk instantly felt he was going to like her. He sat down in front of the two women. "I am Wizard Hermosa, and this is my aide, Helena."

"Hello," Dirk acknowledged them nervously, giving a slight bow. The women looked and smiled to each other. He didn't realize that he was nervous until he spoke.

"Such a gentleman. Now, there is nothing to be nervous about. This isn't a test. It's more of a gauge. There is no pass or fail here. This is just to find your main area of study so that we can use it as a focus for you in the first few months. We like starting with your strongest element first so that we can get you acclimated, then move on to your lesser strengths after a few weeks. Sound good?"

"Yes ma'am."

"Now see that gem in front of you?" Dirk acknowledged her with a nod. "I want you to pick it up and concentrate on its color."

Dirk did as she instructed. The gem was a yellow color. He picked it up and held it in the palm of his hand, concentrating on the gem. Nothing seemed to happen. After a few minutes he sighed.

"Now Dirk, just relax. I want you to close your eyes. Then, without looking at the gem, think about the color of it," the older wizard instructed him.

Dirk felt comforted by her voice, so he did as she instructed him. After a few deep breaths, he felt a warm sensation stirring in his chest.

"Now, that's better. Open your eyes." Dirk did and the gem he was holding was emanating light from its center. It went out almost as soon as he looked at it. Dirk smiled, proud of the fact that he had touched his core easily this time.

The two women started making notes on the parchments in front of them. Hermosa grabbed the gem from him and handed him another. This one was light red. "Now, let's try this one," she told him.

He took the gem confidently from her. His success had given him confidence. He repeated what he had already done and concentrated on the color. Even with his eyes closed this time, he could tell it had worked. He could feel the warmth in his hands and could also somehow see that the glow was brighter than the previous stone.

After he opened his eyes, she pulled out a third stone and exchanged it with the one he was holding. "Now just one more time." He looked at the crimson gem in his hands. It was much darker than the prior stone.

"Okay," Dirk replied. He closed his eyes, and, in an instant, he felt the gem heat up in his hand and a tingling sensation swept through his body. He could sense, more than actually see, that the gem was glowing.

His senses became heightened, and he could hear Tab down the hall talking with a male wizard. He could hear El giggling with another female. It was like time had stopped.

Then he opened his eyes before Hermosa could speak. The wizard and her aide both had identical astonished looks on their faces. The wizard recovered quickly, taking the gem from him, and putting it back in the bag beside her.

"That was good, Dirk." She paused for a moment and then whispered to her aide. Dirk watched as the young girl nodded in agreement. Hermosa looked at Dirk. "I must ask you a favor." He looked at them both and nodded. "I know you have just met me and do not know me yet, but I must ask you to keep what just happened with the crimson ruby a secret for now, especially from the other students and wizards in the school. There are only a few people who have ever made that ruby glow, and this must be handled delicately."

Dirk looked into her eyes. *Trust her*, a voice in his head said. He knew instantly that he could trust her with his life.

Even though he had just met her, he felt confident of his feelings. "You have my word," Dirk responded, putting his right hand over his heart, the sign of honor in the military.

She smiled and both her and Helen bowed their heads to him, accepting the pledge. "Now, Dirk, you can go to room four."

He got up and looked at the women. "Thank you." He bowed.

"No, thank you," the elderly wizard said. "I'm sure we will be spending a lot of time together soon," She smiled. As he walked out the door, Hermosa and Helen started talking with each other excitedly.

He smiled to himself passing Gil in the hall. "How did it go?"

Gil just gave him a *I don't know* look with a shrug of his shoulders.

Dirk headed to the next room to wait his turn. Every room he went into had a different wizard and aide. The only other gem he had gotten to light up was the healing gem, and the glow was just barely visible.

After he finished in the last room, he was instructed to go to the lunchroom and eat. He was told by Wizard Stefano, his last tester, that after lunch the results would be posted on the announcement boards in the lunchroom. As he walked down the hall, he saw that there were signs on the walls directing the new students where every room was. He followed the signs and found his friends at a table, already eating.

"Hey what took you so long?" Tab asked motioning for Dirk to sit beside him.

"I don't know. That last one just barely lit up and they were happy just to get me out," he replied.

"Better go get some food before the line fills up. It starts on the right side over there," El said, pointing in that direction.

Dirk got in line for some food. There were a few people in front of him. Then he heard a voice that made him cringe. He slowly looked to his left. Sitting a few tables to his left was Brock. He was sitting with Skylar and some people Dirk didn't know. They were talking and laughing. Dirk could tell he was the topic of their discussion because most of the table was staring at him. He just turned away and continued waiting his turn for food. The smell of something sweet hit his senses. Dirk felt a warming sensation in his chest.

"Hello Dirk," a melodic voice said. Dirk knew the instant he heard her voice who it was. His hands started to sweat, and his vision blurred a little. He took a deep breath and turned to greet the princess.

"Ah, hello," was all he managed to get out.

"Are you feeling well?" Natia asked as they moved forward.

"Yes, I'm fine, thanks. How are you feeling?" he asked awkwardly.

"I'm wonderful now, thanks for asking. It's just you look a little off."

"I'm fine, it's been a few trying days, is all." Dirk moved forward, trying to get out of the conversation.

"What will you have, dear?" asked a portly lady standing behind the food bar. Dirk was relieved.

"What do you have?" he asked, silently thanking the woman who had saved him from the princess's questions.

"We have vegetable stew, bread, and a few beef sandwiches," she told him.

"I'll have the stew, thanks,"

She turned and grabbed a bowl of soup and some bread. Dirk took it quickly and turned to head back to his friends. "See you later," Dirk said to the princess as he was leaving.

"Yes, you will," she said, smiling at him.

Tab was watching from his seat. He elbowed El forcefully. "Ow, you git! What was that for?" El asked, rubbing her ribs.

"Look," Tab, said pointing.

El saw what he was pointing at. "Well, he isn't wasting any time, is he?" El said, laughing as she saw Dirk talking to the princess. Tab just looked on with concern. He had a feeling Dirk was getting questioned instead of making a move on the princess. As Dirk was walking away, he didn't see that Brock had stuck his leg out to trip him, but Tab did. Tab got up quickly and sprinted to the table in record time.

Just as Dirk started to fall, Tab caught his arm and the hot bowl of stew Dirk had been holding sloshed straight into Brock's face.

"*Ow,* you bastard!" Brock screamed as he wiped the hot stew out of his eyes. He started toward Tab with his fist raised. Skylar grabbed Brock's arm just in time.

"What is going on here?" Wizard Laseous asked, walking up with several parchments in his hands. Before Tab could explain, Skylar spoke up.

"Dirk and Tab threw the stew on Brock intentionally!"

"You sewer skank!" Tab yelled, walking towards the girl. Wizard Laseous stepped between them.

"I see. Thanks, Miss Sweet." The wizard pointed at Tab and Dirk. "I warned you two. Mr. Clearwater, you can join your friend tonight. Be in my office after dinner. Don't make me come look for you two." The wizard turned and walked to the bulletin board.

Dirk grabbed Tab and walked back to their table. "Don't worry, they'll get what's coming," Dirk told him as they sat down. Dirk started to eat the bread that hadn't fallen off his tray in silence as his friends complained to each other. There was another high-pitched squeak. They all turned in the direction it came from.

Skylar was standing up, wiping off her face and robes. "I'm so sorry. I must have slipped on the wet area of the floor," said the princess as she tried to help Skylar clean herself off. Skylar pushed her hands away, her face red. It wasn't just from the hot stew. Dirk could see she was pissed.

"That's ok. Just let me be," Skylar said, heading out of the cafeteria. The princess turned gracefully and walked back to the food bar to get herself another bowl of stew. As she walked to her table, she slowly turned and looked at Dirk. A small smile crept onto her face. Dirk could have sworn he saw a flare of light in her eyes. She sat down with the other elves she had come in with.

"She did that on purpose," Dirk whispered to Tab.

"I think you're right. I think we might like her," Tab responded.

A loud throat clearing brought everyone's attention to the front of the lunchroom. "Now that all of the commotion is over, I want to make a few announcements," Wizard Laseous said to the new students. "There are four sections of parchment I will put up on the board up here. The first is a yearly calendar. It has a breakdown of the terms and the dates of all other events. Special events are noted as well. The one on the top right will be your rooming assignments. The third one on the bottom left will be a list of instructors and their area of expertise. And the final one will have your names on it and the names of your main instructor. They will set up the rest of your schedule after you meet with them on the first day of classes.

"I want to stress one more time to every one of you," Laseous said, glaring at Dirk and Tab, "There will be no shenanigans in this academy. If there are, the ones responsible will be dealt with severely. Do you understand?"

"Yes, Wizard Laseous," the crowd said loudly.

"Now, this afternoon will be the time for you to get familiar with the school and get moved into your quarters. Remember there is no leaving campus until break after today. Make sure you have everything you need today and get back to the dining hall by six tonight for dinner. Any questions?"

No one wanted to test his patience.

"Good, now one table at a time. Starting with the table to the left in the front of the room, go up and check the board. Once they are done, the next table to the right and so on," he told the kids, and then he headed out of the room with a swish of his robes.

Dirk and his friends talked about the mornings events and how they all did on the testing while they waited their turn to go up to the board. Dirk remembered his promise and didn't say anything about the crimson jewel. El explained how she got a reaction from the green and the clear gems. Gil said that he had only gotten a reaction from the clear one. Everyone thought that made sense seeing that his father was the High Exalted one.

Tab said he only got a reaction from the clear gem too. Dirk thought that was strange, seeing what had happened to them, but he didn't say it aloud. Volar had a reaction from the green gem. *That suits him since he lives in a cave,* Dirk thought.

Finally, their time came to go up to the school board. El was the first to get there. She clapped, quietly bouncing up and down on her feet. "I'm so excited, guys! I got Wizard Sahsi as my main instructor. She's from one of the desert dwellings to the south. Look! There are three people to each dorm room, and I'll be rooming with a pair of twins, Vira and Nira Frost. The only thing I know about them is they're from Aarkas." She pointed to their rooming assignments.

Aarkas was an island off the north coast. No one from there had been to the school here for more than a hundred-years. Dirk knew that El loved mystery's and would be excited about getting to know them. He smiled at her and squeezed her shoulder.

It was Gil's turn next. "Aw man! I got Stephano as my main instructor."

"Well, what's wrong with that?" Tab asked.

"Nothing really. He's just a good friend of my father." Gil sighed. "Well, at least we'll be roommates." He slapped Tab on the back.

"What?" Tab pushed Gil out of the way. Disgusted, he just shook his head. "Sorry Gil, I didn't mean it that way I just thought I would be put in Dirk's room."

"That's ok. I know how close you two are." He stepped back so the rest could read the board. Dirk saw that he and Volar were roommates, along with Phil Wark from Pineral.

"Well at least you and El will have the same main instructor," Dirk said, bringing Tab's attention back to the board. Tab stepped back from the board and took a better look. A small grin appeared on his face. Only Dirk and Volar saw it. Dirk was scrutinizing the school schedule while Volar was asking the group questions about Wizard Quentin, his main instructor.

"Hey, did any of you look at this schedule?" El said. The group stepped up behind her to take a look.

"Going to be some early mornings. I mean starting at five am every day?" Tab said. The group agreed with him.

"Yea, working out after breakfast could be disastrous," Dirk said, laughing.

"Well, it's not going to be boring. It looks like our days are busy, with no spare time until it's time for bed at nine every night," El said.

"Boy, there's no time off," Gil said as the group read further.

"Well at least Sunday afternoons and nights are free," Tab's mischievous grin appeared.

"You think that's tough, look at the yearly schedule." Dirk directed everyone's attention to the other piece of parchment.

"You know this isn't going to be an easy schedule," Gil said.

"Well, at least you got Laseous kissing your ass already," Dirk smirked. He knew how Gil hated his father's friends. They all thought they could get in good with The High One that way. None of them really knew him at all if they thought that. He would want them to be extra hard on Gil to make him tougher.

"Ha-ha."

"Okay, let's go check out our rooms then we can meet back in the entrance at three so we can explore the school," El told the group.

Dorms and Detention

When Dirk and the group got to the stairwell that led up to the dorm rooms, they were met by a pair of identical women. They both had dark hair, though one's was a shade lighter, pulled up in a bun. One of them wore glasses, and both wore robes. They smiled as the group walked up. Other kids their age lined up behind them. Dirk looked back to see who was behind them.

Unfortunately, Brock and his group of thugs was there along with a few others that Dirk didn't know. He had seen most of them in the cafeteria though.

At the very back of the group, a pair of twin girls came to a halt. Dirk thought there was a look of familiarity about them. They seemed to be withdrawn, not looking anyone in the eye. They had small frames and held their bags close to their chests, hugging them tight. They both had shoulder-length dirty blonde hair that looked like it needed to be brushed and wore tattered beige robes.

When they stopped, the one on the left looked up towards the women standing in front of them and, for a second, she looked in Dirk's direction. Their eyes met and a hint of a smile formed on her lips. Her eyes, a cool blue, were mesmerizing.

It made him feel nervous, so he looked away. A chill ran through his body. He closed his eyes and shook his body to clear the feeling.

"Now that all of you are here, let me introduce who we are," the twin on the left said. "I am Tilda Pine, and this is my sister, Hilda. We are the first-year girl's and boy's dorm mothers. We will be the ones who help keep you on the right path your first year. At night, we will help with your studies outside of class. I will be with the girls and Hilda will be with the boys on their floor. One rule that you must follow is the only rule you need. Follow all of the rules. Do that and everything will be fine. Now, you already have your room assignments. Once you get to your floor, you will see that your clothes and everything you brought with you will already be in your rooms. Now ladies, follow me to the third floor. Boys, follow Hilda to the fourth. All other questions will be answered there." Tilda turned and headed up the stairs.

The group followed them. Dirk took in his surroundings. The stairs were made of stone, just like the walls.

At the bottom of the stairs, there was a big wooden door on the right. On it was a sign that read PRIVATE in bold letters. It was evidently locked, and it had some kind of sheen to it.

Probably magically protected, Dirk thought as he started up the stairs behind the boys. He was transfixed on the door, so much so that he hadn't noticed that he was being passed by all of the other new students. Before he went to catch up with everyone, he felt a strong urge to touch the door. It was calling to him.

His hand was mere inches from the door when he heard someone clear their throat behind him. He froze and then turned to see who was there. Standing behind him was Master Nabas. He was an older man in blue robes. He had a look of power that radiated around him. His hands behind his back, he stood there with a look of concern on his face.

"Ah, Mr. Storm, I'm glad I caught you before you touched that door," he said, moving closer to Dirk. "You see that door has a powerful enchantment on it and anyone not authorized would be stricken with blinding pain. So much so that if anyone with ill intentions did, it might kill them."

Dirk just stared back in disbelief.

"You see, we have many secrets in the school and we want to keep them hidden from people who don't need to know certain things. Do you understand?"

"Yes, Wizard Nabas, I do. I'm sorry. It just felt like the door was calling to me."

The elder wizard just looked at him with a knowing eye. "I do understand, but you must keep away from certain areas until we feel the time is right for the students to know what they are. Can you promise me you'll stay clear of these areas for now? I don't want you getting hurt unnecessarily."

"I will ignore that urge to keep out of trouble, and any pain that might cause."

"Thank you, Dirk. Now head up to your room for now. I'm sure we'll be talking more as time goes by," Wizard Nabas said, dismissing Dirk.

As he hurried to catch up with the other boys, he noticed each door he passed had signs on them. The first floor had the words *second year- girls*. It was the same type of door without the sheen. The second floor had *second year-boys* written on it. It also lacked a sheen. As Dirk passed the third-floor door, it was just being closed.

Thinking about what he was told by the headmaster, he resisted the urge to let the curiosity get to him, but he had only so much control. He smiled, excited to tell Tab about what had happened. *He probably already sensed it through our connection,* he thought.

When he finally reached the fourth floor, Hilda was tapping her foot impatiently, staring at him as he came up to the door. "Mr. Storm, I hope this isn't how things are going to be. Please make sure you are on time and from now on and keep up," Hilda scolded.

"Yes ma'am. Sorry," Dirk responded. "By the way what's behind that door going to the basement?"

"That is none of your concern and mind me when I say it's better to stay away from it," she said, ushering him into the room and closing the door behind her. "Now, I want to have all of your attention, so gather around me before you go into your rooms. Look at where we stand. On the walls around you are the dorm rooms. In the center, you see the fireplace. It goes through all the floors top to bottom. Don't try going up or down in it to get to another floor. That would be a gruesome death, as one poor child unfortunately found out," she said, lowering her head a little and pulling a tissue out of her pocket to wipe the corners of her eyes.

After a few seconds, she cleared her throat and looked at the boys. "Hopefully, that's all I need to say about that. The left side of the room is where my room, 302, and a guest room are located. In the back center is my personal washroom and beside it is the communal restroom and showers," she said, waving her hand in that direction. "A time will be posted for your allotted use of the showers." She pointed to a schedule hanging on the shower doors.

"Now on the left side is a supply room that you cannot enter without me being present. This will be explained more as your studies begin." She pulled a small piece of material out from under her shirt with a key attached to it. "I have the only key and if any of you get any ideas about trying to get in without me being there, let's just say it will be quite enlightening." She raised an eyebrow, looking at each one in turn to make sure they understood.

After seeing everyone nod in agreement, she continued. "Now the rest of the rooms are on the right side of the wall with a guest room there as well. The study areas are spread throughout the rest of the room with tables, chairs, and couches, as you can see. The small bookshelves contain materials to help with the various studies that each of you will have. Make sure if you use any of the books that they get put back when you are through with them. They belong to this room only. Some of them are very old so be gentle with them when you use them. Now, after your first day of class tomorrow, come to me at the end of the day and I will dispense to you the items you need from the supply room. The first set I give you will be free.

Anything after that you will have to buy."

Everyone again nodded in understanding.

"Since you no longer live at home, there will be duties assigned to each of you, cleaning duties and such. You will be responsible for your own laundry. The laundry room is on the fifth floor that you will share with all students in the north tower. Usually twice a week, I will make it a part of your responsibilities. The schedule will be set and posted on the room bulletin board by the supply door. If you don't have any other questions, the rest of the day is yours to check out your rooms and the rest of the school.

"Do not go anywhere that is prohibited or suffer the consequences. There will be staff and student aides walking the halls to help with any questions you may have. You can leave the school to say your goodbyes to your families, but be back here by dinner, as you were previously told. I will be locking the dorm room door at nine tonight so be here on time." She smiled and dismissed them.

The group went to check out their rooms. Dirk saw Brock and his little group laughing at something Brock had said. They were looking at him, so he figured he was the butt of their joke. He felt his eyes warming up, so he turned away and headed to his room. He was rooming with Volar, and a boy named Phil Wark. Dirk had seen Phil earlier. He was average-sized with brown hair. He seemed like a good guy, but time would tell. Tab was still a little miffed about not rooming with Dirk, but at least he had Gil in his room, along with Dusty Maris, a kid from Venia.

Dirk knew from his studies in primary school that Venia was a town to the south. He had always heard a lot of bad rumors about that town. It was close to where the last battle at Der-Tod had taken place. It was always shrouded with darkness, it seemed. Dirk had never been there but the general always held the land and its ruler in contempt.

Not much was known about Dusty yet, but Dirk was sure Tab would find out everything within a few days. He laughed to himself. Tab was like that. He always had a way of finding out things about people. He was good at mingling with just about anyone, no matter who they were. Watching Tab start to question Dusty, Dirk just smiled and headed to his assigned room.

When Dirk walked in, Volar and Phil were already there unpacking their things. The room was simple, with one bed and a desk by each wall. The beds were singles with pine frames, feather mattresses, one pillow and one blanket. The desk had two drawers on one side and wooden chairs. Dirk could tell by the color and smell of the wood that it was pine, just like the bed frames. It looked very old but still sturdy. There were also hanging cabinets for clothes and one big drawer at the bottom of each. They all had their own.

Dirk went to the center bed since Volar and Phil had chosen beds on the left and the right of him. He was okay with it because the one window in the room was over his bed. It faced towards Mt. Blazire and his home.

He began unpacking his clothes and putting them away. There were two light brown robes, the color always worn by first-years students. He put his pants and shirts neatly in the bottom drawer, his undergarments, and socks in the top and he set his extra boots on the top of the shelf. He hung up his two coats next to the robes. One was his dress coat and the other was his travel coat.

Dirk sat on the bed while the boys finished putting away their things. Dirk saw that Phil's things were simple, like his, except he had boots that looked new. Phil noticed Dirk admiring his shoes.

"My dad is the finest cobbler in the land. He makes the best boots and leather products. He really can make anything out of leather. He has a secret process he uses to make them. The products always look new, no matter how old they are. They're as sturdy as any other, but they're also soft," Phil declared with pride. "Here, take a look at these." He handed Dirk his boots. Dirk was in awe. They were as he said, sturdy but very soft to the touch.

"I bet you guys are rich then," Dirk said.

"Not really. We're from Pineral, so it's hard to get our products to the markets for sale. My dad won't sell to just anyone. He doesn't want anyone selling his product but him," Phil explained.

Pineral was to the far west, close to the elven homeland. They didn't wear clothes made by anyone other than themselves. "I see, but these are really nice. Maybe one day your dad will find a way to get them to market easier." Dirk gave the boots back.

"Thanks Dirk. That's very nice of you to say." Phil nodded with a smile.

Volar walked over and looked at the boots with his appraising eye. "Aye, this is some of the finest craftsmanship I have ever seen." Phil put them away.

"Well I have to go and say goodbye to thine parents. I look forward to learning more about your father's skill," Volar said to Phil, smiling. "I'll see you after dinner. I must dine with them before they leave." Volar patted Dirk on the back and walked out the door.

"Yes, I have to say goodbye to my mother and father as well. I'll see you at dinner, Dirk," Phil said following Volar out. Dirk, not wanting to say goodbye yet to his mother, sat back on the bed and looked around his new room. The walls were gray stone. There were circular orbs on each wall that lit up when touched. Dirk had seen these before at the palace and he knew that they were powered by small yellow gems.

Dirk thought about the events of the past several days. They were still overwhelming him. The things his grandfather and mother had told him made it seem like he was living in a dream. He just couldn't shake that feeling that there was still more he didn't know. He'd just have to deal with it later since Tab was walking toward his room. He could sense Tab's anxiety. The connection they now shared was a little unnerving, even though since they were kids, they had been close.

"You ready?" Tab asked.

"Yes, I am. Let's go. We still have time to get to the farm and back before dinner," Dirk responded. The boys hurried down the stairs and out of the school. They knew the school's layout was basically square with five floors. There was one hallway down the middle of each floor, with classes on the bottom three floors. The fourth and fifth floors were the instructor's offices and living quarters. The military officer's quarters were at the military school apart from the commanding general. His room was next to Head Wizard Nabas on the top floor, which included a huge library that they both used.

Dirk had heard the general talk about it having maps and books containing the uses of magic and military strategies. The recorded history of the school could also be found there. A few religious books were available there, but most of those were kept with Gil's dad at the temple's library. Very few people got to use that library unless the king deemed it necessary. Dirk definitely didn't ever want to go there.

The kitchen and meeting hall were on the first floor. It had been an addition added to the main school twenty years ago since the school was always growing. Dirk already knew all of this from his trips to the school with his grandfather, so he didn't feel the need to take a tour.

It was now a little after two, so the boys wanted to get to the farm to check on Aarya one last time. They wouldn't be able to visit her for a few weeks. *At least not officially*, Dirk thought as they ran through the market towards the farm. As they headed out of the market, Mr. Burk, the baker, was sweeping his sidewalk. He noticed the boys running.

He yelled at the boys as they approached. "Hey, you two come by here on your way back to the school. I have a care package for you and your friends!" He waved as they ran by.

"We'll be around a little before six!" Dirk yelled back over his shoulder.

"Okay I'll have it wrapped up and ready for you." He smiled at them.

It was around three o'clock when the boys came into view of the farm. Dirk felt a little saddened when he gazed out at the farm. He was leaving home and didn't know for sure when he would be back. He just realized that he had never been away from home that long before.

Tab put his hand on his shoulder. "It'll be here when we get done with this school business. Don't worry. The general will make sure she's safe."

Dirk just looked at him and smiled. "You know it's still weird that you're being able to read my thoughts."

"Well, you know, we both have always been on the same wavelength. I guess it's just a little more prominent now."

"Yeah, you're right, but we may need to work on blocking our thoughts in the future. There may come a time when you know... Girls and stuff."

Tab stared at him, slowly realizing what he just said, and cleared his throat. "Yes, you're right, we need to do that. And soon."

"Don't worry, I promise I won't tell El your dream about her."

Tab punched Dirk in the shoulder. "Yeah and I won't tell the princess what happens to you when your eyes meet," Tab said, laughing and running away as Dirk started chasing him. He tackled Tab in front of the barn. They wrestled around for a few minutes. Kira came walking out.

"What do you two think you're doing? You're supposed to be at school."

They got up, laughing. "We just wanted to say goodbye to you and Aarya one last time since we won't see you for a while," Dirk said quietly, in case the new help was close by.

"I see. Well, I've already worked it out so that your friend has a nest in the loft in the barn. A more permanent one than she had before and one on the desk in your bedroom. I'll just leave the window where she can come and go as she pleases," Kira told them.

"That's great, Mom, thanks. We're going up to the loft and spend a few minutes with her before we leave. Then we will come say goodbye,"

"That's okay. Just don't take too long."

They headed into the barn and went up the ladder. Aarya was nestled in her new nest, resting, and looking at them as if she had been expecting them. They grabbed some crushed corn from the barrel and let her eat it out of their palms as they sat beside her.

When she finished, she just looked at each of them. Dirk explained to her that they would be away for a few weeks at school. He wasn't sure if she understood everything, but she squawked at them when he was finished. Tab thought it was an acknowledgement. Dirk agreed. Aarya's eyes began to glow a little. Both Dirk and Tab felt a warmth in their heads. A picture of Linc came to their minds and then they saw a vision of Kira hugging the boys. Dirk looked at Aarya, thinking he understood. She was asking if he was family. Tab thought the same thing.

"Yes, he is family," Dirk told her. She nodded her head then the warmth came back. They saw Linc again, Aarya sitting on his shoulder. A snake was sneaking up on Linc. Aarya flew off his shoulder and killed the snake. Then she landed back on Linc's shoulder. He rubbed her head in appreciation.

The vision finally cleared, and Dirk and Tab just looked at her for a minute until Tab figured it out first. "Yes, please keep him safe as well."

She nodded and her eyes seem to go back to their natural color. Dirk smiled and gave her some more corn. They sat with her, talking about the day's events, and she just looked back and forth between them, understanding everything.

It was getting later in the day, so they said their goodbyes and made her promise not to get into any trouble. She squawked again, and they headed to the house to say goodbye to Kira.

She was waiting at the back door for them. She scolded them for making her wait so long. She finally smiled, hugged them both, and told them to be good. They then headed back to the school.

They stopped by the baker on their way back and he gave them a bag full of sweets. He told the boys to eat them sparingly since he knew they wouldn't be allowed out for a few weeks. He wouldn't take any money from them when Dirk offered, and he told them to make him proud. They gave him their thanks and ran to the school. They just made it to the lunchroom at six on the nose. They were locking the school down as they slid into the school.

The dining hall was fuller this time when Dirk and Tab entered. There were more tables and seemed like the whole school was there. They went to the right side to get their dinner from Miss Heloise, who was in charge of the kitchen. Tab had found out earlier that she was the head cook.

She smiled and gave them each a plate full of roast, potatoes, and a warm loaf of bread with butter. They thanked her, grabbed some cider, and started looking for El and Gil. As they were looking around, they noticed the tables were set up like they had been at the banquet. Third-year students were up front with second-year behind them and first-years at the very back. Dirk noticed Princess Anastasia and Kal James sitting at the center table in the front. Everyone was talking with them, or at least trying to.

Kal looked up and noticed them. Dirk and Tab started to walk over to El, who was sitting with the eerie twins and Gil. When Kal nodded an acknowledgement to them, Princess Anastasia looked up, "Hi Dirk."

"Hello, Stas. How have you been?"

"You know, being the good daughter," she said with a smile. Dirk laughed. She winked at him. Dirk knew what she meant. One of her biggest complaints was that since she was the daughter of the king, everyone expected her to be perfect. She was really a rebellious child. Dirk knew that. She never liked being a royal and was a tomboy at heart. She hated most nobles and always did everything she could to stay away from them. Because of her, he had gone through his own rebellious stage.

"Better watch it. Gil will be after you," Tab said as they made their way to El.

"You know I've known her my whole life," Dirk responded a little uneasily. Truth be told, Anastasia was his childhood crush. He remembered wanting to be just like her when he was younger. She was brave and mischievous. When they were older she had been Dirk's first kiss and he had been hers.

He smiled at that thought. They had just been messing around, practicing for when they got older, and nothing ever came from it. They were still friends. She swore him to secrecy, and he had no problem keeping it.

"Yeah, there's more to that story. Remember, I can sense your thoughts now," Tab whispered.

Dirk totally ignored him and rushed to the table in the back. Gil moved over so they could sit down. Dirk sat by Gil and Tab sat by El. "Where have you two been? We just barely saved you a seat," Gil told them.

"Never mind that right now, Gil. This is Vira and Nira Frost. They're from Aarkas," El told Dirk with a raised eyebrow. Dirk and Tab looked like they had seen a ghost.

The one whose eyes Dirk had noticed earlier in the day started talking. "Don't worry, we won't eat you," she said in a soft voice. "I'm Vira, and this is my sister Nira." The other girl was very closed off and didn't look anyone in the eye.

"Nice to meet you both, and I see you all have met Phil and Dusty," Dirk said. They all nodded and started eating. While they ate their food, Dirk listened while Vira talked nonstop about their homeland. How they almost died making the trip through the Beast's Teeth, the jagged mountains separating the waters between Aarkas and the mainland.

The group pretty had much learned their life story by the time dinner was over. Dirk's heart ached for the twins, after hearing everything they had been through. They had lived a hard life. They had been raised by their grandfather. He had been sort of an outcast on an island where most people still practiced the dark arts and worshipped Zolun. Their grandfather still worshipped Zona. Their parents had mysteriously disappeared when they were very young. People thought they had been raised in the traditional way of the island. In the home, he taught them about Zona and the good in life.

Everyone at the table, enthralled in their tale, asked questions throughout the story. Their grandfather had finally been able to sneak them out when they were old enough to attend the school of magic. He had paid a pirate that he knew to take them.

"The pirate knew if he didn't get us here he would suffer the consequences. So he took good care of us and got us here safely," Vira explained looking around.

After she was finished telling their story, everyone at the table talked a little about themselves. Of course, Dirk knew all of them, except Dusty. He was a farmer's son from Venia. He talked about living close to the desert and how they farmed it even with low water supply. Of course, Tab already had interrogated him.

While Phil was telling his story, El edged Tab back a little and leaned in close to Dirk.

"So, I saw that Princess Anastasia said something to you when you were walking this way." She smiled at him.

"She just said hi. I haven't seen her in a while."

"Okay." El shot him a look she always gave him when she knew there was more to the story. Dirk just ignored her.

"Nira, how do you like it so far?" He asked changing the topic.

"It's ok, I guess." Nira quickly responded without looking up.

"Nira isn't very talkative," Vira said.

Phil, finally getting the courage to look at the twins, said, "Well, does she really get a chance? I mean, as much as you talk, who could get a word in edgewise?"

Everyone at the table fell silent, shocked at his boldness. He just raised an eyebrow and looked at Vira with a smile. Vira glared at him. If Dirk hadn't been looking at Nira, he wouldn't have seen the small smile that cracked the corners of her mouth.

Vira finally spoke, "You're right, I tend to talk too much when I am nervous." She smiled at Phil; the tension finally gone.

"Well, we all are, Vira. Don't think we all aren't," El said as she patted Vira on the shoulder.

She smiled back at El. "We'll be very good friends, El. I know it already."

"That's good because all I had growing up is these bums," El said, pointing at Dirk, Tab, and Gil.

"Hey, we've had to put up with you too," Gil said. They all laughed.

"Yes, we have been through a lot through the years, but there's always room for more friends," Dirk said, looking around the table. He saw Dusty and Phil both shake their heads in agreement. He locked eyes with Vira. She smiled at him, nodding her appreciation. And for the first time, Nira looked up at him and smiled looking deeply into Dirk's eyes. She had the same cool blue eyes as her sister. The stare was so deep that he felt a little uncomfortable and had to look away.

Everyone began talking as one after Dirk's announcement. Dirk looked back at Nira and she gave him a knowing smile. This time Dirk felt comfort from her smile, and he smiled back.

Dirk was amazed that people from all over the country sat and talked as if they had known each other their whole lives. He shared the treats that Mr. Burk had given them with everyone. Phil declared they were the best he had ever had. The rest of their new friends agreed. "Well, I guess we better get going," Dirk said to Tab.

"Where you off to?" El asked.

"You know us," Tab said.

"Yea, we got into a little trouble already," Dirk replied.

"How. You just got here?" Gil asked.

"Laseous didn't like a few things we said. So, he said he was going to explain what's acceptable. We have to be in his classroom after dinner."

"You two never learn," El shook her head.

"See you guys in the dorms. Ladies, see you in the morning," Dirk said bowing to the twins as he and Tab headed to take their plates to the kitchen.

When the boys got to Wizard Laseous's room, which also served as his office, Dirk noticed there were two more boys and a girl that Dirk didn't recognize already in the room. "Well, I see everyone is here now so let's get started. Mr. Storm, Mr. Clearwater, these two boys here are Mr. Fisher and Mr. Maclin, and this young lady is Moira Sloan. They are in here because of a stunt that happened at the end of the term last year."

Both boys began to protest, saying it was Moira's fault but Laseous held up a hand to silence them. "I told you two before. If you antagonize her, you're just as guilty."

Moira just sat in silence and smiled, looking down at the desk. Laseous paced with his hands behind his back, while the kids sat at the tables before him. Dirk listened as he went into a tirade about how rules were there to keep things running smoothly and he would not tolerate mouthy kids and their pranks. He informed them that since they started behind the ball he would use them to set the example for what would happen to those who didn't take him seriously.

He assigned them to dishwashing duty after dinner for the rest of the week and told them if that didn't work, he knew some stables and toilets that could use some sprucing up.

After several groans and complaints from the other kids, Laseous led them to the kitchen and introduced them to Hanks, the head washer. He was a plump, older man with a scruffy, graying beard.

"Thanks, Wizard Laseous. I'll sort them out." Hanks chuckled as he led the kids to the sink.

Laseous left and Hanks introduced them to the dishes. There were hundreds of them along with a mountain of silverware and piles of pots.

"I recognize you three. Been here before, haven't you?" he said to the two boys and the girl. "You two, I haven't. Though you look very familiar to me. You must be firsters. That's what we call first-years."

"Dirk Storm and Tab Clearwater," Dirk said, gesturing to Tab. Hanks let out a boisterous laugh, holding his belly and doubling over. Dirk and Tab just looked at each other, confused by the old man's outburst.

The other three, having evidently been there before, started doing the dishes. One washed, one dried, the other stacked.

"I knew it, I just knew one day those boys would get payback," Hanks said, wiping tears from his eyes.

Dirk and Tab continued to stare at him.

He saw their confusion and explained. "You see these dishes in here," he said, pointing to the dishes in the room. They nodded. "Well, these dishes have been here for forty years. I have been here sixty. I have had a lot of trouble-makers come through here. Some noble and some not. But there was never a pair like the two who came through here twenty-some odd years ago. I think they washed these dishes more than all the others put together,"

"And?" Tab asked, holding his arms out, waiting for the rest of the story.

"You see those two boys are bit of a legend around here," Hank said turning a little more serious.

"Their names were Diron Storm and Thad Clearwater."

Both Dirk and Tab's eyes widened in surprise while he shook his head.

"I loved them boys like they were my own. Now, I'll tell you this because we were close. Don't try to imitate them." He gave them a serious look. "They were good boys, but they had a lot of mischief in them. And you know what happened to them. At least we can only assume. So, I'm saying, be boys but don't turn out like them in the end. They were best friends and good boys, but they got into a little too much trouble," Hanks said somberly.

"Are you through with the history lesson Pops?" Moira asked. "The dishes are piling up."

"Sorry," Hanks said. He showed the boys where the dried dishes belonged on the shelves. Dirk stared at Moira. He hadn't really looked at her until now. She gave Dirk a crooked smile. *Her strawberry-colored hair, deep green eyes, and the hint of freckles on her cheeks definitely make her easy on the eyes. Dirk thought.* She was as tall as Dirk and looked to be in good shape, but he really couldn't tell because of her loose, baggy clothes. Dirk smiled, receiving another smirk from her as she continued to dry the dishes.

Both Tab and Dirk wanted to hear more but they knew there would be time for that later.

"Okay firsters. Put the dishes up when I'm done drying. If that's not too hard to understand." Moira said sarcastically handing Dirk a plate. Dirk and Tab nodded ignoring the remark.

"So, you've done this before?" Dirk was eager to engage Moira.

"You could say that farm boy," Moira said, eying him. Dirk smiled. She was cheeky and he liked her immediately.

There were so many dishes that it took until nine to finish. Hanks assured them before they left he would tell them more about their fathers later. He would, after all, being seeing them the rest of the week.

"I like Moira," Dirk said to Tab as they were heading back to the dorm.

"I think she's a bit crazy. I'm not sure about her. She seems like she has a sarcastic attitude." Tab replied, causing Dirk to laugh.

"I think it's just her way of being friendly,"

"Did the bond addle that brain of yours?" Tab placed a hand on his head, as if checking for damage. Dirk just pushed his hand away, smiling as they walked up to Hilda.

Her arms were crossed, and she was tapping her foot in the door.

"I was just fixing to lock you two out."

"Sorry. We were doing the dishes. Wizard Laseous."

"I know. You still have to be on time, no matter what. Do you understand?" she asked.

"We do," Dirk answered for both of them, heading into the dorm.

Dirk and Tab walked over to a table where Volar, Phil, Gil, and Dusty were sitting. "Well, there you two are," Gil said.

"Yes, we were discussing where you were off to," Volar said in a questioning tone.

"We were just breaking in the detention services," Tab said, laughing. The group all laughed as Dirk and Tab pulled up chairs to join them and then began talking about the day's events. Dirk looked around and saw Brock and his crew huddled together. Dirk and his friends were probably the focus of whatever scheme they were plotting. Brock kept looking at them with a smirk. Dirk just ignored him for the rest of the night.

They kept talking until Hilda told them it was time for bed.

The group said their goodnights and Tab, looking a little perturbed, headed to his dorm.

"I'll see you in the morning," Dirk said, trying to cheer his friend up. Tab just nodded. Volar and Phil had already made it to the room when Dirk heard Hilda say his name.

Diron's Pack

"Mr. Storm, a word!"

"Yes ma'am," Dirk said, turning back. Tab, sensing Dirk's distress, didn't close the door all the way peering through a crack no bigger than a finger's width. Dirk sat down beside Hilda on the couch and looked at his new room mother.

"Dirk, I wanted a word with you alone before you start your training tomorrow. I have some information I feel I need to share with you. I know you'll probably be the leader of this group, except for a select few." Hearing this, Dirk started to squirm. Hilda put a hand on his shoulder to put him at ease. She waited until he nodded before she continued. "Now, I say this not to make you feel uncomfortable, but to educate you on a few things."

Hilda looked towards the fireplace; a tear started to form in the corner of her eye. He watched as she wiped it away with a handkerchief she was holding. *This feels like it's going to be an important moment. Tab stay put.* He felt through their link that Tab understood.

Dirk sat there, waiting.

Hilda turned back, smiled, and put her hand over his. "What I'm going to tell you must stay between us," Hilda said, affectionately looking into his eyes. Dirk felt a deep connection to Hilda the moment she touched his hand.

"On my honor." He focused on her eyes.

"Dirk, you know I told all of the first-years that my sister and I have been here for twenty years."

Dirk nodded.

Just listen, Tab said in his mind. Tab knew just how many questions he wanted to ask. Dirk obeyed and let Hilda continue.

"When your father and Tab's father were here, Tilda and I were here as well. We were all very good friends. In fact, we were almost inseparable. We did everything together. There was seven of us that kind of made up a group. Much like you and your pack." Dirk just looked at her in disbelief. Hilda smiled at him.

"Yes, Dirk, we have kept up with you and your friends most of your life. You see, your father was our leader. Thad was always right by his side during everything. We probably set a record for detention. Usually, when one of us got in trouble, the rest weren't far behind." Hilda talked in a daze as if she were far away. Dirk squeezed her hand, sensing it was the right thing to do. She tilted her head to the side, seeing something in him, and smiled.

"Diron, Thad, Josie Garner, Heath Meric, Solomon James, Tilda and me. We were something in our first year back then, at least until the accident. That's when things really changed for all of us." Hilda wiped more tears from her eyes.

"What accident?" Dirk asked, finally breaking his silence. Hilda looked up at the fireplace for a moment and then back at Dirk. She squeezed his hand, clasping it in between both of hers and looked into his eyes. A subtle warmth flowed through him.

As Dirk stared back into her eyes, a small flame rippled across them briefly. Hilda closed her eyes and took a deep breath.

Hearing light footsteps behind him, he turned and saw Tilda walking into the room. She sat beside her sister and put her hand on her shoulder. The same sensation coursed through Dirk again as Tilda placed her hand on theirs. she took a deep breath and let it out slowly.

When Tilda opened her eyes, she saw Dirk staring at her. Flames rippled briefly in her eyes as well. "How?" Dirk asked both of them. Tilda leaned forward, and a sad smile crossed her face. Tears started rolling down her cheeks.

Hilda took another breath and looked at her sister. "You tell him."

Tilda nodded and looked over her shoulder. "You might as well come out, so we only have to tell the story once," she said quietly to the crack in the door. Tab looked to his left to see that Gil and Dusty had already fallen asleep. He stepped out and closed the door quietly.

Grabbing a chair, he sat in front of the sisters. Tilda grabbed his hand and smiled at him. Tab, already having felt the sensation through Dirk, felt it again as her hand squeezed his gently. He smiled and returned the gentle squeeze.

"I assume you two have a strong connection just as Hilda and I do," Tilda said.

"Yes," they replied.

Tilda and Hilda both smiled. "We could feel it when you both first walked up the stairwell today. We just needed the confirmation. I assume everything Hilda has told Dirk you heard as well?" Tilda asked.

"Yes," Tab responded.

"I'll continue where she left off then. Diron and Thad, like she said, were pretty much our group's leaders, Diron, more than Thad. Everybody else in the group always wanted to prove their worth to them and Solomon and Heath were always trying to one-up each other. Diron tried to stop their antics by telling them that they were just as much a part of the group as anybody else, but they just wouldn't listen. You probably don't know this, but Diron exuded leadership. He was a larger-than-life figure. but he was very humble and the best friend anyone could ask for. Thad and he were like brothers, just like you two are now. As Hilda said, we have kept up with you.

"One time, Heath had broken into Laseous's office and stole a book that was considered off limits for first-years. Solomon just had to prove he was better, so one night at the end of winter, he had the great idea to sneak out of the room after bedtime. The doors are magically sealed at night, but he found a way to get out. He never shared how he did it. Everyone in the group tried to discourage him, but he felt he had to prove himself, regardless of what Diron and everyone else kept telling him.

"The next morning at breakfast, we discovered he was missing. We all thought he had been caught and was with Nabas in his office. We went through morning exercises and drills like normal, but still no Solomon. We finally started worrying when we were finished, and he still hadn't shown up. We hurried back to the dorms to get ready for classes. When we got to the stairwell, it was sealed off and guards stopped anyone from entering. Our room mothers were standing there, waiting for us. Both seemed very upset. They saw us and separated us from the rest of the group, pulling us back the way we came. They took us to a classroom and told us to have a seat."

Hilda couldn't hold back her tears any longer. She leaned forward and sobbed into her handkerchief. Tilda comforted her by rubbing her back. Dirk feeling sick to his stomach, coughed trying to keep it settled. He knew where this story was going from what Hilda had informed them of earlier about the fireplace. Tab stood and squeezed Hilda's shoulder. He wiped the tears in his eyes away. He like Dirk, had figured out what was coming next.

"Do you need to take a break?" Dirk asked, concerned.

Hilda sat up, finally getting her emotions under control. "Thanks Tab. No Dirk, I am fine. Thanks for your concern but we can continue." She smiled and squeezed his hand. So Tilda continued.

"We tried getting information from them, but all they would say was Wizard Nabas would be there any minute. Panic began to build between us because we knew something was wrong. Wizard Nabas finally came in through the door. Just as he started to close it, we could see a body wrapped in sheets being carried away."

"It was Solomon, wasn't it?"

Both twins nodded while wiping away the tears. "He was the boy who died trying to get out through the fireplace wasn't he…" Tab said slowly as the realization dawned on him..

"Yes," they both said in unison.

"You see, there are open airways through the fireplace system that help keep the smoke funneled away from the rooms. We assume he thought he could sneak in and out without anyone being the wiser. What he probably didn't know was that there is a series of shutoff panels that regulate the air flow. We found out years later that he got trapped in between the shutoffs and couldn't get out. He died horribly because he just had to one up Heath…"

"That's horrible. I'm sorry you lost your friend that way," Dirk said, trying to console the twins.

"Yes, we're sorry," Tab added.

The twins nodded their appreciation. After a few minutes, they gathered their emotions.

"Dirk, your father blamed himself for a long time for Solomon's death. I don't think he ever forgave himself. He felt he should have done more to prevent the competition between the two. Heath really took it hard because they had been best friends, like both of your fathers were. I know it's getting late, but Tilda and I agreed we needed to talk to you two tonight before everything gets into full swing around here. That is why we wanted to give you the warning I did earlier," Hilda said.

"There's more to this story. No matter how long it takes tonight, we need to hear the whole thing. I sensed and saw the flames in your eyes, both of you," Dirk said, looking at both of them.

"Yes, I agree with Dirk. I can sense the power you two share with us," Tab touched Tilda's shoulder. The twins looked at each other and a silent agreement seemed to pass between them.

The bell tower rang in the distance. Hilda got up and went to her room and Tilda watched her walk away. Anyone watching what happened next without context probably would have thought it was a little creepy.

She looked between the boys, raised her hands, and put one each on the boy's faces. A warmth spread from her hands into the boys. The sensation contained, feelings of love and loss.

"You boys are the spitting images of your fathers. It seems like yesterday that we were all here sitting and talking together," Tilda said, returning her hands to her lap as Hilda walked up, carrying a small brown book that resembled a diary. Tab looked at the book then at Dirk. Both boys thought it kind of resembled the Book of Storms

Hilda sat down by her sister and they both sat facing the boys. Tab had pulled his chair closer to Dirk. Hilda looked at Tilda and nodded.

"What happened to Arial?" Tilda asked. Dirk and Tab silently made a snap decision and shared the news of Arial's death and the birth of Aarya. They ended up telling them the whole story, including Tab's connection to Aarya even though they weren't supposed to. The ladies just sat and listened.

"But how do you know about Arial?" Dirk asked.

Hilda opened the book she had brought out from her room. Pulling out two pieces of folded silk, she handed one to Tilda and they both unfolded the silk. Inside each piece was a single red phoenix feather. The boys gaped at the sight.

"But Mom and the general didn't tell us anything about anyone else knowing," Dirk said after the shock wore off.

"Because your mother wouldn't expose us unless we were ready. The general never knew. After all we had learned, Diron wanted someone else to know what his mission was. When things started getting bad with all the attacks in the south, he made us agree to stay here in Silver City if he failed in his mission. He wanted someone to be able to pass along what we had learned, especially the mistakes that had been made. He wanted to make sure his heir would know what he did.

"We suspected Nabas knew what was going on so when Der-Tod went bad, we came to him and he confirmed our beliefs. He kept our secret and gave us jobs so when we were needed, we would be close," Hilda explained. Dirk and Tab just stared at the feathers. The twins caressed the feathers, then folded them up and put them away.

"I'll explain more but first, like I said, after Solomon's death, your father changed. He grew very protective of us and told us the Storm family secret. We already knew there was something special about him, but what he shared was so much more than any of us expected. Well except for Thad, who had already known.

"Diron taught the rest of us his knowledge of the Chosen and the protector's responsibilities, and the burdens that had been placed on his shoulders. One thing to know is the longer the bonded are around each other, the stronger connected they are to each other's thoughts. From what I sense, Dirk, you and Tab have been introduced to the Book of Storms?"

"Yes," they both responded.

"Did you notice anything familiar about it and the book Hilda has in her hands?"

"We both felt it looked to be made from the same material and looked similar in color," Tab said.

Tilda and Hilda both smiled. "As I said, Dirk's father was very protective of us. He wanted to find a way to try and end the family legacy and protect the world at the same time. One idea he had was to have our group all meet Arial and see if we could bond with her. Thad had already bonded so he felt it would be successful. And it was. We met that beautiful creature at the end of the first school year before we went home for summer break.

"When we met Arial, Diron communicated what he had in mind, so she landed on each of our shoulders. He instructed us to rub her neck. When we did, we felt a spark from the touch. A single feather came out and each of our palms tingled with a burning sensation. In that spot, a small red shape had appeared."

Both ladies raised their right palms to show the distinctive mark. It was the same as Dirk's birthmark and the one Tab now had on his palm. The boys instinctively showed them their own marks.

"That confirms what we already knew. When the bond is formed, that mark is what makes the connection possible."

"What is it? I've had it my whole life." Dirk asked.

"It is the mark of Zona. It's the connection through which your bond flows," Tilda explained.

"So, anyone with this mark could be one of the protectors of the Chosen?"

"Yes, it means that person is connected to you through it," Hilda clarified.

Dirk mulled that over. He was sure he had seen the same mark on Princess Natia. It would explain a lot of the feelings he had when he was around her. Tab agreed with his thinking.

"Yes, Dirk, Natia is connected to the both of you," Tilda said with a smile.

"But how did you know what I...?"

"The mark, silly boy. Remember what I said earlier. The more you are around people with the mark the more attuned they become to your thoughts," Hilda said, tapping the mark on her hand. Dirk looked nervously at the twins.

"The one thing your father regretted most was that he hadn't bonded us to Arial sooner. He felt that if he had, then maybe Solomon would still be alive because he would have sensed what he was thinking," Tilda said.

Dirk's expression was grim. "That could be true but if it hadn't happened, he might not have decided to introduce you to Arial. There is one concern I have about the connection. Is there a way to block your thoughts from the bonded?"

"Don't worry, we'll teach you how to keep your thoughts from being shared. Now, this book was another one of Diron's ideas. Once the group became bonded, Arial flew off. In a matter of minutes, she was back carrying this book. Diron took the book from her, smiled, and held it up for all of us too see." Hilda held the book so Dirk and Tab could see what was written on it. It was the same writing that was on the Book of Storms.

"In this book, Diron wanted to keep a more detailed diary of what worked and what didn't. He also had strategies and the steps taken to achieve them. Tilda and I are the ones chosen to chronicle our actions in more in-depth detail than the Book of Storms. Anyone in the group could put ideas in it, whereas with your father's book, only the Chosen and protector could write in it."

The boys sat there soaking in what was said.

"How did my mother fit in? Dirk asked.

"We all thought Thad would be his protector. Eventually, that happened, but only after your mother agreed to pass it on to him, after Diron and her fell in love."

Tab and Dirk had more questions than they knew they had time to ask so they just continued to listen.

"We met your mother in our last year at school when we were doing a joint training exercise with the elves. The minute their eyes met; the connection was made. The entire group felt it. It was a magical connection that washed through us. It felt complete. After that, we were determined to help Diron stop Zolun, no matter how long as it took." She paused to let everything sink in

Dirk looked at Tab. They shared a thought, "Go on please."

"Once the exercise was over, a small contingent of elves stayed behind. They were posted with the military due to the uprisings in the southern kingdoms getting more and more often and violent. Kira joined our group and soon it was just like she had been with us our whole lives."

Hilda took over from this point. "What was really important about Kira joining our group was that now we were back to seven in our group."

"Now wait a minute," Dirk interrupted. "I get the feeling that this is really important. You've mentioned seven in the group more than once. Can you explain that a little more?"

Tilda nodded. "Diron had the idea that when we were in battle, the bonded could combine their powers and use them together as one to strengthen our attacks. The power of the seven was a theory that one of the Storms in the past had originally come up with, but he was never successful with getting it to work."

Dirk sat there; eyes glued to the book. "You know, we haven't really had a chance to study the book. All of this just happened, and it's really overwhelming," Dirk said with tears in his eyes. Tab gripped his shoulder for support. Hilda pulled the boys into a hug. Tilda rubbed Tab's back in a motherly way from the side.

Hilda pulled back so they could see her better. "You boys are not alone in this. We'll be here to help you prepare for what is needed."

"We'll work with you and your pack, if you decide that is what you want," Tilda said.

"That is what your fathers would have wanted. It's a heavy burden and we know what everyone in our group went through, ourselves included. We can help you with that. The most important thing to remember is secrecy. No one can know what we're doing, except for the ones in your group. The ones you choose to bring in is your choice. Do not make that choice lightly, for their lives will forever be changed, regardless of what you think. There are just three of you right now, so we will set up a schedule to help," Hilda said.

"Wait, what if I don't want Natia in our group?" Dirk asked.

Tilda raised an eyebrow at Dirk, confused by his remark. "Dirk, I'm afraid you can't do it without her. She is already connected. She has the mark."

Dirk let out a frustrated breath and put his head in his hands.

"Dirk, take some time to get to know her. She is a wonderful girl. I've seen it already and I'm sure you will too," Tilda said.

"I don't know. I feel something when she's around but it's strange, not like the bond that Tab and I feel."

Tilda looked at her sister and smiled. "Every bond is a little different in the beginning. Remember, she was bonded to Arial, just like you in the beginning. The bond you two share is different from any other bond. Just give her a chance to get to know you.

"All bonds eventually grow strong, pretty much the same with all the bonded. Though still a little different, you'll work that out," Tilda explained. "But right now, you two need to get to bed. Tomorrow will be a long, hard day. We will set up a time when we can work together. I know you have a lot of questions, but we just wanted to introduce ourselves and let you know some things you needed to know."

"You're right, that's a lot of information you gave us. It's sort of hard to believe, but the proof you've shown us is overwhelming," Tab said.

"I'll think about everything you've shared and think about Natia," Dirk sighed, hugging both ladies. "Thanks for being my dad's friends. I didn't get the chance to know him, but I feel from what you've told me, that we're a lot alike."

"You are, both of you are," Tilda said. "We'll see you tomorrow after classes. Now get to bed."

Both boys headed to their rooms and through their bond, agreed to talk about everything in the morning.

"Well, that went a little differently than I thought it would," Tilda said after the boys had gone to their rooms. "The one thing that really surprised me was his reaction about Natia. I think I know why that is." They both laughed and said good night.

That night Dirk and Tab had the same dream. Both their dads and five others were sneaking around the halls of the school at night.

"Heath, are you sure we can get that book from Laseous's office?" Solomon asked, peeking around the corner to see if the coast was clear. The five other kids were all crouched behind Heath and Solomon, waiting for the word to move forward.

"Yes, I saw it on his bookshelf when we were leaving class today."

"What is so great about this book?" a girl with jet-black hair asked.

"Are you kidding, Josie? It's the book on teleporting we have been looking for." Heath responded.

"Hilda, Tilda, can you sense the guards," Diron stepped to the front of the group.

The twins looked at each other and grabbed hands. They closed their eyes for a second, then looked to Diron. "The night guard is coming," Hilda said.

"We better hurry. He's close. We don't need to get caught. We just got out of detention yesterday," Tilda suppressed a sigh. She really didn't want to spend any more time in that small room, or with Laseous, than she had to.

"We better go then," Thad said, grabbing Solomon and dragging him back to the stairwell.

As they neared the girls dormitory, Hilda said, "Goodnight."

Diron was about to respond when the dream suddenly ended. Tab and Dirk woke with a start.

A spark through their cores and they immediately sat up. "Linc!" they both said in unison.

Nearby, in the girl's dorms, Natia had been experiencing the same dream and the same reaction. She hadn't really gotten to know Linc, but she knew something had happened.

Laying back down, she tried to calm her breathing. Her dorm room door creaked open. Tilda stood in the doorway, motioning for her to join her in the common room. Natia got up silently and followed.

Tilda sat on the couch with Natia and clasped the princess's hands in hers. "I know you sensed that. We did as well."

"Yes," Natia said

"Did you sense everything that happened tonight?"

Natia explained the gist of what she had sensed, and Tilda listened patiently.

When Natia was finished, Tilda filled her in on what she had told Dirk earlier.

"That explains a lot," Natia said. "But I still sense apprehension from Dirk."

Tilda nodded. "He hasn't grown up like you, knowing what lies ahead. You will have to help steer him in the right direction." She still didn't say anything about Tab because it wasn't her information to share. If Natia hadn't sense it yet, it wasn't the time for her to know. Only Dirk and Tab could decide when the time was right.

Natia had sensed the connection to the twins the moment she met them, and she was glad they were having the talk sooner rather than later. After talking for a while about the challenges ahead, Tilda finally said that they had better get back to bed.

Natia smiled and said good night.

But something was still bothering her. The connection felt different than what she had been expecting. Natia had always been very pragmatic and decided to worry about that later. She snuck back into her room and silently got back into bed closing her eyes and trying to go back to sleep.

After several minutes of tossing, she finally fell asleep. In her dreams, emerald, green eyes kept staring at her. The feeling she got was that they pierced her soul was a little nerve-wracking. The smile that went along with those eyes melted her insides like butter in the midday sun. She smiled to herself, feeling butterflies in her stomach.

Even in her dreams, she felt that Dirk, with his piercing eyes, would one day be more than anyone else had expected, especially to her.

First Bonded

Linc's day after saying goodbye to Dirk and Tab had started as he expected. He met his new crew at the boat. They all stood there looking at the ship before boarding. "LiTaDi Flame," Linc said the ship's name with pride.

River looked at the ship in awe. "I never thought I would be a part of a crew," he said to the group.

"Your first time is always important," Corky said in his brisk voice.

"Aye," Jerle said.

"It's the one you always remember," Kaz added.

"Well, let's not get too mushy now. We have a ship to get ready to sail," Linc said to the crew as they walked up the gangplank. "River, get ready to hoist the lines. Kaz, check on the cargo Mr. Little sold us. The grain from the south and silk he traded with the elves should be weatherproofed. Make sure it's sealed properly. Jerle and Corky, unfurl the sails so we can catch wind as soon as we get out of the main shipping lane. River, when you untie the lines and Kaz has the cargo checked, push us off. We'll use the oars to get us moving." Linc commanded like he had been a captain his whole life. The crew went to work without question.

"Cargo secure, Cap," Kaz said, coming out of the hold.

"Help River with the oars now," Linc told him. Kaz grabbed the oars and handed one to River as he finished untying the lines. *LiTaDi* was fourth in line to cast off.

While they waited, Linc stepped up to the helm and checked the tension in the rudder. It felt a little loose to him. "Jerle, the rudder feels a little loose. Jump over really quick and make sure it's secured to the keel cables,"

"Yes, sir, cap'n," Jerle said a little sarcastically, taking off his shirt and then jumping off the stern of the ship. He went under for a minute and then came back up. He climbed back up on the dock and then onto the ship. Water dripped from his dark hair.

"It's fine, cap'n, I tightened the fasteners on the cables."

Linc gave him a nod of approval. "Help the guys get ready to push off." Jerle nodded and grabbed another oar. Linc tested the wheel again and even though it felt a little tighter, he still didn't like its strength, something he would check personally once they were out on the open water.

Linc paced back and forth until he saw that their time had finally come, and the third ship cleared the main lane. "Shove off!" Linc commanded. The crew went into action. Linc grabbed an oar, pushing with the crew until they had gotten in place, and then immediately headed to the wheel. "Corky, get ready to unfurl the sails once we're in the main shipping lane!"

"Aye, Aye."

"When you're done with the sails, head to the mast and get ready to unleash the jib. River, Kaz, and Jerle once I turn the stern west, start rowing to get us into the main lane."

They were set up on the port side as soon as the ship turned. Kaz moved to the starboard side to even out the rowing. Jerle moved between the two to keep it even, as Linc had ordered them. Once the sails were unfurled, Corky evened the teams out until the wind caught the sails.

"Now shift starboard, Kaz," Linc ordered. Kaz moved quickly.

Corky eyed the young crew, wondering why in all the hells he was here. What he needed was a swift drink. He reached inside his left pocket, pulled out his favorite flask, and took a quick swig of whiskey. He looked around to make sure no one had noticed and put it away just as quickly as he had taken it out.

Looking back towards the docks, he noticed two figures step out from the shadow of the closest warehouse. The two definitely eerie-looking characters seemed very interested in the *LiTaDi*. From this distance, Corky saw the evil grin on their faces and wondered what that was about. He scanned the deck and saw River was paddling with all his strength.

"Good kid," Corky thought.

Linc eyed the waterways ahead, being very attentive to his surroundings. Kaz was paddling just as hard as River. Jerle, though, kept looking over his shoulder at the two figures, or at least in their direction. Corky got a twinge in his gut. That sailors instinct he had always had. He knew something wasn't right with Jerle.

He had never worked with any of them before, but he had heard of Jerle's reputation. Then he saw it.

As Jerle moved back to the port side to help River, Corky saw him wink and nod at the two men on the docks. It was subtle and if Corky hadn't been watching him at that moment, he would have missed it. In that instant, Corky's instincts had proven right. He decided he would keep a close eye on him.

"Unfurl the sails!"

Corky did as ordered and headed towards River. Jerle was already at Kaz's side of the ship. Corky moved as quickly as he could looking back just in time to see the two figures acknowledge Jerle and then walk off. Corky grabbed the other oar, stepped up behind River, and started paddling in rhythm with him.

"Boy," Corky said in a low voice, just barely loud enough for River to hear.

"What?" River asked in a strained voice.

"Do you know Jerle well?"

"Not really, he's been coming into my Da's tavern for years, but I don't know him well. Why?"

"Just an old sailor's gut. Don't say anything to Linc but help me keep an eye on him. I have a bad feeling about him," Corky replied softly. River looked at Jerle and then at Corky.

"All right I will, but if I suspect anything suspicious, I'll tell Linc. We've been friends for years."

"Aye, that's what I expected, but wait until we're sure, okay?"

River nodded in agreement. Linc ordered them to hold the oars because they had lined up perfectly in the main lane and were heading out into the deeper waters towards Oak City.

"Tie the main sails in place and lower the second sail, Corky," Linc ordered. "River, Kaz, secure the oars. Jerle, make sure the harpoon launchers are uncovered with the arrows are ready for use."

"Expecting trouble already, cap'n?" Jerle asked a little too sarcastically.

Linc's brow furrowed, and his steely gaze locked onto Jerle.

"As far as I know, I am the captain of this ship. Right?" he said with a touch of venom. Jerle, startled by the force in Linc's voice, stepped back.

"Sorry cap'n, just making a little light joke. Not being disrespectful," Jerle said, embarrassed he had been berated in front of the crew.

Linc's voice shook with anger. "Look, I know I'm young, and you might question my motives, but remember I grew up mainly on those docks. I have a good sense of when something isn't quite right. I have that feeling right now." Linc eyed the whole crew. "If you didn't notice, two ships that belong to Ram Stockton were in the harbor getting ready to depart. One before us and the other after. So, trust me when I say make sure all weapons are ready, just in case. Understood?"

"Aye captain!" They went back to work securing the weapons and the ship. Linc had noticed Monk and Kumbo standing in the shadows. Since

Ram's meeting the other night with the mysterious character, Linc was staying on the alert. His crew was all new to him. River was the only one he trusted completely. The rest were a gamble. Which, in this business would always be a risk. He was not going to let Tab and Dirk down.

"River, take the helm when you finish securing the fishing nets and poles. Make sure they're ready to use once were out in the straights. It's a five-day trip to Oak City if the weather is good. So that'll leave us time for some fishing on the way. Who knows, we might catch us some reds."

High above the *LiTaDi* Aarya was flying through the clouds, out of sight. She too had sensed danger. Like she had promised, she would take care of Dirk and Tab's brother. In the distance, behind the *LiTaDi*, a sinister-looking ship was just making its way out into open waters. This ship was the main cause of her concern. It had an evil intent about it, so she would stay close.

Monk and Kumbo boarded the Silent Raider, officially known as Wave Rider to the ports, just as Linc's ship had hit the main waterway. Monk had told Captain Sleigh to take off when they could and to follow Linc at a distance. The plan was to attack the third day on the water.

Sleigh was Ram's main captain and one of his main sources of income. He was the most notorious pirate in the waters surrounding Silver City and Lake Fire.

"Captain, we have a man on that ship. He will prepare for our attack." Monk explained.

"We'll finally get that little bastard and end his menace," Kumbo said to Monk with a smile. He hadn't forgotten their recent altercation and was ready for some revenge. Louy was still hurt, but he would return the favor for his friend. Kumbo's knee was still sore, but he had snapped it back into place with the aid of some strong whiskey.

"Yes, his little pain-in-the-ass friends won't be there to protect him this time. We'll deal with them also when the time is right," Monk said, skimming the sharp side of a knife gently across his thumb. A breeze blew across the deck, bringing with it the stench of the harbor.

Monk turned his back to the smell, taking in the scenery.

He thought the water itself had its own smells, depending on where one was. Being so close to the fish warehouse, the smell of dried blood and fish guts overwhelmed him. "Captain, get us the hell out of here fast. I can't stand this smell."

Sleigh looked at Monk with a toothless smile. "Now master, we'll be beyond it in a few minutes. That's the smell that drives seaman, like the likes of us. Be patient."

Monk eyed the captain, who was of a similar build, wondering if he could take him if it came down to it in a fight. He figured he didn't want to find out, so he just sneered. "Okay."

Sleigh was over six feet tall with a scar across the left side of his face that ran from his ear to his chin. His hair was either deep brown or dirty blond. It was so greasy no one could tell. His almond skin was weathered from spending so many years on the water. His hands were scarred, but Monk knew first-hand he had the strength of two men. Monk had shaken his hand before and had actually winced from his grip. He detested the sea scum, as he would refer to him as when talking with Ram.

But he knew Sleigh was Ram's biggest moneymaker and he always swayed towards the captain in the times that Monk berated him. Monk just stood back and let the crew do their thing. The Silent Raider was a fast ship, and he knew they could catch Linc's any time they wanted. Patience was their key to revenge. Sleigh wanted to attack him where there would be no witnesses.

As the ship hit the main waterways, he and Kumbo retired to their room to get some rest while Sleigh did his thing.

Captain Sleigh smirked at the two flunkies Ram had sent as they walked away. He didn't know what was so important about the young captain they were going after, but he would do as Ram wanted. The main reason for that was because he needed Ram to give him safe harbor when his ship came into Silver City. Plus, Ram always bought his stolen goods without asking where they came from.

Ram was a needed tool. He didn't mind helping him when it benefitted him too. He needed a second ship and the one they were chasing would be his just as soon as they killed the crew and took it over.

Silent Raider had been on the water for several hours. Stars were starting to fill the sky. Sleigh took them in as he stood at the helm, as he did on most trips. He had an uncanny ability to need little sleep. Two hours a day is what he had lived on for many years, and he felt no need to change that now. Most of the crew had settled in for the night below except for Matt, who was up in the crow's nest, keeping watch.

Matt had been with him for ten years. Sleigh trusted him as much as he trusted Kelt, his first mate. They both had come on board around the same time, Kelt a few months before Matt. They were both cut throats and didn't mind murder or kidnapping. Nearly nothing was off limits to them.

The only thing Sleigh drew a line at was raping young girls. He watched the ship in the distance. He had a sick sense of honor. He wouldn't let them be raped but had no problem slitting their throats.

Rape was okay, but they had to be of age. His thoughts wandered to the two crewmen he killed several years back as he watched the ship in the distance. They had been attempting to rape a fourteen-year-old girl.

Sleigh drew in a deep breath. The scent of the water always seemed to put him at ease. It was home to him. He was born on the sea many years ago, how long he couldn't even remember.

Suddenly a small light appeared and heard a swooshing sound right in front of him. The captain smiled at Draxen, who was unruffling his cloak.

"Ah I see my mistress's apprentice has come to pay me a visit," Sleigh said to the flamboyant wizard before him.

Draxen just cocked an eyebrow. "Captain, I assume your guests are fast asleep?"

The captain nodded. "I knew you would be here tonight, so I put some sleeping herbs in their food. They will not wake up until after dawn."

Draxen smiled, walked over to the port side of the Silent Raider, and looked out at the water. He truly loved being on the water. That was one of the benefits of living at Ishani's palace. It was high enough in the mountains that the Bay of Muerta was always in view.

He took a deep breath, exhaled, and walked back to the captain's side. He stared at Linc's ship. "She wants the boy captain to survive," Draxen said with a serious look on his face.

The captain grunted, not shocked by these words, "I know, I don't understand either." The captain rubbed his grizzled face and looked at Draxen. "Ishani is playing a more dangerous game than she has ever played before, it seems."

"I know, I fear this will be the death of us if it doesn't go Zolun's way this time," Draxen said, still staring at the back of the *LiTaDi*.

"What is special about the boy captain?" Sleigh asked.

"She wouldn't say, but he's a part of her plan to break the Chosen, I believe."

"What about the two below deck?"

"Well, you can't kill them. They're a part of the plan in Silver City. If we lose Ram's help, that will ruin our plans there. So, find a way to get them off the ship somehow," Draxen turned around and walked away from the captain.

"Draxen, we've both been around for hundreds of years. I will do what is needed, just as you. I can't help but say it feels different this time," Sleigh looked to the spot where Draxen was standing.

"What do you mean?" Draxen asked. The captain looked back at the ship he was tracking and then at Draxen.

He pulled a handkerchief out of his pocket and wiped sweat off his brow. "The power I felt when the young captain and his crew walked by us this morning was brief, but I could sense it coming from two of them. The boy was one of them, I'm sure. The other one's power was fainter, but I still felt it. There definitely is another one. I couldn't tell which one it was when they walked by, but it's there, though, waiting to be tapped. I felt it." The captain paused for a moment.

Draxen looked at the ship. "Then they both must survive. Whatever the reason, we need to find out what this is about. Ishani might already sense it, but let's not destroy a possible ally down the road."

Sleigh agreed and opened the top of a barrel. He grabbed an almost rotten apple and tossed it to Draxen. Draxen caught it with a smile and took a bite. He made a small groan of satisfaction as he chewed the ruined apple, several worms wiggling around while he finished them off. He tossed the core overboard and looked at his friend of many years. "I don't know her plans, but she has always taken care of us, regardless of our failures."

"Aye, the mistress has taken care of the two of us," the captain said just before Draxen smiled and disappeared.

The captain looked up to the crow's nest. Matt was looking at him. He had seen the whole interaction. "You better come down!"

Matt scurried down the rope ladder. "Aye captain." Matt stood in front of Sleigh.

"Sneak down and wake Kelt. Bring him up here now. We have a change of plans we need to make before the others wake up," he ordered. Matt took off to get his friend. *Now, just how do I achieve what we need to do?* Sleigh thought. He gazed out at the water. The tossing of the ship always had a calming effect on him. *Ah that's it. That should work*, Sleigh smiled to himself. He filled Kelt and Matt in on his plan when they returned, and they understood and got to work.

Linc turned the helm over to River and went to do a complete check of the ship. He walked around surveying their work and everything seemed fine to him, though he couldn't shake that nagging feeling that something wasn't right.

Night came around and he and River were the only two on deck. The rest of the crew had eaten their rations and were sleeping below deck until their shift in the crow's nest. Linc had decided to put some backup plans in place.

"River, I want you to do something for me. I want you to make sure the escape boat is loaded with back-up supplies while the others are asleep." River just looked at him. "Trust me we need to be prepared, just in case." River nodded and started to walk away. He stopped, walking back up to Linc and, looking around hesitantly. "What is it River?"

"Linc." River's tone made it clear he wanted to talk to his friend instead of his captain. "Corky said he had a bad feeling about Jerle while we were rowing out today."

Linc glanced back to the door that led to the sleeping quarters and then back to River. "What did he say?"

River stepped closer to Linc so that only he could hear what was being said. "He said his sailor's gut was telling him Jerle was off and asked me to help keep an eye on him. Jerle kept looking back at the docks when we were taking off. I noticed so I agreed, but I told him I would tell you if I suspected anything was off," River stepped back. Linc smiled. River was the right choice to bring along.

"You did the right thing telling me. Thanks, but for now, keep what I'm having you do between us until we're sure, ok?"

River nodded and went to make sure everything that Linc wanted was in the shore boat. Linc watched as River quietly gathered the supplies, including several bows, quivers of arrows and a couple of staffs and swords. When he was finished, he covered the boat with the weather tarp. No one would be able to see what was in there.

"Finished," River said walking back to Linc.

"Good job. Go eat and get some sleep. The next few days may be long, and I don't know how much sleep we'll get."

"Aye, captain," River said heading to bed.

Linc was alone at the helm, staring at the stars, deep in thought. Back and forth, the boat rocked. His thoughts went back and forth between everything River had told him, Dirk, and Tab, and what lay ahead for the three friends. A rustling in the air behind him caught his attention.

Linc watched as a crimson flurry came swooping down, but he didn't move, sensing he wasn't in danger. Aarya slowed just enough to land softly on the ship's wheel in front of him. Aarya trilled, looking at him.

"You're the phoenix, aren't you, Red?" Linc said to the phoenix. She nodded in acknowledgement. He smiled. *The story Dirk and Tab had shared was a little unbelievable until now*, he thought. "They weren't lying, were they?" Aarya shook her head and leaned close to Linc. He caressed her neck.

As soon as his fingers touched her feathers, a spark shot through him. Linc was frozen in that position for what seemed like hours, but it was mere seconds. In that time, Linc was filled with the knowledge that had been instilled in Dirk and Tab. Crimson flames danced in his eyes for a few seconds. Snapping out of his daze, he realized in his hand was a small feather. Aarya eyes flamed.

"Thanks, Aarya," Linc said to her. Since he was bonded with her, he finally knew her name. She trilled back and he caressed her neck one more time.

Communicating to Linc through images. Aarya told him he was being followed by the Silent Raider.

"I'll be ready thanks to you."

She looked at him one more time before taking to the skies. Minutes later, Aarya dropped a crimson gem into Linc's hand. She trilled and took off in a flash of fire. Power emanated from the small gem. He knew instantly that it was a stone of power. It had many uses and that it would be very helpful to him if he needed it. It was smaller than his fist. He put it in his pants pocket for when he would need it and hoped he wouldn't need it soon. But with Aarya confirming his suspicions, he was afraid that he would. Some of the tension Linc had been feeling had been washed away by the bond he now shared with Dirk and Tab.

Brothers I am with you fully now, Linc thought as he stared ahead, caressing the feather between his thumb and forefinger. Putting it in the inside pocket of his tunic, he looked down at the small red spot on his palm. It was quickly taking on the shape of the phoenix. He rubbed it and smiled. "Just like Dirk" he said to himself.

Since he now knew that he was being followed by Captain Sleigh, the vilest captain on the waterways, he immediately began working through a plan. Familiar with their tactics, Linc realized they probably wouldn't attack for a few days. The ship would be entering the straights soon. That meant deeper water. It would give him time to set up a trap. The first thing he did was to wake River up.

Nug Bars and Shattered Gems

The next morning came faster than Dirk wanted. Hilda led the boys down to the dining hall. Dirk gave Tab a look.

"Did you sense Linc last night?" Tab quietly asked.

"I did. It's like Aarya bonded with him." Dirk stated.

They both smiled knowing that's what exactly had happened. Laughing too excitedly about their revelation brought Hilda's ire onto them. After she put a finger to her lip they straightened up and didn't talk anymore. Dirk turned his head slightly and whispered. "We'll talk later." Tab nodded.

The first-year girls were already in line. Tab and Dirk jumped ahead of several boys, receiving glares. They ignored them and walked up to El, who was talking with the twins.

"Hi." El beamed at them. The twins said hello. Vira was especially friendly when she saw Phil. He nonchalantly waved hello. Dirk smiled as Nira rolled her eyes at her sister. Dirk saw the princess was watching them.

Tab leaned over so only Dirk could hear. "Do you think she sensed it as well, considering everything that we learned last night?"

Dirk looked Natia in the eyes for a moment and held her gaze. She had a small smile at the corners of her mouth, and she nodded. He had his answer.

"Oh yeah. She did." He looked away. Brock bumped into him. Sensing what he was about to do, Dirk grabbed Tab's arm before he could push Brock back. "It's not worth it."

"Yeah, listen to your friend, orphan boy," Brock said, his lackeys behind him.

Tab pointed a finger at Brock. "One day, you will get what you deserve, and your loser friends will too soon enough."

Brock stepped a little closer, looked around, and noticed nearby kids watching. He whispered, "Is that a threat?"

Tab smiled and whispered back. "It's a promise!" He turned and moved forward in the line before Brock could respond.

Dirk smiled at Tab. They got up to the counter to get their food. Ms. Heloise gave them a bowl of porridge and they moved to get some juice. They knew they would be training after breakfast, so they only ate a light breakfast.

"You two look like you didn't sleep at all," El said.

"It was a rough first night," was all Dirk said. El just gave them a, *we'll talk later* look and didn't say anything more.

All of the first-years were rushed to the training yards after eating and they lined up in a classic five-deep six wide formation.

"All of you first-years, pay attention. I hope you didn't eat too much today. Because if you did, by the end of our training this morning, you would probably lose it," a stout-looking man in training fatigues yelled walking to the front of the formation. He was average height with a buzz-cut and a thick mustache. Dirk watched him closely as he eyed the first-years. "Now, when I address you, stand at attention with your back straight and your head up, facing forward with your hands at your side and feet together. When I say at ease, place your hands behind your back and spread your feet shoulder-width. Do you understand?"

"Yes sir!" the group shouted back.

"No, no, no. I am no sir. I am Sergeant Giles, and you will address me as such. Do you understand?"

"Yes Sergeant!"

He nodded and then began to pace back and forth, sizing up his new recruits making comments on who was standing right and wrong.

After he examined everyone, he went back to the front of the line. "At ease!" he commanded. Everyone relaxed and assumed the position.

"Bending and stretching your muscles is the most important thing you can do in the mornings before you start your workouts and runs. It will help you strengthen the muscles in your body and keep your injuries to a minimum."

Sergeant Giles showed them what to do. He again corrected them while walking around.

After fifteen minutes of continuous stretching, he told them to grab a back sack from the pile by the gate. "Girls on the left side. The boys on the right."

Dirk ran to the boy's pile and picked up one of the foliage-colored packs. Putting it on, he guessed it weighed around thirty pounds. Some in the group mumbled complaints under their breath.

"Yes, they are weighted," Giles said, grabbing his own pack off the ground. "Today, we run the trails to the east. They're the starter trails. We will run for thirty minutes, where we should reach the trail that circles back. We'll break for five minutes then run back. We'll start at a slow pace today and begin picking up the pace when you start to achieve the conditioning that is expected of you. By then, you should be able to run the whole course in thirty minutes. Once you achieve that, we will move on to the mountain trails."

"Yes Sergeant Giles!"

He nodded and started out the gate with the group following. They walked across the trail surrounded by the military cadets who were practicing their sword and shield training. Jonesy and the rest of the dwarves came into view. They were doing strike and block maneuvers. Tab just laughed because every time Jonesy struck someone, their knees would buckle.

"Poor dwarves," Tab said to Dirk. They both smiled and continued to follow the sergeant.

When they got to the start of the trail at the edge of the woods, Sergeant Giles took off at a brisk pace. Dirk and the group followed. The trail was wide enough for three people to run side by side. The woods were thin at first with very little foliage.

Animals could be heard in the distance. The birds were singing, the squirrels were chittering back and forth. Fresh morning dew still hung on the leaves. The smell of wildflowers drifted along on the slight breeze blowing across the group's path. The deeper into the woods they went, the thicker the trees and underbrush were.

Of course, there were those who wanted to impress the sergeant, like Brock and his ghouls, so they had taken off at a faster pace. Dirk laughed to himself. His group was smarter, and they were pacing themselves.

El began to struggle fifteen minutes in so Dirk and Tab ran alongside her.

"Come on, El! You can do it," Dirk encouraged, pushing each word out. Tab was already sweating and breathing hard.

The twins and Gil were ahead of them. Evidently the run hadn't gotten to them yet. Phil and Dusty jogged just ahead of the twins and Gil. Dirk glanced back and saw that the elves were right in front of Volar. They didn't seem to be struggling at all just pacing themselves. Natia even seemed to speed up. Volar was bringing up the rear, going as fast as his dwarven legs would allow.

When Natia came up behind El, she smiled encouragingly at her, "Steady your breathing. It'll help." She touched El's back. A small spark arced into El's back. Dirk felt it rather than saw it.

El straightened up, feeling a surge of energy. Her breathing slowed and she risked a glimpse behind her. "Thanks for the encouragement! It helped!" With a deep breath she started to pick up the pace. Dirk and Tab both nodded to Natia before speeding up to keep pace with El.

The elves caught up with Natia.

"What was that? "Sirien ask Natia.

"A little encouragement. Sirien, don't ever question what I do again!" Natia said through gritted teeth.

"I'm sorry, your highness. I was just making sure you were ok. Your shoulders slumped for a second."

"You are here to be my protector, I know, but you're just a lookout for my mother. Don't deny it. You must learn to trust me."

Panting, Sirien nodded. The other elves, straight-faced, neither acknowledged nor commented on the exchange. They just kept pace with Natia.

Dirk and Tab had heard the exchange between the elves as they ran. They glanced at each other and shrugged.

Sure enough, a few minutes before Dirk and the gang reached the thirty-minute mark, they passed a very slow-running Brock and his gang. They were breathing heavily and looked like they were about to lose their breakfast.

Dirk and Tab just smiled too tired to put words to their glee. El, with her added encouragement from Natia, kept pushing the boys and came very close to passing the twins and Gil.

When they got to the trail that circled back, Giles informed them they had four minutes to catch their breath before they would be heading back. Volar, huffing noisily, got there with two minutes to spare. Natia, or the other elves, didn't seem to be bothered by the run. Sirien, the male elf, looked at Dirk and gave a curt nod.

Natia walked over to Dirk and Tab, leaning down close to Dirk, who was kneeling on one knee. "Dirk, we really need to talk. Now that there shouldn't be any interference from anyone, we need to have a serious discussion."

Dirk looked her in the eyes. With his elbows on his knee while he caught his breath, he nodded. "Ok, let's sit together at lunch and we'll discuss what's going on, but I will warn you," he said, standing up straight and looking at her, "Tab hears everything I do. We don't keep secrets."

Natia smiled, straightening. "That's fine, you can choose to share, but what I have to say is between us alone for now. After we talk, you can tell him if you choose." She put a hand on his shoulder. The same spark El had received transferred to Dirk and he felt rejuvenated.

"Thanks," he told her with a smile. She smiled back, hesitated for a minute, then walked over to grab some water from the water tank. She brushed shoulders with Tab as she walked by. He immediately smiled and straightened up, nodding a thank you. Dirk noticed that all the elves were eyeing him suspiciously now, especially Sirien. He turned to look at Tab.

"I think she wants something. Better at least hear what she has to say," Tab said and nodded towards Natia.

"I think your right."

Volar walked up, reached into his pack, and pulled out a nug bar. He broke it into enough pieces to share with the pack. They thanked him and chewed very fast. "Won't this break the no stimulants rule?" Dirk asked, his mouth full.

"No, Master Storm, it won't. It is all-natural food that hasn't been enhanced with anything," Volar said smiling.

"Thanks, friend," Dirk said. With the water, the nug bar he received from Volar, and the jolt of energy from Natia, he felt energized and was ready when Giles picked up his pack and started jogging back. Brock and his group had just gotten there, quickly drinking water as the rest of the group started to leave. Dirk noticed Brock reaching into his pocket but thought nothing of it.

"You all have one minute," Giles shouted over his shoulder at them as the rest of the group started jogging back to the academy.

Everyone made it back in the allotted time, even Brock and his group, though they were dead last. Something about them didn't look right to Dirk. They looked too rested, not at all like they had just run miles and miles. He wouldn't worry about that right now.

"All right, not a bad first day. Tomorrow, we'll follow the same routine. We'll pick up the pace and add more exercises as the days progress. So, get plenty of rest tonight and eat right in the morning. Now off you go!" the sergeant ordered.

Dirk and Tab let everyone go before them to return their packs so they could discuss Natia. "That rush of energy she gave us was awesome. We really need to learn how to do that," Tab said, heading to the dorms.

"You're right, it was awesome. She wants to talk at lunch. So, I'll listen to what she has to say," Dirk responded, following Tab. They got there last and had to wait on the rest of the boys to shower and get ready.

Hilda smiled. "How was your training?

"It was rough, but we got through it," Dirk replied.

"It'll get tougher, so you best be prepared." Hilda patted the boys on the back.

They groaned. "Great."

"You'll survive." Hilda laughed as she walked away.

They showered, got into their robes, and ran down the hall to the classroom, they came too fast around a corner. They smashed into Wizard Laseous, knocking books and papers out of his arms.

"Watch where you're going! I don't want to add anymore detention unless I have to," he scolded while picking up the books he had been carrying.

"Sorry sir," they both said, trying to help him. He shooed them away and they walked briskly to their assigned rooms.

"See ya at lunch," Tab said, heading into Wizard Quentin's room. Dirk headed into Wizard Hermosa's classroom.

Dirk was the last to walk in. There were five other students already seated. Two tables were set up in the front of the wizard's desk. Dirk cringed when he saw Brock sitting at a table with Jacko Jenkins and Larkin. Jacko didn't seem to really be paying any attention to what Brock was saying, but Larkin was hanging on his leader's every word.

Dirk's heart skipped a beat when he saw who was sitting at the other table. Natia and Sirien were sitting there, looking at him as he took a seat next to Natia. Sirien gave him a slight scowl that he ignored. He almost laughed as Natia elbowed Sirien in the ribs.

"Look it's the wannabe's leader." Brock laughed with Larkin. Jacko just smiled and looked away. Dirk's eyes felt warm, so he closed his eyes and took a calming breath to get his emotions under control.

Hermosa looked at her time piece tapping her foot. "Mr. Storm, I'm sure that your time is precious, so let's assume ours is as well. Be on time from now on. Do you understand?" She lowered her eyes so that she was looking him in the eyes.

"Yes ma'am, sorry. It won't happen again," he said.

The tables were set up with the first two gems that he had tested out the previous day. The third one he had tested was nowhere in sight. *We'll probably use that one later*, he thought.

"This morning and into the afternoon, we will be practicing how to touch your core. Since there are six of you, we will team up in groups of three. Mr. Little, Mr. Carpus and Mr. Jenkins you three will work with the yellow stone together. Ms. Silver, Mr. Sleigh and Mr. Storm, you work with the red gem. One person in each group will hold the gem while the other two observe. Helena and I will work with each group during the class, and we'll switch back and forth every hour to help instruct and guide you on using your core once you have touched it. Any questions?"

No one asked any so she told Helena to work at Dirk's table and she would work with the other first.

Hermosa pulled a wooden chair over by the group she was working with first. Helena did the same and sat at Dirk's table. She smiled at them. Dirk noticed she had dimples when she smiled. She wore the same robes as the day before. A loose strand of hair fell into her eyes and she pushed it behind her ear.

"Well let's get started," Helena said. "Everyone here understands what the core is, correct?" They all nodded. "Good, what we're going to practice is like what you did during testing. The difference is that you need to hold it longer, staying linked with the gem as long as you can. Now, close your eyes and try to find your core."

After the kids closed their eyes, she did the same.

"Feel for the warmth it exudes. When you find it, hold onto it as long as you can. When you're holding the gem, you'll release a little of your core energy into the gem and try to keep a steady stream between you and it. That stream is what keeps the gem lit up. These gems have been crafted to only light up, nothing more."

Dirk spoke up. "You mean a gem can be crafted to be used only for what you need it for?"

Helena opened her eyes. "Yes, Dirk, all gems can be crafted to do many different things based on their color. Their specific function can only be crafted by a gem-crafter that specializes in doing that." Helena stopped, making sure he understood. "For example, a red gem can be restricted by the craftsmen to produce only light, fire, or even heat. I'm not sure exactly how they do it. I just know they can use their core to block the undesired effects and keep them from being used. Now with that answered, any other questions before we proceed?"

"I got it," Dirk responded. The elves just shook their heads.

"Each of you will do this in fifteen-minute intervals for the first hour. Ladies first."

Natia picked up the red gem and closed her eyes. Almost immediately, the red gem began to glow in its center. It was a steady light that seemed to pulse as if it was a heartbeat. Dirk just watched Natia. She was holding the gem in the center of her palm with her eyes closed and was breathing calmly. He was amazed at her control.

"That's really good, Natia. Now try to let go of a little more of your core and feed it to the gem," Helena told her. Natia took a breath, and as she released it, the light increased to about twice the output it was before, but the pulsing seemed to stop. "After a few more minutes more, you can release your connection."

STORM RISING

Natia did as instructed. When she released the connection, the gem faded, and she opened her eyes. Dirk was amazed and started to clap but stopped when Sirien glared at him.

"I was doing that at the age of ten," Sirien said with disdain starting to say something else when Natia elbowed him again. "Ow." Sirien glared at her, but she glared right back until he apologized to Dirk. Dirk just scowled and turned to face Helena.

"That being said, Sirien show us what you can do," Helena said with a little harshness in her voice. She clearly didn't like his comment either. Sirien, with a crooked smile, grabbed the gem from the table and closed his eyes. The gem lit up, similar to how it had during Natia's turn, but it didn't shine as brightly or pulse.

After a few minutes, she told him to go ahead and increase his core just like Natia had. The gem started to get a little brighter. Beads of sweat started to form on his forehead. He let out a big breath and the light faded. He opened his eyes.

"That's ok, Sirien. Good first start." Helena praised him. Sirien set the gem down and dropped his head.

"Good job," Dirk said. Sirien leaned forward to scowl at Dirk, but he realized he was being sincere.

His scowl dropped. "Thanks."

Dirk nodded and turned to face Helena. His vision seemed to fog up as Helena was speaking. He normally wasn't afraid of anything, but despair crept into him. "Sorry, What?" Dirk's head cleared when he realized she was looking from the gem to him. He picked up the gem closed his eyes and concentrated on his core. He started to panic, trying to remember what he had done the last time to touch his core. *What was it*? He couldn't remember.

With his eyes closed, he heard Helena "Just relax, Dirk. Just like yesterday."

Oh yeah, he thought. "I can do this," he said out loud without meaning to. He heard a snicker from Sirien. Dirk kept trying to think of what worked. Then he remembered "Natia," he whispered, only loud enough for Natia to hear. She smiled slightly after hearing her name and squeezed his leg under the table. Confidence surged through his body. The gem started glowing immediately and he could feel the connection to his core.

"That's good," Helena said in the background. After a few minutes of holding the flow of his core, Helena instructed him to increase his connection. He started to panic again. He tried and tried but couldn't get it to work.

In his mind, he saw a pair of amber orbs floating towards him. When they came closer he could tell they were amber eyes. A small flame danced in them.

"That's it, Dirk," he heard Helena say. He was still focused on the flaming eyes. Dirk felt the pressure on his right leg again and the flow increased. "That's it, Dirk. Now hold it there."

He tried but couldn't seem to slow the flow. It kept increasing. *I can't stop it*, he realized.

The light seeping through his eyes was beginning to intensify. *Dirk, you must relax and ease the flow.* The orbs became clear. In fact, a face materialized. It was Natia and Dirk could hear her voice. *Break the flow Dirk! Now!"* Natia's voice was panicky.

Helena was yelling. Why was Helena yelling at him?

Natia's face disappeared along with the pressure on his leg. The light that was seeping through his closed eyes vanished at the sound of shattering glass. Dirk felt an intense burning pain in his hand. He opened his eyes to see Helena, Natia, and Sirien brushing shards of the shattered gem off of themselves.

"You idiot!" Sirien yelled. The gem had exploded in his hand. Dirk quickly blew the remainder of the gem off his hand. It had left a scorch mark.

"I'm fine Sirien," Natia said as she put a hand on his chest.

"You need to be checked out by a healer. He could have hurt you princess!" Sirien glared at Dirk. He tried to lunge at Dirk but Natia put pressure on his chest and stepped between them.

"It was an accident. You better get used to it. The humans haven't had as much practice as we have. You're just going to have to accept that there will be accidents and I may be in danger, but it is my choice. If you can't abide by that, then you need to leave."

Sirien realized Helena, Dirk, and the rest of the class were watching the exchange. He looked around and relaxed. "Yes, princess. I am sorry. I will do as you wish, but if I feel you are in danger I will do my job and protect you."

"I understand." She then turned to Dirk to see if he was okay. Helena finished brushing the remnants of the gem off her robes and made the three of them sit back down.

"Dumbass," Brock said loudly from the other table. Larkin laughed. Jacko looked a little disgusted. Heat rushed through Dirk's body and he started to get up. Natia put her hand on his shoulder to keep him in his seat. She squeezed tightly. Dirk looked into her eyes and relaxed.

Under her breath, she said, "Calm down and focus your eyes."

Dirk took a moment to register what she had said. He closed his eyes and took some deep breaths, feeling the calm flow through their shared connection. He relaxed and opened his eyes. No one had noticed the interaction because they were watching Wizard Hermosa taking Brock to task for his language. Dirk nodded and Natia removed her hand.

"Dirk, that was unexpected. What happened?" Helena asked.

"I don't know. I just couldn't break the flow. I tried but it wouldn't stop." Helena was staring at him intently and it made him slightly uncomfortable.

"Well, we'll take it easier from now on out until you can learn to control the flow." Dirk nodded. Sirien looked like he wanted to comment but decided not to. "Wait here while I get another test gem." Helena got up and headed to the storeroom.

Natia leaned over and took Dirk's hand. "It looks healed already."

"Yes, it really didn't burn that much," Dirk said, trying to pull his hand away. Grabbing his wrist, she stopped him from getting away.

She rubbed her thumb over his birthmark. "Interesting birthmark." She smiled and opened her palm, exposing it to him. Dirk, realizing she had released him pulled his hand back and looked at Natia's palm. There, in the same spot on her hand, was the same phoenix birthmark that he had. "Lunch." was all she said.

Dirk nodded, and by that time, Helena had returned. They practiced for a few more minutes. Then it was time to switch teachers. Wizard Hermosa took them through the same process, but this time she only allowed them to connect their core and the gem for a few minutes at a time.

Dirk was successful a few more times but thoughts of the accident kept creeping up in his mind and he would lose focus. This went on until it was time for lunch.

Before Hermosa dismissed them for lunch, she told them to eat a hearty meal because, after lunch, the practice would continue. Her gaze lingered on Dirk. "We must maintain focus. You need the food for stamina." He looked away, knowing what she meant. The bell rang, and she dismissed them.

Lunch

The halls filled quickly. Tab caught up with Dirk. "Wow that was horrible. El was the only one in our class to successfully connect to the gem consistently. I did terrible. How did you do?"

"I think things went a little better in our class. That is, until I exploded the gem."

Tab stared at Dirk, then started laughing. "Ow," Tab said rubbing his arm where Dirk had punched him.

"It's not funny. I couldn't control it." Dirk looked around. He grabbed Tab by the arm and slowed down so everyone could pass them. Brock and his group came walking by and Dirk could tell that, once again he was the topic of their laughter.

"Let it go," Tab said after everyone had passed.

"Look, here's the problem. I couldn't find my core until I felt this pressure on my leg. Then all I could see was a pair of amber eyes looking at me. Then all of a sudden, I felt my core." Dirk gave Tab a look.

"Natia?" Tab asked, clearly following Dirk's train of thought.

"Yes. It was her eyes I was seeing. Then when Helena told me to increase the flow. I couldn't stop it."

"Well that makes sense. You're clearly smitten by our princess and since she is connected to us, your feelings for her are more than you want to admit." Tab smirked.

"Ow!" He rubbed his other arm where Dirk had just punched him again. "I'm just saying," he said, holding his hands up backing away from Dirk.

Dirk waved him off. "You're crazy."

"Look, I know how I feel."

"Okay. If you say so." Tab tapped the side of his head.

"You're wrong, but there's one more thing. After the gem exploded, I opened my eyes, she grabbed my hand, and looked at my mark. She rubbed her thumb across it, and I got this tingling sensation from her touch. She said nice birthmark. Then she showed me her hand. The mark is just like ours. I started to ask her about it, and she wants to talk at lunch. I told her I would eat with her so maybe I can get more answers."

"Sounds like a plan. Tingling sensation, huh?" Tab said as he ran away from Dirk's swing. Dirk laughed and followed him.

Natia was waiting at the entrance to the lunch hall. Tab nodded at Natia and went into the lunch hall. Dirk walked up to her with a smirk on his face. "Where's your protector?"

Natia scowled and headed into the lunch hall. They didn't say a word to each other while they waited to get their lunch. The lunch hall was totally full today. All eyes seemed to be on Dirk and Natia as they moved forward. Dirk watched Tab and El head to the same table consisting of the same crowd from the day before.

El was talking with Tab and he pointed towards Dirk as he sat down. El just gave him a quizzical look and smiled. The whole table looked at Dirk. Frustrated, he turned away, moving up in line. He caught a glimpse of Anastasia and Kal. Anastasia waved with a small smile and he waved back.

"You know Anastasia?" Natia asked.

"We've been friends since childhood. We basically grew up together." Dirk laughed.

"What's funny?" Natia asked.

"She used to babysit me," Dirk replied. Natia smiled and turned as Miss Heloise asked her what she wanted for lunch.

"Salad please," Natia told her. Miss Heloise gave her the salad and looked at Dirk.

"Soup please." He received his mutton stew and followed Natia. She headed straight to the back corner of the hall. There was an empty table there. When they got closer, Dirk realized why. The elves had sat at the table beside it and wouldn't let anyone sit there. Natia sat at the back of the table, away from prying ears in the corner. She motioned for Dirk to sit by her. He sat down and started eating. Natia followed suit. They ate quickly without talking. Dirk noticed they were receiving stares from all of the students, not just the first-years.

Moira from detention was sitting two tables over, glancing at him while talking with her friends. Dirk smiled at her and she smiled back. Natia waited politely while Dirk finished eating his last bite of soup and bread.

"It's good, I was starving," Dirk said.

"Using your core for magic uses a lot of energy," Natia stated.

Dirk looked at her curiously. Her beauty was breath taking. The scent of almonds and honey seemed to float around her, it was very pleasing to Dirk's senses. He smiled and finally responded to her statement. "So I've been told, now I have a good idea of what this is about."

"You do?" Natia asked, sitting up straight. Dirk looked down at Natia's hand. She followed his gaze, but then she looked up from her hand to Dirk's. She leaned close to Dirk and looked into his eyes. Little flames rippled across their eyes at the same time. Natia leaned back a little bit. The sensations that he always seemed to feel when he was near Natia started to kick in. He closed his eyes and shook the feeling away.

"Do you know where our mark comes from?" Natia asked. Dirk looked around to make sure no one was listening.

"I have an idea."

"That's what I thought. You don't really know where it comes from. I know you probably understand why we have it, but do you know how we got it in the first place?"

Dirk looked into those amber eyes, lost in thought. "You're right. I know why we have it, but I don't know where it came from, or why."

His breathing was getting shallower the longer he sat next to her. Natia kept his gaze. He could tell by her breathing that her heart was beating faster. She also could feel the deep connection he sensed.

She took a breath, leaned closer, and decided to explain. "When the Chosen and protector die, the next in line receive the mark through a transfer that the phoenix bestows upon them." She let that sink in. Dirk looked at her confused. She placed her hand over his. Her touch sent shivers down his back and legs. "The phoenix was created to aid in the fight against evil. Its primary purpose is to support, heal, and even battle alongside the Chosen and protector. The bond between them is so intense that they feel every sensation, good and bad. So, when a Chosen or protector dies, the next in line receives a visit from the phoenix and it bestows the mark by leaving a single feather in the palm of their hand. That feather's magic transfers the bond."

"Wait a minute," Dirk interrupted. "If that was true, then why didn't Tab receive a mark when his father died?"

Natia smiled. "How much has Aunt Kira told you?"

Dirk looked at her, not wanting to go into great detail. He knew he had to pick what information he wanted to share. "Mom and the general explained the history of the Chosen and protector to me after I witnessed Arial dying and Aarya being born. They didn't really go into too much detail, other than there being a need for our bloodline to become the chosen of Marona. They said there was plenty of time to learn the rest."

"Tell me about Arial's death. I sensed it, then I felt Aarya being born seconds later."

"I saw her falling from the sky. At that time, I didn't know who or what she was. I just knew I had to get to her. Tab and I had found a rock we thought was a gem of power the day before. In the back of my mind, I knew I needed it, so I took it with me and ran out of the house, chasing the falling bird. I didn't even see Tab as I ran by him. Luckily, he followed me. When I got to the base of Mt Blazire, I found her on the ground with an arrow sticking in her chest."

Dirk took a breath. This part was where he needed to be careful.

"As soon as I picked her up, two wood nymphs popped up in the trees behind me. They both had their bows drawn and one of them yelled something like, "Father will beat you this time." The next thing I know, Tab is appearing around the bend and shoots one of them in the chest, killing it. The other one screamed and they both disappeared. Then I sensed the gem in my pack moving so I pulled it out and then this bright light overwhelmed me and Arial. When it disappeared, I had some knowledge of the Chosen and Arial was gone. In the place of the gem was Aarya. Tab asked me what the hells was going on so I explained what I could. That night, we confronted Mom and the general."

When he was done, Natia took a deep breath and wiped a tear away. "Thank you. That explains a lot. And it seems there is a lot you haven't been informed of, but we don't have the time for that now."

The kids in the lunch hall were starting to get up and throw away their lunch trash. Natia looked around and leaned in closer.

"I will say this to answer your question. Your mom was supposed to be the protector for life. When she and your father fell in love, they chose to break the bond that had been set up. The protector was always supposed to be an elf. It is the way Zona made it. That chain was broken when Tab's father became the protector. When he died, it jumped back to the elven people. I was the elf that had been chosen to receive the gift."

Dirk nodded. "You seem to know a lot about this."

She nodded, getting up to dump her tray. She stopped and their eyes connected again. "I have been trained since I was born to be your protector. You're just learning what your destiny holds. The only thing that bothers me is that the connection doesn't feel whole." Natia paused.

Dirk just shrugged his shoulders. "I don't have a clue what it's supposed to feel like."

She gave him a quizzical look. She knew there was more to the story than he was telling her. She would just have to figure a way to find out. "Well, we'll continue this later. We better get to class." Natia took off without waiting for a reply. Dirk got up and followed her. He knew why the connection was different, but he didn't feel it was time to tell her about Tab yet.

As the kids went back to their classes, El and the twins caught up with Dirk. El looped her arm through Dirk's. The twins just giggled behind her. "How was lunch?" El asked in an overly sweet voice.

Dirk glared at her.

"Spill it. I have known you most of my life, and I can tell that was something," El demanded, stopping Dirk in his tracks. The twins halted right behind them. They just stared at Dirk, who was squirming from El's scrutiny.

He pulled her close. "Look, you know she's my mother's niece. She just wanted to talk about that."

El shrugged and gave him a *I don't believe you* look, then took off to her class without saying another word. The twins followed her, saying goodbye to Dirk as they hurried down the hall.

Tab walked up. "What was that about?"

"She wanted to know what I was talking to Natia about."

"You're going to have to tell her, you know."

"I know. But not yet. Let's discuss it after class. I don't want to be late again."

He and Tab both headed to their classes after Dirk gave him a brief summary of his lunch conversation with Natia.

That afternoon, the classes went the same with the exception of Dirk not blowing up a gem this time. They practiced and practiced and before spending the last hour going over the theory behind how the magic of the core worked.

When the days lessons were over, Hermosa told them to study the first three chapters of *The Core and Your Body* tonight. They would take what they learned and put it to practical use tomorrow. Dirk swore under his breath. He had detention again tonight with Tab. As soon as they were released from class, they all headed to the dorms.

Volar and Phil both were already in the room when Dirk got there. "Ah, Master Storm, how was your first day?" Volar asked.

"Well I blew up a gem today," Dirk said with a laugh.

"I kept blowing the teachers desk over so don't feel bad," Phil said after they finished laughing.

A loud obnoxious laugh brought the group's attention to Brocks table. Dirk could tell he was the subject of their laughter again by the way they were glancing at him. Tab started to get up when Volar put his hand on his shoulder, "Let me handle this, Master Tab," Volar said with a slight bow. Brock sneered and started to get up.

He held a hand up to halt Brock from getting the rest of the way up. He walked over and looked Brock in the eyes.

"Let me introduce myself," Volar said with a slight bow.

"What do you want, little man?" Brock scoffed.

Volar just smiled. "You see, Brock, that's where you are mistaken. I, for one, am no human. Second, I am actually one of the biggest dwarves to have been born in over a century. I am Volar Horan, son of the king of the dwarves. I tell you this not to brag, but to inform you so that you will know that I have access to a lot of information. Now, we dwarves do most everything underground, and one of the things we do is harvest the shade violet."

Brock started squirming when Volar mentioned the plant. Volar just smiled.

"You see, I worked with the traders as a part of my training, and one of the things we trade is the powders produced from that plant. Now, it is used for several things, from medicines to stimulants and poisons. I just happen to know that your father is one of the biggest purchasers of a specific powder."

Volar cocked an eye at Brock, leaning forward and resting his foot on one of the chairs. Everyone in the room was mesmerized by Volar words. No one wanted to miss what he said next because now Brock, Stew, and Larkin were squirming. Jacko, who was sitting at the table, just looked confused by their reaction.

"Brock, I can say this for sure. Every one of us saw how you struggled to get halfway through that run this morning. I, myself, was last the whole way until the end when I passed you three. You were throwing up on the side of the trail." Everyone in the room laughed. Brock and his cronies just looked around guiltily. "Now I bet if I checked your room, I would find some sort of stimulant that was made to boost energy. What do you think?" Volar paused for effect. "Because the way you three finished, I think you might have taken something. What say we go to Sergeant Giles tomorrow and see if my suspicions are accurate?" Volar looked Brock in the eye. "Because I seem to remember there being a rule against supplements to increase your abilities?"

Brock stared at Volar. "What do you want?"

Volar looked back at Dirk and smiled. "I suggest you give my friends a break for a while and I will forget about what I know about your father's purchases."

Brock stared at Volar. "I'm not saying you're right, but I think I can lay off the losers for a semester or two."

Volar looked at Brock. "Remember, if I think anything squirrely is happening around them, I won't hesitate."

Brock nodded. He, Larkin, and Stew got up and went to their room. Jacko gaped at Volar. "Hey, I didn't know anything about any of that."

Volar looked Jacko in the eyes and could tell he wasn't lying. "I know." Volar stuck out his hand and Jacko shook it. "Come sit with some real friends, Jacko."

Jacko followed and pulled up a chair. Soon, the dinner bell rang, and they all headed to the lunch hall.

At dinner, Dirk and the group sat together and discussed their afternoon classes. Phil told the story of Volar taking Brock down a notch. Vira hung on his every word twirling the hair over her right ear and laughing at the right times. Nira just rolled her eyes every time her sister laughed. Vira was so loud she got shushed by the second-years nearby more than once. Dusty, who was sitting by Nira, smirked every time she rolled her eyes. El was still miffed at Dirk. She faked a smile, listening to the story while staring at Dirk the whole time and purposefully making him feel uncomfortable. As soon as the end of dinner bell clanged, they all got up to dump their trays.

El stopped Dirk. "Well," she said, staring him down. Tab was waiting by the door, pointing to his arm where a timepiece normally would be. Dirk nodded.

"I have to get to detention."

"I know, but do you remember standing on that hill the other day? Before we headed to the tournament?"

Dirk looked into her eyes. "El, you know I do. I love you. You are my sister, and you know it," Dirk put his hand on El's shoulder for emphasis.

A tear rolled down her cheek. She wiped it away and looked Dirk in the eyes sadly. "I thought I was. The past few days, you've been different, and I want to know why." El waited for Dirk to respond. "I'll give you one more day to tell me the truth about what's going on. After that, if you don't, then consider us not related anymore." She pushed Dirk's hand away and stormed off. She blew by Tab without saying a word.

"El…?" Dirk pleaded, trying to stop her. But she ignored him and kept on walking.

Dirk headed to detention with Tab, summarizing the conversation. "I believe we need to tell her. You know she is part of the Pack. Might as well be now than later."

He stopped, a serious expression on his face. "The danger that will put her in. I don't know if I can risk putting her there this early."

"Look, she is going to find out. Let's tell her so she can train now and be protected."

Dirk nodded and started walking. *I'll think about it.* Dirk decided as they were walking into Laseous's class.

Detention was the same as the night before, beginning with a lecture by Laseous and then being sent off to do the dishes again. Hanks told a few more stories. Moira got pissed off again about them talking too much, so the stories were cut short.

After they finished, Dirk and Tab rushed to get to the room before Hilda locked the door. They made it just in time. She was tapping her foot as they came running up the stairs.

"Just in time," she said, closing the door behind them. The gang was sitting around, doing their nightly reading. Tab and Dirk joined them grabbing books from the guys who had finished. They read as fast as they could, finishing just before they were told to go to bed.

Hilda ushered them off to bed ignoring their pleas and telling them that they needed their rest after a big first day. Dirk and Tab couldn't argue with that since last night they hadn't gotten the same amount of sleep as everyone else. Dirk said good night to his new friends and headed to his room.

"Mr. Storm, a word."

No not again, Dirk thought as he turned around.

Hilda smiled. "Not to worry," she said, tapping her head. "Remember when we're close, I can sense your thoughts." The acknowledgement made him feel a little better. "I just wanted to say that we'll carry on every other night with our special studies. That way, you and Mr. Clearwater can get some rest." Dirk thanked her and turned to go to his room. "See you bright and early," she said as he was closing the door.

Dirk fell into bed as soon as he changed clothes. Phil was already snoring. Volar was tossing. "Can't sleep?" Dirk asked.

"No. I can't get used to sleeping outside the mountain."

Dirk got a funny feeling from what Volar said. "Did you sleep well last night?"

Volar sat up. "Not really, and I think I'm not the only one."

Dirk sat up as well. Looking at his new friend. Dirk started to speak. Just like with Brock, Volar held up his hand, before he could get to far.

"Dirk, there are some things one needs to know, and a certain time when they need to know it. I believe right now in this moment; it is not the time for me to know. I know you and Tab met with Hilda and Tilda last night. And that is your business. When the time is right, you'll share whatever it is that I need to know. Just know this, I feel a connection to you. I feel our paths were meant to converge. And when the time comes, I will be ready to hear what I need to know. Good night." Volar smiled and laid back down.

Dirk was stunned by Volar's honesty and awareness. Thinking about what Volar had just said, he laid down. *Tab is right. I need to protect my friends. Especially El.* Tomorrow, he would inform El about everything. He would always protect her. She was right, she was his family, and her knowing would be the best way to protect her. Gil though, he wasn't ready to tell him just yet. El was the more pressing one. Soon, he fell asleep.

A Spies Confession

Linc was happy with his crew's second day at sea. It went fairly well. They made it to the straights and settled into the long voyage to Oak City.

As soon as the other ship made their move, Linc would act. He would also find out if Jerle was the traitor he suspected he was. They had done some fishing when they got into the deeper waters. Linc had kept his eye on Jerle. He had followed all of Linc's orders.

Kaz was really good at the fishing. They had filled their stores with Blues but no Reds. Corky seemed to constantly have a flask out but he did his duties as expected.

Linc stayed at the helm all day watching the crew. Corky seemed to watch Jerle every time he was around. River kept the sails, ready to adjust them to the different wind currents, keeping an eye on Jerle as well. They had their mid-day rations while sailing smooth waters. Linc knew they had better eat while the waves weren't choppy. Smuggler's Turn would be coming up soon and the water always got rough around the reefs in that area. Plus, he was thinking the ship that was following might try to take advantage of the new crew in that area.

When the sun began to disappear, he noticed that Jerle had started getting antsy. "Cap'n, decided yet which way were going to turn at smugglers turn?" Jerle asked looking over his shoulder at Linc.

Linc glared at Jerle. "Not sure yet!"

"Really. I was just wondering Cap'n cause that's a tricky maneuver," Jerle looked behind the ship squinting Linc noticed.

"I'll tell you when we get closer. I know that the waters are rough around that area. We may actually sail around it through the slower currents." Linc gritted his teeth. He was annoyed by the constant questions from Jerle. *He may not be a spy, but he is definitely questioning my ability as a captain.* Linc thought.

"Okay Cap'n." Jerle, seeming satisfied disappeared for a while. Linc knew River had been tasked with keeping up with him so he wasn't worried.

It wasn't two hours after dark when Linc noticed the lights that had been were trailing him were getting closer. He smiled to himself. The ship following him had taken the bait. He was timing it perfectly and they would reach him right when he wanted them to.

Kaz had a fishing line out. He was still trying to catch a Red, using the hand crank, a series of three small wheels that were attached to a circular piece of wood with a makeshift handle on the right-side on the pole to reel in the line. It was a neat contraption he had created. When he turned the handle away from his body, the line came in. There was a small latch on the same side that, when pressed, allowed the line to release out. It was mounted towards the bottom of the seven-foot-long ash pole by a series of clamps that allowed the wheel to turn when needed.

Linc's head snapped in the direction of a loud ruckus at the back of the ship.

"Kaz, come take over the helm while I see what's going on. Hurry up!"

"Sorry captain," Kaz said, putting his pole up and running to take the wheel.

Linc hurried to the stern to see what the commotion was. Jerle was laid out, struggling to get away from Corky, who had his legs wrapped around the man's torso and his arm holding one of Jerle's behind his back. The other was wrapped around his neck. River was sitting on Jerle's left arm, holding it down. The torches set up around the stern lit up the scene. It would have been comical, if not for the ship closing on them.

"What's this?" Linc asked, staring at the three entangled crew members.

"We caught him, Linc," River said. Jerle tried to protest but Corky covered his mouth so he couldn't speak. "We had been watching him like you told us. Then after dark, he went to the stern and just stared out at the water."

"Then all of sudden, a yellow light flashed three times in Jerle's hand," Corky continued.

"Then in the distance, three flashes of red came back in reply. That is when we saw the lights in the distance seemed to start getting closer," River explained.

"Ow!" Corky screamed, pulling his hand back from his captive's mouth.

"Cap'n, it's not what you think!" Jerle tried to explain. River punched him in the face.

"River, let him talk," Linc ordered.

"Yes sir."

"So, Jerle, explain yourself."

"I had no choice cap'n."

"Why is that? Why don't we just throw you overboard and see if your friends will save you!" Linc's eyes started to ripple with small flames. The mouths of all three crew members flew open.

"Linc, what's wrong with your eyes?" River asked, backing away from Linc trembling.

"Why?" Linc felt the warmth in his eyes starting to abate.

"Well, they look like they're on fire!" Corky said, releasing Jerle and stepping back. The other two members crawled back, as if forgetting their earlier anger toward Jerle.

Relax. Echoed in Linc's mind.

Linc closed his eyes and took a deep breath. When he opened them, everything was calmer, and the heat was gone. "River, look at me." River did. "Now do you see anything wrong with my eyes?"

"No Linc."

"What you saw was the light of the torches in the dark reflecting off my eyes," Linc explained, getting the idea from Aarya's voice in his head. River and Corky quickly grabbed Jerle again and held him in place. "Now tell me, Jerle. I pose the same question. Why don't I just throw you overboard and let your friends try and save you?"

Jerle sighed in defeat. All of a sudden, he started crying. The three witnessing this couldn't believe a grown man was blubbering like a knee-high child on the deck. Corky smacked him in the head. "Stop it. Be a man."

Jerle seemed to gather himself. He looked Linc in the eyes. Even though he didn't quite believe his story about the torches, he was still afraid of him. "Ram kidnapped me daughter. She is only ten and he told me he would sell her to the slavers if I didn't help him." Jerle slumped, defeated. "She is my only child. Her mother is bedridden with the cough and needs her to help take care of things while I am at sea!" Jerle pleaded. Linc, being an orphan, knew what it felt like to be on your own, and for some reason he believed him.

Focusing on the man's body language. Linc could sense he was telling him the truth. "Let him go," Linc commanded.

"But Cap'n…Corky started.

"Let the man go Corky." River grabbed Corky by the arm and pulled him away. River trusted Linc.

Jerle got up, walking up to Linc and thanking him. "Now tell me what we are up against,"

Jerle told him about Captain Sleigh and his crew and how they were planning to attack around Smuggler's Turn just like Linc had figured they would.

Thinking about it, Linc had two problems. One, the ship following them was captained by the most notorious captain in the area. Two, they had to save Jerle's daughter. Jerle told him he thought if Captain Sleigh failed, his daughter would be lost, but Linc assured him that wouldn't happen. He would just have to get word to Dirk back in Silver City. Linc told Jerle his plan.

"I don't know cap'n. How can you do that? It's hard to believe," Jerle looked down as he spoke.

"Look, I'm trusting you. I'm asking you to trust me. I mean, literally with our lives," Linc said, determined.

"Trust him," River said. "I've known him almost my whole life and if he said he can do it, he will."

Jerle looked between them and he could see Linc, and River believed in what they said.

"I still say we toss him overboard!" Corky replied, taking a swig from his flask. Linc just looked at Corky and smiled.

"If I find out he is lying, Corky, you can personally throw him overboard." That made Corky smile.

He pointed at Jerle. "Remember."

Jerle looked at Corky. "Trust me, my daughter's life is on the line. I will not betray you."

"Cap'n, is that the only way? I mean, I'm the only one who will have to literally bleed for this to work."

Linc felt his eyes warming. He closed them quickly to keep anyone else from asking more questions about them. He took a calming breath and then, pinned Jerle with a steel gaze. "You're the reason we're in this pickle!"

Shame washed over Jerle. "You're right cap'n. It's better than losing my daughter." Linc nodded.

Captain Sleigh couldn't wait to catch the sloop he was chasing. He had gotten the signal earlier than expected so he had to move up his plans. "This job is beginning to be a pain in my arse!" Sleigh said to Matt and Kelt. "Did you get the sleeping powder in the food for Stockton's flunkies?"

"Aye, we did as you told us, Captain," Kelt replied.

"Doc and Lefty are putting them in the dinghy right now. They got four day's rations in case we run late picking them back up." Matt pointed towards the boat. "Lefty is going to stay with them until then."

Captain Sleigh nodded. After they made sure the dinghy was off, Matt and Kelt went to get ready to take the ship they were chasing.

"We're within a league captain," one of the crew up in the nest shouted.

He smiled. It was time to unleash the power of his ship. He flipped the top of the wooden box open that sat on the rail by the wheel. It had been a permanent fixture on his ship since he had it. A light blue gem was attached to a series of lines that ran through the ship to the bow. They attached to a pair of hidden propellers in the back of the ship. The propellers were made of a metal he had discovered on one of the islands in Fire Lake. Not much was available, so he made do with what little he had and had the propellers made by a smith in one of the cities to the south.

When he pushed the gem down in its socket, the propellers would come to life, spinning, and moving the ship through water at twice the speed of any other ship on the sea. It was his secret weapon and one of the main reasons he had been so successful. He smiled to himself. He knew they would catch the ship before Smugglers Turn, just like he planned. Then they would board the ship and capture the two he needed, killing the others. The spy's daughter that he had his men kidnap was probably already on her way to becoming a slave in Vanguard. He knew Ram was big on kidnapping children then turning a profit on making them slaves, or whores, depending on their age. Sleigh frowned at that thought. The thought of a ten-year-old girl being whored out turned his old stomach. He did have some limits he wouldn't go beyond.

Sleigh looked around, making sure his crew was ready. "Get ready to fire the front cannons, Matt! Don't hit them, just try to steer them toward the reef." The cannons started firing relentlessly. The persistent waves created by the cannonballs soon effectively steered the ship towards the reef.

That fool, Sleigh thought. He could tell from the way the ship was turning that it was going to try sail through Smugglers Turn. Only a few experienced captains could make that. He was one of the few.

"Fire over their heads! Now we need to slow them down. Don't let them wreck that ship on the run," the captain shouted at Matt. Shots flew over the ship.

Lightening boomed in the distance. The captain looked around. "Where is that coming from?"

"Up ahead of us, captain!" the crewman in the nest yelled.

"Bring me a spyglass Kelt!"

Kelt grabbed the spyglass and presented it to him. The captain looked through the glass in time to see a thick blanket of clouds rolling towards his prize, lightning arcing the sinister, billowing mass in the sky. He heard Matt firing the cannon. By the time the shot got within range of the ship, the clouds were over-taking the ship. The cannon fired again, and an explosion resounded in the distance. The captain's mouth fell open. He couldn't see the ship anymore. There was a cloud of smoke mixed in with the storm clouds rolling in.

"Gods dammit, Matt! You hit their powder!"

Matt looked at his captain in disbelief. "No way, captain. You know I know how to shoot."

"Take the glass and have a look!" he ordered. Matt ran up and confirmed what the captain had told him. All he could see was smoke, clouds and also what looked like a small fire. The captain looked at Matt. He took the glass then picking up the club he always had by the wheel, smacked Matt across the face as hard as he could. Matt hit the deck hard, blood pouring from his nose. Ignoring Matt's groans, Sleigh gave orders to cease pursuit. "Well, I guess we need to wait until this storm passes and we can see what's left of my prize." For good measure, Sleigh kicked Matt in the ribs.

He decided to head back and pick up Ram's thugs. He couldn't let them die in the storm. They needed Ram for the future. Kelt picked Matt up and had two crewmembers take him to his bunk after they cleaned him up. The captain eyed him.

"You know it was an accident, cap."

"Damn it I know, but we just lost a big prize because of him. Someone had to pay."

"Yes, captain." Kelt went about getting the ship ready to turn back and pick up the dinghy.

The Visit and The Shattered Door

Dirk woke to Hilda banging on the door. He and the boys were herded out the door to their breakfast and morning training. It went the same as the day before with no new exercises added. The run was the same, except this time Brock and his cronies didn't take off like the day before. Brock must have taken Volar's threat seriously. This time was almost as grueling, but they made it back in time.

El brushed past Dirk and Tab. Dirk grabbed her arm to hold her back. She whipped around, turning to face Dirk. Hurt blazed in her eyes.

The twins started to stop, but Tab grabbed them and pulled them away, "Family business." Vira started to object but Nira grabbed the other arm and pulled her along with Tab.

After everyone was out of earshot, El said, "Well?"

Dirk stepped closer to her, looked her in the eyes, and put his hand on her shoulder. She flinched, but she didn't move away. "El," he said, trying to figure out how to word what he needed to say. Tears filled her eyes. "El, I love you, but what I need to tell you will take a few hours." Dirk paused to swallow. "You're right, something has happened to us. It's something so big that it will change all of our lives. Yours, Jonesy's, Gil's, and anyone close to us."

El just stood there, some of the hurt easing from her stare.

"I can't tell you right now, but I promise during lunch, I'll start the story, but I'll probably have to finish it at dinner. What I will tell you now is that it involves Tab's father and mine. Basically, we found out what happened and why it happened."

El relaxed. Her hurt look changed to sorrow. The tears still fell but she removed her hands from her hips and grabbed Dirk in a hug. "I'm sorry I've been selfish." El squeezed Dirk.

He hugged her back. "You haven't been, El. I was being selfish for not including you and the others on what I know. I promise at lunch I'll talk with you. I'll make sure we have a spot where we can talk freely." Dirk released El from the hug.

She kissed him on the cheek and smiled. "I'll hold you to it." She wiped the tears away and they headed to the dorms to get ready for class.

Class went well in the morning for Dirk. He was able to hold his core and not lose control over it. Brock's group wasn't so lucky. Larkin had a similar incident to what happened to Phil. The parchment he had written notes on about the core and your body caught fire while he was working with Hermosa. She quickly put them out, but his notes were ruined. Brock chided him about being an idiot but was cut off by the wizard. Brock just sulked, looking embarrassed to be sitting by Larkin.

When the lunch bell rang, Dirk put a hand on Natia to keep her from leaving. "Stay for a moment I need to ask a favor."

Sirien started to protest but Natia glared at him and he left in a huff.

"Do you want to talk some more?" Dirk's eyes were locked into hers.

"Excuse me?" he said after a few awkward minutes.

"I asked if you wanted to talk some more."

Dirk looked at her, finally understanding. "Yes, I do, just not to you. I mean…." He was starting to feel uncomfortable being alone with her. "Not today. We can talk more tomorrow. I just need some privacy with El. You know who she is, right?"

Natia seemed a little hurt but didn't say anything so Dirk continued. "Natia, El is like a sister to me. She's noticed a change in my behavior. I've decided to inform her about what is going on. She's been my family for a long time, and I feel I have to tell her so that she can be protected and alert."

Natia relaxed. "I talked with Tilda the other night."

"I figured she would talk with you. You understand the power of a group verses going against the evil just you and me?" Natia smiled. Dirk saying what he just said was the acceptance she had been waiting for.

"Dirk, I understand. I'll make Sirien and the others save the table for us."

"Wait, I mean, I have to talk with her first and alone."

Natia seemed to think about that for a minute. She raised one eyebrow. "Ok I'll make sure it is set up for you and her alone. But, after today, I need to be involved with anyone that you decide you want in the group. Remember, it's my life that's in danger as well. Agreed?"

Dirk nodded. This was taking longer than he intended. She smiled and took off to the lunch hall. *Wow, this is happening too fast. If she wants to be that involved, fine. I have to try and control this situation though.* He thought, then he took off behind Natia.

El was waiting on Dirk at the entrance to the lunch hall. She had Tab cornered and Dirk could tell he was in evasive mode. He kept shrugging his shoulders. Dirk smiled. He knew how El was. Once she got the scent of something, she didn't let go until she had all the facts.

"Ah, there you are. What took so long?" Tab asked. El turned to face Dirk.

"Just had to make some arrangements." Tab took the opening to escape when El turned.

She smiled, "I was waiting."

Dirk grabbed her arm and headed into the lunch hall. "I was making sure we had some privacy." As the two moved in line to get their food, El was listening and looking around. She noticed the elves had shooed away some people who were trying to sit in the corner where Dirk had sat with the princess yesterday.

"I see you have made some new friends," she said nodding to the corner table.

"A needed evil," he said jokingly. She laughed. She'd always loved Dirk's humor. "I just wanted to make sure we had the privacy to have this talk."

"Does it involve her?" El asked.

"It'll all be clear after we speak but to answer your question, yes, Natia is very much involved." El just gave a look and asked Ms. Heloise for today's soup when they finally arrived at the front of the line. Dirk did the same and they walked to the table in the corner. Anastasia waved and smiled at Dirk when he and El walked by. He reciprocated and this time, Kal said hello as well. El smiled at them. It seemed today instead of Natia and Dirk, everyone was staring at El and Dirk. She felt a little uncomfortable, so she lowered her head and walked a little faster.

Dirk nodded a thank you to Natia who sat with her friends beside the table they had cleared out for Dirk. Sirien scowled again and turned away. Dirk could have sworn he heard him complaining to Natia again, but he quieted down really quick. Dirk smiled. Natia must have shut him down again.

Dirk began with telling El what happened the day he found a dying phoenix at Mt. Blazire. He also told her about Tab so there wouldn't be any secrets. She sat there and listened to the whole story without interrupting. Dirk hoped he told her quietly enough so that no one else could hear because he didn't hold back anything. He had gotten to the part where they were going to confront Kira and the general when they noticed kids start getting up to throw their trash away.

"So, that's about all I can tell you until after class this afternoon."

El was dumbstruck. "I don't know what to say." El put her hand on his arm.

"Well, that's only the beginning. I'll meet you after class and we can talk before and at dinner."

"Okay, let's meet in my classroom. I'll make Tab stay behind and tell Wizard Quentin we're going to do some individual practice. She knows Tab is slow, so she won't mind me helping him," El said as they walked out the door.

Moira walked by snickering. "Dirk can I sit at your special table tomorrow?" She laughed as she and her friends walked by. Dirk smiled at Moira.

"What was that?" El asked.

"That's Moira. She's in detention with us. She has a different sense of humor. I like her but Tab thinks she's weird."

"Oh, ok. I'll see you after class." She hugged him and took off to catch up with Vira and Nira.

Natia was waiting on Dirk by their classroom door. "How did it go?"

"I got about halfway through the story so we're meeting after class, so I can finish telling her. Thanks, I appreciate you helping me with the table."

Natia smiled and put her hand on his chest. Dirk's heart started racing. Natia whispered in his ear. "Anything for you, Dirk." She pulled away and Dirk saw flames ripple in her eyes as she turned and disappeared into the classroom.

Dirk was flustered. He couldn't tell what Natia was trying to do to him. She was sending his body into territories it had never been before. His heart felt like it was going to jump out of his chest. His vision blurred. He shook his head to try and clear the clouds away. He took some deep breaths to relax. After his heartbeat seemed to come back to normal and his vision had cleared, he went into the classroom. He was in a daze for the rest of the afternoon. It went by so fast that he didn't even remember most of it.

"Are you just going to sit there?" Natia asked as she leaned close and squeezed his leg under the table.

With her touch, Dirk finally felt the haze lift from his mind. "Huh?"

"I said, don't you have somewhere to be, or are you just going to sit there?"

Dirk realized class was over. "Yeah you're right, thanks." He got up and headed to the door, extremely confused. He barely remembered walking into class after Natia had whispered in his ear, and the next thing he knew, it was over. The kids in the hall were rushing past him. He opened the door to El's classroom and saw Tab and El waiting on him. He smiled and started to walk in.

"Mr. Storm!"

Dirk stopped at the door. Tab and El had heard Laseous so they got up and moved closer to Dirk. "Yes sir?"

"Mr. Storm, your grandfather is here and needs to speak with you. He is in with Wizard Nabas and wants you to come right away."

Dirk's heart started beating faster. Panic was starting to creep into his mind. *Was something wrong with his mother? That was the only reason the general would be here.* He thought. "Do you know what's wrong?"

Laseous just gave him a sour look. "Mr. Storm, I do not. All I know is that he has requested to speak with you, and Nabas has granted him permission even though it is against the rules. So, get going."

Dirk gave Tab his class books. "You two stay here. Somethings wrong. The general is up in Nabas's office waiting on me. I'll come back after I talk to him and let you know what is going on." Tab squeezed his shoulder. Dirk looked at El. I am sorry." She nodded.

"Tab can pick up where I left off. Just start at the barn with our friend before the confrontation with Kira and the general."

"Don't worry. I'll tell her everything. You better get going." Dirk took off to the headmaster's office.

Dirk knew where the office was, but he had never been there before. He walked past Laseous's office where he and Tab had detention every night. He stopped in front of an old mahogany door. There was a golden nameplate on the door that said, *Wizard Tobias Nabas, Headmaster* carved in intricate letters. Dirk knocked.

"Come in," a calm deep voice said from the other side of the door. Dirk entered closing it behind him. The office was filled with books and parchments of all types. The walls, with the exception of the one he was closest to, were covered in floor-to-ceiling bookshelves. Parchments were scattered on every flat surface, including several small desks that were spread throughout the room. The headmaster's main desk was a huge wooden mahogany desk with small ornate carvings of trees and animals all over the front and sides. There were two very comfortable plush chairs in front of his desk. Nabas, wearing his crimson robe, sat leaning back in a high back chair that looked like it was made for a king with his hands interlocked in front of him.

There, sitting in the one closest to the bookshelves, was the general. He was dressed in his uniform. Now that he was once again active in the king's service, he wore it almost all the time.

"Ah Dirk," Nabas said, motioning to the empty chair.

"Dirk." The General didn't smile. He just nodded.

"Grandfather," Dirk said and sat down. Dirk knew how to act in public around the general. It had been embedded in him since he could walk. At home, things were different, but, in public, Dirk was the respectful and well-mannered grandson. He looked at the general, but it was Nabas who spoke first.

"Dirk, I know you've only been here a few days and we usually like to keep the first-years from any contact with their family for at least two weeks." Dirk nodded. "Good, so since your grandfather and I are who we are, I have the ability to change that if something urgent comes up. Now normally, even though he is over the king's army, I still might have denied his request. Since the king gave him permission, I see that I cannot deny him this meeting." Nabas winked at him and smiled. "I will leave you two to talk." Nabas got up to leave. "Durkon, you still remember how to get out?"

The general nodded and got up to meet Nabas at the door. "Thanks, Tobias. You know I wouldn't be here unless it wasn't important," He shook Nabas's hand."

Nabas looked at Dirk and then at the general. "He is the spitting image of Diron," Nabas said, opening the door.

"That he is," the General said, smiling. "In more ways than one."

Nabas stopped and raised an eyebrow at the general. The general nodded. Nabas took one more look at Dirk before leaving "Well, if that is the case, I'm sure we'll get to know each other very well." He laughed and closed the door behind him.

"Grandfather what in the hells is going on?"

The general put a finger to his lips. He walked to the door, put his hand on it, and leaned forward a little, closing his eyes and mumbling some words. A red glow formed around his hand. Dirk noticed a golden bracelet with every color gem set in it on the generals wrist. The general nodded, satisfied that what he had done had worked. He then sat down across from Dirk. Dirk was amazed at what had happened and just gave his grandfather a questioning look.

"That was a shield I put up so no prying ears could listen to our conversation. You know whose classroom is right beside this office."

"More than I want to, actually."

The general looked at his grandson for a second. "Laseous and our family have never gotten along. It's a long story, one I will share with you at a later time, but I would advise you to stay clear of him as much as possible."

Dirk really didn't want to tell his grandfather how hard that would be, given their stellar track record so far, so he simply nodded. "Why are you here?"

The general walked to the window opening it halfway. Aarya flew in and landed on Dirk's arm. She trilled, rubbing her head on his arm. He patted her head, receiving a light spark. Any fogginess in his head from Natia's touch that afternoon was washed away. At that moment, it dawned on him that Natia had done something to him. His eyes flared to life, causing Aarya to trill. Anger, bordering on hate, rushed through him. *I'll deal with her later.*

The general noticed Dirk's eyes. "What's the matter, son? By the look on your face, you seem like you're ready to explode."

Dirk took a calming breath, realizing what his anger was doing to him. He closed his eyes and laughed. "Elven princesses."

The general laughed with a knowing smile. "They can be manipulative. I know. I've had to live with your mother for years."

Dirk laughed. "It's nothing. I'll work it out. So, what brings you and Aarya here?"

"Aarya disappeared for a few days. Which in itself is normal for the phoenix. This morning she showed back up around breakfast. Kira could sense something was bothering her. She kept trying to show your mother images that she couldn't understand. Kira finally recognized an image of Linc and a ship battle. This bothered her so much that she sent for me. When I got there, she explained some of the images to me. I tried to make sense of the images for several hours without much success. I, like your mother, don't have the bond with her like we did with Arial. Finally, I got an image of you running towards what I could only assume was something dangerous and Linc was motioning you on. I decided I needed to get her and you together so we could find out what was going on."

The general stopped and looked at Aarya. She trilled, shaking her head and immediately began to communicate with Dirk. He spoke as she relayed the images. He was smiling at the first image. "She has bonded with Linc,"

The general just nodded. "Interesting, but that makes sense. Your dad believed that linking several people with different powers would strengthen his chances of defeating Zolun."

"I know," Dirk said. The general raised a questioning eyebrow. "I'll explain later. A whole lot has happened in two days, but I promise I'll fill you in. She's saying that Linc was being followed. That the ship was bad, and it meant harm to Linc. She made Linc aware of it. Linc gave her a plan that when the ship started to attack, she had to cause a distraction. Genius!"

"What?"

"Linc told her to fly as fast as she could in a circle about half a league in front of his ship ten feet above the water. The heat from her flying so fast repetitively would cause a fog to form and engulf his ship so that when the other one attacked, he could disappear."

His grandfather smiled with pride. "Brilliant tactical move."

"You know Linc, always planning and scheming."

"Well, something must have gone wrong if she's here."

"Wait a minute, she's changing images now. She's showing me a small blonde girl tied to a chair. Now she's being led to a ship at the docks. Wait! You're going too fast," he told Aarya.

"What is it?" the general asked, leaning forward in his seat. Dirk rubbed his head for a moment. "What is it, son?"

Dirk took a deep breath. "The little girl is one of the crewmen's daughter on Linc's ship. Jerle, I believe. Ram is involved. He's using her to force Jerle to spy on Linc. Corky, one of the older crewmen Linc hired, was keeping an eye on him because he was acting suspicious from the start. They caught him and he explained to Linc why he was doing it. So Linc sent Aarya to investigate. She found out it was the truth and then she came to inform me about what was going on. I guess so we could save the girl and her mother."

The general rubbed his chin thoughtfully. "What happened to Linc?"

"Aarya doesn't know yet. Linc sent her away as soon as the fog set in. He wanted us to know as soon as we could." Dirk paused. 'I'm not sure how this bond thing works yet. I did sense Linc was in danger, but it didn't feel urgent. I assumed it was just worry, but now that he's bonded, I'll have to figure out how to communicate with him. That is, if he's ok."

The general stood up and patted Dirk on the shoulder. "I'm sure he's fine. Lincoln is a very bright young man. He's streetwise, which makes him that much more cunning. I suggest you send Aarya to find out for sure and then she can communicate back to you."

Dirk nodded. "Well, when do we go?"

The general looked at Dirk. "You're not going anywhere, young man. I'll take care of Ram and hopefully rescue the little girl. I have more than enough soldiers to do the job. Besides, I've caused enough trouble coming to see you. Laseous would blow a blood vessel if he knew you left the school," the general said, laughing. Dirk wanted to protest, but he knew he would lose.

"She's growing fast," Dirk said, stroking Aarya's back.

"She's almost fully grown already," the general said, scratching her neck. "Well, it's almost dinner and you need to get back. I have a raid to quickly plan and a young girl to rescue. I will send you word through Giles of the outcome. He may have to be vague but I'm sure you'll understand his meaning."

Dirk gazed at Aarya. "You did a great job." He said patting her head. *You help the general with getting the little girl back.* He communicated through their bond. She trilled in understanding and took flight. The general shook Dirk's hand and then hugged him. Dirk hugged him back. "Be careful, Grandfather, and tell Mom I'm ok."

"I will." The general went to the door and released the shield. He smiled and walked out with Dirk.

They separated at the hall that led to the entrance of the school. The general gave Dirk a nod and headed for the Door. Dirk just stood in awe, watching his grandfather walk away. He didn't realize until that moment how much he admired his grandfather. The grace and confidence he walked with was breath taking. All of the kids that he passed just stared at him in admiration. That gave Dirk a strong sense of pride. As the general vanished out the door, Dirk headed to the classroom where he had left El and Tab.

When Dirk got to the classroom, El and Tab were in an embrace. Not like lovers, but it was very affectionate. Dirk coughed. It startled them out of the hug. El had tears in her eyes. She pulled away from Tab and ran to Dirk. She pulled him into a hug. "I am so sorry, Dirk. If I had known I would've never behaved like a bitch."

"That's okay El. I should have told you sooner."

"No, that is a big burden. On both of you." She reached with a hand towards Tab and pulled him into the hug. They stood there until Mother El was satisfied she had shown them that she was sorry. El released them and stared at their eyes. She gasped when she realized their eyes were definitely different now. "I should have noticed the change. But I was so concerned that you were throwing me to the side for the princess. I was jealous. I mean it's always been us," El said, motioning to the boys.

"It's still us El. Don't you ever forget it,' Dirk said.

"So Natia is a part of this?"

Dirk nodded filling in any gaps that Tab might have left out. El just listened. Then Dirk told them why he was called to Nabas office.

"What?" Tab said.

Dirk nodded. "Remember the other night when we both felt something about Linc?"

"Aarya bonded with him like we thought." Tab smiled. El frowned.

"What's wrong, El?"

El, like she usually did when she wanted something, looked at the ground "Nothing."

"I know you. What is it?" Dirk already knew why she was pouting. She looked up and before she could say it, Dirk said, "On our first day off, I'll introduce you to Aarya."

El lit up like the sun. "If you insist."

"Well if you don't want..."

El punched Tab in the arm.

"Ow, El!" Tab rubbed his arm and smiled at Dirk, who was laughing.

"Seriously, though, I hope Linc is ok," El said as they headed to the hall after the dinner bell had sounded.

Dirk looked at her. "I think he is. Surely since we're bonded, we would have felt something."

"Surely," Tab agreed.

After they got their food, they sat with their usual crowd with the exception of a newcomer. "Hi Jacko," Dirk said to the new member of their group.

"Glad you finally came to your senses and joined us," Tab said to Jacko, pushing Gil over, so he could sit by El.

"Watch it," Gil pretended to be hurt. Tab just smiled. They both laughed and started eating. Gil knew how Tab felt about El.

"So, Gil, how's your training going?" Dirk asked.

"Much better day than the first." Gil smiled.

"Yeah, he didn't blow the table over today!" Vira laughed. The group had learned fast that Vira was very loud. El had told them earlier that she was loud because she was really nervous about being accepted, since she and Nira came from Aarkas.

Gil said, "We're not all as talented as Vira."

She blushed for the first time since he had met her. Phil, who everyone knew was taken with her said "Yeah, Vira, all I hear from the others is how you and your sister are probably better than the second-years."

Vira started twirling her hair and smiled at Phil. "Thanks, but I'm sure they really don't say that," she said in a much quieter voice.

"I swear, Vira," Phil said, crossing his hand over his heart. She blushed and looked to Nira, who was rolling her eyes. Dusty, who was sitting beside Nira, smiled. They were both quiet. It amazed Dirk how the group he was sitting with was already seeming to pair up.

Volar, feeling a little out of place, changed the subject. "Dirk, did I see thy grandfather walking down the hall earlier?"

"No, I didn't see him. Must have been here on the king's business."

Everyone at the table stared at Dirk, who shrugged his shoulders and started eating his beef sandwich. Volar cocked an eyebrow and dug into his as well. That was the cue for everyone else to drop the subject. The original members of the Pack knew when Dirk wasn't being honest, but they knew to leave it alone. The rest of dinner, Dirk just took in each of the groups conversations that were all going on at the same time. Dinner flew by.

Soon, it was time for Tab and him to go to detention. They told everyone they would see them later. Gil and Jacko started back for the dorms, both in deep conversation about religion. Dirk smiled. He kind of felt bad about not telling Gil about everything, but he needed the information flow to slow down until he could get a grasp on what was going on. He told Tab how he felt about it and they agreed that telling Gil could wait.

"After we get a handle on the training, we can bring him into it more prepared," Tab said as they turned the corner, heading to their favorite classroom.

When they got to the door, there was a note stuck to it. Dirk read it aloud. *Everyone in detention report straight to Hanks tonight. Wizard Laseous.* "That jackass could have told us sooner. We wouldn't have had to leave the hall."

Tab smiled. "Yeah but we don't have to see him tonight."

Dirk smiled back. "You're right, let's go."

They passed Moira and the boys from detention and informed them about the note. Moira pumped her fist in the air. "Yes!" She turned to follow Dirk and Tab. The older boys always seemed to have a sullen look about them. They didn't say anything, and just followed.

That night, they got back to the dorms early since they didn't have to listen to an hour of Laseous berating them.

When Dirk and Tab entered the dorm, Hilda was walking around and helping the boys with their night studies if they needed it. Volar and Gil were on one of the couches discussing the finer arts of earth magic. Phil, Dusty, and Jacko had their heads down, writing on parchment while occasionally flipping pages from a book they shared. Brock and his two friends were at another table doing something similar.

Brock looked up at Dirk as he walked by but didn't say any of his normal taunts. He just went back to his homework. The elves just looked at Dirk without emotion. Sirien just gave him his normal sneer and a nod.

"That elf has issues," Tab said, noticing the way Sirien looked at Dirk.

"His problem, I think, is he doesn't know what is going on with Natia. He is some kind of guard here to keep watch over her." They both laughed at that thought. Dirk knew she didn't need any protection.

Now that the day was coming to an end, Dirk was wishing he could remember his afternoon and what went on after Natia's touch. The more he thought about Natia, the madder he became. "I don't know if I can trust her now since she did that to me," Dirk said after he explained to Tab what had happened. He shared his concern with Tab about missing the whole class. Tab assured him he would get by, that all he had to do was ask Jacko.

Dirk slapped his palm to his forehead. "Why didn't I think of that?"

"That's why you got me," Tab said, punching him in the arm and heading to get the things he needed to do his work. Dirk went to the table where Jacko was and pulled up a chair. "Jacko."

Jacko looked up at Dirk. He leaned closer to Jacko. He definitely didn't want Brock to hear what he was going to ask Jacko. "Jacko, I can't seem to find my notes from class. I think I left them in detention. Can I borrow yours to copy them?"

"Sure," Jacko said with a smile and slid the notes in front of Dirk. Dirk sighed with relief, quickly copied the notes down, and thanked Jacko. After that he grabbed the only free table, nodded to Volar and Gil, and sat down. He looked over the notes then got up to get the necessary books. Tab soon joined him and started doing his work.

An hour and a half later, Hilda was telling the boys to hurry up and get their work finished because it was time for bed. Dirk finished his report, rolled up his parchment, and put his books back. As he and Tab were saying good night, Hilda slipped him a note. She nodded and headed to her room.

"What's it say?" Tab asked.

Dirk read the letter to him. "Meet in the room at the bottom of the stairs. I'll leave the door unlocked. Half an hour after bedtime." They looked at each other.

"Isn't that the door marked private?" Tab asked.

He remembered Nabas warning him about those doors. "Yes, it is. I guess it's time to find out what's down there. See you in thirty minutes," Dirk said as they both headed to their rooms.

After Volar and Phil were both snoring as usual, Dirk got up, put on his tunic and pants, and slipped out of the room. Tab was waiting by the door. "Any problems?" Dirk asked.

"Gil wouldn't go to sleep. He kept on about Volar and his knowledge of earth magic. He finally realized I wasn't paying attention and went to sleep."

Dirk smiled. He knew how Gil loved earth magic and its direct ties to the gods.

They slipped out of the room and headed down the stairs until they got to the door. Dirk reached for the handle and then pulled his hand back.

"What's wrong?" Tab asked.

"Just remembering Master Nabas's warning."

"Since we were invited, we should be allowed to enter."

Dirk nodded and slowly grabbed the handle. As soon as he touched it, he started shaking uncontrollably side to side violently.

"Oh, my gods! Dirk what do I do? Tab looked around frantically for a solution. He didn't see any other way and started to push Dirk with his shoulder. As Tab lunged, Dirk stepped back, and Tab slammed into the wall. Dirk started laughing as Tab rubbed his shoulder and pushed Dirk.

"You *asshole!* I thought you were being shocked!"

Dirk regained his composure and straightened up. "Sorry, I just had to. You should have seen the look on your face."

"Real funny," Tab said laughing. "I will get you back!" He then opened the door himself and headed into the mysterious room with Dirk behind him. The door opened into a small foyer. There were two doors, one to the left and one straight ahead. The door straight ahead was open, so the boys went through it. Another set of stairs led down. The round lights on the wall were spaced evenly apart.

After several flights of stairs, it opened up into a well-lit room about the same size as the dorms common room. Bookshelves lined the walls. Dirk surveyed the room slowly.

Several tables and chairs were spread throughout the room with a few couches. Light orbs were on all the walls. There was a big round table in the center of the room with enough chairs around it for twelve people. Hilda and Tilda were seated at the table, facing each other. His eyes flared to life when he saw El was sitting between them, facing Natia. Dirk had to close his eyes and search for the calm. He was still very upset with Natia.

The women all turned as the boys walked in. Dirk and Tab were instructed to sit by El and Natia. Of course, Tab went straight to El, leaving Dirk the option of sitting by Natia. He still couldn't remember much about that afternoon class, so he was determined to get answers now, especially since he could confront her in front of Hilda and Tilda. He sat beside her with a look of determination on his face.

Tilda nodded after everyone was seated. Dirk watched as Hilda got up to close and shield the door. He noticed she had a bracelet, similar to his grandfather's on her wrist. It sparkled with light when she put her hand on the door. Nodding to Tilda, she sat back down.

Tilda began. "We have decided that, since we have sensed things are starting to change, we need to work with all of you at the same time. Hilda and I can sense that the four of you will play the biggest role in the events that are yet to come. You four need to be the most prepared to train the others as they are added to your group. El, I know you haven't been bonded yet, but you can still learn what we are teaching because of your closeness to Dirk and Tab. Once you're bonded, it will make things much easier for you."

She looked around at each of the kids to make sure they were listening and that she had their undivided attention. When she got to Dirk, she saw that his face was starting to turn a shade of scarlet and his eyes were rippling with flames. Everyone at the table had noticed.

"Dirk, remember we can sense when something is wrong. Spit it out!" Hilda demanded. His closeness to Natia just made Dirk angrier and angrier. He could feel that his body temperature was rising by the second. Tab, starting to feel the anger from the bond, tensed up. Dirk closed his eyes and took a deep breath, and then looked around the room. He slammed his fist on the table so hard that Tilda, Hilda and El jumped back a little. But Natia didn't even flinch.

"There are some things I want to say first," he said, looking around the table at each of them until his eyes settled on Natia. Flames rippled across his eyes. When he locked gazes with her, he noticed that her eyes were having the same effect. "I feel that for this endeavor to be successful, we all need to be able to trust each other with our lives," Dirk didn't take his eyes off Natia. "If I'm gonna trust my life to someone, that means I have to trust my family's life to that person as well. Playing games with each other doesn't build trust. Especially with me. My family is the most important thing in the world to me." Dirk pointed to Tab and El. "And that right there is my family." He was getting angrier and angrier as he spoke. "That game or trick you played on me this afternoon was unacceptable. I can't remember a thing about class this afternoon after whatever it is you did to me. I want to know, princess! Why should I trust you?"

Heat was literally coming off of his body. Natia jumped up and got so close to Dirk that their noses were touching. The intensity that Dirk was exuding was coming off of her as well. Tab and El started to get up and intervene, but Hilda and Tilda both put up hands to stop them. They both sat back down and watched the scene unfold. El put her hand over her mouth. She was amazed but horrified at the same time. Tab's body was producing heat in response to Dirk's anger.

El realized this and put her hand on his arm. Tab turned to look at her. When he saw her face, his body reacted immediately, and his core temperature started to cool. The flames in his eyes that had been raging slowly subsided. He took a deep breath and let it out. He smiled at her, put his free hand over hers, and squeezed. "Thanks," he said affectionately.

She smiled back. "You're welcome." They both turned back and watched Dirk and Natia. Tilda smiled at Hilda and nodded, confirming something they had discussed earlier.

Natia released waves of heat with each breath. *I'm ready to show this farm boy who I am*, she thought to herself. Who was he to say anything about trust? The secrets he was still keeping weren't even close to what she was keeping from him. She had had enough when she jumped up to face him.

"You want to talk about trust, do you?" Natia yelled back. "What about you? The secrets you're still keeping are positively *miniscule* in comparison to any secrets that I might be keeping. And the games, well, what other way was I going to get you to open up to me? Yes, I messed with your head this afternoon, but that was only to make you curious and want to talk more. All I did was cloud your senses temporarily. Just enough that you would still be coherent but not remember everything so that you would be forced to talk with me!" Natia's breath came in shallow gasps.

Dirk's anger was reaching a boiling point. "What the hells do you mean 'secrets'? I've answered your questions so far. I haven't kept anything from you. I didn't grow up like you, training for this. Hells, I don't even want anything to do with it! I just really want to run away and never look back! Secrets, *humph!* I haven't kept anything from you that you didn't need to know!" Dirk screamed.

Natia was tired of Dirk's lies. "What about him?" she shouted, pointing at Tab, catching both Dirk and Tab off-guard. Dirk, easing up, looked to Tab, then to Hilda and Tilda. Both ladies knew what his questioning look meant. They both shook their head.

He turned to face Natia. Some of the anger he had a second ago dissipated. "You think I don't know? No one told me anything. Remember how I told you the connection didn't feel right? I simply figured it out. It really was the only answer. Every time I'm around him, I get a similar feeling inside like I do when I'm around you, nowhere near as strong though.

"I know. I feel the bond Dirk. And it's not from Aarya, it's from Arial. Which means only one thing!" Natia looked around and had everyone's attention. "That he is Chosen as well somehow." The anger slowly disappeared from her voice.

Dirk's shoulders dropped. The flames in his eyes diminished to small embers. He looked at Tab, then to Hilda and Tilda. He still felt he really didn't have to tell Natia anything he didn't want to, but, deep inside his mind he felt the connection and Aarya's urging. He took a deep breath and released it slowly.

Decision made; Dirk spoke in a calmer voice. "Look, part of me feels I don't owe you anything." Before Natia could respond, he continued. "Like I said, I didn't know growing up about this destiny that had been laid out for me. I wanted, we wanted," he said pointing to Tab, "to be traders and merchants until a few days ago. I still want that one day but with every day that goes by, I see that dream slowly slipping away. I have always been loyal to my family, and that's the reason I probably will never be able to fulfill that dream I've had for many years. So, if you will forgive me for not wanting you, someone I just met, to know every secret I have." Dirk sat back down.

Natia somewhat relieved that Dirk finally seemed to be really opening up to her, sat down and put a hand on his shoulder. He tensed a little but didn't pull away. "Dirk," she said in that voice that melted his insides. "I, too, if you look at it, didn't have a choice either. I was just lucky enough to be raised knowing what my destiny was. Believe me, it really hasn't been easier knowing. I was never a child. I never got to play with other elven children, other than Tara and Oriana. My whole life has been a training lesson for me to basically save the world or die," Natia said in the first sign of emotion in her voice that Dirk had ever heard.

Concluding that they were both in the same boat, he looked into her eyes. There was a tear rolling down her right cheek. He slowly wiped it away. The touch sent a brief wave of fear for her to his core. He leaned closer to Natia. Their eyes locked. He kissed her lightly on the cheek, feeling a deeper connection to her. Deeper than he would have admitted an hour ago.

"I'm sorry," he whispered. "I promise I won't ever keep anything from you again." He pulled back a few inches. She was transfixed on his eyes and felt the bond between them strengthen. It almost took her breath away. She could feel and see his thoughts. Not only his. She looked to Tab, who was smiling and already looking at her. She nodded.

He nodded back and put his hand over his heart. She turned back and realized that she and Dirk were still inches away from each other. "I will never keep anything from you either. I am sorry for what I did to you today. I'll never do anything like that again, to any of you."

He smiled and realized everyone in the room was watching the two of them. He released her shoulders, realizing that he had unintentionally grabbed them when he had leaned closer to her. They both sat up. Anxiety filled Dirk.

"Incoming!" was the only thing Dirk and Tab could get out at the same time before the door shuttered and then exploded inward towards them. Everyone covered their heads just in time. Hilda, El, and Tab caught the bulk of the shattered wood. Dirk had shielded Natia with his body, but she still had to pick small pieces of the door off of her. Tilda, who had been shielded by the other three, brushed the few toothpick-sized pieces off of her. She stood up in a defensive position, forming a protective shield around the table.

"A little late for that, sister," Hilda said to her, laughing and pointing at Dirk. Tilda turned and gasped. There sitting on Dirk's shoulder was the second most beautiful phoenix she had ever seen.

"Sorry, everyone. I sensed her getting closer. I think she was worried because I was so upset," Dirk said, petting Aarya on the head.

"You think?" El said. They all laughed.

"Everyone, this is Aarya," Dirk said, introducing her to the ones who hadn't met her. El and the twins had already gotten up and were coming around to see her.

After Hilda introduced herself to Aarya, Dirk watched as she walked over to the exploded door and made a swirling motion with her hand, causing the pieces to gather into a pile. She then made a pushing motion with her hand like a broom and all of the debris was swept into the corner.

"I'll be right back," she said before heading up the stairs. Dirk turned back to the table and saw Aarya nudge Tilda as she rubbed her neck.

Dirk stared at her in shock. "There was no spark."

Tilda laughed. "You were expecting her to bond with me?"

"Yes. I thought that's how it worked."

"Unfortunately since Hilda and I bonded with Arial, we can't be bonded with Aarya. At least that's what I sense from Aarya. We still have a small connection from Arial that allows us to communicate with her, but that's it."

Aarya nodded her head and trilled.

"That makes sense," Dirk replied watching Aarya.

"Well what about Dirk and Natia?" El asked curious by Tilda's response.

"That's different because Dirk and Natia received the power transfer of the Chosen and protector from Arial, not just the bond." Tilda explained.

"I see," El nodded.

"That makes sense," Tab said, rubbing Aarya's neck.

Dirk, Tab, and Linc. Flashed into Dirk's and Tab's minds. Then Natia and El flashed there with Aarya on their shoulder.

"It's time." Dirk said with Tab agreeing.

Aarya nodded her approval and glided from Dirk's shoulder to the table in front of Natia. Natia smiled and bowed her head. She reached out and caressed Aarya's head. There was a spark from the touch and the bond was made. Natia's breathing deepened as she closed her eyes for a few minutes. Tears were leaking from her eyes. Dirk and Tab both took deep breaths and closed their eyes. The emotions were overwhelming.

Tab gripped El's shoulder to keep from falling over. El steadied him. Dirk grabbed Natia's shoulder at the same time. Natia's life passed before Dirk and Tab's eyes while, at the same time Natia was seeing everything the boys, including Linc, had been through in their lives, including the death of Arial and the birth of Aarya. She now felt the deep connection to the pack that Dirk felt.

When the transfer was over, Natia opened her glistening eyes. She then opened her hand, and inside was a single feather. She looked at Tab and El and smiled. They smiled, understanding. Turning to look at Dirk, she took in those emerald, green eyes with a hint of crimson in them. He was staring at her. The bond between them was different from her and Tab. The connection between them was deeper. It was like the sun shining light on a new day, clearing away the morning fog. The thrill of life exploding all around you on a spring day. She saw Dirk differently now. He was the reason she was feeling all of these sensations. His true nature had been shown to her and it took her breath away. He nodded in understanding.

She smiled and placed a hand on his face. Dirk felt a longing for her that made him tremble. Goosebumps had incased his entire body. A passion to protect her at all cost stirred within him. He gazed into her amber eyes, lost in their flames. His face was very close to hers. El cleared her throat. Dirk snapped out of the trance at the sound and shook his head to clear his thoughts.

"Well?" El asked, looking at Dirk. He looked at her and smiled. Aarya trilled. Dirk stood up and motioned with his hand towards the chair. El came over and sat down beside Natia, staring at the beautiful phoenix. She reached out to Aarya. The phoenix leaned closer and nudged El's outstretched palm. The spark was bigger.

Immediately, everyone, except Tilda, closed their eyes. The transfer of the bond wasn't as intense as Natia's but was still overwhelming.

Hilda came downstairs with a wooden door floating behind her on an invisible cloud. She directed it in place then magically secured the hinges. She turned just in time to see the bond completed. The four friends were all in an embrace. She smiled, remembering that feeling. Walking up, she put a hand on her sister's shoulder. Aarya flew up, landed on Tilda's shoulder, and nudged Hilda's hand. She shared with them Arial's last moments and the deep love that she had for them. Flashes of Arial's memories of them passed between them as well as the love she had for them and the happiness they had shared. Tilda and Hilda leaned their heads together and cried for a minute. After their grief subsided, they both mentally thanked her.

After a few minutes, the twins pulled apart. Hilda then chastised Tab and Dirk for not locking the upstairs door, but she was secretly thankful they hadn't or Aarya would have broken two doors. She made them promise to lock it from now on.

"Hilda, where does that other door lead to?" El asked to get her attention off of the boys as she was returning to her seat.

The twins looked at each other, and then Tilda replied. "Tonight is a night of revelations and sharing, but you four are not ready for that yet. And please do not push the matter. You will find out when the time is right." Tilda stared at them. They all agreed.

"El, what's wrong?"

"Nothing," she replied quickly. Tab could sense some distress. El looked at Natia in silent thought.

"What was that?" Dirk asked, sensing thoughts between to the two girls.

"Hilda," Natia began, "I know it's late, but I think the first thing we need to do is learn how to keep the thoughts that we want to keep private blocked." Natia stared at the twins and they seemed to understand. Dirk, sensing weird feelings from the girls, caught on and agreed.

Clueless, Tab said, "Huh?"

"You remember that discussion we had right after we bonded about privacy?"

Tab looked at Dirk quizzically, "Oh yes, I agree." The twins wanted to get the kids to bed but taught them the word and what to focus on to keep their thoughts private. Dirk listened as Hilda told them that the magical word was *privacious*. The word to unblock their thoughts was *unprivacious*.

"That's kind of simple, isn't it?" Dirk asked the twins.

"Not all magic is hard, Dirk, especially with a little help," Hilda answered, handing each of them a silver bracelet that had four thumbnail-sized gems in it. Dirk rolled it around in his hand, looking it over. There was a yellow, red, blue, and green gem set in it. "I want you to wear these under your sleeves. Keep them hidden from anyone not in the group."

The kids all immediately put them on. The gems flared to life as soon as the clasp was closed. "Now that you have put them on, no one else can use them. They are attuned to your core only," Tilda told them.

"I've seen my grandfather wear one of these. He has one," Dirk said to no one in particular.

"What do they do?" El asked.

"The bracelet acts as a power boost to your natural powers you have already in your core. Just be careful with these. I stress not to let anyone outside the group see these. If you need to use them, just focus on the bracelet and your core. The bracelet's magic can kind of sense the need," Hilda explained. "Now, it's late. Tomorrow is a big day. The reason must be clear, but I think you all understand why I wanted to meet you down here tonight. You all needed what happened here. There is a war coming sooner rather than later and you need to be ready when the time comes, especially when you are called upon."

"Thank you," Dirk said to the twins. "If you had not brought us all together tonight, I don't think I would have ever let Natia close." Dirk touched her shoulder. Natia smiled and agreed.

"Now, off you go. We will start doing some practicing and studying our book every other night. We will meet down here at the same time each night. Don't forget to lock the door when you come through from now on.

I'll teach you how to release the shield and set it back up the next time we meet."

Natia and El agreed and said goodbye to Aarya, leaving arm-in-arm like best friends.

"Tab, you go on. I've got to get Dirk to take Aarya up to the top floor and release her. We don't need any other doors being broken," Hilda laughed.

Tab laughed as well, and after caressing Aarya's neck, said goodnight and went up to the stairs. After he left, Dirk said *"Privacious!"* He felt the expected tingle that affirmed the magic had worked. Hilda and Tilda looked at him questioningly. Dirk walked straight to the twins and he hugged Tilda in a tight embrace and then turning to Hilda, he hugged her.

"I don't know if it's the bond or my emotions are getting the best of me tonight, but I need you to know that I love you two and feel very thankful that my father had friends like you. Family is what we are, family is what we will always be," Dirk said, tears streaming down his face.

The twins pulled him back into a hug, causing Aarya to leap onto the table. "Dirk, we love you as well, just like we did and still do your father. We will always be here for you, even after all of this is over. You are so much like your father. It makes our hearts ache from missing him, but also happy because knowing that we can help you eases the pain a little," Hilda said. Tilda agreed.

"Thanks, I'm gonna hold you to that," Dirk said, easing back. He kissed them each on the cheek. Tilda smiled at Dirk, wiping away her tears and then said goodnight and left. Hilda smiled and hugged him one more time. She kissed his cheek.

"I will get access panels put in for Aarya. She will have easier access then to our meetings."

"I would like that very much. Thank you." Dirk squeezed her shoulders in appreciation.

Aarya landed on his shoulder and nestled her head next to Hilda's face, causing her to smile. Dirk squeezed her hand and, after saying 'unprivacious', went upstairs with Hilda. Hilda showed him how to activate and deactivate the shield on the door. With that accomplished, they went up the stairs together. When they reached their room floor, he left her at the door after she showed him how to lock and unlock the door to the dorms. He told her goodnight and that he would lock it when he came back down. She smiled then closed the door quietly.

Anastasia and The View

Dirk had Aarya on his shoulder when he came through the door to the roof. He took in the night view, looking around as he walked to the edge. It's beautiful up here, he thought. The fires from the city and even the countryside could be seen from up here.

Dirk wasn't paying attention to anything but the view when he walked to the edge of the roof. Aarya trilled and nudged him. "You be careful, and don't forget to help the general." Aarya nodded, then peered over his shoulder and took off with a flash. Dirk was startled by the abrupt way she took off and could barely see her flaming through the sky.

"Dirk," came a voice he knew he would never forget. Dirk looked over his shoulder and saw Anastasia walking toward him from out of the shadows. "You're up kind of late," Anastasia said as she leaned on the wall beside him.

"Well, I'm not alone." He smiled and leaned on the wall next to her.

"This is my favorite place in the whole school," she said, staring out at the scenery. Dirk knew something was wrong. He knew she just wanted to talk so he just stared at the same thing she was. Anastasia was wearing a crimson night tunic and pants. She pulled the shawl she was wearing tighter around her shoulders and leaned against Dirk. Dirk sensed she wasn't going to say what was wrong, so he simply asked her.

"What's wrong?"

"You remember when we were kids playing around the palace and we would watch the soldiers doing drills in the courtyard? We would march around, acting like them."

Dirk laughed. "Yes, I remember you ordering me around, telling me what to do. And I was a good soldier and did everything you told me too, even though your father or Grandfather would get on to us."

Anastasia laughed as well. "Yeah those were the days, but you know it was pretend back then, Dirk." She paused staring out over the city. "Tomorrow, my brother is taking the western division of soldiers south. The raids are getting worse, and King Cray is trying to extend his boundaries further north. My father is going to send him a message with a show of force."

"How do you know?"

She looked at Dirk, straightening up. "Thelon sent me word today. He told me he might not see me for a while and what he was heading out to do. He said the third-years might end up joining the campaign if it took too long, but I'm worried about all of this."

"The prince is smart, and he knows how to handle himself," Dirk said, trying to relieve her worries.

"Dirk, you don't know everything that's going on." She turned and leaned back on the wall.

Dirk knew it was late and he would pay for it tomorrow. He felt Natia start to worry through the new bond. He could tell now she could sense everything he did. *Listen, it's important.* He heard Natia in his head.

Do you know about this?

A little but listen, it's *really important.*

Dirk thought he might not be able to get used to this.

Just listen.

So, he did.

Anastasia leaned into him again and laid her head on his shoulder, "The Gore are beginning to gather again, north of Der-Tod, and there are rumors The Screel has been seen stalking the woods outside of Ker. You realize he hasn't been seen since...." Anastasia stopped, looking up at Dirk and seeing the look on his face. She put a hand on his chest. "Dirk, I'm sorry. I was so lost in my loathing that I didn't even think what that might mean to you before I said it."

Dirk touched her shoulder. He smiled, "Stas, its ok. That was a long time ago. Remember, I never met my father. I didn't even know what had happened to him until a few weeks ago. Mom and the general finally explained it to me. They said they didn't want me growing up with the memory of my father dying that way. It's ok really, don't you worry, just tell me what's wrong." Dirk looked into her eyes, hoping he hadn't said to much.

She looked at him for a moment trying see his eyes. He turned away quickly from her stare. She had seen what she had been looking for though and finally smiled and pulled away, looking towards the palace. "You know, I met your father before that mission. I was only two but, for some reason, I remember it like it was yesterday."

Dirk just looked at her. "You never told me that."

"After what happened, I didn't want to make you sad."

"Don't worry," Dirk said, looking towards the palace. "They will get what's coming to them."

She sighed. "At what cost?"

"Is there a cost that's too high to stop evil?" Dirk asked.

"You're right, but promise me this," she said and looked at him with that steel gaze Dirk had seen many times, usually when she was fighting, "that if something happens, you won't go gung-ho and do something stupid!"

He smiled, "Don't worry, Stas, you know me."

"That's what I'm afraid of." She gazed into his eyes trying to verify what she had seen earlier. The stars and the moons were high, lighting the roof up like early morning and he could see her face plainly. Dirk felt uneasy since she stared at him so long. He smiled at her and she finally relaxed. "It's late. Thanks for listening."

With those words, she turned and headed to go back into the school. She stopped before she opened the door and looked back at him. "You need to go to bed. Remember, the Chosen needs his rest."

Dirk's mouth fell open. She winked and hurried into the school. *Who the hell else knows?* Dirk thought, following her.

She is the King's daughter, Natia thought.

You know that's creepy, right?

Natia snickered in his head. *Yes, I agree but beneficial. Besides, she probably heard her father and the General talking in the past.*

You know I bet the whole royal family knows.

Mine does.

That makes sense.

Dirk closed and locked the dorm room door. *Good, no one is up. We'll talk about this tomorrow.* He snuck into his room. Volar and Phil were a chorus of snores. Dirk laughed to himself as he got into bed.

Goodnight Chosen.

He smiled. *Good night protector.*

For all the gods, will you two go to sleep? Tab thought back. Dirk had assumed that Natia was the only one awake.

Sorry, they both said in unison. Dirk lay his head on his pillow and, after several minutes, despite his thoughts racing, finally dozed off.

Down at the docks, twelve people were gathered in the shadows. The men and women both wore masks to cover their faces. They were watching Ram Stockton boarding a ship with one of his thugs-toting what looked like a small body on his shoulder. The general was among those standing in the shadows, watching the two board the ship.

After confirming what Aarya had told Dirk, he had given his team the go-ahead signal. Aarya, flying overhead as promised, was taking in the scene below. She watched as the general, dressed in his camouflage fatigues, followed his team who were walking silently through the streets towards their target. Soon, the sound of swords clashing, and muffled grunts could be heard echoing off the water.

Aarya could sense the general smiling. She knew that was a sound he hadn't heard in a long time. The outcome was not certain to the general, but he and his best unit was on it. Aarya, knowing everything about Durkon from Arial, didn't have a doubt in the outcome.

Disappointment and Rewards

Dirk had barely gotten out of bed when Hilda came in to personally make sure he got up. He went to the food hall with the rest of the first years and ate a quick breakfast. He would have sworn that he was dreaming until he found himself in front of Sergeant Giles, listening to him scream at everyone who was stretching the wrong way. That snapped Dirk out of his daze.

Soon, he and the group were all picking their packs up and heading for the training trail. Dirk, Tab, and El ran together, with Natia and the elves on their heels. Dirk could hear Natia in his thoughts, encouraging him. He smiled and picked up the pace. El brushed her shoulder against his. Dirk felt the spark and the jolt of energy the spark brought with it. She smiled at him. El now knew what Natia had done for her on the first day. Natia smiled as well. Dirk couldn't see her, but he felt it.

The run went the same as the day before. Volar came in last at the halfway point. He shared a nug bar with the Pack, Jacko included this time. When they made it back to the training area, everyone was bent over and breathing hard. Even the elves were pushed to their limits. Giles had started picking up the pace as promised. He walked around the group, telling them they were in the worst shape out of any of the first years he had ever seen.

"I swear those packs are heavier today!" Gil said beside Dirk.

"What's that, Mr. Jamous? The packs are feeling heavier, are they?" He smirked at the group. "That's probably because they are. Oh, didn't I mention that they would get heavier every day until they reached one hundred pounds?" Giles laughed. "I must have forgotten to tell you. Oh well get over it! There are surprises in war and battle. You must prepare for the unexpected." He laughed again. "Off you go. Class awaits!"

As he walked by Dirk, he stopped. Dirk looked at him. "Dirk, you like fishing?"

"Yes sergeant!" Dirk answered, wondering where this was going. He stood up with his hands over his head, taking deep breaths, looking at the sergeant and waiting for him to speak.

"You know, I used to go fishing with your grandfather back in the day.

We used to fish down by the old docks sometimes for the elusive Claire fish. I never thought there was one. I thought he was just spinning a yarn like he always liked to do back then. Then I got a message from him this morning. He said I wouldn't believe it. His note said that last night he decided to try and catch one again and damned if he didn't catch one down by the docks where we used to fish. A healthy, forty-pound one. He said it took an hour to reel it in, but he finally got it safely landed. Tell him I want to see it before he takes it home," Giles said, patting him on the back walking off. Tab, Natia, and El were standing by him listening. They all smiled at the news.

The general had saved Claire, Jerle's daughter. This gave Dirk a great sense of pride. He hadn't been there, but he was still a part of the successful mission.

Tab squeezed his shoulder. "Our first victory against evil."

Dirk squeezed Tab's shoulder. He smiled at Natia and El. "Our first in many to come." They all agreed.

Then they hurried off to get ready for class. With what Anastasia had told Dirk last night, he had been feeling depressed. Now with some good news, his spirits were lifted. He headed to class with a better attitude.

"Captain, we are coming up on debris!" Kelt yelled over his shoulder. Captain Sleigh and the crew walked up to the edge of the ship and peered into the water by Smugglers Turn. There was debris from a ship floating everywhere.

"I told you, idiot. You must have hit their powder." Sleigh glared at Matt. Matt, with his black eyes, just looked away.

Monk glared at Sleigh. "If you hadn't veered from the plan, this wouldn't have happened either!"

Sleigh just ignored him, looking at the wreckage. Looking at the two big rocks that made Smuggler's Turn possible, there was blood smeared on the one on the left. About three feet above the water was a bloody hand-print. Floating in the water below, pieces of a shirt clung to some floating wood from the ship. Kumbo recognized it.

"That's the shirt Jerle was wearing. I recognize it from when he went on the boat." They all stared at it.

"Poor bastard must have been trying to escape," Sleigh said.

"Well, it wouldn't have mattered. He would have died anyway after we told him about his daughter being whored out." Monk laughed.

Sleigh sneered at Monk. "You know how I feel about that."

Monk just laughed even harder. "It really doesn't matter how you feel.

Turn the ship around and get us back to Silver City."

Sleigh started to reach for his knife. Kelt caught him by the shoulder. Angered, Sleigh sliced at him. "Ow," Kelt said, snatching his arm back before he could be cut too deep. Blood was dripping from his arm.

"Put a bandage on that, Matt. Turn the ship around. We've lost our prize. Might as well move on," Sleigh ordered, heading back to the helm. He stopped and pointed his knife, dripping with blood, at Monk, and then he pointed it at Kumbo. "Remember, you two could disappear out here and there is nothing Ram could do. Ye best be on good behavior till we get back." He turned and walked to the helm. Monk swallowed so hard it made a sound across the water. Kumbo looked away, not saying a word as the crew got ready to turn the ship around.

Over halfway to Oak City, the *LiTaDi* was making good time on smooth water. Linc was thinking it had cost them both of their dinghies and one of the smaller masts. Not to mention some of Jerle's blood and a shirt, but their ruse had worked as far as he could tell. He didn't think anyone would be the wiser until they got back to Silver City, which was several weeks away.

He would deal with the consequences then. They could repair the ship in Oak City. The cannon firing had been an unexpected gift that had allowed them to set the plan in motion. Aarya causing the fog and lightening was sheer genius. No one else on the crew knew what had caused it. They thought it was just good luck. Linc smiled, listening to them discuss it. His first sea battle. He had run away, but at least he survived. He couldn't wait to tell Dirk and Tab the details.

Last night, while trying to sleep, he kept feeling strange sensations coming from Dirk and Tab. Then, all of a sudden, he felt a new presence. After working through what he was sensing, and the flashes of memories he was seeing in his mind, he knew it was the elven princess.

Then, much to his excitement, he felt El. He was overjoyed feeling her presence. El was his sister. Not by blood but by deeds. He knew right away that the bond had grown. The feelings he was getting from El was a little confusing at first. Then after the rush of emotions from her he was now experiencing settled, he smiled.

Tab you lucky dog. I always knew she loved you. Linc laughed out loud. He really wanted to get back to Silver City now. He knew though, he had to finish his first journey. Linc was very pragmatic and tended to take things as they came.

After the crew had their lunch rations, Linc sensed Aarya was near. They were halfway through the Wilds Run that edged closer to the area known as The Deep. Linc knew this area was dangerous so he had to be alert. The ship had already passed one of the islands that was half in the Deep and half in the Wilds. He had heard screeches and moans floating across the water as they neared it. The island had no name that Linc was aware of, so they just referred to it as The Half-Deep based on its location.

Linc made sure the crew stayed sharp. He let Jerle take it easy, due to him donating his blood to the cause, even though it was partially his fault. Linc couldn't blame him though. If it were his daughter, he would probably take on Zolun by himself.

Linc looked up. Aarya was on the crow's nest. A small parchment dropped from her talons. It landed in front of Jerle and Linc. Jerle looked up, but Aarya was already gone. Linc smiled at the sailor's confusion. "What's it say?" he asked. Jerle looked confused. If he hadn't seen it drop out of nowhere, he wouldn't have believed it had happened.

Luckily, Jerle was a sailor who could read. Linc watched as Jerle unrolled the small parchment after he untied the crimson string that held it closed. "I can't believe it!" Jerle shouted. The rest of the crew came running up to see what the fuss was about.

Corky, still not trusting Jerle, snatched the parchment from his hands. He handed it to River because he damn sure couldn't read. He just glared at Jerle. "What's this say River?"

Linc laughed. He was starting to have a soft spot for the crusty old sailor. River looked to Linc and he nodded to go ahead. Linc already knew what it said. He had sensed the meaning from Aarya.

"To Linc, the captain of The *LiTaDi Flame*. Received your message. Just wanted to let you know, I and a team of twelve engaged the target last night. It saddens me to say," River paused for effect.

Kaz punched River, though he wasn't the only one who wanted to. "Go on mate. Don't leave me hangin' like one of them cheap whores at the brothel." Corky smiled at that but still gave Jerle the evil eye as he took a drink from one of his many flasks.

River cleared his throat. "It saddens me to inform you that you are not the one who will be putting a beating on Ram Stockton. Last night, we arrested him and killed three of his men while he was attempting to sail away with a beautiful young girl by the name of Claire."

Jerle shouted his glee. Corky shushed him before he could say anything.

"Furthermore, Mr. Stockton will be spending some time in the stockade for the attempted enslavement of the young girl and inform the concerned party that he doesn't need to worry about her or her mother's welfare. I have taken a personal interest in them and moved them to my farm where my daughter Kira will be taking care of them until the mother is well again and can take care of herself. The girl can help around the farm to help pay for the cost. It was signed by General Storm. commander of the king's guard." River smiled. Jerle was dancing around in circles. Corky just *blah'ed* him and walked off.

Kaz congratulated Jerle then asked, "Captain, how did this get here?"

Linc smiled. "Why magic, of course." Kaz just stared dumbfounded and walked off.

Jerle walked up to Linc and hugged him with his good arm. "Thanks, cap'n. I owe you everything."

Linc gently pushed him away and looked him in the eye. "Don't you forget it, either."

Jerle nodded. "You can count on it. Always. I am in your debt." Jerle, with pep in his step, carried on watching the waters for any danger. River walked up and handed the parchment to Linc and gave him a quizzical look.

"Dirk?"

Linc nodded.

"How?"

"River, there are things that can't be explained. The best answer is magic." Linc paused, rolling the parchment up and putting it in his belt.

River smiled and headed off to finish making repairs from the cannon fire that had actually hit the ship.

Linc tried to send a mental message to Dirk or anyone who could sense it. *Thank you, brother!* he thought. He didn't know if they would get it or not. He hoped they would and know that he was okay. He stared at the waters ahead.

A loud screech sounded from the island they had just passed. It was so high-pitched and loud it sent chills down Linc's spine. "River, hurry up with those repairs. We need to reach full speed as soon as possible. I want to get far away from that island."

Linc looked back in its direction. He could see flocks of birds flying away from the island. Whatever had made that sound was wreaking havoc. The sooner he was in Oak City, the better. He would get with Lord Saint and request some upgrades he had been thinking about since the attack.

He wanted the upgrades for the return trip. He had enough coin to pay for what was needed. Hopefully, Lord Philias Saint would agree with Linc's ideas. He took a deep breath to ease the edginess he was feeling about the island.

After letting Jerle take the helm, Linc and River started working as hard as they could to get the repairs done. Soon, the island was out of view and that in itself was a victory for Linc. He continued helping River late into the night.

Training and Class

The next few weeks went by fast for Dirk and his friends. The training got more extensive. They actually started training with the military when it came to weapons and tactics. Jonesy and the dwarves had become closer. El was happy to see her brother three days a week now.

Brock had actually lived up to his word and had been tolerable. Dirk watched as he actually got into a fight with Skylar in the lunch hall one day about how he was acting. Dirk overheard the whole thing while he was in line with Natia. Skylar's burning hatred for Natia hadn't cooled since the soup incident the first day and she wasn't subtle about it either.

"Why are you putting up with him?" Skylar asked, pointing to Dirk. "Just because he hangs out with that wood animal doesn't mean you have to accept him." Dirk could sense Natia was going to punch Skylar and he grabbed her arm when she started to ball up her fist. Skylar raised an eyebrow at princess.

"Keep calm. Remember, we get to practice sword and shield attacks tomorrow," Dirk whispered. Natia smiled. She knew who her partner would be. Skylar was actually good at combat, but she was no match for Natia.

"You're right." Natia relaxed and smiled at Skylar.

"What's so funny?" Skylar retorted. Natia just smiled again and turned away. Dirk could hear Skylar yelling at Brock for not defending her. Brock tried to calm her down, but she wouldn't have it.

"If you've lost your balls, then I know a few boys who would like to show me theirs," Dirk heard her say before she stormed out of the hall. Brock yelled at her to come back but once Skylar had her mind set, she wouldn't do anything else. Dirk knew her well enough to know that.

The class lessons were going better for Dirk. He was starting to get the hang of connecting to his core. The first-years had even started training in other classrooms on the third week. Even though Dirk had bonded with El and Natia, he still had problems using the other stones of power. The bracelet the twins gave him helped him touch his core, but he just couldn't connect with some of the gems.

He was getting better with the red and yellow gems, but he had barely any luck with the others. He could sense them in his core, but he just couldn't get them to work. El said it was because he was putting too much pressure on himself.

Training with Hilda and Tilda was going slow. They were trying to teach the four of them some of the things that had worked with Diron's group. Hilda always stayed positive, explaining to the group that it took years for their group to get any of the things they were trying to teach them to work.

"Don't give up. You must learn to combine your powers and make the connection solid for it to work. When you come back from your weekend break, we will start working in pairs. Let's see if that will strengthen the bond between pairs first."

They were all frustrated, Dirk especially. He had seen Anastasia the day before and she had informed him that her brother hadn't returned yet and she had heard that the third-years were going to be joining the military campaign soon. She was actually upbeat about joining them in the field.

"Remember what I said on the roof," was the last thing Anastasia said to him before Kal greeted him and pulled her away.

Dirk was planning on asking her about the Chosen comment but, between training and classes, he hadn't had time. Detention had finished finally. The only thing he regretted about that was he would miss Moira's nightly torture. Dirk actually liked her quirky attitude. It was refreshing.

"Don't worry. Knowing you, we'll both be in here again soon." Moira smirked.

"Well, at least try and be good. That's what I am going to do," Dirk said to her their last night of detention.

"Dirk, you know me by now." She waved as she left.

Dirk laughed. "I like her Tab. I think she would be a great asset to our team."

Tab looked at Dirk, confused. "She is a psycho you know."

"Come on Tab, she's a little strange, but she is a smart. Yes, she is a little sarcastic, but I think it's a self-defense ploy by her. I don't know what it is. I sense something happened to her to make her that way. I mean take a look at how she dresses. Baggy clothes, nothing ever tight fitting like all the other girls her age wear."

Tab tilted his head and looked Dirk in the face, trying to read Dirk's thoughts about Moira. "Okay what's this really about. I know you don't *like her-like her*. So, what is it about her?"

Dirk smiled and grabbed Tab's shoulders. "I get the feeling we are going to need her one day. I don't know what it is, but my gut is telling me we will.

And besides, I do really like her. And you're right, not in that sense." Dirk smiled and released Tabs shoulders.

Tab let out a big sigh. "I think you're still crazy or your brain is still foggy from when Natia addled your head that day." Tab then shook his head. "I don't think we could trust her. That's the way I feel." Tab said and walked off.

Dirk knew he would win Tab over eventually. He followed him. "Okay, we can talk about it later. Let's head up and see what everyone else is doing." They then headed to the dorms like the discussion had never happened.

"Gil, are you coming out to the farm this weekend?" Dirk asked him at lunch after another grueling morning of training and class. Giles had lived up to his word and added weight to the backpacks daily. Dirk was sure they were up to at least one hundred pounds by now.

"No, I can't. Dad has some traveling priests of Zona in town, and he sent me a note through Laseous saying that I needed to help with their visit." Gil just frowned and rested his head on his arms. Dirk felt sorry for Gil. He knew he hated that kind of stuff. Dirk believed that Gil down, deep inside, hated his father, but then again, who wouldn't?

He was an ogre to Gil. Dirk had seen the bruising where the High One had dealt out punishment before. Gil had made Dirk promise not to say anything to anyone when he saw it. Dirk agreed but still shared what he had seen with the general.

The general told him, "One day, the High One will get what is coming to him. I promise, and it might be me who gives it to him."

Dirk knew the general was serious, so he didn't say anything else about it, but with the bond now, he was sure Natia knew and probably Tab and El. They just didn't say anything.

"I'm sorry, pal. You know the whole crew is gonna be there. The twins are staying with El and Jonesy but will be over to campout. Phil, Dusty, Volar and the dwarves are coming as well. Even some of the elves are spending the weekend there. You know, Mom is Natia's god aunt."

Gil just huffed. "I'll try to come Saturday night for dinner." He tried to sound convincing.

"Great, I hope you can come. I can get the general to request it. If that will help?"

When he looked up, Gil's eyes were huge. "No, don't do that. You remember what happened the last time he tried to help," Gil pleaded. Of course, Dirk knew. He just didn't think about it that way.

"You're right, Gil. I'm sorry."

Gil just shook his head and slumped forward against the table. *Idiot,*

Dirk thought. It suddenly clicked that after Dirk has asked the general to help Gil out with his father, soon after Gil had received those bruises he had seen. He felt Tab's and Natia's eyes on him. He looked up and they both looked away, starting conversations with the twins and El.

Dirk, realizing that they both knew, looked to Volar. "So, friend, are you coming over in the morning?"

Volar nodded. "Yes, I am very interested in seeing Mt. Blazire up close and personal." Dirk nodded. One thing they were going do with the dwarves was explore the mountain. At least Tab and he would. He wasn't sure Natia, and the others would want to do that.

Natia would be staying at the farm, but the rest of the elves would be staying at the palace the first night. She had convinced Sirien that she would be with her god aunt and that he didn't need to worry for her. Of course, that hadn't stopped him from telling Dirk that he knew over a hundred ways to hurt a human if anything happened to Natia. Dirk took his threat lightly.

There was always a delegation of elves at the palace, that included Sirien and some of the other elves parents. The twins were excited about meeting El's parents. Vira couldn't quit talking about it for the last few days. Nira had made everyone laugh at dinner last night when she actually told Vira to shut up before they were uninvited. The whole table sat there, shocked that Nira could actually speak. Vira, being Vira, just laughed and told her sister not to worry and that she would control herself. Nira rolled her eyes, and everyone laughed.

Dirk could have sworn he saw Nira actually smile at him. He could tell Nira was excited. Dusty had told Dirk that she loved sleeping out in the fresh air. Dusty was the only one Nira actually talked to. Nira and Dusty were both quiet and seemed to get along really well. Phil and Dusty would come to the farm with El and Jonesy. Dusty's father was in town and he wanted Phil to meet him. Jacko had kept his plans secret but gracefully apologized for not being able to go and promised he would come hang out with everyone next time.

The day to visit the farm was finally here. Afternoon classes were short since it was a free weekend. Dirk was really excited because he was planning on taking advantage of the general's building. He had come up with a plan to tell all of their friends about the Chosen by planting ideas in their heads then using the power of the building to make them forget what they had been told. Then when the time was right for them to know, he would already know how they were going to react.

"Dirk that's silly isn't it?" El asked about his plan.

"Well, I'll know how they're going to react before they really need to know. I think it's a good idea, besides, you get to keep your memories," Dirk replied.

El looked at Natia, who only shrugged. "I get to see The Book of Storms, right?"

"Yes." Dirk squeezed her arm.

"Okay. It's a good plan then." El smiled.

El was itching to see the Book of Storms. Hilda and Tilda even said they might drop in and see their old friend Kira. Dirk thought that might be a good idea, as long as the general wasn't around when they showed up. Dirk was fairly certain he would be at the palace anyway.

"So, the plan is this," he told the group at the table. "Tab, Natia, and I will head to the farm as soon as class is over. Vira and Nira, you come out in the morning with El." The twins nodded. Vira started to speak when Nira elbowed her.

She looked at Dirk while rubbing her ribs. "Yes Dirk that is the plan," she whispered.

"Dusty and Phil, I've given you directions, so you can come tomorrow whenever you're ready. Come early if you want to hike to Mt. Blazire with us."

"Yes, we will. My father is heading out early and we will come after he leaves," Dusty said.

Dirk then turned to Volar. "Volar, you and the other dwarves are coming in the morning, right?"

"I believe it will be only me and Raga. Jonesy has promised the others to get his father to show them the finer workings of smithing in the morning. They will come out tomorrow afternoon before you fire up the smoking pit."

Dirk nodded. "Ok."

"Sounds like a plan," Tab said. Dirk looked around the room. The lunch hall was buzzing with conversations. The group got up when the bell sounded and headed to classes after putting their trash away. Dirk waved to Miss Heloise and Hanks and told them he would see them Monday. He felt sorry for them. They still had to work since some of the kids from far away didn't have anywhere to go.

Dirk was glad the afternoon classes were only two hours long. He spent it in Wizards Hermosa's class. He listened impatiently as she recapped everything that they had learned over the past few weeks.

"I want you all to enjoy your weekend. Be prepared to step it up when you come back. The morning training class will begin on Tuesday since you don't have to be back here until ten on Monday."

The class seemed to be excited about that, except for Brock. He was starting to look distant, Dirk thought. Even Stew and Larkin were having a hard time getting him to talk. Dirk figured it was because Skylar had been hanging out with some second-years and had completely avoided him since the lunchroom incident, just like she had told him she would.

Dirk actually started to feel sorry for him for a few moments. "Nah," he said to himself. "He's an asshole. He deserves it for the things he's done to the Pack over the years."

"Nah, don't waste a single thought on that loser," Tab said as they headed to the dorm to get the packs they had gotten ready that morning.

The Hill and Family

They met Natia at the front gate of the school. Sirien was busy lecturing her. "Sirien, I will remind you one last time who I am and that I will be in good hands." She smiled and glanced at Dirk.

Sirien noticed and let out a deep sigh of disgust. He glared at Dirk and stormed off with the rest of the male elves towards the palace. Tara and Oriana were a little more accepting of Dirk and said goodbye to the three.

"They actually smiled at me," Dirk said as the three headed down the streets of Silver City towards the market.

"Tara and Oriana are actually coming tomorrow with Volar," Natia informed him.

"That's fine, there's plenty of room and maybe I can get to know them better."

"Don't push it. I mean, they are accepting, but not because of you. They are accepting you because of me and will show you respect, but if they see anything they don't like, they'll change their opinions. Don't worry about Sirien or the others. They'll come around when the truth is known."

"Even Sirien?" Tab asked.

"Haven't you figured it out yet?" she asked the two. They both shared emotions with Natia but she was very good at hiding certain things and the boys accepted that now. Some things concerning the elves they didn't need to know.

"Natia?" Dirk insisted.

"He's in love with me, idiot!" she said, punching Dirk so hard he almost fell over. Tab laughed. Natia looked at Tab and he stopped immediately, not wanting to be on the receiving end of one of her powerful punches. He had been on the receiving end of several of them when they had sparred, so bruised that she felt the need to apologize to him.

Dirk straightened up, rubbing his arm. He just laughed, standing a few feet away, safely out of her reach. "I should have known."

"You're damn right you should have. He doesn't understand what's going on and thinks you're a threat," Natia explained.

"Well, you told him there was nothing to worry about, right?"

"Of course, but he's so untrusting of humans he doesn't believe me," Natia said, a trace of hurt in her voice.

Tab, wanting to change the subject, shouted at the group hanging out in front of Burk's Bakery. "I knew this would be the first place you would go!"

Dirk looked to see who Tab was shouting at. In front of Burk's Bakery was El, Jonesy, Gil, and the twins. Dirk smiled as he walked up to Mr. Burk and his wife. They were out front, giving away sticky honey buns to his friends.

"Ah Dirk, Tab, I knew you would come here when you got out," Mr. Burk said, turning the tray towards them.

"Mr. and Mrs. Burk, I would like to introduce Princess Natia Silver," Dirk said.

"Nice to meet you Your Highness," Mr. Burk said bowing. Mrs. Burk attempted to curtsy when Natia smiled and stopped her from finishing the proper bow.

"The name is Natia. And there is no need for that among friends. From what Dirk has told me, you are practically family and that is the way I want it to be as well." She smiled receiving one in return from the Burks.

"I have heard so much about these sticky buns. I'm truly glad to finally try one!" She took one from the tray. Mr. Burk beamed at the look on Natia's face after she took the first bite.

Dirk and Tab grabbed one for themselves and scarfed them down.

"This is the best treat I have ever had," Vira said, licking her fingers after she finished her bun off in seconds. Nira was nodding enthusiastically while trying to finish her bun.

The group all agreed and thanked him. Vira was itching to say more, but Nira glared at her. So Vira just smiled and nodded.

Natia got Dirk's attention. "Dirk, is that your tree on the hill?" she asked, pointing to the Pack's favorite place.

He looked at where she was pointing. "Yes. Do you want to see it?" Dirk asked to the group. They had all heard about the pack's favorite spot.

"Yes!" they answered at the same time.

El smiled. "Let's all go up now, then. I've missed our spot."

Gil felt a sudden sense of dread wash over him. He looked around, searching for the cause. Through the crowd, he could see his father heading towards him. Gill wished at that moment he would disappear in the crowd. Like a leaf in the wind, he would just float away. He didn't want a confrontation in front of his friends so with an exhale of his frustration he turned to Dirk. "I can't, I've got to go." Gil said averting his eyes.

Dirk noticed The High One. "Ok but try tomorrow night."

"I-I will." Gil said, watching his father's hulking form. He locked eyes with his father, his palms started sweating. His heart felt like it was going to beat out of his chest. The High One glared at Dirk and then turned away. Dirk felt his eyes warm. He clenched his fist and was about to say something, but El's hand on his arm stopped him. He closed his eyes, took a deep breath, and exhaled slowly. He looked at her. The fire raging in his eyes had disappeared. He turned towards Gil and saw his shoulders slouch as in defeat, so he didn't want to embarrass him.

"Let it go," Dirk heard Tab say. He followed El, who was leading the group up the hill to their tree.

When the group got to the top of the hill, Dirk watched as his new friends admired the view.

Vira stood arm in arm with El. Vira smiled. "I can see for miles,"

"It is breathtaking." Nira squeezed El's arm.

"It's an overwhelming sight. I understand why it's your favorite spot in the whole city," Natia said as she took a deep breath and released it. She smiled at Dirk. Their eyes met and she felt her heart pounding in her chest. Her emotions were taking control. "I…" She turned away from his gaze realizing she had to get control before she lost total control. The farm boy had won her heart. Intentionally or not. Thoughts of the mission brought her out of her reverie.

While Vira and Nira were still looking over the city in awe, Natia was desperately trying to find a way to get her emotions under control. She looked at the tree and noticed the carving. Walking over to it, she brushed her hand over it respectfully. Dirk matched her step for step. Natia closed her eyes and whispered, "I understand even more now," Dirk looked at her quizzically. She opened her eyes "Family."

Dirk smiled at her as their eyes met. He didn't want these feelings for her. He was drawn to her but stopped mid-step when Natia put a hand on his chest. She could sense what he wanted to do. She wanted him to but couldn't allow him to do it.

"Not now," she whispered and smiled. She turned away because if she didn't, she would have removed her hand.

The rest of the group seemed to be watching them. Vira smiled and came over to see what Natia was looking at. Dirk stepped back so Vira, followed by Nira, could see the carving. Natia stepped back to stand beside Dirk. El followed the twins and told them what it was about.

"*Privacious*," Dirk whispered. Natia followed suit and said it as well. Dirk felt the sensation of the magic.

"It's for the best," she whispered. Dirk nodded in understanding, taking a deep breath. "We'll talk tonight," she said and stood beside El.

Tab looked at Dirk giving him a *what the hell* look. Dirk just shrugged. When El finished the story, tears were flowing freely from Vira's eyes. "I've just never felt this way about any of my friends," she said in between sobs. Dirk watched Nira rub her back, tears in her eyes as well. "Until now, I mean," Vira finished. Dirk stepped up to Vira. He put his hands on her shoulders and turned her to face him. Nira turned as well.

Dirk felt a little warmth in his eyes as he gazed into both Vira and Nira's eyes. "Sisters, you never have to worry about that again." He put one hand on Nira's shoulder to make sure he had her undivided attention too. "You will never be alone again. I will not stand by and let anything, or anyone ever hurt you. You both are in our family now." Dirk smiled at the twins. "Family is what we are, Family is what we will always be."

Vira and Nira at the same time rushed into Dirk's arms, squeezing him tightly. Dirk didn't know what had caused him to say that. He just realized he truly meant what he had said. The two sisters had become family over the last several weeks and he felt they needed to know.

El was crying. Jonesy had pulled her into a brotherly hug. Even Natia was tearing up by Tab's side. He had put his hand on her shoulder. If one looked close enough, they could see a tear or two in his eyes.

"That's why we all love you Dirk," El said.

"She's right, Dirk. You all have accepted us, even though we came from the vilest place in all the land." To everyone's shock, it was Nira who had said this.

Dirk eased the sisters back so he could see their eyes and wiped away the tears. "It doesn't matter where you came from. It's what's in your heart that makes you who you are. I can see in yours the shame you hold. Well, it's time for you two to let that go and be the people you are and were meant to be, not the people you come from. Your grandfather believed in you and now it's time you believe in yourself. I believe in you." Dirk smiled.

Each twin smiled back and kissed him on the cheek. Dirk looked to El, Tab, and Jonesy. They knew what he was thinking. Jonesy pulled out his knife and handed it to Dirk. Dirk handed it to Nira first. She looked at it and noticed Dirk looking at the carving.

"I insist. Every one of us insists," He motioned to the tree. El and Tab both agreed. Nira smiled, walked over to the tree, and carved her initials under Gil's. Vira smiled really big and carved her initials under El's. Dirk looked at Natia and she moved forward. She took the knife and carved an N that connected to the bottom of Dirk's D. Then she looped her S through

Dirks S. He smiled when he saw what she did.

She handed the knife back to Jonesy and smiled. "Family," Dirk said. "Even though Gil and Linc are not here right now, I know without a doubt they would feel the same way."

"I agree," Tab and El said in unison.

"I don't know you as well as the rest of the Pack. But if you're okay with them, then it's fine with me," Jonesy then grabbed the twins in a hug. He released them and looked at each in turn. "Sisters." His words had the whole group in tears.

"Let's get going, Mom is going to be wondering where we are at," Dirk said satisfied that the future just got brighter.

With that being said, they all headed down the hill to go their separate ways. El, her brother, and the twins headed home. Dirk, Tab, and Natia headed towards the farm. "See you tomorrow, sisters," Dirk said over his shoulder as they were departing.

Nira and Vira, walking arm in arm with El smiled. "See you then, brother."

Dirk's heart warmed. He felt like he had just taken a big step closer to leading his group to victory in the future. Natia was overwhelmed by Dirk. He was totally different from what she had expected. She realized that he was a very special person. Not because he was the Chosen, but because of who he was inside. The goodness in his heart was extraordinary.

What he had done with the twins was unexpected, but then, even more unexpectedly, he had let her carve her initials into the tree as well. Natia was so glad she had used the privacy magic, because if she hadn't, Dirk would know without a doubt that she was deeply in love with him. She didn't know how it happened. It just did.

This worried her because she knew the importance of what her mission in life was and she didn't want to jeopardize that. She couldn't stop these feelings, no matter how hard she tried. She had resolved herself to let the events of the future unfold naturally from now on. She would just deal with the consequences, whatever they be.

Home and Heart

Dirk was relieved when the three finally got within sight of the farm. He felt as though he had been away for ages, not just a few weeks. Dirk waved to Bart, the farmhand his grandfather had hired. Bart's wife, Carly, was standing by her husband. They looked like they had been working with the sheep. They both waved with a friendly smile. Tab and Natia waved back as well.

"Ho there, Dirk," Bart said as Dirk and his friends were walking up.

"Hello," Dirk said, shaking his hand.

"Tab." Bart nodded and shook Tab's hand as well.

"And who is this lovely lady?" Bart's wife asked.

"Oh sorry. This is Natia Silver, a friend of ours from the school. And she is my mother's god niece," Dirk told them.

Bart and his wife introduced themselves.

Natia smiled, "It's nice to meet you."

"How is the farm?" Dirk asked.

"It's been running smoothly with the exception of some wolf troubles here lately. They got into the sheep pasture and killed about five sheep before I could run them off."

"That's not like the wolves around here. They usually stay far away," Tab said, looking around.

Dirk looked to Tab and they both smiled. "Sounds like a wolf hunt later."

Tab nodded in agreement. "I miss the woods. It'll be good getting in there and finding out what's stirring them up,"

Dirk saw Natia staring at the woods with concern. "Oh, you can come also!"

She turned back and faced him. "Let's see how Aunt Kira is and then I'll decide," Natia replied.

"Well, she's had her hands full for the past few weeks," Bart said with a smile. Dirk looked at him with concern.

Carly spoke up. "She has been taking care of Ulny and Claire since your grandfather took them in. Ulny has been in poor health, not really getting any better. And that Claire is a handful," she said with a laugh. Bart laughed and agreed.

"Oh yeah, that's right. I forgot about hearing something about that," Dirk said. He had completely forgotten about the general rescuing Jerle's daughter. He didn't know the general had taken them in though.

"I haven't told Mom yet, but there are at least eight of my friends coming to stay for the weekend. They won't be here until tomorrow. I wanted to let you know so they won't worry you when they show up."

"No problem. I guess they will be camping out around the pits?"

"I think that would be best. But don't go to any trouble. Tab and I can get them set up."

"No, I'll take care of it. You three see your mom. She has missed you. Plus, it'll break up the monotony of doing the same thing. It won't be a problem," Bart replied.

"Thanks for that, Bart. I really appreciate that. Well, we better go check in. It's good to see the farm is in good hands," Dirk said, patting Bart on the shoulder. Bart smiled his appreciation. They said goodbye to Carly and headed to the house.

As they got closer to the house, Tab felt a pain in his right shoulder. "Ow, what the hells was that?" He looked down at the stone lying at his feet. Dirk and Natia stopped and scanned the area. A blur of brown aimed straight for Dirk's head. Natia snatched it out of the air right in front of Dirk's nose. She opened her hand. In it was a small, round, brown stone.

"Hey! How did you do that?" came a small, high-pitched voice. The three looked to the entrance of the barn. Out of the shadows, a small girl revealed herself. She had shoulder-length blonde hair with sparkling blue eyes. She was wearing a pair of tan pants and a brown shirt. Dirk recognized them as his old clothes from when he was a much younger.

The little girl was walking fast towards Natia with her fist balled up. Dirk smiled. Tab was rubbing the spot where the rock had hit him. Natia just raised an eyebrow at the little girl stalking towards her.

"And who are you?" Dirk asked as she got closer to the three of them.

"None of your business who I am! You're strangers and General Durk told me to protect this house from strangers!" Dirk kneeled down so he was eye-level with the little girl. She stopped and pinned Dirk with an evil stare.

"Now, why would General Durk have you guarding the house?" Dirk asked gently, trying to get the little girl to relax. She looked at each of them and then back at Dirk.

Her brow furrowed. "Because two strangers took me away from my mommy. And they were bad, so the general told me to be vigilant. Don't know what that means, but he said to make sure bad people didn't come here and try to get me again. I told him I would."

Dirk laughed under his breath.

"Who taught you to throw rocks like that?" Natia asked, gazing down at the little girl. She looked up at Natia and decided maybe they weren't bad people because they hadn't done anything mean to her.

"Miss Kira did. Why, what's it to you?"

Natia smiled and kneeled down next to Dirk. She held out her hand with the rock in it. "I believe this is yours."

The girl snatched it back. "That's my favorite," the girl said, rolling it around in her hands.

"You know, Miss Kira taught me how to throw rocks too. I'm her son, Dirk." He held his hand out for her to shake. The girl stared at it and then looked at Natia. Natia was nodding to the little girl. Tab, who was still rubbing his shoulder, just looked at the little non-committal devil.

"I'm Claire," she said, shaking his hand.

Natia extended her hand as well. "I am Natia. I'm Kira's god niece. And this is Tab."

"I'm sorry I hit you with the rock," she said to Tab, looking ashamed.

Tab finally knelt down, picked the rock up that Claire had hit him with and handed it to her. "That's ok, you were doing your job. How is your mother feeling?"

She smiled, "She's better than she's been in months. Miss Kira is a great healer!" The little girl beamed.

"Well, I haven't seen my mom in almost a month. Do you think you can take us to her?" The little girl didn't wait before she took off running to the house. The three just laughed and followed.

By the time they got to the door, Dirk could hear his mother admonishing the little girl for not taking off her boots. "But…but Miss Kira." Kira looked up and could see Dirk through the screen door. Kira patted Claire on the head and ran out the door, grabbing Dirk in a motherly hug.

"Mom…," Dirk could hardly get the words out of his mouth because his mother was squeezing him so tight. She finally released him and noticed Tab waiting beside Natia. Kira was confused for a second, but then grabbed them both in a hug.

"Good to see you too Mom," Tab said.

She smiled and released Tab, looking him over. "You have grown," she said kissing him on the forehead. Then Kira wrapped both arms around Natia. "I didn't know you were coming. It's so good to see you!" She held Natia by the shoulders and looked her over.

When she saw Natia's eyes, she put a hand over her mouth, Natia smiled. Kira grabbed her again in another hug. Finally, she released her and looked at the three. She started to ask something, but Dirk nodded.

"El and Linc too," Tab said.

"Dirk Storm, Tab Clearwater! I told you two to keep that to yourselves as long as you could. Just how in the hells did Linc get bonded?" she said with one hand on her hip, the other pointing at the two of them.

"Mom," Dirk said, walking up to her, "Aarya is the one who bonded Linc. She must have felt the need since he was in trouble."

"Who am I to question her, then?" Kira said. She looked around and noticed Claire standing at the door. "Claire, go check on your mom." Kira smiled at the little blonde girl. Claire nodded and took off. Kira turned back to Dirk, "Talk quickly."

"Mom, there's no way to make it quick. Let's just say that some things have happened quicker than we'd hoped. I'll explain later, I promise."

Kira laughed at that answer. "I guess I deserved that." They followed her into the house after taking off their boots.

Kira prepared some snacks and put them on the table with a pitcher of cider. Claire came out of Dirk's grandfather's room. "Sit down and have a snack, Claire," Kira said sweetly. Claire smiled, sitting in Kira's lap, and happily ate cheese and grapes off the tray. "So, tell me how your first weeks have gone."

The three of them told her about the training they were going through in class and in the field trying to keep it basic. Claire finished her snack.

"Miss Kira, can I go out and play until dinner?'

Kira squeezed her shoulders lovingly. "Yes, you can. Just stay away from the woods."

"I will, thanks." She then looked at Tab. "Again, I'm sorry I hit you with my rock,"

Tab smiled at her. "It's okay."

With that said, Claire took off. Kira watched her until she was out of hearing range. Her smile vanished as she turned to face the three who had finished their snacks. She looked at Dirk then Tab. "Now we can talk, and I want some answers." Dirk looked back towards the general's room.

"She's asleep. The herbs she's taking as a part of her treatment make her sleep most of the day. When the general found her, she was almost dead. He brought her here and I've been treating her with fire shrooms and water violet powder."

Natia nodded, familiar with the treatment. "She is getting better, but it is a slow process." She paused.

"Tell us about Hilda and Tilda."

Kira's stern look turned into a sad smile. "They must have sensed it was time if they have told you their story,"

"You mean your story, right, Mom?" Dirk said.

She raised her head and looked her son in the eyes. Little flames were rippling there. As she looked at the other two, she saw similar flames flickering in theirs as well. She felt a small wave of relief wash over her, then she smiled, and her mood immediately lightened. She knew the sands of time were in motion now and the best thing she could do for these kids was to be there and help answer any questions they might have.

"I guess you already know so, without any secrets, tell me how and why. I'll fill in any blanks." Dirk looked between Tab and Natia and there was an agreement between them. So, Dirk told his mom everything that happened from day one at school.

After several hours, Dirk, with the added help of Tab and Natia, finished their tale, leaving a few things out that they felt needed to be private. Kira just sat there listening and tearing up when certain details about Diron and his group's story were told. "I am so sorry this is happening so soon,"

Natia put her hand on Kira's. "Aunt, it's not your fault. Our destinies lie beyond your control, no matter what you try to do to change it. I know my mother pushed you to tell Dirk before he was ready. And I'm sorry for that. I wanted badly for Dirk to know as soon as we got here, but now, after bonding with Aarya, I realize that what you were trying to do was probably the right thing. Dirk wasn't raised like anyone who has ever had this burden put on them before. I, myself, you know, was raised just as you were."

Natia paused, sensing Dirk's emotions.

She looked back to Kira. "But I also know that since we have bonded, Dirk has grown to believe that what we were destined to do was inevitable. As much as I now would have wanted to delay the knowledge getting to him, I know that we can't wait any longer and with some of the things happening in the world, we must be ready sooner than later. Hilda and Tilda felt the same way. That's why they told us and have started preparing us for what's to come. You made your choice when you released your bond as protector. You had to know that your child would fall into that destiny if anything happened to Diron."

Kira squeezed Natia's hand and looked at her. "After Diron died, my world was shattered. The night Harbinger appeared by Dirk's bed, part of me died as well. I vowed that night I would protect Dirk as long as I could."

Kira paused, looking to her son, then to Tab. Kira smiled at Tab. "Then the unthinkable happened. The other child I swore to protect on his mother's deathbed got dragged into the fire as well." Tab leaned forward and grabbed Kira's other hand.

"I panicked when they told me what happened. When they both were bestowed the power of the Chosen, another piece of my heart died. I wanted to still shield them from what I knew would eventually be evident. I made a mistake. I see that now. If I had trained Dirk earlier and made him aware of the Storm family destiny, he would be prepared, and Tab might not have been involved." Kira stopped and stared out the window.

It was getting later in the day and it would be time for dinner soon. She didn't realize that she was lost in thought. Tab was the one to bring her out of her trance. "Mom, you know no matter how hard you tried to keep me away from this, it would just make me more determined to get involved."

Kira smiled back at Tab "You're right, son. Like I said, I was wrong in how I handled it, but things are different now. I will help you anyway I can, to make sure you stay safe. When El gets here tomorrow, we'll all meet. Linc will just have to wait until he gets back to find out any answers to his questions. If you have any lingering questions, I'll answer all that I know. I'll come up with a way to communicate with you at school, so that we can correspond any information that needs to be shared."

"That's a great idea, Mom, but there's one thing I need to tell you about," Dirk said, smiling.

Kira frowned at her son. "What else?"

"There's more people coming this weekend. Actually, they're coming tomorrow when El comes. Vira, Nira, and several of the guys from my dorm are coming."

"You know I don't mind, but why so many?"

Dirk had already discussed his plans with El, Tab, and Natia. They nodded for him to continue. "I want to use the general's workshop to tell them about my destiny. I want to see how they react. Then when they leave, I won't let them keep their memories. When it's time for them to know, I'll restore them because I'll already know how they will respond," he explained.

"Mighty risky. Do you two think it will work?" Kira asked Tab and Natia.

They both smiled. "We came up with the plan together," Natia said confidently.

"And you're sure it'll be safe and that you can make them forget until the time comes where they need to remember?"

"It worked on me," Dirk said.

Kira nodded. "Yes, but your mind was young. Some of the people you intend to bond minds with will be stronger and it might not have the same effect."

"It's a risk we're willing to take," Tab said.

"Mom, you know about the buildup in the south, right?" Dirk asked. Kira nodded.

"Then we must get ready now," Natia said, hoping Kira would understand.

"I do and, like I said, you have my full support." The kids were happy Kira liked their plan. "Then you three need to put your things away. It sounds like we have a busy weekend. Natia, you can take the room across from Dirk's. Tab, you know where to put your things. I need to get dinner ready, then we can have a more relaxing evening."

"I talked with Bart as we came onto the farm. I told him about the group coming. He said he would get things set up for us, but I told him we would do it. He wouldn't here it and said he would handle it. Sorry I wasn't trying to give him extra work."

"That's ok. He likes making sure everything is handled. He and his wife are great," Kira told Dirk.

"That can wait until tomorrow Dirk. Now go put your stuff up so I can get dinner ready,"

"Yes Mom."

Natia followed Dirk and Tab up the stairs, and he showed her to the room.

"I got the bath first," Tab said, putting his things away hurriedly and going to the bath.

"I guess chivalry is dead?" Natia smiled.

Dirk smiled back and shrugged his shoulders. "What do you think?"

"About what Kira said?"

Dirk nodded. Natia leaned her back against the door. She smiled at Dirk, pulling her braid over her shoulder, and untying it while she stared at him.

"I didn't really know her until we met after the tournament. I mean Mother told me all about her. There is a record in Elmwood of who the protectors were, along with a little history about them. But nothing more." Natia paused, looking at the auburn hair in her hands. *Privacious*, she thought.

"*Privacious*," Dirk whispered. The bracelets they both wore flared with a small light and then it disappeared. The strange sensation washed over them. Natia smiled. Dirk stepped closer.

His heart was pounding so loud that he would have sworn Bart and Carly could hear it out in the fields. Natia, feeling Dirk's closeness, looked up into his eyes. Dirk started to say something, but Natia put a single finger on his lips to stop him. She then slowly moved it on to his face in a loving caress. Her touch had Dirk wanting more.

She edged closer. Their lips were only an inch apart. "Don't speak, just listen." She waited until Dirk nodded.

Natia's heart was beating just as hard as Dirk's, almost in rhythm with his. She inhaled, breathing in the scent that he always seemed to have, regardless of how clean or dirty he was. She closed her eyes. The smell was woodsy with a hint of cinnamon.

"Cedar and cinnamon," Dirk said. "Mom uses it to clean my clothes."

Natia's eyes widened slightly. "How did you know what I was thinking?"

Dirk smiled. "Ever since the bond with Aarya, I can sense what you're thinking and feeling sometimes."

Natia's eyes sparkled. "You know, I think you're right. I've sensed your thoughts as well."

"I think it's that way since we were the original Chosen and protector. At least I believe that's why," Dirk said confidently.

"Almond and honey," Natia said, responding to Dirk's thought.

He smiled. "I thought so. Every time I smell either almonds or honey, I get a flash of your amber eyes in my head," Dirk said, caressing Natia's face.

"You know we have to fight these feelings," Natia pleaded.

"You're right," Dirk said, moving closer, their lips barely touching. "I can't quit thinking about you," Dirk whispered, his lips brushing Natia's again. She gazed into his eyes, her body giving into the feelings she couldn't fight anymore. She ran her fingers through his hair.

"And I can't quit thinking about you either," she responded. She pushed closer, tasting his lips.

Tab, at the moment yelled out, "I'm almost done. Who's next?"

Dirk pulled back from Natia just as Tab opened the door.

Shaken out of the moment, Natia smiled, "I am."

"Take your time. I'm looking forward to a cold shower."

Natia turned, brushing past Dirk with her butt teasingly, put her pack into the room and grabbed a change of clothes before heading for the bath. She looked back and smiled at Dirk as she passed Tab. "Good, because I'm sure I'll use the remaining hot water." She entered the bath and closed the door. Tab acted like he didn't understand the comments and followed Dirk into the room.

After Dirk took an extended cold shower, he got dressed. Kira was already yelling up the stairs that dinner was ready. "Great I'm starving. I've missed Kira's cooking," Tab said, jumping up from the bed and running down the stairs. Dirk smiled and followed. He almost bumped into Natia as she was coming out of her room. Dirk's breath caught in his throat. Natia had not put her hair back in a braid. She had instead put a headband on, pushing her hair back from her forehead. The headband was almost the same color as her hair. Her hair was straight, all the way down her back to her waist. She wore an aqua-colored tunic with matching pants.

"*Wow!*" Dirk said, finally starting to breathe again.

Natia smiled. "Yes, those dingy colors we wear at the academy are boring. It's good to get to wear something different and lighter. This is made from the silkworm silk in northern Elmwood."

Dirk touched her sleeve and rubbed the fabric between his fingers. The clothes they wore at school were made from a mixture of cotton and wool. "You're right. This feels great."

Natia pushed his hand away. "I'll have to see if I can get you something made from there if you like it so much."

"I definitely do. We better hurry. Mom gets cranky if we're not at the table after she calls." Dirk motioned to let Natia go first. She kissed him gently on the lips, then curtsied and led the way.

Great, I'm gonna have to take another cold shower, Dirk thought as he followed Natia.

When they got to the kitchen, Kira was smacking Tab's hand and scolding him to wait. He just smiled and gave her a hurt-puppy look.

"Couldn't wait, I see!" Dirk said, sitting by his friend. Tab just shrugged, wearing a cynical smile.

"Nice digs," Tab said to Natia. She nodded. Claire was sitting at the table, fidgeting. Kira set a baked chicken, some fresh steamed vegetables, and a bowl of salad with several fruits added to it on the table, along with a pitcher of cider and some fresh, hot baked brown bread, and a bowl of freshly made butter. Kira sat beside Claire and put a hand on her leg to get her to quit fidgeting. Claire looked up at her and smiled.

For the first time, Kira looked up and saw Natia's hair. Kira raised an eyebrow. Natia tilted her head towards Kira. Kira's smile changed to concern. "We'll talk later, niece."

Natia nodded. Dirk and Tab, oblivious to what the two were talking about, assumed they were talking about elven family business. Dirk sensed a little distress in Natia but waved it off after his mom told everyone to grab hands.

When Natia and Dirk clasped hands, a calming sensation washed over him. Natia held Claire's tiny little calloused hand in hers. Natia looked at the little girl and smiled. Kira was rubbing her thumb over the other little hand affectionately. When Tab grabbed Kira's hand, Tab sent a spark of love through the touch. She turned away from Claire and smiled gratefully at Tab.

"Now," Kira said, turning back to get everyone's attention. "Since Claire and her mother have been here, we have started each dinner with giving thanks to the gods."

Dirk raised an eyebrow, which Kira ignored. Claire started "Thank you Marluna for sending General Durk to save me and my mom. Also, thank you for Miss Kira who took us in and is making my mom better each day." She eased down a little in her chair after she finished.

Natia beamed at her. "I'll go next if that's okay, aunt?" Kira nodded. "Thank you, Mother Luna, for all your blessings. Thank you for my new friends." She squeezed Dirk's hand as she said the last part. "Thank you, Zona, for all you have given us and please watch over all of us in the days ahead. May we do as you would and make wise decisions." There was an approval from everyone at the table.

"Thank you Marluna for my mother. Thank you for protecting my friends. May you keep them healthy in the days to come. Thank you, Zona, for all that we have been given. I hope in our endeavors in the future that you watch over us as we strive to keep Marona safe." Dirk said and the table agreed.

"Thank you, Zona, for allowing me to learn the truth about my family. I hope you watch over everyone and that at the end of our journey we can all be here where we're at and spend the rest of our lives in peace." Tab got a *yes* response from the table.

Kira started next. "Thank you, Marluna, for bestowing upon me these healing hands. Thank you for bringing Diron into my life. Thank you, Zolun, for bringing my family from afar back into my life. Even though you are pure evil, it is because of you we have come together again. Lord Zona, I know we don't talk as much as we used to, but I have one request. Please ease Diron's suffering."

Dirk looked up at his mother. "I will explain later," was all she could get out.

Someone's stomach, growled loudly. The tension was broken by everyone looking at Claire, who smiled.

"I'm starving, sorry."

Laughter ensued as Kira started passing the food around. Dirk, still bothered by his mother's last comment, didn't eat a whole lot. Natia kept sending him probing thoughts. She had pulled her sandal off and was running her toes up and down the back of his leg. Dirk was distracted by her touch and didn't know what to tell her.

"I will find out though," he said lowly enough so that only Natia could hear.

Tab, too hungry to be worried by Kira's last words, was staring at the food. "Finally," he said as Kira passed him the chicken. "Dirk?" Tab asked, sensing Dirk's worry.

"I'm fine let's eat. Really, I'm fine." Dirk smiled and started eating.

The group ate their dinner. Everyone was asking Claire questions. Did she like it here and would she be ready for school when it started back up? The regular schools didn't start until a month after the military school and the academy did.

"I've never been to school," she said, looking scared.

"You'll be fine, and you'll make a whole bunch of friends," Dirk said with a smile.

Claire shrugged. "Hey, don't worry. I used to be an orphan. I met almost all of my friends at school. I was really afraid at the beginning. It was scary. I met Dirk first, then after that, we started making new friends every day. You'll be just fine. Just don't throw rocks at them," Tab laughed, getting one in return from Claire.

"You will get to meet most of them tomorrow. They're all coming here for a cookout," Dirk said, smiling. This seemed to ease Claire's worry after Kira assured her what Tab and Dirk had told her was true. Claire relaxed, and she was in a happier mood.

Kira and Natia talked about Elmwood and people Kira had grown up with. Dirk paid close attention to the names being said. He hadn't known much about his mother's childhood. Tab, after his conversation with Claire was over, ate two more servings of food. He pretty much had ignored the conversations from then on out.

Claire would ask Dirk or Natia a question every now and then about their school and they would answer the best they could. "Magic sounds awesome," Claire said after Natia explained how it worked.

"Don't worry, little one. You'll get a chance one day to see if you can use it," Natia assured her. This made Claire smile through the rest of dinner. Her smile was infectious. It also made Dirk's stomach roll. The thought of what almost happened to her was sickening. That thought alone, if his mind hadn't already been made up, would have sealed what he would do in the future. He would do all he could to prepare himself and his friends to destroy evil. Whether it be man, or the gods, it didn't matter anymore. He had his mind set now.

He felt a wave of relief from Natia. He smiled as she squeezed his leg under the table, getting a little too close to his crotch. Dirk fidgeted a little and Natia removed her hand, smiling. He looked up at Tab and realized he was looking at him. Tab nodded an agreement.

In his mind, he heard Tab say, You're damn right. We'll have plenty of time for trading after.

Dirk smiled and tilted his head questioningly at Tab. Oh, you think you can block me out completely? Tab thought back at him. Maybe when it comes to the princess, you two together can block your shared thoughts, but other than that, I guess what I would call intimate things. I can read your mind just as easily as talking.

Dirk smiled. Tab winked and continued eating. Natia looked at Tab and cocked her head, but he hadn't seen her.

After they finished eating Kira told Claire to make her mom a plate and they would go sit with her while she ate. Dirk and Tab washed the dishes while Natia cleaned the table off and put the leftovers away in the cold box. She was fascinated by the box. Dirk explained to her that it was made of wood lined with some material that his grandfather had brought home. He didn't know what it was, but it kept food fresh for several days after it had been put in it.

He also showed her the deep blue gem that was attached to the back of the box. Thanks to his lessons, he now understood that the gem was what made it cold. She nodded.

When they finished, the moon was coming over the horizon, lighting up the night. He knocked gently on the door to Claire's mom's room. Kira opened it slightly and peered out. "We're going to build a fire in the pit out back."

"Ok" Kira said softly.

Dirk touched his mom's shoulder and looked into her eyes. "When you're done, and Claire is in bed, come join us. I want to know more about what you said at dinner to Zona."

Kira looked back over her shoulder. "I will try. It's been a long day. If I don't, I promise we'll talk in the morning. Remember I told you, no more secrets." She smiled and closed the door.

The three went out back behind the main guest house to where one of the fire pits was located. Dirk and Tab gathered kindling and placed it in the pit. There were two fire pits on the farm. The other was over by the fields where all of the kids would camp out the rest of the weekend. The one behind the guesthouse had more privacy.

Natia was used to things like this. That was one of the things about her that Dirk loved. She was definitely no pampered princess. Anastasia was the same, but her father, the king, tended to dote on her more.

They then stacked some bigger logs around the kindling in a teepee formation. Natia saw that there were big logs spread out evenly around the pit in a circle to sit on, far enough back that the fire wouldn't burn them but close enough to feel its warmth. Natia suggested they try and start the fire using the bond. Dirk agreed, twisting the bracelet around his wrist. They sat next to each other and decided that each would try individually first.

"If you don't mind, can I try first?" Tab asked. Natia and Dirk agreed. Tab settled in and focused on the kindling. Beads of sweat started to form. After a few minutes, a little trail of smoke drifted into the night sky. "I give up," he said after nothing more than the smoke happened.

"That's ok, Tab," Dirk said.

"You haven't had that much practice with that part of your core," Natia said, patting his shoulder. He smiled gratefully at her. "Dirk, go ahead."

"Ok I'll try." Dirk reached for his core and stared at where he thought would be the best spot for the flames to sprout. After a minute, his bracelet's yellow stone flared to life. A small flame started at the spot where he had been staring. His elation soon ended as a breeze blew the flame out. Natia and Tab were both laughing by his side. "Hey that's not fair! Who did that?" he asked, insinuating one of them had caused the breeze.

Tab just shrugged his shoulders.

Dirk smiled, "Ok *princess*," he emphasized, nodding towards the fire. She wiped a tear away from her eye, faced the kindling, and began to concentrate. Immediately, a flame started at the base. Dirk sent her a thought since he knew Tab still couldn't hear the ones he sent to Natia. *Do you know how beautiful you look tonight*? He saw her smile and began to squirm a little. He smiled and sent her a thought that was more than a little inappropriate.

The flame went out immediately and Natia punched him in the arm so hard it knocked him off the log. Tab started laughing so hard he fell off it too. Natia stood up and pointed a finger at Dirk. "You wish!" She put her hands on her hips the way Kira did when she wanted to get a point across.

He smiled back at her, rubbing his shoulder. "Yeah you're right. I think I do." She gazed at him for another moment and then began to blush. She smiled, put her hand out, and helped him back up to the log.

She sat down and whispered in his ear as Tab finally got back up and sat down. "Maybe one day," She let her lips brush his ear.

That sent chills all through his body. He looked her in the eyes and then looked to the fire.

"I'm not gonna ask," Tab stated from the side.

Natia looked at Tab, still blushing, "You needn't worry. I wouldn't repeat to anyone what he said." Tab caught the gist.

"Ok, let's get this fire started. I'm getting chilled," Dirk said.

"I have an idea. Let's join hands." The boys each took her hand. "Now close your eyes and focus on your core. Let your mind spread into each other through our hands," Natia said.

Tab interrupted. "I know where you're going with this. Like we practice at school with Hilda and Tilda?" Natia nodded. "I have an idea about why we haven't been successful and want to try something with the three of us. It's something that Hilda read from their book."

"Go on." Dirk was curious as to where this was going.

"Remember when she said something about how they were more successful once they got to seven in their bonded group?" They both nodded. "Whatever gave your father that idea, he was adamant that there had to be an uneven number for them to be successful. We've been practicing with El at school and we haven't had much luck." Tab paused to let what he was saying sink in.

Natia, starting to understand finished his thought. "You mean we have to have an odd number for it to work, right?"

Tab smiled but held up a hand, so he could give them the biggest revelation. "That's right, Natia, but were all here to help the Chosen. We have to surround ourselves around him to protect him." Tab raised an eyebrow, anticipating her response. She looked him in the eyes and turned to Dirk, who was looking more confused by the minute.

"I am the Chosen, but Tab is a part of that as well," Dirk said.

"That's true, Dirk, but I wasn't Chosen at birth. I was Chosen and received the bond just because I was there at Arial's death and Aarya's birth." Tab smiled.

Natia and Dirk both realized what he was saying. "You mean that the reason it wasn't successful is because the Chosen has to be in the center of an odd number of bonded." Tab nodded. Natia smiled back.

"Well, let's try." Dirk got up and sat between the two. They took his hand. Immediately, they closed their eyes and concentrated on what Natia had said earlier. There was almost an instant connection to their cores. The warmth spread from Dirk into Natia and Tab equally. All three gasped. It was exhilarating.

All three opened their eyes as one thought passed between them. They looked at the wood in the fire pit and it immediately burst into flames. A smile crossed their faces. They looked to each other with glee. Their eyes were rippling with crimson flames and not because of the raging fire in the pit. Dirk squeezed their hands. Natia and Tab squeezed back.

"We have to make sure we share this information with the twins. This will help us pick up the pace in our training." Dirk said. Tab released his hand, got up and started pacing around the fire. Natia released Dirk's hand after a squeeze of reassurance. Dirk squeezed back and released her hand.

"Say it out loud." Dirk could sense what he was thinking. Natia looked to Tab as well. "There are four bonded right now. Now we know why we've had the problems. We have two choices. We need to add one or three people into the training."

Dirk sighed. He was feeling the same way. "I say three," Natia said.

"That's where you're wrong," Dirk said, looking at the elven protector. She raised an eyebrow at him. Tab looked at him as well. "Linc."

Tab realized he had forgotten about their other best friend. "Well, it worked tonight," Natia said, bringing their attention to her.

"What do you mean?" Dirk asked. Natia paced around the fire with her hands behind her back, her head down, deciding how to phrase what she was thinking. She stopped finally.

"There are five of us now, but there has been ever since that night in the room under the dorms, right?" she asked as Tab sat down next to Dirk on the log bench. "Well, maybe that's where your father's group got it wrong. It's not seven that's powerful, it's the fact that it's an odd number. No matter how many bonded there are, only an odd number of bonded can combine to make their cores connect. Sure, with even numbers I'm sure it can work the longer we are bonded, but the odd number is what matters," Natia said with confidence.

Dirk and Tab could see the logic with what just happened with the fire. "But from your logic, it has to be at least three," Dirk said, understanding.

"That's right. I believe I heard a story once when I was growing up that the power of the odd favored the gods. I can't remember exactly what it was about, but the gist of it was some greater power tied to the gods. Since there were three original gods, Zona, Marluna, and Garga," Natia said, sitting down by Dirk. He nor Tab added anything. They had never heard the story before.

"We can ask my mom," Dirk suggested.

Tab started laughing. "What?" Natia and Dirk asked.

"Don't you see what that means?" They both looked at him. "I know we don't want too many people involved, but if you decide, Dirk, you can bond more than seven."

Dirk finished Tab's thought. "That way if something happens to one of the bonded, then another person will be ready to step up."

Natia smiled, understanding. "But we have to make sure that only an odd number are trying to connect at the same time. There's one more thing. Whatever the odd number is, Dirk has to be in the center of the bond," Natia said, satisfied with their revelations. The three took a satisfied breath. They then discussed the options that were possible.

"Tab, great thinking," Dirk said. "You know that's something that El would have come up with."

"Like the twins say, the longer we're bonded, the more our thinking becomes alike, especially with the feelings Tab has for El," Natia said.

Tab looked at Natia in an understanding way and smiled. "You said that in the tone of our teachers," Dirk said, breaking the small tension that had been formed.

Dirk and Tab laughed at her terrible imitation of the sisters. "Yes, and you know what else they say? The stronger the feelings or how intimate you are with one another, the easier the traits come through."

Tab, realizing what Dirk just said, threw a stick at him that had been lying on the ground beside his foot. Natia, again showing her quickness, caught the stick in midair right in front of Dirk's face. Dirk looked stunned. He thanked her, scowling at Tab.

He smiled. "Sorry, it's my strength. I'm still getting used to it."

Natia threw the stick into the fire. She looked at Tab and a corner of her mouth twisted into a smile. "Well if that intimacy gets any stronger, you won't have to worry about your strength." Tab just looked at her, his mouth open in shock. Dirk said nothing and just watched Tab.

Tab finally closed his mouth and looked Natia in the eyes. "Well if that is the case, then I'm sure Dirk will be eating a lot of salad soon." He smiled sarcastically and turned to head back into the house.

Dirk couldn't believe Tab had just said that. "Wait, Tab."

"Sorry. I'm just tired. I'll see you two in the morning," Tab said over his shoulder, not wanting to look at Natia.

Natia threw another stick into the fire. It crackled and orange sparks floated on the light breeze up into the sky. She slid to the ground off the log and leaned back to gaze at the stars. Dirk watched Tab walk off and then sat on the ground beside Natia leaning back.

"I think he's right. I never would have made a comment like that before I came to Silver City." Dirk turned his head and saw Natia was looking at him.

"What do mean?" Natia turned onto her side to face Dirk. He did as well, leaning on his arm.

"I'm becoming more like you in the way I act. I'm saying things that I normally wouldn't think to say." She smiled and her amber eyes sparkled. "I was raised to be your protector. I was warned many times about the feelings that came with the bond and the dangers of it. I was taught to keep them in check or face what the consequences might be." Natia gazed into Dirk's eyes and placed a hand on his face.

"Natia, I can't explain the way I feel, either. Let me ask you a question though. I know that after the first time I saw you I've felt different. I first thought it was just intrigue but knowing now what I know, I know what I feel," Dirk said, running his fingers through the hair that had fallen over her shoulder.

"What's the question?" she asked.

"This has been going on for hundreds of years, right? My question is this, then. Why?"

Natia raised her head. "I don't understand?"

Dirk twirled her hair between his fingers, pulled it towards him and took a deep breath, smiling at the scent. "If everything you have been taught is from the lessons of the past, then why do we do things the same way? What if we do it different this time? I mean, they all lost, sort of. Who's to say that when my father and mother fell in love, if she had stayed by his side instead of giving up her role, they might have succeeded?" Dirk asked sincerely. Natia stared at him with a questioning look on her face. While Dirk waited on an answer, the fire crackled in the background. An owl hooted in the woods. "Probably a predator roaming the woods," Dirk said, looking to the woods. Dirk turned back to face her.

She put her hand at the base of his neck and pulled him closer. Dirk's body reacted to the sensual move. His breathing became shallower. Natia's eyes were rippling with flames. Dirk tensed a little when his anatomy started to react. Being this close to her, the smell of the almonds and honey that he hadn't been able to stop thinking about for the last few weeks was sending his body into a spin.

Without any further hesitation, Dirk leaned in and their lips touched fully for the first time. He kept his eyes open. He wanted to see her face when they first kissed. Natia kept her eyes open as well. Giving in to the desire that had been growing, Natia slid her tongue into his mouth, finding his. It was soft and gentle. Dirk, not experienced in this kind interaction, let her take control. Her tongue twisted around his and he copied her movements.

Natia slid closer and wrapped her leg around his waist, pulling him tighter to her body. She ran her fingers through his hair while rotating her mouth to take in every sweet taste he was giving her. Dirk grabbed her at the waist and pressed her closer to his body. She moaned when her crotch was pulled tighter to his. Dirk's stiffness made him feel uncomfortable but hearing the pleasure in her moan from his squeeze, he decided not to worry about it anymore.

Dirk's pants weren't as soft as Natia's. He was wearing his regular clothing, but he could feel the heat her pleasure was emanating. Natia put her hands inside Dirk's shirt. The tightness of his body made her body ache, wanting him to take her that much more.

Natia pulled one hand out and with a wave at the fire the flames settled down to a small dim light. Dirk pulled back from her lips. She put both hands on his face. The flame was barely rippling in the pit, but the flames that were rippling in their eyes gave off enough light that Dirk could see her face. Natia looked around. The pit was between the guest house and the horse fields, so they had privacy.

"Are you sure?"

Natia smiled, "Without a single doubt."

Dirk got up off the ground and picked her up into his arms. Natia smiled. She was in the arms of the man that she knew she loved. Dirk carried her to the guest house that Kira always kept ready for guests. He gently opened the door and closed it while still holding Natia in his arms. The guest house had a small kitchen with a living room and two bedrooms. Dirk knew Kira always kept the finest sheets on her guest house beds. He wanted the best for Natia. Dirk took her to the room that was furthest away from his house.

He pointed his fingers towards the logs in the fireplace. Dirk's bracelet flared. The flames burst into existence. Natia smiled and shivered in his arms. Dirk pulled the blankets back on the bed. He gently laid her down on the silk sheets. Natia waved her hand and the door closed gently. She waved again and a red light flared over the door.

"For our privacy," she said as Dirk leaned forward and kissed her on the neck. The taste of honey again sent fire through his body. Natia pulled Dirk's shirt over his head. She ran her fingers through the hair on his chest. Dirk leaned down and started undoing the wrap she had tied to her waist. Natia trembled as Dirk opened her tunic and slipped it off. He took both sandals off, kissing each toe, sending chills throughout her body. He then slipped her pants off slowly, laying them on the floor with her top.

Natia's eyes flamed as Dirk took in her body. "You are the most beautiful women I have ever laid my eyes on."

"Dirk Storm, if you don't take me soon, I'm going to go crazy." She gripped the sheets in her hands and looked deeply into his eyes. "Dirk, I have never been with anyone before."

"I've never been with anyone either," Dirk said as he leaned over and kissed her passionately. He pulled back and gazed into her eyes. "I'm sure we will figure it out." Dirk kissed her again.

For the next several hours, they spent their time exploring what each other enjoyed the most, as new lovers do. After they were too tired to carry on, Natia laid her head on Dirk's chest. Her auburn hair hung down, surrounding his face. "I love you Dirk Storm."

Dirk, finally able to move his arms, lifted his hands up and cupped her face. His eyes flashed flames. He knew because he saw the reflection in hers. "I love you too, and I will never let you go." A tear fell onto Dirk's face.

He noticed she was crying. He kissed her cheek and then pulled her close. "I won't let you go, either. Anywhere you go I go, in life and death,"

"Agreed," he said before they dozed off in each other's arms.

The young lovers laid there until a sense of urgency came over Dirk's thoughts.

Where are you?

Dirk started waking up, becoming aware of Tab's message. He woke Natia up. She was snuggled up next to him. "What time is it?"

They both realized they had fallen asleep. They both jumped up in a panic and hurriedly put their clothes on. Natia removed the shield and waved her hand at the fire, putting out the small flames that still burned. Dirk quickly made up the bed, deciding to change the sheets later. Natia stopped his rushing around and grabbed his face to force him to look at her. Seeing she had his attention, she kissed him passionately receiving the same in return.

Hurry! With the urgency of Tab's message, Dirk and Natia slipped out of the guest house quietly. They ran in the light of the morning sun. He sent a mental note to Tab and ran with Natia by his side until he got underneath his bedroom window.

"I have an idea. Trust me and do as I say." He told her to step into his hands that he had clasped together at his waist. "When I push you up, jump to my window!"

Natia understood. Tab was leaning out, mouthing for them to hurry. "Now!"

Natia jumped with all her strength as Dirk lifted her up in the air. Natia grabbed Tab's hands as she got close to the window. He pulled her through into the room. Natia thanked him and rushed to her bedroom as Kira was coming up the stairs. She quietly closed the door and fell into her bed.

Dirk made the jump, barely catching Tab's arms. Tab pulled him through the window and Dirk and Tab both crawled into bed as Kira came in.

"You two sleepy heads better get up. We have a big day." She turned after seeing that the boys were stirring in the bed and quietly knocked on Natia's door. Dirk heard Natia reply, and he smiled with relief.

Hearing Kira going down the stairs. Tab leaned on one arm and stared at

Dirk. "Tab, Natia was just poking fun at you."

Tab looked at Dirk then smiled. "I know she was. I was just jealous that El wasn't here."

Dirk smirked. "She will be later on today."

"I'll tell her later that I'm sorry."

"She will probably beat you to it. She felt so bad."

"It wasn't that bad, was it?" Tab asked with a devious grin on his face.

Dirk threw his pillow at him so hard feathers busted out of the seam on impact.

Both boys laughed so hard it caused Kira to come back up and scold them for being so loud. It didn't help when she saw the down floating around the room. "You two will clean this mess up and I mean every single feather. Before breakfast." She almost ran into Natia as she was leaving the boys room. "Oh, Natia, dear, I hope you slept well?"

Natia hugged her aunt. "The best night's sleep I have had in a very long time. Thanks. I'm just going to wash up before breakfast if that's ok?"

Kira looked at her god-niece and smiled. "That's fine, dear. Just stay out of that room until those two fools clean up their mess." Kira motioned towards the boy's room. Natia raised an eyebrow and looked in the room to see the boys cleaning up feathers.

Tab noticed her and smiled. "Good morning, Natia. I just wanted to say I'm sorry for being an ass last night. I was missing El really bad and I was jealous of you two getting to spend time together."

Natia walked up to Tab. "Tab I understand. I shouldn't have been kidding with you like that. I am sorry, too." Natia hugged Tab and he hugged her back. She whispered. "And if you talk about last night with anyone, I will demand that we be practice partners the next time we have weapons training."

He pushed her back and frowned. "I'm hurt."

She looked at him and studied his face. "You will be if you don't remember what I said."

Tab mimed buttoning his lip. She smiled and winked at Dirk and headed for the bath. Dirk wanted to follow her badly and pick up where they left off, but he was slammed in the head with a pillow.

"Payback," Tab said. Dirk fell back on his bed, took a deep breath, and let it out, gazing at the ceiling. "Dirk, stop."

He looked at Tab, confused.

"Remember, I can sense your thoughts this close, and I don't need to think about what you're thinking about when we see her downstairs."

Dirk smiled. "Sorry, let's get this mess cleaned up. I'm starving."

Tab mumbled under his breath, "I bet." They both laughed. The boys finished cleaning up the room before Kira could yell at them a third time.

Diron's Warning and a Grizwolf

After breakfast, Kira sent Claire out to see if she could help Bart and Carly. She fussed, but when Kira told her to remember that everyone had to help, she begrudgingly agreed. Dirk, Tab, and Natia helped clean up the dishes while Kira checked on Ulny.

When she came back from checking on her, Dirk and his friends were waiting on her at the table. "Sit down, Mom."

Kira knew what this was about. "I'm sorry I didn't get to talk with you last night. I'm just so tired lately. There's so much to do around here now, especially with a ten-year-old girl living here. Then there's her mother. Don't get me wrong, we owe her father. If it hadn't been for him, we might have lost Lincoln."

Natia looked at Dirk. "Linc. Mom and the general call him by his full name," Dirk explained. Natia nodded. "Mom, why don't you get some more help? Grandfather can afford it now that he's working for the king again."

Kira shook her head. "It's not that. It's just been a long time since I had a little one running around, and the other issue you asked about last night." She stared at Dirk and squeezed his arm.

"So, tell us. We're all family here," Dirk motioned around the table. Kira sighed.

"Lately, your father has been appearing to me," Kira began.

Dirk, concerned for his mother's safety, leaned forward, and grabbed her hand. She smiled and put her free hand on top of his.

"It started out with him appearing for a few minutes. He was translucent and I couldn't understand what he was saying to me. Then it started getting more frequent. His words started becoming clear. I didn't understand why it started after all this time until I finally started understanding what he was telling me. He was urging me to become more forthcoming with you about your destiny. It all made sense then. You had officially become the Chosen. That's when I knew for sure it was him. I thought at first it might be Zolun trying to trick me," Kira took a deep breath. Dirk could tell this had shaken his mother. He squeezed her hand.

"It's ok Mom. We're here,"

Kira smiled at her son. Then looked at Tab and Natia. "It was him. There's no doubt. I felt it in my core. Once I started believing who I was seeing, he became clearer. He just kept telling me to get you ready. That a war was coming, sooner than later. I tried to get him to tell me how he was appearing, but it was like he would say what he wanted to say then he would disappear. Then, lately, he became really cryptic with what he was saying."

"What do you mean more cryptic?" Dirk asked.

Kira squeezed Dirk's hand, smiled and then she looked at Natia whom she noticed, had a certain glow about her this morning. Kira, without Dirk or Tab noticing, raised a questioning eyebrow at Natia. Natia immediately felt like she was being probed.

"Aunt Kira, finish telling us. The sooner you tell us maybe we can help." The diversion worked.

"He kept saying, 'Make sure Dirk knows he is being forced'. It's not his fault. It was like he was in a loop."

The three looked at each other. Tab spoke up first. "That sounds like we may have a traitor amongst us." Dirk and Natia agreed.

"But no one that's bonded can be a traitor. There's only five of us and two are girls. Linc is so far away, he can't harm us. Tab and I are always together so I know it's not Tab," Dirk said and Natia and Tab nodded.

"Natia, what have you been taught about visions?" Kira asked.

Natia paused, thinking about how to say what she needed to say without hurting anyone's feelings. "They can come from a spirit in distress that can't pass into the afterlife for some reason or other. I mean, what little I know is that sometimes they can be unreliable because the spirit is confused. They also have knowledge about the future events I was taught."

Kira nodded. "That's what I was taught as well. And nicely put, dear." Kira patted Natia's hand.

Dirk looked at Tab. "Wait a minute." They all looked at him. "The night the general introduced us to the Book of Storms, there was a man in my dreams saying the same thing." Before Kira could respond, he continued. "I think that was Dad." He described what he could remember from the dream.

Kira teared up. "That definitely was your father. Do you remember anything else, Dirk?" He shook his head. "Tab, do you remember anything like that from your dreams that night?" Kira asked.

"I remember a group of men and women, human, elves, and dwarves sitting around a fire. And Mom, you were there also. You all were listening to a dwarf tell a story. The part I remember is that it involved a goat and a cleaver. Then everyone was laughing. It's all kind of hazy."

Kira laughed. Tab frowned at her. Kira squeezed Tabs shoulder. "I'm not laughing at you, dear. I'm laughing about that night. We were at the base of Jover Mountain. Hilda, Tilda, Josie, Heath, Diron, Thad, Naira, Askin, and I were there with a group of dwarves who were showing us survival skills to use in that kind of terrain. Gunnar was the one telling the story about the goat. He was a funny dwarf. He was going to kill the goat, and the way he went after the goat, it scared it so bad that it squirted him in the face with its milk, which made him fall down and roll on the cleaver. It stuck in his butt." When Kira finished telling the story all of them were laughing. Kira smiled.

"So, what are we gonna do about this traitor?" Dirk asked.

"Be vigilant," Kira said. "You can't worry about what might happen, you just need to keep an eye on who you choose to bond with. Visions are like prophecies. There is always more than one meaning and that doesn't mean it will happen."

"Mom, I think there could be another answer," Dirk said. She looked at him questioningly. "It could be a sorceress or even Zolun himself trying to give us false information." Dirk let that sink in.

"Tab spoke up. "Yeah Mom, they might want us to not trust anyone. They'll make us so untrusting that we won't follow through with a plan for fear it might be compromised." Natia agreed.

"That could very well be. But I am still going to communicate with Diron's spirit when it shows up. That way I can gain as much information as I can."

Dirk dropped his head. He didn't want his mother taking any unnecessary risks. He looked her in the eyes. "I agree. But promise me you will be careful."

Kira placed a hand on Dirk's face and smiled. "I promise,"

After that, they discussed their hypothesis from last night and told her how it worked with the three of them. "You know, we never tried that. Heck, I don't even think we thought of trying it with more people," Kira said. The three of them smiled, proud of their accomplishment.

Dirk turned to the window when he heard the pounding of hoof beats on the dirt road. Kira got up and looked out the window as the horses stopped in front of the barn.

Claire rushed to the door. "Ms. Kira. Strangers are here," She said from outside the door, then she took off running.

"She takes her job seriously," Tab said. They all laughed.

"I better go rescue your grandfather. Claire probably didn't realize it was him in the king's carriage," Kira said and went out of the door, yelling at Claire.

"The king's carriage?" Tab asked. They followed Kira out to see what warranted the general coming home in the king's carriage.

The general was standing beside Claire, smiling. What really got Dirk's attention was the man leaning down, talking with Claire. He was wearing brown pants and a crimson tunic with a brown belt around his waist. His dark hair had streaks of silver running through it. "By the gods!" Dirk stopped halfway before he reached them. Kira was straightening her hair and talking to another woman who had gotten out of the coach.

"What, Dirk?" Tab asked.

"It's the king," Natia stated.

Queen Thea was wearing a simple pair of beige pants with a shirt that matched the kings. Her raven, silver-streaked hair was pulled back into a bun. Thea smiled and waved at them. They were standing there looking dumbfounded. Dirk then noticed Anastasia getting out of the carriage and heading his way. She had a grin on her face, but Dirk knew that look all too well.

"She's pissed that she's here I bet," Dirk said. Natia looked curiously at him. "I told you what she said that night on the roof."

"Yes," Tab said.

"Yesterday, she seemed like she would be leaving today going to join Thelon."

"I guess that isn't going to happen now," Natia stated, smiling as Anastasia walked up and she hugged her.

"Hi Dirk."

"Hi Stas." Dirk looked at her inquisitively.

"I'll tell you later but first, don't you think it's time I met your friend?" she said nodding toward Tab. Dirk introduced them.

"H-hell-o. It's nice to meet you," Tab said in a quivering voice.

"Relax, Tab. I'm one of you. I'd rather be hunting in the woods than hanging around a bunch of giggling girls at the palace." She smiled and patted his shoulder.

Natia smiled at the comment. Tab relaxed and finally said. "I would love to practice the bow with you sometime."

Anastasia smiled. "Well, from what I remember from the tournament, you did well for yourself."

Tab couldn't believe she remembered that. "I do ok, but El still beat me."

"Yeah, but just barely. Is she here yet?"

Dirk responded first. "She and the others will be here soon. Again, what are you doing here?"

Anastasia motioned to her father. "Let's go for a walk." She cleared her throat loudly. "Father?"

The king stopped talking with Claire, stood up, patted her head. He bowed to Kira and kissed her hand. She smiled, looping Thea through the arm. The king kissed his wife on the cheek and told her he would see her later. She said hello to the kids as she walked by with Kira. The general, right behind the king cleared his throat as they walked up. Claire ran to catch up with Kira and Thea and waved as she ran past.

Anastasia smiled at her as her father said, "Yes dear?"

"I just wanted to let you know we were gonna go for a walk. We haven't really had a chance to talk since school started and Natia wants to tell me about what they have been learning. And the boys wanted to show us the farm."

"Hello, princess Natia." The king bowed.

Natia curtsied back. "Your Highness."

Then he looked at Dirk and Tab and smiled. "Hello Dirk, hello Tab."

Both boys bowed. Or at least tried to.

The king stopped them. "We're all friends here, boys. Remember what I told you at the banquet, Dirk."

"Yes sir," Dirk said. Tab was freaking out that the king knew his name and just stood there before finally saying hello.

"That will be fine but there are some things that Natia, Dirk and I need to discuss sometime today. Don't forget."

"Yes Father," Anastasia grabbed Natia and headed towards the back of the house. Dirk and Tab followed after saying hello to the general.

Dirk stopped. "General, have you seen El and the rest of my friends? You should have past them on the road here."

The general and the king were walking towards the general's workshop. The general looked back and said, "Oh, they all decided to come a little later."

Dirk nodded. He knew something was up by the general's tone but knew not to ask. He and Tab rushed to catch up with the girls who had made it to the fire pit. Dirk would remember last night for the rest of his life. Natia beamed as he and Tab sat down on the log, facing Anastasia and herself.

Anastasia flicked her hand in a circling motion and a red shield formed around the logs surrounding the pit.

"First, Dirk, if my father asks, you invited Kal to the camp-out tonight."

Dirk smiled, "I will if you tell me what in all the hells is going on."

She took a deep breath and looked at Tab for a moment. "I guess you two are really close?"

Tab answered for Dirk. "Brothers."

She smiled and relaxed a little. "I thought so. I could tell the way you two were never apart growing up. I'm just sorry, Tab, I didn't get the chance to know you like I did Dirk."

Tab looked at her with confidence. "It's not too late."

She frowned at that comment. Tab thought he had offended her by her remark. "Unfortunately, it may be." Before he could apologize, she started talking again. "Father is worried about the skirmishes in the south. It's going bad for us. We've lost thousands of soldiers and Father is going to send more troops to support Thelon. After we get back on Monday, all of the third-year students and remaining military cadets are marching out to replace the soldiers who are leaving to join the campaign in the south."

"What about the elves?" Natia asked.

"From what I understand, they're sending a legion south from Elmwood to participate, but they will have to travel north first, then head south to join Thelon."

Tab looked at Natia. She read his mind. "If they traveled south, they would have to go through Dead Swamp. Then they would have to skirt the Screel's territory even though he hasn't been seen since Der-Tod." Natia paused, giving the boys a sympathetic look. "There are rumors he has been building his army up again." Anastasia nodded.

Tab finished what Natia was saying. "So, they are traveling north first to go around any potential threats." Anastasia nodded again.

"That still doesn't explain why you're here," Dirk said.

Anastasia's intense stare made him a little uncomfortable. Natia started to fidget a little, feeling Dirk's uncomfortableness.

"He knows that the school and academy will be depleted by a whole grade when we leave. Oh, hells, Dirk, he wants to make sure you and Natia are well on your way to being trained." She stopped, leaving it hanging in the air for a minute. Dirk cocked his head to the side and looked at Anastasia. "Don't be daft, Dirk, he knows your family's legacy. For the gods, he and your grandfather were best friends growing up. Who do you think the Chosen answers to, anyway?"

"Ah!" Tab said.

Dirk looked at Tab. *Don't mention our connection to anyone yet. Not even the king.* Tab sensed his thoughts and felt Natia agreeing.

"Natia is the obvious choice as your protector. I'm sure her parents informed Father the day they got in town."

"That's the first thing they would have done," Natia confirmed.

Dirk finally said what he had been thinking. "That night on the roof, you hinted that you knew, didn't you?" She smiled.

"Yes, I've known a long time. I just didn't know what it meant until recently when Father explained to me what the Storm legacy was, and that if anything happened to him or Thelon, I would know whom to turn to when things got bad."

"Thelon knows too?" Dirk asked, feeling the heat in his eyes come to life.

"Yes, he was working with your grandfather before he left. Your grandfather helped him set up the plan to combat the advancing forces in the south." Anastasia paused and looked Dirk in the eyes. She put her hand over her mouth when his eyes rippled with flames but quickly composed herself. Her shoulders tensed, and she did the shoulder roll that she always did to ease the stiffness. "If something bad happens and it comes down to us, I just want to make sure you do as I ask. Not as your princess, but as your friend. Don't do anything rash and stupid if something happens to me!" she said pointing a finger at him.

Dirk raised his shoulders back a little and smiled at her. "You know me, Stas."

She glared at him. "Fortunately, I do, and I will order you if I have to!" Dirk smiled.

"Stas, if it gets so bad that something happens to you, I can promise you that I won't do anything stupid. Though I will not stand by with these gifts and let the girl I first kissed be hurt." Dirk let his words sink in while he and Tab got up and moved closer to her and Natia. "I'll tell you," he started, grabbed Natia's hand and put his other hand on Tab's shoulder, "that we'll have a good plan and I assure you we'll have the right people with us."

Anastasia finally relaxed, stood up, and hugged Dirk. "Hey!" she said, pushing him back. "I thought you said you'd never tell anyone that." She then pulled him into another hug.

Natia observed Dirk and Anastasia embrace. Her eyes rippled flames. A wave of jealousy started to overtake her. Tab sensed her uneasiness about Dirk and Anastasia's relationship. He placed a hand on her shoulder and squeezed. Natia snapped her head around towards Tab like a viper fixing to attack. He smiled. *Friends only.* Her eyes cooled instantly after realizing what She already knew. *Oh, my gods. I was about to be the psycho girlfriend, wasn't I?*

I think you're more than a girlfriend. I think you know that. Tab thought

Natia smiled and squeezed Tab's hand. *Thanks.*

He squeezed back. *You're welcome, sister.* A tear formed in Natia's eye. She quickly wiped it away before Dirk and Anastasia could see it. She smiled and turned back to the discussion.

"Well, I think that's enough for us to think about right now. Do you have any more lingering questions?" Anastasia stared at Dirk and then looked into Tab's and Natia's eyes. Tab looked away because he didn't want her to know his secret yet. She assumed Tab was just saying no. Amazed at seeing the flames in Dirk's and Natia's eyes, she was satisfied with how their conversation had gone. She then looked towards the house and smiled. "Good, since Kal seems to have arrived." She waved two fingers. The bracelet she was wearing glowed red for a few seconds and the shield disappeared as Kal was striding towards them.

Kal carried himself the way Dirk hoped he would someday, tall with broad shoulders and confident. His blond hair was pulled back into a ponytail and his piercing green eyes scanned the area. He wore light green slacks, a white traveling shirt, and a brown leather vest buttoned halfway up. He carried an air of strength about him with each stride that Dirk definitely wanted.

Kal smiled when Anastasia put her arms around him and kissed him in greeting. Dirk noticed Kal was looking around uncomfortably. "Don't worry. He and the general are still in the general's workshop."

"Whew, I'm glad but you could have warned me before that most welcomed kiss," he said lightly.

She smiled, "Kal, I know you've heard me talk about Dirk." She waved an open hand towards Dirk.

Kal reached out and shook Dirk's hand. "By the way, thanks for the invite. I've heard stories about the Storms my whole life and to be here at the farm is a bit overwhelming." Dirk wanted to scream from the firmness of Kal's grip but bit it back. Tab snickered under his breath. Natia just sent one thought to Dirk.

Yummy!

He looked at her with an *are you kidding me?* look.

Don't worry, farm boy. You're the only thing on my menu. He smiled back at her.

After finally catching what Kal said he looked at Kal and responded. "It's nice to meet you, but you stirred my curiosity. What stories?"

"My grandfather and father both served in the military. So, you see, I was raised hearing about their time served in the military." Then Kal turned and bowed to Natia. "Princess Natia, I am at your service."

She curtsied. "It's, just Natia. That's what my friends call me."

Kal straightened. "Natia it is." He then turned to Tab, "If it isn't one of the archers that almost made us looked bad, Stas," Kal said, smiling and shaking his hand. Tab couldn't handle the grip quite like Dirk had so he pulled his hand back, shaking off the pain.

Anastasia punched Kal "Sorry Tab, I was always taught that a firm grip is the biggest impression you can give. I apologize."

Tab smiled "That's ok, I just wasn't ready that's all."

Dirk laughed inside. *Tab, you would never be ready for that grip!*

"Well, it looks like several people are starting to arrive, Dirk. Since you're the host, I guess you have duties to perform. If it's ok, Kal and I will hang out here until Father gets done with the general."

"That's fine." Dirk, Natia and Tab headed to the front of the house. Dirk stopped and looked back at Anastasia. "Hey Stas, where is your dad's guard?"

Anastasia smiled. "Oh, they set up a perimeter around the farm. He wanted to keep this trip low-profile, so he didn't bring that many."

Dirk nodded an ok and headed towards his group of friends, who were walking down the trail to his home. El was the official guide.

As El was telling the twins, Phil, Dusty, and the dwarves where everything was located at the farm, she smiled to herself. She saw that Dirk, Tab and Natia were walking away from Princess Anastasia and Kal James. She wasn't surprised since on the main trail, they were all but accosted by the king's guard. El knew that the general and the king grew up together and were close friends. She also noticed Dirk and Natia were walking really close to each other, practically holding hands. She smiled and looked at Tab, who was happily walking and talking. He was just so natural.

That is the only thing he would ever be. Probably why I love him! El thought. Tab whipped around and stared at her.

"Oh Shit! *Privacious*," El muttered under her breath, the strange sensation clouding her mind for a second. Tab smiled and waved. Vira, who didn't miss anything, eased up to walk beside El since Nira was only interested in what Dusty was saying.

"El, dear," she said, grabbing El's hand and squeezing it, "did I just hear you use a privacy spell?" El looked at Vira. It surprised her how different Vira had become in one day.

After Dirk had solidified their friendship on the hill, both twins seemed to have expelled any doubt about being liked and just relaxed into normal people.

"El?" Vira raised an eyebrow and looped her arm through hers.

"My mom taught me that when I was younger. She told me you never knew who might be listening to your thoughts, so she showed me how to protect my thoughts and feelings." Vira just nodded.

"You know that's the first spell my grandfather ever taught Nira and me." Vira slowed El down so they could talk. The others sensed them slowing and Jonesy took over the tour guide's job, leading the crowd towards his friends. Vira turned El so that they were facing each other. "I want you to know that if there's anything you ever feel like talking about, that I'm here for you, anytime, anywhere. What you and your friends have done for us is so wonderful. We never had any real friends before. I mean, sure, when we were little, we had several but the older we all grew, those damn evil bastards started sinking their hooks into every one of them. Teaching them to think they were better than all the world and that one day they would return back here and take back what was taken from them."

Vira looked off in the distance, clearly remembering a bad time.

"You're talking about the council of Aarkas?"

Vira nodded. "If it weren't for Grandfather, we would have ended up like our parents," Vira said with tears in her eyes.

El held Vira's hands. "I have a feeling, Vira, that one day we will make them pay for what they've done to you and Nira." The use of *we* made Vira smile.

"Remember what I said. I know that word you used is powerful and I won't ask why, just know I'm here." Vira kissed El on the cheek. El nodded.

"What's this?" a voice asked a few feet away. The girls turned and saw Dirk. Tab was talking with Jonesy, Volar, and Raga. Natia had been pulled off to the side by Tara and Oriana, her childhood friends who had shown up with the rest. "El, you wouldn't be keeping my new sister to yourself, would you?" Dirk stopped in front of them, staring at El.

El smiled back and hugged Dirk. Vira practically knocked El out of the way so she could hug Dirk too. El snickered. Vira, after squeezing the life out of Dirk eased him back. "Sorry, I have been wanting to do that again since yesterday. I wanted you to know what you mean to us." Dirk hugged Vira again with one arm, which she accepted, and then they started walking toward the house. El stepped to his other side. Dirk put his free arm around her, and she listened to Dirk as they walked.

"I can't wait for you to meet Mom," Dirk said to Vira. He saw her grin get bigger the closer to the house they got.

"Will she like us?" Vira asked.

"Let's find out." Dirk released El and pulled Nira away from Dusty, who was standing with the rest of the group off to the side. He told Dusty he would return her soon. Nira, embracing Dirk, walked with him to the front door. Dirk stopped and explained they had a sick guest in the house, but he would elaborate on that later. He knocked on the door. "Mom, can you come out and join us for a few minutes? I have someone I need you to meet."

Vira was surprised when a little blonde girl ran to the door and stared at her. Vira looked at Dirk then at the girl. Dirk laughed. "No Vira, that's not my mom. This is Claire. She lives with us. Actually, she and her mom do,"

Vira realized Claire's mom must be the sick guest and leaned forward and introduced herself and Nira. Claire said "Hello," and took off into the house.

Nira laughed out loud, still in Dirk's hug. Dirk looked at her and smirked. "I guess Vira isn't the only one in the family with a beautiful laugh." Nira covered her mouth with her other hand and squeezed Dirk. Kira finally must have left Claire with the queen because she walked out of the house.

She beamed at her son. "And who are these two lovely women you have at your side, son?" Kira smiled.

"Mom I want you to meet your new daughters. I have adopted them into the Storm family and want your approval."

Dirk could sense that Vira and Nira were really nervous. "What will we do if she doesn't like us?" Nira said so only that Dirk could hear.

"Don't worry. She will love you, like I do," Dirk said and gave the twins a squeeze before releasing their embrace.

Kira looked at the twins while walking around, inspecting them. "I don't know son. They look a little thin." She stood in front of them. Dirk had told his mom all about the twins and their life story. At least the version Vira had told. After getting to know them better, he sensed there was more to the story.

Kira knew what Dirk was doing. "What do you think, Thea?"

Dirk had seen the queen come out of the house and walk up to see what was going on outside. He smiled at her. She hinted a smile back. Claire was glued to her side. The other kids, who had been talking, stopped, and bowed. They all knew who she was, but they didn't know that she was inside the house.

Thea waved them off and they all stood watching her. She told Claire to stay put for a minute and walked around the twins, eyeing them. She stood beside Kira and looked them in the eyes. Thea walked with such grace that crowds would just watch with awe. When she spoke, even the king was amazed.

"Kira, I think they need some fattening up but other than that, they are absolutely beautiful." The queen smiled.

Kira, who had been deep in thought, finally smiled. "You two are welcome into our family."

Vira squealed. Nira did her eye roll, but she had been holding her breath. They rushed forward. The queen held her hand up to pause the elated twins. They stopped mere inches from the queen's hand.

"Vira and Nira of Aarkas."

"Yes, my lady?" they both said bowing.

"Do you swear with your life, that you will be honest, trustworthy, and loyal to the house Storm and my husband, the king of Silver City?" The queens face was stern. It had a stone coldness to it. Her demeanor sent a chill through the twins that even Dirk could sense. Even though she was presenting a chilling exterior, Dirk knew, and the twins knew, she meant well. After all, it was that important to be a part of the Storm family.

"We do, on our lives," they said in unison.

The queen's face relaxed. She smiled and moved her hand. "Then I officially name you Vira and Nira of the house Storm. Let the hugs begin." They rushed forward, embracing Kira, who was shocked at what Thea had just done. Regaining her composure, she hugged them back. Thea got pulled into the embrace a moment later.

"Well, I guess I'm not needed anymore?" Dirk said, pretending to be hurt, dropping his head, and closing his eyes. Thea pulled Dirk into the hug and he smiled.

Thea whispered in his ear while the girls were talking nonstop with Kira. "Take care of your sisters and they will take care of you." She pushed him back so she could look him in the eyes. A look passed between them. Dirk nodded. Thea, satisfied with what she saw in Dirk's eyes, released him, and walked back into the house with Claire in tow.

Kira, finally breaking free of the twins, was led over to the other group by Dirk. He introduced her to the ones she didn't know.

Natia sent Dirk a thought. It was an image not words. *The bed in the guest house.*

His face turned so red that his mother checked his head to see if he had a temperature. He assured her it was just from the excitement of everyone being there. She finally relented.

Dirk went to show the group where to stow their packs, and where they would camp-out tonight. As Dirk was leading them to the second fire pit, he looked at Jonesy and Raga, "I thought you were staying at home with the dwarves, not coming until after they learned some things from your father?"

"Thelgra, Fernen, and Jangoo stayed back to work with him. Raga wanted to come on out here with Volar, so I came too. I think they will be busy all day and possibly tomorrow, seeing how my father was excited to learn some of their techniques," Jonesy replied. Raga nodded affirmatively.

Dirk patted his big friend's shoulder. "I've missed you not being around, big guy," he said to Jonesy. Jonesy returned the sentiment and the group followed Dirk to the pit.

Back at the fire pit behind the guest house, Kal and Anastasia were watching the group of friends come together. "Look at him."

Stas smiled. "He is a natural leader."

Kal agreed. "If what you tell me is true, we will need him to be that one day."

"Soon Kal, much sooner than I'm afraid he will be ready for."

Kal squeezed her hand. "My love, we will be there as well, right by his side."

"Well, we better be or that would mean we were dead," Anastasia said flatly.

Kal sighed. "I'll make sure that doesn't happen."

She kissed his cheek. "Well, time to go, Father and the general are coming out of the general's shop."

Kal got up and offered Anastasia his hand. "I'll retract one thing." Anastasia stopped and looked at him. "I'll be there if your father doesn't kill me first." He smiled, motioning towards the king who was scowling.

Anastasia smiled and waved, walking toward her father. "He's a big teddy bear."

Kal laughed. "Yeah, with the fangs of a grizzly," Kal said as he followed her.

After Dirk had finished getting his friends set up where they were going to sleep, he met up with Kal and Anastasia. They had just finished talking with the king and the general.

"There has been some wolf attacks here lately. I was thinking, how about a wolf hunt?"

Kal looked at Anastasia and smiled. "Sounds great," Anastasia replied.

"General, I think my friends and I are going to go out and take care of that wolf problem Moms been having. Is that ok?" Dirk asked.

The general looked to the king who shrugged. "See if you can kill some boars while you're out. That would be great for dinner," the king replied. The general nodded.

"Our pleasure," Dirk replied.

"So, lets split up in two groups. Kal, you and Stas can take one group south, and I'll lead another one from the north. Tab, you, and El go with Kal's group. Nira, Jonesy, and Dusty can go with you. I'll Take Natia, Vira, Volar, Raga, Oriana, Phil, and Tara. We'll try to push them south towards your group and get them in a crossfire." Dirk said with everyone nodding.

Dirk's group headed off into the woods with their weapons of choice for the hunt. Volar and Raga carried hand axes. Jonesy carried a spear. The elves all had bows. Tab, El, Vira and Dusty had selected bows as well. El was itching to try her new bow. Dirk wanted to help chase out the game, so he only carried a dagger. Natia carried her twin katanas. Nira had chosen katanas as well. Kal and Anastasia carried the bows they had received at the award banquet.

Tabs group would take the trail that led them close to the old wolf's den the pack had discovered earlier in the year. Tab wanted to follow up on the wolves with his group and see if they really were starting to get brave and venture to the farm. Dirk agreed. Dirk led them north closer to the dark forest, north of Silver City. Tara and Oriana were Natia's best friends and were good trackers. He wanted to learn how the elves tracked. Volar and Raga didn't really care about the hunting. They just wanted to visit Blazire. Both trails eventually led to the mountain anyway.

The general and the king were tempted to come along with them but decided to let the younger adults have their fun, at the urging of the queen.

As soon as Dirk and his group were a hundred yards into the woods, he could sense a predator was near. He stopped at the first curve of the trail and bent down, looking, at the tracks in front of him. Oriana and Tara kneeled down on each side of him, arrows already nocked.

"What is it?" Natia asked as Volar, and Raga stopped behind them with their axes ready. Vira and Phil also had their weapons drawn. Phil had a spear; he didn't like the bow. Vira had a bow that was made of a wood Dirk had never seen. It was black, and the bowstring was made of a type of red leather. She could fight with katana's but preferred the bow.

"These don't look like wolf tracks. They're too big," Dirk said, touching the paw marks on the ground.

"Are they a bear?" Volar asked.

"No, they're too small for that," Dirk replied. Natia and Tara just looked at each other.

"I'll scout ahead," Oriana said. Before Dirk could say no, she took off at a stealthy pace. She was smaller than Natia and seemed to glide through the woods.

Damn, Dirk thought. I wished I had brought my sword now.

Natia sensed his thoughts, *Don't worry, love, I am here.*

Dirk looked at her and smiled. "Ok let's move ahead but be on alert." They all agreed.

"Sister, keep our backs covered in case whatever this is tries to sneak up on us."

Vira couldn't keep from smiling. "Don't worry, brother, Phil and I have our backs." Dirk and Natia smiled and moved forward, watching from all sides for any threats. Tara followed right behind them with Volar and Raga at her side, and Vira and Phil brought up the rear.

Dirk took in the view as they searched for any threats. The foliage was thicker on this side of the farm. The maples and pines seemed to be intertwined, making it hard to see through them easily. The trail was narrower than the one Dirk usually trekked through to Blazire. The trail was covered with fallen leaves and the broken limbs of trees.

"Everyone watch your step. There's a lot of debris on the trail."

Dirk didn't want them stepping on any stray leaves or twigs, giving away their presence. The group continued on, following Dirk for an hour but not seeing anything that warranted any further investigation. Oriana had snuck up on them several times, causing Volar to swear to Garga. She reported that she had indeed found wolf tracks and they seemed to have been circling for a while and then they had headed south.

"Damn the gods," Dirk swore.

"What is it, Dirk?" Natia asked, grabbing his forearm. Tara and Oriana stared at the princess, shocked she was showing affection towards Dirk. Natia just stared them down.

"From what Oriana said, it means the wolf pack is heading towards Tab and his group and coming from this way. They'll never see the wolves coming because the trees are so thick." The realization of who was in that group came to everyone at once. "Princess Anastasia!" Dirk shouted and took off running.

The group took off after him. Volar and Raga told them to go on and that they would catch up. Vira stopped in front of the dwarves, lowered her head, and started mumbling some words. After she felt what she had done was successful, she told the dwarves to hurry and took off behind Dirk.

Volar looked at Raga. "Was she glowing?" Raga asked Volar.

"Aye, thine brother. I believe she was. We better hurry."

Tab and his group had not seen any sign of trouble until they found wolf tracks not far from the dens where the wolves had been known to stay. Within a few hundred yards of the caves, Tab started seeing the bones of dead animals everywhere.

Kal immediately took charge. "Tab, is this normal?" he asked, stepping up to examine the bones with Anastasia by his side.

"No. These are way more bones and the tracks are much larger than normal."

Anastasia jumped into action and began ordering the group. "Nira and Dusty watch our flank." Nira had drawn her katanas and Dusty had his bow in hand. "Tab, you and El take the sides. Let us know if you see any movement. Jonesy, beside me and Kal. We'll move forward and try to flush out what is waiting."

Jonesy moved forward immediately. Kal started to move, but Anastasia put a hand on his arm to stop him. He looked at her. "What is it?"

Anastasia nodded to Kal's bow. He looked at it. The runes were glowing. She pulled hers out. It had also begun to glow.

"Wolves!" Nira shouted. Kal turned and saw a pack of wolves running straight for them.

"Gods, there must be fifty of them," El said, drawing her bow.

Tab stood beside her. "I'm with you," he said while aiming at the onslaught of teeth. Jonesy moved to El's other side.

Kal and Anastasia seemed to move as one person. They started unleashing arrows as fast as they could nock them. This caused the rest of the group to fire. The first arrows started taking down wolves from a few hundred yards out. Anastasia watched as the wolves split in to two packs after their first brethren went down. One was coming from the north and the second coming from the south. Kal and Anastasia followed the northern attack.

"Jonesy with us," Kal ordered. Jonesy moved beside them.

"Tab, the rest of you take the southern attack!" Anastasia yelled. Tab and El spread out by Dusty and Nira. El heard Jonesy let out a battle cry.

El turned and saw her brother take down two early arrivals with one swing of the spear. She smiled. *The berserker's getting into battle mode*, she thought. She barely had time to worry before she heard the paws getting closer.

Dusty and Tab had started firing. She looked over at Nira. Nira had her arms over her head, mumbling. El could have sworn the girl was glowing. She then turned and released a volley of arrows.

"Pulver!" Nira screamed, clapping her hands together towards the oncoming wolves. A thunderous roar sounded, and a wave of wind burst forward from her towards the wolves. The force from her clap ripped through the trees, taking leaves and bark with it as it swirled towards the wolves. When it hit them, they were blown back, their fur ripping away from their bodies. The heap flew into several behind them.

Nira collapsed to the ground. Dusty stepped in front of her and continued firing at the wolves who had dodged her attack. Tab and El didn't have time to worry about Nira. They kept firing. There were six left, and they were still coming. El took down one while Dusty kept missing his shots. Tab took down two more. The remaining three wolves bounded towards Tab and El. They seemed to have dismissed Dusty since he had seemed not to hit any of them. One was within biting distance. It was ripped away from El slamming into the other one at her right. El quickly looked around to see what had yanked the wolf away from its attack. Nira still on the ground, had her arm outstretched towards the fallen wolves. El pulled out her dagger and quickly cut their throats.

Dusty helped Nira to her feet. She yelled at El, pointing. El turned in the direction Nira was pointing. Her eyes flared to life with flames. Her heart felt like it was going to beat out of her chest. The horror of what she saw made her gasp. Tab had been tackled by the remaining wolf, its fangs dangerously close to his throat. El took off running to save him. When she lunged forward to stab the wolf in the back, her hands were trembling.

Kal and Anastasia had put down half of the wolves when they heard the rush of Nira's spell. Jonesy had killed four. They all turned at the sound. Still, the wolves kept coming. Kal, realizing his mistake, pushed Anastasia.

"KAL, NO!" she screamed as she quickly reached her hand out, pulling him back toward her. The wolves ended up snapping at empty air. Jonesy took out the two coming at him. The remaining wolves halted their attack and started to stalk Kal and Anastasia. They both had dropped their bows in the chaos. Pulling out his knife, Kal got up, placing himself in front of Anastasia, ignoring her protests. The wolves ran at the same time and jumped.

Thump, Thump, Thump, Thump, Thump, Thump.

The two leaping wolves dropped to the ground, dead, before they could tear into him. Kal just stared at the dead wolves. Anastasia looked around their feet at the dead wolves. There were two arrows a piece sticking in the wolves hearts.

As El started to stab the wolf that was attacking Tab, she heard the sounds of arrows hitting flesh. Someone had shot the wolf with two arrows, knocking it over dead.

She bent down, tears falling from her eyes, and threw the wolf's corpse away "Are you ok?!" she asked, checking Tab for bite marks.

"El, I'm fine," he said grabbing her face in his hands.

"I thought you were dead, you bastard." Tab just looked at her, staring at the rippling flames in her eyes. Then he kissed her. Thrown off by his reaction, she pushed him back and looked into his eyes. She smiled and then kissed him back.

"Ahem," came a voice from behind her. El broke the embrace and looked up to see Dirk and Natia. He smiled. "And here I thought you were in trouble."

They both got up and wrapped their arms around their friend pulling Natia into the hug. Kal, after helping Anastasia up, walked over to the four with Anastasia on his heels. The four, realizing they weren't alone, broke the group hug.

Natia looked around at the elves, who were just staring at her. "I'll be back," Natia said and pulled the elven women to the side. Vira and Phil were checking on Nira and Dusty.

"Looks like we owe you our lives," Kal said to Dirk. Dirk shook Kal's hand then hugged Anastasia.

"It wasn't me who took the shots," Dirk said pointing over his shoulder to the elves. Then he turned and pointed at Vira. "The elves shot one shot a piece, but it was Vira who fired the other four shots." Dirk smiled at Vira, who was walking up with Nira, Dusty, and Phil.

"Well, Vira, it seems we owe you and your sister our thanks," Anastasia said, coming around and hugging the twins. They hugged her back.

Dirk looked questioningly at Kal. "It was Nira who performed some kind of wind magic. That took out a lot of the wolves at once."

Dirk smiled. "Well, they are Storms, you know." They all laughed at Dirk's words, but he really had meant it. Vira and Nira, knowing what his words meant, hugged him.

The group began spreading out to make sure that all of the wolves were dead. Dirk worked his way closer to Natia, who had finally separated from the elves. Tara and Oriana had taken up with the others.

Dirk and Natia walked away from the group towards the wolves' dens. "What was that about?" Dirk had just gotten the words out of his mouth when a ground-shaking growl filled the air, rustling the trees. Dirk stopped and looked around. Natia did the same.

From out one of the dens came the biggest wolf Dirk had ever seen in his life. It jumped between the two and the rest of the group separating them. Dirk pulled out his knife and Natia pulled out her twin katanas. They positioned themselves for an attack. A red shield formed behind the giant beast. Its jet-black fur bristled and its red eyes glowed.

"What are you doing?" Dirk asked Natia, who had thrown the shield up.

"This one is ours," she said.

Dirk could sense his friends trying to break through the barrier. Their muffled shouts echoed through the forest. He knew they were desperate to get in. Dirk smirked. "Well, it would have been better if I had my sword."

"You have me, love," she said and kissed him.

The beast attacked at that moment. Dirk rolled right and Natia rolled in the opposite direction as the beast landed, attempting to pounce on them. They sliced the beast's sides as it slid by. Blood gushed out of the wounds. The beast howled with anger, ripping the ground up as it twisted around, trying to sink its teeth into Dirk. Dirk dodged left and then flipped onto the wolf's back as it ran past.

It's the size of a horse, Dirk thought.

Natia rolled to her feet, hacking at the wolf's hind legs. The beast spun, not knowing which one to attack. Dirk repeatedly stabbed it in the neck. It finally tossed Dirk off its back, causing him to hit the mouth of the cave. He fell to the ground, dazed.

He sensed Natia probing him for injuries. A wave of heat coursed through his body; the fuzziness cleared as the wolf bounded towards him. Natia leapt over the wolf and landed beside Dirk, tossing him one of her katanas. They grasped hands; each shoved the katanas up into the open mouth of the wolf as it bit down. Their eyes rippled with flames as their magic came to life. Fire coursed through their blades as the katanas sliced into the beast's brain. The dead beast landed on top of them with a smoking hole in its head. They pushed the heavy beast off of them just as the rest of the group came running up, having finally gotten through Natia's shield.

"What in the gods!" Anastasia exclaimed, examining the huge wolf.

Kal leaned down beside it as well. "I have never seen anything like this before." He ran his hand over the pelt.

"It's a Grizwolf," Vira said, walking up and examining the wolf.

"Did it have red eyes?" Nira asked, kneeling beside Dirk, checking the bite marks on his arms.

"It did," Natia answered. Nira looked at Natia's arms then grabbed her and Dirk by the wrist. They just watched as Nira started mumbling some words they couldn't make out. She began to shimmer a light blue color. Dirk and Natia began to get dizzy, but the dizziness quickly faded. They stared at Nira. She looked exhausted.

Vira put her hand on her sister's back, lightly shimmering. Nira looked up at her sister. "Thanks."

"That animal is very deadly. It secretes a poison that paralyzes you, then makes you think you're going crazy until you finally die." Vira looked at Dirk sternly with tears in her eyes. She pointed at him. "Don't you ever do that to us again. If you do, you will learn why I am from Aarkas, I, we just found you and we can't lose you. Either of you."

Dirk got up and pulled her into a hug. Nira stood up and put her arms around the two. "If I face anything without you two by my side again, it will not be by my choice," Dirk said.

Nira pulled back and punched him hard. "You better not." Then she smiled and helped Natia up.

Vira released Dirk, looked him in the eyes and said "Promise?" Dirk nodded.

Vira looked to Kal, "This means that at least one bad wizard from Aarkas has to be here if the animal is."

Natia hugged Dirk after confirming he was okay. He saw the elves looking at him. They nodded and went back to checking the wolves. Tab and El came up and hugged them both.

"What were you thinking?" El asked no one in particular.

"Doing what we are supposed to do," Natia said. Tab just looked at her.

"But not alone!" El demanded.

Dirk finished what Natia was saying. "We had to see if we could fight together. It might have been stupid, but we didn't want any of you in danger. Especially after the battle you'd just been through. Do you understand?" He grabbed their arms and sent the love he felt for them and the deeper meaning of his words into them through the touch. El looked at Tab and they both nodded. In that connection, El felt the love Dirk had for her, but she also felt the deep connection he had with Natia. She sensed their love for each other was deeper than it had been the day before. She smiled a knowing smile and pulled Natia into an embrace. She whispered to her. "I love you."

Natia squeezed El back. "I love you too, Elyse." They smiled.

Jonesy finally came down from his battle rage with El's help and started skinning the huge beast. "Take its head, also. Then burn that hideous creature," Anastasia told him.

"Aye, princess," Jonesy responded.

"Hey where is Volar and Raga?" Dirk said looking around. Volar and Raga showed up a few minutes later.

"Sorry we're late. From the looks of things, you handled it without us. We dwarves aren't very fast when it comes to running, you know. As we were trying to get here, we came across a pair of wild boars. So Raga and I decided to make sure we had something to put on the spit for tonight," Volar smiled and nodded. The group laughed.

"Well, it's a good thing we didn't die while you were looking for dinner kin-son," Tab said.

Volar bowed to Tab. "Tab Clearwater, you honor me with thine humble name. I knew you would never let anything happen to our friends."

Tab patted Volar on the back and said "You're right, friend. Let's go get this dinner and head back. We have a hell of a tale to tell you."

They went to round up the boars after telling Dirk where they were going. "Take Phil and Dusty with you," Kal ordered.

"Okay."

El watched Tab walking away. "He will be ok," Dirk said.

She smiled. "I know, I just can't believe it took almost dying to get him to step up."

Dirk hugged her "But he did." She walked over to help Jonesy finish the skinning. After Vira and Nira finished talking with Kal and Anastasia they went to the pile of dead wolves, chanting words. All of the wolves in the pile started burning.

Anastasia walked over to Dirk as Kal went to talk with Natia and the elves and looked into Dirk's eyes. "I knew it."

He just looked at her. "I could tell earlier there was something between you two."

Dirk started to deny it.

"Don't bother. You look at her the way I look at Kal. And let's not forget that kiss." She smiled then grabbed his hand and started walking towards Kal. "Just remember what we are fighting for."

He stopped and that made her stop as well. He pointed towards Natia, who could sense his burning anger from the attack. "That is what we are fighting for!" His eyes flaring. Anastasia didn't back away.

She glared at him. "What?" She wasn't used to Dirk getting upset with her.

"Love, Stas. Without it, nothing is worth fighting for, and I'll tell you there is nothing I wouldn't do to protect her."

Anastasia looked at him, relaxing her glare. "Remember Dirk, every race will depend on the two of you. Don't make a decision in battle that could jeopardize us all." Dirk looked at her questioningly. "Kal made a decision earlier that almost cost us our lives. He worried about me instead of finishing the fight with the wolves, and if it hadn't been for you showing up, we all could have died. Finish the enemy first, then make sure everyone is ok."

Dirk held her gaze for a minute, "Stas, that's the mistake many dead soldiers have made in the past. We have to remember what and who makes us who we are. Kal did the right thing. You just don't see it because you're pissed someone had to protect you." She looked at Dirk considering his words, and a look of realization came across her face.

She grabbed Dirk's hand and squeezed it. "Dirk, you're right, I'll follow your lead."

"Remember, Kal loves you as I do Natia." She smiled at Dirk and he let her go. She walked straight to Kal and pulled him away from the group. Dirk followed, watching her, and smiled to himself, thinking about what he had said. He felt deep down that those feelings would be the reason that, this time, they would win.

After making sure the other dens were clear of any wolves, the group headed back to the farm. "I have told Tara and Oriana about our feelings for each other. They realized something was different by our actions today. They told me they sensed it and would honor my choice and keep it to themselves." Natia squeezed Dirk's hand.

"Well, I'm sure that once we got back to school they would've figured it out anyway." Natia nodded.

Kal was walking ahead of Dirk, toting the beast's head. He looked back at Dirk. "Vira has taught me how to check for dark wizards. I have, and there are none around now. That's the reason the wolves were so bad and probably the reason they attacked the farm's sheep. Vira feels with the general's importance, that's why they were left so close to the farm."

Dirk looked to Vira and smiled. "I trust Vira with my life, and if she says that's what happened, then I agree." Dirk nodded at Vira who beamed from the praise.

Dirk and his group got back at the farm the same time as Tab and Volar's group did. The king and the general came out to the noise. After seeing the beast's head, the king made them tell him everything that had happened. When they were done explaining, he walked around, scratching the stubble on his chin that had formed during the day. The king knew he had to keep his thoughts to a select few.

"Volar, can you take Raga, Jonesy, Phil, and Dusty and get the boars ready for the pits?" Volar nodded, and, with the help of the ones the king suggested, hauled the boars to the slaughterhouse. It seemed to the king that everyone deserved a good meal tonight. He then asked Durkon one question. "Durkon, my old friend, is it time?"

The general looked around at the young men and women in front of him before he answered. "Thurmond, as much as I wish it wasn't, I believe it is."

The king nodded. Kira, who had come out with Thea to see what all of the commotion was about, sniffled in the background. Thea held Kira in her arms. The king looked at Kira with sadness in his eyes. "I'm sorry, Kira. You know more than I do what is at stake."

She nodded. "I know, Thurmond. I'd just hoped they had more time."

"Me too," he said. The general told the group remaining to follow him to his workshop. At the door to the shop, the king took a breath and released it. He looked at the young adults gathered around. "It is time to finish what was started a long time ago and looking at you in front of me, I believe we might have the combination to make that happen this time. Everyone, follow me in," the king said. Kal and Anastasia stared at the king, mouths agape. He stopped and grabbed his daughter by the shoulders. "Trust me. Durkon and I have been planning a long time for what we are about to put on your shoulders." He looked at the rest of the group." Trust me, I will explain. Follow me."

The Prophecy

The General led them all into the shop. The king and the general motioned for them to sit around the table Dirk and Tab had seen on their last visit. The room seemed bigger to Dirk than it did the last time he was here. Tab thought the same thing. Dirk heard a knock at the door. The king opened it and Volar was standing there.

"Is it time?" Dirk heard Volar ask. Dirk had suspected Volar knew more than he had let onto that night in the dorm. The king nodded and let Volar in.

Dirk was positive the room was bigger now. There were four couches with five chairs around a table in the center of the room. The walls were the same with the exception of a door on the left wall by the weapons. The king walked over and said something into his hand. The ring on his finger glowed red and he touched the door.

"It will take a few minutes for them to come," he said, sitting in the biggest chair at the center of the circle of chairs and couches. He instructed everyone to have a seat. Tab and El sat on one couch with Anastasia and Kal. Dirk and Natia sat on another couch with Vira and Nira by their sides. The rest just filled in the empty seats, leaving only four empty seats.

The general got up and opened a window, then sat back down. Dirk noticed on the center table that the book of Storm was sitting there in the open. Dirk nudged Natia and motioned towards the book. She noticed it then and looked at El, who elbowed Tab lightly nodding at the book. The four all had the same thought: *What the Hells?*

They all shrugged. Then there was a knock on the new door in the room. The general got up and opened the door. He stepped back and to Dirk's surprise, Hilda and Tilda came walking in, followed by Wizard Hermosa and Head Wizard Nabas. Everyone in the room except the older ones were shocked by their entrance. The king introduced the four just in case anyone there didn't know who they were.

"Already?" Wizard Nabas asked looking at the king.

"I'm afraid so, my old friend." Wizard Nabas nodded and then the four took the seats the general had motioned them towards. The king looked around, satisfied that he had everyone's undivided attention. "Let me tell you a story and about a prophecy," the king said to the gathered group.

He began by telling the Storm family history from the start. Dirk heard some things he didn't even know, like the part about him and even the general knowing what Diron was trying to do with the power of the Odd.

Then he began on the prophecy. "The prophecy I am going to tell you about started with this story. In nine ninety-nine AZ, the Chosen, Durk Storm, had a daughter named Rebea. She was a little different from the other Storms. She had an extra power, you see. She was the first in her line to have visions. She secretly kept a diary about the visions, or prophecies, as they became to be known as. At least until she married and had a daughter. On her death bed, she told her daughter about the prophecy diary she had been keeping. She told her it was her duty to pass along the prophecy diary down through her family until the signs of the prophecy started coming true. When it happened, she, or whoever her descendant was, should share the prophecy with the Chosen and protector." He paused, making sure he had everyone's attention.

Dirk couldn't stand it. He had to ask a question. "My king, I must ask a question." The king nodded for him to go ahead. "How is it my grandfather isn't telling this story. I mean no disrespect, but he was a Chosen," Dirk stated.

The king smiled. "Dirk, I am getting to that. I have to set up what you are about to learn." Dirk nodded and sat back. "As I said, the reason for this was so if the signs showed up then the prophecy would be shared. The reason, Dirk, that I am telling this story is because your grandfather didn't know anything about this until after your father died. You see, that was one of the signs. The family that knew this information was descended from the Storm bloodline but not through the Chosen line. You see, Rebea wasn't a Chosen, her brother was, so it was her direct line that carried the prophecy through to this day."

The king stopped and looked at his wife. Everyone followed his eyes. "Mother?" Anastasia asked.

She smiled and continued the story. "You see, Dirk, I am a descendant of the Storm line. The women in my family, since the day Rebea died, have had at least one visionist in the family. That's what we are called. I know what the prophecy says so here is the way it's been told for generations. Hopefully, you will understand." She paused and Dirk nodded.

"When the protector gives his life for the friend or brother and the father willingly falls on the sword, the beginning of the end is near." Dirk sat there in shock. Natia held his hand. Thea continued. "When the flaming bird flies its final flight and willingly yields to her newborn, the dark sisters will come forward to undo that which has been done. The time of the mountain will be here to join the hunt till the end. The daughter of the seer will join the final battle so that the Chosen and protector, deeply in love will join the hunter, making thirteen warriors able to prevail over the evil from underneath. Beware though, if the one who was a rat is not there to join the final battle, all will be lost." She stopped and put her hand over Kira's.

The group just sat there. Dirk put his hands over his face and wiped away the sweat, sitting up. "So, you're saying that Tab's father dying for my dad started the prophecy coming to fruition?"

The general looked at Dirk. "Think about the words of the prophecy. Tab's father, Diron, the way he died. You know from the dreams, I'm sure by now," Dirk nodded. Kira openly started to cry, and Thea comforted her. The General continued. "Arial dying and giving birth to Aarya. Vira and Nira returning home from Aarkas. I believe it is obvious to everyone, why they are here. They came to make amends for what their people have done." Vira and Nira both had their hand on Dirk's shoulder now, confirming the general's words. He smiled at them. "The seer's daughter entering the fight. Anastasia battled with you today against evil. The Hunter," he said, looking at Kal. Kal came from a long line of hunters. "Volar has come from the mountain and let's not forget what Lincoln was before Agnes saved him."

Dirk looked up "A wharf rat."

And it was Kira who stated the last fact. "The Chosen and protector deeply in love," she said smiling at how tightly her son and Natia were holding hands. Dirk looked at Natia, who was smiling at him. "I've known since yesterday that the two of you were in love. I knew once I saw Natia with her hair down. It's a sign that an elven female has accepted her life mate." Natia nodded.

Dirk looked around the room at Tara and Oriana. They smiled then nodded their heads in a sign of acceptance. At that moment, Aarya flew in and landed on the book of Storm in front of Dirk and Natia. The others, who had never seen a phoenix, gasped. Dirk saw the amazement in their eyes. She looked around the room at the gathered group and trilled. He reached out and caressed her head.

"And they are here too?" Dirk said, pointing to the other students while looking at the king.

"Isn't it obvious, Dirk? They're here because like I told you I have a plan." The king smiled. "First Dirk, and the rest in this room, will you accept the challenge that has been laid out before you?"

Natia, breaking her silence, started first. "Let me say this to you, Your Highness. I know I speak for Dirk, El, Tab, and Linc who could not be here." The three there agreed. "I feel we have already given our lives over to our destiny. Whether we meant to or not, that will not change. The rest in this room need to understand that not all of us will survive this. Some of them will not be here when this is over. Hells, maybe none of us will be."

She stood up and looked around the room, making sure everyone understood what this commitment would mean.

"Any of you who don't want to be a part of this, now is the time to back out. I, nor anyone, will think any less of you," Natia said. All four of them grabbed hands, looking around the room. Vira and Nira were the first to confirm their commitment by standing and joining hands with the four. Anastasia and Kal were next, linking hands with a firm nod.

Volar stood next to Tab. "I wouldn't let you do it without me."

The elves walked up to Dirk. Tara, with Oriana beside her, took a knee, bowed, and said. "We will be honored to follow you until the end."

Dirk released the hands holding his. He walked around the table and put his hands on the elves, beckoning them to stand. He stared into their eyes. The reflection of flames rippled in their eyes. "No, Tara and Oriana, it is I who would be honored." He knelt down and bowed to them. They put their hand on his shoulder and he stood up. They both nodded their appreciation. He then turned and the group of eleven all clasped hands.

Aarya looked around the circle, flames blazing in her eyes, and let out a war cry that would have shook the heavens. The group stared in awe at her. "If Linc was here in person, he would say 'Let's get started.' Why wait?" Dirk nodded to Aarya.

Tab and El laughed when they heard his thoughts. El said "You're damn right! He just confirmed it to us through our bond." Dirk, at that moment, sensed Linc's eagerness to be back.

"We still need one more though," Tab said and looked at Dirk. Dirk and Tab had the same thought.

"Gil will be the thirteenth. It's too bad he couldn't be here today," El said.

Dirk frowned. "I'll get Aarya to bond him when we have our next break," Dirk said. Tab agreed. "I do want to warn all of you though. The king only told an abbreviated version of what it's like to be bonded. It's so much more intense. I do promise we'll help you adjust to the way it feels, but there is one side effect I can't prepare you for." The group looked inquisitively, waiting on Dirk to finish. He looked at Natia and she nodded. "Every sensation, every feeling, every joy and every pain you have will be shared." Anastasia raised an eyebrow. Dirk looked to Kal and then back at Anastasia. "Every one of them. Know that this even means that when one of us dies, we will all feel that as well."

Hilda, who had been watching without saying a word, decided to chime in from behind the circle. "It is a feeling you will never forget. It has stayed with us, to this day," she said, hugging her sister.

Everyone in the group looked to Dirk but it was Kal that said, "To the end, I will be there." Anastasia and the rest repeated his sentiment. He looked at Aarya who flew up and landed on his shoulder.

"Let's begin then," he said and Aarya began bonding the group. Everyone in the group felt the same sensations. Every pain, every joy, and every doubt that any in the group had was shared at that moment. By the time she was done, everyone's resolve was that much stronger. They were emotional, having had their innermost secrets and desires shared, but the bond also shared the love that came from each individual.

Dirk looked at Vira and Nira. The bonded all turned their way, sensing Dirk's intentions. "Vira and Nira. You now know through the bond that I truly do love you both. I understand even more now the pains you two have gone through, seeing the true way your parents died," Dirk said with tears in his eyes. He wiped their tears away. "I promise you this, sisters. I will kill the ones responsible for taking them from you."

"I love you, Dirk," Vira and Nira said in unison, hugging him close. The bonded all felt the love Dirk was sharing now with the whole group.

Dirk looked at the bonded all gathered in a circle, holding hands, and smiled. "Family is what we are, family is what we will always be!" The bonded repeated his words with love in their hearts.

After the emotions were all shared and dealt with after Dirk's assurances, he turned to the king. "So, what's the plan? I suppose they're here for a reason," he said looking at the wizards and the twins. The king, snapping out of his thoughts, willed away his tears before looking at Dirk. Though he had been preparing his daughter for war for a while now, he still hadn't come to terms with the thought of actually losing her.

With his emotions under control the king told them the plan.

The general filled in the gaps when he needed to. Everyone had gathered around them, listening. Dirk looked at the group. "Any questions?" No one spoke so he assumed they all understood.

"I have a question." Dirk dropped his head because he knew what Tab was going to ask. Everyone smiled, sensing what Tab was going to say. The king just looked confused. "When do we eat I'm starving?"

Everyone including the older adults, laughed. With the tension having been eased by Tab's question, the king said, "Well, those fine boars that Master Volar killed today should be ready by now. We will talk again tomorrow. Agreed?" They all nodded.

"Okay now listen up. There is a spell you need to know to retain your memories of everything you have learned in here. This shop has a protection placed on it, so that if anyone ever came in here and learned something they shouldn't, their memory of it would be erased. Unfortunately, I've had to use it over the years. So, to remember what you have learned you need to focus on your core, and say, *Rememoria*. Once you feel the tingle, you can walk out the door," the general explained. The group all nodded again.

Dirk waited on Kira. She walked up, teary-eyed, and hugged him. Natia walked up as they were separating, and Kira pulled her into a hug. "I'm sorry aunt, we just couldn't fight it."

Kira put her hands on Natia's face and looked her in the eyes. She kissed Natia on the forehead. "I know." She then pulled Dirk into the circle with her and Natia. "You two don't make the mistake Diron and I made. Stay by each other's side until it's over. Don't get me wrong, Dirk. The day you were born was the happiest day of my life and I wouldn't change that. The saddest day was when Diron died, and I wasn't with him." Natia and Dirk, both crying, just squeezed Kira tightly.

"Never, Mom. I love her, and we have agreed to stay by each other's side until the end."

Kira released them. "Good. Time for children will be after." They both agreed, and after saying *Rememoria*, followed her out of the building towards the fire pit. "Oh, Dirk, dear, do me a favor before we eat. Make sure the guest house has fresh sheets. No one has stayed there in so long I want to make sure the king and queen are comfortable."

Dirk and Natia stopped once they realized what she said. "I'll help him aunt."

Kira just smiled. "I figured you would." She turned to catch up with Thea.

"*Privacious*," they both said as one. When the sensation of the magic cleared, Natia smiled, and Dirk smiled back.

"So, maybe we can make sure the sheets are really dirty before they're changed." She grinned and they took off to grab some clean sheets.

As soon as they got to the guest-house with the fresh sheets, Dirk closed the door as Natia was getting ready to pull the old ones off. Dirk's bracelet flared. The bond to the others had strengthened his connection to his core making it easier for him to touch it. A red shield formed on the door behind him. She looked up at him and raised an eyebrow. "You wouldn't dare."

He smirked. "Wouldn't I?" Dirk tackled Natia onto the bed. She finally pinned him on his back after rolling around for a few minutes. She straddled his waist and smiled down at him. She tossed her hair braid back over her shoulder. Then the passion took over.

"I wanted you so bad after we fought that beast," Natia said, kissing Dirk's neck and ear viciously. She ripped his shirt open down the center and began kissing him the same way she had the night before.

"I wanted you every second of the day. Even while we were fighting that beast," Dirk said, running his hands slowly under her shirt and sliding it over her head. Natia took control of the situation.

After half an hour in the realm of the gods, as Dirk would put it, Natia moaned a sigh of relief and Dirk just fell back, trying to catch his breath. Natia put her arms across his chest and kissed him passionately again. "We better hurry."

"Are you kidding me? Can't we just lay here for a minute?" Dirk complained.

"No, we have to get back before they miss us too much." Dirk hesitantly got up and then they hurried to open the windows to let some fresh air in. After changing the sheets, they headed to the house to drop off the dirty sheets. They both went up to freshen up and then headed to the pit.

Dirk and Natia had been gone only a little while so they were relieved that no one questioned them when they came strolling up. Everyone was spread out around the pit, already eating. No one spoke. They just looked up and acknowledged them. "Let's grab some food and head over there," Dirk said, pointing to where Tab and El were sitting with the twins, Dusty, and Phil. They sat on the log beside the group once they got their food. Vira smiled when they sat down. Everyone else greeted them.

What took you so long?

Dirk stared at El, who had sent the thought. She was smiling mischievously at the two. Natia smiled and lowered her head to take a bite from the boar she had decided to try. Since the bonding, she had been having the urge to eat meat. Phil and Dusty were finished eating already so they both got up and said they were gonna go talk with Jonesy and Raga, who had become very close at the military school.

"All right, we will see you two in a little bit," Vira said to them as the boys walked off. She immediately moved to the ground in front of Dirk and Natia. Nira was right by her side.

"Girls, how do you feel?" Dirk asked them. They looked at each other and giggled. Dirk's face flushed from their thoughts. Tab was confused.

"What? I didn't quite get that."

Nira moved closer so no one else could hear "I said we feel horny." She winked at him. Natia choked on her food and El busted out laughing. Shocked, Tab just looked at her. Then he smiled and joined the rest of the group as all six of them busted into fits of laughter. The others of the group who weren't sitting with them stopped talking for a moment to see what was so funny.

Soon, the group went back to their own discussions after the laughter died down. "Sister, you have changed," Dirk said, finally calming down.

It was Vira this time who looked Dirk in the eyes, "Well, what did you expect with you and the princess here rutting around like a couple of wild dogs. Surely you knew there would be some aftereffects brother." El covered Natia's mouth with her hand since it was just hanging open.

"How?" was all Dirk could mutter.

Vira put her hand on his knee affectionately. Flames were rippling in her eyes now. "You didn't think you could block out two dark sorceresses, surely." She smiled and turned back to Nira and they both giggled.

"Well, Dirk, I guess that answers that," El said as she smiled at the two. Feeling like all eyes were on them, Dirk and Natia looked to the twins.

Vira smiled at the two. "All right, remember how everyone gets affected differently? Like Natia, we've been trained since we were born, basically. Our powers are less susceptible than others to certain spells. The *privacious* spell being one of them." Dirk looked up with a concerned look on his face. Nira placed a hand on his knee. "Don't worry, though. I think we are the only two that were affected."

El was feeling mischievous. "Well, now since that's out of the way, do you girls need to go take care of those feelings?" She looked to where Dusty, and Phil had been sitting. She smiled at the girls.

"Nah, I'm satisfied at the moment." Vira looked at Dirk. "Dirk was enough for one night." Everyone busted out in laughter again. Even Dirk smiled, though he was embarrassed. Natia smiled and made sure her eyes rippled at Vira, who smiled back.

"What's all this laughter over here?" Anastasia said, walking up with Kal hand-in-hand.

"Nothing just giving Dirk a *hard* time," El said.

Dirk squirmed a little. "Uh, Kal, Stas, how are you feeling?"

"It's still a little confusing, but I feel exhilarated. I sense feelings from all of you. Like right now, I'm sensing confusion in you and Natia, but happiness from everyone else."

Dirk didn't want this conversation to go on any longer. "Well, with us being the original Chosen and protector, it's a little harder to sense our feelings." Vira and Nira busted out laughing again. Dirk pushed Vira into Nira, knocking them over. "Ignore them. I think their brains got rattled a little with the bonding."

The girls sat back up and agreed with Dirk.

"Nira, I have a question for you or Vira." They both looked at Kal. "During the fight today, I swear I saw you glow."

Volar just happened to be walking up and heard that question. "And you Vira. I saw you glow as well after you mumbled some words before you took off running after the group this morning."

They looked between each other and Vira stood up. "Everyone, form a circle around us." The group stood. Vira and Nira stood directly in front of each other after the circle was completed around them. Nira shook her head and they both dropped their robes to their waist, each blocking the frontal view of their bodies. Kal whistled. The group walked around in a circle, looking at the twin's backs. There were gems imbedded in them.

It's in the shape of a cross, Dirk thought. Though he had already seen most of what had happened to them from the bonding, seeing their backs actually made him even angrier than he originally had been. Natia, sensing his feelings, squeezed his hand, sending a calming wave through her touch. He calmed himself then took in the sight of the twin's backs, starting at the small of the back, the gems were imbedded up to their necklines with a line across the shoulders that intersected with a huge gem in the center where they met. They were all different colors with a deep crimson stone half the size of Dirk's fist in the center. "That's just like the gem that Hermosa tested me with the first day."

Everyone looked at Dirk. He explained about the testing and how she made him swear not to say anything about it.

"That's a God Stone," Anastasia said after the twins said she could run her fingers over the stones. After that, the girls pulled their robes back up and everyone sat around them.

"It is a God Stone. That is the main reason the Dark Wizards went to Aarkas. It is said to be where the first volcano before Blazire was formed. All it is now, though, is a big lake. The reason we came back is the wizards there, are close to procuring enough of them to fulfill their goal. Their powers will be almost impossible to stop once they achieve their goal. Grandfather knew it was time to warn the king or anyone who would listen to prepare for what is coming. Sorry, Dirk, that's the only thing we didn't share." Vira had tears in her eyes, pleading to be forgiven.

Dirk grabbed her in a hug. "It's ok, sister. I already knew that."

She leaned back. "How?"

He smiled and tapped the side of his head. "There are no secrets from the Chosen. When the bond takes place, I feel all of your thoughts. All of them," he emphasized as he held her gaze. She smiled. "Well I think that's the case, but I don't think I know all of your powers, but I do know all of your thoughts."

Vira knew he was referring to what Nira and her had sensed when he and Natia had embraced earlier. Natia just nodded when the girls looked at her. "It's a gift that we were bestowed at birth in the original transfer," Natia confirmed.

"You think that they will attack soon?" Kal said trying to get back on subject. What Dirk and Natia just revealed had made him feel uncomfortable.

Dirk took the lead in the conversation since the twins were feeling a little uncomfortable themselves. "Not yet, but soon. I believe we have time to put the king's plan into effect," Dirk said to Anastasia since she was looking around and not making eye contact with anyone.

She looked at him. "That's good because we have a lot to do."

Dirk cocked his head at her to get her attention, looked her in the eyes and sent a thought to her. *Don't worry. Only Natia and me know. Your secret is safe with us.*

She smiled. *Thanks.* She hooked arms with Kal. Something passed between them and he sighed in relief. He nodded to Natia and Dirk.

"Ok, let's get something straight." It was Tab who spoke up. Everyone looked at him. "No more secrets from this point forward. Don't forget, I can sense as well as the other bonded when something is being left out. Don't try to explain. I understand we all have secrets that need to remain ours, but we all have been through a lot today. But I have one important question that no one is asking." Kal nodded for him to go ahead. He looked at the twins with love and sadness in his eyes. "Did it hurt, sisters?"

Two things happened when the twins heard his question. Everyone who didn't ask felt like horse's asses and the twins felt the connection to Tab grow almost as strong as the one they had with Dirk.

Vira put her hand on his arm. "Dear, no. It was done with magic. It felt a little uncomfortable, but there was no pain."

"I assume they strengthen your core magic?" Volar asked just as Tara and Oriana were finally able to get away from Kira and came over to see what was going on.

"It does, but you have to use it sparingly until you can build up your strength," Nira responded. Natia explained to the elves through the bond what they had missed. They nodded in understanding and just listened.

Tab looked relieved. "That's good. I'd hate to have to go to Aarkas and kick some Dark Wizard ass tomorrow."

Vira and Nira, feeling the love he projected through the bond pulled him into a hug. "Don't worry, brother, I am sure you and everyone else here will get the chance sooner than we want," Nira said after Tab released them from the embrace.

The group all sat down on the ground and discussed the new revelation that had just came up. They talked for hours about Vira and Nira's childhood and what was done to them. They also talked about the new feelings racing through each of them until the king gathered them all up.

"Thea and I are going to bed. I expect you to as well. Tomorrow will be a big day of planning." The king nodded and he and Thea headed towards the guest house.

Jonesy looked to Raga and shrugged his shoulders at the king's comment. "What the hells are they talking about?"

"I haven't got a clue, but it's probably got something to do with why they were gone after we started the boars on the pit." Dusty guessed and Phil nodded.

"Aye. Gentlemen I believe this conversation isn't for our ears. Let's go get some more food. I'm still hungry," Raga stated and took off towards the food. The boys agreed and followed Raga.

Wizard Nabas strolled over after he said goodnight to the king. He looked at the young adults who had gathered around him. "I know you know the importance of the task that has been thrust upon you. I remember when I found out about the Storm legacy. I was no older than you when Durkon told his friends about it. I know the strain it can put on you and your relationships. But know this. I will be there to help in any way I can." He looked to Wizard Hermosa, who was standing by his side.

"Classes will change for most of you when we get back. I will personally be instructing the bonded. I think it will help you develop faster and become stronger, quicker." Hermosa looked to Hilda and Tilda.

"I guess our night class just got bigger.," Hilda said.

Dirk smiled. "Earlier than you planned."

They both walked up and hugged Dirk goodbye. "That's the problem with plans. Sometimes things happen that you don't expect, and your plans go to hells in a handbasket," Hermosa said. She hugged Dirk and the rest of the group as well. The four wizards followed the general to the shop. Dirk had an unsettling feeling as Tilda and Hilda were walking away. Tab sensed his dread.

"What?" Tab asked Dirk, concerned.

"Our fathers," Dirk said. Tab understood.

"We're not going to end up like them," Natia said, grabbing Dirk's hand.

"You're right," El said, grabbing Tab's.

"Well, Dirk, I think it's time for some alone time," Kal said pulling Anastasia close to him and walking away from the pit. She just smiled and went willingly.

Vira and Nira walked around to their side. "You know what, El?' She cocked her head and looked at the twins. Vira smiled. "I think you were right earlier." Then Vira and Nira hurried away, grabbing Phil and Dusty away from Raga and Jonesy, leading them from the pit towards the woods.

Dirk laughed, realizing what they were going to do. "Make sure you shield your thoughts!" Tab yelled to the girls. Nira looked back and winked. Volar patted Tab on the back and went to join Raga and Jonesy. Tara and Oriana said they were gonna lay down and went and settled by the logs away from the fire. That left Dirk and Natia and Tab and El alone. El hugged Natia then Dirk. She shared a thought with Natia and then grabbed Tab and pulled him away as well.

"Let's go for a walk." Natia dragged Dirk over and grabbed their sleeping bags.

"Where are we going?" he asked.

"To the other pit, of course. It's too crowded here." Dirk smiled and told everyone good night and that they were sleeping by the other pit to give them more room.

"Don't get any ideas. The king will be sleeping thirty yards away." Tab said, walking away with El.

Dirk frowned "Damn." Natia laughed as they walked to the other pit. Dirk joined the sleeping bags making them one while Natia lit the fire. Dirk made them comfortable.

"Make sure we're on the side by the logs that are closest to the house so they can't see us," Natia said. Once that was done, they both took off their boots and snuggled into the bags close to each other. Natia laid her head on his chest, feeling the beat of his heart. It was racing. Dirk rolled to his side and stared into her amber eyes. She gazed into his emerald green and crimson eyes. Thoughts passed between them. Dirk kissed her passionately. Natia returned the favor.

"I love you, Natia Silver, and I swear when this is over we will be standing."

She took a deep breath. "Good, because I love you too and I want us to live a long life together. I want you to be the father of my children and I want to sit on the porch here at the farm and watch them grow."

Dirk smiled. "Your wish is my command, Your Highness." They kissed one more time. The day's events had taken hold and they both fell fast asleep in each other's arms.

Oak City

Linc was glad when LiTaDi finally made it to Oak City. It had taken them longer than he had originally planned. The repairs they had had to make after the pirates had tried to sink them were only makeshift and had to be fixed daily. He wasn't happy that they had to spend several days off the coast of some wooded area they didn't know so they could go on land and try to find a second mast. They had lost one in the barrage of cannon fire the night of the battle.

After finally finding a similar tree in height, which was a tall white oak, they cut it down, spent time peeling the bark, and smoothed it out. Then they had to drag it to the beach so they could build a fire big enough to dry it out. Not to mention that they then had to get it to the *LiTaDi* without it getting too wet. After that was finally achieved using their spare dingy, they set sail again, trying to make up the lost time.

Linc was happy when Oak City finally came into sight. "River and Kaz, man the oars and get ready to slow us into that third dock on the port side, I believe that's Lord Saint's warehouse."

"Aye, captain."

"Corky take the wheel so Jerle and I can get ready to tie us down."

Corky cut his eyes at Jerle, still not trusting him, "Aye Cap'n Linc!"

"I look forward to at least one night at an inn with some hot food," River said.

"The warmth of a local girl wouldn't be bad either," Kaz said, smiling. Corky agreed but warned River not to catch the crabs. Linc chuckled to himself. He knew Corky wasn't talking about the kind one would eat. Everyone laughed. River just waved away his comment.

Two employees of Saint Trading met them at the dock to help tie the ship down. "Batten down those lines. Furl the sails. Kaz, Jerle, and River, get the cargo ready to unload," Linc commanded before getting the paperwork from his cabin. Lord Saint was waiting for him as he walked down the gangplank. Linc looked back over his shoulder. "Jerle, make sure everything that gets unloaded gets checked off."

"Aye, Cap'n Linc," Jerle said, helping the others getting the cargo ready to unload.

"Thought you were dead?"

Linc smiled and shook his hand. "Damn near would have been if those damn pirates would've gotten their way."

Lord Saint gave Linc a questioning look. "Follow me," he said and turned towards his office. Linc followed him into the trading offices and sat down at a chair in front of his desk. Lord Saint sat back with his hands together. "I am glad you're safe. Tell me what happened."

Linc told the story from start to finish. Lord Saint listened and when Linc was done, he informed Linc about the news he had received from Silver City.

"Ram in jail?" Linc laughed.

Lord Saint smiled, "And his henchman who were probably on the ship trailing you. The city guard got two coming off the wave runner. That Captain Sleigh is smart one though. He got away before anyone else could get arrested."

Linc smiled. "Monk and Kumbo."

Lord Saint shook his head. "Louy and Junker were killed by the attack force that rescued the little girl."

Linc felt slight satisfaction hearing about Louy, but Junker was just a dope who followed Louy everywhere. "So, you think it was Sleigh, huh?" Linc asked with concern. Sleigh was Ram's man and Linc knew how dangerous he was.

"Had to be. No other captain will work with Ram anymore, so he had to be the obvious choice."

Linc rubbed his hands over his face and through his greasy hair. "Well, if Sleigh comes after me again, I need to be ready."

Lord Saint looked at him for a moment. "I agree. I have invested in you, Linc, and I don't intend to lose. After you get the cargo unloaded, I'll get my shipmaster to look over your ship and design some improvements. Come by tomorrow and let me know if you like what he's come up with and we'll see if you have any more suggestions."

Linc thought about it for a moment and then shook his hand. "That sounds great. Thank you. I'll see you tomorrow after a much-needed bath and some hot food tonight." He got up and turned to head for the door to follow up with the crew.

"A warm woman might not be bad either."

Linc turned. "You're probably right, but I don't have time to get entangled right now."

Lord Saint had walked up beside Linc and put a hand on his shoulder. He walked with him out the door. "Don't make it complicated, Linc. There's plenty of willing participants in this city. Remember, it is a port city," he said and winked, releasing Linc. "Oh, by the way, this came for you." He handed Linc a rolled-up parchment and took off towards the shipmaster's office. Linc took the parchment and looked at it. It had the Storm family seal on it. Linc thanked him again, putting the parchment inside his tunic, and headed to where the cargo was being unloaded.

The crew had finished unloading when he got there. Linc settled up with Burnie, Lord Saint's foreman. "Where's the best place to stay in town?" Linc asked.

"There's several inns in town, but the Broken Spear is the best. It's on the other side of town. The best ale in town though is at the One Eye Jack's," Bernie pointed down the main street.

"That be where the best women in town are at," Mickey, another worker said, winking at River. Linc thanked them and the crew grabbed their packs.

"Here's your pay. Try not to spend it in one night." Linc eyed Jerle and Corky. "Remember, we'll probably be here for a couple of weeks getting the repairs done. I'll be staying at the Broken Spear if you need me." Linc turned and started walking to the other side of town.

Corky smiled. "Aye, Cap'n Linc. See you in a few days." Kaz smiled and followed Corky to the best ale in town. Jerle and River followed Linc.

It wasn't a long walk to the other side of town. They passed several businesses, just like they had in Silver City. *They're much smaller*, Linc thought. The market for trade was about a third the size, but still busy.

Finally, they reached The Broken Spear Inn. It had a typical sign that said its name and a spear sticking through the sign with the tip barely hanging on. Linc smiled at the sign.

"I guess we're here." He looked at the two following him. "I'll pay for everyone's rooms so just watch out for your food money." They thanked him and followed him in. It was a typical inn with tables and chairs spread throughout. An older man was behind the bar, serving ales and food to men and women at the bar. There was a jolly plump lady walking around serving the tables. A young boy, a little younger than Linc, was cleaning tables where patrons were departing.

A tall, slender female came walking up, carrying a tray. She was wearing a red skirt with a low-cut cream top that exposed her vitality. She stopped and eyed the three of them. "We don't serve pirates in here," she said, taking a step forward, blocking the view of the rest of the inn.

Linc's eyes rippled flames. He felt perturbed at being judged. "Well, it's a good thing we're not pirates."

"Oh really? You look like pirates to me," she said, taking a defensive stance. Irritated, Linc looked her up and down. She was almost as tall as him with fair skin and flowing, jet-black hair that complimented her gray eyes.

River started to protest and Linc put a hand on his chest to stop him from saying anything else. Linc stepped up close in front of her. She didn't flinch.

"We've been on the water for three weeks. We've battled real pirates and the elements and all we want is a warm and dry place to stay while Lord Saint's shipmaster fixes our ship."

Linc's eyes were roaring flames now, "I am too tired to put up with anyone's shit right now, especially a judgmental bitch."

Her glare didn't waver. "Prove it."

"Prove what?"

"That your ship is at Lord Saint's. I mean, how do I know you're not some water rat just trying to get past me?" He relaxed at the words she used to describe him. Linc pulled out a piece of parchment and handed it to her. She grabbed it and read it. "Humph." She handed it back to Linc. "Rooms are two coppers and a bronze a night. Meals are a copper each and ales are a bronze each." She paused and looked Linc up and down. "Baths are three coppers, but yours is on me tonight because you reek of a stench I don't recognize. You better get that bath before you eat. Harry won't feed you if you smell. See Tank over there." Linc followed her gaze to the young boy cleaning tables. "He will get you rooms and then the bath," she said, not changing the way she looked at Linc and walked away.

Linc watched her glide away. He smirked. Come on boys let get those rooms and a bath.

After they talked with Tank, they found out he was Harry's son. He got them their rooms and set them up with baths.

It was a simple room with one bed, table, and a chair. Linc dropped his pack off and put his papers away and headed to the communal bath down the hall. After he bathed and got out, the water was covered with slime.

"Damn you. This bath is disgusting!" The matron shook her head with disgust.

"I'm sorry. It's been weeks since I was able to take a bath. Here take this silver for the extra work I've caused you." He tossed it to her, and she quickly changed her attitude. He went back to his room and pulled out his best leather pants and gray shirt.

He put on his boots and examined them. They were ragged from the journey. "I guess I need to get some new boots soon," he said to himself. He then got up and headed downstairs where River and Jerle, who had beaten him to the baths and were already eating their beef stew. "Is it good?" he asked.

River stopped. "I don't know if it is but it's the best I ever had." The portly lady was walking by when he said it.

She stopped and beamed at him. "Well, thank you dear," she said in a motherly voice.

"I spent hours making that today." Jerle looked up and told her it was great also. She smiled and looked at Linc. What will you have, dear?"

He smiled back. "The stew, please."

She patted him on the shoulder. "Good choice." She took off to the kitchen.

Linc sat down, looking around the room and sipping the ale that the boys had gotten for him. *Typical crowd*, he thought. He saw a pair of seedy-looking men sitting in the corner talking. It reminded him of that night in Ram's place before he left. Linc watched the two, not realizing when his stew had been placed in front of him.

"I said, do you want any bread?"

Linc turned and looked into the gray eyes of the mouthy brunette. He smiled at her. "Yeah, toots, that will be great."

She glared at him and leaned close to his face. "The name's Mildred, not toots." She bumped his ale into his lap. "Oh, I'm sorry, rat."

Linc didn't even move. He just picked the mug off his lap and set it back on the table. "Oh, and Millie, I'll need another ale."

She huffed and walked off towards the bar.

"Linc, you better watch out for that one. She has the eyes of a demon," River said. Linc just wiped the ale off his lap with the towel Tank had brought over after witnessing the confrontation.

"Thanks Tank," Linc told the cleaner. Tank nodded and went back to cleaning tables.

"Yeah cap, I knew a woman once with gray eyes and she was *craaaazzzzyyy*," Jerle said, eating the last of the bread.

"All women are a little crazy Jerle." He looked back to the corner where the two seedy characters were. They had left during his encounter with Mildred. "Damn it to hells," he said, sensing danger. River and Jerle looked up at Linc with a questioning look. "Nothing," he told them.

"Here's your ale and your bread," Mildred said, throwing it in front of Linc and walking off. He watched her walk away, swinging her hips with each step. A hunger pang ate away at Linc, but he shook it off.

Maybe it's because I'm hungry or... He let the thought trail off as he watched the girl who intrigued him walk away.

After diving into the stew and bread, he found out it was really good, and he told the portly woman when she came back by.

"The name is Sally, love," she said before she thanked him and left.

The boys said their good nights after they ate. River and Jerle were going to go find Corky and Kaz and tell them about the rooms. Linc told them he was tired and wanted to get a good night's sleep. They left and Linc headed to his room. As he turned away from the boys, he bumped into Mildred, causing her to drop her round of drinks.

SMACK!

Her punch was the last thing Linc felt before Tank was helping him off the floor. Tank was laughing. Linc shook off the dizziness.

"Why are you laughing, Tank?" he asked.

"Mildred, she must really like you to waste any time knocking you out."

Linc rubbed his jaw. "I would hate to see her if she hated me." He laughed and got up with Tank's help. He thanked Tank and stared at the bruiser who was getting an earful from Harry. Linc shook his head and went up the stairs.

Linc laid on the bed and closed his eyes. He sensed a stirring in the bond with Dirk. His mind seemed clouded, then it cleared, and he was in Dirk's grandfathers shop. He saw the interaction between the king and the group gathered through Aarya's eyes. He was overwhelmed with what he was seeing. Then he sent a message to Tab and El. "You're damn right. Let's get started," he said aloud, answering the thoughts of his friends and smiling as he felt El and Tab grin. Linc felt every bond that took place.

He fell asleep, drained from the day's events. All of the emotions that swirled through his head, like a storms gusting wind. He woke him up with a sweat halfway into the night, reliving every sensation he had felt earlier.

"I really need to get home. I need to find out what in the hells is going on," he said aloud. Getting up, he quickly opened the window.

Aarya landed on the windowsill. He rubbed her neck, receiving a spark of clarity. "Is that smart?" he asked her. Aarya relayed what had happened and why. "I guess that makes sense. What was that part about the rat again?" She relayed the queen's prophecy.

Linc and Aarya could communicate as good as Dirk and Tab could now. He sat on his bed and Aarya landed right beside him.

"Well I guess we better get ready." Aarya trilled an agreement. Linc just laid down and held the covers up and Aarya snuggled down beside him. "You're tired, Red. Get some sleep." Linc covered her up to her neck. He fell asleep, thinking about three things. Dirk, the bonded and those damned gray eyes.

New Boots

The next morning, Linc awoke, and Aarya was already gone. After stretching away the stiffness of the long journey, he got up and got dressed. He needed some caf. Caf was a black bean that grew in certain areas. The bean would be picked and left to dry out for a few weeks. When it was just right it would be ground down to a fine dust and could be mixed with hot water into a strong drink that would wake a person up in the morning. Some people swore it gave them energy.

He went downstairs. Harry, the owner, was wiping down the bar. "Ah, early riser, I see," the man said to Linc.

He just nodded. "Always have been. You got some caf back there?"

Harry nodded and put a cup in front of Linc, who had sat down at the bar. "Sorry about Mildred," Harry leaned on the bar.

Linc took a sip of the hot brew. "No need. I can't blame her. We looked pretty rough when we got in last night." He looked at the cup curiously.

Harry frowned. "I just made it fresh. Is something wrong?"

Linc shook his head. "No, I believe this is the best caf I have ever had!"

Harry smiled. "It's me own brew. I grow the bean plants myself. I do it all at my farm. It's something about the soil there that gives it that robust taste."

Linc smiled and ordered another cup as soon as he finished the first. A few seconds later, Linc got an idea. "Do you sell it to anyone else?"

Harry smiled. "There was one who tried awhile back but I told him I wasn't interested."

Linc took another sip of the caf. "Well, if you ever get interested, I bet I could sell a thousand pounds of this in Silver City." He took another sip. "Linc Kane. Captain of The *LiTaDi Flame*. I'm a trader. I just became partners with Lord Philias Saint." Linc reached over to shake Harry's hand.

Harry grasped Linc's hand. "Interesting partner you have there. I know he is an honest man. He must have a lot of trust in you to be doing business with a man so young. No offense. I just know he doesn't choose partners lightly. That's saying a lot about you. I assure you I'll think about it." Harry nodded. With introductions out of the way, Linc ordered some breakfast.

While Harry was getting his breakfast, he pulled out the parchment Lord Saint had given him the day before. He smiled as he read it. Dirk had written him and told him about school, the twins Hilda and Tilda, El and Natia, and the things they had learned.

That confirmed the sensations he had been having lately, even though Aarya had communicated some of the information already. And from the things he had heard through their thoughts, he was getting an idea of everything that was going on.

"It's a wonder you can read," said a sultry voice from his left. Linc rolled up the parchment and put it inside his vest. He turned and looked at the gray-eyed demon. He snickered at the thought. Mildred squared her shoulders. "What's so funny, rat?"

"I was just thinking, I haven't been hit that hard since I was a lot younger," he said, rubbing his jaw.

"I'm surprised a scoundrel like you hasn't been hit a lot more than that."

Linc could sense her tension. *A bonus gift from Aarya*, he thought. "Look, we got off on the wrong foot last night." Linc stood, bowed at the waist, and then straightened, holding out his hand. "Captain Linc Kane of the *LiTaDi Flame*."

Mildred eyed him up and down. She offered her hand. "Mildred Swon."

Linc took her hand and kissed her knuckles. She chuckled. "I am not wrong often, but I will see if I'm wrong about you," she said, taking her hand back. She turned back to the bar. "Harry, have you got those cafs ready?" she asked the inn owner.

Linc bowed again and sat down to eat the eggs and bacon that Harry had just put in front of him.

"Here you go, Millie. Did you apologize to our patron here?"

Millie just looked at Linc and then turned to Harry. "Maybe later," she said and took the two tubes of caf Harry handed her, swinging her hips as she walked out the door without saying another word to Linc.

Harry laughed and looked at Linc. "What is it?" Linc asked while eating his breakfast.

"You be careful with that one. She might look tough, but she's even tougher than that. I think she might have taken a liking to you."

Linc took another sip of caf. "What makes you think that?" he asked, rubbing his jaw.

"Son, I've known her since she was a little girl running around the streets. She grew up an orphan, so she had to learn to fend for herself. She always seemed to beat the crap out of the boys she liked the most, and with the way she just looked at you, I'm afraid she might like you a lot." Harry said, laughing.

Linc thought about what Harry had told him and then, finishing off his caf, he asked for one more cup. "An orphan you say?" He smiled.

"What's that?" Harry asked, hearing intrigue in Linc's voice.

"I was an orphan too and I know what kind of life that can be." Linc stared in the distance, lost in thought, but he let it go after his third cup of caf was poured.

"So, what brings you to Oak City?"

Linc really liked Harry so he told him his story, about Dirk and Tab and the business they wanted to start. He told him about his journey to Oak City and all the dangers and perils they'd faced.

"Wow, hell of a first trip," Harry said. Locals had started to come into the bar for breakfast.

"Yeah, it wasn't what I had planned for the maiden voyage."

Harry patted Linc on the shoulder. "Well, at least you got a good partner in Lord Saint. He is the most respected man in our city."

Harry had to leave at about the time River and Jerle came downstairs. "Have some breakfast on me, boys," Linc told the two. They thanked him and ordered the same thing Linc had.

By the time they had finished, Linc had told them if they wanted to see the city to go ahead. He had to find a cobbler to get some new shoes and clothes. Linc left soon after the boys had gone out to find their two missing crew members that hadn't been seen since the night before. He figured they would find them somewhere today.

Linc asked around town for the best place to buy some good, durable boots. Everyone told him that Madam Swon's trading post was the place. Walking down the middle of town, he came to the trading post fairly quick.

It was a typical trading post, with everything from dried foods to clothes. Linc walked up to the counter. A girl was bent over, putting something under the counter. There was a familiarity about her.

She stood up. "Can I he…" She stopped when she came face to face with Linc. He smiled at those gray eyes. "What do you want?" Mildred snapped, realizing Linc was standing in front of her. She just stood there, glaring at him with her arms folded across her chest. She was dressed in tight, tan leather pants with a tan vest and red shirt. Her long hair was pulled up into a bun on top of her head.

Linc laughed, holding up his hands. "Hey, I didn't know you worked here. I was told this was the best place to buy some new boots." Linc held up one of his boots.

She looked over the counter and saw he was telling the truth. She relaxed. "Follow me." Linc watched her tight leather pants lead the way. She stopped at the back wall of the room. "Have a seat." Linc sat down in front of a wall that had several boots spread out on shelves. "Ankle or knee-height?"

"Ankle."

Grabbing a couple of pairs and then sitting on a stool in front of him, she asked him to hold his foot up so she could judge his size.

"Take off your boot and place your foot here." She pointed between her legs to the board on the stool. It had a flat piece of wood attached that was angled down for him to rest his foot on.

Linc complied. "I probably need some new socks as well."

After Linc pulled off his boot, revealing several holes in the sole, she agreed and told him she would be right back. Linc pulled off his old sock, took off his other boot, and pulled off the other sock, tossing them in the trash can beside his chair.

Mildred came back and sat on the stool. "I'm glad you decided to take those nasty things off," she said, looking at the discarded socks with a raised eyebrow.

"They have seen better days," Linc said, seeing Mildred smile for the first time since they met. She rolled his pant leg up to his calf, her hands brushing his skin. Linc's senses were set on fire with her touch. He cocked his head to the side looking at her eyes.

She just looked back, almost as if she felt something too. She started to say something but stopped before putting one of the new socks on his foot. Her fingers brushed against his leg again. Linc squirmed a little.

She looked up at him, genuinely smiling. "Ticklish I see."

Linc, not wanting to say too much, replied, "Well, I am a little nervous around you. You did knock me out last night, just for accidentally bumping into you."

She put the other sock on and looked up at him. "I was on edge last night. I've had some bad dealings with pirates and seeing your crew, and the way y'all looked, brought back some bad memories. I'm sorry about that."

She genuinely looked sorry. Flames were beginning to ripple in his eyes, so he looked away to calm the small storm brewing inside him. *What is this girl doing to me*? He looked back at those gray eyes after the flames dissipated. "That's ok, no apology needed, but I would accept a drink from you."

Mildred took a deep breath and released it. "Let's get you some boots, then we'll discuss that drink." Smiling, she continued to measure Linc's foot. "My, what big feet you have!"

Linc did have big feet for his size, but he thought she was just trying to make conversation. "Yeah, the kids at the orphanage use to kid me about having big feet," Linc said, trying to bait her into talking more. As she was picking up the first pair of boots, she stopped and turned to face him, boot in hand.

"You're an orphan?"

"Since I was two. My parents were killed by pirates on a trip to Silver City," Linc said with bitterness in his voice.

Mildred put a hand on Linc's knee and squeezed. "I was orphaned as well. I barely remember my father before he went off to fight in the war at Der-Tod. I never knew my mother." There was sadness in her eyes.

"Well, we have that in common, I guess." Linc's plan was starting to work. He just sat there, waiting on her to continue.

Mildred stared into Linc's eyes. *What the hell.* "I'm off tonight. I'll meet you at the One-eyed Jacks. We can have a drink there."

Inside, Linc was bursting with anticipation. He really was intrigued by Mildred. "Sounds great," he replied, containing his excitement.

Mildred started fitting him with some boots. He didn't like the feel of any until the last pair. They were sturdy and flexible, like they had been worn a hundred times, but they were brand-new. Linc really liked them "These are the ones," he told her. "Where did they come from. Does someone here make them?"

"No, a merchant came through here a few weeks back, saying he lived in Pineral. Said he and his wife had just dropped their son off at the school in Silver City and thought since he rarely got out this way, he would try to sell some of his wares while traveling back."

Linc walked around in the boots for a minute. "These are amazing!"

"Yes, they are. He only had five pairs and you're getting the last one."

"Do you know his full name? I'd like to get in touch with him and see if I can set up a trade agreement. These will really sell in Silver City." He felt there would be a huge market for the products.

"On one condition."

Linc smiled. She wasn't just beautiful. She was intelligent. He thought he knew what she was going to say so he waited.

His guess has been right. "Make me a partner on the goods you buy and sell from him, make Swon's the only place that you sell to in Oak City."

"I have partners already," Linc said, knowing he was going to already agree.

Mildred's mind was made up. She walked up close to Linc, putting a hand on his chest. "Are they as smart as me?" she teased, rubbing her hand across his shoulder and down his arm.

"No, but Dirk is handsome. Tab not so much, but both are lifelong friends."

"I'll make it worth your while." She pulled her arm back and stepped back a few paces.

Linc, feeling his insides turn animalistic, whispered, "How?"

"Well, extra benefits, you know."

Linc just looked at her.

Mildred laughed. "I will make sure you always get the best room at The Broken Spear and I promise you'll always have someone to have dinner with, other than those rogues you travel with."

Knowing she meant more, Linc smiled. "Well, how could any man with a sane mind ever turn that down?"

Mildred smiled. "Then it's a deal." She held out her hand to shake.

Linc grabbed her hand and pulled her close, looking into her eyes. "Deal," he said, feeling her chest rise up and down with each breath. He released her, much to her disappointment, and headed to the counter to settle up.

Regaining her composure, she went behind the counter and told him two silvers. Linc normally would have tried bartering, but these boots were phenomenal. He smiled and paid her.

"I look forward to our partnership. I'll see you at dusk for that drink."

She smiled and waved goodbye as he was turning to leave.

After Linc left the trading post, Mildred sat down on the stool behind the counter. "So that was him?" came a voice coming down the stairs.

"Yes, Elanor, that was him."

Elanor Swon walked up, pulling up a chair next to her adopted daughter, and sat down. She patted Mildred's arm with affection. "A bit roguish, isn't he?"

Mildred looked at her and smiled. "He is, but I sensed something in him. A connection the first time I laid eyes on him."

Elanor looked at Mildred. "Dear, be careful with your feelings. Whatever this sense is, you must be careful with it. We don't know what it is or how it works so it could mean danger."

Mildred thought for a moment. "I think this is different. I mean, when I was younger and would get that feeling from boys or men who meant me harm. It was a dull ache. This sense feels like a warm and happy feeling."

"Well, dear, your instincts have almost always been right, so I trust you. But be wary that you don't share this information too soon until you're sure of his intentions."

Mildred squeezed her hand and kissed her on the cheek. "I'm going to the backyard and practice with my sword."

"Ah, is Lord Saint coming by to practice today?"

"No, he said he would be tied up with business affairs for a few days, but he made me promise to practice while he was gone."

"Well, I will say this, if he is in business with the lord, maybe he's ok," Elanor said.

"My thoughts as well," Mildred said, grabbing her sword by the back door and heading out.

After three hours of going through stretches and a vigorous workout, Mildred went inside to bathe and get ready for her drink with the mysterious Linc, He had taken her breath away earlier when he'd pulled her so close. She could have sworn his eyes looked like they had flames in them at one point in the conversation, but it had probably been a reflection of the light.

As Mildred headed back into her house and closed the door, two figures who had been in the shadows watching her, peeled away from their hiding spot, and headed down the trail that lead into the woods surrounding Oak City.

"You see, it is as I said. She has the gift," the man said. He was wrapped in robes that seemed to blend in with whatever colors surrounded him at the time. The female looked at him and stopped, grabbing his arm to force him to look at her. He turned, making sure they weren't in view of any onlookers.

"She has to have it if we're ever to be free, my love." He put his hands on her face tenderly and he kissed her passionately, receiving passion in return.

"We will be, and we will make up for our lies and mistakes. She is our daughter. She has our blood running through her veins. The power is there. I sense it." She nodded and the two faded into the woods, heading down the trail out of Oak City.

That night, Linc and Mildred met for a drink, which turned into several. Linc finally found his two lost crewmen, Kaz and Corky, who, it seemed had been hanging out and staying at the One-eyed Jack. They had met some women and been privy to their rooms.

Linc told them about their own rooms waiting for them at The Broken

Spear and they were happy to hear the news. They left, much to the complaints of the whores they had been hooking up with. They liked their money more than they liked the women. Kaz and Corky promised they would come back after a day's rest and a bath.

They left early in the night. River came in for a few ales and seemed enthralled with a waitress by the name of Flora. She was a petite, young girl about River's age and it was apparent she didn't work in the whoring trade. She was just a drink server.

Linc told Mildred about his life as a wharf rat and the orphanage. Mildred laughed at the nickname. Linc told her that was really what had gotten his attention. He told her about Dirk and Tab and their plans and basically told her his entire life story. Mildred gave a brief description of her life, explaining very little about her father than what he already knew. She told him how Elanor Swon had been a friend to her when she was in the orphanage and had adopted her after a bad incident with a pirate by the name of Sleigh.

Linc's eyes flared up when he heard the name. He knew how evil the man was first-hand. He didn't ask her to explain. "Sleigh was the pirate who attacked my ship on our voyage here. We narrowly escaped his attack. If it hadn't been for some great maneuvering from my crew, we wouldn't be here tonight. I promise you this. That scumbag will get what he deserves one day, and I plan on it being me who gives it to him."

"Thank you, but if I get to him first, it will be me that gives him what he deserves. The scum's death is in my hands," Mildred proclaimed, staring into Linc's eyes."

Linc tilted his head to the side, trying to break Mildred's death glare. She noticed the movement and smiled. "I'm curious, what do you mean? I've told you why I want to kill him, but you've been vague."

Mildred took a drink from her ale. She rested the glass to her lips, deciding what to tell Linc. She set it down on the table. "Let's just say that it was bad enough that I have been training for the last five years with blades and staffs so that one day when I do come across him, I'll send him to the underworld alone!"

Linc, sensing the tension in Mildred's voice, quickly changed the topic. "I would very much like to practice with you," Linc said out of the blue. Mildred just looked at him. "The sword and staff," he explained.

"Ok, but I must warn you my tutor is very hard on me and I am pretty good."

"If I can last in a match with Dirk Storm for as long as I do, then I think I can handle a girl." Linc laughed as Mildred punched him in the arm and knocked him off the stool. He got up and Mildred joined in his laughter. "I should have remembered that right hook of yours," he said, sitting down and ordering another pitcher of ale, satisfied his diversion had loosened her up.

"We'll start tomorrow but I must warn you I practice for hours and it's intense," Mildred declared.

"I look forward to it."

They finished their drinks and Linc, wanting to be a gentleman, walked her home. He kissed her hand goodnight and said he needed to get in bed early. She smiled at the manners that he was affording her and kissed him goodnight on the cheek.

As Mildred was locking up and heading to bed, one thought from the conversation just wouldn't leave her mind. *Dirk Storm. Why does that name sound so damn familiar?* She knew it would come to her. She never forgot anything. Sometimes it just took a while for her to remember.

As Linc walked back to The Broken Spear, he kept feeling as though he was being watched. His senses were on alert. Aarya hadn't been around all day but he was sure if it were real danger, she would appear. He shook it off and got to the inn in time for one of Harry's cups of caf. He then went to bed soon after that, anxious to see Mildred's moves.

A Warning from Beyond

Dirk could sense the sun rising in the east. Yesterday had been an extremely long day. He felt stiff and sore. He was lying flat on his back, feeling trapped when he tried to move. As his eyes came into focus, he looked to his left and the scent of honey filled his senses. Natia was sleeping on his shoulder with her hand on his chest. Her breathing was soothing. He felt weight on both of his hands actually. Now that he was more awake, he felt weight on his right shoulder as well. He turned to see what was on his right shoulder and saw a head of brown hair snuggled up next to his side. The smell of pine and roses caused him to smile.

He raised his head to see over Natia and saw a similar head of hair sleeping on his other hand, snuggled up in a spooning position behind Natia. Smiling and wanting to laugh, he laid his head back down. They were under the sleeping bags with Natia and him.

"They came in the middle of the night," Natia whispered. Her amber eyes filled him with love as he gazed into them. Dirk pulled them all closer, feeling movement from the twins as he embraced his new family. Vira snuggled up closer. Nira put her arm around Natia's waist, resting her hand on Dirk's chest.

Dirk, who was gazing into Natia's eyes again, said, "I love you."

Natia smiled and kissed him on the cheek. "I love you too."

Vira snuggled even closer, putting her hand on Natia's side. "I love you both," she said and kissed Dirk's cheek.

Nira kissed Natia's cheek after leaning up and looked at the two. "I love you too, but can we sleep a little longer?"

They laughed quietly. Dirk pulled them tighter. "I love you as well, sisters. Sure, a little while longer."

Natia rolled on her back. She pulled her arm free and put it under Dirk's head and the other under Nira's and pulled her tighter. Vira thought, *I guess it's a good thing we didn't sleep like we normally do.*

Dirk, intrigued, asked out loud, "And how is that sister?"

Nira yawned and whispered, "We usually sleep in the nude." Natia and

Dirk were still getting used to Nira's ever-evolving personality. They just laughed.

Vira was so close to Dirk now that she was right by his ear. "Seriously we do." Then she went back to sleep.

Dirk enjoyed the warmth of the growing closeness of the twins. Natia agreed with his thoughts and leaned her head closer to Dirk, falling back asleep as well. Dirk gave in to the light snores and dozed back off.

Being this close with the twins, Dirk now shared their dreams and the horrors that the two had lived through from their childhood until the time they fled that horrible island.

When he finally awoke an hour later, the rest of the group was starting to stir. He sat up when the others did and looked into the twin's eyes. "I swear by the time this is over, I will make every one of them bastards pay."

Natia hugged Nira as Dirk was hugging Vira. "We all will, this I swear." She had seen everything Dirk had.

The twins just squeezed them back and said in unison. "We know."

"Who's hungry?" Dirk asked.

"I'm starving," Nira said, getting up and stretching.

"Mom probably has breakfast started," Dirk said, separating the sleeping bags and folding them up. Natia put the fire out and noticed another pair of sleeping bags on the other side of the pit. Anastasia and Kal were starting to get up.

"I'm glad you four finally shut up. I thought I was gonna have to order you to be quiet earlier," Anastasia said, smiling while grabbing her gear and packing it up. Kal was doing the same.

"You say something about breakfast?" Kal said, slinging his pack over his shoulder.

"Yeah, follow me," Dirk replied. When they got to the house Kira had set up some tables outside the back door. Carly and Kira were setting out plates for twenty people.

"Morning," Kira said as the group came walking up. Dirk hugged his mom, followed by the group, who now felt a connection to Kira. Carly watched the scene and said good morning to each of them as well. After Vira finally released Kira from the hug, she sat down as the last of the food was set on the table. Knowing they had to be careful with what they said in front of Carly, Dirk asked his mom if the king was still there.

Kira looked around, "He wants a word with several people before he left." Anastasia nodded, knowing she was one of them.

Several minutes later Claire came running up from the other pit and informed Kira that everyone else was headed to the house. She sat down and started digging into a plate of eggs, sausage, and bread.

"Mom, do you have any fresh caf? I have a serious craving for some this morning."

"I'll get some." Kira started to go get the caf. Before she could take two steps, Natia, who never had any caf in her life, said, "I think I'll have some as well." The whole table excluding Claire, said the same.

"That's weird, I've never wanted caf before," Dirk said, leaving what he was thinking unspoken since Claire was there. The group caught on and nodded in agreement.

Linc? Natia thought.

Dirk smiled. "Probably. Since the bond is stronger now, we may experience cravings that someone in the bond has," Dirk whispered to Natia, putting a hand gently on her leg under the table.

Thwack!

"Ow!" Dirk looked around to see who had thrown the biscuit at his head. Anastasia was staring at him with a raised eyebrow. "Thanks, Stas. I needed a reminder," he said while the rest of the table laughed.

"Remember," she said, tapping the side of her head. Everyone else started eating, ignoring the conversation between Anastasia and Dirk. It didn't seem to bother Natia. She just smiled and nodded to a now-smiling Anastasia. Claire, oblivious to the reason the table was laughing, just laughed right along with them. Tab and the rest of the group came walking up soon after that.

"Great! I'm starving!" he said, taking a seat at the table with El sitting beside him. Everyone else found a seat and started eating. Kira brought out the caf and said good morning to the rest of the group. She had food for everyone, fruits and even fish for the dwarves.

After everyone finished eating, the king and the general came out to greet them. The king said good morning to all of them and hugged his daughter.

"Now, what say we do some training since we have a good-sized group here today?" the general announced, looking at the gathered students. When all eyes were on him, he continued. "Especially since Kal and Anastasia are here, I think you first-years can get some valuable training from them that the rest of your grade will miss out on."

The group expected this, minus the four who weren't aware of what happened in the shop the day before and agreed.

"Let's divide up into two groups. One led by Kal, who will train with the staff. The other led by Anastasia, who will train with knives. Remember, no contact, just forms practice and maybe some formations," the general instructed. They all agreed. "Then, after lunch, we can do some sword and bow practice."

Dirk knew the practice yard was set up already. He helped Kira clear up the breakfast table first. The group all thanked her and then went to the training area behind the general's workshop.

The general had plenty of wooden swords, shields, and staffs for practice. Dirk, Tab, and Linc had used these many times in their youth. Both groups went through an extensive stretching exercise led by Kal and Anastasia. It was even more intense than the one they did with Sergeant Giles.

After thirty minutes of this, they separated into two groups. Dirk, Natia, Vira, and Nira went with Anastasia, along with Tara and Oriana. Tab, El, Volar, Raga, Dusty, Phil, and Jonesy went with Kal. Both groups went through blocking and footwork. Anastasia showed the group several feint moves, ending with a leg sweep and thrust to the heart. Kal showed similar moves to his group, making sure everyone learned that the staff should be used as an extension of their arms. They then squared off with partners.

Dirk was partnered with Anastasia. "I forgot how good you were," she said to him after twenty minutes of practicing.

"It's been a while since we sparred." Dirk panted.

The sound of knives became louder and quicker by the minute, stopping everyone but the two involved. The match between Natia and Vira became a blur to most watching. They were moving with beautiful rhythm and speed. After a few minutes, they stopped, with Natia stopping her practice knife an inch from Vira's throat. They were both drenched in sweat, breathing hard and smiling at one another. Natia pulled her knife back and bowed as Vira stood and bowed.

"That was bloody brilliant," Tab said. The group of students and the adults who had been watching, began to clap.

"Vira, I didn't know you were that good with a knife!" Dirk exclaimed. She nodded in acknowledgment.

"Let's switch group leaders now," the general suggested.

Vira, walked up to a stunned Dirk. "Really, I just channeled your abilities through the bond. It made my skills better than normal," she said for his ears only. Dirk hadn't thought of using their abilities that way.

"That was awesome Vira," El said giving her a high five as she walked past to switch over to Anastasia's group. Kal took Dirk and his group through the same exercises that he had taken the first group through. Natia paired up with Vira again and it was another great presentation.

Lunch time came around sooner than expected. Kira had put out sandwiches and fruit for all of them. Before Dirk and Natia could sit down, the general and the king came up to them.

"Dirk and Natia, might I have a word?" the king asked. They agreed and followed him to the general's workshop.

The general let them in and followed behind the king. Today the room seemed smaller to Dirk. There was a couch with two chairs facing it with a small round table between them. On the table was a bag about twice the size of Dirk's backpack. The king motioned for them to sit on the couch as he and the general sat in the chairs.

They listened as the king began to speak. "I am glad everyone seems to be handling this situation better than I'd anticipated they would." Dirk and Natia both agreed. "Now there are things for your ears only since you're the Chosen and protector. If you decide to share this information with the other bonded, that is up to you." The king paused and the general took over.

"The two of you are the original heirs to defend against Zolun and his evil. So, when the time comes down to it, one of you has to deliver the killing blow. The only way to deliver the blow is with Harbinger or an arrow shot from Luna's Tears. When you leave here tomorrow and go back to school, the two of you will know how to come here to get them when the time comes. That is a secret that you can share but remember, you two are the only ones who can open the doorway."

The general glanced at the door by the weapons cache. He got up and motioned for them to follow. He placed his hand on the door and said a few words. The door glowed yellow for a moment. He then instructed Natia and Dirk to put their hands on the door. They did as he instructed and the door warmed at their touch, flashed yellow one more time and then cooled. The general pulled away and told them to sit back down.

"Now the other side of that door is at the bottom of the stairwell that leads to the dorms."

Natia and Dirk looked at each other. "The door on the left after you enter from the stairwell?" Dirk asked.

The king nodded. "Yes, it leads to the basement, but that's not the only door down there. I had Nabas set up this passage during your father's first few years at school. We wanted a way for him and others to escape if the school was ever attacked."

"All you have to do is place your hand on the door and it will activate. You step through it and you're instantaneously transported to the other side," the general told them.

"That's cool," Dirk said.

"There are several others throughout the school that leads to other places like the palace, the guard tower at the south gate, and one at the palace that takes you to the Silver City outpost."

Dirk and Natia nodded.

"Now the general has a map of doorways that he will give you before you leave."

The general held up a folded piece of parchment that Dirk assumed was the map.

"There are some things that the two of you need to be made aware of. There is a set of armor that was made by the dwarves for the Chosen and his protector. The elves inscribed runes of power on them with powerful gems encrusted throughout the armor. Two sets. One for you, Dirk, and one for you, Natia. The armor is made of Mythril. It is five times harder than any steel ever made yet it's like wearing a light tunic."

The general motioned to the door beside the weapons cache. "You can see it after we get through talking." The king opened the package in front of him. He pulled out four bracelets and two necklaces, similar to the ones Hilda had given to them but much grander. Dirk and Natia both had looks of awe on their faces.

The king laughed. "I did the same thing the first time I ever saw these as well." Dirk and Natia just sat there anxiously. "These were made by the dwarves. The gold was given to them from me and again the elves inscribed runes of power into them. The gems were mined from Blazire, another gift from us."

Dirk and Natia stared at the beautiful craftsmanship. "You need to put these on so your core can attune to the runes, which will enable you to use their power. They are like everything else. The power is limited but will regenerate over time." The king handed a set of bracelets to Natia and a set to Dirk.

"I have a question," Dirk said.

"Go ahead son," the general urged.

"What if I wanted to give one of these extra bracelets to someone else to wear? Would they be able to use the power?"

The general rubbed his mustache. "The only thing is this, you will need all the power you can muster when you finally come face to face with Zolun. Other than that, I would think they could use it."

Dirk and Natia took off the bracelets Hilda and Tilda had given them and put on one bracelet a piece. As soon as they wrapped them around their wrists and clasped them on, the runes lit up and the gems flared to life. They felt a power they had never felt before. Their hearts synchronized with the pulse of life itself. They instinctively grasped hands. In that moment, they were one.

Time stopped as far as Dirk and Natia were concerned. He saw the beauty of her soul, her very essence joined with his. They both had one thought: *I love you*. They both took a deep breath and exhaled not realizing they had closed their eyes. Then they opened them and looked immediately at the other. Tears were falling down their faces.

"That must have been one hell of a connection," the king said, bringing their attention back to him.

"Yes, it was exhilarating," Natia said, and Dirk agreed. The king then handed them the necklaces.

"Now you have to wear these too," the general said. They put them on, and the same intense connection happened, only this time they both passed out from the power flowing through them.

The Chosen and protector's history flashed before their eyes. The happiness, sadness, and the love they all shared. It would be memories that one day they would be able to access, but right now, Dirk knew from the connection that it was all jumbled emotions.

After a few minutes, they came around. The general gave them each a glass of water. "It will ease the dry mouth, trust me." He smiled.

Dirk and Natia still had their hands grasped. "That was overwhelming," they said in unison.

The general laughed. "It is, but it'll eventually unjumble itself and usually when you need it. Now, those are linked to the bracelets. If you ever take them off, you must secure them so no one will see them. That would bring questions that you might not want to answer. If anyone tries to put them on other than you, they will die from excruciating pain. That is the defense mechanism the elves inscribed in the runes. The bracelets, as well. Those you are wearing now are tuned to your core and your core only. The ones you give away will be attuned to the ones that put them on."

Dirk and Natia thought for a minute. After a mental conversation, Dirk spoke. "With the plan you have laid out, we would like Kal and Stas to have the other bracelets."

The king smiled. "That might be wise since your missions in the beginning will have you separated." The general nodded, went to open the door, looking where the group was still eating lunch, and called Kal and Anastasia to join them.

Anastasia and Kal entered the shop, and the general closed the door. Anastasia looked around and sat beside Dirk. Kal sat down beside Natia.

"Dirk and Natia have been given some tools to help with the battles to come. A set of necklaces and also two sets of bracelets. They have been infused with runes to make them stronger. These were gifts from the three races. Dirk and Natia have put them on already, linking them to their cores, with the exception of a set of bracelets. They want to give you each a set of bracelets to wear. I think this is wise because when you set off on your journeys, you will be separated. This will allow you to communicate, no matter how far away you are from each other. This is a high honor, that they bestow upon you," The general nodded, looking at Kal and Anastasia. Anastasia, grasping the significance of these gifts, touched Dirk on the shoulder appreciatively.

Dirk and Natia gave them the bracelets and Kal and Anastasia put them on. Dirk and Natia felt the connection immediately. Kal and Anastasia had a similar overwhelming sensation as Dirk and Natia had. Feeling the deeper connection to them they hugged.

"I explained to Dirk and Natia that once you put those bracelets on that no one else can. Only you two can wear them because they are attuned to your cores. If someone else tries they will die an excruciating death."

All four nodded and began to get up. "One last suggestion," the king said as the four were walking to examine the armor.

All four stopped and looked to the king.

"What's that, sire?" Dirk asked.

"Don't put that on until you're ready to announce to the world who you are. Because once you don that armor, it will be obvious to all who you are," he said, walking out, saying *"Rememoria,"* with the general, before exiting.

Dirk opened the door to the small closet that housed the armor. He pulled out each set. They were mounted on wooden statues. "Wow that is beautiful," Anastasia said, admiring the armor and running her hand over Natia's breastplate. It was a dark silver plate with a phoenix engraved in the center. It had no sleeves, and the leg greaves were one connected piece. The backs of the plate and the leg armor were open with runes engraved down the sides of each piece. The eyes of the phoenix were crimson gems with smaller ones set into the armor down the seams, all different colors the size of Dirk's thumbnail.

Dirk's armor was the same. They both had crimson capes made of a soft mesh material that also had a phoenix on the back painted in colors that reminded them of Aarya. Dirk touched the armor; at his touch, the gems came to life, pulsing with light. The eyes of the phoenix seem to flare, recognizing his touch. Natia touched hers and the same thing happened. There were two clasps at the top and bottom of each piece for securing them in place. They had small crimson gems in each of them as well.

"This must be what seals them on," Kal said, looking at the clasps.

"How do the knees bend?" Natia asked, picking up one of the leg pieces. She felt the gems come to life in her hands as she tried to bend the armor. It bent in the knee area with little effort.

"That's amazing," Dirk said.

"Now I see what Father meant about not putting it on until you're ready to declare who you are," Anastasia said. They all agreed.

"Look, we need to all talk before we go back out there. There are some things we need to make sure happen for the plan to work," Dirk sat on the couch with the others in tow. "Kal, when you and Stas leave next week, you're going to replace the soldiers in the north border, right?"

Kal and Anastasia both agreed that was part of the plan. "Like Father said, our real mission will be to train with our group on tactics and covering an advance," Anastasia said. "Two weeks later, a contingent of one thousand more troops will be put under our command to provide support. That will include the first-years like, Jonesy and the dwarves' class."

"Right. They will be shipped out, as if on a training exercise, and brought into the fold," Kal finished. Dirk nodded.

"Kal, I think they need to know the truth. Let's face it, they'll be more prepared if they know what's coming."

Kal looked at Anastasia and she nodded. "Dirk, we already decided last night on our walk that we would tell them the truth," Anastasia said.

"That's good. I agree with that, and besides, we were going to tell most of our class ourselves, regardless of what we were told the plan was. It's the best thing we feel." Dirk stated and Kal nodded his agreement.

"We will have attention brought to us as soon as we start our special classes with Hermosa anyway. At least we'll tell the ones we need to so they can help prepare for what's coming. Plus, I need to prepare Gil for the bond. I can't do that to my friends and leave them unprepared if something happens before we're ready."

Kal and Anastasia agreed. "There is one thing nobody knows, except grandfather, Mom, Hilda, Tilda, Natia, El, Tab, Linc and me."

"There's something we don't know, Dirk?" Anastasia asked, perturbed.

He took a calming breath. "When Arial died and shared the power with her dying breath…" Dirk paused, looking into Natia's eyes for permission. She blinked and nodded. "Tab was with me."

Kal raised an eyebrow. Anastasia just smiled. "He received part of the power transfer, didn't he?" Dirk nodded and told them the true story of that day. After he finished, Anastasia got up and rolled her shoulders.

"Look, let me say this. I am the one who bears the burden of the Chosen and for one, I don't really like it, so we decided since nothing has really worked over the past five hundred years that maybe keeping this a secret can work for us."

Anastasia sat back down and said, "You're right, Dirk, but keeping that from Father could've been dangerous."

He looked at his friend, who he now knew better than he actually wanted to thanks to the bond and dropped his head. "Anastasia, I love you. We've been good friends a long time. Some of the secrets we've kept from our parents would have gotten both of us in deep trouble. We were kids then, though. Now, we're having the fate of the world put on our shoulders, and I personally would like to have an ace in the hole. Let's face it, going by the Book of Storms, or even the book my father and his friends made is only a history of what didn't work. Let's make our own plan and end this madness. What I'm saying is, we learn from the history but since it's our asses that will actually be in life-and-death situations, shouldn't it be our plan?" She stared at Dirk, flames rippling in her eyes.

Kal put a loving hand on her shoulder. "He's right, Stas. I agree with Dirk. We need to keep this a secret and use it when the time is right."

She looked into his eyes. Her shoulders relaxed. She grabbed Dirk's hand and Kal's in the other. Dirk grabbed Natia's hand and Natia grabbed Kal's free hand. Standing in a circle, they agreed to keep Tab's secret safe until the time it needed to be known. They decided it was time to get back to practice after they put the armor away.

Dirk and Natia decided to leave the necklaces with the armor and get them when it was time to fight. Right now, it would be harder to keep them hidden. They put the bracelets the twins had given them on their opposite wrists. Saying "*Rememoria*," they all headed out to the waiting group.

The king told the group that he and Thea had to get back to the palace. They said their goodbyes and headed out. Anastasia and Kal had a brief meeting with him before he left, and then they headed back to the training yard where the group was gathered. Now that the young adults were alone, Anastasia did as they had decided. "All gather around. Dirk, go ahead and tell the ones who don't know, why we're truly here."

Dirk nodded and told everyone to sit. He told the basic story to everyone still there, the bonded filling in when one of the not-bonded asked a question.

Jonesy stood. "I knew there was something going on with you." He pointed at Dirk. "You have been my brother since we were kids. I love you and will follow you anywhere." Jonesy wiped the tears away as he finished.

El was the first one to her brother and embraced him. "Dirk knows. That's why he wanted to tell you the first chance he got." El released him as Dirk grabbed Jonesy in a hug.

"I couldn't do it without you big guy," Dirk said.

Jonesy released Dirk and nodded. Dirk looked around at Phil, Dusty and Raga.

"I haven't known you as long Dirk. I do know that I am very impressed with you. I will be there as well," Phil said with Dusty agreeing with his sentiments.

Raga laughed. "Aye. If kin-son is involved, the dwarves will be there as well. You have my axe." Dirk smiled.

"I appreciate all of you. I just want to make sure you know how dangerous it will be. Our lives will change from this point forward, also it is very important that you don't talk about this with anyone outside our group."

They all nodded. "Good, now let's take advantage of Kal and Stas while their still here and get some training in. We're going to need it."

They practiced archery techniques that afternoon. Dirk even brought out Midnight and a few other horses from the barn so they could practice shooting while on horseback.

Before dusk, they called a halt to practice. Kal talked to the group, reminding them how serious their training over the next few weeks and months would be. Then they all separated for the night, with some of them going to the pit by the hay fields, following Kal and Anastasia for dinner.

The others went to the pit behind the guest house with Dirk. Bart had already put a couple cows on the pits earlier in the day when the group was training so they would be ready when they finished.

Having this many guests, Bart had engineered four temporary showers at different locations around the farm. *That's actually genius*, Dirk thought when he saw them. He had taken a metal barrel and put it on a platform with a hose running down through a water spigot with holes in it, forming a shower head. He had attached a chain to a lever that would release water when it was pulled down. Depending on how far down the lever was pulled determined the flow. There was a small fire lit under the barrels to warm the water. Each were set up at the specific locations for extra privacy.

"I'm going to shower before I eat," Dirk said, pointing to Bart's invention.

"Ladies first," Natia said, bumping into him as she ran to get there first. Dirk laughed and chased after her, slinging his pack over his shoulder. The rest of the group laughed and started eating.

"I guess we can shower later," Tab said eying the food, making everyone laugh. Dirk went around the corner of the horse barn and Natia had already beaten him to the shower. Bart had made some benches and had set some towels on them.

Natia stepped behind the tarp and started undressing. Dirk sat on the bench, waiting his turn. The tarps weren't tall, around shoulder height. Natia had unbraided her hair and was washing it with the homemade soaps and shampoos that Kira had made.

"Oh, my gods," Natia moaned as the warm water rinsed the shampoo and soap from her body.

"What's wrong?" he asked, jumping up.

"Nothing. This is just wonderful." She stared at him standing there, water dripping from her hair and face. Taking one hand, she brushed the hair out of her face. Their eyes locked and she smiled. "Get in here and wash my back, but no funny business, mister."

Dirk saluted her. "Yes, ma'am. On my honor." He looked around to make sure they were clear. He quickly took off his clothes and joined her. She had her back to him. She pulled the lever as he got close and water poured over his head, soaking him. She giggled, made him turn around, and she put shampoo in his hair massaging it in while he washed his body and face with the soap. She pulled the lever again and rinsed the shampoo and soap away. He then turned her and washed her back. As promised, he was a gentleman, even though his anatomy wanted otherwise.

He pulled the lever, releasing the water to wash away the soap. She spun around, surprising him, wrapping her arms around his neck. He reached his around her waist. She kissed him passionately until they heard someone clearing their throat. Dirk looked over his shoulder and saw Kal and Anastasia sitting on the bench, waiting on them to be through.

Dirk smiled. "I thought you were on the other side of the farm."

"We wanted some privacy, so if you don't mind, hurry up." Anastasia answered.

Natia laughed and grabbed two towels. "Come on, lover, let's give them some privacy." They dried off and put on some fresh clothes that they had in their packs.

As they were leaving, Anastasia winked at Dirk. "Remember, I am still your princess, Chosen!" She put a single finger to her lips. Dirk nodded then kissed her on the cheek. He waved her off as he and Natia walked to the pit for some food.

After Dirk and Natia had their fill of ribs, the group talked about how anxious they were to begin their other training with Wizard Hermosa. They knew she was powerful and wanted to see what she would show them. Dirk calmed them down with one small reminder. "Remember why we're training. I'm glad you each are enthusiastic about learning new powers. Just keep in mind why we're learning them." The group stared at him.

"You don't have to be a buzz kill Dirk," Tab said throwing a stick at him. Again, Natia caught it in the air right in front of his face. Natia glared at Tab. He just smiled. "We know, Dirk. If we don't make up some reason to be excited, then we would die of worry. What's better?"

Dirk shook his head. "I know. I'm usually not the one to take a responsible role." He looked at El.

She shook her head. "It's a nice change for you, but Tab is right. We are young and if we don't find a way to relax and have some fun, then we've already lost. Wouldn't you agree?"

Dirk's eyes rippled. A wave of calm washed over him. He noticed Natia's hand on his knee, smiled at her, and looked back at El. "You're right, El. I just care about all of you so much." El got up and sat beside Dirk. She put her arm around him and pulled him close.

"We are in this together."

Dirk hugged her and smiled. He released her and said in a serious tone, "You know, those showers work well." She punched him in the arm, and everyone laughed now that the serious Dirk had left, and their loose friend had returned.

"Well, I would have taken a shower already, but it seems a certain few people took them over first, Besides the water is probably cold now that Stas and Kal are done," she said, tousling his hair before returning to her spot beside Tab.

"Oh, I'm sorry, I thought you were supposed to be a magic wielder," Dirk said sarcastically, feeling his eyes ripple with flames. El just looked at him and shook her head. She grabbed Tab and headed for the showers, laughing. The whole group, other than Dirk and Natia, hadn't even realized the simple things that they now could use their magic for.

After the rest showered, they all sat by the fire and talked about their childhoods more. At least the parts that weren't shared through the bond. By the end of the night, everyone was finally getting ready for bed. Some departed to their own sleeping areas. Again, Dirk started to set up the sleeping bags together when Vira and Nira came walking up and handed him theirs. He smiled and connected the four sleeping bags together. Dirk and Natia nestled together in the center with Vira on Dirk's side and Nira on Natia's.

After everyone was settled in, Dirk said, "You know I don't think I'll be able to sleep once we get back to the school."

Natia, who had her head on his shoulder raised it up and stared at him with a questioning look.

He looked at the twins and then at her. "I'll be lonely," he said seriously.

Vira leaned on her elbow, "Well, we can always sneak into the downstairs room and throw our sleeping bags on the floor."

They all laughed and got closer. Vira kissed Dirk on the cheek. "I always wondered what it would be like to have a big brother." Nira agreed.

"Well, you don't have to wonder anymore." Dirk kissed her cheek in return and squeezed Nira's hand.

Natia looked at Dirk when he finally settled in to sleep and whispered, "I'm going to miss the showers."

His eyes rippled from the affection. "We'll have to see if we can prevent that." Then he kissed her gently on the lips. Some of the horrors the twins had gone were revealed through their shared dreams, only this time it was a little different. Every time a bad memory entered their nightmares, Dirk would save them. He didn't know how it happened; it just did. The twins were really scared of an Aarkas wizard named Asher, who was tormenting them. Dirk would materialize to vanquish him with crimson fire.

He awoke in the middle of the night drenched in sweat. Actually, all four of them were. Natia awoke at the same time as he did. "Did you feel that too?"

"I witnessed it all," she whispered.

"How?"

She put her hand on his chest. "I don't know. That's a question for Hilda and Tilda." She pulled him back down beside her and soon as she did, Vira mumbled in her sleep.

"Thanks, brother, for saving us."

Dirk pulled her closer, still feeling the effects of the fear Vira and Nira had shared with him. He swore to himself that if he ever got the chance, he would make this Asher pay for what he had done to his sisters.

Dirk stared at the stars, wondering how any of the things that had happened recently were possible. He was anxious and couldn't sleep now. Listening to the twins and Natia sleeping was starting to calm him down. Then, out of the corner of his eye, Dirk saw a glimmering light beside the guest-house. He eased Vira's arm off of him and slid out from under Natia without waking either of them. He quietly went to investigate, his knife drawn as he went around the corner of the house. His hands fell to his side at what he saw. There, at the side of the guest house, was a glimmering silhouette of a man. Dirk knew in an instant who it was. He had seen him in his dreams a lot lately.

"Father?"

The shadow nodded and smiled, stepped closer, almost touching him. "Hi son," Diron said. It was more like a whisper.

Tears fell down Dirk's cheeks. "Father, I have so…"

Diron held up his hand. Dirk knew that familiar gesture immediately. He had seen his grandfather and mother do it many times in his life.

"I don't have much time, son. I can't hold this connection long and I don't have time to explain, but I do need to tell you this so, listen and don't speak." Diron waited for Dirk to nod before continuing.

"I am so sorry I didn't finish Zolun when I had the chance. I hate that this burden has fallen upon you and your friends, but I can't change that now. The most important thing for you to remember is this: Keep all of your friends close to you. Don't let them get separated from you when the final battle begins. I made that mistake and it cost us all our lives. The battle is coming sooner than anyone expects, and you have to be ready."

Dirk wanted to scream hearing this. He had been thrown into this destiny not even a month ago, and to top things off, he was now finding out it was coming even sooner than he expected. Dirk bent over with his hands on his knees, frustrated. Diron saw the pain and turmoil in his son's face. He reached to console his son but pulled back when he realized he wouldn't be able to comfort him through touch. He was nothing but a spirit projection with no solid form. He knew Dirk and his friends were going to go through the toughest thing they would ever face in their young lives, death possibly, and the only thing he could do at this moment was to give him a hopeful look.

"Dirk.... Son, I need you to listen. We don't have much time left," Diron said. Dirk stood back up, looking at his father."

"What I tell you, keep it to yourself for now. No one can know we've spoken. I assume your mother shared with you my warning that one of your friends will betray you. I can't tell you who it is right now. That might alter events in the wrong direction. Believe me when I say that they have no choice. It will be very difficult for you to understand, especially with what they will do, but you must find a way to forgive him. He will be needed for you to defeat Zolun. You will have to forgive that person for what they have done. If you don't, everyone will die. Promise me to try."

Dirk was so confused by this information that he just nodded.

"When the first attack comes, there will be a sign. When it comes, you and your friends will eventually need to travel south to the lands of the nomads. Again, I stress that you can't tell anyone, or all will be doomed. Do you understand?"

Trying to comprehend everything he was being told, he nodded again.

"You must find Garrick. He is the leader of the nomad nation. He will get you to where you must be. He has been planning for almost two decades, so he should be ready."

Dirk couldn't stand it and, he had to ask. He fell to his knees and looked up to his father, "Father, what do you expect of me?" Diron's spirit felt his son's anguish. He grimaced, hearing the despair in his son's voice.

He kneeled beside his son. "Dirk Storm, look at me," he demanded. Dirk took a deep breath and looked the spirit of his father in the eyes. Crimson flames rippled within his father's eyes. "You are my son. Generations of the Storm blood pumps through your veins. You have access to all their successes and failures. When in doubt, use the common sense that your grandfather and mother have instilled in you since birth. I believe in you. Zona believes in you. Remember that when you start to doubt your ability."

Dirk felt he had been given a pep talk for the first time in his life by his father. He stood with determination. "I will," he responded.

His father smiled at him, evidently feeling pride in his son's determination. "One last thing I have to say. Don't make the mistake I made with your mother. Keep Natia by your side always. She is your strength and you're hers. You won't make it through the trials that are coming your way without her. I feel I'm being pulled back. I love you, son."

Diron started shimmering again and before Dirk could say anything else, he was gone. He looked around, hoping he would come back. Finally, he let his head drop.

Hearing a twig snap, he turned and raised his knife. Natia and the twins were standing in the shadows behind him. "Did you see him?" All three nodded.

"Did you hear what he said?"

It was Natia who spoke. "Yes, love. Even if we hadn't been here watching, I believe we would have sensed every word."

Vira spoke next. "We all woke up when we felt you sneaking away. We sensed the unease in you and followed. We were worried."

Dirk nodded, "It's okay Vira. I understand."

"For some reason, we four seemed to be more bonded than the others, Dirk. I don't know why. But I know there is a reason." Nira said. "I mean, there is a strong connection between us, and I don't mean the way you and Natia are connected. It's a kindred love Vira and I feel for you and Natia." Dirk stared at Nira. What she had said really made since. He was actually feeling the same way about them.

"Dirk, I'm sorry. We didn't mean to intrude on that moment with your father. Please forgive us for that. But know this, it was out of concern and love that we followed," Vira said.

"I know, sister. I feel the same way you do. Remember, we are family and I think you know how important that is to me by now."

Both twins squeezed his hand, acknowledging they understood and that they felt the same way. "And I as well," Natia agreed.

"I don't understand this any more than any of you and I have been trained my whole life." There was a moment of thought between the four.

"Dirk, I must confess one thing that Nira and I have kept from you." Dirk looked through the darkness at Vira. Her eyes, rippling with flames, reflected her tears.

He walked up and hugged her. "I know, sister." Nira stepped into the hug. "Remember, I sense everything in the bond. I know you know about Tab. You have to keep that to yourselves for now. No other bonded can know until the time is right."

They agreed and Natia joined the hug. "Let's get some sleep. We can discuss all of this later."

They quietly headed back to the pit. Before they got to the sleeping bags, Nira said, "Thanks for saving us from the demons brother." Dirk was taken back by what she said.

"I thought it was a dream."

"It was, but you still saved us," Vira said. Dirk was lost in thought as the four all got back into their sleeping bags *I wonder what else is possible with this bond.*

There is no telling, love. Good night. Natia thought.

Yeah, no telling. We love you, Vira and Nira thought. They all snickered and were finally able to get a good night's sleep without any night terrors.

Consequences

The next day, everyone was awakened early by Kira, who had made them one last big breakfast before they went back to school. After they finished eating and getting packed up, Kira hugged all of the visitors before they left. Vira and Nira had to be pried away by Dirk, who promised they could come back on the next free weekend. Dirk and Tab took a little longer saying goodbye.

"I love you, Mom. Remember what we discussed. Be careful," Dirk stressed.

She assured him she would. Dirk said goodbye to Claire, Bart and his wife and thanked them for all that they had done. Natia received an actual hug from Claire. The little girl seemed taken with Natia.

"Be good and do as General Durk has instructed you and protect the farm."

"I swear I will," Claire said smiling.

The group then headed back to Silver City. Dirk and Tab walked behind Natia, El, and the twins. "I wonder what people will say when they see this contingent traveling back into town together?" Tab said as they were walking slowly into town.

"Yeah, I mean twenty of us. Elves, dwarves and humans, all lead by Princess Anastasia and her handsome man, Kal," El said.

"Hey," Tab replied, squinting his eyes, and sticking his lower lip out.

She smiled, "Well, maybe he's the third handsomest man in the group." Tab puffed his chest out. El slapped him on the shoulder. "Don't get cocky, I mean, there is Dirk and my brother." Tab acted hurt and hung his head. Everyone in the group laughed.

El let it go on for a little while longer, then lifted his head and kissed him on the lips. Dirk, caught off guard by El's reaction, just stared at her. Tab, smiling, said just loud enough for Dirk and Natia to hear, "You're not the only one to have confessed your feelings this weekend."

Dirk smiled at his two friends. "It's about damned time."

Jonesy, who was walking in front of the group, looked back over his shoulder. "Thank the gods. I don't have to listen to the two of them anymore, asking me what the other one thinks. It's a god's damn blessing." He smiled and turned back. "And now if I can just convince Gil that Stas isn't in love with him, my life would be better."

Dirk and the original Pack laughed. "What was that Jonesy?" Kal asked, smiling at Anastasia who had heard every word.

Jonesy realized what he had said a little too loudly and tried to backpedal. "Nothing really, Kal, just talking about Gil."

Kal smirked. "Okay, Jonesy,"

Anastasia started giving Kal an earful for asking that question. They knew how Gil felt about Anastasia.

"I wonder why he didn't come," El said.

"His father," Dirk replied with disdain.

"Yeah, you're probably right." El had a sad look in her eye.

"I'm just gonna say it out loud," Tab said. "His father has to be related to Zolun. I mean he is a bastard and the beatings he gives Gil. I swear, one day, I will kill him." There was an unspoken agreement between Tab, El, Jonesy, and Dirk on that.

"I'm with you friend. After all of this Chosen mess is over I'll be right by your side brother," Dirk said.

I'll be there too, my brothers.

Dirk looked at Tab and Tab looked back at Dirk.

"Linc," they both said in unison. Natia and El smiled at each other. Everyone else, hadn't heard Linc through the bond.

"Well, once Gil is bonded, he'll be more protected," Dirk said.

"Yeah, we might not get a chance to kill him then. Gil will probably do it himself," Tab said jokingly. The four who had heard Linc laughed. Dirk explained to the rest of the group what had just happened with Linc.

The group led by Princess Anastasia stopped at Mr. Burk's bakery for a treat before heading back to the school. Rumors about the group walking through the city started to make its way through the market by the time they got within a few hundred feet of the school, everyone in the market seemed to be watching and waiting for them to walk by.

After the group all said their goodbyes, they headed their separate ways. Dirk, Natia, Kal and Anastasia were the last to enter. Anastasia hugged them both. After Kal and Dirk shook hands, Natia hugged Kal. A few passerby students eyed them skeptically but didn't stop walking.

"You two be careful. Remember the training out there. When the time comes, we will need you at our sides," Dirk said.

"I assure you we'll be ready. Make sure you're ready. Don't forget we can communicate if something happens, and you need us." Kal twisted his bracelet.

Dirk nodded. "And the same for you."

Kal and Anastasia headed to the third-year dorms. Natia and Dirk turned and headed to their dorms, holding hands, oblivious to the stares of everyone they passed by. The first person they saw was Sirien. He saw them holding hands and a look of hatred came across his face. He turned and walked away.

"See you soon," Dirk said as Natia entered the girl's dorm. Dirk knew he would be confronted by the elves the first chance Sirien got. Dirk made it to his room without an encounter. Volar and Phil had already headed to the commons room. Dirk put his pack away and headed out to sit with them. That's when Sirien, Alian, and Aaric confronted him. Sirien stood in front with the other two.

"You, human scum, what did you do to her?" Sirien yelled looking down at Dirk.

"Sirien, you need to back off. I didn't do anything to Natia."

"I know you did. She wouldn't like you if you were the last person alive." Sirien poked Dirk in the chest for emphasis.

Wait. He heard Natia's warning in his head, but it was too late. That poke had sent several people into action all at once. Volar bounded over a chair. Tab came running out of his room, knocking Brock and Larkin, who had walked out of their room to see what the commotion was about, on their collective asses. Tab reached the scene as Volar was grabbing Aaric by the elbow. Dirk had grabbed Sirien's wrist and twisted it at an angle. Sirien fell to his knees.

Tab stepped between Alian and Dirk and put his hands up, "Stay calm Alian."

"I told you I didn't do anything to her, Sirien. You need to talk to her. I don't want to hurt you," Dirk said, flames starting to warm his eyes.

Sirien just stared at him with more hatred than Dirk had ever seen. Just as Sirien was drawing his knife, Natia came bursting through the door to the boy's dorm and screamed at the two. "Stop this instant!"

Sirien, hearing Natia's voice, released his knife. Dirk released his wrist and stepped back. "I tried!" Dirk held his hands up.

"I know." She motioned for the three elves to follow her. They obeyed their princess and followed her out of the room.

"Well I guess that could have gone better," Tab said. Brock punched him in the side of the face. Tab's vision blurred as he went down. The sucker punch had caught Dirk and the rest of the boys off guard. Larkin went to swing at Dirk, but Volar tackled him, putting him in a head lock. "If you move, I'll have no problem breaking your neck. Well, maybe just a fracture." Larkin didn't move.

Dirk faced Brock. His inner hatred for Brock burned inside of him. "That was cheap even for you, Brock."

"That orphan deserved it. He ran over me and didn't even apologize or say excuse me. I'm sick of holding back. I will not be blackmailed by that half-ass dwarf anymore!" Brock balled his fist, ready to punch Dirk.

"You know what, you goat's ass? I'm sick of you Brock!" Dirk stood calmly.

"What? You half…" was all Brock had the time to get out. Dirk moved so fast Brock didn't even see the punch that landed on the left side of his jaw. Brock's head spun. He was spitting blood and teeth as he fell to the floor unconscious.

"DIRK STORM, WHAT IN THE NAME OF ZONA?" Hilda screamed, running to check on Brock. Volar released Larkin, who scampered away while Volar helped Dirk pick Tab up off the floor. He was starting to come around. The rest of the room was staring at Dirk in shock. The three elves had returned and were standing in the entrance of the door, observing what had just happened. Hilda sent for Wizard Stephano, the wizard in charge of the healing arts. Brock was coming around and sitting up, blood all over him and around where he had fallen. He was unaware of what had just happened.

"Dirk, you three go and sit down and wait on me until I'm done cleaning up your mess," Hilda said furiously. "The rest of you get to your classes. Jacko, tell Wizard Hermosa Dirk and Brock will not be there until after lunch. Gil, tell Wizard Quentin the same for Volar. I'll tell Wizard Stephano about Tab. Now the rest of you go!"

The rest of the boys headed out. Gil gave Dirk a high five as he walked by. Luckily, Hilda didn't see it. Wizard Stephano was there in a few minutes and quickly healed Brock. He put his knocked-out teeth back in and sent him to the infirmary to be looked over by one of the regular healers. Brock gave Dirk and Tab a look that said, *This isn't finished yet.* They just smiled and waved. Hilda's stare made them lower their arms.

Are you ok? Three voices asked simultaneously. He felt Natia, Vira, and Nira's distress. He eased their minds by making sure they knew he was okay.

"Now tell me what in the hells happened," Hilda said in a calmer voice.

"I don't know. I was keeping the elves from jumping on Dirk and the next thing I know, Dirk and Volar are helping me up off the floor," Tab said.

"Aye. That's what we were doing, keeping Alian and Aaric from jumping on Dirk with Sirien. Then Brock came out of nowhere and blindsided Tab knocking him out," Volar explained.

"That's what happened. Then Brock smashed Tab's face without warning. Then he started to jump on me, so I defended myself," Dirk said.

Hilda raised an eyebrow at Dirks brief explanation. "Well it sounds justified, except, Dirk, you have to control your temper. You know you could have killed him just as easily," Hilda said with a little fear in her eyes.

The world would be a better place... Tab started to think.

Let it go! Dirk stared at Tab.

"You do understand that don't you?" Hilda asked Dirk.

"I do, but you don't know the shit we have had to put up with from him through the years and when he suckered punched Tab, all I could see was red," Dirk said, realizing what Hilda had said was true. He put his head in his hands and leaned on his knees. Hilda came over and patted Dirk's shoulder.

"Son, that trivial bullshit means nothing to what you and your friends will face in the future. You have to learn to let things go. Now what Brock did was unforgivable, and he will be dealt with. You, especially now, have to keep that temper under control. Remember what's at stake. You two have to make sure he does," Hilda said to Volar and Tab.

"Okay," They said in unison.

"I'm sorry Hilda," Dirk said, standing up.

She squeezed his shoulder and gave him a motherly, understanding smile. "Now go get something to clean up the mess you made spilling Brock's blood on my floors." The three did as she said and by the time they finished, the lunch bell was ringing.

The lunchroom was buzzing when Dirk and his two compatriots in the fight walked in. All the first-years were staring at them, even some of the second-years were pointing and talking. The third-years weren't there at all. Natia made a beeline for Dirk when she sensed him walking in. Tab and Volar knew it was time to get their food. "See you later."

Dirk saw fury in her eyes. "It's not what you think," Dirk said before she could say anything.

She glared at him, then as he was moving up the line. "You have to be careful. These childish vendettas have to cease. There's too much at stake!" She quietly berated him.

"Look I've already had this lecture from Hilda. I don't need to hear it again," Dirk said, a little heated. Natia didn't say anything else. She just turned and went back to sit at the table with the elves.

Great, now I have two Els in my life, Dirk thought sarcastically, watching Natia walk away. El, who had been talking with Tab and Volar, evidently had sensed his remark and stopped talking, and looked at him, raising an eyebrow. Dirk just smirked and turned away. He got mutton stew from Ms. Heloise, thanked her, and then went to sit with his friends at their normal table. He got evil looks from the twins as he sat down. Phil and Dusty were telling them what happened. Dirk just smiled and started eating.

Dirk, you have to be more careful, Nira thought. He looked at her and nodded.

I know. It just happened so fast. Strike that earlier thought, Dirk thought to himself. *Now I have* four *Els in my life.*

El elbowed him without looking away from the conversation she was having with Tab. Dirk rubbed his ribs. Vira looked at him, totally ignoring Phil, probably for the first time ever. She gave him an understanding smile, placed her hand on top of Dirk's. He nodded to her, squeezing her hand back. *Don't let him off that easy, Vira.*

Vira looked over her shoulder at Natia, who still looked angry. *I'm not. It's just it was Tab who was ambushed, and if it weren't for Sirien being such a dick, it would have never happened,* Vira thought back.

I agree about Sirien and have dealt with him. Dirk, you have great powers now and you know, or at least you do now, what can happen when you lose control. Natia replied in their thoughts. Dirk dropped his head and quit eating.

A few minutes went by and then he felt a hand on his shoulder. He knew that touch. His insides melted whenever she touched him, and now with how close they had become, it was worse.

El scooted over to let Natia sit beside Dirk. The whole table had stopped talking. He looked into her eyes. She leaned her head forward and he did as well until their foreheads were touching. The table started talking again, but Dirk and Natia seemed to be having a private moment.

Everyone at the table knew of the bond, except Gil and Jacko. Gil just shrugged. He had already been informed about Dirk and Natia getting together so he assumed it was just an elven thing and continued to talk with Volar.

"I love you. I worry now that your strength is uncontrollable." Dirk raised his head back.

"I do too." Natia caressed his face.

"We'll talk with Tilda and Hilda tonight." Dirk agreed. She hooked her arm through his and started talking with Vira and Nira.

Dirk finished eating and then asked Jacko what he'd missed in class.

"Basically nothing. She just did a recap of the first few weeks. Hermosa told us that she has been assigned a new special project to her by Wizard Nabas. She'll be teaching several students four days a week in a different class. Helena will be working with the rest who aren't in the new class."

Jacko said he was okay with that. He seemed to have a thing for Helena the group had discovered. Of course, everyone at the table, except Gil and Jacko knew what the special class was.

After lunch, Dirk went to class and it was normal, other than Brock and his ghoul friend not being there. This didn't bother Dirk in the least. Hermosa told the class that everyone in the new class would start the next day. The classes would be on Tuesday, Wednesday, Thursday, and Friday and the other students on those days would be working on their regular training. She dismissed the class but before Dirk could leave, she said, "Natia and Dirk I need you two to stay behind for a moment." They stayed seated while the rest of the class left. Sirien gave Dirk a mistrusting look as he walked out. Hermosa went to her desk and leaned against it and looked at Dirk. "I assume you have learned a lesson on self-control?"

Dirk nodded.

"Good, now starting tomorrow, we will meet with you two and the other seven here at ten a.m. After you have fulfilled your responsibilities to your daily exercise with Sergeant Giles. We will start with a short summary of where each of you are at in progression with your magic, then we will discuss your plan and what you have come up with since you last met with Hilda and Tilda. They will continue to work with you on Monday, Wednesday, and Friday as before. That way, they can still advise on your training. Now, I know there are others that know about your secret, but the training has to stay with the core bonded, agreed?"

They both agreed.

"When the time is right you can decide when to share with the rest of them." She then dismissed them.

"We have to deal with Sirien today. I'm not gonna keep looking over my shoulder, waiting for him to attack me," Dirk said as they were walking to the dorms.

"I agree. Let's do it after dinner. I'll get El and all of the elves to come and you bring Volar and Tab. The twins, I'm sure, have already sensed your plan."

Obviously, they both heard them respond.

"We can meet on the roof," Natia said.

"All right, I'll bring Gil on board as well." Dirk stopped and looked Natia in the eyes. His mind made up he told her, "Let's just bring the rest of the class up to speed on what is going on, except Brock, Skylar, and their friends."

Natia looked at him, raising her eyebrow, then smiled and said, "Okay."

He kissed her cheek, and they went upstairs. The room was buzzing when Dirk walked in. "What's the deal?" he asked Gil about the excitement in the room when he sat down beside him on the couch.

"Brock got kicked out of school."

Dirk just stared at him. "Shut the hells up."

Gil just nodded and laughed. Dirk felt a tremendous weight lifted off his shoulders the moment he realized Gil wasn't lying.

Tab came over "Did you hear?"

"I did."

Tab just laughed.

"Yeah, it seems his only shot at redemption is to join the military and if he conducts himself honorably, he can get readmitted next year," Gil explained.

"Stew and Larkin left with him," Tab said. "Poor Brock." Dirk just smiled. Red Granger and Daven Burke were sitting with Volar, listening to the story of the three departed. They laughed and smiled at Dirk. Red came over and sat with Dirk and the rest of his group.

"It's a shame about Brock," Red said, genuinely sad. Dirk just looked at him. "I really wanted him to be my practice partner the next time we had sword practice." Red smirked. Dirk and Tab laughed. Dirk knew how hard Red could hit with a sword. "I'll see you later." Red got up and joined Daven at a table by their room.

Conversation at dinner throughout the entire hall seemed to be about the incident in the first-year's boy's dorm. Skylar was shooting daggers with her eyes at Dirk and Tab the whole time. Dirk had to stop Natia and El from going over to where Skylar and her friends sat. Dirk told them, "Her time will come." Dinner went on as normal after a few moments. Dirk had to keep the girls in check. He was starting to feel anxious.

After dinner, as planned, Dirk, Tab, Volar, Phil, and Dusty met Natia, El, the twins, and all of the elves on the roof. Sirien just stared at Dirk when he walked out onto the roof.

"Well, I'm here, princess. What do you want to explain?" Sirien asked. The elves, who didn't know why they were there, had the same question.

"Wait Natia," Dirk said as Natia was fixing to take Sirien to task about his attitude. "There are a few more people still coming to join us. Sirien, if you will be patient, I will explain."

Sirien glared at Dirk, but Dirk just ignored him.

A few minutes later Gil, Jacko, Red, and Daven came through the door. Gil looked around at almost the whole first-year class on the roof. He gave Dirk a questioning look. "Gil, just come over and listen. If you would have been able to come to the farm this weekend, you would have already known so please don't interrupt and I'll explain everything."

"Ok," He went over and stood by Tab. Red and the others went to stand with Volar. Dirk looked at Vira and she nodded. She raised her hand at the door and a red shield formed over it to keep them from being interrupted as they had planned on the way up the stairs.

Dirk walked to the center of the group and asked them all if he could have their attention. The all agreed and gathered around him. "Sit please, this may take a few minutes to explain." They did, even Sirien did after being prompted to by Natia.

"Sirien," Dirk began in a loud and commanding voice, looking at him. "I want you to know that I am sorry if I hurt you today." Sirien just scoffed. "Let me finish and you will understand." Sirien caught a glare from Natia, and he nodded. "First, Sirien, let me ask you a question. What do you know of the war that has been waged over the centuries against Zolun?"

Sirien laughed. "Everybody knows this."

Dirk smiled. "Go ahead and educate us on your knowledge then." Dirk got a glare from Natia. He ignored the look.

Sirien explained the basic history that there had been a long feud between him and his parents over the rule of the world.

"That's the history that is taught to all of the races, which is right but incomplete," Dirk said, making sure he had everyone's attention.

Vira and Nira, who were standing beside him, put their hands on his shoulders for strength. They felt his apprehension about sharing his pain again. Dirk thanked them mentally and they smiled.

"The story that isn't told is that five hundred and twelve years ago, Zona decided he couldn't protect the races by himself anymore. See, Zolun had started creating monsters to attack on his behalf. Zolun, in the agreement with his parents, was limited to only attacking every twenty years." Dirk paused for a minute.

"Wait a minute, Dirk. How do you know this?" Red asked.

"Red, give me fifteen minutes and all will be clear."

"Ok, Dirk, you got it. Go ahead."

"So, Zona and Marluna decided to choose a so-called guardian for the races. One that would be around in his and Marluna's absence to protect against these creatures Zolun had created. Zona searched and searched for one that was pure of heart and selfless. Finally, after years of searching, he had almost given up until one day, he witnessed an act of selflessness and bravery. An act so brave that it made him, and his wife decide to choose this man as the protector of Marona. Zona approached the man and told him what he wanted of him. The man didn't even have to think about it. He just agreed. Zona brought the leaders of the humans, elves, and dwarves together and explained to them what he had in mind by making the Chosen. They all pledged their support in any way they could. The only thing Zona did was make them promise to keep the information about the Chosen limited only to their leaders and they all agreed.

"Things went the way Zona wanted it to for a while, but The Chosen, always eventually fell short of succeeding. So Marluna came up with an idea to choose a second line of defense, a protector for the Chosen to help in the battles. The two together became almost invincible against the evil Zolun was producing. It never failed. When Zolun was allowed to enter the battles, he always defeated the Chosen and protector but still fell just short of overall victory. You see, when a Chosen or a protector died, their responsibility was passed along to their first born or their bloodline."

Dirk stopped and looked at the ones gathered around. Their eyes told him he was having the effect he had wanted. He took a deep breath and continued.

"This has repeated itself for the last five hundred years. One last thing that Zona did was to create a companion for the Chosen and protector to help keep an eye on the evil all over the world."

Sirien laughed. "If this has been going on for so long, why we haven't ever heard about it?"

It was Natia who answered the question. "Because Sirien, only the trusted few knew about it. Listen to what Dirk is saying and you will see it's true."

Sirien nodded for Dirk to continue.

"As I was saying, they created a companion." Dirk looked around to make sure everyone was still paying attention after Sirien's interruption.

"The phoenix," Gil blurted out. The group looked at Gil. "I've read stories about the phoenix and how they just appeared, and no one knows how or why."

"Not they, Gil, *she*. Her name was Arial. She has been around for the last four hundred and some odd years. At least, until the day she died. Her last act was to pass along her remaining power to her unhatched egg." The group that had come up with Gil just looked shocked. "She fought beside the Chosen and protector until the day she died, or should I say, was murdered. There is still a phoenix left to carry on her responsibilities. Ariel's offspring's name is Aarya. She has stepped up to fulfill her mother's role."

Dirk paused. Still feeling the pain her death had caused, Natia urged him on.

"Like I said this has been going on for a long time. The phoenix bonded with each and every Chosen and protector. That connected them in thought and in ways no one ever thought possible. They shared feelings not just thoughts. Love, pain, happiness, and sorrow, and with the bond came special abilities and powers along with the responsibility that was passed down to each new generation. I know everyone hear noticed the third-years leaving the school today?"

The group nodded.

"The reason they left is because the war is starting up again. The raids and attacks are getting so bad that Prince Thelon had to call for reinforcements. This is just the beginning of far more sinister things to come. The third-years left to take over patrols in the areas where there were no conflicts going on so that those soldiers could join the prince." Dirk again looked around and saw concern in the entire group. "So, our generation, us gathered here will be called into this conflict sooner or later. I, for one, having lost family to one of these battles, wants this to end. We need to be the generation that ends the madness of Zolun forever. I will not sit idly by and let my future children have to deal with this," Dirk said, his voice becoming stronger with each word.

"I put it to you, each and every one of you, all of you gathered here on the roof tonight. Will you stand together with me? Will you be the spear that shatters that evil?" Dirk stepped into the center of the group.

"You make it sound like you're the one who's gonna lead us, Dirk," Sirien said sarcastically. Dirk lowered his head.

In the distance, a war cry reverberated through the air, causing the hair on everyone's arms and necks to stand. The group all looked around to try and find the source of the sound. Dirk looked directly at the ones in the group who didn't know his secret. He could tell they were starting to figure it out. "Not by choice, Sirien, but by destiny. You see that family that was Chosen those many years ago…" Dirk paused for effect. "Was the Storm Family and I have no choice." He raised his head, his eyes rippling in flames as Aarya swooped down and landed on his shoulder.

There were gasps from the ones who hadn't seen her. Everyone stood up to get a better view of the majestic bird. Natia stepped up beside Dirk, her eyes rippling flames as well and she grabbed his hand. "And my family was the bloodline that was chosen to be the protectors." Her eyes rippled with intense flames as she focused on the elves. "As Dirk has asked, will you stand with us when the time comes?" Natia stared directly at Sirien. All of the elves, including Sirien, fell back down to a knee.

Gil's mouth was hanging open.

"Gil, you might want to close that," Tab said, smiling at Gil and pointing to his mouth. Gil smiled.

Dirk looked around at the gathered group. "Can I count on you, when the time comes, to be my brothers and sisters in arms against this evil?"

Red was the first. "You have my sword and shield."

Dirk nodded as the rest of the humans did the same as Red.

Gil just said, "I knew something was different about you." He patted Dirk on the back. "The Pack forever."

Dirk hugged his childhood friend and whispered, "My friend, as soon as you're ready, I would love for you to be our thirteenth bonded. I will explain to you later what that means. What do you say?"

Gil looked at Dirk and then at Aarya. "Do you even need to ask, brother?"

Dirk nodded. "As soon as we can, I'll gather the other bonded and we will do just that." Dirk squeezed Gil's shoulder. "There are some things only for the bonded to know." Gil nodded in agreement.

Dirk then looked to the remaining elves. "Well, Sirien?"

Sirien got up, followed by the rest of the elves. When he got to Dirk, he bowed, crossing one arm across his chest, the elven salute of honor and respect. "I am ashamed of my actions. I only hope you will forgive my jealousy."

Dirk put a hand on Sirien's shoulder, forcing him to face him. "You need to forgive me. I am the one who is ashamed of how I acted today."

Sirien smiled. "No need. I will be with you and the princess until the end."

"Until the end," the elves all said in unison.

Dirk swelled with pride as he looked around at the gathered group. He raised his head and got everyone's attention. "You all don't know how proud it makes me that we have only known each other a short time but have already become friends, brothers and sisters even. Hells, we have become family." He looked at the bonded and they knew what he was going to say.

"Family is what we are! Family is what we will always be!" the bonded chanted, with the others soon joining in. Tears rolled down Dirk's face because of the love he was feeling. The fear for their safety started to get to him. Natia squeezed his hand, washing away the fear. He smiled a thank you to her.

"I love you," she said for everyone to hear.

"I love you too." He then kissed her.

Dirk turned to the gathered group and thanked them all and explained what they had planned. He left out the part about Anastasia and Kal. There were a few things the original bonded only needed to know. That was why he left out the part about the group of bonded. The rest would find out when the time was right. Now he just wanted to get everyone here on the same training routines. Natia stepped up and told everyone that this information was for this group only. No one else could know what Dirk was since it might endanger him sooner than necessary, especially around any of Brock's friends still left at the school like Skylar. They all swore they would protect his secret.

After a lot of individual questions and answers, Aarya sensed it was time to leave and took off. "Gil, I guess we can do it during the next weekend off if you have time," Dirk stated as the group headed to the stairwell.

Gil was disappointed he didn't get to bond with the rest of his friends when Dirk explained what it was. He was eager now to know more though. "When did it happen? How did you find out? What was it like?" Dirk filled him in on everything, except Tab. He explained how Arial had died and Aarya was born. "Gods, Father would shit his pants."

"You know you can't tell him."

Gil looked hurt. "I wouldn't tell that bastard anything. You know that!" Dirk knew Gil wouldn't say anything, but he just got a weird sensation from Gil when he was asking for more details. He brushed it away. It had been a trying day.

"I know, brother. Just had to say it. I mean, this is a damn big secret, and we have had to keep it quiet for a while now. You will understand as soon as your bonded."

Gil put a hand on Dirk's chest. "Linc?"

Dirk nodded. "He's known since the beginning."

Gil had a pained look. Dirk patted him on the back. He told Gil about the incident with Ram's thugs and how Linc wouldn't let it go until they confessed what was up.

Gil agreed. "I bet El was on you too. I mean the way she mother-hens us if she thinks one of us has pulled a nail." They both laughed at that.

"She badgered me until I explained why I was acting different."

"I remember a few weeks back when she was all standoffish with you." Dirk nodded.

As they all were being hurried to bed by Hilda. Gil stopped and grabbed Dirk in a hug. Dirk, used to the hugs by now hugged him back. "Remember, brother, I am here for you always. Remember that, whatever happens in this life." Dirk squeezed his friend and he flinched.

Dirk pushed him back a little. "Your father?"

Gil knew what Dirk was referring to." "Leave it alone, Dirk. It won't change who he is." Gil smiled and rushed off.

Something has to be done about him. Natia thought.

You're right. But we have bigger fish to fry right now. Dirk thought.

See you after everyone goes to bed.

I almost forgot about that. See you then, Dirk headed to his bed to wait on the training the nine would get from Hilda and Tilda in the basement.

Mildred's Bargain

Linc's night had been a very pleasant surprise. He found out Mildred was actually a lot like him. She liked to drink and have fun, and actually didn't mind the occasional bar room brawl either. After they had said good night, he couldn't wait to see how she handled herself in combat.

The disturbing thoughts he had shared with Dirk and the bonded about Gil's father made him angry. It made him a little too aggressive with Mildred when he first started sparring. She had a look of determination on her face after he'd knocked her weapon out of her hand a third time.

"I'm sorry. I'm just agitated today, and I am not doing a good job controlling myself." He helped her up after knocking her down.

She brushed herself off, picked up the wooden staff, and smiled. "That's ok. I was taking it easy on you until I was sure you could handle yourself." She stood ready for another round. Linc thought it was a lot of bravado until she advanced twice as fast as she had the first three rounds. When she reached him and started to swing, Linc went to block, but before he knew it, she had reversed her momentum. She clipped his legs out from underneath him, knocking him on his backside.

Walking around, she held out her hand. Linc just brushed it away, annoyed that she had been playing him. He looked away, keeping the flames in his eyes hidden from her and then he got up without a word.

"So, it's gonna be like that," she taunted with a smile.

He motioned her on. That was the last time either of them touched the ground again until they practically collapsed, drenched in sweat, and laughing together. They both had moved at speeds a normal person probably couldn't follow. Blocks and swings were the routine. Jump and parry. They were evenly matched in skill and they both put in every ounce of energy they had.

"I have never had a match like that before," she said, the back of her head resting on his chest.

Linc was still breathing heavily, "You haven't met my brother, Dirk Storm. We're not blood brothers but might as well be since we grew up together and are so close. Tab, our other brother, and I trained with him growing up. Dirk's grandfather, the general, worked our asses off in the training field in his back-yard. Dirk was always just a little faster than us though," Linc said, running his fingers through her wet black hair.

She raised her head up to look at him. He told her how they all became friends first and then basically family. She stared into Linc's eyes, listening to him tell his story in detail. Linc was thankful the workout had calmed the flames in his eyes, or she would have clearly seen them, being this close. Talking about Dirk and Tab had helped calm his nerves as well. She propped up on an elbow, still locked on Linc's eyes.

"You know you talked about Dirk Storm last night. Not much about Tab, though. There is something about that name Storm that seems familiar. Especially when you say his grandfather is a general."

Linc pushed a lock of hair behind her ear. "Well Dirk's father was in the military just like his father, the general. You might have heard of a little battle at Der-Tod?"

She thought for a moment. "No, I don't think that's it. It'll come to me." She was still locked on his eyes, catching Linc off guard. She leaned in and kissed him. Even though it shocked him, he put his hand behind her head and pulled her closer, kissing her passionately. She leaned back, satisfied with the softness of his kiss. "Slow down, tiger. Mom is home and I really don't want to start something we can't take at least an hour or two to explore." She kissed his shocked face again, then pushed herself up and helped him up off the ground. She pulled him towards the house. "Besides, I've got to work at The Broken Spear this afternoon. Maybe we can play later." She shoved him through the gate goodbye.

He smiled at her and before she could close the gate, he said, "Maybe." Then he laughed after she kicked at him. "Yeah, we'll see if you have time. See you tonight," Linc said as she closed the gate and headed into the house. He whistled all the way back to the inn.

In the shadows, the same two figures were watching the girl and the boy again. "I think he is the one," the female said to the male.

"You may be right, my love. He has the aura about him. Did you notice his eyes?" the male asked.

"I did. The phoenix bond is there."

The male agreed. "I felt the connection, but something is different about it than I remember."

The female shrugged. "It has been years, dear, since you came into contact with another bonded," she said to the love of her life.

"That's true but still it feels different." They kissed briefly, not wanting to bring any attention to themselves.

"Remember our plan. Do your part and I will do mine. When the battle comes, I know we'll be free this time," she said as they headed towards the trail that lead away from the city. As soon as they entered the woods, and no one was around, they vanished as fast as they had appeared hours earlier.

Linc was happy when he arrived at The Broken Spear. Jerle and River were eating lunch. He walked over and took a seat beside them.

"How did your practice go this morning?" River asked.

"Very surprising."

"Really?" Jerle asked.

"She definitely is in the Dirk Storm-area of expertise."

"No way she's that good," River said. River had grown up with Linc and Dirk. Everyone their age knew how good Dirk was. Linc just nodded and smiled.

"Put me on my ass," Linc said, causing River to laugh. Linc continued to tell them about the workout while he was waiting on the stew he ordered from Sally as she came by.

"Wow, she must be good if she put you on your ass, cap'n" Jerle said, finishing his stew.

"I think we might try to make a trip upriver before we head back." Linc was seeing if he had their attention. Linc put his boot up where the boys could see it. "Touch this boot and tell me what you think, River."

River did, looking at the seams and the durability.

"They look new but there's no way. They're too broken in," Jerle said, checking them out himself.

Smack! The sound rippled through the room. Sally put Linc's soup and bread down. "You put your foot down, Linc. Don't you dare put that on my table," Sally said after slapping Linc on the shoulder.

"Sorry, Mrs. Sally, I was just showing them my new boots. I was thinking about heading upriver to see if I can get a trade agreement for some."

Sally looked at the boots. "That's them boots that man from Pineral sold to Madame Swon, isn't it?" Linc nodded. "We wanted to buy Tank and Harry a pair, but he didn't have their size."

"Yes ma'am, I bought the last pair from Mildred yesterday. I think I'll travel to Pineral while repairs are being made on my ship and see if I can get an agreement with him."

"You know, that's a week's travel on the water," Sally said.

Linc thought about what she was saying. "I thought it was closer than that."

She smiled. "Sorry dear, but it's a little longer trip than you think."

"Thank you, Mrs. Sally, for the information, and again, I am sorry for putting my boot on your table," Linc said as Sally smiled and walked off. "Guys, after you eat, go try to pull Kaz and Corky away from One Eyed-Jack's so they can meet with us this afternoon. I'm going to see Lord Saint and see about renting one of his ships. If he agrees, we can prepare for a trip to Pineral and see if we can meet this Mr. Wark, who makes these boots,"

River and Jerle left while Linc finished his soup. He then asked Tank to set him up with a bath. While Hank was getting his bath ready for him Mildred came into the inn to get ready for her afternoon shift. She winked at him and walked up to the bar to talk with Harry and Sally. Linc asked her to come over when she got a chance.

After a few minutes, she came over and he told her his plan.

"I want to go,"

Linc just looked at her as she sat down.

"I think since we are partners in this venture it wouldn't hurt to have me along. Especially since I know him," Mildred stated. Linc thought about what she said.

"Have you ever been on a ship?"

"I have. I spent one summer on one of Lord Saint's ships. We only did local trading, several days out at a time."

"Everyone on my ship works. You know, I can't take it easy on you since you have the hots for me," Linc said ducking when Mildred slapped at him. "Just kidding," he said, receiving a glare and then a smile from her. "Sure, but can you get off from work?"

Mildred looked at the bar and then turned back to Linc. "Yes, I believe I can. It's the slow time of the month and Mom has been telling me to get out more. So, I'll tell Harry tonight, then I'll tell Mom in the morning. Hopefully, Lord Philias will let us use the *Smooth Trader*. That's his fastest ship, and I know it's just been refitted." Mildred was getting excited.

"Maybe you ought to come with me to see Lord Saint. It might make him more agreeable since he's known you longer."

Mildred nodded and went to check to see if she could take off for the afternoon since it was slow. Linc watched as she convinced Harry to let her off for a few hours but told him she would be back for the dinner rush. Harry told her it was okay.

Linc passed by Mildred on the way upstairs. He told her he wanted to take a quick bath and then he would meet her downstairs. She smiled a cynical smile. He headed up to take his bath and get changed.

Linc had just gotten into the steaming water when the door opened.

"Bath's taken. I'll be done in a few minutes," he said to whoever had opened the door and walked in.

"I know I just wanted to make sure you didn't need a healer after that beating I gave you earlier," Mildred said, walking up and kneeling on the floor beside the tub. Linc didn't flinch. The water was warm and steamy, but Mildred could still see the drain plug through the water. Mildred looked down at him and a smirk settled on her face.

"Well, what do you think? Do I need a healer?"

Mildred acted like she was looking him over. She made him lean forward. Then she pushed his shoulder-length hair back and checked behind his ears. "Well, from what I see, it looks ok to me, I guess."

Linc stood up to Mildred's surprise. He turned so she could get a good look. He stopped spinning around, leaving his ass in her face.

"Well…" Mildred smacked his butt hard.

"You're fine." Linc sat back down, and Mildred moved to the back of the tub. "Lean forward and give me the soap." Taking the soap she washed his back.

"Did you like what you saw?" Linc asked after she was through rinsing his back. Mildred got up and held out a towel for Linc. When he got out of the tub, she wrapped it around him.

"I guess you will do in a pinch," she said, smiling. Then she left the room while Linc finished drying off and getting dressed. Mildred was waiting outside the door when he came out. He looked her in the eyes.

"Tease," he said, laughing.

"Some things are worth the wait." She turned and headed downstairs with Linc following. They left the inn and headed to Lord Saint's office.

As they were walking to Lord Saints business, Linc realized something. "Isn't Lord Saint out of town?"

Mildred had a mischievous look on her face. "I lied about that. I just wanted to spar with you alone today."

Linc nodded. "You didn't have to lie to me."

"I know that. It was him I was worried about. I didn't want to hurt his feelings." Mildred liked that Linc was easy going. He just took things in stride. She punched him in the arm. He just brushed it away.

"You know you can spend any amount of time with me you want," Linc told her.

"Oh, I am so lucky," Mildred scoffed.

Linc just rolled with it. "So, what do we say first. Oh, I lied to you today, so I could spar with Linc. Or can I just borrow your most prized boat for two weeks?" Linc said seriously.

She smiled "Let me handle it."

Linc just stared straight ahead. "Okay, I'll leave it up to you."

They got to Lord Saint's office about ten minutes later. Mildred walked right in through the front door. Linc followed her and saw that there was a lady sitting at the front desk, reading over some reports.

"Kiley!" Mildred said to the woman. She looked up and smiled.

"Mildred, it's been too long." The lady got up and hugged her. After a few seconds, she released her from the motherly hug and turned towards Linc. "Who is this handsome man you're with?"

Mildred put a hand on Kiley's shoulder.

"Kiley, this is Linc Kane."

"Well it is a pleasure to meet you. Philias has told me so much about you."

Linc bowed.

"Linc, this is Duchess Kiley Saint, Lord Philias's wife."

"It is a pleasure to meet you as well, Duchess," Linc thought she had a motherly look to her. She was dressed in the finest shirt and pants Linc had ever seen.

"Is he busy?" Mildred asked after the introductions.

"I think he just got through with Jorgen. Go right in." Linc nodded and followed Mildred into Lord Saint's office. Lord Saint was closing the other door into the ship builder's warehouse as they walked in.

"Ah, Millie, and Linc, what a surprise."

Mildred walked over and hugged him. "Have a seat. I am intrigued as to why you two would come and see me."

Mildred and Linc took a seat in front of his desk. Mildred sighed. "We've come here to ask you a favor." Lord Saint raised an eyebrow. Mildred smiled then continued. "you remember Mr. Wark who came through here several weeks back?"

"I seem to remember him being a cobbler?"

"That's right. I bought several pairs of boots from him. Yesterday I sold Linc the last pair. Linc liked them so much that he wants to go to Pineral. Linc wants to buy some of them, so he can sell them to Silver City traders. Of course I convinced our young Captain here to make me a partner or I wouldn't tell him where they came from." Mildred lowered her head grinning.

"That's a long way to travel by Land. Since the *LiTaDi* is being refitted right now," Lord Saint replied.

"Well, that's why we're here. Can I convince you to allow us to use *Smooth Trader* for a few weeks while his ship is being refitted?"

Lord Saint stared at the two. "Who would be going on this trip. You know the Gore have been seen close to Mt. Jover lately?"

Linc responded sensing he was close to saying yes. "Me and my crew would be going, along with Mildred of course. Since she has already met Mr. Wark, it would be good to have her along for the introductions."

Lord Saint looked around the room in thought for a few minutes, and then back at the two. "Mildred, can I talk with Linc for a few minutes before I give you my decision?"

She smiled, "Sure." She got up and went out to talk with Kiley. Lord Saint closed his eyes for a minute, and then took a deep breath, and looked at Linc.

"I find it pleasing that you two have met. I want you to know that I have watched her grow up from an unfortunate childhood to become a very strong young woman." He paused, got up, walked to the window, and looked out over the water. "I assume you have just met her, Linc, but can I ask how you feel about her?"

Linc thought it was a weird question, but Lord Saint had been very good to him so far. "I think she is the most intriguing woman I have ever met. I believe in the short time that I've known her that I'm starting to have strong feelings for her." Linc was astonished that he had opened up so easy.

Lord Saint turned and smiled at Linc. "Good. If I say yes, will you protect her with your life?"

Linc looked at Lord Saint, then turned and looked at Mildred through the office window. He grinned and looked back. Lord Saint sat back down in his chair.

"I think she would be the one protecting me. You're the one who trained her with a sword and staff," Linc said.

"Ah that I did. So, you have sparred with her."

Linc nodded. "But to answer your question, yes, I would,"

"She is very special to me. You have no idea how important she is." By his words, Linc could tell he really cared about her.

He just nodded. "She is very special. I can tell that." Linc watched as Lord Saint rubbed the stubble on his face in thought. He put his hands on the edge of his desk and looked Linc in the eyes.

"It should take you twelve days to sail there, meet with Mr. Wark, and sail back."

"That's about what I thought as well," Linc replied.

Lord Saint got up and went to the door to the ship builders warehouse and called Jorgen back to the office. Jorgen came up to the door and he and Lord Saint talked for a minute.

Lord Saint came back and sat down. "It will take fourteen days to finish your ship so hopefully you won't run into any trouble that would delay your trip."

Linc sensed the meeting was over so he got up and shook Lord Saint's hand. "Thank you. We will be leaving early tomorrow morning if that's ok?"

"That will be fine. I know Jorgen is excited about working on your ship. Now he won't feel as rushed. Safe travels and take care of Millie, like you said you would." Lord Saint raised an eyebrow.

Linc smiled. "It will be my pleasure." He turned as Mildred was coming back in the office. Linc told her that Lord Saint had agreed.

She hugged Lord Saint. "Thank you so much. I'll see you when I get back."

They said their goodbyes to Kiley, who hugged her and Linc as well.

After they left, Lord Saint called Jorgen back into the office. "Yes sir?"

"I want you to get *Smooth Trader* loaded with all the new special weapons and have it fully stocked with backup."

Jorgen never questioned Lord Saint. "Aye. I'll have the crew get it ready by nightfall."

"Mildred and Linc will be taking it on an adventure. So make sure they have at least a month's supply of rations for the trip. They're going to need it. They just don't know it yet," Lord Saint smiled.

"Yes sir," Jorgen replied and turned to go get started..

"And Jorgen." Jorgen turned back. "No need to hurry on the *LiTaDi Flame*. They probably won't be back for it for a long time." Jorgen nodded and went off to work.

Lord Saint walked over to the window and looked out at the water again. It was always so calming to him. "Is it time?" Kiley asked, walking up and putting her hand on his shoulder. She turned to stare at the water with him.

"I am afraid so. All of the signs we were told would come to pass are happening as we speak."

She sighed. "When I saw him walk in with her, I knew it. It was all I could do to keep from screaming to both of them, 'Run both of you, as far away from here as you can.'" A tear ran down her cheek. Lord Saint pulled his wife into a hug.

"We were tasked with a hard job, my love. We have brought them together. Let's trust the gods know what they are doing." He kissed her cheek, and they remained that way for several hours, just staring, until the sun started to set.

Long Time Coming

As the *Smooth Trader* sailed away the next morning, the two figures that seemed to always be watching Mildred were standing in the woods, once again watching her. "Marluna protect you, my child," the female said.

"May Dirk Storm and the protector be the ones who bring us our freedom," the male said. The female agreed. They both vanished immediately after the *Smooth Trader* disappeared over the horizon.

The night before, Linc had received another letter from Dirk, confirming what Linc had already felt. Dirk told him about his plans to tell most of the first-year students about the Chosen and what lay ahead for them so they could be better prepared. Gil would be the final bonded, but he had to wait until the next free weekend to be bonded. Linc laughed to himself for an hour over Brock getting expelled.

Linc agreed with Dirk's plan and wrote him back:

Brother, I agree with your plan. I have met someone here. I know you and the Pack would love her. Her name is Mildred. She has a certain fire about her. I don't know what it is yet, but she stirs something inside me, every time I look at her. She works for her adopted mother. She owns a trading business. I bought the best pair of boots I have ever had the pleasure of putting on my feet from her. I decided to travel to Pineral and meet the man she bought them from. His name is Wark. You may know his son. I believe he is a first-year student as well. Mildred convinced me to take her with us to meet him. Also, I hope you and Tab don't mind but I decided to let her be a partner on this deal. I really think this deal will make us a lot of money, so I'll split my shares with her. Got to get ready for bed. I miss you guys so much. I can't wait to get back. I'm excited about meeting my new brothers and sisters in person. Give El a hug and kiss from me. Tell Gil to be strong. We'll get that bastard father of his one day, I swear. And tell Tab not to muck this up with El.

Your brother, Linc

Linc, satisfied with his response, sealed it with a wax seal and sent a message to Aarya. She must have been close by because she landed on his windowsill a few minutes later.

He petted her head affectionately and asked her to take the letter to Dirk. She trilled, took the message in her talons, and was gone in a flash.

Watching her vanish gave Linc a thought. He would have to find out if messages were the only thing Aarya could carry.

That night, Linc's dreams were a mixture of feelings, love, fear, apprehension, and determination. He could feel his love for the bonded growing stronger, even though he had never met many of them. Linc had been all alone at one point in his life with no family. Now he wasn't alone and had a big family. It seemed to be growing by the day. He smiled, thinking that if he ever had had children, he had no doubt that they would never have to worry about being alone.

Dirk awoke the same morning that Linc and his crew set sail for Pineral totally exhausted from the events of the previous few days. The night before, the group of nine had spent a long time with Hilda and Tilda working on joining powers. It seemed to work when Dirk, Natia, and Tab would join, but very few attempts worked with the whole group. They had more luck when Vira and Nira joined them, but not every time was successful. Dirk was getting frustrated, and he was beginning to question leaving the necklaces the king had given him and Natia at the farm. He thought that since they weren't being successful that they might help. The bracelets seemed to give him and Natia a boost, but they felt incomplete without the necklaces. Natia assured him that they could get them anytime, but he had decided that they needed to do it on their own first.

The twin room mothers decided to finally call it a night after more than a few taxing attempts.

That morning, he and the first-years went to breakfast like normal, but soon after, they found out that Sergeant Giles had definitely ramped things up for their training that day. They were given only twenty minutes to the halfway point and twenty minutes back. Only the elves and the twins made the deadline. The ones who didn't had to run it again.

Dirk thought he would die before he got back an hour later. Sergeant Giles lectured them on making sure they stayed in shape on their weekends off. After he released them, they had to rush to get to Hermosa's new class. Dirk and the bonded got there five minutes late.

Hermosa began her first class after a lecture on punctuality. She then laid out what they would be focusing on. "Now that we all are here, Natia, please put a barrier up on the four walls." Natia materialized a barrier with little effort. "Is that your best barrier?" Hermosa asked and Natia nodded.

Hermosa closed her eyes and raised her hand at the back wall. She made a fist and Dirk could see she was wearing a ring with a yellow stone in it. The stone started to glow, and a lightning bolt shot out of it and straight into the wall. It glowed red for a moment and then the barrier disappeared.

The class gasped and turned to face Hermosa. "Now what Natia did with her barrier would have been quite sufficient under normal circumstances, but your group will be facing very powerful wizards. I couldn't have done what I did without this," she said, holding up her ring. She passed it around for the class to examine it. "What do you think could have made the barrier stronger?"

El was the first to speak up. "Combining powers, casting the barrier spell together."

Hermosa looked at El. "Very good, Elyse. Is there anything else?" No one answered. Hermosa stared at the ring Dirk was now holding.

"There are objects you can use to strengthen your abilities, right?" Hermosa asked.

"Yes, Wizard Hermosa."

"Right, so now you all have had lessons about how certain people have the ability to change a gem for certain uses. If you have a gem that has been adjusted to strengthen your barrier power, then that would work as well." She had the class's attention. "Let's take what we have learned. Natia, pick two people to join you this time and raise the barrier again."

Natia looked at Vira and Nira and they stood together. Vira and Nira each put a hand on one of her shoulders. "Ready?" Natia asked.

"Yes." The twins responded. They closed their eyes for a minute. Natia felt the twins connected to her core. She raised her hand and pointed at the wall.

A bright red barrier formed on the wall this time. Hermosa told them very good and to take a seat. Dirk handed her the ring after she asked for it back. Once again, she attacked the barrier.

This time, the lightning hit the barrier and it crackled on impact. Hermosa held it for a moment then gave up, lowering her hand. "Everyone, give them a hand." The class clapped. "That is a perfect example of how to build a barrier from now on. Remember, the stronger your enemies become the more people you will need to build the barrier," Hermosa said, smiling at the group. "Now, after lunch, I will have you team up and practice this.

"Remember, just as you saw how joining together can strengthen the barrier, you can do the same with other aspects of magic. I know you have been practicing joining your cores but haven't been very successful in your efforts. We will be working on these things for the first few weeks until you can achieve that ability effortlessly."

Lunch time was always loud, but today, when the nine, who had been chosen for the special class, came in, the whole lunchroom stared. After the initial shock wore off, though, everything went back to normal with exception of the whole third-year class still being absent. Dirk and Natia walked side by side while having to endure Skylar and her friends.

Dirk had to grab Natia's elbow to stop her from reacting to one remark Skylar made. He whispered to her, "Now what was it you said to me yesterday about the responsibilities of power?"

She cut her eyes at him. "Well, I wasn't gonna knock her out. I was just going to inflict pain." Dirk smiled and laughed. They got their lunch and headed to the back. Dirk saw that today the entire first-years, except Skylar and her friends, had all set up the tables so Dirk and the nine would sit in the center while the other tables surrounded them. The tables were close enough that they could easily discuss what Hermosa had taught them that morning. Dirk told them it would be easy for everyone to learn from the lesson they had today, and he would try to work out a way to do that.

"Invite everyone to the farm the next free weekend," Tab suggested, El agreed.

Dirk looked up and smiled. "That's a great idea." They passed the word around and before lunch was over, the weekend group would be much bigger than before. He just hoped Kira wouldn't mind. Dirk looked around the lunch hall as everyone else was talking and couldn't help but notice Moira staring at him. He smiled and waved at her. She returned the gesture with a raised eyebrow. He just shrugged at her.

At that moment, he realized he wanted to bring her into the fold. Deciding to keep that to himself for now, he would deal with the consequences of what Tab would say when it happened. He mouthed the words; *I'll talk with you later*. She stared at him for a minute then nodded an ok. Dirk waved again, and this time she smiled and waved back.

Dirk caught Tab staring at him. "What?"

"I know what you're thinking."

Dirk gave him an innocent look. "What are you talking about?"

Tab looked to Moira then back at Dirk. "Don't even think about it. She is a psycho."

"You underestimate her, Tab. But I wouldn't do anything without discussing it with you first."

Tab gave him a hard look. "You, better not. Remember, I know you better than the rest of the bonded," Tab said, looking around at the group.

Dirk squeezed his friend's shoulder. "I promise I won't do anything without your consent," he said, teasingly. Tab smiled back, accepting him at his word.

Saying "*Privacious*," as quietly as he could, that familiar sensation washed over him, and he squeezed Natia's leg under the table. She had been listening to the whole conversation. In Dirk's mind, he heard her thoughts. *I think your right about her from what you've told me. But let's wait and see how the training goes first. There should be time to bring her in whenever we need* to.

Dirk nodded in agreement. He didn't want to say or think too much, since Tab could pick his thoughts up easily. As Dirk was leaving the lunch hall, he pretended to stay back and say hi to Hanks before going back to class. Tab was in an in-depth discussion with El so he told him he would see him there.

Just like Dirk thought, Moira was back in the kitchen talking with Hanks when he entered. He smiled at Hanks and shook his hand. "Hello Hanks. How have you been?"

"Been good. Workload has been less since the third-years are gone. Well, it looks like you two wanted to talk so I'll leave you be." Hanks smiled and looked at Moira, "You be good."

She smirked. "Always." Hanks shook his head and left them alone.

Dirk looked at Moira, who was waiting with her hands on her hips. "Look, I know you want to know what's going on," he said.

"You know me, Dirk. I have to keep an eye on you. First, you and the princess have first-year table all to yourselves a few weeks ago. Then you and Elyse, I believe is her name, had the table the next day. Now I hear there was a very exciting weekend at your farm." She paused and cocked an eyebrow at him. "The whole first-year class is set up in a big circle, except those crags you don't get along with. So, what's up, Mr. Storm?"

He smiled and put a hand on her shoulder, thinking of what to say to her without saying too much. "Moira, I need to make this quick so here is what I can tell you. You noticed the third-years are gone."

"Duh!"

Dirk laughed. "That's what I like about you, Moira. Here's what I can say, and I really need you to trust me. Do you trust me?"

She looked at him with her hand on her jaw. "Dirk, I knew the first time I saw you that there was something special about you. Not because of who you were, but by how you treated me and the others around you. Yes, I trust you."

Dirk squeezed her shoulder. "There are things happening down south with Vangaurd and the Der-Tod again. You know about Der-Tod, I assume." She nodded. "Sometime in the future something might happen to bring certain things to light. I want you to know that when it does. I want you with us. Please don't ask what that means right now because I can't say. Just keep your eyes open and your ears listening for anything that seems out of the ordinary. And if you think I need to know, please find me. I promise as soon as I can tell you more, I will." Dirk waited anxiously for her response.

She looked at him, taking in what he had said. Finally, she let out a breath. "You got it, friend. Just don't leave me in the dark too long. You know how antsy I can be." She smiled as she said it.

"I promise. And try to stay out of trouble. Trust me, enough trouble is coming our way to keep us all busy." Satisfied with what he had told her, he said goodbye and they both headed off to class.

Hermosa separated them into two groups. Dirk was chosen to use the ring and cast the lightening at the barriers the first hour, though he couldn't maintain the lightening long enough to do any real damage.

"That's okay Dirk. You don't need to worry, your abilities will grow the more you practice, and get more experience," Hermosa explained.

The second hour, it was Vira. She decimated the shields very quickly, so Hermosa kept her casting the spell the rest of the afternoon. Dirk's group, which consisted of Natia, Nira, Volar, Tara and El, was the only group to keep their barrier up after five minutes of Vira attacking it. It was so good that Hermosa ended class early so everyone could focus on the other homework.

"Hey, let's go to the roof and watch the military practice drills. We can watch Brock get his butt handed to him," Tab suggested. The whole group decided to since the rest of their classmates were still in class. Dirk was starting to get used to having all of the bonded around him. Dirk knew Oriana and Tara had been Natia's best friends her whole life, and since becoming bonded, he could now see why. They were just like Tab, Linc, and himself in a lot of ways. They, for one, were a little mischievous. Oriana was a big flirt. Tara was the more calm and cooler one, who always thought things through before she decided. Natia kicked ass first and asked questions later.

Dirk laughed to himself when he realized the three were just staring at him. "Sorry ladies, just letting my mind wander."

Oriana winked at him with those silver eyes. *So damned sexy,* he thought. Natia punched Dirk in the arm. "Hey, you know what I mean," Dirk said.

Tara laughed and followed Natia, who had walked off. "Sorry Dirk. If you weren't already taken..." Oriana bit her lip playfully, then slapped him on the butt as she followed Tara and Natia.

"Man, some thoughts you just have to keep private," Dirk said to Tab and Volar as they were heading to the roof. Both of them laughed at him the whole way up. Natia knew Dirk was just doing some harmless thinking. When he walked up beside her, she grabbed his hand and pulled him to her side. She smiled at him, letting her eyes ripple flames. "I know."

They watched the military trainees running through their obstacle course, and just like Tab thought, Brock and his two cronies were last and catching an earful from Sergeant Giles. The group watched for a few minutes.

Since this had become their official meeting place, they all sat down on some chairs that Vira and Nira somehow arranged to be put up there. There was a small portable fire pit in the center of the chairs. It was made out of a small metal barrel. It looked to be cut in half and was supported by several cinder blocks underneath to keep the heat away from the roof.

The weather is starting to chill so it'll be a nice place to come and relax by the fire at night before we get shut in by the twins. Dirk thought. El was becoming closer with Tara and Oriana, who were telling El about what happened on the way to the roof. El gave Dirk her El look. The three started having a serious discussion and seemed to have forgotten about Dirk. Tab and Volar sat together, also talking. Dirk, Natia, and the twins settled in a group of chairs.

"How did you sleep last night, Dirk?" Vira asked.

He looked at her, wondering where this was going. "To be honest, not very good."

"Me neither. It felt…" Vira paused, searching for the right word.

"Lonely," Natia finished for her.

"I know, but what can we do? We're at school and the doors are magically locked."

Nira smiled at Dirk's comment. Dirk looked at the three girls he was sitting with. Vira and Nira kept looking at each other, as if having a private discussion. The bond was strong between them. Dirk could pretty much read everyone's thoughts when he wanted to, but Vira and Nira seemed to be able to keep him out whenever they wanted.

To get their focus back on training, he said, "That was a good lesson today. We really need to focus on that kind of thinking. I mean what about swords and arrows? Does that concept really work?"

"We used items similar to the ring for growing food at Elmwood. I don't see why it won't work on any object," Natia said, leaning her head on his shoulder.

A breeze blew the smells of the city across the roof. Dirk looked out over the obstacle course. They were finishing up. A satisfied smile crossed his face as he watched Brock get chewed out by Giles. *He deserves it,* Natia thought. Dirk agreed.

"You know, I think we're constricted in our training," Vira said, smiling.

"I think I know what you mean." Nira replied, following up her sister's thoughts.

"We need to convince Hermosa of this. I mean, we really need to be free with our practice," Natia said.

"We need to be out in the field training, in all seriousness." Dirk thought about it, then asked the others in the group what they thought.

Volar spoke up. "When we were traveling here, there were acres of land just north of the great forest with no inhabitants around. I know it's an uncontested area where there haven't been any conflicts for years and to my knowledge, nobody lives in that area that far north. It would be a great place to practice actual tactics."

Tara chimed in. "I think I remember the study of an abandoned city somewhere around there."

Dirk looked around at each of them, feeling the group's growing need to be uninhibited in the way they trained. Being bonded for only a few days, they were already starting to think similarly. Today was a small sample of their potential. Dirk started to come up with a plan. When the rest of the group got out of class, he would run it by them and see what they thought. The only problem was Skylar and her friends and the rest of the school.

"We will have to come up with a way to deal with them," Natia said answering Dirk's thoughts. Everyone agreed.

Aarya flew in right before dinner and delivered a message from Linc. The ones who hadn't really had a chance to see her up close were astounded. Dirk confirmed with Aarya that Gil would be the last to bond as soon as they could get to the farm.

"Dirk, she's so majestic," Gil said while Aarya was perched on his arm. The bond wouldn't happen just through a touch. Aarya would have to initiate the bond herself. Anyone could touch her safely without bonding unless she allowed it to happen.

Dirk felt a little guilty about Gil not being bonded yet. "I wish you could have come for the weekend."

Gil smiled. "Maybe it's for the best, with Father being so demanding. I mean I would have loved it, but I would hate to think that I might mess things up if Father needed me." He hung his head in defeat.

"Gil, as soon as we can get to the farm again, you will be bonded..."

Gil stopped Dirk from finishing what he was going to say. "It's okay, brother. All will be fine in the end. I know as soon as I can, I will bond with Aarya." Gil said, then held his arm out to Red, who was waiting patiently to see Aarya up close. "I'm gonna head down to dinner early. I have a lot of studying to do."

Dirk, trying to get Gil to stay said, "I got a letter from Linc."

Gil stopped and sat back down. "What is our wayward traveling brother doing?"

Dirk read the letter, then told him about Linc's adventures and that he had met a girl in Oak City.

"What's her name?"

"You'll like this. Her name is Mildred, and she was an orphan," Dirk said, smiling.

Gil laughed. "I bet Brock would have a field day with that. Oh, wait, he's not here to find out." The group laughed.

"Believe it or not, they're on a trip with his crew to meet none other than Phil's father. He bought some of his boots at the place Mildred works and he wants to try and convince him to trade with him."

Phil stepped up after hearing what Dirk was saying. "I doubt he will, Dirk. I told you he's real untrusting when it comes to traders." Phil sat down.

"Linc can be persuasive," Dirk said.

Phil nodded. "I could send him a letter informing him of who Linc is and that might make him want to do it."

This gave Dirk an idea. "Phil, how fast can your father make, let's say, forty pairs of those boots of different sizes?"

Phil thought for a moment. "Maybe twelve days."

Dirk was pleased with Phil's response. "Let's give your father an incentive. I'll place an order for those, and as many more pairs as your father can make, before Linc gets there. Can you send that information, plus Linc's introduction to him in the letter?"

"How will it get there before him?" Gil asked.

Dirk nodded to Red. Phil turned and looked in the same direction. "Air Aarya," Dirk said, smiling.

"You bet. I'll gather shoe sizes, then give it to you to send with the letter."

"Tell him that Linc will have the silver to pay for them when he gets there."

Phil nodded and headed off to collect the sizes. Gil said he needed to go, and he left before anyone could stop him. Dirk would have stopped him, but felt he needed to leave him alone.

Tab came over and took control of Aarya. Right then Skylar, Sylvie, Skylar's best friend, and the rest of the girls who weren't in the group busted through the door. "Oh, I see, you think since you're in 'The Special Class', that you can just do whatever you want?"

Aarya vanished in the blink of an eye. "No, Skylar, we just wanted a place for us to hangout other than in the dorms," Dirk responded.

Skylar walked straight up to Dirk and stopped right in front of him with Sylvie and her beak nose right behind her. Skylar looked around. "You think that just because Brock is gone, you can just treat me anyway you want?"

El stepped up with Tara and Oriana right beside her. "I got this Dirk," El said, basically pushing Dirk out of the way. She poked Skylar in the chest a little harder than necessary, causing Skylar to flinch. "You, two-faced, sorry bitch. You have the nerve to talk as if Brock and you were still together. Or don't you remember the scene you caused in the lunch hall where you told him he had no balls?" El's eyes were starting to feel warm.

Skylar was shocked by El's force and the fact that no one had ever really stood up to her until Natia had come along. "Well, that is none of your business. For your information, we made up on the long weekend and he told me he was being blackmailed by the half-man."

Tab grabbed Volar to keep him from getting in between El and Skylar. "This has been a long time coming. Let El handle it," Tab explained. Volar nodded.

"Oh, you're talking about Brock using banned substances for his benefit, are you? Well, you know what, you two losers deserve each other, and by the way, it's none of your damn business what we do. If you try to start trouble, I will personally kick your whore ass back to the gutter you crawled out of," El said, stepping nose to nose with Skylar. Sylvie took a step back.

Skylar probably shouldn't do what I think she'll do next. Dirk thought as he watched the scene unfold.

She took a step back and swung at El. El caught her arm and flipped Skylar over her back onto the ground. El, still holding her twisted arm, put her boot on her throat. Skylar's friends started to step up, but Oriana and Tara stepped in front of them.

"Do we have a problem?" Tara asked, itching to punch someone. El's feelings had gotten them ready for a fight.

Sylvie realized she and her friends were outmatched and started to retreat back. "No." None of them were as brave or as stupid as Skylar.

"I said, do you understand me?" El asked putting more pressure on Skylar's throat. Skylar nodded. "Good, now, I'm going to let you up and you and your friends are going to leave and never come here again unless invited."

Skylar nodded again. El looked to Skylar's friends. They all looked scared. She let Skylar up. Skylar rubbed her shoulder and left, fussing at her friends for not helping her.

After the door closed, the roof erupted into applause. El was everyone's hero. She just took several breaths. "By the gods, that felt good."

Tab grabbed her and hugged her. The rest of the group patted her on the back, congratulating her on knocking that bitch on her ass. Dirk walked up and smiled. "Wasn't it yesterday I was the one being chastised for using my strength?" He looked between El and Natia. They blew him off and sat and talked with Tara and Oriana.

Dirk shrugged and went to sit with the twins, who had very mischievous looks on their faces. Dirk stared at them. "What are you two up to?"

"Now brother, you are so mistrusting," Nira said with a smirk. He sat with them, realizing he wouldn't get anything out of them for now. He started talking with them about his plan to get the training moved until it was time for dinner. Phil came up and handed him the letter.

"Thanks, Phil. I guess Aarya had somewhere to go when Skylar showed up. I'll get it to her when she returns. I'm sure it will get to your father and to Linc in time." Phil nodded and went to talk with Dusty. Vira leaned in and whispered to Dirk as Phil was walking away. "Tonight, bring Natia up here with you after everyone goes to sleep. Nira and I will be waiting," Vira smiled at his look of confusion. "Trust me," she replied, and he nodded.

Phil and Volar were having their nightly snoring duel when Dirk snuck out of their room. To his surprise, the door had the certain glow that meant it was locked.

It's ok. It'll let you through, Vira's voice echoed in his head. Dirk turned the knob, and sure enough, it opened. Natia was waiting outside the door.

"You ready?" she asked.

"As ready as I will ever be, and by the way, you look very beautiful tonight." She smiled and kissed him. "Whew, I have been dying to do that for two days," Dirk said, grabbing her waist and pulling her into a more passionate kiss. After a few minutes of kissing, they headed up to the roof. When they got up to the door that lead to the roof, it had the same glow, but Natia turned the knob and it unlocked for them.

Dirk laughed at the sight before him. Natia smiled. The chairs were now gone. Several logs were spread out around the fire pit, almost identical to the way it had looked at the farm. There were four sleeping bags attached to each other. Vira and Nira were sitting in front of the small fire on top of the open bags. Dirk and Natia joined them.

"I guess this is the thing you two were scheming earlier?"

Vira and Nira smiled. "We thought of it this afternoon. We went to Hilda and Tilda and told them how you two had helped us with the night terrors, and how important it was for us to be at our best in training. Much to their doubt and hesitancy, they agreed to let us sleep up here at night as long as we keep it to ourselves. They also said very strongly that no funny business would be tolerated. Of course, we swore that we had no intention of that. And you know, we were only talking about Nira and me," Vira told them with a smile.

"I agree. It really is for the best. We haven't been able to sleep since we've been back because of the night terrors," Nira confirmed.

"Well, as long as you two don't do any funny business," Dirk said, laughing while taking off his shirt and then laying down.

Sweat formed on Natia's brow. "Naughty thoughts sister," Nira said, smirking at her.

Natia smiled. "Well, while Dirk fills your dreams killing the night terrors…" Natia paused, looking between the sisters. "He fills other things in my dreams," She winked at Nira and Vira. They laughed. "Are you hot?" Natia asked Dirk. He looked at her confused. "You normally sleep with your shirt on."

He caressed her face. "That was just at the farm with everyone there. I usually sleep without one at night." He smiled, then looked at the sisters. He had heard everything they had said to each other. "I usually sleep without any undergarments as well, just like you two." He winked at them.

Vira just stared at him before laying down behind him in her new favorite sleeping spot. Natia had already laid down beside him and had her hand on his chest, running her fingers across it. Nira lay behind Natia and snuggled.

"You know, Dirk," Vira said getting his attention, "if you want to do that, it's fine by me. Besides, I like having something to wrap my hand around while I'm sleeping." Natia looked up at her. Dirk just stared. Nira giggled, knowing her sister.

Vira laughed. "That look is priceless. You know I'm joking, right?" Natia smiled. Dirk didn't respond.

"Well I'm just saying," she said and laid back down beside him, still laughing. He finally realized Vira had been pulling his chain. He laughed and put his arm around her pulling her close. He also put his arm under Natia, pulling her and Nira closer.

"Vira, can anyone come through that door?" Vira laughed.

"Of course not. Only the four of us, Tab, and El. If someone does try to, it is spelled to cause an illusion, so they won't see anything there."

Dirk moved so he could see her face. "Can you cast the spell in a way to make everyone see whatever you want them to?" Vira nodded. "That's awesome. I know how to handle the other first-years now if we want to train outside of school."

"An illusion is one thing, Dirk, but I believe I have something better for that," Vira said.

"What?" he asked, causing them to sit up.

"What if I told you that Nira and I have a way for a person to be at two places at the same time?"

"Tell me more," Dirk grinned as she explained the Miraga stone and its uses.

Dirk was really enthusiastic about their chances now. Especially now the twins had explained how the Miraga stone was used as a doppelganger. He planted a quick, loving kiss on her lips. She returned it and smiled. "This will definitely work better."

Dirk smiled then adjusted his idea with the new information and shared his idea with the girls. They all agreed it should work. Dirk thought now they just had to convince Hermosa to let them go through with their plan.

Finally, after the excitement of their revelation, they settled down and talked for hours, planning. On the verge of passing out, the twins were soon snoring quietly.

Natia sniffed Dirk's neck. "Mmmm, I love that smell." She rubbed his chest slowly and started moving slowly down to his stomach. He tensed a little since the twins were there. "Don't worry, they won't mind." She kissed his ear, then started running her tongue around its edges.

Dirk stifled a moan. Natia slid her hand down his pants and found what she had wanted to wrap her hand around, remembering Vira's joke about it. She kissed his cheek, said good night, and pulled her hand back out, placing it on his chest. "When we're alone. It wouldn't be right doing it up here when they promised."

Dirk sighed. "Where's a cold shower when you need one?"

Natia laughed quietly, kissed him goodnight and dozed off. Dirk would have fallen asleep right away, if it hadn't been for Vira, who had wrapped her arm around his waist while they were sleeping and had accidently brushed his manhood with her hand. He adjusted her arm away from his crotch and finally went to sleep. As soon as he did, he was in the twin's nightmares, destroying the evil creatures that tormented them. Dirk felt their relief. They smiled in their dreams. They were finally safe now, thanks to their brother.

They awoke before the rest of the first-years and headed downstairs before anyone else could get up. Vira and Nira kissed dirk on the cheek. "Thanks. That was the best night sleep we've had since the farm."

He smiled "Me too."

They all snuck back into the dorms. Hilda was already up. "Did it work?"

He nodded then he told her about the twin's night terrors.

"That's what they said."

"Well it is very real," Dirk told her. She then ushered him off to get ready for the day. Dirk got to the showers before anyone else for the first time. The day went much the same as the day before. Dirk felt that Sergeant Giles ran them half to death in training. Several of the students made it under the forty-minute mark. Dirk and El made it, but when Volar and the others that didn't had to run again, they decided to run it with them. Following Natia's lead, the elves got up and followed her. This seemed to get Sergeant Giles attention and he decided to run it with them too.

Skylar and two of her friends that had made it in time just sat and waited for the group to return. When the group got back, Giles commended the ones that ran with the ones who didn't make it the first time on teamwork. He looked at Skylar and her two friends, sneered, and then dismissed the class.

Hermosa's class went the same, with doing more practice with barriers, only this time it was against a freezing blast. This time, she had a staff with a blue gem on the tip of it. Dirk and the group caught on quicker today. Hermosa was ecstatic at the way the class picked up on the lessons by the end of the day.

"That's a great day of training. Tomorrow we will start with shield and barrier combinations. Class dismissed," Hermosa said. The whole class stayed in their seats, per the plan Dirk and the twins had conceived. Hermosa noticed and leaned against her desk. "Dirk, what is going on?"

"Wizard Hermosa, I would like to explain an idea we as a group have had and wanted to run it by you," Dirk stated getting encouragement from Natia. Hermosa pulled her glasses off and let them dangle, raising an eyebrow. Dirk felt courage pouring into him from everyone in the class. "I think that what we are starting to do here is great and has started us down the right path for success."

Hermosa smiled "But?"

"What we need to do is go to a place where we can practice in the open and not be restrained in a classroom." Hermosa absentmindedly bit down on one of the ends of her glasses.

"Do you have such a place in mind?"

Tara stood up since the idea had been hers to begin with. "Wizard Hermosa when elves are young we learn a lot of ancient history. One thing we learned was that a long time ago there was a great city that something devastating happened to. It caused the inhabitants to abandon it, even though there was nothing physically wrong with it. That abandoned city is just twenty leagues from here, just southeast of Oak City and in the great forest, and it is still uninhabited." Tara sat down.

Hermosa thought about the information she was given and stared out the window. "It would be a good place to train uninterrupted and it is still in fairly decent condition, I have been told," Volar added.

"That city was abandoned a thousand years ago. Did you know that?"

Hermosa asked. "There was a great catastrophe there, but history has decided to forget why. What would you do about the other students in your year?" Dirk had been waiting on this question and smiled.

"Wizard Hermosa if you will give us a minute, I'll show you what we can do about the other students," Natia nodded to Vira and Nira. They got up and left the class.

Hermosa just watched and waited. Dirk when he felt they had enough time. "All we ask is that you keep an open mind Wizard Hermosa." She nodded.

Dirk, satisfied Hermosa was willing to at least see what their plan was, looked to the door. "Ladies, you can come in now."

Vira, Nira and Natia walked back into the room and sat back down. Hermosa just stared at them. She heard someone clear their throat, so she turned her head and could see the three of them standing outside the door.

"How?" Hermosa asked. Vira walked over to where her doppelganger was sitting.

She looked at her and said, "Do you mind?"

"Not at all, gorgeous," the doppelganger said. It got up and stepped to the side. Vira's double, handed her a red stone half the size of her fist. Vira held it up for the class and Hermosa to see.

"Miraga Stone. It creates a mirror image of the person it is linked with. The mirror image looks and acts identical to that person. It has to be touched and repowered once a month to continue the mirage. It's not very sentient but can think and respond the same way the person it is linked with would. It pulls power directly from the world's core and the person it is connected to. If used right, it can last up to two months," Vira explained, handing it to Hermosa.

Hermosa looked at the stone. "I've heard of these. They were used by..."

Vira cut her off. "The Droc used them in the last war. Our grandfather was forced to make them. While he was being used by those evil bastards, he taught us how to make them."

Hermosa studied the stone, then tossed it back to the real Vira. "How many do you have?"

Nira smiled. "Twenty right now, but we can make double that in a few days. We just need the right stones to convert. And we'll need to train a few people to help us."

Hermosa chewed on the end of her glasses again, seriously thinking on the issue. "Where do you need to go to get more of these stones?"

Dirk victorious as he answered, "Mt. Blazire has those scattered all around its base. Tab, Linc, and I have seen them our whole lives but just thought they were normal stones."

Hermosa asked Vira to show her how they worked. Vira rubbed the stone with her thumb and her mirror image disappeared. Then Vira rubbed it again and the doppelganger reappeared. "Hello gorgeous," Vira Two said, winking at her.

Vira, anticipating Hermosa, rubbed the stone and again Vira Two disappeared. She tossed the stone to Hermosa. "Rub it with your thumb." She did and Vira Two appeared.

"Wizard Hermosa," she said and bowed. Hermosa rubbed it again and she disappeared again. Natia and Nira did the same and theirs disappeared as well. Then they sat down.

"Anything else?" Hermosa asked, looking around.

Dirk smiled. "There are other things we need to work out, but we feel with your guidance, we can make it work."

Hermosa chewed on her glasses for a minute looking around the room. "Is this a unanimous decision?"

The whole class as one said, "Yes!"

Hermosa smiled to herself. "Well then, I agree with your plan with one addition. There has to be more than just students going."

Dirk nodded in agreement. "I agree. We will need several of the teachers to go with us to help us train, especially if we get stuck. Their expertise can guide us in the direction we need to take. I would really like it if several of the military staff could go as well to work with us on what we have planned."

Hermosa paced in front of her desk back and forth for a few minutes. "Tomorrow, we will make a field trip to Mt. Blazire and collect the stones you need." She held up her hand to stop their cheers. "As long as Wizard Nabas approves of it," she said.

"There is one more thing I need to tell you. We as a group decided to tell everyone in our class, with the exception of four girls in our class that I don't trust." Hermosa looked confused. "Before you chastise me, it was my call. I, for one, want to end this circle of death once and for all, and I feel the more people that I include in our plan, the more likely we will succeed."

Hermosa let out a breath. "You're right Dirk, it is your decision. As long as everyone knows what they are getting themselves into."

Oriana stood up. "We all freely made this choice as did all of the others that was told. Dirk made sure they knew everything. The only thing he didn't do was bond them. That he kept to the original group." She bowed and sat down.

"Very impressive, Dirk. You seem much more grown up at your age than your father was." She laughed and looked between him and Tab. "Your fathers, at this age, were both a thorn in Laseous's backside." She smiled at the two. "Don't get me wrong, he was very determined, but he had a mischievous side to him. Thad, as well, Tab. That group of theirs was probably the most troublesome group to ever to come through here.

"But that's a conversation for another day," she said, eyeing the boys. "All right, tomorrow, if he permits, we will take a trip to the mountain. Then we will plan and practice the rest of the week while the twins teach you how to make the stones. Then, on Monday, if everything goes as planned and we are prepared, we will start the trip to the Forgotten City. There is still a lot of planning that we need to do, but I agree with the plan." She looked at the group, slightly sad. "There are many of us, not just at the school, who want to end this as well, Dirk. We all have lost loved ones." He nodded.

They told the rest of the class about their discussion with Hermosa after class and went to dinner a little while later. Dirk could tell everyone was excited about their plan. As they were eating it was clear Skylar had gotten the message. She and her friends barely looked at the group. Moira came over to Dirk as she was leaving the hall. "Haven't seen you in detention lately." Dirk smiled.

As he and Moira were walking back to class after lunch the day before, he had told her she needed to act like she didn't know anything about what was going on. So, he kept up the charade. "Hi Moira, how have you been?" Tab scooted over so she could sit.

"Pretty good. Laseous has really been on me lately. I've been in detention for a week now with a couple of my friends." She pointed towards the table she had come from. Two girls and a guy at the table waved." Dirk waved back. "That's Olive, Annise, and Noah."

Dirk laughed. "What did you do?"

She smiled. "I'm not saying we did it, but someone kind of rigged Laseous's office door to lock when he went in and wouldn't open until someone, mainly me, would let him out. I came to his rescue, but he didn't believe me for a moment. Those damn boys we were in detention with the first week turned us in, I believe, but that's ok I'll get them back." she smiled. "How have you been?"

"Just training and trying to keep out of trouble," He replied.

She gave him a; *I've been watching* you *look*. "Well, got to go, see you."

"See you later. And try to stay out of trouble," She winked at him, laughing as she went to catch up with her friends.

"She is so weird," Tab said, scooting back over.

"She's all right. I like the way she thinks," Dirk said.

"No."

Dirk just looked at him. "No what?"

"Remember what we talked about. I know how you think," Tab said, tapping the side of his head.

Dirk shrugged. "I was just thinking she's very resourceful."

Tab shook his head. "I know ultimately it's your call, but we have enough to worry about. Remember, there is someone among us who will betray us," he whispered. Dirk nodded. He had already planned on telling Moira everything when the time was right. Since they were leaving soon, he wanted Moira to know what was going on since she would still be at the school. He would just have to tell her before he left, regardless of what Tab thought.

Dirk and Sorey

That night, Dirk and the bonded trained with the twins. Dirk told them about their plan. They were a little hesitant but agreed with Hermosa. It needed to be planned out carefully. They practiced on linking with five people and were successful every time Dirk was involved. But without him, there was less success. Dirk could tell they were still improving though.

An hour later, they stopped working to get some rest. Hilda and Tilda had started to let them lock up by themselves. Dirk held Natia and the twins back as everyone was leaving. "What is it Dirk?" Natia asked.

He made sure everyone else was gone. "Follow me." He grabbed Natia and Nira's hand. Nira grabbed Vira's as Dirk pulled them to a door at the top of the stairs that they had never gone through. "Vira, put up that barrier on the entrance. We won't be gone long."

She did as Dirk asked, and he touched the door. The door glowed crimson for a second then he turned the handle. There was a stairwell that went downward. The walls had the same lights as the other stairwell, the lights came on as they passed them. After a few minutes, the floor leveled out and they came to a stop.

"There're three of them," Natia said, pointing at the doors. Dirk was confused as well.

"Remember, the king said Grandfather had a map," Dirk said to Natia. She agreed. "But I think he forgot to give it to me."

Nira listened and then walked to the center of the room. She mumbled some words. The gems in her back came to life giving the room a haze. She held her hand up in front of each door without touching them. The door on the left glowed yellow. The door in the center glowed light green and the one on the right of her glowed crimson. Nira smiled pointing to the door on the right. "This is the one." Dirk just shook his head.

"What is it, Dirk?" Vira asked.

"I think I know what powers you two have and then, out of the blue, you surprise me with something new." He laughed.

"And you're just beginning to see what we can do regardless of what you think you sensed in the bond," Vira said. Dirk smiled.

"Where do the other two go?" he asked Nira.

"This one on the left, I believe, goes to the palace, and the one in the center, I can't really tell. All I know is that it's a really old and dark place,"

"The old outpost," Dirk said to the group. and smiled. "All right then, let's go."

They followed Dirk as he touched the door on the right as his grandfather had showed him. The door glowed crimson and he turned the knob. The door opened. They all held hands and stepped through the door, feeling a pulling sensation in their cores. Suddenly, there was a flash of light so bright they had to close their eyes. After the light and the pulling sensation disappeared, a whooshing sound that had accompanied them on their trip, disappeared. They had stopped in front of another door. Dirk tried shaking off the sensation of being transported. After their sense of balance came back, Dirk turned the knob and entered the general's shop to see the general sitting at his desk looking over some maps.

"Hello Grandfather," Vira said. He looked up and smiled at her. He got up and gave them each a hug.

"I can say that I'm not surprised to see you. I felt the doorway open at the school."

"Hello general. I wanted to come tell you what I wanted to do with your approval of course."

The general motioned for them to take a seat. "I know already. Tobias sent for me this afternoon and asked me what I thought about your plan." The general grabbed what he had been looking at and put it on a table in front of the four of them, who were sitting on the couch by his workbench. It was a map.

"What's this?" Dirk asked, not expecting what the general had placed in front of them.

"It's the map of the Forgotten City." The four of them looked it over.

"This is wonderful General Storm," Natia said. "How did you get it?"

He pulled the Book of Storms out and flipped halfway through the book. "Ah, here it is." Dirk looked where the general was pointing.

Seventh Chosen 1081az-1119az Dirk Storm Chosen. Protector Sorey Silver. Dirk looked up at his grandfather as did the girls.

"Really?"

His grandfather nodded. "Your namesake had an idea that there was an ancient power there that he could use to help defeat Zolun. He went with his best friend and protector, Sorey Silver and Tadon Clearwater. They went there to find this ancient power. I know they found it and used it to help defeat Zolun but didn't destroy him."

They all looked over the map and there was a small X marked at what looked like a temple. Dirk pointed to the X. "I don't know what it is. His blood has faded away almost to nothing. When I was young, I tried to read his history, but it was bits and pieces, not a full story for me to understand. I never had to go there, but since this is the place you're going to train I thought it might be worth a look," the general said. They all were excited. "So why did you come, son?"

Dirk looked up at his grandfather, pointing to the book. "I wanted to get your approval and see if I could take it with me so I could study the history while I'm training,"

The general nodded. "Makes sense, but, son, you don't need my approval. You are well on your way of becoming the man I always knew you would be. If you need it, it's yours." Dirk embraced his grandfather. The general grabbed Dirk by the shoulders and looked him in the eyes. "But I ask one more thing. Before you go, come by here one more time. I want to give you some things to take with you on your trip. You need to say goodbye to your mother anyway."

Dirk agreed. So, they talked a little while. The General asked Vira for more information about the Miraga stones. Vira and Nira told him everything they knew. "Those might be very useful. Do me a favor, granddaughters."

The girls smiled. "Whatever you need."

"Make me about twenty of the stones, will you?"

They looked at each other, "We might be able to make twenty extras before we leave."

"That would be great." He hugged the twins and they kissed him on the cheek before they left.

Just as Dirk was about to turn the knob on the door he looked back at his grandfather. "General, the middle door in the basement goes to the old outpost, doesn't it?"

The general smiled. "Ah, I guess you figured out the other one goes to the palace then?" the general said, giving Dirk the map he'd forgotten to give him last time.

"You're serious?" The General nodded.

"That means it will be a shorter trip to the Forgotten City than we thought. Who put it there?"

"I did. I wanted a way to get across Marona faster than normal and King Jerard and Nabas allowed me to make it, but I only went there once. I didn't even explore where it went other than into the basement of the old outpost."

"Will you teach me how to make a doorway?'

The general pointed to the book. "Check out Daron Storm 1259az-1298az. That will tell you everything you need to know,"

They told the general they would see him in a few days. Before they knew it, they were being pulled back to the school.

After closing the door, Dirk snuck back into the dorms. He grabbed his sleeping gear and headed to the roof. Tab and El were up there tonight, taking advantage of the privacy. Dirk was a little uncomfortable when he walked through the door. They were making out passionately. Dirk cleared his throat.

El got off Tab and covered up quickly. She smiled sinisterly. "You couldn't be twenty minutes later I guess?"

Tab looked a little frustrated. "Twenty minutes?" She winked at him. "Maybe thirty." He smiled.

"Don't worry, I can take care of that," Nira said. She said a few words. Her back glowed, and then an obscure barrier appeared. Once Dirk and the three walked to their side of the barrier, they couldn't see or hear Tab and El. He told Nira to remove it for a minute. She did. "Sorry guys, this should make it private. See you in the morning," Dirk said. Tab and El smiled and returned the reply. Nira waved her hand, and the barrier went back up.

Dirk laid the map out after setting up the sleeping bags. "Dirk what do you want to do with the book?" Natia asked. She thought she knew the answer but had to ask.

"I want to see if the four of us can see what happened when I touch the thumbprint of my namesake." He looked around.

"But there is four of us. It might not work," Vira stated.

Dirk nodded. "The connection we four have is strong. I think we can do it." Natia agreed. "But let me warn you, we'll sense their deepest feelings and some of those could be intimate."

Nira smirked at Dirk. "Really, Dirk? Remember we felt … how do you put it…" She looked at Vira and received a smile in return. "Every thrust from you and Natia back at the farm. Intimacy doesn't bother us."

Dirk just laughed. "You're right, I guess we have shared everything since the bond, and I do want to apologize for that," he said sincerely.

Natia grabbed their hands. "Dirk, we love you as deeply as Natia. Anything we have shared with you, no matter what, just makes the bond that much stronger," Vira said. Dirk leaned forward and kissed them both on the forehead. They smiled. "Let's go."

Dirk opened the book and flipped through the pages to where his namesake's thumbprint was. "Let's go see what this great power was, if we can."

They agreed and sat in a circle. Dirk opened the book and laid it in the center. They all held hands except Dirk and Nira. Nira grabbed his arm so he could put his thumb over the blood print.

He looked around and said. "Close your eyes and when I feel we are connected, I'll put my thumb on the print." They all did, and it was an instant link.

Dirk felt the emotions and love from all three girls. He opened his eyes and placed his thumb on the blood print. Every one of them gasped from the connection. It was cloudy at first, then they all were transported back in time. There, in front of them, were two men and an elven female with silver hair. *She's breathtakingly beautiful,* Dirk thought.

There was no doubt who Dirk Storm was. He was Dirk's blue-eyed twin without the pointed ears. Tab's relative was similar to Tab, although shorter. They were walking in a tunnel, each carrying a torch. The cloudiness returned and a minute later they were standing around an underground tomb. The elven female had a silky voice. "I swear the parchment that we read shows this as the tomb."

"But Sorey, I thought it was in a man's tomb. That looks like a woman."

She laughed, then kissed the older Dirk on the lips. *I guess it's natural to have these feelings,* Natia thought. Young Dirk agreed.

"My love, that is a man. The first Maronans all looked similar." He nodded then the clouds came again.

"Run!" Tadon yelled looking back over his shoulder. Dirk and Sorey were running ahead of him with a bag in Dirk's hand.

"We got it! We just have to survive getting out of this tomb alive," Sorey said between gasps. There was a screech and several growls in the background.

Their thoughts clouded again. When they cleared, Dirk and Tadon were standing at the tomb again, both crying. The older Dirk waved his hand and the top of the tomb slid over to the side. He put the bag he had been running with back inside the tomb and closed the top. "She died to save us all," Tadon said with tears in his eyes.

"My love and I will be together again." Dirk had tears rolling down his face.

"Brother, you have to take care of the children now. You must train Alliese so she will be ready," Tadon said. The older Dirk nodded.

The clouds came again and the four came out of the trance at the same time.

They were all crying and clutching each other so tight that their hands were turning white from their grip. Dirk gripped Natia's hand.

"What do you think?" Vira asked, breaking the silence after a few minutes.

Dirk looked up. "I don't know."

"I think that whatever they used was dangerous to get and definitely dangerous to use," Nira said, wiping away her tears.

"You're right. The good thing is the link worked." They all smiled at that.

"That was amazing. She was my great, great grandmother's sister. I've always heard how beautiful she was, but she was breathtaking," Natia said. They all agreed.

Dirk closed the book and set it to the side. "We need to think about the implications it might have. But first we need some sleep. It is so late." The others agreed. "The link was not only emotional, but it was also exhausting," Dirk folded up the map, grabbed the book and put them away. He took off his boots, got into his sleeping bag. Taking off his shirt to Natia's pleasure. She smiled. "Be good," he said. She frowned but nodded and snuggled up next to him.

Tonight, Nira spooned up behind Dirk and Vira did the same to Natia. Dirk smiled at Nira, gave her a kiss on the cheek, and pulled her closer. She laid her head on his shoulder and told him she loved him. Vira echoed the sentiment. Soon the sisters were sleeping. Natia looked sadly into his eyes.

"What is it?" She shook her head and said nothing. "Tell me."

Natia kissed him gently, the taste of tears on her lips. "I would give my life for you, but what she did makes me sad. Make me one promise. If either of us has to die, that we do it together. I don't mean to sound selfish. I just don't want to wait for you in the afterlife. I want you by my side throughout eternity," Natia pleaded.

He kissed her. "I love you with all the essence of my being. I will never leave you alone. I promise that our ending will be the same no matter what." She smiled and closed her eyes.

Dirk was soon fighting the night terrors again. This time, they were a little stronger. It took him longer, but soon the twins were free of the nightmares and sleeping easily. Dirk was soon dreaming of a long tunnel lit by torchlight. Natia, himself, and the twins were running for their lives from what sounded like an angry creature.

Unexpected Help

Linc knew not all of the crew of the *LiTaDi* were happy about leaving on another voyage so soon. Kaz had hooked up with a bar waitress at One-Eyed Jack's named Gretchin. She was a single mom and she and Kaz had hit it off really well. River had wanted to hang out with Flora longer. Corky had actually met Mildred's adopted mother, Ms. Swon, one night at the bar. Jerle was the only other one besides Mildred that was excited to get sailing again.

Everyone accepted Mildred after she showed them how much she knew about sailing and was willing to do whatever the crew needed her to do. Corky really liked her when he found out who she was. He couldn't quit asking her questions about her mom.

Linc was shocked at the armaments on the ship. There were two forward cannons. Two rear cannons and three per side. There was enough ammo for a small war and also swords, shields, and five bows with enough arrows for thirty people. The armory on the ship housed all the gear, four staterooms, a captain's quarters, and a small galley, along with a big cargo hold with three dinghies. The ship was wider and longer than *LiTaDi Flame* but with the way it was set up, four people could handle the ship easily.

"This is pretty awesome," Linc told Mildred after the inspection. She smiled.

"Like I said, this is the best and fastest ship around. Lord Philias likes his comforts," she said.

"Well, the sleeping arrangements should be nice," Linc said casually. He was at the helm, watching the water currents and adjusting his course.

Mildred looked at Linc. "Don't get any ideas, mister." He didn't acknowledge her comment. She walked up and punched him in the arm. "Don't take nothing for granted."

He smiled. "I didn't say anything about sleeping with you. I just said they seemed nice." He looked her in the eye with a mischievous grin. "You're the one that assumed I was talking about us sleeping together." She leered at him and walked off. He smiled to himself. *She thinks she's playing hard to get.*

The sleeping arrangements really didn't matter to Linc. He was starting to get a sensation again that something wasn't right. He stayed at the helm all but four hours the first two days. It wasn't until after they passed the back of Mt Jover on the third day before he could make sense out of what he was hearing and feeling.

The sounds of rattling weapons and shields echoed through the woods. He could hear branches being broken and the guttural cries of beasts as they ran. A large group was paralleling them in the woods close to the bank.

"River, get up in the nest and check out the woods starboard and see if you can make out if we're being followed."

"Aye cap'n," River said shimmying up the ratlines. Linc felt Aarya was close and knew she was concerned. She would be watching. "Can't see anything cap'n. The woods are too thick!" River yelled down.

"Kaz and Jerle, man the bow cannons. Make sure they are ready to fire if need be."

"Aye cap'n," the two said. Mildred went to the armory and grabbed her sword, a set of bows, and a couple bolts of arrows. She walked back up from the armory and handed a set to Linc. He watched her position herself between the starboard cannons, gazing intently into the woods. Linc closed his eyes and started to sense what Aarya was seeing. There it was. What he had sensed.

A band of thirty wood nymphs led by what he figured was a Gore with twelve of his kind as well. The wood nymphs were setting up something a league down the river, close to the bank. It looked like some kind of catapult. They had arrows already aimed and were lighting some kind of ball made of a wood and mud mixture, getting ready to launch it when the ship came into range.

The thirteen-Gore had some kind of barge they were loading onto. He relayed what he saw. "cap'n are you sure? I don't see anything," River yelled down.

"Just keep an eye out. When you see them launch, give me a vector," Linc instructed.

"Yes sir."

"Corky, take the helm." Linc grabbed the arrows and bow Mildred had brought him and stood beside her. He looked her in the eyes. "I'm going to ask you to trust me. If I tell you to do something, do it. okay?"

She stared into his eyes and clearly saw the flames rippling in them. "My life is in your hands," she said, nodding. As Linc started to turn away, she grabbed his elbow. Linc looked back at her. "But after this, you're going to explain that" she said, pointing to his eyes.

He thought for a minute and knew he could trust her. Placing a hand behind her head, he pulled her into a deep kiss, which she didn't resist. "I'll tell you everything after we kill these monsters." She nodded and released his arm and then followed him up to the front of the boat. *Aarya, I'm gonna shoot arrows at the balls of flames when they're coming towards the ship. Can you help destroy them when I do?*

Aarya sent him a vision of an exploding ball.

Yes, he thought back.

In the distance, the crew heard a war cry from a distant bird. Linc smiled. Aarya agreed. "Do what I do," he said to Mildred. She nocked an arrow at the same time he did. "Jerle, get over here and man this cannon. When their little trap comes into view, I want you and Kaz to rain holy hells on them."

He received a nod. It wasn't long before River was yelling, "Incoming! Ten degrees north!" Linc turned and searched in the distance for the flaming ball coming their way. His eyesight was sharpened, thanks to Aarya's bond. He lifted the nocked arrow in the direction of the flaming ball. Mildred copied his movements, seeming to have locked onto it too.

When it got within a few hundred yards and was starting to come down, he released his arrow and Mildred did the same. The arrows soared into the ball at about the same time Aarya blazed through it, destroying it in midair.

Mildred just looked at him. She seemed to come to an understanding of what was going on. "You have magic, don't you?"

He smiled. "You could say that." She smiled, accepting what she had already sensed. They both shot flaming balls out of the sky until they came into full view of the barge full of Gores trying to cut them off. "River, get down here and grab a sword." Jerle and Kaz had started firing cannon balls at the catapult.

After more than a few shots, the catapult was destroyed. The wood nymphs that had survived were all loading into canoes and heading for the ship.

"Start aiming at the canoes," Linc ordered. "You ready?" He looked to Mildred as he drew his sword. Mildred drew out her own twin blades. They were a little bigger than katanas.

"I haven't exactly been honest with you either." Linc turned to look at her, waiting for an explanation. "Well, let's just say, when I told you I had experience on ships with Lord Philias..." Linc nodded, keeping an eye on the approaching barge full of Gore. "This is what we did. We hunted these animals down and killed them. That's why he trained me so well. He wanted me to take over for him one day, keeping the waters safe for merchants. He trained me to kill these creatures."

"There's more to you than meets the eye as well." Linc said, smiling.

"We both need to have a long talk after this."

"Agreed," Linc replied.

At that moment, the cannons started firing. An explosion rocked the ship. Two of the canoes exploded. Wood and body parts flew through the air in all directions. To the dismay of the Gore commander, the third canoe of wood nymphs was retreating to the riverbank.

The Gore's voice was deep and reverberated through the air. "You sleazy cowards!"

"They're big and strong, but slow. Their weak spots are under the chin and the back below their ribs. It's a soft spot," Mildred informed the crew. They were too close for cannon fire now. Ropes with wood hooks were thrown over the rail of the ship as the barge came up alongside them.

Linc and Mildred both fired arrows at it until it was too late. They took out three of the Gore before any of them tried boarding.

"Cut them down before they can come over the rail!" Mildred yelled. Two Gore tried coming over and Linc hacked both down, taking their heads off. Blood splattered all over his body. Their leader shouted an order and two Gore jumped with amazing agility, landing behind Linc and Mildred with a thunderous thud. The ship rocked from the sudden change in weight. They roared at Linc and Mildred.

They don't need any weapons. They're huge, Linc thought. Their teeth were pointed like tiny daggers. Their thick, muscled bodies were covered with black hair, like a cross between a bear and a jungle ape. They used wood weapons with steel-pointed heads. Every swing would cut through a body like butter.

The first one attacked River. Linc blocked the swing before it connected with River's head. River took the moment to thrust up, killing the Gore instantly. Linc turned to see that Mildred and Jerle had downed one a-piece. There was a head rolling around the deck. That left five Gore.

The leader, evidently tired of his group's efforts, landed on the deck. "He's got wings?" Kaz asked, stepping back. He didn't see the one who had just boarded. It roared, Kaz stumbled. It was driving the weapon at Kaz's chest when Corky tackled the creature. Kaz jumped up in time to see Jerle decapitate the Gore.

Kaz looked around and saw that Corky was down. Blood ran down his chest. The Gore had bitten him on the neck before Jerle could get there. Corky waved them off as the last of the Gore boarded the ship. The deck was covered in blood, making it hard for the crew to keep their footing. River slipped just as a weapon came sailing through the air where his head had been.

Kaz blocked the second jab then spun around, using the momentum to stab the Gore under the ribs where Mildred had instructed. The Gore roared, swinging its claws at him as it fell, raking him across the chest. Kaz fell with a sickening thud.

The other Gore went down leaving the leader alone. He was in a battle with Linc and Mildred, who were swapping blows. It wielded two weapons easily. Linc bled from a gash going down his left arm. Mildred had a cut across her left cheek.

Jerle was trying to get behind the Gore, but the Gore kept swinging at him, not letting him pass. Mildred jabbed the Gore in the thigh. The retaliating swing pushed her back.

"Screw this," Linc said tired of the ongoing fight. Jerle caught a claw to the shoulder. He rolled away, clutching his shoulder. Linc pulled out the gem Aarya had given him.

We're with you brother, Linc heard in his mind. He pointed the gem at the beast.

The beast stopped swinging and laughed. "Oh, you're a powerful wizard, are you?" the beast boomed.

Linc smiled, feeling the bonded urge him on. "That's right, ass-breath." His eyes rippled crimson flames. The look of shock on the beast's face was priceless when a crimson beam blasted from the gem, burning a fist-sized hole straight through the beast's chest.

It was dead in an instant. It didn't even have time to roar.

Linc fell to his knees exhausted. Mildred helped him up by his shoulder. "Corky!" River screamed. They ran to Corky's side.

Corky was gasping for each breath. Linc knew he couldn't save Corky, even with help from the bonded. Corky's breathing was getting weaker by the second as he pressed his hands against his neck in an attempt to stop the blood from gushing out. The Gore had ripped a chunk out of it. The hunk of flesh was still in the mouth of the dead Gore.

Linc tore off a piece of his already ripped shirt sleeve and held it over the wound. Jerle came crawling over. Corky looked at Jerle and motioned him closer. "What can I do, Corky?" Jerle asked with tears in his eyes.

River saw Linc was handling Corky, so he hurried over to check on Kaz. River tried to tend to his ripped chest but knew he couldn't do much for him. He could hear Corky struggling with his words. River watched as Corky nodded at Linc. Linc understood.

Corky looked Jerle in the eyes. "I was wrong about you, lad. Thanks for trying..."

His eyes glazed over, and his arms dropped to his side. Jerle started crying.

"Linc, I think Kaz is dying too!" River yelled.

Linc ran to his side. He looked Kaz over. At least he could try and save Kaz. He didn't get to Corky in time, but by the gods, he would save Kaz. He still had the gem in his hand and placed it over Kaz's open wound. Closing his eyes, the gem began to glow. Kaz, who had been gasping for breath and choking on blood, started to heal slowly.

Linc didn't know how long he held the gem there, but he could see Kaz was opening his eyes and trying to sit up. His wounds had healed. *Linc, Linc hold on*, Linc heard in the back of his mind, his vision blurring. He passed out and hit the deck with a thud.

Healing and Explanations

Linc's senses felt off. *Linc, Linc hold on*, was the last thing he had heard.

"Dirk?" Linc asked, trying to clear his head and sit up. He tried opening eyes, but he felt dizzy.

"Take it easy, big fella." Linc felt a pressure on his chest, keeping him from moving. With his vision starting to clear, he realized he was in the captain's quarters, lying on the bed with Mildred sitting at his side, wiping his face with a wet cloth.

"How long?" Linc asked.

"Two days. I was beginning to think I'd lost you," Mildred said, helping him sit up slowly and stuffing a pillow behind his head. At that moment, Aarya flew through the window and landed beside him.

Mildred gasped and sat back a little. "It's okay. She's a friend," Linc said. Mildred nodded and scooted back closer to Linc. Aarya looked up at Mildred and trilled. Linc smiled. "I think so," he said, rubbing her neck. The touch sent healing, rejuvenating waves through him. He closed his eyes and grabbed Mildred's hand. She gasped, feeling the power. He let out a breath, opening his eyes, and smiled. "Thank you Aarya."

She trilled and took off after leaving a message from Dirk. "She healed you completely didn't she?" It was more of a statement instead of a question.

"I think it's time we have that talk." Mildred nodded. Linc told her his tale, leaving out only the part about Tab as they had agreed. Mildred got up and walked to the window, swaying with the ship. She put her hands on the ledge and looked out at the water, the same way Lord Saint had done in his office.

She's taking in everything she just learned, Linc thought. He got up, still a little stiff and sore even after Aarya's healing and walked slowly behind Mildred putting his arms around her waist. "Too much?"

She shook her head and turned around in his arms, putting her hands on his face and looking him in the eyes. "I haven't told you everything about me, so let's wait on judgement until you hear my story."

Linc gazed into those dark gray eyes, "I don't need to know anything else about you. I mean, if you feel you want me to know, then by all means tell me, but I'm falling in love with you and your past don't mean a damn thing to me."

She smiled and kissed him. Then she pulled back. "I will tell you, but we've had enough things revealed on this trip. Let's wait until we secure the boots and head back."

Linc kissed her again. "Ok."

"By the way, you know your butt ass-naked, right?"

He smirked. "I know, but you've seen me naked before." Mildred laughed.

"You're right. I was the one who took your bloody clothes off of you after you passed out." She reached around and grabbed his butt, pulling him closer. She kissed him again, feeling the response she wanted.

"Now's still not the time. I want at least a few hours alone when this happens."

He laughed at her remark. "How's the crew?" he asked, releasing her, and getting dressed.

"They're still a little freaked out. They decided to go ahead and give Corky's body back to the sea."

Linc nodded. He would say his goodbyes when he felt he could. He had grown to like the crusty old sailor. "You healed Kaz completely. Jerle's shoulder could probably use some of that healing magic but, other than that, River's taken over giving orders in your absence. No more attacks, which is good sign because that means word must have got out by the fleeing wood nymphs to keep away from us with the way we decimated their raiding party." Linc, now dressed, sat on the bed, and put on his favorite boots.

"Aarya took them out after they made it back to the riverbank," Linc said, picking up the letter from Dirk.

Mildred's jaw dropped open amazed. "She's very useful to have around."

"Very." Then he read the letter and smiled. "You won't believe this."

"Where did you get that?" Mildred said pointing to the letter Linc was reading.

"Aarya," Linc said, seeing the shock on Mildred's face. "She carries messages between us when something is urgent."

"Like I said, very useful. So, what won't I believe?" Mildred asked.

"One of Dirk's roommates is Phil Wark, the son of the man who made these marvelous boots." They both smiled at that. "He has sent a letter to his father, introducing us, and asked him for an order of boots on top of what we want to buy, and he told his father he can trust us." They both were excited about this turn of events.

"Well, maybe we can be real partners now," Mildred said. Linc got up and grabbed her hand. "I had already decided whether this worked out or not, to make you my partner."

"I know," she said. He didn't tell her the rest. He figured that could wait until after they got the boots and were heading to Silver City. "Come on, you have some explaining to do to your crew and then you need to heal Jerle."

"Ok let's go," Linc followed her up to the top deck. The crew was glad to see he was okay.

"Thanks cap'n. You saved my life," Kaz shook Linc's hand.

'If you hadn't killed that beast, we would all be dead. Thanks Linc." River replied with Jerle agreeing.

Linc walked over to Jerle and pulled out the crystal. "Stay still Jerle. Let me fix your wound." Jerle nodded as Linc placed the gem over Jerle's wound. He closed his eyes, and the gem began to glow. Healing Jerle was a lot easier this time since he was fully restored.

Linc then told the crew an abbreviated story of Dirk and the legacy he had inherited. He told of how he had gained his powers through Aarya, who was perched on the wheel at the helm. The guys were all little overwhelmed, especially River, but they accepted what had happened and why.

After checking on the cleanup from the fight, Linc took over to give River a break. When night came, he was still there. Mildred came out and just stood by his side. She wrapped an arm around his waist and leaned against him.

"What's next," Mildred asked.

"We continue to Pineral and get that trade agreement. Then after that we will decide."

Mildred kissed his cheek. "I trust you and whole heartedly agree. We get that contract first, Then we'll see what's next."

The Miraga Stones

Dirk woke up sweating and breathing hard. Natia sat up and put a hand on his back. "Did you see it?"

Natia shook her head. Vira and Nira woke up drenched in sweat as well. The only one not totally drenched was Natia. She looked at them. "What was it?"

"Either it was a nightmare or a vision. I don't know. We were running down that tunnel that our relatives were in," Dirk said, looking at Vira and Nira expectantly.

"That's what we saw. It was so real. I thought we were gonna die," Nira said.

"I was so scared something horrendous was chasing us," Vira said.

"Did you see what it was?" Natia asked, a little disappointed that she didn't have the dream.

"No, all I know is that it was huge and the sounds it made sent fear through every bone in my body," Dirk said, trembling. Natia looked at the twins, who were trembling as well. She pulled them into a group hug and sent a wave of confidence through their connection.

"Thanks. I needed that," Dirk said. The girls thanked her too.

"Why do you think I wasn't in there?"

Dirk shook his head. "Natia, you were there. I don't know why you didn't dream it with us, but you were there. I think maybe you might have had the dream but just don't remember it," Vira said, getting up and taking off her sweat soaked clothes. She had her back to Dirk, so she didn't think anything about it. Dirk, not thinking anything about it either, got a good look at the gems that had been embedded into her back. They were glowing lightly. He squeezed Natia's hand to assure her that there was a reason she didn't remember.

He's probably right, she thought.

Dirk turned his attention back to Vira's back. "Vira, do the gems in your back glow all the time?" He walked up to take a closer look. Natia was right beside him.

"No, not unless our power is being accessed," Nira said, standing beside them. "Oh no!" She took off her soaked clothes. "Dirk, look at mine."

Dirk and Natia both looked at Nira's back. Vira turned to look at her sister's back. "They're glowing also," Dirk said, running his fingers over the implanted stones.

"Are they warm?" Nira asked.

"A little. Vira, turn around."

She did and Natia ran her fingers over Vira's gems. "They are too. What does it mean?"

Vira physically trembled. Her eyes opened wide in fear "It can't be him," She said, biting her lip looking at Nira.

Nira lowered her head. "He is supposed to be in Aarkas." Dirk and Natia just looked at the two.

Dirk was getting frustrated. He grabbed the twins by the shoulders. "What the hells are you talking about?" Vira sighed.

Nira looked at him. "There was someone accessing our thoughts. That's why the stones are glowing and warm," Vira said.

"And there is only one dark wizard powerful enough to do that. The wizard who put them there when we were younger," Nira said, wrapping her arms around her stomach as if she was gonna be sick. Dirk hadn't really thought about the sisters being naked up until that point because Nira's boobs seemed to grow out of nowhere, her arms wrapped around her stomach.

Dirk turned away. "Ah ladies, I love you like sisters, you know… but maybe before you finish, you can put some fresh clothes on." The girls finally realized why Dirk said what he did. Natia hadn't really thought about it either until Dirk mentioned it.

"Ladies, though you both have gorgeous bodies, I believe he is right." Natia smiled.

Vira and Nira laughed, easing a little of their fear. "Sorry brother, you know we don't think anything of it. You're our brother."

Dirk laughed. "I honestly didn't either until Nira put her arms under them and it kind of brought attention to the fact." Dirk turned as the girls bent over to get a change of clothes. He smiled at Natia and she smiled back before Dirk slapped both of them on their bare asses.

"Ow!" they both said rubbing the spot where Dirk had slapped them.

"I will say, though, very cute asses." He smiled at them.

"You'll pay for that," Vira said mischievously while putting her clothes on.

"Brother, payback is a bitch." Nira smiled at him. Dirk held his hands up in surrender.

"My love, I think it's too late for that and you deserve whatever they dish out," Natia said, laughing.

"All right but I'll keep a watch on you two," he said, trying to calm them down a little more. The girls sat down. "Tell me about this dark wizard."

Vira took a deep breath and the group all grabbed hands. "Asher. He's the wizard who put these gems in our backs when we were young. Back then, he was one of the faction leaders on Aarkas. He was our faction's leader, to be specific.

"He came up with the idea of infusing gems in children's backs. He always thought that they would bind with the young person's core easily and make them grow stronger and more powerful as they grew older. In the beginning, there were forty of us kids in our faction around the same age. He took us all and tested his theory on us," Tears filled her eyes. She took a shaky breath and continued.

"Dirk, he's the one who killed our parents. They didn't want anything to do with his crazy ideas so when he came to take us, they resisted. He and four of his council destroyed our home and obliterated Mom and Dad. There was nothing left of them when those evil bastards were through,"

Dirk already knew parts of the story from the bond. He hugged Vira as she cried freely now. Natia squeezed the girl's hands for support. "I am so sorry," Dirk said, feeling their pain. It caused his anger to rise. "We can stop."

The twins both shook their heads. "No, you have to know what he is capable of now," Nira said, finishing the story. "After he killed our parents, they took us to the main village. He put us in one of the buildings where he conducted all of his experiments. I don't know how long we were out for the procedure but when we awoke, we had these in our backs. The pain was excruciating. I know we told Tab there was no pain. But I didn't want him to worry about us. He was so sincere when he asked that night if it hurt." Vira lowered her head.

"Neither of you need to worry about that. I am sure Tab would understand why you didn't feel the need to tell us." Dirk squeezed their shoulders affectionately.

Vira and Nira nodded. "So he told us he would use magic to reduce the pain, but we had no way of knowing whether he did or not because it hurt really bad for several weeks. After we were healed enough, he started testing us. It didn't work at first. Several of the kids died in the first few days of testing, and over the next month, all but six of us died. I don't know why anyone else survived, but being twins, Vira and I together have always been stronger than most. He trained us to link with the gems and use that connection to touch our core and release the power by focusing on an object. We were the best out of the group that had survived.

"The others were successful, but not like Vira and me. I mean Raven one of our friends was doing good but not as good as us. After a year, we could pretty much control every aspect of the elements. Raven, who we thought we could trust, turned out to be his favorite student. She did everything he wanted. Even helped when it came time to dish out punishment to the ones who didn't act the way Asher wanted them to. It still hurts that she turned on us the way she did."

Dirk squeezed their hands. "Sisters, you know we will never turn on you." He had tears in his eyes.

"We know Dirk," Nira said, squeezing his hand back. Seeing that the girls were settled now, Dirk asked them to continue. "Then one day, out of nowhere, our grandfather showed up, demanding to see us. Asher refused him at first until grandfather, who was a powerful wizard himself, showed his strength by defeating two of his main apprentices. He threatened to kill all of them if he didn't get to see his granddaughters. He told Asher that he needed to know we were ok. Asher finally agreed, but before he let us see him, he told us that we would never escape him. He was speaking about the gems in our backs. He said he would always know where we were and how to find us. He then showed us his back. He had twice as many gems in his back as we did. He caused pain through the connection. It was a blinding pain that made us fall to our knees. We told him we understood, and then he let us see Grandfather. As soon as we saw him, we both ran to him and hugged him. He grabbed our hands and told us to hold on.

"We vanished in an instant. He had transported us to the far side of the island. He gave us these bracelets to put on just as soon as we appeared," Nira said, looking at her empty wrist. "Grandfather said it would keep Asher from finding us. He then raised us for the next seven years, teaching us about Zona and the good in the world.

"We moved around and stayed far away from Asher. We heard that he had finally won over the rest of the council. At least the ones he didn't kill. He became the High Dark Wizard over our people. When Grandfather heard about this, he finally decided to get us off the island. He paid a pirate friend of his to smuggle us here,"

Nira wiped her eyes. Dirk's and Natia's eyes were blazing now. They both knew most of the story, but to hear it with the twin's emotion sickened them both.

"You think that bastard is the one who caused the dream we had last night?"

Vira nodded. "Vira, do you think he is the one who causes your and Nira's night terrors?" Natia asked.

"I believe he has gained the ability not just to do that, but somehow he was able to read our thoughts while terrorizing us. That's probably how he found out about you and Natia," Nira said.

Vira nodded. "He can probably sense how we feel about you two now since we bonded. That also means he has probably stolen some information as well. That's the only way he would have known about the tomb passageways."

Dirk, finally letting the flames in his eyes ease up, had a thought. "I bet he can only get pieces of what we share since the only thing I remember is the hallway and nothing else from the dream."

Vira and Nira looked at him. "You're right."

Dirk nodded and looked out over the city. The sun was coming up. He closed his eyes and let the sun warm his face. "Can you block him?"

"I don't know," Vira said.

"I bet Hermosa or Nabas would know how," Natia added. "What happened to the bracelets your grandfather gave you?"

Vira frowned. "We left them on the island. We didn't feel we needed them anymore," Nira said.

They all looked at Natia, considering what she had said about Hermosa. "I was thinking the same thing," Vira said with a smile. Nira agreed.

At that moment, all four of them felt a plea for help. Dirk laughed. "Nira, can you lower the barrier? I believe Tab and El are ready to come out."

She nodded, mumbled the usual words, and waved her hand at the barrier. It glowed briefly and then Tab and El were standing there, looking frantic.

"It's about god's damn time," Tab said.

"We have been trying to get out for the last thirty minutes," El said.

Dirk just shrugged. "You wanted privacy and you got it."

She glared at him and pointed that motherly finger at him. "I bet you have been laughing at us the whole time." They all shook their heads and Dirk told them about what had happened when they touched the thumbprint in the Book of Storms.

After they discussed those feelings, he told them about their dreams and what he had been doing to help the twins with the night terrors.

"That's amazing. Think of what we can do with the bonded," El said, staring at Dirk, who nodded.

Vira then told them about what they discovered about the Dark Wizard and their night terrors. This had Tab wound up now. He, like Dirk, couldn't wait to find Asher and, as Tab put it, "Kick his Dark Wizard ass." Nira and El calmed him down and promised he would probably get the chance.

"I am sorry we lied to you Tab. You were just so sweet. We didn't want you worrying any more than you seemed to already be doing," Vira replied.

Tab hugged the twins. "Sisters I understand. But you know you can tell me anything. I am here for you." Tab kissed them both on the forehead.

Dirk hadn't told the twin's whole story. He saved that for them to share if and when they wanted. El forced herself into the conversation. She hugged them and asked what the plan was to fight against Asher entering their dreams. They explained they didn't know but they were going to ask Hermosa.

El agreed that would be the best course of action. She then looked out over the city. "It's beautiful up here."

"Yes, it is."

"Look, you can see our tree from here," She pointed in the direction of the hill. Dirk hadn't notice that before. He smiled at the hill. El got up and walked to the wall ledge. The rest of the group followed her. Dirk stepped up beside her and put an arm around her.

If anyone would have been able to see the roof of the tower at that moment, they would have seen a strange sight. Six young adults, arm in arm, leaning over the edge.

Dirk kissed El on the cheek. "You look radiant this morning." She had a glow about her.

She leaned her head against his. "This is one of those moments."

The twins agreed. "Most definitely, El."

Natia couldn't read their thoughts. "El, please explain,"

El looked at them and then back to the tree. "This is one of those life moments where you'll always remember the moment in time and the place you were at and who you were with. I mean, here we are looking at our favorite spot from one of our favorite spots and being with the ones we love the most in the world." She turned, and Tab looked at her, smiling. She kissed him.

Dirk smiled. "Ah I understand." Natia finally understood. She had that special moment also. She turned and looked Dirk in the eyes.

The twins pulled them all into a hug. "I'm afraid this feeling will be a fleeting one if we don't take care of what we have been charged to do," Dirk said somberly.

"Natia still gazing into his eyes "That's why we must and will win my love."

"Anyone else hungry?" Tab asked. Everyone laughed.

"You're always hungry, brother," Nira said to Tab. He just shrugged and they all headed downstairs to grab some breakfast before their morning exercises.

Later that morning, when everyone except Volar had made it on time running the trail, the group, including Skylar and her friends ran it again. Dirk could hear Skylar explaining to Sylvie, "If we don't we'll become total lepers, and I am starting to feel tired of not getting along with the rest of our class. I mean, this whole 'me against the world' thing is tiring." Dirk wondered if it was a ploy because she said it pretty loud, but he decided to let time tell the tale. They finished in time for a shower before class.

They ran into Laseous on their way to Hermosa's class. "Mr. Storm, a word." Dirk felt his eyes start to flame. Natia squeezed Dirk's hand, silently telling him to calm down. After the rest of the group had passed by, Laseous stepped closer. "Mr. Storm, I hear your little special class is going on an excursion today," he said, his words dripping with disdain.

Dirk, not wanting to end up in detention, just said, "Yes sir."

Laseous scowled. "Why?"

"Sir?" Dirk asked.

"Don't be daft, boy. Why are you going on a field excursion?"

Dirk now knew why he had stopped him. He figured he would get under his skin and it would cause him to blow up, so he had a reason to put him in detention again.

"Sir, you need to ask Wizard Hermosa that question. It was her idea anyway," Dirk said.

Laseous turned three shades of red at that answer. He pointed his finger, almost poking Dirk in the chest. He then turned and stormed off. Dirk laughed inside and ran to Hermosa's class.

Hermosa was waiting for Dirk in the hall. "What did that weasel want?" she asked. Dirk told her what he asked. "He did, huh?" She patted Dirk on the back. "You did well. You know not to trust him, right?"

Dirk nodded.

"Good. Hurry up then and get in to class." Vira and Natia had saved a seat between them for him. He sat down and waited on the announcement that he and the girls already knew was coming. "Class, I have had the discussion with Wizard Nabas about your planned training trip." She paused for effect. "He has approved it with the added blessing of the king and General Storm."

The class erupted into cheers. She smiled, letting them enjoy their victory.

After a few minutes, she calmed them down. "Next Sunday evening, we will depart for the Forgotten City, but there is a lot we have to do first, so I need every one's undivided attention." She then laid out the week.

After Hermosa explained the plans and who was responsible for what, they left the school and went to the stables. They got a wagon for hauling the stones with two horses. Hermosa climbed up in the wagon and taking the reins. "Everyone, follow me," she said, as the wagon moved forward. The class followed her to the northern trail.

The kids had all gone to the lunch hall and picked up a travel lunch from Ms. Heloise for the trip. Hanks had waved at Dirk and Tab and told them to come see him soon.

The group walked behind Wizard Hermosa, laughing the whole way because she sang almost the entire time. She had a good voice. Dirk had never heard the song before. It was about a woman who had lost her love to a war.

It took them forty minutes to get Blazire and as soon as they did, she made them eat their lunch before they got started. After a lunch, which consisted of a beef sandwich and water, Vira and Nira showed them the rock to look for.

The group, at Hermosa's instruction, paired up and headed out in search of the rocks. It took them four hours to gather nearly a hundred stones. Vira and Nira told them that what they had gathered would be sufficient.

As they headed back, a shadow passed above them, and they all looked up. Aarya was flying overhead. "She'd probably been there the whole time," Dirk said.

"She is very protective," Tab said. Aarya landed on the wagon seat by a surprised Hermosa. After the surprise wore off, she smiled and petted the phoenix's neck, receiving a trill in response. She stayed with Hermosa until they were a few miles from town. Trilling one more time, she took off.

They got back in time for dinner. Hermosa told them to work with Hilda and Tilda tonight on the travel plans and report the status tomorrow. They had four days to get ready. Dirk was mad at himself for forgetting to give Aarya the letters for Linc and Mr. Wark. He knew he could call her back but was sure he would see her again soon.

That night the whole group came up on the roof to learn how to create the Miraga Stones. It was a three-step process, but they told the group that everyone could help with the first two steps which would make things go faster. The third step could only be done by the twins themselves. Chipping the stones into round objects was the first step. The twins had already laid out the tools to do this. The second step was to smooth them using the gem-smoothing wheel they had set up. All they had to do was pump the wheel with the attached pedal, smoothing the stone until a glassy outer shell formed. The twins had demonstrated this step.

They had explained to Dirk beforehand that they weren't willing to share their knowledge on the third step of knowledge yet. Dirk knew the twins were aware someone would betray them, so he was glad they wanted to keep that information for a select few. Soon after the explanation, they all got started and spent the next three hours working on the stones.

The group was able to get over half of the stones rounded that night. Hilda and Tilda met with the nine bonded and told them their main priority should be working as one to practice on their barrier protection magic, moving on to attacks with wind, water, lightning, and fire.

"You aren't coming with us?" Dirk asked, surprised.

"We need to stay here and make sure the stones stay active," Hilda said. Dirk wasn't expecting that. His sadness showed when tears formed in his eyes. Hilda pulled him into a hug. "You'll be fine."

"I don't know if I can do it without you. It's been us from the start of this journey," he said emotionally, wiping away tears. Tilda came over and pulled Dirk away from Hilda, hugging him herself. She held him in front of her looking him over.

"Dirk, your father is in you. There was nothing Diron couldn't do. He believed in himself. That was his strongest power. Now you remember whatever happens, promise me you will believe in yourself as much as we believe in you as much we did your father." She kissed Dirk on the forehead. "We have grown to love you as we did your father, and we have no doubt that you will succeed. Believe in yourself."

Dirk nodded and pulled both of them close. "I'll miss you."

Hilda laughed. "Well, Dirk, you'll only be gone for a month or two. We will be here when you get back."

He nodded, but down deep inside, Dirk knew after he left on the trip, he would never see them again. He didn't know why. He just felt it.

That night, instead of faking where they would sleep, they had brought their sleeping gear to the roof with them. Dirk said goodnight to the group and went up with the others. Even El and Tab didn't pretend.

The stones on the roof had been separated, stage one and stage two, into piles off to the side. El, whose power had been getting stronger, waved her hand and the fire blazed to life. Her bracelet didn't even need to be used. Dirk was amazed at how she had grown.

She started to get undressed next to the sleeping bags that Tab had set up, stripping down to her undergarments without a thought. Dirk knew that was one of the side effects of the bond. Modesty was almost gone from the bonded. Tab was doing a similar thing, though he was a little more discreet. Vira and Nira, who had taken over the duties of getting their pallet ready had almost finished. Dirk just stared at El in awe. The little girl who had been so motherly to him and the boys since they were young had grown into a young and beautiful woman. He smiled.

"El," Dirk said. El turned and looked at him. She had no top on, and she was barely able to cover her breasts with her hands. They were bigger than the average girl their age. Her legs were toned from the training they all had been going through.

She had also started to let her hair grow longer over the past month. Her blonde hair was past her shoulders and she had begun to braid it similar to Natia. When she had turned without moving her hands, Dirk had no doubt that Tab was a lucky man.

"Well are you gonna gawk or speak?" she asked, sensing Dirk was seeing her as a woman for the first time.

He snapped out of his admiration. "I just wanted to say that I think you have grown into a breathtakingly gorgeous woman and I love you, sister. I haven't told you lately and I wanted to make sure you knew how I felt. Thank you for everything you have done, and I appreciate your sacrifices that you've made."

She turned around and put on a sleeping shirt, then ran over to Dirk, who was sitting in one of the chairs, she sat in his lap and wrapped her arms around his neck, nearly breaking it from squeezing it so hard. He felt tears on his neck.

"You're right. I needed to hear that from you. I have felt the last few days that we are getting kind of distant. Not in a bad way, but I don't feel that we spend enough time together anymore." She pushed him back to look in his eyes. All eyes were on them. "I love you, but we're starting to group up, it seems. Even though we are bonded, we have to stay strong together as one, not as groups."

Tab came over and kneeled down beside her. "El, you're right. We need to stay strong together." Natia kneeled down on the other side while Vira and Nira squeezed into the circle.

"I agree, El. We need to stay united together, not as groups," Dirk said, wiping away his own tears. "I am sorry I'm so sensitive tonight." He looked away from them and at the stars, trying not to let his emotions get the better of him. Finally composed, he turned back. "Hilda and Tilda told me they weren't coming with us."

Natia cocked her head. "You will see them when we come back," Natia said. He looked into those amber eyes and then at his closest friends. He knew he needed to tell them what he was feeling.

"I don't know how to say what I'm about to say, but I need to say it. Just listen before you say anything. Ok?" he asked, waiting for a response.

El, still sitting in his lap, gave him a stern look. "Spill it." God, he loved

El's demeanor.

"I've had a dread growing in me." Dirk picked El up, kissed her cheek, then sat her in his chair. He knelt down between Natia and Vira, grabbing their hands' and the group all did the same with each other. "Let me show you. I want you to close your eyes and link with me."

They all did as he asked. The fear deep inside of Dirk was felt by all almost instantly since he wasn't blocking it anymore. Vira gasped and Nira squeezed her hand really tight. "Do you feel it?" They all opened their eyes and nodded. "I thought you would. El, I'm glad you said what you did. I wasn't going to mention it until you said that you felt we were growing apart. I know that's not exactly what you said, but that is what you meant."

She nodded. "I'm sorry. I used to have all of you boys to myself, and it's not that I'm jealous of you, Natia, Vira, and Nira. At least not since the bond. I love you dearly as I do Dirk. It's just felt different the last few days and I miss you, Dirk. I know you have been right here, but you feel far away," El said, lowering her gaze."

Dirk smiled at her. "Go ahead."

She wiped away some tears. "I am here for you as well, don't forget that." Dirk nodded.

"I think that something or someone has been causing these feelings," Vira replied.

"You think the Dark Wizard Asher is doing this?" Tab asked.

Dirk shook his head. "I think it's something more powerful than him, but it could be. I don't know if it's a warning or someone using powerful magic to cause me to feel this way," Dirk said with uncertainty.

"Dirk do you think the Chosen of the past are sending us a warning like the one your father sent?' Natia asked.

"I think so. I think they are sending us a warning that danger is coming. I think we shouldn't ignore it."

"What do you want to do about it?" Natia asked.

"I think we should warn as many people as we can to stay vigilant. El, you should tell your parents before we leave. Tab I think you need to tell Mother Agnes as well. We should give a warning to everyone we care about. Tell them that at the first sign of danger that they need to head to the farm," Dirk said, staring out at the city.

"Do you want me to tell my parents everything?"

Dirk nodded. "El, think about it. Who is the best smith in all of Marona? Do you think the king would trust anyone but your father to make the bracelets we wear?"

El thought about it for a minute. "You're right. He has to know about your family's legacy."

Dirk smiled at her realization. "But they don't know about you. You need to tell them just in case." She agreed. Tab joined in and said he would tell everyone that needed to know in the city, especially River's family and Mr. Burke.

"Something is coming, and Father said there would be a sign. I think this is it. I don't know how long we have but it will happen soon."

"Are you going to tell your grandfather and Mom?" Tab asked.

Dirk said he would before they left. Dirk looked at Tab and Tab knew what Dirk was going to say next.

"I am going to tell Moira as well. At least one of the students will know and be able to keep an eye out. I trust her Tab, and before you argue with me you know I'm right."

Tab shook his head. "Just make sure she knows not to blow it out of proportion. We don't need all of the students going crazy or thinking we're crazy," Tab said, smiling.

"I'll handle it brother."

"I believe in you Dirk, and with what we had happen last night, I believe you are right about all of it," Vira said. She looked at the group. "We really need to finish as many stones as we can before we leave."

"I agree," Dirk said.

"We can teach you how to finish the Miraga stones. It should be easy with us being bonded and we should be able to make them faster," Nira said. They all agreed.

"Well, let's get some rest for now and make sure we get the other bonded involved tomorrow. No one else yet, though, for now. If I'm wrong I don't won't the teachers and others who have supported us to lose faith in our mission," Dirk said, and they all agreed.

"Do you need a barrier tonight, El?"

El looked at Nira. "We're good." She smiled and went over to the other side of the fire with Tab.

"Are you sure about this?" Natia asked. Dirk looked at her. She had laid down beside him.

"Put your lips on mine, and don't move once you do." Natia did as he asked. Once their lips touched, Dirk let his consciousness slip into hers. Natia was overwhelmed by the feelings she received from him.

The responsibility of their safety. The love he had for her and his friends made tears run down her cheeks. Then he fully shared the dread he had inside. The darkness was there but still felt distant. Natia noticed it was growing bigger. She sensed something else, also. It was distant as well, but it was clearly a light. It was pulsing like a beacon.

Do you sense it more clearly now? Dirk's thoughts filled her own.

I do.

The beacon pulsed brighter for a few minutes then it was gone. Natia, having seen enough pulled away from Dirk. She stared deeply into his eyes. "How long has this been happening?"

Dirk was consumed by Natia's beauty. He had to look away to answer. "It started after Father appeared."

Natia turned his face so he'd look at her. "And you didn't tell me?" She rubbed his chest.

"I didn't know at first if it was real, or if I was imagining it. That is why I didn't say anything."

Natia kissed him. "I understand but, like El said, we're in this together, so no more keeping things to yourself."

He smiled. "The light is the warning of the darkness approaching, I believe."

"I agree," Natia said.

"Dirk, if we are going to make Miraga Stones tomorrow I need some sleep," Nira said, laying her head on his shoulder.

"Point taken. We can discuss this tomorrow. By the way, what did Hermosa tell you about keeping Asher out of our heads?"

"I almost forgot." Vira, got up, and grabbed her bag. She handed all of them a leaf that was shaped like a white oak leaf. "It's the white Enda leaf. She told me it will stop certain functions of the brain that control our imagination. The only side effect is slight grumpiness. Just chew it up and don't swallow it. Spit it out before you go to sleep, or you'll make several trips to the bathroom for a while." She snickered.

They all chewed it. "Argh, this taste like horse dung!" Dirk's face twisted as if he was in pain. He looked at everyone and they too agreed with his sentiment. Dirk couldn't take it anymore and spit the chewed-up leaf into the fire. The others followed suit.

"Pass me a water skin, Vira." She did, and he drank some and shared it with the group.

"I hope we come up with something better than this. That was awful," Nira said.

"Let's see if it works first," Dirk said, laying down with his three girls. He smiled at that thought. They were his girls. It made him happy. He always wanted a sister. Now he had two. The woman he loved was also in his arms.

Dirk, Vira, and Nira had their best night's sleep in days. No night terrors came. They just had a good night's sleep with no dreams.

Dirk woke before the sun came up. Nira had slept so hard that she had drooled all over his shoulder. "Sorry," she said wiping it off with her shirt.

"It's okay. I slept great! How about you?"

Nira stretched. "It's been a long time since I slept so good."

"I can't believe I slept so good," Vira said, stretching.

Natia frowned. "At least you three did. I had two of you snoring in my ears all night."

Dirk feigned innocence.

"Well, it wasn't Nira," she said grumpily. Dirk patted her shoulder.

"Someone is suffering from the Enda leaf I believe." Natia scowled and got up to take a shower. "I'll see you at breakfast."

Dirk was shocked at the abruptness. "Do either of you feel edgy?"

They shook their heads. "Nope, I feel fine," Vira said, scooting over and putting her head on Dirk's shoulder.

"I do as well. Actually, I feel great," Dirk said, wrapping his arms around the twins.

"I wonder why she is so edgy and we're not?" Vira asked.

"I don't know, but you know how she is. Better let her get it out of her system," Dirk said. They talked for a little while before they decided to go get ready for the day. El and Tab got up as well and went with them.

Dirk showered and then went to breakfast with the rest of the guys and girls from class. He smiled when he saw Natia. She smiled back when she saw him. She walked up and grabbed his hand. "Feeling better?"

She nodded. They ate a light breakfast and headed to the training field for their daily run.

After everyone did the morning stretching drills Sergeant Giles gathered everyone around. "Today we'll be advancing to the harder trail. The only difference in time. You have thirty minutes to the halfway point, then only twenty-five back." A chorus of complaints started and ended abruptly when Sergeant Giles put his hands on his hips.

"I know how tough it can be, but like I said in the beginning, your training will step up. The same rules apply. Anyone who doesn't make it back in time get ready to run it again." He took off without giving them time for questions.

Dirk picked up his pack and felt it was noticeably heavier. He just looked at Gil and they both shrugged. No one bothered complaining anymore because it would do no good. Everyone struggled with the run.

The new course was much steeper, and the terrain was more treacherous with smaller trails and bigger obstacles, such as jagged rocks and vines that they had to duck under. The vines had razor-sharp thorns on them that cut several of the students, including Dirk and Tab. Everyone except Volar made it on time so when he started running the trail again, everyone in the class followed suit without complaining, even Skylar and her friends.

Dirk thought back to what she said. *Maybe she was being sincere and not playing her usual game. Time will tell,* he thought.

After the grueling two runs, any effects Natia had from the Enda leaf were gone. Walking back to get changed for class, Natia couldn't explain why she had been so irritated. "I guess it was just the effects of the leaf. I wanted to rip all three of your heads off. For no reason."

Dirk laughed. I'm glad you didn't." He smiled and rubbed her shoulder.

"Me too." She kissed him and told him she would see him at class.

Dirk was getting excited, but he was still nervous about their plans. He knew a lot was riding on him and his friends. He definitely didn't want to let anyone down, especially since the decisions he made could mean life or death.

In class, they went over where they stood with preparations for the trip. As the supplies were getting sorted and ready, the training they would go through was still being discussed. The status of the Miraga Stones was deemed important enough that Vira and Nira were dismissed to go work on them.

Hermosa informed the class that Helena was being brought along to help with the training. Dirk didn't mind. He liked her, and she was smart. Wizard Stefano would also be coming as well to strengthen the group's healing abilities.

Dirk got a surprise when Hermosa said that the military first-years had been chosen to meet with Anastasia and Kal to start their group training as well. Fifty second-years and first-years were chosen through their merits and ability. The only concern for Dirk was that Brock had been picked.

He was very skilled when it came to the fighting, but Dirk questioned his trust. Hermosa guaranteed him that the vital information of the mission would be kept from most of the cadets.

After lunch, they were just starting to practice with combining their core with sword and shield defenses when, all of a sudden, Dirk and Tab both grabbed their arms, yelling out in pain.

"Dirk, Tab, what's wrong?" Hermosa asked concerned.

Dirk kneeled down on the floor, dropping his shield. Tab dropped beside him, laying his sword down. They looked at each other and then closed their eyes trying to calm their breathing.

"Linc is in trouble," Dirk said. The bonded quickly gathered around, sensing the danger. "All of you join hands with us and form a circle." Dirk ordered. Vira and Nira came busting through the door.

"Linc!" Vira said.

"We know. Join the circle." Natia grabbed Vira's hand and Nira sat on the other side of Dirk between him and Tab. "Everyone, link with me and let me guide our thoughts."

They did and when Dirk thought of Linc, he felt the group join in his thoughts. *Linc, we're with you.* Dirk sent the image to Linc.

The group collectively gasped as they all connected with Linc and could see through his eyes. Linc was fighting a humongous Gore. The girl with Linc had been knocked away. One of his crew was holding his neck. Another was holding his chest. Another crewmate had just taken a Gore's head off.

Dirk felt Linc grab a crimson stone out of his pocket. The Gore was laughing at Linc.

Linc let us focus the beam combined. Let us guide you.

Let's kill this big bastard, Linc thought back. Linc held out the crimson stone.

The beast laughed. "Oh, you're a powerful wizard, are you?" Aarya's trill filled the group with calm and certainty. They felt Linc smile and the urge from Aarya. Hermosa was watching and listening the best she could.

What she was witnessing had never been recorded in history, for that fact even been done.

"That's right, ass-breath!" the group said with Linc. They all wanted the gore dead. Their joined power released the stone's magic and they watched in awe as the crimson beam cut through the shocked Gore's chest. The look on the Gore's face was priceless. Linc fell to his knees. Their combined power had left him drained.

Take deep breaths and let us feed you energy, El thought to Linc.

"Corky!" They heard River scream. They felt Linc get up and walk to Corky's side.

We can't help him, brother. Sorry, Vira said. It looked to the group that Corky had died. Linc looked to River. He was trying to stop a crewmate's chest wound from bleeding, but he looked to be in dire straits. Linc ran to River's side. One clear thought came through the bond.

Help me!

Vira took over for Linc. *Let me guide you through this.* Linc agreed and laid the stone on the crewman's stomach.

He could feel Vira, Nira, and El guide him though the healing. The sailor was getting better right before their eyes, but Dirk could feel Linc slipping into darkness.

Don't stop, Linc pleaded.

It might kill you brother, Tab relayed

It doesn't matter. It's my fault.

No, Linc, it's not. The darkness is rising. You should be able to feel it.

I sensed something but didn't know what it was.

They could see Linc was at his limit. The crewman started to come around just in time. The group felt Linc's vision blur then the impact of him hitting the deck.

Hang on, brother. We'll heal you. All you need is sleep, Natia communicated.

Hold on, Linc!

After a few minutes of sending him energy, they let go. *Hold on, brother,* was the last thing Dirk thought before their connection was lost. The group all exhaled when the connection was broken, and they opened their eyes at the same time, looking at each other and smiling. Every one of them were drenched in sweat.

Hermosa, who had been watching with anxiety, said, "Well, don't just sit there. Tell me what happened." Natia stood up and helped Dirk to his feet. The rest of the group got up as well.

Volar spoke up. "May I explain?"

Dirk, feeling drained himself, said, "Be my guest."

Volar told the experience from start. The whole group added in their own feelings they had during the experience when they felt they needed to. Hermosa was so overwhelmed she called Nabas and Helena to the classroom. She recapped what Volar and the group had shared.

Nabas was excited by the news. He asked about what they sensed when it was happening. He asked each member of the group. They all said they had similar experiences except Vira and Nira. They seemed to have a clearer memory of the surroundings on the ship.

"Like what?" Nabas asked the twins.

They looked at each other. *Dirk is it okay to discuss what we realized about Mildred?*

Go ahead just don't give too much detail about Mildred. I sensed that she has special abilities.

We did too. That's why we asked.

Everything else is okay then.

"There were dead wood nymphs floating in the water around the ship." This made Tab pay closer attention to what Vira was saying as he thought about the small run-in with those creatures months ago. "There was some kind of destroyed weapon like a catapult on the bank, and there were destroyed projectiles of some sort floating in the water as well."

Nabas shook his head. "Anything else?"

Vira spoke before Nira could answer. "No that was it," she said, staring at Nira, who agreed finally.

Nabas looked at the girls. "Well, I will share everything with General Storm. I'm sure he will be happy with your group's first real success with the connection. I'm pleased as well, but I will say one more thing that you all need to be aware of. This sounds to me like a coordinated attack, especially since the Gore and the wood nymphs were working together." Nabas, satisfied that they had told him all they could, told them he would see them off Sunday night.

"It's getting late. Vira and Nira you need to have at least ten of the Miraga stones completed tonight. Do you think you can do that?"

"Absolutely."

She then dismissed them from class. They gathered their gear and when Dirk was walking out the door with the girls, he ran into Laseous trying to get into Hermosa's class.

"Out of the way. You think you're so special and can ignore me. I'll have all of you in detention. Now move!" Laseous, turning red-face, screamed at the kids.

"Wizard Laseous! What in the hells do you think you're doing?" Hermosa screamed back at the weaselly wizard. Hearing her tone, he stopped his berating of the young adults who were just trying to leave class.

"I had some questions about some supplies you have requisitioned," he said smugly. Dirk and Natia slowed down and stopped beside Tab and El who had also stopped walking to watch Hermosa rip Laseous apart.

"I don't think that it's any of your damned business what I request, Elger," Hermosa said, walking past him and ignoring him as he followed her down the hallway.

The four laughed. They turned and headed to the roof. "That was awesome. I bet Laseous crapped his pants when Hermosa yelled at him in front of us," Tab said, walking hand in hand with El.

"I bet," Dirk responded.

"Do you think Linc is okay?" El asked Dirk.

Dirk closed his eyes for a minute. He nodded. "Mildred has him in his bed already." All three of them looked at him with a how the hells do you know look. He laughed. "Aarya is keeping an eye them." Closing their eyes, they could feel Aarya there.

"Smartass," Tab said, slapping Dirk on the shoulder as they walked away.

"Dirk, you could have just said Aarya is with him," El said, giving him that stern look of hers.

"Sorry," he said, laughing. "Wait a minute." The group stopped. Dirk closed his eyes for a minute. "All right, we can go now," Dirk began to walk away.

"What the hells was that about?" Tab asked.

"I forgot to give Aarya the letters the other day when Skylar barged in, so I asked her to come get them as soon as she could. She said she would as soon as she was sure the rat was ok."

The group laughed at Linc's unofficial nickname. When they all got to the roof, Dirk told everyone about what Hermosa said to Laseous. Volar loved it. He didn't like Laseous either. He'd always felt the wizard was condescending. They spent the rest of their time working on the stones until dinner.

After a quick dinner, Dirk told the group to go on ahead. He was going to talk with Moira. Tab looked at him, "Okay, I'm with you." The rest of the class, excluding Skylar and her friends, hurried back to get to work on the Miraga stones. Dirk walked over to Moira's table and sat down beside her, talking with her and her friends while they finished eating.

Moira figured it was time to hear the rest of the story, so she told her friends she would catch up with them after detention. Dirk said goodbye to them then made sure they were the only ones who could hear the rest of his story. Moira just sat there and listened patiently.

When he was done, she smiled, He was getting more use to that smile. "So, let me break this down. There's a big bad guy that you and your friends have to defend us from because Zona picked your bloodline."

Dirk smiled. "Yes, basically, and we're leaving the school to train soon. I wanted you to know so that you can keep a look out for anything that doesn't seem right."

Moira looked at him questioningly. "How will I let you know if somethings wrong if you're not here?"

Dirk patted her shoulder. "You are going to love the answer to that question," He looked around to make sure no one was listening. He then told her about the Miraga stones and how they worked. He knew what she would say to that.

"Oh, you know I've got to have one of those," she said, smiling. Dirk could already see the trouble she would get into with if she had one.

"Maybe when we get back," he told an unhappy Moira. She agreed and said she would keep the secret. If she saw anything that he needed to know she would tell his doppelganger. She then surprised him by pulling him into a hug.

"Be careful."

Dirk hugged her back. "You, too. I'll see you before we go. I just wanted to talk to you about it before this weekend."

She told him she was glad he did and then left in a hurry to get to detention.

Vira and Nira wanted to get all of the stones prepped so that when everyone else went to bed, they could teach Dirk, Tab, El, and Natia how to complete the stones. Volar hung around after everyone left. Dirk knew something was on his mind.

"What's up, Volar?"

"I didn't want to say anything, but I believe I can help lengthen the time the stones are effective." Dirk motioned for the remaining group to all sit and listen to what Volar had to say. "I'm sure the third and final step will include the Cretoria magic?" Volar looked at the twins. They nodded. Dirk gave him a questioning look.

"It is a process using the Cretoria magic, but it has a little Droc magic mixed in with it," Vira said.

Volar shook his head. "I assume you haven't told Dirk or anyone else how dangerous this magic is?"

Dirk looked concerned. Vira responded. "It's only dangerous if you do it by yourself."

Volar rubbed his beard. "If the stone doesn't reject the change, right?"

"Yes, that's why we do it in pairs. The more power we use allows us to overcome the will of the stone if it doesn't want to change." Nira replied.

Dirk stopped them right there. "Why didn't you tell anyone, Vira, when you offered to do this and why in the hells is that dangerous?"

Nira put her hand on Dirk's knee. "Listen, it is simple magic to us. We were trained to do this kind of magic from an early age. Let me finish, Dirk Storm," Nira said sternly when Dirk started to interrupt. He nodded for her to continue. "All magic has a cost. It takes from you when you use it, but the more you use, the stronger you become, like we were taught our first week. Now when you change an object from its original state, there is always a chance that the object will reject what you're trying to do.

"Remember, all objects have magic in them. That magic comes from when the world was created. The gods had to use magic to create everything, so for it to remain the way it was created, it had to retain some of that magic."

Dirk thought about the information. The way Nira had worded it made it sound simple. "So why is it so dangerous, Volar?" he asked looking at the dwarf.

"In order to change an object, you have to open yourself up to the object, leaving you vulnerable to an attack if it rejects your attempt. It could actually kill you, whether you mean it harm or not. Natural survival instinct is instilled in everything that was created."

"That's why we do it in pairs, Volar. One person can protect the other if the object tries to reject the change."

"Natia, what do you think?" Dirk asked.

"I think Volar has given us something to discuss, but I feel we have no choice now. Our whole plan depends on the Miraga stones. Vira, I'm surprised that Dirk didn't sense what you kept from us," Natia said, glancing at her.

Vira dropped her head for a moment, trying to calm the anger trying to take over. She raised her head after several deep breaths. Then she looked at the three who were questioning her and Nira. She pointed her finger at Dirk and Natia. "Look here, you two. Let me make one thing perfectly clear. We are not the only ones who kept things from each other. Nira and I didn't think about it that way. We were raised doing this and it's just the way it works. Dirk kept the darkness to himself. And you princess, my sister, there are still a few things you haven't shared, so don't talk to us about not telling the whole truth," Vira scolded them. Natia lowered her head.

"You're right." It was Dirk, not Natia, who spoke. He looked at Natia and put a hand on her shoulder. "Volar, I assume you had another reason to bring this up other than that it was dangerous."

He nodded. "There are few who know what I'm about to tell you, so I trust beyond the twelve, soon-to-be-thirteen this will not be shared." They nodded.

"When Garga created the dwarves, he instilled in them the Cretoria magic to make stone obey dwarves. All dwarves have this power when under Mt Jover." He looked around. "Only the royal lineage has the power to do it anywhere in Marona." Volar smiled as the rest of the group realized what he had just told them.

"Let's get this straight. You have the ability to make it safe for the Miraga stone to be created?" Dirk asked.

"Well, why in the hells friend, didn't you say something earlier?"

"I wanted to see how far the twins would put themselves in danger before I spoke up. I wouldn't have let them start the final stage without saying something about it though, but now hearing how they planned to create the magic, I may have been wrong about the danger," Volar said apologetically.

"No need to apologize, brother. I understand your concerns," Dirk said. He smiled. "If you hadn't come forward, turning the stones would have taken twice as long. After Vira and Nira teach us how to do the third step, every one of us can do it with your help," Dirk looked at the group. Vira and Nira were nodding in agreement.

Natia was still disturbed by Vira's accusation. "I agree, but there is one thing I need to say before we go further."

Everyone looked at her. She stared at Dirk and grabbed his hands. "My love, there is one thing I haven't told you that you should know. At first, I thought you would know from the bond but since you haven't said anything about her, I assume you don't know," Natia said, searching his face and thoughts.

Dirk smiled. "It's ok. Aarya has met Sora. I figured when the time was right, and you felt the group needed to know, that you would introduce us."

Natia exhaled. "You're right. She's a creature of magic that was born the same year I was, but she's not as friendly as Aarya."

Dirk kissed her. "She'll be fine once she gets to know us all. Let's just make sure she's not hungry when Tab is around." They all laughed, except Tab, who didn't get the joke.

"Huh?" Tab shrugged looking at the group.

"Don't worry, dear, I'll explain later," El said and kissed him.

Tab satisfied with a kiss, said, "Continue before I get hungrier." The group laughed at the irony of Tab's remark.

Dirk looked at the twins. "Anyone else have a secret they think I should know?" Vira and Nira looked guilty. "I'm not talking about who…, or should I say what…, Mildred is. I sensed her as soon as we connected with Linc. I don't think Linc knows fully who she is, but I'm confident she'll tell him when she's ready. If she doesn't before we meet, then I'll force the issue. There isn't much that I don't sense anymore. That's the last secret that I haven't shared. My powers are growing every day and it's kind of hard to take it all in. Even though I am a little surprised by Volar and the fact that you two didn't tell me first."

Vira and Nira looked apologetic. "Now we will talk about these new revelations once we're on the trip, but until we create these Miraga stones, we aren't going anywhere." Dirk looked around.

"I'll convince the stones to open up," Volar said.

"We'll teach everyone how to make them," Nira said. Vira agreed.

"The first part of step three is to open your mind to your core. Once you find it, you need to open your mind to the stone to show your intent. The stone accepting what you're going to do is the hard part, but since Volar will change all the stones to accept their fate you merely need to show your intentions. Then you should say these words: *Cretoria, formus, accepta, change. Imatatata, core. Bind these words and accept the change of who you bond. Remember the form from which holds you, until the power they've release to you binds their knowledge to you until you're released or until death or their magic runs dry.* Once that's said then you make an offering of your core's magic into the stone. Once it has accepted it, release the stone from your thoughts." Vira looked at the group. "Understand?"

"That's a mouthful," Tab said looking at the twins.

The group laughed at Tab's summation of the magic. He hadn't even noticed he tied it in with food.

"Huh?" Tab asked.

"Don't worry brother. I'll write it down for you," Nira stated patting his shoulder.

"Thanks."

"Understand?" Nira asked again since Tab had interrupted her explanation. Everyone nodded. "Now the stone will glow dark red then become crystalline once the glow disappears," Nira added.

"Now here is the added Droc step." Vira pulled out a knife. "You cut your thumb with the tip of the blade. Squeeze three drops of blood onto the stone. After the third drop touches the stone say, 'bind in blood and regenerate'. Then heat the stone with your magic until you can't hold it anymore. The blood will seep into the stone and disappear. That causes the stone to regenerate on its own for around thirty extra days. Heal your thumb or have someone else heal your thumb and start on a new stone. Any questions?"

Everyone started asking questions at once. Vira and Nira held up their hands to halt the questions. "One at a time, starting with Dirk," Vira said.

He looked disturbed. "Cut your thumb?"

Vira nodded. "The blood from a person who has power is like an energy booster. That causes the stone to regenerate. Your blood runs through your body and is linked to your core. Imagine what blood from one of us will do to the stone."

Dirk tilted his head. Natia answered what Vira was saying. "Our blood has been bonded with all of the group and Aarya." Dirk had a look of awe on his face.

Natia shook her head. "There is no telling how long our blood will affect the Miraga stones then," Dirk said.

"That's right. Next question," Vira asked. One by one, they voiced their concerns. "We will be with each of you until you feel comfortable doing them." Everyone was relieved, knowing that the twins seemed to know what they were doing.

Volar started working the dwarven magic on the stones and soon they all had been made compliant. Vira and Nira worked with each person on their first few stones until they felt comfortable. That night they completed over thirty stones. Dirk was amazed at the change in each stone as the once-gray stone turned a shiny dark red. He felt every drop of blood from the group.

"Why do you think the stones are turning Red, Vira?"

"It has to be a side-effect of the bond," Vira proclaimed.

It eventually drained him to the point that they had to stop for the night. El had been the resident healer and helped everyone after they cut their thumbs.

When they were done and satisfied with their efforts, Volar told them the blood-enhanced stones would probably work better, extending the life of the stones rather than his original idea of forcing the stones to regenerate faster.

"One question I haven't asked," Dirk said, looking at the twins. "How does the person bind the Miraga stone to themselves?"

They looked at each other. "Droc magic again."

Dirk dropped his head. "Let me guess, it involves blood?"

Vira smiled. "The person wanting to bind the Miraga to themselves just has to cut their thumb and place it on the stone. Then say '*Miraga stone, I bind you to me*', and then heat the stone until the blood dissolves into it. Then pressing that stone with that same thumb will activate its magic. After that, anyone can turn on the Miraga stone. You turn it off by pressing on it again."

Dirk shook his head. "The Droc do everything with blood don't they?"

"The Droc are sick, power-hungry people and they feel blood magic is the strongest. That's why we left."

Dirk squeezed both of their hands. "We will straighten them out, I promise."

The twins smiled. "We know, brother. That's why we are here." They both hugged him.

El and Tab looked at each other after Volar left and stood up. "I think we will need a barrier tonight," El said, looking a little guilty.

Nira nodded. "El, you know you can do it yourself."

"I just want to make sure it is strong enough." She paused, looking at Dirk.

He smirked. "El, you make all the noise you want. I am happy for you two and you don't need to worry about that anymore. I love you and want you to be happy."

El hugged Dirk and kissed him on the cheek. "I still do worry."

"Don't. If I wasn't so drained, I might be busy myself with a certain elf and trust me, she is loud." Natia punched Dirk in the shoulder.

El grinned. "I love you all. Good night. I'll make the barrier then. That way, I can at least lower it when we're ready to leave."

El's barrier went up after she and Tab had gathered their packs. It was so strong that the four on the opposite side of it had to cover their eyes when it formed.

Vira passed out the Enda leaf. Natia refused it, saying she didn't really need it because of the way it made her feel. Vira, Nira, and Dirk chewed on the leaf and spit it into the fire, causing green flames to fill the air for a few seconds. After drinking water to get rid of the taste, they all lay down.

"I'm ready to get to the Forgotten City," Natia said. Vira and Nira agreed.

Dirk was a little apprehensive. "I'm afraid that when we come back, everything will be different."

Natia snuggled into his shoulder. Vira did the same. Nira snuggled into Natia's back and grabbed Dirk's hand, wrapping her arm around Natia's waist.

"Everything is going to change, Dirk, sooner or later. And you have to accept that," Natia said lovingly. Nira squeezed his hand tight. Vira grabbed Natia's hand and pulled them tight as well.

"We will be here for you don't forget, and we will do our best to protect everyone we can." She kissed his cheek. "You're tired now. It has been a taxing day with everything that has happened with Linc. Your power will rejuvenate tonight, and you will feel better tomorrow," Vira assured him. He kissed her forehead and closed his eyes after gazing into Natia's for a minute and telling them all he loved them.

Dirk woke the next morning to a happier Natia. "Sleep better?" She nodded and kissed him passionately. He smiled at her. They were thinking the same thing. When would they get to be alone?

"Soon." She nodded.

"Would you two just do it? Act like were not here," Nira said, kissing Natia's cheek and getting up. She smiled.

"Yes, please, the tension is killing me," Vira said, kissing Dirk's cheek and getting up also. "It's not like we won't feel it, no matter where we are." Vira grabbed Nira's hand, and they headed down to the showers.

Thirty minutes later, Natia was feeling guilty as they headed to the showers. She had broken the promise that Vira had made to Hilda and Tilda about the funny business, but then again, she was relieved. The tension with what they were doing was building and she and Dirk both needed some relaxation. They walked, holding hands down the stairs. Tab and El followed behind them.

"How was your night, El?" Natia asked smiling.

"It was very relaxing. How was yours?" El asked.

"Well, I slept like a rock all night, but my morning was also very relaxing," she said, winking at Tab. He laughed and El smiled.

"I guess it's a good thing I didn't drop that barrier any sooner."

Dirk smiled back and grabbed El's hand. All four went down the stairs, hand in hand.

The Old Outpost

The next few days went by fast. Making the Miraga stones had been their main focus. Hermosa informed the group a few days before they left that the supplies had all been gathered. The gear and weapons needed had been loaded on the supply wagons. Dirk was glad to hear that the wagons would leave a couple of days before them and escorted by twenty soldiers, a commanding officer, and one sergeant. The rest of the non-bonded group that would leave with the soldiers. Sirien and Red had been put in charge of keeping the group together.

Dirk met with Sirien and Red before they left and gave them the coordinates for the Great Forest outpost explaining where they would meet. Since the information about Dirk's family history had come out, Sirien's attitude had changed. He was now very supportive of Dirk and Natia's relationship. Dirk was disappointed when he found out Gil had to stay behind. His father had conveniently requested him home for a family matter the night before they left.

Dirk had told him it was okay, and that he could take the doorway with them on Sunday night when the bonded left. Anyone could go through the doorway as long as Dirk or Natia opened it. He told Gil that as soon as they got to the outpost, he could become bonded with the group. Gil left on Friday, disappointed to be leaving but excited to get to the outpost.

The Miraga stones were working better than Dirk could have imagined. He had carried on a conversation with Red's double just like he was there. It worked so well that Dirk's first thought was to get a couple of the stones to Linc. He had Aarya carry a note and a couple of stones back to him.

"See you at the outpost," he told Aarya, rubbing her neck before she flew away. Dirk hoped he would get it before he got to Pineral. Jonesy and the other dwarves had left with the first-and second-year cadets to meet up with Anastasia and Kal for the maneuver training the same day the wagon train left.

Dirk and Natia met with the general, Wizard Nabas and the king the night before they were supposed to leave. Dirk gave the general the twenty stones Vira had promised.

"Dirk, I have been updated on the experience your group had with Linc. I am very excited by the success," the king said.

Dirk told him he was too and that they hadn't expected it, but it was a great test. "It taught us a lot about the bond that we didn't know before. I wrote it all in blood in the Book of Storms, in case something goes wrong," Dirk said confidently.

"That's good, but hopefully we'll never have to rely on that book ever again," the king said. Then he updated him on military movements and that Prince Thelon had started having success with the increased troops that had been sent. They had started pushing the Vangaurd back.

"Yes, it seems that Thelon is finally getting the upper hand."

"I'm glad. That attack definitely seemed coordinated," Dirk confided.

He still didn't share what he had sensed about Mildred. He wanted to meet her before deciding.

"Dirk, Thea wants to meet with you before you leave," the king informed him. "Alone. I'm sorry Natia. You'll have to put up with us men a little longer." She nodded.

"I'll be back to say goodbye," Dirk told the general.

Dirk was then escorted to the queen's private sitting room.

"Hello Dirk, how are you?" Thea asked him.

"It's going better than expected my Queen."

"That's good, Dirk. Everyone else you can leave. I want to talk with Dirk alone. Come sit by me." Dirk sat beside the queen. She grabbed his hand and placed her other hand on the side of his face. "My dear boy, I have asked you here because there is one last thing I must share with you before you leave. It is for your ears only."

Dirk looked into the queen's eyes. Her beauty was breath-taking. She had teared up. Dirk could sense the dread behind what she wanted to tell him.

"My queen, I would do anything you ask."

She smiled. "Such a father's son you are. Diron said those same words to me the last time I saw him." Dirk turned his head to the side, taking in what she said. A faint smile came to her lips. "The family legacy that has bonded you to your family's line has also bonded me to mine. We are related in that way, not just in blood. I have one last vision that I must tell you about before you go. I might not get the chance to again, I'm afraid." She squeezed his hand. "I know you have sensed the darkness growing ever closer. No need to speak until I have finished."

"As I said my queen, anything you ask."

Thea began to tell him the vision she hadn't shared with anyone, taking a quivering breath. "When the final battle comes, the Chosen will have suffered great losses. Ones dear to him will be gone. The Dark twins will hold true to their brother, for without their faith in him, all would be lost.

The past and the present will join and the one who was forgotten will deliver the final blow to end the evil once and for all. When good turns evil, and evil turns good, the world will finally be released from the turmoil that has stricken the land. The Chosen must stay strong after the final battle, for the seer's heir will have to build the world a new."

Dirk was shocked. He knew what part of that meant, but the rest was very confusing. "Can you be more specific?"

The queen shook her head. "Dirk, this time it seems clear that there will be much devastation and death before this war is over."

Dirk slouched his shoulders. "I'm not ready, am I?"

"Maybe not at the moment, but you will be," she said, pulling him into a hug. "Protect her, for she will need you."

"I will, Thea. I would die for her."

She pushed him back. "I know you would. I have seen it. Dirk, our family blood is strong in magic. It has always been strong but not strong enough. I believe with the steps you are taking now that you will be the strongest Chosen ever, but that might not be enough. Keep your friends close. Stay together, even when you don't want to. You must, son, for they are the ones that will make the difference. You might not understand now, but I promise you will when the time comes. I love you, Dirk, just as I loved your father, just like a son." Thea was crying openly now and hugging him close.

Dirk embraced Thea just like he would have Kira. He hadn't ever realized how good she had always been to him until that very moment. She had always been nice to him, even when he and Anastasia were getting scolded by the general or the king. Thea had been their protector without Dirk realizing it.

He looked into her eyes. "If it's the last thing I do in this world, I will end this madness."

Thea, finally composed, looked Dirk in the eyes and smiled. "Son, I do believe you will." Dirk hugged her one more time. "Now make sure you see your mother before you leave. She misses you and it could be a long time before you see her again."

Dirk kissed Thea on the cheek. "I will, and I have given Grandfather enough Miraga stones that there should be one for you if you need it."

The queen nodded. She kissed Dirk's forehead and said goodbye.

Dirk clenched his fist, opening and closing them as he walked away. He had every doubt running through his mind. *I'm not ready for this. What if everyone I love dies.* A trill echoed in his thoughts. "Aarya," he said out loud. Her voice caused him to stop and take a deep breath. He knew Aarya believed in him. She basically had just said it without words. He now knew that he would figure it out.

He and Natia left through the door behind the throne and stepped into the school. Dirk had an idea.

"Let's get the twins and go see my mother now." Natia looked at him questioningly. "I just feel we need to do it now."

Vira and Nira walked down the stairs as if summoned. "Ready?" Vira asked.

Dirk smiled. "You two always seem to amaze me. Just when I think I've got you figured out."

Before they left, Dirk told the three about Thea's last vision. "Part of that is easy, but the part about when good turns evil and when evil turns good. I don't know," Natia said.

"Well the part about the loss and suffering is what bothers me," Vira said. Dirk agreed.

"Let's go see my mom then we can talk about it tonight."

Dirk laid his hand on the door that led to the general's workshop. It glowed crimson. Dirk opened the door and they stepped through. Feeling the pull immediately landing behind the door that opened into the general's workshop. After the dizziness and whooshing had dissipated, they opened the door and stepped into the workshop. Kira and the general were waiting on them. The twins about knocked Dirk over rushing to hug Kira and the general. Natia laughed.

They all sat in the living room talking when Natia asked where Claire was. "Claire is in the room with her mother. She has stopped responding to treatment. I don't know what else to do," Kira said.

The twins sent a thought to Dirk. He nodded. "Mom, did the General tell you what happened with Linc?"

"Yes. That was extraordinary. We were never able to do anything like that," Kira responded.

Dirk looked to the twins and they shared a thought. "I believe we can heal her," Nira said, stepping up. Kira was shocked at the change she sensed in Nira. The confidence and forthrightness she spoke with was astonishing. Kira looked into Nira's eyes. She could see the flames rippling in them. Kira sensed that Nira believed she could really help.

"All right, it can't hurt. I'll go get Claire, then you can do what you can for her mother." Kira got up and went to the room. When she came out, holding Claire's hand, Dirk and the girls went in.

The sickly smell in the room made Dirk cough. Ulny was laying in the bed in a sweat-drenched nightgown, breathing heavily and moaning.

"We better hurry," Vira said. Dirk and Nira went to one side of the bed while Natia and Vira stood on the other. They grabbed hands and then closed their eyes. The bond connected instantly. Vira started searching for Ulny's core.

"There it is. It is very weak and clouded," Vira said, directing the groups thoughts. Natia gasped.

"I see it," Dirk said.

"Oh, my gods, it's the darkness," Nira said.

"That's what I thought."

"Well, that explains the beast you two fought," Vira said.

"I don't understand."

"The Dark Wizard Asher has infected her. That's why the beast was near. The Dark Wizard knows who you are, Dirk. He would have wanted his presence close so he could sense when you were here."

At that moment, Ulny started shaking. A voice much deeper than Ulny's came out of her as she spoke. Vira and Nira felt chills when they heard it.

"I sensed you were here, my little twin pets," Asher's voice said.

"What do you want?" Dirk asked.

He laughed. "The Chosen speaks. Well, I'll make it simple. I want my world back. It was stolen from the Droc before you were born. I will be taking my two pets back from you as well. I will destroy everything and everyone you love until I get it all back."

"The hells you will. I'll tell you what will happen." Dirk's eyes flamed with crimson and green fire. "I will find you and I will kill you for what you have done to my sisters, and I promise you I will take my time and enjoy every minute of it."

Asher laughed again. "Don't worry, you'll get your chance soon." Ulny started shaking and convulsing.

"We must destroy the darkness in her quickly," Vira replied. Dirk blocked Asher from everyone's thoughts. He didn't know how he did it. He just thought it and he was gone.

Then they all focused on the darkness in Ulny. The gems imbedded in the twin's backs began to glow. They started chanting words Dirk didn't understand, but he just joined in, following his instincts. Dirk felt a wave of light form in his core, then it rushed out through all of them and attacked the darkness in Ulny. Dirk would have sworn that he heard Aarya's war cry in his head when it happened. The darkness fought back but stood no chance against the four of them. The crimson light wrapped around the darkness. Dirk heard voices in the light. He could also hear the darkness screaming as it died. It didn't last long, and then, with a flash, the darkness was destroyed.

STORM RISING

The group felt a wave of relief. Ulny relaxed and stopped convulsing. Her breathing normalized, and she opened her eyes looking around the room. "Claire?" she asked Dirk.

He smiled and helped Ulny sit up. "I'm Dirk, Kira's son and this is Natia, Vira, and Nira. It's so good to finally meet you."

Natia poured her a glass of water. "Thank you for saving me," Ulny said to the four.

"It was our pleasure," Nira said.

"Claire is waiting for you in the living room." Ulny started to get up. Dirk stopped her. "First, can you tell me what you remember?"

She nodded. "That night, Jerle, Claire, and me were eating dinner. These five men busted through our front door. One of Ram Stockton's men pulled Jerle up out of his chair and put a blade to his throat. I was so scared I grabbed Claire and pulled her into my arms. This dark robed figure came in and told Jerle to help Stockton's men out or we would die. He then raised his hand and a dark, clouded ball formed in it. He shoved it towards me and my whole body trembled. I felt the dark cloud enter my body. Claire was jerked from my grasp. I remember every now and then getting the urge to fight the darkness that had overtaken me. But it didn't last long. I tried so many times. I got weak and could no longer stay focused on any one thing." Ulny was sobbing now. Natia and Vira comforted her.

"Ulny, Jerle and Claire are both safe now," Dirk told her.

She looked up, wiping away the tears. "Thank you so much."

Dirk patted her shoulder. "You're welcome. Now go see your daughter, she's been missing you," Dirk said helping her up.

"Mom," Claire said, running to hug her mother when she walked out of the room. Kira smiled with tears rolling down her cheeks. Kira helped Ulny to the couch and told her she would get her some food. Kira then went into the kitchen where Dirk and everyone were sitting at the table, discussing with the general what had happened.

"You four are so much more than I ever would have dreamed," she said, pulling them into a hug. Dirk explained what and who had caused Ulny's sickness.

The general's mouth was set in a firm line, not giving away his thoughts. Tapping his fingers on the table he sat in deep thought. "I have to leave. Things are in play that the king needs to know about." He kissed the girls goodbye and told them he would see them soon.

Dirk grabbed his grandfather and hugged him. "Be careful."

The general hugged him back and whispered, "I will do what is necessary, as you will. Remember, we are here for a reason." The general looked at all of them gathered around. "Family is what we are..."

"Family is what we will always be!" Dirk and the girls finished the general's words. Pride showed in his smile. He hugged them all one more time with tears in his eyes and then shook Dirk's hand firmly. He released his grandson. "I am very proud of you." He looked at the girls. "I love you all."

Ulny and Claire were led into the kitchen to eat and Kira got them set up with some food. "I'm starving. Thank you for the food, Kira," Ulny said gratefully.

"What was that about?" Natia asked.

Dirk said one word. "Darkness."

Natia and the twins all grabbed hands. Kira had walked back into the living room while Ulny was eating and saw how close the four were. She sat down in front of them and put her hand on Dirk's and Natia's. "Why are you here early?"

"Mom, the darkness is coming and soon. You know what that is right?"

Kira nodded. "Dirk there is always a darkness that lingers. Your father and grandfather always said to be weary of it. Sometimes it's nothing more than a few skirmishes. Sometimes it's bigger. I know that this Dark Wizard has you worried." Kira caressed his face. "Try not to rush into anything. Stay focused on your training that way when the battle does get here, you'll be ready."

"I will Mom. But to be safe I made you this," Dirk said, giving her a Miraga stone. She took it and immediately felt the stones power. "It's a Miraga stone and I personally infused my blood into it. It is stronger than any of the other's and I wanted you to have the best." Dirk looked intently at her.

"I heard about these. Shouldn't someone more important get this?"

Dirk shook his head. "There is no one more important to me."

She kissed her son on the cheek. "Thanks." Vira explained how to use it and the part about it being used to communicate with them. "That's amazing." Kira looked at it with awe.

"Another precaution I've taken is I've had Tab make certain people aware that this is a safe haven for them to come to. That is if anything happens," Dirk explained.

"I'll be here for them if needed."

"If anything happens, we will be here soon after," Dirk told her. "Mom there is one last thing I need to tell you."

Kira looked her son in the eyes. She shrugged her shoulders, waiting on him to explain.

"The last night we were here on our visit," Dirk paused looking at Natia.

Tell her. She needs to know.

"I saw Dad in the middle of the night. He told me what he has been telling you. That someone will betray us. But it's not their fault." Dirk said.

She paced around the room. "What do you think?"

Dirk got up and stood in front of her. "My powers are growing, and I can sense things now. I believed him."

"Just remember what we discussed. Keep your plans to a select few. That way you control the information flow." Dirk nodded.

"There is one more line of protection I would like to leave with you," Natia told her god aunt. Natia and the group walked outside after saying goodbye to Claire and Ulny who thanked them for healing her.

"Sora," Natia said as the group came to the door of the general's shop. There was a loud feline roar and Dirk saw a pair of yellow eyes before something came pouncing out of the darkness. Dirk smiled, as did the twins. Kira took a step back toward Natia. "It's okay."

A giant black panther, whose head was as high as Dirk's chest, walked up taking in the twins, Dirk, and Kira. She stood a few feet away and stared at Natia.

"Aunt Kira, this is Sora. She has been my guardian since I was a child. I decided to leave her here for now to help protect you and the farm while we are gone," Natia said, standing beside the panther, who licked the side of her face. The panther looked at Kira.

"Kira of the house Fleur Ian, I am honored to do my companion's bidding and protect everyone here while they are gone," the panther said in a deep voice.

Kira, shocked that it could talk, smiled, and bowed to the noble panther. "Thank you, Sora. I'm honored that you'll be protecting us."

"Sora, thank you," Dirk said, bowing on one knee.

"Dirk Storm, I will hold you accountable if anything happens to my companion," she said with a hint of a growl.

"Sora, I would as well, and I assure you, anything bad would have to go through me first."

Sora, pleased with his answer, licked Dirk's face. The twins petted the panther giggling when she licked their faces.

After that, they said goodbye to the majestic feline. They all received big hugs from Kira and then stepped into the workshop.

"Let's go ahead and get our necklaces before we leave," dirk said opening the cabinet that they were stored in.

"I agree. It will be good to wear them while were training." Natia replied.

They got back at dinner time. Since they were leaving the next day, everything had been prepared. The Miraga stones had been given to everyone that needed them. Vira had about ten spare ones that she wanted to keep.

They ate dinner with the doppelgangers and the rest of the bonded on the roof. Dirk sat with the real Natia and twins, watching their doppelgangers eating and talking across from them.

"It's a little weird, isn't it?" Dirk said.

The real people and doppelgangers looked at him and, as one, said, "Yes." Of course, Vira's doppelganger added her usual 'gorgeous' at the end and winked at him. They all laughed even Dirk.

After seeing how well it was working, Dirk decided there was no sense in waiting. He went and told Hermosa and Nabas that the class would leave that night. Hermosa agreed and since Gil wasn't back, Dirk asked if he could come with them. Dirk felt a little guilty about leaving him behind, but it was only for one day. Tab agreed that he would understand.

Nabas agreed and said they could go ahead and set up at the outpost and wait on the wagons to get there in a few days. They gathered the bonded then told their doppelgangers that they were going to leave.

"Okay gorgeous, but you know we already know," Vira's double said. Dirk felt silly that he didn't think that they would already know. Since it was his idea, his doppelganger had already informed the others. Dirk was amazed at his double. It was like looking into a mirror.

The doppelgangers took off and went about their normal activities as they got ready to leave.

The bonded met Hilda and Tilda down at the doorway. Dirk hugged the twins and handed them each one of the spare stones. He held up a hand when they started to complain. "For me, please!"

"Okay," Hilda said, hugging Dirk and all of the class goodbye. Tilda did the same.

"I'll go through first with Natia and the twins right behind me," Dirk said to the group. With tears in his eyes, he looked at Hilda and Tilda one last time. *Thank you. I love you both*, he mouthed to them. They nodded.

When he opened the door, a brisk breeze blew past them. "Here goes..." He kissed Natia and stepped through. The pull was instant, but it seemed to take a little longer for him to stop. The whooshing sound faded, and his dizziness cleared. It was a small room that he had been teleported to, he felt the sides of the walls with his hands trying to get his bearings. It was totally dark. He pulled Harbinger from his sheath. He had decided to bring it, Luna's Tears, and the twin blades with them on the trip. Natia had the bow and he had given Nira and Vira each a dagger.

The room lit up as Dirk's magic flowed through the blade. He opened the door into a basement and looked around. There were cobwebs hanging from the rafters and boxes everywhere. The musky scent of death floated around the room. Dirk was kicking a dead mouse into the corner when there was a whooshing sound behind him.

Natia and the twins walked into the room. Tab and El right on their heels. "Nice place," Vira said, looking around. Vira and Nira both produced a hovering ball of light to help light up the room.

"Thanks," Dirk said. They nodded and headed to the staircase. "Be careful. They look a little rotted." They heard the whooshing sound again when Volar, Oriana, and Tara came walking in. Natia sealed the door behind them. "Everyone here?" Dirk asked. El nodded. Dirk gave the same warning to the rest of the group before he started up the stairs.

All eyes were on Harbinger. None of the bonded, other than Tab and Natia, had ever really looked at it. The stones were pulsing, reacting to being in the Chosen's hand for the first time in several decades. The stairs creaked with each slow step he took. He used Harbinger to cut through the cobwebs as he ascended, laughing to himself. *I'm using a god-killing weapon to kill spiders. I hope Zona isn't watching right now,* Dirk thought.

There was a door at the top of the stairs. It made a loud creaking sound as he opened it. He smiled and looked at Natia, who was right on his heels. "Guess that hasn't been opened in a while."

"You think?" Tab said sarcastically. Dirk gave him the look. Tab shrugged and smiled back. Dirk emerged into the kitchen of the outpost and looking around.

After everyone had finally made it up the stairs and into the kitchen, they split into three groups to explore the long-since used outpost. Dirk and his girls went searching to the left. Tab, El, and Volar went right, Oriana and Tara searched the path that went straight-ahead. Dirk and his group found a meeting room connected to a hallway that lead to the front door.

He went outside to look around. There was a wall made from thick logs that surrounded the perimeter, along with a small barn and a courtyard with a well in the center of it. The front gate was in need of some instant repairs. Securing the outpost while they waited on the rest of the group to get there was vital. Dirk turned back to the building and saw lights through the windows as the others searched the rooms. Tab and El came out of the building.

Tab whistled at the view. "Wow look at the size of those trees."

They're old and majestic, Dirk thought. They were very tall with large branches, twice as tall as the trees in the forest that surrounded Storm farm. "Come on, Tab. Let's see if we can secure that gate," Dirk said, heading off to the broken doorway. El and the girls walked the perimeter while Dirk and Tab tried to find a way to fix the gate.

The outpost was a good-sized fort. The main building was half the size of the school with only three floors. The top two floors had rooms for the troops who used to be stationed there. One hundred could be housed in the outpost. The courtyard was twice the size of the training area at the academy. Dirk found a building beside the stables. Someone had stored away extra wood, tools, and nails. Dirk and Tab repaired the gate and a few of the timbers that the girls had found that had fallen due to age.

Tara and Oriana had started cleaning up the sleeping quarters when the girls came back. Volar had cleaned the rotten food out of the kitchen cupboards and gotten a fire started in the fireplace in the common area on the first floor. While checking the well, Volar found the rope had rotted through so he went to the storage building and found at least a hundred feet of rope, along with a spare water bucket. Once the well was fixed, he tested the water. It was still safe to drink.

After the boys finished the repairs, they headed into the house. The smell of something good hit their senses. Even though they had already eaten an early dinner, Tab had hinted that he was still hungry, so Oriana and Tara had cooked a vegetable stew and made some fresh bread from their supplies. That made Tab very happy.

"You're always hungry, brother," Vira teased. Tab looked around at the bonded, all eating the stew.

He cocked his head and looked at Vira who had a spoon to her mouth. She smiled at him. "It's the bond, you know." She laughed.

They had a hodgepodge of chairs seated around the table. Crates, buckets, and a few good chairs. Dirk thanked the two elves. He knew they enjoyed being able to help their group in any way they could.

They had decided it would be better to sleep on the floor after discovering that the beds were all moldy. "I prefer to sleep under the stars anyway," Vira said.

"We know." Tara smiled at Oriana and she laughed. Vira raised an eyebrow at the elves. They giggled, very unlike elven women. Natia smiled. Dirk sensed what Tara and Oriana were thinking.

"Tara, you and Oriana aren't jealous, are you?" Dirk asked.

They looked offended. "Well, Dirk, I can assure you, if it weren't for Natia, you wouldn't have time to sleep with anyone else. You would be very busy every night," Oriana said, smiling at the twins. The table laughed. Dirk smiled at the two elves.

Tara had long blonde hair with green eyes that sparkled when she smiled. She was built the same as Natia. Oriana was smaller with silver hair and silver-white eyes. She was a little curvier but was just as athletic as Natia. She rarely smiled at him but since the bond, she had taken on more human traits.

"I am sure I would have enjoyed that thoroughly," Dirk said, receiving an elbow from Natia and glares from Vira and Nira. Oriana winked at him.

Tara looked at Natia. "You better keep an eye on him, Nat," Tara replied. Natia, Tara, and Oriana had been good friends their whole lives. They were the only ones allowed to call her Nat. Natia smiled, taking another bite of the soup.

"Tara, you or Oriana didn't put Haine berries in the soup, did you?"

Tara smirked. "Unfortunately, I didn't bring any with us."

Tab looked up, confused by the comment. "What are Haine berries?"

El grinned, "You'll never need them," The elves laughed.

"They're used for building stamina, but they can also make you want to mate, more often than not," Nira explained.

Volar laughed. "When mating season comes around at Mt Jover, many of our women slip them into their mate's food."

Tab smiled. "Volar, are your women so ugly they have to drug the men to procreate?" he asked, trying not to laugh.

Volar smiled. "Ah, Mr. Clearwater, ever the comedian. Thine bride Valia is more beautiful than your Elyse, believe it or not. No disrespect. Elyse. You are very beautiful, even for a human," Volar declared.

El smiled and thanked him for the compliment. "Wait a minute, Volar. You're married?" Tab asked, shocked.

Volar nodded. "Just before I left for Silver City. I look very much forward to seeing her again."

Dirk looked at Volar. "I can't wait to meet her myself," Dirk said. Volar nodded. Dirk had some serious questions about the Haine berries. "So, we could use these for stamina in times of need?" Dirk asked.

"I say we get some of them berries and prepare them for that use." Tab smiled and whispered something to El who blushed.

"And that's the reason it will be prepared the right way only, Tab," Dirk shook his head.

Tab gave him a *who me?* look. Dirk raised an eyebrow. "I bet the plant is in the great forest," Oriana said grinning.

"We can look for some when we're hunting tomorrow," Tara replied.

"Fine, that's settled," Dirk confirmed.

They cleaned up and decided it was time for bed. "I suggest we take turns keeping watch tonight. There are nine of us, so we can do it in two-person teams every two hours," Dirk said. "Me and Volar can take first watch, El and Tab second, Vira and Natia third, Oriana and Tara can take fourth, then Nira and I can take last," Natia wanted to complain but let it go.

Dirk helped build a fire in the courtyard and set up the sleeping bags for the girls. Tab and El had decided to sleep in the outpost with the rest of the group. Vira and Nira were pouting while looking at Dirk.

"I'll be with you ladies shortly." He kissed the twin's foreheads and kissed Natia on the lips. They pulled out the Enda leaf and handed one to Dirk, who said he would use it later.

"Ready, Master Storm?"

Dirk nodded and then he and Volar walked the perimeter in the agreed upon pattern. They talked while making sure everything was ok.

Time passed quickly with them keeping their eyes open for anything out of the ordinary. It was time to change watch, so Dirk went to wake up El and Tab while Volar kept watch.

Dirk knocked on the door. Tab answered. "We're coming," A few minutes later, Tab and a grumpy El came out.

"See you in the morning," Dirk told them as he went to try and figure out how to get into his sleeping bag. Vira and Nira had Natia sandwiched between them.

Dirk took off his boots after chewing up his Enda leaf and spitting it out. He pulled off his shirt and scooted in behind Nira. He figured it was best since they had last watch. She fit perfectly against his body. He wrapped his arm around her waist and grabbed Vira's and Natia's hand falling asleep immediately.

He barely remembered hearing someone wake up Natia and Vira and saying it was their turn. Although, he felt Natia kiss his cheek. Nira rolled over and wrapped her arms around Dirk after the other two got up. She dug her nose into his shoulder and went back to sleep. Dirk smiled. The way he was holding Nira so close made him feel he was protecting his little sister.

He got very little sleep and was grumpy when Tara and Oriana woke them up for the final watch. Natia and Vira had situated themselves into their normal sleeping positions. He got up, deciding to let Nira sleep instead of waking her. It was only an hour until sunrise. He felt he could hold down the fort by himself. She woke up when he moved.

"Lay back down. I got this," he said to a sleepy Nira. She frowned and moved closer to Natia. He covered them back up and walked the perimeter, listening to the creatures outside making their nightly calls. There was a scent in the air he couldn't recognize. He would have to ask the group tomorrow if anyone else had smelled it.

Dirk, can you hear me? Dirk stopped. He leaned against the corner of the outpost building and smiled.

Stas?

Yes, it is good to feel your thoughts. How are you? Anastasia asked.

Good. How are things going? Dirk rubbed the bracelet the king had given him thinking of Kal and Anastasia. They had the identical bracelets to the one Dirk and Natia wore.

The military cadets got here yesterday. We started drilling them in different formations. It was slow going at first, but after they understood what Kal was telling them to do, it got easier. Where are you at?

Dirk explained to her what they had come up with on training outside of *the school.*

That's brilliant. We sensed something to that effect was happening, but we couldn't quite make out what you were planning.

That's really good because you won't be far from our position once you get to the Forgotten City. I think we will plan an excursion to see you when you get there.

Dirk told her that was great then he told her about the incident with Linc.

Kal and I both thought we felt something the other day, but it was cloudy. That's why I wanted to contact you to make sure you were okay.

Yes, we're fine. After everyone else gets here we should be in The Forgotten City in a few days.

They made plans for her and Kal to meet them there in six days. Dirk told her about Asher and him invading the twin's dreams. He also told her about the Enda leaf and what it could do. They talked until the sun came up.

Well, I got to go. We are about to wake the cadets and take them on a long training run. Giles would be happy. Anastasia laughed.

Well you can tell him all about it. He is one of the instructors coming. She was glad to hear that, and she was sure Kal would be also. They said their goodbyes. As they did, Natia and the twins came walking up.

"Anastasia?" Natia asked. Dirk nodded and kissed Natia. Vira and Nira hugged him.

"I missed you," Nira said.

He smiled. "I was right here."

"I wonder if you can rig up one of those showers?" Vira asked.

Dirk looked at her. "I bet we can come up with something."

They sat by the dying fire and went over the group's traveling plans.

After the rest of the bonded joined them, they all talked about what they wanted to accomplish that day. "First order of business should be to scout out the trails. The wagons should have a clear path in tomorrow," Tara said. She volunteered herself, El, and Oriana to do the scouting. After the day was planned out, they ate their rations for breakfast.

When Tara, Oriana, and El went out on the scouting mission, Volar and Tab went to gather supplies to build a makeshift shower system since not one in the outpost worked.

Dirk, Natia, and the twins finished getting the rest of the rooms ready. Dirk knew they were only staying one or two more days, but there were a lot of people heading their way and Dirk wanted to make sure that the were rooms were ready for them.

Several hours later, they were sitting around the firepit when Tara, El, and Oriana came back with a couple of deer they had killed. Dirk was amazed at how resilient the elves were. They had carried the deer by tying the deer's legs together and ran two sturdy tree limbs between the legs. They carried them on their shoulders easily.

After setting the deer beside the building, they sat with Dirk and the girls. Tara informed Dirk that the surrounding area was mainly regular wildlife, and they didn't see any indication of anything dangerous close by. Trees had fallen across the path in a few places, but they had already cleared them away.

Dirk went to inspect the shower while all of the girls stayed and talked around the fire. Volar and Tab had thrown together a makeshift shower, consisting of a metal barrel that had been used to water the horses. They also had found some tubing made out of some kind of soft, waterproof material. They used the shower head and chain system from the broken-down shower from the outpost.

No need for a fire to warm the water now that they all had good control over their powers, and they could heat the water up as hot as they wanted. Dirk, satisfied that the girls would be happy with the shower, went back to inform them it was ready.

He watched as Tab, El, Tara, and Oriana cleaned the deer. Dirk, after filling the water barrel of the shower, helped Volar build a bigger pit to cook the deer over. The twins and Natia took advantage of the shower while the rest of the group took care of the cooking.

Tara took Tab and El out after the deer was cleaned to look for the Haine berries. They found a couple of bushes not far from the perimeter wall and collected enough berries to last a month. They also found some wild mushrooms and tubers to cook alongside with the vegetables for dinner.

Volar wanted to make some dwarven bread for dinner. He asked them to look for some wild oats while they were out. They came back with enough to satisfy Volar's needs. Once they all had showered, they had about an hour before the venison was done. Dirk and Natia went downstairs to wait for the arrival of Hermosa, Helena, Wizard Quentin, and Gil. Dirk was anxious to bond Gil.

Dirk and Natia entered the basement. Dirk touched the door, activating it, so they could come through when they were ready. It glowed, and Dirk felt the connection to the school was ready. Not long after, there were four whooshing sounds in quick succession.

The door opened and a disheveled Hermosa came through. "Dirk and Natia glad to see you," she said. Her entrance was followed by Helena, Wizard Quentin, and an Aide Dirk didn't recognize. Dirk looked around, waiting on Gil to come through the door.

"Wizard Hermosa, where is Gil?" Dirk asked, concerned.

"My dear, his father has suffered an illness. I am afraid it is grave, and he requested Gil to stay home from school for a few weeks."

Dirk hated Gil's father, but he didn't want him to die. "I'm very sad to hear that. I should go back and see him."

Hermosa put her hand on his shoulder. "There is nothing you can do."

"There most certainly is something we can do." Dirk clenched his fist, his eyes blazing.

Hermosa with her hand still on Dirk's shoulder, shook her head. "You can't let your secret get out, Dirk." She looked to Natia for help.

Natia put a hand on his chest. "Dirk, I am with you with whatever you decide, but what would Gil want you to do?" Dirk hung his head. The turmoil in his heart was ripping him apart.

"Did he say anything about us coming to his father's aid?" Wizard Quentin, who knew Gil well, and his father even better, spoke up. "Dirk, he has the best healers. Gil told me to tell you not to sway from your mission. It's more important than anything else in this world. He was badly shaken up, but he said he knew you would want to come. He made me promise not to let you."

Dirk shook his head. "All right," he said but something didn't feel right about abandoning Gil. He would talk with Tab and El about it later. Natia sensed his doubt and squeezed his hand.

"Dirk, this is Apprentice Geraldo. He has my utmost trust." Hermosa said, introducing the aide. Dirk shook his hand.

"Nice to meet you," they both said to each other.

"We also have a surprise for you." Hermosa waved her hand toward the door and two crates came floating in on a gust of wind. Dirk tried to lift the top of one of the boxes, but Hermosa stopped him. "You'll get to see them at the same time."

Dirk nodded and then showed them up the stairs. The rest of the group was waiting in the common room. Tab was complaining about having to wait until Hermosa got here to eat. Dirk shook his head at his best friend. He didn't always have the best timing.

Tab looked away as Hermosa and the rest of her group came in.

She motioned at the crates and they positioned themselves in the center of the room. After she introduced Geraldo, and Wizard Quentin, everyone's attention was on the crates. "I am glad to see you all. The king has one gift for you that he hopes you will wear with pride when the time comes to disclose who you are."

Geraldo asked Dirk to help him. Dirk bent down and lifted the top of the first crate. He whistled when he saw what was in the crate, reached in, and pulled out a leather top. It was flexible and soft to the touch. Something told him it wasn't easy to cut though.

He held it up for everyone to see. There was a crimson phoenix emblazoned across the chest. The Silver City crest was behind the phoenix. There was a hood, that could be used to conceal the identity of whoever wore it. The Storm family crest was sewn onto the right shoulder. It filled Dirk with pride.

The other crate contained matching leather pants. Natia held up the pants so everyone could see that there were flames down the side of the legs and included a belt to store knives or other weapons. Small gems were sewn into the leather in varying places into the waistband of the pants.

"Wow," Tab said, forgetting he was hungry.

"Try them on. There's also female armor and male armor for the four that aren't here," Hermosa said. The bonded, being as close as they were, stripped down to their underclothes right there. Hermosa, having been around them more than Quentin, Helena, or Geraldo explained. "Their bond to each other opens them up to each other's most intimate and secret thoughts so they are not bashful in front of each other."

Geraldo just nodded and turned away. Quentin and Helena did the same. Helena's face was turning red from embarrassment. Hermosa had told Dirk on the way up the stairs that Geraldo was a third-year student. Dirk noticed Geraldo couldn't stop checking out Oriana. Dirk smiled, knowing the effect she had on men. She did look very exotic.

Geraldo was from Seafare and was used to seeing elves because he lived close to them, but she was built differently. Her curves were a little more extensive, her breasts were twice the size of a normal elf's and her almond skin was flawless. Dirk heard every thought Geraldo was having. Dirk had started sensing other people's thoughts as his powers were developing further, but it was still new enough that it weirded him out slightly.

"Geraldo," Tab said, noticing him constantly peeking at Oriana. Geraldo looked at Tab innocently. "I would be careful. My sister Oriana there is probably better with a dagger than anyone else here. She isn't too particular about what appendage she cuts off when she gets annoyed." Tab pulled his pants up and winked at Geraldo.

"Tab, leave that poor boy alone. I think he is kind of cute," Oriana said, smiling at him, mesmerizing him with her silver eyes. Geraldo turned away and didn't look at her again.

Dirk enjoyed that Tab was giving Geraldo a hard time. They knew he was joking, and it was a good way to break him into the group.

After they finished getting dressed, Dirk looked around at his brothers and sisters. *We look like an elite group of assassins*, he thought.

Hermosa clapped at the group "Absolutely fabulous! You all look amazing. Now, there is one more surprise. Pull your hood over your heads. There are snaps at the bottom of the top and the top of the pants. Snap them together and snap the hood to the front of your top."

As soon as the last snap was fastened, they all disappeared. Hermosa smiled. "Does anyone see anything different?"

"No," Dirk said.

"You're invisible to anyone not wearing that armor. You can see each other, but we can't see you. It lasts about thirty minutes but will recharge when not in use by pulling from your core magic." She held up a mirror and showed them that their reflection was gone.

There were giggles and laughter from the group. "This is great," Tara said. Everyone agreed.

"Now unsnap the hood and you become visible. And now for the last test. Master Volar, will you please take your axe and hit Dirk as hard as you can in the stomach.

Dirk looked at her, alarmed. Volar grabbed his axe and, before Dirk could complain, he swung as hard as he could and hit Dirk in the stomach, knocking him back a little. Other than that, he didn't feel a thing. Dirk looked at Volar, who was smiling, and looked at Hermosa.

"That was amazing. Who made these?"

"That is a secret to be told another day," she said. Before too long, the group had each hit each other with their swords testing it out for themselves. After the excitement wore down, Hermosa suggested that they change back into their regular clothes. Geraldo got another eyeful of Oriana's breasts as they changed.

Tab chided her. "You're teasing the poor boy!"

She winked at him, "Hey, you got Elyse." Tab smiled and nodded. With that, they ate dinner finally to Tab's relief.

Hermosa was impressed with the way the group had organized the old outpost. They had set up tents around the courtyard. The whole group then sat by the fire and talked until it was time again for bed. They talked about setting up watch and Hermosa suggested to just to set up a barrier for the night.

"Why didn't we think of that?" Tab exclaimed. Dirk just shrugged.

The Traitor

After everyone said good night, Dirk asked Tab to sleep outside. He gave Dirk a strange look. Dirk didn't want to think too much on it, fearing the rest of the bonded would catch on to what he had planned. Tab agreed. Dirk settled down between Natia and the twins, waiting for them go to sleep. As soon as the girls drifted off to sleep the boys got up, and quietly walked to the side of the outpost.

"So, are we going to check on Gil or what?" Tab asked. Dirk felt guilty about it, but he had to see how Gil was. Dirk nodded.

"Let's put on our new armor first, we can wear a cloak to cover it up. It will help us sneak in," Dirk said.

After putting on the armor, they went to the basement. When they got there Natia, El, and the twins were waiting for them. Dirk laughed. Vira and Nira had a murder in their eyes.

El just said one word. "Really?"

"I have to try."

"I know that's why we're coming with you," Natia said, revealing her armor under the cloak she was wearing. The girls all had on similar dark cloaks and revealed their armor as well.

"What's the plan?"

"We'll use the armor and sneak through the school. Once we get to Gil's house, Tab and I will go in and check on him. We can do the same thing we did for Ulny if we need to," Dirk explained.

"I don't like it," El complained.

"El, I'll make sure Gil knows your there. I promise." Dirk squeezed her shoulder.

El stared at Dirk and finally relaxed her shoulders. "Okay. As long as he knows the rest of us are there if he needs us." Dirk nodded then touched the door to open it and stepped through, feeling the pull instantly.

Dirk knew immediately something was wrong. There were explosions in the distance. The ground shook, almost knocking them off their feet. "Aaaaahhhhh!" Vira and Nira both fell to their knees, holding their heads in their hands.

Dirk and Natia bent down beside the sisters. "What's wrong?" they both asked. The twins were shaking and trembling, tears falling freely. Dirk grabbed their hands and joined them through the bond.

"I told you I would come for you!" Dirk heard Asher's voice in their heads.

"No, I want let you!" Dirk boomed.

"How?" Asher was outraged that this mere boy would interrupt him when he was busy getting his revenge.

Dirk, now linked to the twins let go of their hands and grabbed Natia, and El's hands. "Join with me. Tab, stand guard."

Tab nodded. The three went deep into Vira and Nira's thoughts. "Come back to me, sisters. I can't make it without you." Dirk sent his love to them.

"Dirk, we're trapped... He won't let us go..." Vira whimpered. Dirk felt Asher sending night terror after night terror into the twin's minds. He also felt El and Natia's resolve, and it gave him strength. Aarya screamed a war cry. Dirk, emblazoned and filled with love and strength from the bond, sent a wave of green fire at the creatures attacking Vira and Nira. The twins were curled up in fear.

The magical fire incinerated the creatures. Asher appeared in front of Dirk. He was a big man with cold, dark eyes and hatred was etched into his face. "You will get what you deserve, Chosen. I know who you are and who your family is. I will torture and kill every last person you love," Asher hissed.

Dirk felt the power burning deep inside of him. The necklace the king had given him was pulsing, as if asking for release. Dirk knew the whole fight was just inside the twin's head, but he still wanted to destroy the vermin. "We'll see about that dirt bag," Dirk said, his eyes flaming. He lifted his hand and crimson-green flames leapt forward, burning through Asher's form. Asher screamed, as if he truly were on fire, and then disappeared.

The twins, now released from his magic, hugged Dirk, clinging to him. "Brother, you came for us."

He kissed both girls. "I love you. I told you I would never let anyone hurt you again. I'm sorry it took so long to get rid of him and the terrors." Dirk opened his eyes as the girls sat up.

"What was it?" Tab asked.

"The Dark Wizard is here," Vira answered, wiping tears away.

"And he is not alone," Nira said. All four of them staggered, as if hit by some wave of dark magic. Dirk steadied himself by grabbing Natia. When his head cleared, he noticed the entire group was holding onto each other.

"Our doppelgangers are all dead!" Vira exclaimed.

Dirk nodded. "I thought that was what I felt," he growled, fear washing over him. He looked at El and grabbed her hand. "El, I love you. I need you to do me a favor." El looked at Dirk. "Go to the farm and make sure my Mom is safe." El nodded.

"I'll go with her," Nira said.

"Are you sure?"

Nira nodded. "Vira will be with you." Nira kissed Dirk on the lips. "I love you, brother. Thanks for saving us."

Dirk smiled. "I love you too, sister. I'll see you both when we find out what is going on." He reminded them to use their new armor and pulled El into a hug.

She squeezed him tight. "I will take care of Kira."

Dirk told her he loved too and then released her to Tab. Tab kissed El. Natia put her hand on the door to the General's shop and it glowed. She opened the door then told Dirk she would be right back. El and Nira followed Natia. Dirk knew that only he and Natia could open the doors safely, so he waited a few minutes. Hearing the familiar whooshing sound, he saw that she had come back. He kissed her.

"Your mom was already in the shop. She knew something was wrong but didn't know what. I told her we would be back in a little while to explain," Natia told the group. Dirk kissed Vira and hugged Tab.

"Remember, together we can't be beat."

Tab wrinkled his nose, "You aren't kissing me."

Dirk smiled "Let's go." They took off their robes, pulled their hoods on, and snapped the buttons, becoming invisible. Dirk opened the door into the academy and what he saw made his stomach turn.

The school was in chaos. Students were running around fighting with wizards in dark red robes. Dead bodies littered the hall. Destruction was everywhere.

"We can't help them now!" Natia said, holding Dirk back.

Dirk thought quickly. "We need to go to the palace first. But wait, I need to do something first." He closed his eyes. *Moira, I'm here. Protect yourself until I find you.*

Hurry... was all he heard back. He was sure it was Moira responding.

I have to go somewhere first, but I promise I will be back as soon as I can. Dirk opened his eyes and then turned around and went back through the door.

"Moira?" Tab asked.

"She's okay right now, but I felt her fear."

Tab squeezed Dirk's shoulder. "You were right about her. She'll be fine until we get back," Tab assured him. Dirk was glad Tab was finally seeing Moira the way he was. "Those powers of yours seem to be getting stronger," Tab remarked.

"Since we got to the outpost, I'm starting to be able to sense thoughts from anyone I am near. Not just the bonded. I sensed every emotion Geraldo was having tonight about Oriana. It was weird. It felt very unsettling. Like I was eavesdropping on his private thoughts. And Moira, I think it's the friendship we have that allows me to sense and even communicate with her. I don't understand it, but now is not the time to discuss it."

"It's probably because now that you're bonded with eleven other people, our powers are growing rapidly being linked. There's no telling what any of us will be capable of as time goes by," Vira explained.

"We can discuss that later. We better hurry!" Natia urged, bringing their attention back to the moment. They hurried back down the stairs. Dirk placed his hand on the door that lead to the palace.

As soon as they entered the throne room, Dirk saw the king's soldiers fighting with soldiers that were wearing black and gold armor.

"Vanguard scum," Dirk said, pulling his hood back. The others did the same. He wanted these scums to know who was going to kick their asses.

The king was surrounded by eight of his guards, who were fighting off twenty of the Vangaurd soldiers. The king had his sword out and was helping fight off the combatants. The king caught a glimpse of Dirk, Tab, Vira, and Natia behind the throne. Sadness filled his eyes. He shook his head and mouthed *No*.

Dirk knew what he meant so they reluctantly stepped back in the shadows.

With tears in his eyes, Dirk watched the last of the king's guards fall. They had taken out all but five of the invaders. Two robed Dark Wizards walked into the room. One of the attackers wore shiny black armor. He was a terror with the sword, striking down the last guard and disarming the king, holding the sword to his throat.

Tab and Natia gripped Dirk tightly to keep him from running to the king's aid. Vira put her arm around his waist, holding him back. Natia put her hand over Dirk's mouth to keep him from screaming. The Dark Knight turned to the doorway that the wizards had used.

Someone else was standing in the shadows, but Dirk hadn't noticed them. Vira gasped and pulled Dirk tighter against her body. Dirk felt his heart shatter into pieces when he saw the body laying by the entrance.

His grandfather was lying on his side, facing Dirk and the group. His eyes were open and cloudy, a dagger sticking out of his back. Tears were streaming down Tab's face. Vira was starting to convulse, trying to hold her tears back, as Natia tried to muffle Dirk's heart-wrenching cries of pain.

The man, who had been watching the fight from the sidelines, moved towards the captive king. Hatred swelled in Dirk's chest. The darkness in his heart grew in that instant. It was starting to overtake him to the point that he would probably never get it all out. The figure was a man he had hated most of his life. When he spoke, Tab released his grip, overwhelmed with shock.

Walking beside his father was Gil. He didn't look like a captive to them. He looked like he had been a willing participant in the bloodbath that was taking place all over the school and inside the palace.

Natia released Dirk and covered her own mouth. Vira pressed her face into Dirks back, silently crying. "Thurmond, I have warned you for a long time that this day would come, but you wouldn't listen, my old friend. Instead, you listened to that old fool lying over there, like you have since we were kids." The High Cleric of Zona shook his head in disappointment.

"Romus, have you lost your mind?" the king yelled.

"No, my old friend, I have finally come around. Zolun promises a better life. He promises that my son will rule and that we won't have to put up with those damn Storms anymore." The king glanced at Dirk quickly, trying to make sure he was still hidden.

"Romus, I feel sad for you, my old friend. Durkon never trusted you, and I can now safely say that since your son has killed him, he was right."

Dirk went limp in Vira's arms, numb to everything around him. He felt dizzy and his thoughts had gone blank after hearing the news.

Gil had killed his grandfather.

The darkness swelled inside him even more, threatening to burst. If it hadn't been for that small beacon of light pulsing inside him, he would have probably lost it all together. Tab gripped his brother's wrist, holding him tight. Dirk snapped out of the darkness that was consuming him.

"Enough, my old friend, when I find Thea, I will force her to marry me, making me the king and my son heir after your pathetic children are dealt with," Jamous said.

The king laughed bitterly, not of fear but in amusement. "You are truly mad, you fool. Thea would kill you first." He smiled.

Romus face turned scarlet red. He clenched his fist glaring at the king. "Kill him!" he screamed.

"Father, no!" Gil shouted as he approached his father. A second later, he was sent flying across the room.

Before Dirk could move, the black knight had stabbed the king in the heart. The king's body went limp, and Dirk felt Anastasia scream in his mind. His rage sent him into action. Dirk felt the numbness subside, his eyes burning with rage. Breaking free of Vira's grip, he moved to where he could be seen.

"I will kill all of you and end your pathetic family line for your betrayal!" Dirk promised gravely, stepping out from behind the throne, throwing off his cloak, and unsheathing Harbinger. It lit up the room, the war cry of a phoenix echoing throughout the room when he pulled it from its scabbard. The shock on the High One's face would have been priceless if Dirk hadn't been so sickened by his actions.

The two dark wizards started to cast a spell. "Send my regards to Asher when I send him to you!" Vira said, eyes blazing. The gems in her back lit up the room even brighter when she threw a hand each at the Dark Wizards. Two bolts of crimson lightening left her fingertips and burned the two wizards in half.

Knowing his family had his back, Dirk looked straight at Gil. He pointed his sword at him, tears streaming down his face. "You were my brother. I can't believe what you have done. Why?" Dirk pleaded.

Gil couldn't say anything. Fear and shame filled his eyes. "I make a vow this day. I swear before everyone here that I will kill you and make you suffer for the pain you have caused me and my family. You have broken my heart, brother." Dirk's eyes blazed and then the black knight charged. Catching his enemy's sword on the downswing, he pushed it to the side with ease and punched the knight so hard that he knocked the knight's helmet off his head.

The man had black, cropped hair and yellow eyes. Dirk knew it was the king of Vanguard's son, Julian. "I have been waiting a long time to kill a Storm. Too bad the little brat got to kill your grandfather. I wanted that privilege," he said, goading Dirk.

"You will go to the underworld disappointed still, I'm afraid," Dirk said through gritted teeth, attacking with such viciousness that Julian had no time to block the blows.

Julian tried to change the momentum and lunged forward; Dirk laughed inside. "You fool." Twirling around as he lunged, his sword swept around, cutting the Vangaurd prince's head off with one swing. Blood sprayed all over his body, the headless body twitching on the floor. Dirk wiped it away, seeing that Tab, Natia, and Vira had taken out all of the other guards.

Gil was gone, but his father was on his knees, at the mercy of Natia and Tab's swords. They were pointed at his throat. Vira held a ball of crimson fire in her hand. He wore a smug smile as he looked at Dirk. "You idiot. Who do you think this will be blamed on?" the High One proclaimed.

Dirk's eyes flared. "Romus Jamous, I, Dirk Storm, protector of Marona and the Chosen of Zona, do here by find you guilty of treason."

Gil's father laughed. "You little fool. You don't have the authority or the balls."

Dirk stared at him. "For what you have done to the kingdom, and for what you have done to my king, for what you have turned my friend into... All the beatings you gave him, it's no wonder he turned out the way he has. Trust me, I do have the balls."

In one fluid motion, Dirk and Tab stabbed him in the heart. Natia swung her katanas right after and took his head off, spraying them all in his blood. Vira released her ball of fire and burned his whole body to ash, leaving his head.

"Dirk..." The king's low voice reached Dirk's ears. Dirk and the three-bonded ran to the king's side. Tab propped him up. Natia held his hand. Vira closed her eyes and tried to heal his wounds, laying her hands on his chest. Dirk knelt down and placed a hand on his shoulder.

Dirk looked to Vira. She shook her head. "Poisoned, as well."

Blood was running from the corner of the king's mouth as he tried to speak.

"Yes, my king," Dirk said.

"Finish what your family started. Protect Anastasia, like you promised. Thelon is lost, I'm afraid. Protect her, Dirk."

Dirk nodded. "My king, where is Queen Thea?"

The king smiled. "The safest place in the world. With your mother." And those were his last words, King Thurmond Jerard closed his eyes.

Dirk screamed at the heavens, hearing Anastasia's scream. His head fell to his chest as they laid the king down. He grabbed Natia's hand and walked over to kneel beside his grandfather's dead body. Dirk pulled the dagger out of the general's back and put it in his belt.

Vira came over and turned the general over slowly. She closed his lifeless eyes, laying her head on his chest and crying. Dirk knelt beside her and laid his hand on her back. Dirk closed his eyes. Tab joined them. Natia grabbed his hand and comforted him. She knew the general had been like a father to Tab as well.

Tears welled in Natia eyes. "Why didn't they use the Miraga stones when the attack came?" Dirk asked, pulling the stones out of the general's coat pocket.

"Maybe there was no warning with that piece of shit traitor amongst them," Tab suggested, and the others agreed.

The sound of fighting could be heard from the hallway. It brought them out of their reverie fast. Dirk's training took over as Stavers came running into the throne room. Twenty palace guard were fighting off ten black-and-gold armored Vangaurd soldiers. Several dark wizards were not far behind the Vangaurd soldiers, blowing up the palace as they strolled toward the throne.

Stavers gasped and fell to his knees when he saw the king on the floor. "NOOOOOO!"

The captain of the guards took in the scene. "Jamous?"

Dirk nodded. "He has paid for his crimes." He pointed to Jamous's head and the pile of ash beside it. "I'm sorry I couldn't get here in time."

"Your orders?" the captain asked. Dirk looked to Stavers, who was still in shambles from the king's death. Dirk noticed the captain looking at him expectantly. "Your orders sir?" the captain asked again.

Dirk wiped the tears away. The guards, still fighting, yelled, "They're getting closer!" Vira raised her head. She looked at Dirk and then Natia.

They rose and Tab did the same. Dirk, realizing, he was now in charge, looked to the captain. "Secure the king's body. We'll take care of this," Dirk commanded his eyes blazing. The bonded moved so they were in front of the group of guards.

Natia waved her hand and three Vanguard soldiers slammed into the wall, splattering blood everywhere. The four bonded grabbed hands with Dirk and Tab in the middle. Vira raised her free hand, and a crimson barrier came up. The advancing wizards shot lightning and fire at the barrier, but the attacks just bounced off.

The wizards parted, and a big man wearing a dark cloak came forward and held his hands up for them to stop. He laughed as he approached the barrier.

"I knew I would find you, my lost child," Asher said, leering at Vira. Dirk was restraining himself. He knew that the barrier required them all to stay focused. Vira glared at Asher. "And we're graced with the Chosen and his protector," Asher said, eyeing Dirk and Natia. He looked at Tab then turned back to Dirk. "Vira, I'll deal with you and your sister as soon as I get through with this pretender."

"I'll give you one chance to leave Silver City alive," Dirk said.

Asher laughed. "I guess you haven't been outside the palace, have you? Silver City has fallen. The soldiers who didn't die have fled the city and that so-called wizard school of yours is mine now. The wizards are all dead, as you will be soon too for what you did to me."

Asher turned his head to the side, revealing the burn marks on one half of his face. He glared at Dirk.

"From the looks of things, your king is dead, and you have nowhere to run. Surrender, and I will kill you quickly. Fight, and I will kill you, then rape your mother and your whore a hundred times before I kill them."

Natia looked ready to explode with rage. Dirk had finally had enough. The group's power was seeping out of their fingertips. Their eyes were blazing crimson flames, which Asher couldn't see through the similar-colored barrier.

"Now!" Dirk shouted. The barrier fell and all four of the bonded threw their hands forward, releasing the power of their building hatred.

Flames leapt from their hands with such a thunderous force that Asher, who must have had his own shield up, was blasted over the other wizards, who were roiling with the flames as the fire ripped through their mediocre shields. Dirk hoped he would remember their screams of pain for as long as he lived. It was a little bit of payback for what they had done to his family.

The bonded all fell to their knees, exhausted. Dirk held his head up and looked around for any more immediate threats. The wizards were burning to ash before his eyes. The release of power had nearly sent the bonded into unconsciousness. The captain of the guards and his men came running to their aid. They grabbed them all under their arms and lifted them to their feet.

"Thanks," Dirk said. "That took more out of us than we were prepared for." The sounds of soldiers running brought their attention back to the hall.

"We have to go," Tab said.

"I think we might have to fight," the captain said. Dirk pulled out Harbinger and a wave of energy rushed through the four bonded. They were rejuvenated by the power of the blade. The war cry of the phoenix was heard even by the approaching Vanguard soldiers as Harbinger flared red.

While Dirk set up in attack position, Natia pulled both katanas out as did Vira. Tab pulled out his sword, as did the rest of the soldiers. Fifty soldiers were charging. Asher had seemed to escape the blast of the bonded unharmed this time. He stood back behind several soldiers and said "Kill them all. Except that damn Storm boy. I want him."

Vira flung a burst of air at the soldiers. It slowed them but didn't stop their charge. The first six soldiers who were closest to the bonded paid with their lives quickly. Harbinger tasted blood as Dirk sliced the first one in half. He spun, decapitating two at the same time after they had tried to overpower him. Natia parried a strike from a long sword then slid off to the side, disemboweling the soldier. Blood flowed freely off of their swords.

A rage filled Dirk. He sliced, he cut, he beheaded, and he gutted every soldier that got too close. Natia and Vira were by his side the whole time. Tab had taken a spear to the thigh from the third wave of attackers that had somehow pierced his armor. He had been pulled back by one of the palace guards.

When the last head rolled, the three were covered in Vangaurd blood. Bodies piled up in front them like a wall. Blood dripped from their weapons. Three of the palace guards lay dead. Dirk wiped the blood from his eyes. The rest of the guards just stood in awe as they had watched the three bonded work in unison, cutting down all fifty soldiers.

They had fed off each other's moves, cutting when the other had pulled back. Dirk felt they had fought as one. He was breathing hard trying to ignore the smell of excrement and burnt flesh. The stench caused him to reflexively gag. He heard more soldiers coming. Asher had retreated and was leading a bigger contingent with wizards as well. Fire sailed over their heads, licking at their hair as it crackled overhead. A lightning bolt slammed Natia in the chest and sent her tumbling backwards.

Enraged, Dirk released all of his anger in a crimson flame, cutting through dead bodies and the first twenty soldiers unlucky enough to be at the front. Vira unleashed a cloud of black lightning, striking several soldiers. Their skin began to boil and then they lay dead in a pool of blood.

The dark wizards threw up a barrier. One of them couldn't have stopped Vira's attack so they must have combined barriers to keep the death lightening out, Dirk thought. "Time to go!"

"Where to?" the captain asked. Dirk motioned to the side of the throne. He had sensed Volar, Tara, and Oriana coming through the doorway behind the throne. The captain ordered his men and Stavers to follow Dirk.

"We'll cover your retreat," Oriana said with a chilling, murderous look that Dirk would always remember. Her silver eyes were rippling crimson and green flames as she pulled her bowstring back.

The Vangaurd will shit their pants when they see Oriana, Dirk thought. A goddess with silver hair and silver eyes raining death down on them with her bow.

Tara right beside her doing the same. Volar had his war axe ready. They, too, had their new armor on.

"Grab my grandfather and the king's bodies and grab that traitor's head. It's the least we can take to the queen to show her punishment has been dealt to the traitor," Dirk ordered. The soldiers did as he ordered and grabbed the two bodies with reverence. One of the soldiers stabbed Jamous's decapitated head with his sword and then carried it out with him, following the soldier who was helping Tab to the hidden door.

Dirk smiled inside. A few brave, or stupid, Vangaurds came around the corner and were caught between the eyes by Tara and Oriana's arrows. A third met the dwarf at full speed. Volar dispatched them with a side cut and a chop to the juggler, almost beheading the dead soldier. Twenty more fell to the trio and Dirk, who had refused to leave anyone behind. Dirk was the last one through the door.

Rescue and Retreat

After they stepped through the doorway Dirk closed the door and the pull took him away. He felt drained when he walked into the basement at the academy.

He sent most of the group through the portal to the outpost after making sure Natia was okay. He kept Captain Sinclair and ten of his guards along with Natia, and Vira, to the anger of Oriana and Tara. They had wanted to stay and fight.

"You have to protect the outpost in case they know we were there," he told Tara and Oriana, holding each of their hands and looking into their flaming eyes. "I love you, sisters. Now go."

They embraced him, already feeling his pain. "We love you too, brother," Oriana and Tara both said, turning to hug Natia, then grasping hands with Vira. They went through the door to the outpost that Natia had already opened.

Dirk knew they had to go the farm. He didn't want to, but he had to inform Kira and the queen of the bad news, and somehow convince them to come to the outpost with him. He stopped before he turned the knob. "Moira." Dirk bent over and leaned on his knees. Grief had already ripped his heart apart earlier. *Have I left her to die? Are there any other survivors? I have to know, regardless of what I find.*

"Captain, I need you to wait here. I have to make sure that no one else is left behind in the school."

"Sorry sir, I was ordered to stay by your side should anything ever happen to the general."

Dirk shook his head. "We'll talk about this later. Don't get in my way."

The captain saluted him. Dirk opened the door to the school once they got to the top of the stairs. He pulled Harbinger from its scabbard, the blood still fresh, dripped from the former pristine blade. The war cry echoed throughout the halls.

"Well, a secret search-and-rescue is out of the question now," Vira said with a stern face. Dirk grimaced.

They were immediately attacked by two wizards. Vira put her shield up just in time. Natia threw her katanas at lightning speed, and they buried themselves in the hearts of the dark wizards. She pulled the blades out after making sure the wizards were dead. Natia wiped the blood from her blades on the dead wizard's robes.

They moved out, the soldiers trailing behind them. "We need to check to see if Nabas is alive or dead. Then, check every room to see if anyone is hiding or..." Dirk left it at that. The group nodded.

They snuck through the halls until they came to the head wizard's office. The door had been blown off its hinges. They couldn't hear anyone in there, so they crept inside. There was no one there, but the office was destroyed. The floor was covered in shredded parchments, books had been burned and the stench of fire still drifted through the air. The desk had been turned to kindling. The bookshelves had been ripped from the walls, as if someone had been searching for a hidden safe or compartment. "Let's go. There's nothing here." Dirk turned and furtively headed to the lunch hall, with Natia, Vira, and the soldiers close behind, checking all of the rooms they passed.

As they snuck around the corner, Captain Sinclair stepped in front of Dirk and squatted, taking a quick look at the entrance of the lunch hall. There were four wizards guarding the doors.

"There are four wizards guarding the doors. I don't see any soldiers," The captain relayed.

Dirk nodded and motioned for Vira and Natia to move closer. "Natia, you and Vira take the two on the left. I'll take the two on the right. Captain, you follow my lead." Dirk held up his hand with three fingers up. He counted them down. When he got to zero, they attacked.

Natia and Vira shot fire and lightning at two of dark wizards. Dirk moved so fast that the other two wizards on the right didn't even see him. With two quick strikes, Dirk ripped the two wizards from crotch to throat. Blood spurted from their bodies, drenching him even more in blood. He wiped it away from his face as they gurgled on their own bile.

Six Vanguard soldiers came rushing out of the lunch hall. The captain and his soldiers dispatched them with ease. Dirk and the two bonded burst into the lunch hall.

There were six wizards holding about thirty of the students in the hall. The captured students were bloody. The had bruised eyes and gashes across their faces. Their clothes had been torn and most of the girls stayed clutched close together. Dirk didn't want to think what they had been through. They looked like they had been tortured. Harbinger sent a thrill through his body. He and the sword had tasted the blood of its enemies and they both wanted more. Dirk knew they would get it as soon as the wizards saw them enter. They spread out, using their hostages as shields. *Cowards.* Dirk felt as if his whole body were about to burst into a tornado of flames.

"Vira, shield. Natia, you and I will attack after they do."

Vira joined with the two. The barrier went up as three attacks hit the shield. Vira lowered it and Natia sent fire into the one as Dirk took out the other, leaping over the hostages and slicing through the wizard's body. The third was screaming in pain. Vira had attacked him with black lightning. Some of the hostages had taken advantage of the distraction and taken down one of the wizards, leaving two standing.

Vira shielded her and Natia, but Dirk was too far away for the shield's protection. The two wizards shot lightning at Dirk and he instinctively raised Harbinger. The sword absorbed the lightning. This effect recharged Dirk's drained body. His eyes flamed, and he aimed two green flames at the wizards. They screamed as the fire ate through their bodies like paper.

Dirk looked around. The hostages who had broken free were releasing the others. A wave of relief washed over him. He smiled when he realized that it was Moira leading the group. He was glad she was safe.

"It took you damn long enough," Moira said, hugging him.

He squeezed her tight, covering her in blood. "Sorry, I got tied up at the palace." Moira nodded and left to help the rest of the hostages. Dirk wiped the blood away from his face as he looked around and saw a distraught Skylar. He ran over and freed her. "Captain, help free the rest of the captives and show them to the doorway. We'll be right behind you."

All of a sudden, Skylar grabbed and pulled him into a hug. "How? We saw you die in the attack!" Skylar exclaimed, looking into Dirk's eyes. She saw the flames rippling in them.

"Skylar, you're in shock. You must follow these soldiers. I promise I'll explain later."

Skylar shook her head. "You saved us, Dirk. I don't want to go without you."

Dirk removed her hands from his shoulders. "The captain here will protect you."

Skylar looked up at the captain and finally took his hand. "You promise, Dirk?"

He nodded. "I do."

Skylar then smiled. "I know you're as good as your word, Dirk. Be careful."

Dirk grabbed her arm before the captain took her away. "Skylar, where are Hilda and Tilda?"

Tears rolled down her face. She shook her head. "They tried to protect us."

Dirk felt the air leave his body. He lowered his head. He had known the answer, even before he'd asked. "Where?"

"The stairwell to the dorms."

Dirk wiped away a tear. "Captain, hurry, we won't have much time."

The group headed back to the stairwell after Dirk found Hanks and Miss Heloise, both dead in the kitchen. *Too much death*, Dirk thought and then screamed his anger, causing the dishes to rattle. Natia ran to him, grabbing his arm and squeezing it. He stared at her. "I understand," was all she said.

He bowed his head for a second and then started towards the dorms explaining what Skylar had said about Hilda and Tilda.

Natia teared up and grabbed his hands and put her head to his. "Remember." She shared her thoughts of the twins, which only saddened Dirk more.

After all of the captives were out of the lunch hall, they went to the stairwell to go see where their teachers were.

Dirk and the girls found Hilda and Tilda in front of the girl's dorm. They both had matching scorch marks on their chest.

Dirk fell to his knees and cried, grabbing their hands, and holding them to his chest. His heart had been torn apart tonight. Natia and Vira were both crying beside him. Natia closed the twins eye's. They were still clasping each other's hands, even in death.

"Vira, can you bring them with us?" Dirk asked after he couldn't cry anymore. She nodded, and their bodies floated off the ground. The bodies followed Vira, as if being pulled like a wagon. After the remaining students were sent through to the outpost, Dirk sealed the upstairs door and they went downstairs, lying the twin's bodies on the floor. Dirk crossed their arms over their chest like they were sleeping. He then turned, and they went to the farm.

When Dirk stepped through the doorway, Nira and El were sitting with Kira and the queen.

"Dirk!" Kira said, running to embrace her son. She noticed he was covered in blood. All three bonded were. Tears fell as she hugged him and then pulled the girls into the hug. El and Nira were right behind her.

"Durkon?" Dirk's tears told her all she needed to know. Vira and Natia were crying as well. El broke down as Nira and Vira hugged.

"I'm glad that you are okay, sister," Nira said. Dirk turned and kissed Nira on the forehead and El on the cheek and hugged them tightly.

El was sobbing. "Tab?

"He's okay. He got speared in the leg, but he'll be okay. He has already gone back to the outpost."

Dirk noticed Queen Thea still sitting like the beautiful lady she was. Dirk's heart broke even more as he walked over and kneeled in front of her, bowing his head.

She put a hand on his head. "I know, son. You don't have to tell me," she said, wiping away tears. "Who?"

Dirk looked at her. "Romus Jamous was the traitor."

El gasped, placing a hand over her mouth. "Gil?"

Dirk stood up and frowned at El. "He was in league with his father."

El shook her head. "No, Dirk, that just can't be! He's our friend! How do you know?" she asked between sobs.

"Because he is the one who killed my grandfather," Dirk said gritting his teeth. Shock passed through the room. Kira doubled over, falling to her knees. The queen lowered her head. El started hitting Dirk in the chest hysterically. "That can't be! No, Dirk you're wrong! He would never do that!"

Dirk grabbed her and pulled her into a hug, holding her. "The king told us, or rather, we heard him say it before he was killed."

El cried-on Dirk's shoulder until Natia pulled her into a hug. The queen stood. "The traitor?"

Dirk looked her in the eye. "Gil got away, but his father has paid for his crime. Natia took his head before Vira incinerated his sorry-ass body." Dirk lowered his head realizing he had just sworn in front of the queen. His anger had gotten the best of him. He stood there, waiting on a rebuke that never came. Letting out a breath he continued. "We killed him before the king died. He saw justice before he passed into the underworld,"

The queen nodded. "I never liked that weasel."

Dirk looked around. Kira had finally gotten a grip on her tears. "Where is everyone else?" Dirk asked.

"I sent them south with Garrick. It was the plan we already had in place in case of a catastrophic outcome. He will take them north of Feriah where our soldiers will regroup. I will head there myself," Thea said.

Dirk shook his head. "No, my queen. You'll come with us first. Then we will make sure you get to where you need to be." Dirk's voice rang with the authority of a king. The queen raised an eyebrow but said nothing. "My queen, we retrieved the king's body and have sent him and my grandfather's body to the outpost," Dirk said, feeling guilty for talking to the queen that way.

She walked up and hugged Dirk. "Thank you, son. You're right. I will go with you first."

El, finally getting a hold on her pain, asked, "Hilda and Tilda?"

Dirk couldn't bear to see her cry anymore. He looked away.

"Their bodies are waiting on us at the doorway to the outpost," Vira said. El lost it again.

Kira took her hand. "Elyse, look at me." El did, eyes red and tears freely flowing. "It is time to be strong. You will likely see more of your friends die in the future, and I will tell you from experience, it doesn't get any easier."

El nodded and leaned into Kira's shoulder. Dirk decided after a few more minutes that it was time to head back to the school basement.

Dirk and Natia grabbed their armor and all of the weapons they could carry. "We 'll come back and get all the books and anything else we can carry tomorrow." Dirk opened the doorway and Natia led the group through.

Dirk was the last to leave. He felt the pull when he closed the door right away. He noticed that El didn't even glance at Hilda and Tilda's bodies. Dirk then opened the other doorway to the outpost, bending down and gently picking up Tilda in his arms. Natia, imitating Dirk, carried Hilda's body. They then went through the doorway, followed by the rest of the group. He sensed that the rest of the bonded were waiting there to help the group up the stairwell.

Wizard Quentin and Geraldo took the twin's bodies from Dirk and Natia. "The king's and the general's bodies have already been put in a room off the kitchen," Volar informed them.

"The traitor's head has been bagged and put in the building by the stables," Captain Sinclair told them.

"Mom, you and the queen go ahead with Volar, he will take you to the rooms with the bodies. I'll join you when I know we are secure," Dirk then started up the stairs. Dirk, after making sure that everyone else was ok, went to the room to be with his mom. Natia stayed outside of the doorway to give them some privacy.

After about an hour, Dirk sensed the sun was about to rise. He and Kira came out arm in arm. He grabbed Natia and asked her to find his mother a room. "How's Tab?"

"Quentin healed him," El responded.

Dirk nodded. "All the hostages get taken care of?"

She nodded. "Tara and Oriana got them set up with tents and some food." Dirk sighed, exhausted.

"I'll be back in a few minutes," Natia said, taking Kira to find a room. El hugged Tab as he walked up to her. El then pulled Dirk into the hug.

"I'm so sorry." She couldn't cry anymore. Tab hugged his brother and they for the first time, let their emotions go as El held onto both of them.

Tara, Oriana, and Volar gathered around the three. Natia came back after finding Kira a room. The group was soon joined by Nira and Vira. They had been helping with healing the injured students.

Dirk looked at his arms and realized that he, Vira, and Natia were all still covered in blood from the battle. Just then, Thea walked out of the room that her husband was in. She wiped her tears away. The group all bowed.

She told them to stand. "I appreciate the gesture. I know Thurmond and Durkon would be very proud of what I hear every one of you faced tonight. The captain filled me in on how wonderfully you worked together."

Dirk looked down. "It wasn't enough. I had a chance to save him."

"No, Dirk. He shook his head at us. He wanted us to stay hidden," Natia said.

"Natia is right, Dirk. He would have wanted you to have the best chance. I am sure he wanted you to have as many facts as possible before you announced you were there," Thea said, grabbing his shoulder. Dirk still shook his head. "You look at me, Dirk Storm!" the queen demanded. He obeyed her. She grabbed his face in a motherly manner. "You are so much like Diron. And Durkon, as matter of fact. I grew up with your grandfather and I practically raised your father when Durkon was away. I know how hard-headed they were, and I am sure you inherited that trait." She had tears in her eyes.

"I have watched you grow up just the way they did, and I have no doubt you will still blame yourself. But you can't. It's not your fault. It's those evil bastards who did this. If you want to blame someone, then blame them."

Dirk nodded. She kissed his cheek.

"Promise me one thing more."

"Anything."

"Kill them all."

Dirk's eyes flamed. "We will," the bonded said as one.

The queen looked around and saw every eye was rippling with flames. She smiled. "Thank you all. Now, I think I need to lie down for a little bit."

Natia asked the queen to follow her to the room she set up for her and Kira. The queen nodded and followed Natia down the hall.

Natia came back soon after. Dirk looked at the group. He hugged every one of them and thanked them for their help.

"Dirk, we love you. No need to thank us," Oriana said, grabbing him in an embrace.

"How did you know it was the right time to come?" Dirk asked her.

"We sensed you leave, and it wasn't soon after we felt the doppelgangers disappear. We sensed your distress and knew we had to come," Oriana said, releasing Dirk from her hug.

He grabbed her face and kissed her forehead. "You three worked brilliantly together," Dirk said, looking at Volar, Tara and Oriana.

"We felt the flow you three were using," Tara said.

"It integrated with us through the bond," Volar told him.

Dirk smiled. "That was truly brilliant. You saved us at the right time."

He looked at his own armor, then at Natia and Vira. "Natia, Vira and I need to clean up. After that, all of us need some rest as well. I love you all," Dirk said with love in his eyes.

"We love you too brother," they said in unison.

"One question though," Dirk looked at Volar. "How did you get through the doors?"

Volar chuckled. "Royalty has its privileges. The king had the general allow me access to the doors the night we arrived in Silver City." Dirk nodded.

"Later, we are going to go back to the workshop to gather all of the general's books, and anything we can take with us. I would like for some of you to stay here and coordinate with the rest of the group. I'm sure that the queen will want to discuss what we need to do with the king and the general's bodies," Dirk stated, looking around.

"Stas?" El asked.

"Kal and her are already on their way here. They will be here tomorrow."

"We also need to coordinate and find out what all happened out there, so we need to discuss some intelligence missions as well," Tara said, and Dirk agreed.

With that planned, Dirk headed to the shower with Natia and Vira right beside him. They all held hands on the somber walk to the side of the building, acknowledging the soldiers that passed by. Volar had built a makeshift wall for privacy. Good thing he did. There were several tents set up around the courtyard now, but none in sight of the shower.

When they got to the shower the three helped each other take off their bloody armor. Vira conjured up a fireball to warm the water in the barrel. Volar and Tab had set it up the same as Bart had back at the farm. There was also a pull chain with a hook on the wall to keep the water falling freely. The three didn't think anything about their nakedness. They were all still in a state of shock. The water was checked repeatedly until they found it was just right.

Dirk then pulled the chain down, releasing the water. He hooked the chain to a nail on the wall. He looked down and noticed the wooden floor had a hole in the center for the water to drain away. Dirk let the girls step under the water first. When they had gotten wet enough, he stepped under and let the water rinse away the blood and whatever else was on his body. A little of the tension seemed to ease from him.

Natia put shampoo in her hair then Vira's. Natia then washed Dirks. The scrubbing of her fingers in his hair released more of his tension. The three then washed each other's backs. While Dirk was washing Vira's, he really noticed the gem formation on her back for the first time.

"Vira, did you know the shape of your gems resemble a sword?" Vira looked over her shoulder.

"No, we always thought they were placed randomly," Vira replied.

"The stones seem to be in the same place as the stones in Harbinger. Or very close," Dirk said, running his hand gently over the stones. They lit up at his touch. Goosebumps formed on her back.

Natia reached around and started washing Dirk's chest and shoulders. He turned to let her scrub the blood off his face. He did the same for her then turned and washed Vira's back and then her hair again. The blood would not come out easily.

"We need to look at Nira's as well. It might have a meaning," Natia said. She rinsed off under the water, then let the others take their turn. Nira was waiting on them, holding a towel for each of them when they finished rinsing the shampoo and soap off. She had also brought them some fresh clothes.

After Dirk had gotten his pants on, he asked Nira to pull up the back of her shirt, so he could see her gems. She did without hesitation. Dirk ran his fingers over them, just like he had Vira's. They lit up the same way and her gems were imbedded in the same shape. Vira and Natia looked and finally saw what he was talking about. Nira lowered her shirt.

Dirk explained what he had noticed, and she looked at Vira's differently for the first time since they had been embedded. "We can discuss that later. Come with me, I have set us up a tent at the back of the house. The captain and his men will make sure we aren't bothered for a few hours," Nira said.

Dirk was glad when he finally laid down. He had been awake for at least thirty hours and his body was drained. They didn't bother with the Enda Flower. Dirk had stopped Asher from being able to enter their dreams when he burned him the night before in the basement. Dirk's green flames had destroyed his connection. He wasn't sure how he knew. He just did.

Dirk felt empty, but the closeness of his one true love and his two sisters eased the pain a little. They laid huddled together, Vira on one shoulder and Natia on the other. Nira was wrapped around Natia, holding Dirk's hand. They all had tears in their eyes when they fell asleep.

In the back of his mind he felt the connection to Linc. *I am so sorry brother. I'll be there in less than two weeks.*

Thanks, brother. Dirk answered him.

Be careful, they will be on the lookout for you now.

Don't worry about me. Take care of Kira. I'll pick up the boots and then head straight to the Forgotten City. Hopefully, we'll get there around the same time. I love you, brother. The general was too good to die that way and I want to be there when you face that slimy bastard who used to call us friend.

I love you too brother and we will have our revenge. Dirk promised, and then sleep took him away.

Pineral

Linc woke the next day very irritated for not being able to be there with Dirk and Tab. "What's the matter?" Mildred asked, rolling on top of him. Linc half smiled. The sheets fell off her shoulders, exposing her very ample breast.

Her gray eyes have a sparkle to them this morning. Linc thought.

"I know you want to be with your, what do you call them, bonded?

"That's right, but we are five days away at best speed and we still have to stop in Pineral." Linc frowned. "It's just the general raised us three, Dirk, Tab, and me. I must get there some way, if I can, for the funeral," He had an idea on how to get there faster but was a little hesitant to share his idea with Mildred.

With his mind finally made up, he asked her, "Do you know anything about the phoenix?"

Mildred lay on his chest, her breast pressing on his. "Now how would I know anything about the phoenix?" Linc ran his fingers through her jet-black hair, and then he ran his hands down to the small of her back where he felt a light patch of baby hair.

Mildred giggled and scooted side to side to stop him. "Stop, I told you I'm ticklish there!" Her twisting from side to side in the position she was in got an inadvertent reaction from Linc. Of course, this led to a replay of the night before when they both had finally given into their feelings for each other.

"You are amazing," Linc said to her after they had finished, careful to be as quiet as they could.

She smiled and, after catching her breath, said, "You're only as good as your partner."

"You're pretty awesome yourself." Linc laughed. Mildred laid her head on his shoulder and kissed his ear.

He laughed again. *Sorry. I'll remember next time.*

Mildred raised her head and stared at him. "Excuse me?"

He smiled. "Oh no I wasn't talking to you," he said caressing her face with the back of his hand. "The bond. I explained how all of the bonded are connected and share our deepest and most personal feelings sometimes."

She blushed. "You mean?"

Linc nodded. "I think we just had sex with all of the bonded. A few were ok with it since I don't know how to block them out yet, but El chastised me anyway."

"Well, I guess when I meet them, they'll know me intimately right off," Mildred said, smiling.

He laughed again and nodded. *I'll tell her.*

Mildred knew there was a communication going on between Linc and one of the bonded. "Well?"

He looked at her. "Oriana said not to pay any attention to El. She has Tab, but some of the elven females truly enjoyed what you shared. She said to tell you she looks forward to meeting the two of us in person,"

"I am sure that will be interesting," Mildred said. Linc, finally through talking with the bonded, washed up and headed to the deck.

River had taken over running the crew since Linc had been hurt and was doing a good job. "Where are we at, River?"

River looked at Linc. "According to the last reading I got from the stars last night, we're about half a day out of Pineral." Linc was surprised. "Yeah, we got a big tail wind last night," River said pointing to the crow's nest. Linc followed his gaze.

Aarya was sitting on the ledge of the crow's nest. Linc had told the crew everything the morning he awoke after recovering.

Jerle was so excited when Aarya landed on his shoulder his sun-dried skin cracked from his grinned. It revealed that he probably had never used a toothbrush a day in his life. He asked Linc if she had anything to do with rescuing his family.

"Without her taking the letter to Dirk, you probably would haven't have ever seen them again."

Jerle had become Aarya's biggest fan, making sure she had food every time she was on the ship. Linc felt the crew was still trying to recover from Corky's death, but they were barely getting by.

Kaz hadn't been the same since the attack. He had almost died as well, and if it hadn't been for Linc, he would have. He was grateful but acted a little distant now. He still did his job but, wasn't very talkative nowadays.

Linc was glad when they docked in Pineral that afternoon. He paid three silvers to the port manager and Kaz volunteered to stay and keep watch until they came back from the meeting with Mr. Wark. The rest of the group followed Linc through Pineral looking at the town.

"It's just a smaller version of Oak City." Linc observed as they walked through the town. "I guess that they're all basically the same. Look there's a bakery. They even have all of the local shops like dress makers and smiths." They passed an inn called the Angler's Hook. Then they saw the cobbler shop.

Linc and the crew walked into Wark's Cobblery. He saw an older, brunette man sitting on a bench, working on some belts. He looked up as the four came in.

"Afternoon," Mr. Wark said. He stopped what he was doing and got up, wiping his hands off on his shop apron. "Hello Mildred." He smiled at her.

She nodded. "Hello, it's good to see you again."

"And you, how's your mother?" he asked.

"She is fine," Mildred smiled, noticing Mr. Wark looking at Linc's boots.

"How do they feel?" Linc smiled.

"The best boots I've ever owned. You are a master shoemaker." Mr. Wark smiled at Linc's remark. "Linc Kane." Linc said, holding out his hand. Mr. Wark shook his hand. "This is River and Jerle. Mildred, you already know." Mr. Wark shook the boy's hand.

"Call me Larry," Mr. Wark said.

"Larry, did you get the letter from Phil?"

He nodded. "I did, and I have the amount Phil requested made, but I haven't decided if I want to finish the other part of the order."

Linc nodded and thought about the best way to get Larry to agree with the partnership. "Let me ask you one question, Larry. Do you trust your son?"

Larry smiled. "I do."

"He is roommates with my brother. Not blood-related, but we grew up together and are family. Larry, once I tried on your boots, I knew they were probably the best pair of boots that I would ever own. Now it's obvious that I want to sell your shoes. Only to a few select places though. Mainly, it would be Swon's selling them. But I would like to try and sell some in Silver city and maybe even a few other places once I get trading routes established. Not too many at first though, just enough to make us both a little silver. I'm not interested in stealing your secrets, Larry. I just want to set up some trade routes, like I said, with my new trading company. So, what do you say?"

Linc could sense Larry was leaning towards agreeing with him by the thoughtful expression on his face.

Larry sat down on a stool beside his work bench. He looked at the crew and rubbed his chin with his hand. "I'll do it, but only forty at a time,"

Linc smiled. "Deal."

Larry shook hands with Linc and Mildred. "I have them ready I just wanted to see you in person and judge you for myself. You have the money, I suspect?"

Linc had River put down the backpack he had been carrying. He paid him in silver. Mr. Wark grinned from ear to ear. "I have never made a deal this big before," Larry said with a twinkle in his eye.

"You're going to be a rich man," Mildred said. Larry smiled at her.

"Can we buy a pair for the crew?" River asked Linc.

Larry stood up. "Give me your sizes and I'll give the rest of you a pair."

Mildred patted him on the shoulder. "Thank you, Larry." Larry walked to the back of his shop to get something to write their sizes on. As He walked off, Linc realized he had made his mind up.

He looked at River and Jerle. "I want to let you two know that I have decided that I will be leaving tonight." They looked questioningly at Linc, and he gave them a, *I will tell you after* look. They nodded. "Larry, can you have them delivered to the ship?" Linc asked as he came back. Larry looked at him curiously, but finally agreed.

"Urgent family business. I can get there quicker traveling across land," Linc said to River and Jerle.

Mildred, caught off guard, scowled at him. Linc ignored Mildred's stare and told Larry the slip number the ship was in and paid for the labor and deliver fee. Linc said goodbye to Larry after everything was set up and then they departed.

"Linc, why are you leaving us?" River questioned.

Linc hadn't told them yet what had happened in Silver City. There were a few things he needed to know before he told them everything.

When Aarya had delivered the note and the Miraga stones Dirk had sent, she stayed with the crew until this morning. Linc then sent her to check on the group the queen had sent south. He confirmed through the link with Aarya that several of the families had made it out and he wanted to make sure the crew's families were with them before he told them.

"I'll explain after we get some hot food at the inn. First, I better explain to Mildred before she kills me." Linc told River.

"Okay," River replied then he and Jerle went to gather their gear and lock away the silver.

"I'm waiting," Mildred said. Linc pulled her to the corner of the building where no one would bother them.

Linc explained his theory about Aarya being able to transport more than just letters. "I think she can carry us to the Great Forest outpost. She believes she can as well. That is, if you want to go?"

Mildred looked into his eyes. "Will it hurt?"

"I don't know," Linc said honestly and caressed her face.

Mildred gazed into his eyes. "I think I would follow you anywhere Linc."

She pulled him in for a kiss. Linc's heartrate tripled from her touch. He gripped her by the shoulders and gazed into her gray eyes. "Good, because I would be heartbroken if you didn't come with me."

Mildred smiled at his response. "I'm not that easy to get rid of, my dear."

They held hands as they walked the few yards to the Angler's Hook to meet the boys for lunch. He told her he didn't think River would have any problems running the ship and then he explained the Miraga stones to her. Mildred just listened and realized that, somehow, she was not afraid of Lincs plan after he had explained everything. They would each make doppelganger and leave the stones for River to activate if he needed help.

"I want to help River hire at least two more people for the crew. Especially since we're leaving. We'll plan to meet them in Fork city in three weeks. It's not far from the Old Outpost. River can deliver the boots there and we can get them to Dirk. I have to be there for Dirk and Kira." Linc explained.

"Oh, my dear, I understand." Mildred placed a hand on his heart. "I know what they mean to you. I want to be there as well." Mildred kissed him.

"Plus, I think I can get help understanding this bond more and join in on the training they will be doing," Mildred nodded.

When they got to the Angler's Hook, Linc paid for the crew's rooms. Linc then sat down with his crew and told them what had happened in Silver City. The three crewmen stood there in a state of shock.

"Don't worry, I've sent Aarya to find out about your families. You know how trustworthy she is by now." The crew nodded and sat down. "That's why we're leaving. I need to be with Dirk and Kira. River, you know what they mean to me." Linc looked to River.

"I do. I know they're your family." Linc nodded.

While they waited Linc talked to the owner of the inn, and he pointed him to a few trustworthy crewmen looking for work. River and Linc interviewed the former soldiers. They had experience on naval vessels. River agreed to let them guard the ship that night and if they did a good job, he would hire them for the crew. They agreed and went back to their table.

Linc then explained to River about the Miraga stones. River sat and listened patiently while Linc explained how to use them, and that they would leave the stones in the captain's quarters.

Linc smiled. "River, Aarya has just confirmed that your family is safe and traveling with the people who met at the Storm farm. Jerle, Ulny and

Claire are with them. Kaz your father and mother are with them as well. They all made it out of Silver City thanks to Dirk and his friends warning them." They sighed in relief. Their families were safe.

"This bond I have allows me to communicate through the other bonded. What I tell you, you can't share with anyone. Okay?" The crew all nodded. "I can't explain it all. It's just certain thoughts we share. That's how I knew that Tab got word out that if an attack happened, that they should head to Storm farm. El's parents knew about the bonded, so they were already traveling with a group of first years to meet Dirk and the rest at the old outpost. So, they were safe. Your families had been warned so at the first sign of trouble they all hurried to the farm. Of course, Ulny and Claire were already there, Jerle." He smiled.

"That's all I can tell you now," Satisfied, the crew all agreed.

"Let's get some lunch, then Mildred and I need to get going. River, I trust you. You have proven to be a leader among men. Your father will be very proud of you I know," Linc grasped River's hand.

"Thanks, Linc. That means a lot to me. We'll take care of the merchandise and the ship. We'll meet you in Fork City on time. I promise," River confirmed.

Linc ate, thinking about how proud he was of his friends. They had saved a lot of lives by having a good plan in place. Being brought back to the present by a question from River, Linc realized he hadn't even heard the question.

"Sorry River, what did you ask?"

"How long will it take you to get there?".

"It should be almost instantaneously. At least that's what Aarya thinks." Linc smiled at the looks on his crews faces.

"Linc, I'm sorry for the way I've been acting since you saved my life. It's been really hard dealing with what I saw, and then what you told us after," Kaz said, lowering his head.

Linc grasped his shoulder. "No need my friend. We have a more serious things to deal with now." Kaz agreed.

The crew finally finished their lunch. Linc and Mildred got up to leave, telling everyone they had to get going so they could meet Aarya at the ship. River assured him they would be prepared. They said their goodbyes. Linc also wanted to send Lord Saint a letter explaining what he was doing and that he couldn't return his ship as soon as he thought but he would once they got through at Fork City.

"He won't mind, will he?" Linc asked Mildred.

"I don't think he will. Especially after he hears what happened in Silver

City."

Reunited

The sun was getting ready to set for the day. Linc had written the letter and dropped it off at the post.

"We better hurry. Let's head to the ship, bind the Miraga stones and get our packs. She will be back soon." Mildred followed him back to the ship and Linc showed her what to do to bind the stones to them.

After they did, he put the stones in the desk beside the bed. They then grabbed their gear and left River a note how to activate the stones in case he forgot.

Linc knew he had put a lot on his young friend and wanted to make sure he had the clear instructions. He grabbed the gem Aarya had given him and put it in his pocket not wanting to forget it. They both grabbed their weapons, secured them in the straps over their backs, headed to the deck, and held hands as they waited.

When Aarya landed on Linc's shoulder, he smiled at Mildred. "You ready?" She smiled and stepped close to him, wrapping her arms around his waist. Aarya sent Linc a mental message. He nodded to her. "Put one hand on her side like this," Linc said, laying a hand on the phoenix's back. Mildred imitated Linc. Aarya shrieked a war cry that shook the ship.

Linc hoped the surrounding vessels hadn't felt it. Aarya trilled to Linc and then she began to glow with a golden crimson light. Linc and Mildred both felt a surge of power engulf them and then felt a pull in their chests.

With a flash of light, Linc's eyes blazed, and they both disappeared. It lasted no more than a minute. They appeared, kneeling, with a flash of crimson fire, in the outpost courtyard in the middle of a circle that had been formed by the nine-other bonded.

Linc took a deep breath and stood. Mildred did as well. Linc's eyes were a little blurry, but they cleared when Dirk said, "I am glad you're here safely, brother."

He turned as Dirk embraced him in a hug. More tears fell. "I am so sorry, Dirk."

Dirk released him, smiling. "Me too brother. The pain is barely tolerable." Linc understood because he felt the same way. "I'm just glad you're here now. Looking a little rugged with that long hair, but you look to be okay."

Linc smiled and nodded. "I thought you might sense what I was planning."

Dirk nodded. "Aarya," he confirmed. Linc held his hand out to Mildred, who stepped to his side.

Dirk embraced her. Mildred took the hug. "I am sorry for your loss. And thank you for helping us with the Gore. I don't think we would have survived without all of your help."

Dirk was doing more than hugging her as she spoke. He was sensing her core. He wanted to make sure he didn't feel any darkness in her. There was a little but no more than a normal person.

Still hugging her, he whispered to where only she could hear. "Have you told him yet?" Mildred tensed a little. Dirk felt the power in her come alive. "Don't worry, we are friends here," Dirk assured her.

He pushed her back to look in her eyes. There was a sparkle of light in the center. Mildred trusting Dirk, said, "I am going to tonight." She smiled. Dirk nodded.

Linc, who was busy being lectured by El for his irresponsible actions, grabbed her and hugged her. "I missed you, Elyse."

She gave in and hugged him back. Tab got his hug in, pulling her away. "It's good to have you back with us brother," Tab said.

Linc nodded and returned the sentiment. "Everyone, this is Mildred."

"Yes, we know her very well," El said, smiling while embracing her. After El released Mildred, Dirk covered the smile on his face as the scene played out in front of him.

Oriana walked up and put her hands-on Mildred's face. She looked into those gray eyes and then planted a kiss on her lips. Oriana leaned back and said, "Thank you. That was amazing." She turned and kissed Linc as well. "Better keep an eye on her. If you're not careful, I might steal her from you." Oriana winked at her and slapped Linc's butt as she walked away.

He smiled at her. "Maybe we can share," Linc said, receiving a punch from Mildred and a scowl from El. "Hey, I was joking!"

Oriana, on the other hand, wasn't and smiled back at Linc. After a formal greeting from the others in the group, Dirk took Linc and Mildred around the house. Kira was waiting at the door. Linc stepped aside everyone and ran to her. She held out her arms and Linc embraced her.

"Lincoln, I am so glad you're safe!" Kira said. The group just stood back and let him take his time with Kira. Mildred stood next to Dirk. She grabbed his hand and squeezed it.

"All he thought about for the last twenty-four hours was getting here to you." Dirk squeezed her hand back. Vira and Nira, who were standing behind them, each put a hand on Dirk's shoulder. Mildred saw Vira and Nira were giving her a skeptical look.

Dirk could tell they sensed what Mildred did when Dirk had confronted her. "They will be fine once everything is out in the open," Dirk said to Mildred.

"How did you know?"

"I am sure Linc told you my family's history?" Mildred nodded. "I have an ability to sense just about anything from people. I can tell when they're being honest and when they're not. I can even sense things in their past," Dirk said, watching Kira and Linc.

"And we can as well," Vira said, flames dancing across her eyes.

Mildred nodded again. "I never wanted to have to admit where I came from honestly. I promise I love him, and I will be truthful," she said, looking into Dirk's eyes. Vira and Nira relaxed, and Dirk could feel it.

"Good. I like you and I know that Linc has strong feelings for you." Linc and Kira were finally through talking and queen Thea was talking with Linc now.

"Party approaching!" one of the soldiers, who was on the gate towers, shouted.

"Stas," Dirk informed the group. The bonded all turned and went to greet their bonded sister in her time of grief.

"Open the gates!" Tab shouted, running through the crowd to the gate. They moved out of the way, making a path for the approaching soldiers. Linc told the queen that Anastasia was approaching so he walked over to Dirk. She nodded and went to meet her daughter. Dirk wrapped an arm around Linc as they stood beside Kira. She was standing beside Natia and the queen.

They watched as the gates opened and saw Kal and Anastasia were leading the soldiers they had been training. The soldiers stopped in formation behind Kal and Anastasia after they had filed into the outpost.

Anastasia stopped her horse and dismounted to greet her mother. Dirk watched them tearfully embrace. Kal came over and greeted Dirk and the group with a salute. Dirk returned it and they hugged. "I'm glad you're safe, Dirk. We sensed everything you went through. I am sorry for your loss. He was a great man," Kal said sincerely. He hugged Natia and turned to Linc. "I am glad to finally meet you both in person, Linc, and Mildred."

Linc nodded. "Kal, were your travels safe?" Linc asked.

Kal looked around. "Let me get these soldiers situated and then we will talk."

Before Kal walked away Dirk asked, "They have been informed?"

Kal nodded. "Just as you wanted." "Brock?"

Kal frowned. "He hasn't said anything outright, but I could sense his disbelief."

Dirk nodded "I will talk to him after they get situated. Get with Captain Sinclair of the royal guard. He will get the soldiers set up." Kal nodded and went to give the soldiers their orders.

The old outpost is filling up too fast, Dirk thought, taking in all of the new soldiers. He knew they really needed to move to the Forgotten City as soon as possible, but they had waited on Anastasia to decide where she wanted to hold the funeral pyre. Dirk and the group still hadn't gone back to the shop to retrieve the general's books or any extra weapons. They had been busy all day, helping get the students situated. Dirk knew they had to make new plans with Hermosa since the size of their group had grown extensively.

Skylar and the rest of the students had been watching their arrival. The attention and respect shown to Dirk by the wizards and now Kal, had dissolved any doubts she might have had about who was truly in charge.

Kal introduced Captain Sinclair to the soldiers. Captain Sinclair told the soldiers where to go to set up for the night, food and water were available, and that they would receive instructions from Kal in the morning. Kal then dismissed the group. Dirk listened, and then he watched as Skylar made a beeline for Brock when the group was released. They embraced. Dirk smiled at their reunion.

They had been enemies most of their lives, but with everything that had happened, he needed everybody he could get that was willing to fight. If making peace with Brock was what it took, then so be it.

After Anastasia and her mother were through talking, she headed straight to Dirk, and they hugged. "Thank you for getting revenge for him," Anastasia said, crying on Dirk's shoulder.

"I should have saved him."

She pushed him back. "Dirk, you did what he wanted. I saw him shake his head."

Dirk still felt guilty.

"I am sorry for the general. That hurts almost as bad as losing my father."

Dirk squeezed her. They shared a moment. They had grown up together and Dirk and Anastasia both lost the most important figures in their lives on the same day.

"We will do the funeral pyre here tomorrow night. I have sent a messenger for the wagon train to make haste. We need to be moving on to the Forgotten City as soon as we can," Anastasia said. The bonded had all gathered around and were listening to her talk.

Dirk nodded. "Any word on Prince Thelon? Before your father died, he told me he was lost." Dirk was concerned that there had been no word from Thelon and his troops in three days.

Anastasia shook her head. "I'll send out scouts tomorrow and see if they can find out where he is. I hate doing this without him, but we need to think of the future," She looked around.

"Princess Crystal had already traveled back to Feriah before the attack. Maybe he and the troops were diverted there," Kal said.

"The group we have traveling south to the Silver City outpost may be in contact with them by now. Both of you look very tired. I have a shower set up behind the building. Go wash up. We'll eat and discuss what to do after the pyre," Dirk said, hugging her one more time and then shaking Kal's hand.

Dirk wanted to talk with Brock. He also wanted to see Jonesy and the rest of the dwarves. He went with Natia, Volar, Linc, Mildred, Vira and Nira to find them. El and Tab had already gone off to find Jonesy. Dirk saw Brock and Skylar talking by one of the tents by the east wall.

"Hold up here for a minute. I have something I need to do first." They sensed what Dirk was going to do, so they watched. Linc ignored his request to hang back and was by his side when Brock noticed them coming towards him.

Skylar looked up and smiled. "Well, that's a different Skylar than I remember," Linc whispered to him.

"She has been through a lot. I felt bad for her when we saved them. They were being tortured," Dirk said. Linc just nodded.

Out of nowhere, Tab walked beside his two best friends. "Not without me." Dirk looked at him and gave a small nod. Brock stood up and met them halfway. They stopped a foot apart from each other. Skylar got up and stood beside Brock.

Brock looked at the three in turn. "Any word on my family?" Brock asked Dirk directly.

He nodded. "Your father and mother made it out before the attack got bad. They were warned by Tab if anything happened to head south to Feriah. That's where all the evacuees are heading. I'm told he got six of his ships on the water before it got bad." Dirk said stone faced.

Brock nodded. "I am sorry about the general. I know I have always been a dick about your family, but truth be told, I was always jealous of your relationship with him and my father," He turned to Tab. "I am sorry for sucker punching you the way I did." He held his hand out. Linc nudged Tab.

"We have more sinister things to deal with now than childhood jealousies," Tab said, shaking Brock's hand.

"I agree. Linc, I hear you had a rough trip?" Brock said, turning towards Linc.

"It was an experience. The Gore are real monsters."

"Dirk, thank you for saving Skylar. She told me if it weren't for you and your friends, she would probably be dead."

Dirk shook his head. "It was the right thing to do. Like Tab said, childhood foolishness has no place here. I look forward to being allies in what is to come." Dirk held out his hand.

"I will be there. You can count on that the day we take back our city," Brock said, clasping Dirk's forearm.

"Good. Skylar have you got everything you need?"

"Yes, Dirk, thank you again," Skylar said, giving the first sincere smile Dirk had probably ever seen from her.

"Skylar," Linc said. She looked at him. "I am sorry about Sylvie. I never liked her, but she was your friend, and I am sorry she didn't make it."

"Thanks."

They departed for the first time since they were very young as possible friends.

Dirk and his two brothers joined the group. They found El and Jonesy over by one of the fire pits. They were sitting and discussing what Gil had done.

Jonesy saw Dirk and he got up and grasped his friend in a bear hug. He dwarfed Dirk in size. "I know," was all Dirk said.

He was tired of being told how sorry people were. He was ready to make the ones responsible for the attack sorry. Jonesy understood. Tab, encouraging everyone that they should eat, went in search of food. All of the bonded, including Mildred, got some leftover venison and some ale that Anastasia and Kal had brought with them. They all ate around the fire pit that had been made especially for them. Anastasia and Kal, after taking a long shower, were glad to sit and eat.

"Tomorrow, Natia the twins and I will go back to the farm and retrieve various books and maps from the general's shop that might come in handy while were away. I want the rest of you to help with getting us ready to travel. Tara, Oriana, Linc, and Mildred, I need you to scout the trail that leads to the forgotten city. That will make us aware of any obstacles that could hinder our trip," Dirk said looking to the four.

"Sure Dirk. We can do that," Linc replied, and the girls agreed.

Dirk pulled out a map. "This is the trail for you to check out," Tara and Oriana inspected the map.

"No problem," Tara said taking the map and looking it over with Oriana and Mildred.

He then looked at Tab. "Tab, El, and Volar, I need you to get with Captain Sinclair and work out the logistics for the trip. He'll know the best way for such a big group to travel." Volar nodded.

"El you need to be here anyway for when your parents arrive."

El nodded and squeezed his arm.

"Kal, you and Stas, I would think would stay here making the arrangements for the pyre. Kal, I know the general thought highly of you and I am sure you will make the right decisions helping my mom."

"I will be honored to help." Kal bowed his head.

"Stas, it's a big day tomorrow and I think your mother would like you around."

"You're right, we'll handle the arrangements."

Kal looked at Dirk. "Dirk I…"

"Go ahead Kal. We might as well talk about it now with everyone here," Dirk stated.

"I'm curious about the enemies' tactics. I've never faced the Vangaurd nor the Aarkas wizards. I think it would be a good idea to understand how they move."

"The wizards attack as one. They simultaneously throw spell after spell at you. We used a reflective spell against them. It's a good strategy but it left them unprepared for when we struck back. They were unprotected. The Vangaurd just attacked without rhyme or reason. It was easy to take them out. That could be because we killed their leader at the beginning of the engagement. We'll learn more from future engagements. That's really all I can tell you right now."

Kal nodded. "Linc any insights on the Gore or the wood nymphs?"

"The Gore just use brute force. They wear no armor. They used wood swords with metal tips. They have a weak spot under then chin and under the arm above the ribs. They're huge. They had a commander giving orders, but we only faced a small squad. We took out most of them before they boarded the ship.

"The wood nymphs I can't tell you anything on them. After we destroyed two of the dinghy's they were on, the rest retreated," Linc finished.

"Thanks. Every bit of information I can share with the soldiers, the better chance of success we will have." Kal smiled then nodded to Dirk who looked like he had more to say.

"Kal, the last thing I need to ask is that I need a couple of volunteers."

Kal knew that was coming. "I have been thinking the same thing. We need a couple of soldiers who can blend in and find out what is going on in the city."

Dirk nodded. "I have one suggestion. I believe I know someone who can blend in, and she is smart enough to get out of trouble if she needs to."

Tab knew he was thinking about Moira. "I don't know Dirk. Can she handle it?"

"You should have seen her take charge during the hostage rescue. She outwitted a dark wizard while she was subdued. I know you don't like her, but she is smart."

"I wasn't there. But if you say she can handle it, then I agree," Tab conceded.

"Kal you'll need to get one person who his quick thinking and smart. I know Moira will want to do it," Dirk said.

Kal nodded. "I'll send Raiden with her."

Anastasia looked at Kal.

"You know how good he is. He will know what to look for," Kal said, determined.

Anastasia frowned. She ran her hands through her hair, took a deep breath, and released it with a sigh. She laid a hand on Kal's knee. "He is your best friend, and you may be sending him to his death."

"We're all probably, already marching towards our deaths," Kal said, squeezing her hand.

"That's settled then. Anyone have any questions?" Dirk asked, looking around at the group. Everyone shook their heads no. "Well, I'm ready to get some sleep. I love you all."

Everyone said good night but didn't go too far. Dirk had tents set up for the bonded. The tents had enough room for four people each. Oriana volunteered to sleep with Linc and Mildred.

"That's fine, sister, but we are going for a walk first,"

Oriana smiled, "I'll keep the sleeping bags warm for you."

Linc laughed as he and Mildred headed out. Mildred had told him she wanted a quick word before they went to sleep.

Dirk had been contemplating an idea. One that he had actually been thinking about since the night they bonded at the farm. Natia suspected something else was up with the way he had been acting. She knew it was more than the general's death that was on his mind. Dirk had been closed off to everyone pretty much since the events at the palace.

When they got inside their tent, they sat in a circle and held hands. It was something Nira had suggested they do to help share their pain and clear their thoughts. She felt it would make it easier to deal with the deaths.

Dirk agreed but knew he would have to open up about his idea. "Before we join, I want to ask you a question, Vira and Nira." They looked at him. Natia raised an eyebrow at him.

"Go ahead Dirk," Vira said a little sternly.

He nodded. "I think it would be a good idea to explore the idea of getting the gems put in my back like Vira and Nira."

Natia was shaken. "That is too dangerous!"

Dirk pointed at the twins.

"They were young!" Natia said.

Dirk had to concede that point. "But think about it. Vira held her power a lot longer than we did at the palace." Dirk was pleading with the twins to help him out.

Vira looked away. "Of all the stupid..."

Nira scowled at him. "You do remember me telling you that most of the children died from the procedure," Nira said.

Dirk pulled his hand free from Natia's and placed it on the side of Nira's face. "I would have the combined power of the bonded and Aarya to protect me." She felt Dirk's love come through the touch.

"I don't know, Dirk. It would be very dangerous, and, besides, we can't do it here. We would have to travel to Aarkas and do the imbedding there," Nira said.

"Have you lost your damned mind?" Vira asked angrily. "There is a whole island full of dark wizards there. Do you think you could just waltz up to Asher's lab and say, 'Hey, I'm Dirk Storm. I'm here to borrow your lab."

Natia smirked at the comment. Dirk put his other hand on Vira's face. "It's a good time to go. Asher isn't even there. He would never think that we would go there, so it's probably not defended and if it is, it would be minimal."

"What do you hope to gain?" Natia asked Dirk.

"An edge. Think about how much more power we would have. I think the shape of their gems has a meaning, and it's the only place I think we can go to find out why."

Natia squeezed Dirk's shoulder. "Dirk, we have so much to do, so many things to plan. We can't leave right now. I agree we may have to eventually go there but right now is not the time," Natia said, gazing into his eyes. Dirk agreed but he didn't want to forget about that option.

Vira looked at Nira and they both nodded. "Dirk, when the time is right, we agree that we should go there. I promise we will help you, but only when the timing is right. Agreed?" Nira squeezed his hand.

Dirk's shoulders dropped. "I guess that's better than a flat-out no. But I agree." Dirk relented.

After a few minutes he was too ready join their cores. "Everyone, hold hands."

Their bond linked them immediately when they closed their eyes. The pain they were all feeling was shared with each other. The love for each other began to ease the pain.

While the twelve were all bonded to each other, he felt there was a special connection between himself and the girls. The intimacy the four of them shared was strong. It was a deep love that transcended beyond family. There was nothing they wouldn't do for each other without hesitation.

Natia was Dirk's soulmate, but the feelings he had for Vira and Nira were just as strong.

"I love you all with my heart and soul." He embraced them each.

"We love you too." They responded in unison.

Dirk, after sharing his feelings and knowing theirs, felt more at ease since he came clean about wanting to go to Aarkas. He laid down with Natia at his side and Vira and Nira huddled around them.

Linc found a quiet spot in the back of the outpost. Linc sensed Mildred wanted to tell him something, so he leaned against the outer wall. Mildred hesitantly looked around. "Just say it. It doesn't matter, you know, if there is some dark secret from your past."

She put a hand on his chest. "This may matter," Mildred said.

Linc shook his head. Mildred held her hand out. A small flame appeared in her palm. Linc casually glanced at it then back at Mildred. He shrugged. She let the flame disappear. "My mother was a dark sorceress. I don't know who she was. I just remember she was really evil until she met my father. I really don't know who my father was either. I barely remember him. He disappeared when I was five years old. I remember him talking about a person named Storm a lot, but the memory is vague. He was friends with Lord Saint, that I know for sure. Lord Saint would never really tell me who he was.

"Lord Saint would tell me that one day, I would find out who they were, but it wasn't his place to tell me. When my father vanished, Lord Saint felt responsible for me. He thought it would be best in the beginning to let me grow up in an orphanage to keep me safe. He kept close tabs on me though. I never went without anything because of him. He was the one who convinced Elanor to adopt me. I told the story about my parents being killed by pirates because Lord Saint felt it would cause me less grief from the townspeople. I mean, they wouldn't want a dark sorceress child living near them, now, would they?"

Linc clasped her hand. "Like I said, it doesn't matter. I sense what's in your heart." Linc looked down at her breasts. "And from the looks of things, it's a pretty big heart," He smirked.

She punched him in the chest. "You should know then, I guess." She leaned into him.

He wrapped his arms around her. "Is that the only thing you can do?"

She shook her head. "There are a few other things but nothing really extraordinary. I sense there is more. I just don't know how to reach it."

Linc kissed her cheek. "Well, now that we are here, I'm sure Vira and Nira can help you with that if you want."

She leaned back. "You understand why I didn't tell you don't you? I mean with your story and who you are I was afraid you would push me away."

"Never," he said, his lips a few inches from hers.

After a brief kissing session, they walked back, holding hands. When they got to their assigned tent and went through the entrance, they stopped and stared. The sight of Oriana sleeping on her belly, half covered up, was breathtaking.

Her almond skin is flawless, Linc thought. Mildred smiled. "I guess she'll have to wait to show us how happy she is that we're here," Linc said jokingly. "That's a shame. She is rather exotic, and those eyes are unnerving."

"They kind of left me defenseless when she gazed into mine," Mildred said. Linc closed the tent and then they both stripped down to their under clothes and snuggled next to each other. Oriana must have sensed their presence because she rolled over, pressing her breast into Linc's back, throwing an arm around him and resting her hand on Mildred's hip.

"We'll get better acquainted tomorrow," she mumbled. Linc and Mildred laughed before falling asleep.

Ishani's Reprieve

In the depths Der-Tod, Zolun was listening to Ishani make excuses again. "My Lord, we have taken over Silver City and killed the older Storm. The king is dead, and we are searching for the young Storm and his friends now."

Zolun turned towards Ishani. Before she knew it, she felt a crunching sound in her jaw as she flew into the wall. She healed her broken jaw and picked herself up off the floor. With her shoulders held high, she walked back up to her master and bowed.

"Ishani, you disappoint me. I can't believe I have let you live all these years," Zolun said, resting his hand on her head.

"My lord, I have always done my best to serve you in every way possible," she said, staring at the ground.

"I know you say that Ishani, but I sense that you are growing tired of serving me," Zolun's deep thunderous voice boomed, sending chills through Ishani's body.

Ishani fell to his feet. "My lord, the Chosen will show his face soon and when he does, I will know," Ishani pleaded.

Zolun looked at her. "Screech." There was a hissing pop. Ishani didn't move.

"Yesth Masther," Screech said, going to a knee.

"Silver City has been taken over?" Screech shook his head yes.

"Have you sent your forces west?" Screech nodded again.

"What of the young prince?"

"His forces have scattered. He has not been found, but there are rumors from our captives, he headed to Feriah," Ishani answered.

"Again, another failure," Zolun said, disappointed.

"My lord, we have them on the run. We will have them soon. The Vanguard puppets will continue doing our bidding. They will keep us informed. I have the Gore and Wood nymphs out searching everywhere. They will find them definitely. They want revenge for the death of their leader by the river rat. Give me the chance to finish this," Ishani pleaded. Zolun looked at the two leaders of his forces.

"My lord, I have thirty thousand Gores, Wood Nymphs and Ratkes marching towards Elmwood as we speak. I am needed there to make sure we take the elves. Ishani has to be here to finish the east," Screech pleaded to save his friend's life. Zolun glared at Screech.

"You side with Ishani, Screech?"

"No, my lord, I side with you. Asher is the only other one who could lead, and he has been bested by the young Storm twice now. Ishani is our best chance for winning," Screech said, lowering his head.

Zolun lifted his hand off of Ishani's head. "Rise." Ishani let out her held breath, and stood, Screech standing right beside her. "Punish Asher for his disgrace, but don't kill him. The young Jamous did as good as you said he would, I suppose. I want the Storm boy and his protector dealt with before Screech reaches the Elmwood, Ishani. These smaller towns are of no concern. Take control of Silver City yourself and have your ship captain patrol for anyone who escaped Silver City."

Ishani bowed, "Your will be done lord." Ishani turned to Screech and looked at him. He smiled. She didn't trust him. He had other motives for saving her life.

She thanked him and disappeared. "Keep your spies on her. I don't trust her anymore." Screech bowed and disappeared with a pop.

Zolun went to his favorite torture room of late. He opened the door and stared at the chained spirit of Diron Storm. Diron's spirit had been held captive since that day at Der-Tod when he gave his life to keep Zolun from taking Harbinger. Zolun had instructed Ishani to capture his spirit before it had left his body.

"Where would your son go to escape me?"

Diron smiled at Zolun for the first time in his eighteen years of captivity. "Oh, great one, do you feel it?" Diron asked. Zolun scowled. "Your demise is soon." Diron laughed.

The magical chains that restrained Diron's spirit ignited, causing him to scream.

Zolun laughed. "You will tell me eventually," Zolun said, walking closer.

Diron smiled through the pain. "Never!"

The Thirteenth Bonded

Dirk and the bonded got up the next morning and went about doing what they had discussed the night before. The first thing Dirk did was find Moira. He found her with her friends that he had met at the school. They were sitting around their tent, eating some rations. Moira saw him approaching and she stood up and hugged him. "Thanks Dirk."

Her friends repeated their gratitude. "You're all welcome. I just wish I could have gotten there sooner," he replied.

"You got there. That's what counts," Moira said. Her friends agreed.

"Moira, you might not want to thank me yet. I have a favor to ask," Dirk said, dragging Moira away from her friends so they couldn't hear what he had to ask.

Moira gave him that knowing smile. "This involves something dangerous I suppose?"

Dirk looked at her. "Your kind of thing I believe," he smiled.

"Tell me more." Moira eyes lit up with intrigue. He told her what he would like for her to do. She didn't even have to think about it. "Danger, getting back at those bastards who tortured us, you bet your sweet ass I'm in."

Kal walked up with Raiden as they were finishing their discussion. "Yummy," Moira said, leaning close to Dirk. "Fringe benefits too, Hell yeah, I'm in."

Dirk smiled. He stood up straight, grasped Kal's hand, and then shook Raiden's, who was eyeing Moira, his light blue eyes taking her all in. Moira stood back and eyed Raiden like a bull would cattle during breeding season.

"Dirk, I am honored to take on this mission," Raiden said.

"Moira, this is Kal and Raiden, but I'm guessing you know that already." She nodded. "You two are going into the lion's den to find out what is happening in Silver City. We need intel and fast."

They stood beside each other listening to what Dirk wanted. "How are we getting in?" Raiden asked.

"Let me guess," Moira said. "The same way we got out,"

"Yes," Dirk replied. "I'll meet you both in the basement in one hour. Don't share any of this with anyone. You never know we may have a spy here as well." They agreed.

Kal and Raiden then left Dirk and Moira alone. "So, you definitely are the Chosen the legends are about?" Moira asked, crossing her arms over her chest.

Dirk shrugged. "I told you before I left, remember?"

Moira gave him that look that she always seemed to be giving him. "I know just hearing it and seeing it are two different things you know?"

Dirk agreed. "I was kind of born into it without a choice."

Moira looked at him. "Well, for what it's worth, I saw what you and your friends were able to do in the lunch hall, and if I had a choice of who the Chosen would be, it would be you," she said with a sincere smile on her face.

"Thanks. Go find Captain Sinclair by the front of the outpost building. He'll get you geared up with what you need for the mission. I'll meet you in the basement in an hour." He started to leave, but she grabbed his arm.

"Thanks for believing in me."

He smiled at her and grabbed her shoulders. "Tell me that when you get back safely," he replied hugging her. "And don't molest your partner while you're there," He laughed.

"You know me," She smirked and walked away.

"I do, that's why I am saying it!" he shouted back.

An hour later, as most of the bonded were off doing their own tasks, Dirk, Natia, and the twins had changed back into their armor. They met Raiden and Moira in the basement. Kal and Anastasia were in the basement when they got there.

"Nice armor," Raiden said, touching Dirk's magical leather.

Dirk nodded. "It is and hopefully one day, we will have more of it, or at least something similar, for the rest of you."

Anastasia walked over and hugged Raiden. "Be careful."

He hugged her back. "I will princess. You know, it's not too late to change your mind," he said, looking at Kal.

Anastasia smiled. "Raiden, you will always be my second choice."

He smiled at Kal, and they embraced. "Be careful, my friend," Kal said. He nodded.

Dirk looked at Moira. "Be yourself and you'll be fine." He hugged her.

"I will. See you in a few days," she said. They said goodbye to Anastasia and Kal because they had arrangements to finalize for the funeral pyres.

"I'll go first," Dirk said. He touched the door and then stepped through it. The pull took him away. He materialized in front of a door. He opened it and stepped into the basement of the school. There were several whooshing sounds and then the rest of the group came through.

Dirk and the group went up the stairs. The door was still locked so Dirk held up a hand for them to stop. He touched the door, releasing the barrier, and had them all squat down. Vira closed her eyes and nodded. Dirk opened the door slowly. The hallway was empty.

The group went up the stairs, past the dorms to the roof and Dirk looked out over the city. The fires still burned from the attack. The palace had a gloom about it. The flag of Silver City had been ripped down and the flag of Vangaurd was flying high in its place, which made the darkness in his heart start to grow again. He estimated thousands of soldiers were spread throughout the city. Dark wizards patrolled along with them.

"Now you know your mission. Just gather intel about what's happened. Do not engage them unless it is life or death. See if you can find any kind of hidden resistance. If you do, make contact. They could be valuable later when we take back our homes. If you have to leave quickly, go to the farm. There are plenty of places to hide there until the rendezvous time."

"I understand," Raiden replied with Moira nodding.

"Don't carry any heavy weapons. I think that would only bring attention to yourselves. Use only the daggers for now. I understand, I won't be there, but if you have to engage, it's your call on what to use."

Vira told them to look at her once they were back on the main floor. "I am gonna cast an illusion spell on you. It will tingle at first but will fade away in an hour or two. This will allow you to walk right out of here without being noticed. You'll be invisible to them but not to each other." They nodded.

"Good luck," Dirk said, hugging Moira and shaking Raiden's hand. "I will meet you in two days at the Storm farm. Be at the door by my grandfather's shop out behind the house at noon,"

Vira casted her spell. Moira and Raiden felt the tingle then slowly faded away from their sight. "See you in two days," Moira said, and then they were gone.

Dirk squeezed Natia's hand. "Let's go." They entered the basement doorway and resealed the door, going downstairs and to the general's shop.

The group began loading all of the books and parchments into the rough sacks they had brought along. "Look at this," Natia said, going through one of the general's drawers of his desk. She held up an old book. The language on the cover was a language Dirk didn't recognize.

"It's Drocuian," Nira said, stepping up to take the book from Natia carefully.

"The language of the lost," Vira said standing next to her sister.

"Can you read it?"

"A little, but this language is a thousand years old. The Droc got away from it long before the banishment," Vira said. The twins were flipping through the pages carefully. The book was nearly crumbling. "Wait," Vira said to Nira as she was about to turn a page. Vira read over a few lines. "I'm not certain, but I think this is a text about the tomb of the lost in the Forgotten City."

Dirk beamed at her. "Anything else you can translate."

Vira shook her head. "Maybe if I had a chance to study it more using the words, I know to translate the rest of the letters." Nira agreed.

"Put it away carefully for now. That will be useful and you two can study it on the way to the Forgotten City."

Natia grabbed Dirk's hand. "This was under it." She picked up a note written in the general's handwriting. Dirk grabbed it from Natia's trembling hand and read the letter aloud.

Dirk, I found this in the old library at the palace the other day. If you're reading this, then Thea's prediction has come to pass. It is in the language of the Forgotten City. I believe it was the Droc's center of power when they ruled the world. Use it carefully. I know your father had this at one time and used it. I didn't know what had become of it until I ran across it looking for more maps for the trip you were planning. I am glad I discovered it before my departure. Remember, I love you son. I am very proud of the man you have become, and I know Diron would be as well. Take care of your friends and family and one day we will all be reunited. Love, Grandfather.

Dirk grabbed Natia's free hand. Tears were rolling down all of their faces. Vira and Nira grabbed the two in a hug. Between tears, Vira said, "I swear, Grandfather, we will avenge you." Nira repeated her words.

Dirk squeezed them tight. "I love you," he said to no one in particular. The words were repeated by all.

After a few minutes, Dirk folded the letter and placed it in the book. "Let's grab everything we can carry. We will come back for the rest." Dirk sent a mental message to Kal to meet them in the basement.

Kal met them with several soldiers. Brock being one of them. They handed over their bags and were handed empty ones. Dirk instinctively said, "Brock come with us." He looked at Kal.

Kal nodded, "He is in charge."

"Okay," Brock followed Dirk and the girls through the doorway. He was disoriented when they stepped through to the basement of the school.

"Where are we?" Vira briefly explained the process to him. "Wow. I didn't know that was possible."

Vira nodded. "There is a lot that will amaze you. Ready? We have one more door to go through." Brock nodded. They felt the pull and were standing back in front of the doorway to the general's shop. After Brock cleared his head, he stepped through the door with Dirk. Dirk went to the window and looked out. He could see soldiers searching the grounds and told everyone what he saw. They couldn't see into the shop or get in since it was magically sealed.

"What do we do if they are still here when Moira and Raiden come to the farm?"

Dirk smiled. "Then we send some more of them to the underworld."

"Dirk, I want to be here for that if you will allow me. I want to get the blood of those bastards that killed Larkin and Stew on my sword." Dirk nodded. He understood. Larkin and Stew had been jackasses but didn't deserve to die that way either. They had left with Brock when he was expelled from the wizarding school but had been cut out of the military training.

"That's it, Dirk, unless you want to look yourself," Nira said. He took one last look, and they were off. After they went through the last door, Kal was waiting on them when they returned. The soldiers grabbed the bags and took them to the kitchen where the others had been placed. Vira and Nira immediately got out the old book and began trying to decipher the other book.

His mother came in and sat with them. Dirk handed her the letter. She read it and a few tears sprung to her eyes. "He knew."

Queen Thea came in with Kal and Anastasia. Kira looked at her. "Why didn't you tell me?"

Thea held her hand. "He made me promise not to. You know how he was, stubborn as a mule. Him and Jerard both, two peas in a pod. Once they made up their minds about something, you couldn't change it." Thea had tears streaking down her face and her voice trembled as she tried to explain.

Kira squeezed her hand. "I know, damn him."

Thea hugged Kira. "I'm sorry, but you know I couldn't deny my old friend." Kira nodded.

"I've got something here," Vira blurted out. She and Nira had been engrossed in the book. They all turned to look at her. "Sorry. I didn't mean to interrupt."

"That's okay, dear, go ahead," Thea said.

Vira began. *In the tomb of the Priestess Siala, we placed the Mulga stone in her body in place of her heart. It was the most destructive stone we have ever encountered. No one person should have the power to control the stone. It was a beginning to the end of our society. So, we few, who were dedicated to saving our culture, decided to hide it away from the rest. Beware any who would try to find and remove the stone. A powerful curse has been set with the stone. The beast...*

"The rest of the page is too hard to read. Sorry."

The four immediately recognized what she was talking about. They had been there with Dirk and Sora when they touched his blood in the Book of Storms. Kira noticed the four eyeing each other.

"What is it, Dirk?" Thea asked. She had noticed also.

Natia nodded to Dirk. He told the ones gathered about the night he, Natia, Vira, and Nira had gone into the memories of his namesake. There were questions asked. The group answered the best they could.

"I don't know, it did seem very dangerous for them. Sora gave her life for that stone. I wouldn't think it would be worth the risk," Thea said.

Dirk looked at her. "You know something, don't you?"

She looked away. "Mother?" Anastasia asked, getting her mother to look at her.

Thea relented to her daughter's stare. "It was a vision I had, but it was incomplete. That's why I didn't say anything about it." She sat down beside Kira. She looked at Kira and then told them what she saw. "Natia was lying on the ground, bleeding. Dirk and the twins were there trying to save her. It was in a dungeon-like room lit with torches. Then the vision disappeared,"

"That's why you did what you did at the farm with Nira and Vira, isn't it?" Dirk asked.

The queen looked at the twins. "Yes, Dirk, it is a part of the reason. I knew they would be very important to your quest, and I wanted to make them loyal to your cause."

Vira shook her head. "My dear queen. I could never repay you for what you did for us. Regardless of the reasoning behind your actions, Dirk made us feel like family long before you did that at the farm. We were already loyal to him even before we knew of his destiny." Vira lay her hand over the queen's.

Thea smiled and patted her hand. "I had to be sure."

Vira smiled. "We understand."

Dirk loved his sisters. They never seemed to disappoint him. He smiled at the two of them. "I think that is useful information but, it might need to be a last resort."

Natia looked at Dirk, sensing his deception, and smiled. He wanted Kira and the queen to think they wouldn't pursue the power that might give them an edge, but she knew he would seek it. She sensed him send a thought to the girls.

We'll discuss this later. Vira, hold off on disclosing any more information about the book.

Vira smiled and gave a quick nod.

"Is that everything you can translate, dear?" the queen asked.

"That's all I have been able to for now. It's an old language and difficult to translate," Nira said.

The queen nodded. "Well, it's been a busy morning and going to be a difficult evening. I suggest you rest, and we will see you this afternoon." The queen grabbed Kira's hand and the two of them left the bonded at the table.

"Let's eat, then reconvene where we can have some privacy," Dirk said.

Hermosa, who had been busy trying keep the rescued students busy, walked into the kitchen. "Before you all leave, I want to ask a favor." She looked mainly at Dirk and Anastasia.

"Go ahead, Wizard Hermosa. You needn't have to ask. What do you need?" Dirk replied.

She had tears in her eyes. She had lost a lot when the academy and school fell, lifelong friends and Nabas, who was rumored to be her true love.

"I actually have two. I would ask that Hilda and Tilda have a pyre of their own tonight. Most of the students who are with us feel their loss. They were very important to them," Hermosa said, wiping some tears away.

"Absolutely. I will see it's done," Dirk said.

She smiled and thanked him. "The second thing is I know you have a reconnaissance mission going on right now in the city. I would ask that we send one west as well. There may be survivors who escaped through the mountains, and we need to get the word out to the towns where we will rally."

Anastasia answered. "I have already ordered several soldiers to head out when we leave for the Forgotten City. They will carry word of my father's death and rally any survivors and volunteers to there."

Hermosa smiled. "Anastasia, you always think ahead. Thank you." She nodded and left to take care of travel plans.

"Wagon trains approaching!" a soldier yelled from outside. They all got to greet the overdue wagon train. Tab and El were waiting as the gates were opened. Jonesy stood beside his sister as Dirk and the group walked up beside them.

"They don't know yet," El said, wrapping her arms across her chest.

"Stas will address them once they enter the compound. Then you and

Jonesy need to see to your parents," Dirk told her, putting an arm around her.

She rested her head on his shoulder. "Dad isn't going to take this well. He was very close to your grandfather and the king."

Dirk squeezed her close. "They will deal with it as we did. I mean, as we are doing," he said dryly. A fog started to slip into his thoughts.

"Dirk!" Vira yelled, turning him to face her. Her eyes were blazing, Nira and Natia were staring at him as well.

"What is it?" he snapped, irritated. Natia touched his face. He hadn't realized that El and Jonesy were already embracing their parents. "What happened?" Dirk asked shaking his head.

"We lost contact with you in here," Vira said, placing a hand over her heart, referring to the bond.

"I don't know, El said something and then I felt like my thoughts were clouded."

Vira and Nira closed their eyes. "It's gone now," Nira said, opening her eyes.

"What's gone?" Dirk asked.

"The darkness. Dirk, you have to be careful with your emotions. If you aren't careful, the darkness we sensed back at the farm can creep in and cloud your judgement," Natia said.

He looked at them. "Seriously?" They nodded. "I was irritated with El, but not really at her. I'm just so sick of everyone saying they're sorry. I'm sick of talking about what we are gonna do. Let's freaking just go do it." Dirk's eyes were flaming, and he was breathing hard. Anastasia walked up. Dirk had gotten very loud. She put a hand on his shoulder.

He turned at the touch. "Wha..." He stopped when he realized it was Anastasia.

She squeezed his shoulder. "I feel your pain, and your annoyance, but we have to be patient and put up with the bullshit of everyone's apologies. They feel the need to let us know they care. Remember, it is a loss for them as well."

Dirk felt a big weight lift from his shoulders. "Thanks, Stas. I got a little worked up."

She nodded. "I know how you feel, Dirk." If it had been anyone else, Dirk would have probably not been affected by their words, but she was in the same situation he was. He thanked her again.

She then walked towards the wagons to greet the ones she hadn't talked with. Dirk looked around, feeling angry at himself. He watched as Kal helped Anastasia get up on the main wagon. Kal gathered the soldiers and the group who had traveled with them. The gathered listened to Anastasia explain what had happened in Silver City. Dirk could tell by the way their shoulders slumped and their heads dipped that she had just told them about the king.

After Anastasia was through, she stepped down and talked with several of the group's leaders. The first-year students, who had been traveling with the wagons, made a beeline for Dirk.

He tensed but felt Natia and Vira grab his shoulders. "Relax, love. We have to get through this one more time." He nodded as Natia released his shoulder and grabbed his hand.

"They look like they had a rough trip," Vira said, squeezing Dirk's other hand.

"Thanks," Vira. You're my compass. You keep me pointed in the right direction."

Nira laughed. "Not an easy job brother." He laughed.

Red was the first to reach him and he told him how he was sorry. Dirk thanked him and listened to their tale. They had been attacked by fifty or so Vanguard soldiers three leagues outside the city.

"They thought they were attacking merchants." Red laughed. "We killed every one of them, and when we lost connection with our doubles, we figured something was up. We stayed on guard, but then travel was a little slower." Red's information was vital. It meant that the attack probably didn't come from one direction.

"Thanks, Red. That answers some questions I had."

Red headed off to get some food and catch up with the rest of the bonded as Dirk shook hands and received condolences from the rest of the group. He was glad to see Phil. He hugged him and told him things went as planned with his father. Phil was glad. Dusty and Phil pulled Nira and Vira away after they were through talking.

"Be good," Dirk said, raising an eyebrow at the girls. Nira laughed and they went off with the boys. "Dirk, I'm sincerely sorry for your loss. It is a loss to the world," Sirien said, bowing his head.

"Thank you Sirien. That means a lot. Tell me about their soldiers. They weren't really using any formations, just randomly fighting, right?" Dirk asked.

Sirien nodded. "Red took out their captain in the first five minutes, so they were unorganized." Sirien told Dirk about the whole ordeal. He truly admired Red's tactics.

"Thanks, that's how they fought us as well. Go get yourselves some fresh food and shower. We set up some showers behind the outpost building,"

He had seen Sergeant Giles and several other soldiers from the academy waiting to talk with him.

Sergeant Giles stepped up. He had a somber look on his face. "Dirk, I knew your grandfather a long time. I won't say that I'm sorry. You already know that. It is a loss to us all. That being said, let me introduce Commanders Dorian and Cailyn, Colonel Thibaut and Sergeant's Brooks and Valentina."

Dirk shook all of their hands. "Kal has told us we will be leaving out tomorrow and that we will have a briefing in the morning on strategy and assignments," Commander Dorian said.

"Yes, Commander. We have already planned several operations. Mainly intelligence gathering, and we have one in operation right now in Silver City," Dirk said. Commander Dorian took in the information, then he said, "I see you have the general's keen sense of protocols. I'm glad."

Dirk smiled. "He was very astute when it came to the planning of details," he said laughing. The commanders agreed. "I would like you to coordinate with Captain Sinclair your efforts for the rest of the day. You all need to rest and get some food in you. I have no idea what we will face in the Forgotten City, but I am sure now that you're here, you can look over our plans and make adjustments accordingly." He sensed doubt from the commander.

"That sounds like a good plan." The soldiers all left, except Giles and Brooks.

"Anything else, Sergeant?"

He patted Dirk on the back. "Not to be sentimental, but I know Durkon would be very proud of what I heard you did in the palace. I hope you have been keeping up on your conditioning, because when we all get to the Forgotten City, we're going to have to step it up to third-year level." Giles smiled. Dirk nodded, and the two sergeants went to get some food.

Dirk saw El, Tab, and Jonesy still conversing with the Glans. He walked over and El's mother, Eleanor, met him halfway and embraced him. She was El, only twenty years older with slight graying in her hair. "I'm sorry sweetheart. Your grandfather has always been a close friend. Anything you need just let us know."

"Thank you. I will. How's your husband holding up?"

Eleanor looked at him. "He lost two dear friends. The king really never was like a king to Jonas. He was a father figure to him." She rubbed Dirk's shoulder while she talked.

"Well, I know one thing for sure. The king always trusted him to make the best wares," Dirk said, twisting the bracelet the king had given him." She smiled.

"Figured that out, did you?"

Dirk nodded. "If I could only figure out who made this armor, then I would really be figuring something out," he said, exposing his armor he wore under his cloak. He had a hunch and wanted to see if he was right. Dirk didn't go anywhere without it anymore.

Eleanor smiled. "That's some mighty fine armor."

Dirk agreed. "It saved our lives in the battle at the palace."

She smiled wide. "I'm glad Dirk, but I think I can help you with who made that if you really want to know," she said as her children and husband came walking up with a girl Dirk didn't recognize.

Dirk looked at her and nodded. "I sure would. I would like to get as many made as we can. Maybe not the invisibility thing but the armor for sure," Dirk said, excited for the first time in a few days.

"Well, I'm not sure how fast I can make anymore, but if I can get the supplies and the gems, I can get started as soon as we get set up where we are going."

Dirk smiled, glad that he was right, as El's mouths fell open, Eleanor smiled at her daughter. "You didn't think your father was the only talented one with magic, did you?" She laughed. It felt good to hear her laughter.

It was decided after a brief talk of what materials were needed that Dirk and Kal would get a group to start searching for supplies when they arrived at the Forgotten City. Dirk, wanting to find out one more thing before they separated, asked, "Mrs. Glan, the armor worked great for us at the palace and the school. The only thing that has us confused is Tab's armor allowed a spear to go into his leg. Do you know how that could have happened?"

She looked at Dirk thoughtfully. "The only thing that could have pierced that armor would have been something magical. I'll take a look at it when we get settled and see if I can solve that question and hopefully prevent it from happening again."

"Thanks. There were a lot of dark wizards there we were fighting, and I assumed that might have been what happened," Dirk said.

After that, the Glans went along with Aalana, Eleanor's assistant, whom she didn't go anywhere without, to get some food. "Can you believe my mother made the armor?" El said proudly.

Dirk nodded. "I sure do. She made you, didn't she?"

El hugged Dirk. "Watch it fella. I've got a man now," she said eyeing Tab.

He smiled. "Anyone hungry?" They went to get some food, laughing again at Tab's metabolism.

Natia whispered in Dirk's ear, "I believe this is the first time we have been without Vira or Nira in a while."

Dirk laughed. "Yes, I believe you're right. It feels weird, doesn't it?"

Natia hated to admit it, but she did miss them as well. "Kind of lonely. Come on, let's go drag them away from Phil and Dusty and eat. I'm actually hungry," Natia said goodbye to El, Tab, and Jonesy.

That night, the funeral pyres were lit with Queen Thea, Anastasia, Kira, and Dirk all giving small speeches about the lives and the influence the two great men had had on everyone they met. Anastasia lit her father's pyre with a wave of her hand. Dirk did the same with Generals. The pyres were built in the back of the courtyard where they wouldn't disrupt the tents the group had set up for their ever-growing population. There were close to five hundred adults, soldiers, students, and civilians now being housed here.

Hilda and Tilda's pyre was built to the side of the king's and the Generals pyres. Dirk let anyone who wanted to share a story talk. Several students and adults came forward, sharing stories of the way the twins had helped them get through difficult times. The real jaw-dropper came when Dirk stood up in front of everyone and shared that the twins were bonded with his father and if it hadn't been for them making him see the importance of his destiny, none of them gathered, would be here tonight. He said this with tears running down his face. He then turned to the twin's bodies that had been wrapped in the traditional silk funeral wrap and raised his head to the stars.

"Hilda and Tilda, your spirits will be with us until the very end. Thank you for giving us a chance and spreading your light on us all."

Vira and Nira stepped up and two balls of fire appeared in each girl's hands. Dirk nodded, and the flames flew. The pyre started blazing immediately. A war cry vibrated through the air. The gathered, who had never seen Aarya before, gasped as she landed on Dirk's shoulder.

Dirk looked up at her. "Thanks." She shrieked into the sky. Dirk turned to the group and took his time to look around at all of the gathered. Crimson and green flames were blazing in his eyes and a crimson aura surrounded him. Everyone could see it. He felt the position of every bonded and searched the crowd for the ones he wanted to see. Brock and Skylar were halfway to the back, standing close together.

He needed everyone there to believe what he was about to say. And if he could convince his worst enemy, he could convince anyone.

Go ahead, brother. We are with you.

He felt Linc's words sink in, and he took a deep breath before he began. "I see a lot of faces here tonight. Some, I have known my whole life. Most, I have only known a few months. Some, I really don't know at all, but we all have something in common. We have all survived one of the biggest and most sinister betrayals in the history of our world."

He paused, gazing into the crowd to make sure he had their attention. Satisfied that he did, he continued. "We have been separated from our friends and loved ones for no other reason than greed and the lust for power, but I want you to know, each and every one of you, that we will all be reunited with them again. We are sending several two-person teams out tomorrow to search for survivors and warn the rest of the world about what has happened in Silver City. First though, I must tell you I am no leader. I was forced into this position due to the blood that runs through my veins. I ask that you be patient with me and the leaders of each group. I have asked a lot of them in the short time that we have had here, and there are several of you we will probably ask more of than we should. We start a long trip tomorrow. Several of us are going in different directions but we will rejoin the rest of you when the time is right."

Aarya flapped her wings, stretching. "I will make you a promise." Dirk looked straight at Brock. "I promise you this. If we all stick together and work hard, one day we will march straight back into Sliver City and take what was taken from us and kill every one of those bastards that was responsible."

The crowd roared with approval. Dirk, feeling the passion of the crowd, continued, "The main leader has already been dealt with. It was the High Priest of Zona, Romus Jamous. Natia, Tab, Vira, and I personally killed that piece of shit the night he had my grandfather and the king killed."

Dirk then pulled the head of Romus Jamous out of the pack he had beside him and raised it high in the air for everyone to see. The crowd already worked up from Dirk's speech, shouted their glee over that announcement. He then tossed the head in the air.

Anastasia, who had been waiting, cast a blaze of crimson and green flames from her hands and incinerated the head before it could hit the ground.

The crowd chanted, "Revenge!"

Dirk let them get that out of their system for a few minutes and then held up his hands to quiet the crowd. He turned back to lock eyes with Brock and continued. "And I personally will see every one of them dead if it takes every drop of the blood that runs through my veins. This I swear on my life. FAMILY IS WHAT WE ARE! FAMILY IS WHAT WE WILL ALWAYS BE!" Dirk shouted and pulled Harbinger out of his back strap and raised it in the air. Flames leapt from the tip of Harbinger into the sky. The phoenix's war cry reverberated through the gathered crowd as the bonded and the crowd repeated his words.

Aarya shrieked and flew into the air high above the crowd with crimson, green flames leaping off her wings. Dirk was still holding eye contact with

Brock. Brock smiled and nodded.

When Dirk was done, the designated group of commanders started getting the crowd to break up and get ready for bed. "No leader, huh?" Anastasia said, stepping up beside Dirk and putting an arm around his shoulders. "You just started the spark we needed with that speech. No leader, my ass Dirk. You are a natural leader, whether you believe it or not. Hells, I would follow you into the underworld after that."

She kissed his cheek and grabbed Kal's hand as he walked up. "Great speech, Dirk. See you in a few minutes," Kal said as he and Anastasia walked off to tend to queen Thea. Kira hugged Dirk and told him she loved him and would see him before he left in the morning.

Dirk turned and watched the flames of the pyres burn. He sat down, crossed his legs, and contemplated what tomorrow would bring, gazing into the flames of Hilda and Tilda's pyre and reflecting on the twin teachers.

He smiled, remembering them. He had only known them a little while, but they were almost as big of an influence on his life as his grandfather had been.

After ten minutes, he felt their approach. He slid around on the ground and faced the bonded and Mildred, who had all sat in a half circle around behind him with the exception of Kal and Anastasia, who had to take a bewildered queen Thea to her bedroom. They all held hands. Dirk closed his eyes. The group all imitated their leader, even Mildred. Dirk sensed there was something familiar about her. He also sensed a connection. He welcomed her to the link and felt her warm inside.

"Ah, that's it, isn't it? No wonder," Dirk said to himself. He had finally figured out the connection. She was, without question, the daughter of Heath Merrick. *But how?* he wondered. She was connected to the group the same as Hilda and Tilda were, but should she be more?

Dirk sent a thought to the group. He felt a unanimous agreement. The rest of the group opened their eyes and looked at Mildred. They had felt it also through the connection. Linc squeezed her hand and Oriana, who was sitting on the other side of her, did as well. Kal and Anastasia came back and joined the group, squeezing in between Volar and Tab.

"We agree," Kal said. Dirk nodded and turned to look at Mildred.

"Mildred," Dirk said, bringing her attention to him. The bond was a beautiful thing. The emotions they all shared and felt were universal between them. The sorrow was washed away from each of them as Aarya landed in the center of the circle. The bonded felt her presence before she landed and felt the love, she had for them. He looked back at Mildred. She was still looking at Aarya when Dirk brought her attention back to him. "We would like you to become our thirteenth and final bonded. That is, if you are willing to join us?"

The group all smiled at her. "There is a prophecy. I am not sure if Linc told you that part or not, but it says basically we need thirteen bonded to be successful in our quest to destroy Zolun." Dirk pushed down his anger for the next part. He closed his eyes then continued, "Gil was going to become our last bonded, but seeing how he betrayed us and everything we love, we feel you are the one to fill that spot. I have looked inside your heart. I know how you feel about Linc, and I assure you we all feel the same. Would you do us the honor and become bonded with us?"

Mildred looked around at the bonded. She smiled at Linc and kissed him, then took a breath. "I would be honored to be a part of this group." Dirk smiled and looked at Aarya. She trilled and bounced onto Mildred's shoulder. Mildred touched the side of Aarya's neck, and the spark leapt into her body. The group all took in a breath when Mildred's core joined theirs and her memories flooded into them. This time, it felt different. The word Dirk would have used was "complete".

After a few minutes, the group all opened their eyes and looked at Mildred. The revelations from the bond confirmed what Dirk had already sensed. Mildred grabbed her chest. "I feel the love," she said, tears rolling down her face. All of the girls were crying now since they felt what she was feeling. The feeling of acceptance overwhelmed her. Even the guys were feeling it.

Dirk looked at her. "You're home now, sister." Mildred got up and ran to Dirk and he hugged her.

"I promise I won't let you down."

"I know," he said as he released her. She went around the circle and hugged them all. Volar was misty-eyed when she hugged him. Linc grasped her hand when she had made the full circle and they sat back down.

"Did everyone feel that?" Dirk asked, looking to the group. They all nodded. "Yes, I thought so. We are complete now." The group agreed. "Tomorrow, we will separate for the first time in a while. Natia, Vira, Nira, and I can't leave with you yet. We have to wait on Moira and Raiden. As soon as our friends are safely back, we'll catch up with you before you reach the city."

They all nodded. Dirk sent ripples of flames through his hands, and they passed through the groups touch. Mildred's was astonished as the flames appeared on her hands as they passed through the group. She was bonded with them now and she enjoyed the feeling of the connection. It didn't burn, it was a warm and affectionate connection of love. The phoenix bond burned through them all.

A circle of flames coursed through them, filling them with Dirk and Aarya's love. The group closed their eyes and took in the feeling. "I love you all, my sisters and brothers. Be careful and protect each other until we are together again," Dirk said. The flames disappeared. The group got up and talked with each other for a little while. Eventually, they all hugged each other and told Dirk and his traveling companions to be careful.

Dirk, Natia, and the twins would be leaving before sunrise. They wouldn't see the bonded in the morning before they departed. Dirk looked at the group as they separated, tears forming.

"What is it, brother?" Nira asked, squeezing Dirk's hand. Natia and Vira were saying goodbye to El and Tab.

As they walked off Natia and Vira stepped closer to Dirk and Nira. "What is it, my love?" Natia asked, wrapping her arms around his waist. Vira grabbed his free hand and squeezed.

He looked all three of them in the eyes. "I will admit to you three that I am scared. I'm afraid I will let everyone down."

Natia looked at him with concern. "Dirk Storm, we are all in this together and if one fails, we all fail. You are the bravest man I know, and I have no doubt that when this is over, we will all be together back at the farm, remembering what we went through to get back there. As for you letting anyone down, I very seriously doubt that. We believe in you" Natia kissed him.

"You could never let us down, brother. We love you and wouldn't allow it to happen," Vira said, squeezing the three in a group hug.

Dirk smiled at them. "I don't know how I ever made it without you three in my life." He suddenly felt better about their future.

Nira smiled. "We don't either." They laughed and headed to the tents.

Epilogue

Aarya, after bonding with Mildred, took off flying west. She had sensed that evil was washing through the land in that direction but didn't share her thoughts with Dirk. She wanted to find out what was causing the evil, then after she confirmed what it was, she would let him know.

She flew west over Mt Jover then headed south towards Mere City, letting the wind carry her. The smell of the Mere waters hit her senses. *I'm craving fish*, she thought. She would have to get a snack on the trip back.

As that thought left her, she sensed, and smelled what she was searching for. A darkness was covering the land from south of Mere City past Vinely Post as far as the eye could see. It was night-time, but her eyes were actually sharper at night. She flew lower to try and distinguish what was forming the wave of darkness. When she got to within five hundred feet above the ground, she finally could make out what was making the dark wave.

Thousands of wood nymphs, Ratkes, and Gore marched in formations. They stretched out as far as her eyes could see. The Gore, with their beast-like bodies, were threatening. They carried weapons like the Gores Linc had fought. The Ratkes were about half the size of the Gore, wore brown leather, and carried small spears. Some of them even had crossbows. Then there were the wood nymphs. Slimy, dark creatures with lanky arms and long black hair, only a cloth covering their midsections. They carried spears and bows as well. In the front leading the thousands of Gores and Ratkes was a grayish bald creature. He oozed death as he rode his black horse west.

The Screel caught sight of Aarya. A smile crossed his face. Aarya could see broken fangs and yellow teeth, even from this height. He said something to a figure beside him. The figure nodded then turned faster than Aarya could have thought possible. In the blink of an eye, a cross bolt blazed across the sky towards her. She didn't have time to get completely out of the way. The bolt ripped through her right wing, breaking several bones, causing Aarya to go into a nosedive. Her last thought as the ground came speeding towards her was *Dirk. I have failed you.*

Dirk jumped out of his sleeping bag. Startled by his movement, Natia and the twins jumped, looking at him. "Dirk, what is it?" Vira asked. Dirk doubled over in pain.

Natia went to his side. "Love, what's wrong?"

He looked at the three with tears in his eyes. "Aarya."

This is the end of book one of the Storm Rising Series, The Beginning of the Storm.

Book two, Storm Fury, will be coming soon.

I have added a preview of book two below.

Thanks for joining Dirk and his friends on their first journey.

Storm Rising

Storm Fury

The musky scent of oil torches burning in the confines of the tunnel was enough to make Harper want to turn around and run out as fast as he entered them. *I would follow you anywhere, Shae,* he thought. He had followed her from Aarkas island and that trip in itself was enough danger for a lifetime. He figured following her into the Grand Temple of Drocillia wasn't any different. He would have followed her to the ends of Marona if she had asked him to. He was definitely in love with her. That's just how he felt about her.

Shae was their leader. He and several hundred Droc had left Aarkas to follow a prophecy written a long time ago by a citizen of the very city they were underneath right now. The Droc, at the height of their power, without any explanation to its trade partners, had just up and deserted Drocillia, leaving Marona all together for the island of Aarkas. He knew they fled the mainland to go to Aarkas in search of a greater power.

It was a treacherous island and almost impossible to reach. The living conditions on the island were a bare minimal for existence when the Droc arrived there, but in the last thousand years, they had cultivated it into a very habitable island. The whole story was never known by the general population, but it was deemed necessary for the Droc's survival to move there.

The Drocillians were very loyal to their leaders. Most did whatever the leaders of the high council mandated without question. But there were those who still didn't do what they were told, without hesitation.

There was a faction during the 'Times of Enlightenment', which is what those days were referred to in Drocillian history, that still did things their own way in secret. That was one of the reasons Harper found himself following Shae down this musky cavern. Harper bumped his head on one of the broken beams that hung down from the old ceiling. The sound of his cursing echoed through the tunnel. Shae held the torch towards him to make sure he was okay.

After confirming he was, she turned to continue down the dark path.

Frustrated that they hadn't reached their destination, Harper decided to voice his concerns. He knew Shae was a good leader, but she sometimes got them in situations without thinking things through.

"Shae, you know I'll follow you anywhere, but do you have any idea where we're going?"

Shae stopped. She turned and looked at Harper. He could see her green eyes flare, even in this dark tunnel. "Harper, I told you before we left that I had an idea how far it was to the tomb, but I wasn't exactly sure how long it would take. Do you want to give up so easily? I mean, as far as we have traveled, do you want to turn around and give up? By now, Asher has totally taken over the council. I am sure he will welcome us back with open arms," she said, not really expecting Harper to answer any of the questions the way she had asked.

Harper, feeling berated by Shae, just grunted, "No. Lead on."

Shae smiled, turned, and headed deeper into the tunnel.

An hour later, when the torches were getting low, they finally saw a pulsing light a few hundred feet ahead of them. "Do you see the flickering light?" Shae asked Harper excitedly. Harper stepped closer to her.

He squinted; his eyesight hindered in the dark tunnel. "I do," he said and smiled.

Shae grabbed his shoulder and squeezed. "It's like the prophecy said. Follow the tunnel to its deepest depth. In the depths of the darkness, salvation and redemption is close at hand."

"You left the part out about 'Beware thy curiosity, the evil that protects thy salvation is darker than the reward you seek'. That part is what worries me," Harper said, still looking at the flickering light.

"Harper, that's just to keep normal Drocillians from seeking the stone."

Harper laughed. "If you say so. We came this far, might as well see what's down here." He agreed as she knew he would, so they continued until they came to stand in front of the source of the flickering light. They stood there, looking shocked.

"Someone has been here before," Shae stated, looking at the granite wall in front of them. There was a fist-sized crimson gem in the center of the wall. It was the source of the flickering. It had a small flame burning on the inside of it.

"Oh my," Shae said after reading the words carved above the crimson gem. Disgusted, Harper stared at the words carved into the granite wall as well.

"If you seek salvation hidden inside, turn away and never enter this tomb. The cost of salvation is too high. Find a better solution."

"That's not what I suspected," Shae said. Harper read the words again out loud to see if it was a trick of some kind.

"I don't know, it seems real."

Shae slowly reached out and touched the gem, letting her curiosity get the better of her. As soon as she touched the gem, a spark leapt from the stone to her fingers, knocking her to the ground.

"Are you okay, Shae?" Harper asked, rushing to her side. She shook her head, clearing the effects.

"The prophecy is true," she stated. Harper squinted at her. He couldn't see her face.

"Well, tell me."

"The time will come for salvation when the great phoenix appears with the Chosen."

Harper knew this part but didn't really understand. "I don't understand."

"When I touched the gem, a vision flashed in my mind. It was of a phoenix circling the great temple and it swooped down and landed on the shoulder of a half human half elven male."

Harper turned and looked at the words one more time. "What of the warning?"

Shae got up and looked at it as well. "I think that it was put here to keep out anyone who doesn't belong. We will just have to prepare and wait for the Chosen to appear."

Harper looked at her. "How long do we wait?"

"I guess we wait until a halfling shows up and can tell us who this was that put the warning up."

Harper agreed and read the writing again so he would remember who had given the warning. Satisfied, he said, "We will prepare until the Chosen comes along and can tell us more about Dirk Storm."

To be continued